long way down

KRISTA & BECCA RITCHIE

ADDICTED SERIES
Recommended Reading Order

Addicted to You (Addicted #1)

Ricochet (Addicted #1.5)

Addicted for Now (Addicted #2)

Kiss the Sky (Spin-Off: Calloway Sisters #1)

Hothouse Flower (Calloway Sisters #2)

Thrive (Addicted #2.5)

Addicted After All (Addicted #3)

Fuel the Fire (Calloway Sisters #3)

Long Way Down (Calloway Sisters #4)

Some Kind of Perfect (Epilogue Novel)

A NOTE FROM THE AUTHORS

Long Way Down is the second book in Ryke & Daisy's point of view. However, you **must** read **Fuel the Fire (Calloway Sisters #3)** before reading **Long Way Down (Calloway Sisters #4)**.

A NOTE FROM THE AUTHORS: PART DEUX

Long Way Down—like most of our novels—is heavily character-driven. This is the longest book in the series and concludes the Addicted series & Calloway Sisters series arc. You could even say…that this is the end of an era. Before we start crying all over again, we'll leave you here and meet you one more time at the close. So take care, open your hearts, grab some tissues, and enjoy the ride, provided to you by Ryke Meadows & Daisy Calloway.

xoxo Krista & Becca

A NOTE FROM RYKE

Fuck off.

‹ Prologue ›

Ryke Meadows

The longest blonde hair caught the wind, splayed wildly and fucking madly. I watched her grip onto the railing of a wooden ramp, suspended midair towards a bungee jump. She rocked back and forth like she was squeezing in early morning pull-ups for the day.

She wasn't. Doing pull-ups for the fucking day, I meant.

She just couldn't stop moving.

And I kept thinking, *this girl is off her fucking hinges.*

We stood near the back of the bungee line, and as she peered over the railing again, she lifted her hips onto it, hanging her head further down.

Fucking A.

When everyone bailed on bungee jumping, all but Daisy, I didn't think she'd pretend to be a bird and crawl over the railing. I had no clue what sixteen-year-olds usually did, but for some fucking reason, I thought she would've complained about the long line or lack of cellphone reception.

I'd only known her for short spurts of time, and I was still trying to understand who she was at her core.

6:30 a.m. in the tropical climate of a foreign country.

My first real time alone with Daisy Calloway. Without her sisters or my brother present.

And my fucking issue: in the back of my mind, while I watched her hang headfirst, I thought, *that looks like fucking fun.*

And then, *any farther over that railing and I'm grabbing her.*

I rebounded between wanting to protect her and wanting to do crazy shit with her. I tried to block out whatever thoughts continued to churn, and I just went on impulse.

"What the fuck are you doing, Calloway?" I sidled next to her and rested my hand on her shoulder, but I didn't pull her down. I leaned my waist against the wooden barrier and saw the answer in her green eyes.

She perused the landscape, as though appreciating the expansive view of Cancun, Mexico. The current location of my college Spring Break. Even though Daisy wasn't in college, she tagged along to spend time with her older sisters, who were all happy by her presence.

Daisy tucked a flyaway strand of hair behind her ear. "They're missing out."

"They won't fucking think so." Most of them didn't want to wake up this early, and Lily was too scared of heights to even contemplate the idea.

The line moved forward. "You coming with me?" I asked her, raking a hand through my unkempt brown hair.

She finally met my eyes, something devious behind hers. "Do a lot of girls come with you?" she asked.

My expression stayed in the same fucking darkened state. "If I'm with them," I said vaguely, treading the line between the sexual innuendo and the safer space.

Daisy set her feet on the ramp, and despite her flirty fucking question, there was true intrigue behind her eyes and some confusion that I couldn't read past. "So you've never had a girl not come with you?"

My head pounded, and I rubbed my lips. "Move, Daisy."

I was twenty-two.

She was sixteen.

I would've never—in a fucking million years—taken advantage of Daisy, but I always had a hard time shutting my mouth when someone asked me for advice in so many words, in so many fucking ways. This wouldn't have been the first time I talked to her about sex, but I worried that she would've started relating these conversations to me and concluded that I thought about her in a sexual way.

Daisy skipped up the ramp while she walked two of her fingers along the railing. "I was just curious." She glanced at me with a sincere apology on her face. "Sorry."

"You don't have to fucking apologize for asking me something."

We stopped again, the line at a standstill. Her hair flew in every direction, and she tilted her head, like she struggled to rephrase her first question. Daisy's expression could be summed up as pained confusion, and in my very fucking core, I wanted to help her. I just hoped I could.

"What's eating at you?" I asked.

"Mosquitos." She wafted invisible bugs. She always tried to lighten the mood when she felt it going sour by her own hand.

My jaw hardened. "What's fucking *bothering* you?" I didn't fucking care about whether or not the air tensed or discomfort passed between us. I just cared about her.

"Nothing." *It's not nothing.*

I rubbed my eyes in annoyance. "Daisy—"

"It's not a big deal." She wore that uncertainty again.

"Yeah? Why do you look like you need to throw up?"

She crossed her arms in a very Rose Calloway fucking manner. "You're so pushy. You know that, right?" She'd reminded me of that before. "Are you like this with everyone?"

Only people I care about. "Look, I'm going to annoy the fuck out of you like you're annoying me right now, so you might as well do us both the favor and give it to me, Calloway." I waved her on.

Her lips lifted a fraction. "Do you want it hard or soft?"

"Hard as you want to fucking go."

A gust of wind whipped her hair in her face, blonde strands sticking to her mouth. She looked frustrated by her waist-length hair, and so I helped comb it back so she could see. She grunted in irritation at the tangled mess.

"Give me." I gestured to her hair tie.

She snapped it off her wrist, and I collected her fucking hair, putting it in the messiest bun. She said *thanks* and sighed in relief before I even finished.

I stepped back one foot. "You asked me if I've ever had a girl *not* come with me. Why does that fucking matter to you?"

"It's not about you personally," she said quickly.

"I never thought it was."

Her brows scrunched, her expression fucking killing me. "I just wondered," she began, "if maybe there's something wrong with me." She took a long pause.

My jaw locked. *Nothing's fucking wrong with you,* the words sat like a pit in my throat.

"Or maybe," she continued, "...maybe there's something wrong with the guys I've been with." She then hiked herself on the railing, sitting and swinging her legs.

At six-three, my head was still higher than hers, so I stared down while she looked up at me. I would've sat next to her, but I wanted to meet her eyes.

"Some girls are hard to get off," I told her. "Some guys are fucking terrible at pleasing women. You're not going to know which category you fall into, sweetheart. Not until you find someone that you're fucking attracted to."

She nodded a few times, looking crestfallen and incredibly fucking sad. When she sensed me staring, she gave me an *I'm okay* smile that I didn't believe.

There was nothing I could do to fix how she felt, and that was the hardest part of the entire thing.

"Have you been bungee jumping before?" she asked, changing the topic so I'd stop worrying.

"A few fucking times. What about you?"

"Mostly at theme parks." Daisy skimmed my features, her green eyes flitting over the carabiners on the belt loops of my jeans, rising up my green crew-neck to my unshaven jaw, hardened gaze, and thick, dark brown hair.

She wasn't discreet about the once-over, but she wasn't exactly being suggestive either. Just fucking curious.

She hopped back on the ramp, and we walked up the shortened line, tension winding between us.

"Can you say no?" I asked her suddenly.

She nodded and knotted the bottom of her loose fitting white shirt, a neon-green bikini beneath. No shorts.

"What if I was just some guy and I tried to pull down your bathing suit, what would you fucking do?"

Daisy shrugged. "I don't know—a lot of factors would have to go into it, I think."

"It's not a fucking trick question," I retorted, pissed—not at her. I was pissed because I knew what made her think like that. She'd started modeling at fourteen. She'd been touched and manhandled and told to get dressed in front of people, treated like absolute fucking shit. I'd heard snippets of stories from her sisters, and their mom was forcing her to stand still when all this girl wanted to do was run.

Right now, she could barely even keep two feet in one place.

"Why does it matter to you?" she asked me what I'd asked her.

I shook my head, thinking about how much my mom silenced me, and it'd taken me a long time to find my voice. I wouldn't have wanted that rough road for anyone, but I started seeing pieces of my life inside of hers. And why the fuck were we the only two people here?

Why the fuck did I bungee alone all three other times in my life?

My head hammered again. *I care about you. I want you to be safe. Please don't fuck anyone that makes you uncomfortable. It's going to kill me if it kills you.*

Every word bled into my brain, but I fought myself from saying them out loud. I just kept shaking my head.

I rubbed my jaw and then noticed two twenty-something guys ahead of us. Staring at her ass. I ended up moving forward in the line. In front of her. I blocked them from view, and she spun around to face me once more.

She began to smile, understanding what I just did.

It was a better fucking smile. I liked those because I knew she was doing okay.

And then abruptly, I said, "You can ask me anything." The phrase was weighted. *Ask me anything.* I rarely shared personal facts with people. I barely opened up to my own brother beyond the subject of addiction. And I was letting her ask me anything.

If I dug deep enough, I would've realized that I wanted her to know me.

I felt so fucking compelled to strip a layer away, and I'd never been drawn to do it. I had no idea why. I didn't stand there and list out reasons on a diagram or chart like Connor Cobalt would've. I just followed my gut this time.

My stomach tightened as I waited for her to speak.

She wore confusion again. "I don't know what to ask."

Realization hit me in a second or two. She was still afraid of offending me or hurting my feelings if she asked the wrong thing.

We moved up the line again, and I said, "Maybe next time, Calloway."

"Didn't you hear?" She wagged her brows at me. "I may not be here tomorrow. Life could take me at any moment and then *poof* you'd be here again with another girl, in another time and asking her to ask you anything." She said theatrically, "The unexpectedness of it all."

My gaze darkened and muscles bound. "That's not fucking funny, sweetheart."

"You'd call her sweetheart too." Sadness lingered behind her fleeting smile. I saw it before. Flickering inside of her. Like she would've been alright with dying. Like she was searching for something more that kept slipping out of grasp.

I rushed to say the first thing in my fucking head. To make her feel better. To fix *this*. Something I doubted could be changed by my hand. *Light is dimming behind your eyes; do you fucking see that, Daisy?*

So I said the truth. "You know, you're the only girl I've ever called that."

I didn't tell her that it was the first term of endearment I'd ever used with anyone. I found *baby* and other pet names too fucking patronizing, but "sweetheart" fit Daisy completely and in a sort of nonromantic context. I would've never said it condescendingly or backhandedly. Always just kindly. How it should be used.

Her lips almost pulled up. "You think I'm sweet?"

"I think you're out of your fucking mind. And I'm going out of mine." At that, I focused on the line, but I felt her smiling fully beside me.

Good.

Only two guys were ahead of us, already harnessed and on the platform. About to take their turn. An employee reached us and asked, "Are you jumping together or separate?"

Daisy nudged my waist and joked, "If you're scared, I can jump with you. Lily said I'm a pretty good hand-holder."

I thought about everything she'd been telling me along the ramp, and this underlying function inside of me said, *don't leave her alone.*

"We're jumping together," I told the employee.

Daisy's lips parted in shock. There was no way she could believe I was scared, and if she did, I didn't honestly care. After her surprise wore off, she rolled with the new plan.

The employee gave us instructions and helped Daisy with her harness. Maybe because I had carabiners on my belt loop or because I looked like I knew what I was fucking doing—he never hovered over me.

In the passing minute, Daisy and I repeatedly glanced at each other. I watched her smile gain more life, which actually pulled my lips upward too.

Over the screaming of guys who just jumped, Daisy retied her hair into a pony, and I wondered what she was thinking. If she was *overthinking* what I just fucking did.

I decided to be blunt since I requested to bungee tandem with her. "You know that I don't like you like that, Dais." The words were fucking static and actually hard to produce.

I thought it might hurt her, but she just gave me a knowing look—like she understood more than I gave her credit for. To lighten the mood, she said, "It's okay; you can admit it."

"What am I admitting?!" I had to raise my voice over the next guy's fucking screams.

We were ushered to the empty platform at that point, and two employees checked our harnesses, attaching more straps to our legs and clipping me to her. Face-to-face. They locked us together with another carabiner on our waists.

"That you're scared." She motioned to the descent, a playful look in her eyes.

"Cute."

"Cute because it's accurate." She wagged her brows again.

"Cute because it's fucking inaccurate." My hand slid to the back of her head, and I felt her body react in a way that surprised her. I drew

❋⋎ ⸹ ⋏❋

back only a fraction, my lips close to her ear. I whispered, "I'm not fucking scared of you." If she wanted to dive headfirst, I was going to dive right behind her.

She knew that was true.

She inhaled deeply, her chest rising against mine.

When the employees finished tethering us together, they instructed, "Hold onto each other. The tighter, the better, so your limbs won't smack into hers."

I wrapped my arms firmly around her shoulders, not hesitant about it. Hers slipped around my waist, not cautious either. Her heartbeat thudded against my chest. Racing with each passing second.

With Cancun as our landscape, we hugged each other in the sky. She rose and dropped on her tiptoes in crazed anticipation. I watched her focus descend, contemplating the distance between her feet and the ground.

So I pointed at the sun ascending in the horizon. Just as the darkened sky began to lighten. "Keep your eyes there."

Her green ones flickered to me before following my finger. Her pulse picked up speed. "And what happens when it disappears?"

I would've loved to tell her that it never would. That no matter where we were the sun would always be present. But it wouldn't have been true.

The only thing we could count on was that the sun would rise again.

"Wait for it to return," I told her.

She gave me the saddest smile I'd ever fucking seen. "That's an awfully long time."

For some people, I knew a minute could seem like infinity. So maybe one night seemed like forever for Daisy.

"Hey, Calloway," I said softly, tucking a flyaway strand of hair behind her ear, one that escaped her pony.

"Hey," she whispered back.

"You ready to feel your fucking heart burst out of your chest?"

Her features illuminated tenfold. And she said quietly, "Yes."

I barely heard the instructor tell us to jump before we both charged off the platform together. Our bodies pressed close, my chest against hers, hers against mine. We sliced through air, and she hollered fucking happily. Like she was in the front seat of a rollercoaster.

She laughed.

I smiled. *Fuck*—I was really smiling.

I never bungee jumped with another person, and doing it with Daisy had suddenly beat every fucking time I did it alone. As we slowed— hanging upside-down, spinning some—we met each other's gaze.

She wore this honest smile that I hated to see leave. "Thank you," she panted, out of breath from excitement and adrenaline.

"For what?"

"For doing this with me," she said, "so I didn't have to be alone."

It was then. That I fucking knew how much I really understood her. How much I related to the loneliness in her eyes. I felt closer to her in a way that I couldn't articulate. It wasn't physical. Or mental. It was spiritual, something I couldn't shake.

I nodded a couple times, and she practically radiated. As though she felt the air shift, brighter and lighter.

I felt it too.

And I fucking thought, *thank God.*

Thank God the sun will rise again.

FOUR YEARS LATER

< 1 >

Ryke Meadows

I've scaled mountains with my bare hands, no harness or rope. I've sped down freeways at over a hundred miles per hour. I once dove off a forty-foot cliff, swam with sharks, jumped out of a fucking plane, whitewater rafted class five rapids, ran an ultra-marathon in a remote Chilean desert, and some months ago, I underwent transplant surgery.

All of those moments combined are easy compared to what's happening now. I rock on the balls of my feet—for *fuck's sake*, I can't remember the last time I rocked on my feet.

I stop and run my hand through my hair for the millionth time. I scan the backyard as the sun falls behind spruce trees. The pool is empty, only water wings floating on the surface. *Water wings*—I'm used to seeing these things everywhere.

It happens when I'm living with my brother, his wife, and their one-year-old baby. Though lately, seeing high chairs, diapers, stuffed toys, and rattles sends my mind into a fucking tailspin. I exhale and wipe my forehead with the end of my gray T-shirt, restraining the urge to jump in the pool and cool down from the August heat.

The glass door opens, and I look over my shoulder. My little brother and Connor stroll through with these really fucking annoying smiles. My blood pumps harder in my veins.

"Shut the fuck up," I tell them.

Connor's grin pulls wider, stretched so far that I think it should tear his face apart. It doesn't. He's still good looking. *Fuck him.* And he says, "Shutting up would require talking."

"You are now." I have my hands on my head. I'm really close to pacing, and I don't pace either. Rose paces. Loren paces. Lily sometimes even fucking paces.

I don't pace...do I?

I'm losing my mind.

Lo places a hand on Connor's shoulder, cutting in before he responds. "Let's not make this into a lecture. He already looks like shit."

Fucking A.

"Should I shave?" I ask, running a hand down my jaw. I usually trim more, especially in the summer, but I've kept the scruffy, *I've-been-outdoors* look since March.

"You could start with that," Connor says, his shit-eating grin blinding me. He stuffs his fists in his khaki shorts. "The hair needs some work too." His blue eyes flit to my unkempt brown hair, the thick strands just doing their natural fucking thing.

When I don't argue with Connor but instead rake another hand through my hair—attempting to flatten the strands—his composure shifts.

He arches a brow. "You look like yourself. Just leave it alone."

"So you're saying I always look like shit?" I flatten the longer pieces over my forehead. I don't even know what the fuck I'm doing.

"Yes," he says easily. "And stop touching it."

Lo scrunches his face at the bangs I just created. "Who are you? And where have you taken my brother?"

I don't have a fucking answer.

Connor approaches me, confidence in every deliberate step. When he's inches away, eye-level with me, I piece together his plan.

He's still grinning as he says, "Don't bite me."

"Don't give me a fucking reason to."

Without hesitating, he starts fixing my hair. I cross my arms over my chest. The last time I was *this* close to Connor Cobalt, I punched him in the face. It was as complicated back then as this is now. I don't hate the guy, but never in a million fucked-up years did I think I'd let him play with my hair.

"Jesus," Lo says, laughing. "Please let me record this."

"If you want a fist to your face," I mutter.

Connor is practically gloating. I'm seconds from shoving his chest, but he wouldn't purposefully make me look worse—not today. Not for this. We may not always seem like friends, but we are. We're probably better friends than most.

And why do I even care this much about *hair?*

Loren cocks his head at me, his arrowhead necklace against his black V-neck shirt. "I'm your brother," he says dryly. "You wouldn't hit me." He flashes a sardonic smile. His lightheartedness lives somewhere beneath all of that edge.

And yeah, I have hit him. In the dead heat. In the Utah desert. Until red dust covered us both in exhaustion and fury. All that's in the past, along with any bad blood between us.

He just says shit to say shit.

Connor touches the longer hair by my forehead, and I push him off now. He barely sways. Instead, he purposefully takes a single step back.

"Just leave it," I tell him. Then I comb my hand through my hair without realizing. Fucking fantastic.

Connor arches another brow at me. "You're a lost cause. I don't know why I even try."

I flip him off and just do my natural hair thing. Messy. Disheveled. No system or order. I know I look more like myself, but this day has me disoriented, more than I've ever fucking been.

With a dissatisfied once-over, Connor gestures to my clothes: jeans, a plain gray tee, and a waterproof watch. "Your attire needs work."

"I'm not going on a date with you, Cobalt."

"Of course you're not. I have high standards. Ones that you can't meet."

I shake my head at him a couple times and then I jump a little on my feet, shake out my hands, and crack my knuckles. I just struggle with letting things out, verbally, and if I ever need to do it *right*, I'd want to do it today.

"You need a drink?" Lo sinks down onto a patio chair, his forearms resting on his kneecaps. "It'd help those nerves."

I meet his amber eyes, and he gives me another half-smile to show that he's kidding. I never find the humor in these jokes, and maybe that's why he keeps it up. Anyway, I've grown used to this fucking nonchalant offer of alcohol, and I've never seen him as healthy as he's been in the past year.

If we flashed back to Paris at that bar, I think the Loren Hale today would shake himself for taking a drink and giving me one. In fact, I know he would.

If that's not strength, then I don't fucking know what is.

"Is that a yes?" Lo banters.

"Fuck off."

Connor chimes in, "Fifty-two *fucks* in twenty minutes. Just so you know how redundant your vocabulary is."

My phone vibrates, saving me from talking to Connor. I slide my cell out of my pocket and check the text.

Lunch tomorrow? — Dad

My stomach overturns, and I quickly text back: no.

I let out a tense breath. "This is a fucking sign." I hold up the phone to show Connor and Lo the message. "He texts right now? It's not a good time—"

"Since when do you buy into superstition?" Connor asks me in one of his annoyingly calm voices.

"Yeah, you sound like Rose." Lo doesn't even focus on the text. His eyes are right on me, and I see more sincerity in them. Something that says, *don't be afraid.*

I'm afraid of watching the people I love get hurt. I'm afraid of hurting the people I love. Sometimes I feel like no matter what I do, I'm going to fall into one of the two.

I end up shrugging and then pointing at both of them. "You know what? I'm going inside. You two can fucking stay out here."

I step over Moffy's plastic Batman car, a toy that Lo complained about for a good week before conceding. Lo's love for Marvel was finally trumped by his son's love for a DC toy.

I hear Lo speaking *loudly* as I slide open the door. "You think we hurt his feelings?" *Asshole.* Even as I think it, I nearly smile. I love my little brother. Truth is, I thought we'd kill each other by living together, but it's brought us even closer in the past year and a half. He's also a lot less aggravating to live with than Connor Cobalt.

I wasn't that upset to see Connor move down the street. It mostly sucks in early mornings when I'm in the gym. Connor used to spot me since Lo doesn't wake up that early.

Do I miss him nagging me for information about Daisy's therapy sessions? No. Do I miss him quizzing me about literature and languages? No. Do I miss his constant need to make everything a fucking cock show? Absolutely-fucking-not.

But yeah…sometimes I miss that motherfucker.

Not today though.

I shut the sliding door. The sun has already disappeared outside.

< **2** >

Daisy Calloway

I pack double fudge ice cream onto a sugar cone. Three scoops. It melts a little and drips down my knuckles onto the hardwood. While I suck it off my hand, my white Siberian husky perks up from her curled position, nestled beside the cupboards.

Uh-oh.

She excitedly nears the droplets of chocolate and tries to lap them up with her tongue.

"Coconut, no." I squat down and push her back a little. "I know it's a *horrible* fact—gruesome really—but chocolate is toxic for dogs." She stares at me with a blank look. "I can tell you're taking this hard." I insensitively lick my ice cream cone, but it's melting fast. "I bet in dog heaven you can have all the chocolate you want." I add, "But don't think about leaving me that quickly, okay?" I scratch behind her ears with my clean hand.

She sits down in obedience and delight, nudging her head closer to my palm to keep going. I love her a lot, maybe because her temperament is a mixture of sweet, nurturing, and fearless. I wish I could be all of those one day, without compromise or hesitation.

I go still and listen to the growing sound of footsteps, but I don't jump or panic at the noise. Partly because of Coconut's presence—but mostly because I believe in this moment that no one can hurt me.

I just rise to my feet, and Ryke Meadows emerges into the kitchen. I haven't seen him all day, which isn't unusual. Some weeks we're together twenty-four-seven and others we're doing our own thing, staying in communication by text and phone calls.

Earlier I went shopping and out to dinner with Lily, Willow, and Rose, and they're all back at Rose's house down the street. It's hard for me to be around my sisters' babies so much lately, and since both Jane and Moffy are there, I just left.

I think they knew I would anyway.

Ryke passes the bar counter and nears me.

Six-foot-three with a darkened gaze, scruffy jaw, and brooding brows—he's utterly handsome. The kind of handsome that screams *danger*, yet I know his heart is soft and warm and a place I always want to be.

We don't speak.

We just look at each other, the silence spinning tension in my core. I smile as I lick the ice cream, and I watch him watch me, his gaze descending to my long bare legs, to my banana-print bikini bottoms, to my navy tee that says *Adios Pantalones*, and up to *his* blue baseball cap, turned backwards on my head. My tangled, naturally brown hair is let loose, stopping in layers at my chest.

When his eyes finally lock on mine, I pretend to appear perplexed. "I don't think we've met before."

He almost smiles, which makes mine grow wider before I take another taste of ice cream.

"Are you fucking sure?" He steps closer, only a few feet apart. "Because I have a girlfriend who looks a hell of a lot like you."

I tilt my head, feigning confusion. I sweep his body with one long glance. "You know, it's not clicking for me." I playfully lift up the corner of his gray T-shirt and inspect his abs, a six-pack that's basically an eight-pack if I'm being technical. His hard gaze bores into me, as though fastened on any inner-beauty I possess.

An electric current zips up my arms to my neck, the tiny hairs rising.

"What about now?" he asks huskily. His deep, gruff voice nearly melts me. I drop the corner of his shirt.

"My boyfriend has a ten-pack," I reply, trying to hold my seductive composure but I'm close to laughing.

His brows rise. "Oh really?"

"Yep," I tease.

"That sounds fucking impossible."

I mock gasp. "Are you making fun of my boyfriend?"

He swiftly pushes my hand at my face, and the cold ice cream smashes against my lips and nose.

I immediately laugh, my smile widening. "You must be him," I determine. "Ryke Meadows would totally do that." I try to lick my nose, but my tongue won't reach.

He nears me even more, his feet right beside mine, his chest pressed against me. My breath shallows. And he says, "Would he do this?" He kisses my nose, licking the chocolate, and then he sucks my bottom lip, the force winding an ache inside of me.

I kiss back just as strongly, and we collide into each other like we haven't made out in ages. His hand rises up the small of my back; my free one clutches his thick, disheveled hair. *God, I love his hair.* I keep the ice cream extended so it doesn't smash between our bodies.

My pelvis eagerly curves towards him, and his hand falls down to my ass, my thigh, hoisting my leg around his waist. Our lips never part, and we hungrily attack with an animalistic, carnal desire that seeps into my veins. I explore him with my hand, running my palm across his unshaven jaw, his shoulders—down his biceps.

He lifts my other leg and then pins me against the counter. A high-pitched noise breaches my throat in one breath, and his chest rises and falls heavily. My head rocks back for air, and I take a moment to catch my breath while his eyes flit across my features. Mine dance along his.

"Hi," I murmur.

"Hi," he says and then effortlessly lifts me higher, securing me against him, my body bouncing with the abrupt movement. Then he carries me out of the kitchen. I wrap my legs tightly around his waist and beam in curiosity. The thrill of the unknown place and destination excites me, but not nearly as much as being this close to the man I love.

I peek over my shoulder. We're headed towards the backyard. When I turn to Ryke, I catch sight of a smile that lifts the corners of his lips. It's a beautiful sight, even if it's momentary.

I bring my ice cream cone to my mouth and lick the side. Then I hold it closer to him. With his hands beneath my ass, he takes a bite of the cone and chocolate.

He raises his brows at me and then he swallows. "That's too fucking sweet."

"That's why it's the best tasting thing in the entire world."

He takes one hand off me and opens the door, the outside already dark. "I know someone who tastes better."

I grin wide, a pulse thrumming inside of me. I want to tease him, but he sets me on my feet.

He leans his head down and takes another bite of my overly sweet ice cream and crunchy cone. I finish it off and then wipe the sticky residue with the bottom of my shirt while he guides me around the pool, his hand on my head. The water looks black without any backyard lamps on. Stars blanket the sky, but the house windows behind us are the best source of light.

"We should go night swimming later," I say as though the act is entirely daring and dangerous, even if it's not. I lick my sticky fingers. "We can play sharks and minnows."

He just kisses the top of my head and then he opens the black iron-gate. This is when I realize we're leaving the pool area and heading towards the woods. I hesitate, and he clasps my hand, watching me carefully. It's not like I've never been in the backyard woods before. It's just that we rarely go out at night, at least not without a flashlight.

I glance back at the house for Coconut. She's sitting patiently by the glass door, eyes on me.

"I can go get her," Ryke says. He's not put off by the idea of bringing her along on our mysterious adventure.

I bite my lip in thought and look between Ryke and our husky. I trust Ryke more than any other person, and while Coconut is extra security, I don't want to rely on her all the time. I'd rather her be more of a friend than a lifeline.

I squeeze his hand. "I'm fine."

His eyes flicker to the darkened woods, filled with pine and spruce trees. I can't really read his expression, but it's like his thoughts are churning hard. "We can go back inside if you—"

"No." I refuse this option and then tug him forward. "Let's go. An adventure awaits."

He easily catches up to my side and then wraps his arm around my shoulders. The grass is damp from the sprinklers, and in the dark, I can barely make out the tree line where the woods begin.

I step on something…strange. I stop and nudge it with my foot. A cord? "I stepped on something," I tell him.

Ryke bends down. "Hold on."

I wait.

And then, suddenly, dangling bulbs illuminate. *What.*

Rounder and bigger than Christmas lights.

Dozens of them. All at once.

My lips part. They're strung horizontally along trunks, creating a bright pathway into the thicket of trees. Leading somewhere.

I lose my voice to the beautiful atmosphere, like something from a fairytale. Lightning bugs even blink in and out tonight. I notice the orange extension cord beneath my feet, extending back into the pool area. The switchbox is beside Ryke's boots.

He stands and gauges my reaction.

I'm stunned to silence. I wouldn't consider Ryke a romantic Scrooge. He sweeps me off my feet in his own way, packing picnic lunches, riding to the mountains for the weekend. Taking an early morning dip in a hot spring. Making love on the roof.

It's all very romantic to me, but this is on another level. This took major planning and time. It's not my birthday. It's not Valentine's Day. But I have been sad lately, and Ryke would put in more effort if he thought it'd cheer me up.

Mission success. I practically float forward in wonderment, my body and spirit weightless and airy. I glance at him again. "Where does it lead?"

He takes off my baseball hat and messes my hair with affection. "I'll show you." He sets my hat back, and then he guides me straight ahead. "Be fucking careful where you step."

I forgot to put on shoes, and he curses beneath his breath, pissed that he didn't remember this detail. He even looks back at the house.

"I don't need shoes. It's mainly pine needles." He's really trying tonight. I attempt to peer forward as we follow the lit path, weaving between trees. I contemplate running ahead and having him run after me, but he seems more nervous than usual, his fingers constantly combing through his hair.

Maybe he's really aroused, and he's worried that I won't be tonight. "I want to have sex," I tell him bluntly. I do want to, not just to please him but because the kitchen make out session ended quickly and my blood is still pumping.

His brows scrunch, caught off guard. It takes him a second to regroup, and he asks what he always does, "For me or for you?" *For me* is the right answer.

I've been known to try to please him when I'm not feeling it as much, my sex drive never as high as his. The problem: Ryke is really turned off if I'm not receiving pleasure, or at least on my way to being aroused.

It's just difficult sometimes to reach that place, but I know he'd rather not have sex if I'm not into it. I love that he cares so much about what I feel.

"For both of us," I say truthfully.

He searches my eyes for a second and then nods. I get the sense that he wasn't even thinking about sex until I brought it up. He kisses my cheek, the one with the long scar, and then we step into a circular clearing, the bulbs forming a border around the outside trees.

I can't miss what lies in the middle. Pink rose petals strewn over feather-light bedding: a white comforter with white fluffy pillows. All raised off the ground like an air mattress rests beneath.

I detach from Ryke, nearing it in a daze. A box of expensive chocolates sits right beside binoculars. I look up, the stars twinkling, perfectly clear.

I inhale the fresh, crisp air, crickets chirruping in the distance. It's magical. "You did all this yourself?" I wonder, still scanning the lights and chocolates.

"I had help."

He had help. My sisters, I realize. Lo and Connor. They were all in on this. I think…maybe, I'm beginning to have an idea why now. Why today.

I slowly turn to face Ryke. I detect the earnestness in his gaze, in his opened stance, and our pasts seem to rise from the grave. Two people who weren't allowed to love each other. Two people who now unapologetically do.

He walks towards me, my heart racing with his lengthy stride. I watch his hand disappear into his pocket, and I can't speak, a soulful force tugging locked parts of me.

For a rare moment, I am utterly still.

"I've been alone for most of my life," Ryke starts. I hang on every word. He's almost twenty-seven. I can see the hard, lonely years behind his eyes, but he never wears exhaustion. Ryke belongs with nature, able to withstand the seasons and time just like the rocks he climbs. He keeps going, he keeps moving, and he picks everyone up when they've fallen behind.

It's this unyielding strength that I *feel* now, drawing us closer.

"And then I met you," he says huskily. He holds my face with his large, calloused hand. *I really love those hands.* He pauses to gather his thoughts, and the longer he takes, the more my eyes begin to well.

"I made your life crazy," I whisper.

He nods like it's a good thing. "Yeah, Dais. You made it fucking crazy, and I've been so crazy in love with you." He breathes deeply with me. Every time he pauses, our gazes roam each other, saying just as much in silence as we do in words.

His fingers brush through the side of my hair, skimming my ear. He removes my baseball cap again, this time stuffing it in his back pocket.

"In college," he says, "I used to want weeks to myself. I used to just fucking check out and leave."

My lips lift, remembering him telling me how he'd go climbing and turn off his cellphone for a few days, so no one from college bothered him. So he was mentally at peace, just for a while anyway.

He grew up relying on himself. He grew up in solitude. Being around people, constantly, gave him a headache back then. I can understand wanting to be away from all the noise. Modeling was like that for me. I just wanted out, to stop. And breathe.

After another moment, I can tell he's gathered his thoughts, focused and assured. I rise on the tips of my toes, like I can reach his voice, like I can meet his love head-on.

"I go two days without seeing you, Dais, and it fucking kills me. I never thought I'd love someone this way." His hard eyes almost soften. "I never thought I could, but you've made me *love* my life more than I ever fucking have. I can't even imagine spending the rest without you."

I'm filled with earth-shattering sentiments that vibrate my bones, my legs weak but my body weightless.

He removes his hand from his jeans, revealing a black box. And I suddenly worry—I clasp my hands around his.

"Wait," I say, my stomach in knots.

Ryke pales, more than I've ever seen from him. He's frozen cold, and a pain already twists in my core, burrowing through me. I never want to be the one that hurts him, but I also can't bar him from a fulfilled life either.

"You want a family," I remind Ryke. My voice breaks at *family*. I blink once, and the suppressed tears slide down my cheeks. Hot trails, dripping off my jaw and chin.

His features toughen, making sense of why I stopped him now. "Don't, Daisy."

"I may not be able to give you that—"

"It *doesn't* fucking matter," he says passionately.

I swallow a lump in my throat, recalling what the doctors said about the cysts on my ovaries. How my chances for children are slim. How I could start trying, the sooner the better, but it's a bumpy road that might end without success or hope.

"You need to be sure," I say quickly. "You *have* to be sure. We can always wait, to see if I can have a kid first. You don't have to commit in case I can't."

I want to give him an out. I don't want to bind Ryke to me if later on he realizes that he wants *more*—more that I can't ever offer him. He deserves everything he's ever dreamed of, and I couldn't live knowing I prevented him from that.

He cups my face with both hands, tugging me closer to his body in a forceful, Ryke Meadows way that says *listen to me, sweetheart*. "I fucking love you." Tears build in his eyes. I'm crying more, and his thumb brushes my cheeks. "All I need is *you*."

I try to cover my face, used to shielding my emotions, but if anyone has ever seen them, it's been Ryke. He gently pulls my hands down, and he presses his forehead against mine. He hugs me tightly, his body warm and safe.

He says affectionately, "You're my family, Dais. And if it's only the two of us in the end, I'd be just as fucking happy."

When my tears drip again, they belong to a different place in my heart. I nod and then kiss him, inhaling his declaration. I grasp his hair, clinging to him, his strong-willed energy feeding into mine. He kisses back with just as much force and vigor.

I don't expose what originates deep inside of me. *I want babies in the future.* He knows I do. I know he does too. We've talked about it too many times to think differently.

I pull away first, my hands on either side of his face, his gaze diving straight into me. "I love you," I say with a tearful smile. "I love you so much."

He kisses me lightly, and as his lips travel to my ear, his unshaven jaw skims my cheek, tingling my senses. While wrapped in his arms, he murmurs deeply, "Will you fucking marry me?"

My smile widens. "Yes." There is no other answer in my heart than this one.

As he pulls back to see my expression, he wears a wide, full smile of his own. It's a rare sight, filling me with raw happiness. I welcome every ounce of these passing sentiments, in total bliss for this moment, for tonight.

No one jumps out of the bushes or from behind trees, and I'm really glad he didn't invite my parents or sisters and make it a spectacle. This belongs to us.

He opens the velvety black box and procures a delicate ring, not too large or too gaudy. I hold out my hand, shaking as he slides the gold band on my finger. It fits perfectly, and I bet that he confided in Rose about my size. As I hone in on the ring, I go quiet, stunned by the unique design. Rectangular diamonds form rays around a circular, yellow diamond.

It's the sun.

And I'm speechless all over again. I keep nodding like *this is perfect; this is really happening. I'm engaged to Ryke Meadows.*

He murmurs another "I love you" before kissing my cheek, then my lips. Mine swell beneath his. My body sings as his hands roam and settle on my hips, guiding me towards the fluffy comforter. My arms are draped around his neck, as though slow-dancing while he walks me backwards.

Our lips never break, his tongue tangled with mine in a natural rhythm. Everything with Ryke feels that way. *Natural.* And in the woods, I pretend that we're wild, primitive things. Alone in this world together.

I smile against his lips, and then he lifts me up by the waist and sets me in the middle of the bed.

He climbs on, our legs threaded, my blood hot and my hair in disarray. We stare at each other for a second, and I pulse simply by his intense gaze.

"I have this theory," I begin, and his smile returns.

"Let's hear it." He spreads my legs wide with his knees, and then he rests his palms on either side of my head. My wolf is staring down at me.

I prop myself on my elbows, nearing his face more. "Magical things happen in the woods." The first time I truly enjoyed sex was my first time with Ryke—and it happened in the woods. Now this. I know it's more about the person than the place, but I can't deny the primal energy that surrounds us, which shouts jubilantly, *we are alive!*

"I like it," he says, lifting up my shirt. He goes halfway, revealing the bottoms of my small boobs. He pauses and raises his brows at me. "What the fuck were you wearing, Calloway?"

I gape. "You don't like my bra?" I'm not wearing one, of course. His brother lives in the same house with us, but Ryke doesn't care if I go bra-less as long as I'm comfortable.

He almost smiles and then removes my shirt, the air nipping my skin. His lips warm my nipple, kissing then sucking. Gently.

I run my hands up the ridges of his abs and take off his shirt.

He massages my other breast, and the sensitive bud hardens beneath his tongue. My hamstrings constrict.

"Ryke...*ahhh.*" My cry turns into a sharp gasp. I hold onto his broad shoulders. While he pays attention to my nipples, he slides his jeans off, now only in black boxer-briefs. I kiss the base of his neck. A deep noise sticks to his throat, and then he hoists me in his strong arms.

He steps off the bed with me pressed against his chest, and before I make sense of anything, my back meets rough bark of a tree. My pelvis is lined with Ryke's. His hardness presses against my bikini bottoms.

I'm dizzy; my nerve endings alight. "Ryke," I moan his name, my voice needy, and my legs sway on either side of him, always in motion. Even if there's nowhere to go.

His hands are all over me. Mine are all over him, and his mouth trails my neck, my breastbone. His fingers slowly dip down my belly, diving beneath my bikini bottoms and to a bundle of nerves. As soon as he touches, I breathe rapidly, the build-up electrifying me whole.

I cry out, lips parted, and I buck into him. He digs into me, rocking as though we're making love now, even when two articles of clothing separate us. I slip my hand down his boxer-briefs, his toned ass flexing beneath my palm as he pushes forward.

Oh God. Oh God.

"Come on, sweetheart," he whispers, encouraging me to reach this peak and let go completely. I hope to feel it. I want to be soaked. I want him inside of me.

The way he touches me everywhere, the way the force of his body barrels into mine—it dizzies my head. I cry out again in pleasure.

"Ryke!" His fingers slip *deep* into me, his thumb still massaging my clit. Mixed with his rocking, I begin to lose my bearings. I moan into his shoulder, gripping his back. "Ryke..." My high-pitched noise turns breathy. I tremble against him, and he moves harder, bark grinding into my shoulders.

I raise my head in a daze, and he kisses me, his tongue slipping into my mouth the same time he thrusts forward. Sweat builds on us both, and I pulse and pulse.

I come alive.

As my back arches and my climax binds my legs, he frees his cock, stepping out of his boxer-briefs. He's rock hard. He knows exactly what he wants and how to please me. He's much older, my protector and my best friend. He's my future and my happiness.

He's everything that I wasn't sure he'd ever be, and I want him all, right now. Filling me. Loving me.

I begin to pull off my bottoms, but he finishes undressing me. He moves away from the tree, rubbing my shoulders. He gives me a single look that asks, *you okay?*

I nod at him and kiss his reddened lips. He kisses back. With his hands firmly on my hips—with my body still hoisted around his waist—he masterfully lowers me onto his erection. So slowly that I feel every inch fill me.

I moan halfway there, and he pauses, tormenting with his hardness. I look down, my hands tugging his hair. The image of him in me works its magic. I tense up, in the best way. My mouth opens and refuses to shut.

He uses his insane upper-body strength to keep me upright, and I descend further and further onto his shaft, watching him disappear inside of me. I shake my head a couple times, the sensations overwhelming. "I can't..."

I can't come again this fast. I can't. I can't. I can't...it's too—

"Ryke, Ryke...*ahhhh ohmygod,*" I burst with a breathy cry, tears squeezing out of the corners of my eyes.

"*Fuck*," he grunts. He holds back so this lasts much, much longer, and he bounces me on his cock, building me up *again*.

I struggle inhaling enough oxygen to my brain, light-headed and sublime. We end up back on the bed. He combs my hair out of my face, kisses me, and thrusts in a melodic, deep movement. "Fuck," he says beside my ear. "Dais…"

I love how this looks. Our naked bodies beneath the stars. My legs spread apart. Ryke between them. I love how this feels. Our pelvises grinding together, his hardness giving me pleasure. I love him most of all. His darkened, protective gaze. I latch onto him, my hips bucking up as he digs down, every inch gained between us.

He pulls me swiftly, until we're both upright. He does the work, pushing up into me while we kiss, and as I moan against his lips, I smile. He smiles too because this is *it*.

Bliss.

Happiness. I sense it all around me. For however fleeting it may be, I grasp it now. I hang on and I ride this moment out.

< 3 >

Ryke Meadows

Daisy rests her head on my chest, still for a brief moment, her long, bare legs tangled with mine beneath the white comforter. About two hours ago, I shut off the lights using a second switchbox near the air mattress—the stars more vivid without them.

We've been quiet for the last thirty minutes, but every time her eyelids attempt to shut, she snaps them open and glances over her shoulder at the pitch-black woods.

I keep one arm around her waist, hoping she'll let her mind doze off since she's fucking exhausted.

Then she shifts, propping her body on her forearm. "Do my parents—"

"They know," I tell her. "I asked them."

Her brows shoot up in surprise. "For permission?" She's about to sit up, but I seize her waist and pull her down, her back thudding to the air mattress. She grins as I quickly straddle her waist. I'm not planning to do anything to her, other than create the illusion that I am. *The danger*, I hear her gasp in my head.

I think she wants to stay awake for two reasons.

1. Tonight is a big fucking night, and she's the kind of girl who'd want it to last until morning.

2. She's scared of the dark.

Ever since she switched therapists, she's been a lot better, sleeping around six to seven hours a night. Camping is always harder for Daisy, the woods carrying erratic, odd noises. She's told me multiple times that she loves being outside too much to let fear push her away.

The goal is always sleep. Even the night we just became engaged.

I try to explain more of what happened with her parents. "At Janie's first birthday party, I asked them if they'd be okay if I married you." It was back in June. I've been trying to figure out *how* to fucking go about doing it. Lo said he thought it'd take me six more months to finally pick a day since I kept bailing at the last minute. I wasn't afraid that she'd say *no*. I wouldn't have asked her if I thought she didn't want to take this next step with me. We've both talked about it offhand and in depth, so I knew her feelings.

I was just fucking worried that it'd go wrong somehow—that something would ruin it, and I wanted this moment to be perfect for Daisy. I wish I could give her a million perfect fucking days.

She grins more, her legs rocking back and forth. "You asked them just like that? No *fucks* attached?"

My brows harden, having no clue whether I cursed or not. It slips out like any other word, and I barely notice when I say it. "That's what you're fucking concerned about?" I teasingly mess her hair.

She bites my wrist just as playfully and says, "It's the most important detail." She's restless, her hands continuously moving, and she places a strand of hair above her upper lip and quirks her brow.

She's really fucking cute.

Though I know my jaw is tense and my eyes dark, the opposite of how effervescent she is beneath me. "What about whether or not they said yes?" I ask.

I've never wanted to create animosity between Daisy and her parents. I've tried fucking hard to be accepted by her dad. He sees her as his youngest baby girl, and he saw me as a brute who has more or less defiled her—and it wasn't a good feeling for me. Not when I love her and would protect her from every fucking guy like that.

"Didn't you hear?" she smiles. "Lily said that I have special powers of the mind after I predicted the color of Moffy's eyes. So I already know that my parents said *yes*." She blows the strand off her upper lip.

I give her a look. "Almost everyone guessed that he'd have green eyes."

Daisy feigns shock. "So I'm not special? Because I thought I gave you a really special..." she trails off, unable to say the fucking word. She didn't give me a blow job, so I'm not sure where she's headed.

"Go on, Calloway. What was that?" I shift so I'm kneeling between her legs, pushing them open. We're both naked, and even though I really fucking love her small boobs, long legs, and round ass, I'll harden more by the sight of her infectious smile. The one that pulls the scar along her cheek.

She's too tired to have sex again, so I'm trying not to think with my cock, which wants to stay deep inside of her. I don't like making Daisy sore, but whenever we continuously fuck, there's no avoiding it. So that's also keeping me from pushing my erection between her bare thighs.

"Hmm?" She stares right up at me but plays dumb to keep our conversation alive.

"Hmm," I deadpan. "You gave me a really special..."

"Orgasm," she finishes in a silky voice. "A very special orgasm that defeated all the others." She reaches out and takes a chocolate from the opened package, eating it whole. It's cuter than anything, and I can't help but think—*I'm going to have this for fucking ever.*

I kiss her cheek and then shift onto my side, pulling her into my arms, she whispers in my ear about opossums in an episode of her favorite show, deflecting from whatever emotion she doesn't want me to see. I comb her damp hair back, her forehead perspiring from more than the sex we had.

She's fucking scared.

"Dais," I cut her off, and I have her so close, I can feel her heart pounding against my chest.

She tries to appease me with a small smile. "I'll be okay, really." Her foot runs up and down my leg, mostly antsy. She peeks over my shoulder, her face falling, and then she tucks her head closer to my chest.

"What do you need from me?" I ask, my fingers lost in her hair by her temple.

Daisy whispers, "Can you keep talking?" I strain my ears to pick up her next words. "I hear something out there."

I don't want to discredit her fear and tell her that she's crazy for hearing noises that aren't really there. They probably do exist, on some fucking level, but her mind is making her believe it's worse than it is. That it's not an animal—a deer or a squirrel—but a person.

"Close your eyes first," I tell her.

She takes a deep breath before shutting them, her hands sliding from my shoulders, to my arms, back up to my shoulders. I press her more to me, and she nuzzles her head into my chest again.

If I tell her an interesting story, she'll force herself awake, so I end up talking about climbing techniques: the importance of balancing weight between your entire body, footholds as vital as your core and arm strength; when blood flow is restricted, a fucking pump sensation circulates to the fingers and forearms (a build-up of lactic acid), and I go in detail about how to get rid of it while climbing—using G-Tox (gravity) and a shake out method.

I actually think I've bored her to fucking sleep, and I take a short second to scan the woods.

She jolts against my body, her eyes snapping open. "Did you hear that?" She immediately sits up before I can ease her back. The comforter falls to her waist.

I'm about to say something, but she grabs my arm. "Shhh," she says in panic.

Fuck. I immediately reach over Daisy to her side of the bed and grab a black hard-shell case.

"Ryke," she says. "Do you hear that?"

I've been hearing the same thing. "It sounds like a fucking animal to me." I open the case. "Dais, look at me."

Her widened eyes barely blink, and her face pales in dread.

"Daisy, *look at me.*" I'm about to hold her jaw, but she finally tears her gaze away from the woods.

She whispers in a shaky voice, "I think something's out there."

I take out my Glock and load the gun. It's more for her peace of mind than for whatever animals lurk in the dark. "Do you see this?"

She nods, inhaling a short breath.

"I'm not going to let anything fucking touch you. Okay?"

She nods again, eyes welling. "I'm sorry—"

"Hey." I kiss her cheek and then whisper in her ear, "You have nothing to be sorry ab—"

The lights turn on.

All the ones strung around us, the ones that lead a trail from the house to where we sit—I didn't touch the switchbox by our side. Which means someone touched it by the house.

Daisy's collarbones jut out, struggling for breath.

I touch her cheek with one hand. "Dais, breathe. You're okay. You're fucking safe." It physically pains me to leave her side, but I'm starting to believe someone is out there. I can't just fucking sit here. I pull the comforter up to her neck. "Hide for me?"

She shakes her head. "…I can't…" She's going to have a full-blown panic attack, and I'm fucking pissed at myself for not bringing our husky along, a PTSD dog trained to calm Daisy down.

"Then hold onto this," I instruct.

Her grip tightens around the blanket, clutching it like a safety net. I climb off the bed buck-naked and grab my boxer-briefs, putting them on quickly. I listen to the crunch of pine needles. With the Glock taut in my hand, I step forward, about fifteen feet in front of Daisy.

I distinguish a shadowy figure, moving at a moderate pace. I extend my arm, gun pointed at the person, blood rushing through me. "HEY!" I yell, fury overtaking any kind of minimal fear. I'm fucking *livid*. Fuming in place.

My jaw hardens, my stance closed and lungs ready to explode. And then I recognize the person in the light.

You've got to be fucking kidding me.

I boil over, and my fingers nearly *push* the trigger.

< *4* >

Ryke Meadows

He stops about twenty feet away, not even attempting to raise his hands in surrender. He has them casually stuffed in the pockets of his black slacks. It's ballsy because right now a huge part of me wants to blow out his fucking kneecaps. The only reason he gets a pass is because I don't want to explain to my brother why I crippled our dad.

"What *the fuck* are you doing here?" My jaw aches from clenching my teeth. I check on Daisy with a quick glance. She breathes more normally, her face less flushed, and she has the comforter wrapped around her body. Reminding me that she's naked. I'm practically fucking naked. We just had sex.

I just proposed to her.

And here's my dad. The one person who I can't stand to look at right now.

His hair is graying by his temples, and he has a light layer of stubble, his eyes constantly narrowed and his face set in severe, strict lines.

"No one was answering the door, so I went around back," he explains in a sharp voice, like *I'm* to fucking blame. "I saw the power cord, turned it on, here I am." His tone is almost bored now. He gestures to me and then the lights. "Do you really think I expected to walk in on this?" He leans sideways to gain a better view of Daisy. He glances between her, me, then the lights, the bed, the pink rose petals, back to me. "I can't say I've ever interrupted someone fucking in the woods."

"What do you want?" It takes all my fucking energy, but I drop my arm. I can't shoot him, no matter how much I see my dad like a poison.

He doesn't break his eyes from me. "I came for your advice, but seeing as how there are two girls waiting at your doorstep, I think that's more of concern."

I shake my head, confused. "What the fuck are you talking about?"

"They arrived when I was knocking on the door. Said they're friends of Daisy's and need to speak to her." He barely glances back at Daisy. "They were going to follow me back here, but I told them to wait on the porch or else they'd be trespassing on private fucking property." He smiles bitterly. "You're welcome, by the way."

I run a hand through my hair. What the fuck is going on? First, why the hell would my dad need *my* advice? Second...

I look back at Daisy, and she's already standing up, clutching the blanket around her chest and hugging onto it tightly. She sidles next to me. "I'm going to change and then talk to them," she says. "Maybe it's just Willow and Maya or something..." Her voice trails off, knowing it can't be those friends.

Willow fucking lives with us. And she's spending tonight at Connor and Rose's because she knew about the whole engagement plan. Fuck, she helped Lily and Rose string up the lights in the trees. There's no way she's on our doorstep, waiting around.

My muscles constrict when I think about Daisy's *other* friends.

"Why don't you take Nutty and get dressed," I suggest, "and I'll see what the girls want. If it's something important, I'll come get you."

Color returns to her face, maybe even just by the mention of Nutty—or Coconut. I call the husky by a different name, only because the first week the dog stayed with us, she kept sliding across the waxed hardwoods with this silly *what the fuck is happening* expression. Lo, Connor, and I couldn't keep from laughing, and it's an image that's stayed with the three of us since.

So she's Nutty to us and Coconut to the girls.

Daisy nods once. "Okay, yeah…" She frowns suddenly. "Are you sure you want to talk to them? I can handle it."

I feel my dad's steely eyes dart from her to me.

"I know you can," I say lowly, setting my hand on her head.

She lets out another breath but doesn't declare whether or not she wants me to confront the girls before her. I interpret her silence as *you can greet them*, and we both trek back towards the house.

My dad follows like a shadow, and all of us exit the woods together. I make sure Dais isn't wedged between my father and me. I keep two hands on her shoulders while she gingerly steps on the damp grass.

When I open the pool gate, I can't hold it in any longer. "What fucking advice do you want?" I need him to fucking leave. The sooner, the better.

He cocks his head towards Daisy, his hardened gaze saying, *not in front of her*.

"Speak," I force.

He pushes through the gate, not about to be left behind or locked out. I can barely look at him without popping a fucking blood vessel. So I follow Daisy around the pool, my hand dropping to hers. She trips on her blanket once, and I catch her around the waist, pulling her against my chest so she doesn't accidentally flash my father.

"Oops," she whispers, trying to knot the blanket better.

Fuck this. I lift her in my arms, and her smile returns but fades faster than I like. As soon as she sees Nutty's nose pressed against the sliding glass door, her expression lights up.

I carry her through the doorway and then she taps my arm to set her down. The moment I do, she spins towards me, planting a warm kiss on my cheek.

"I'm going to change while you talk to your dad."

I hate leaving her when we're both fucking confused about what's going on.

She must see the concern in my eyes because she says, "I'll be okay on my own. I have Coconut. She's a badass."

"You're a fucking badass too, you know?"

She smiles. "Enough to be a pirate?"

I kiss her tenderly on the lips, then more aggressively.

She gasps halfway, and when we break apart, she says softly, "Today has been perfect."

It almost makes me feel better, even if it's not completely fucking true. I watch her leave, our white husky's tail whips from side to side, and she keeps stride with Daisy.

I return to the pool area, shutting the sliding door. The water is still black in the dark. And there's my dad. Standing by the grill with his hands stuffed in his slacks.

"I'll make it quick," he tells me. Then he shifts his weight, uneasy. He can face the barrel of my gun with barely a blink, but right now, he fucking wavers.

What's going on?

I comb my hand through my hair. For fuck's sake, we've gone through a lot. My dad and me. Growing up, I despised him for practically disowning me and raising Loren Hale. Then I buried him with all my fucking demons. My dad, as far as I was concerned, was dead to me. When I met Lo, it all changed. My hate for Jonathan resurfaced. I hated how he treated my little brother. I hated him for being a shit father.

Years went by. Struggles. Talks.

Then I forgave him.

And I think that's the hardest fucking thing about all of this. I forgave the bastard. I gave him a part of my liver. I saved his fucking life.

And then a few months ago, he shit on his second chance by trying to hurt Connor, outing his sexuality to the media—all for what? To gain power over Lo again? To protect Lo from Connor? It's all warped and wrong in his head.

I'm the one who believed he'd turn into a better man, only to be whiplashed by the vindictive, spiteful father I've always known.

Now it's just fucking complicated. I don't have energy to hate the guy like I used to, but I can't stand here and be *okay*. We're just not okay.

And I don't know what will get us to that place again.

So right here, beside my pool in the middle of the night, waiting for him to ask for some sort of advice is the weirdest fucking thing that has happened to me in a while. I imagined my first time alone with him would be more volatile. Yelling. Screaming. Maybe some fists flying.

But things are always different in our minds, amped up to the thousandth degree. In reality, he almost seems feeble. Like a king who has abandoned his throne.

"I came into some information yesterday," he tells me. "You know Emily Moore?"

Do I know Emily Moore? Not personally. "Lo's birth mom," I say with a shrug. "Willow's mom." Only Emily raised Willow up in Maine, before Willow moved down here to be closer to her half-brother.

"I've been in contact with Emily here and there to hand her checks for keeping Loren's birth quiet," my dad explains. He takes a deeper breath and scratches his neck. "Apparently, Emily decided last night was a good time to tell me that Willow was also my daughter." He rolls his eyes. "All this time I should have just forced a paternity test. But she had no reason to lie to me." He points at his chest. "I'm the billionaire. But she chose a life in goddamn Caribou, Maine with an average man and an average family. It's pathetic."

My mind is reeling, but I don't try to stop him. He gesticulates wildly as he talks, animated, like I'm the first person he's vented to.

I think I might be.

He snorts into a dry, bitter laugh. "Willow ran away to Philadelphia to meet up with her long lost *half*-brother—my son, Loren. And that... that did it." He shakes his head. "Whatever world Emily wanted for Willow, she failed at protecting. That middle-class life. Gone. And now she sees her daughter struggling in this lifestyle, surrounded by the rich, and she knows I have the means to give Willow a better life. I can offer the handout." He looks back at me, his eyes dark. "I should have raised her to begin with. That selfish cunt."

It's an endnote that almost impales me, and my nose flares. I swallow a *fuck you* for his last line, though I'm fucking brimming to just unleash hell. My hands curl into fists.

I'm too concerned about Willow and my brother—who are both tangled in this fucking news—to ignite a fire off something else. I want to ask if he's sure that Willow is his daughter, but that's something Jonathan would have already confirmed a hundred times over.

This really may be true, and if it is...

Willow is Lo's full sibling.

Willow is *my* half-sister.

Right now, I just go for the most logical question. "What the fuck kind of advice do you need from me?" If he opened the door to anything, I'd start with *stop degrading women*. It makes me physically fucking sick. But it's not like I haven't screamed at him for saying that word before. I used to lay into him when I was seventeen for calling my mom that and worse.

There is worse. I've heard it.

He glares sinisterly, but I don't cower. "You've been down this road before," he says like we share something together. "You've had to reconnect with someone. You and Lo, you're close now..."

"He's my brother," I snap. "Not my fucking child. It's not the same thing." I motion between us. "Don't try to compare this. It's not fucking comparable."

He rolls his eyes, frustrated. "I came here to ask what you think I should do, not so you could piss all over me."

A shrapnel of guilt lodges in my stomach. He's trying. It seems like it, but for fuck's sake, if I even take a moment to think about what Willow's life will look like with Jonathan Hale in it—I go cold. His so-called "love" is layered in iron blades. He cut up his other son. I don't want to see what he can do to a daughter.

I'm fucking afraid he'll cannibalize Willow's happiness.

"She's doing fine without you," I say quickly. "My advice: leave her the fuck alone."

He guns me down with a sharpened scowl. "She's my daughter. I want to be in her life. That's not up for negotiation. I just need to know *how* to go about it. The only thing I have close to raising a daughter turned out to be a sex addict, so you can see, I'm willing to take some tips."

Mention of Lily hurts more than he understands. "Fuck you," I say, feeling my brother's pain from that comment.

"I'll let you think about it," my dad says. "Like I said, I wanted this to be quick. You have company." The girls on the porch. *Fuck.* He heads towards the back gate. "I won't confront Willow until you come up with a plan. I just..." He pauses, his hand on the iron. "I want to do this right."

Is he manipulating me into liking him again? Is that his ploy? He gives me all the cards because he knows what I think of his relationships with his children. They're all tainted with something dark and black and maybe he thinks this is his apology to me. I'm not sure.

Before he leaves, I call out, "Wait!" He stops just outside the gate. "What about Lo? Did you tell him yet?"

"No." Jonathan shakes his head. "Just you."

Just me.

❀ ❀ ❀

I CHANGE INTO A pair of jeans and a T-shirt before heading back outside. I hike around the house instead of opening the door. It gives me time to assess what the fuck I'm walking into.

When I reach the front stoop, I spot two girls, seated on the brick steps. A fairly short blonde stands and crosses her arms with hostility, impatience all over her long face.

I recognize her.

Only she was four years younger with less makeup, also tanner from lounging on a yacht. At Daisy's sweet sixteen birthday party, years ago.

Cleo.

The other girl has darker, straighter hair and a more annoyed scowl. Her black dress contrasts Cleo's preppy pastel sweater and white shorts.

Harper.

I never pictured confronting these two—never let myself construct an idea on what I'd do if I did. My nose flares again because *everything* that they did to Daisy scours my brain and my fucking heart.

I stand rigid, my blood blistering.

They terrorized her in a fucking elevator, for fuck's sake. They *demanded* that she stick a dildo inside of her. *Some of the guys wanted to know how many inches would fit inside of you. We told them we'd find out.*

Cleo said that to her, and I hear Daisy recounting all of this to me, bawling. I see the girl I fucking love breaking down.

Daisy has PTSD. Not just from the Paris riot or because some shit photographer broke into her room during the reality show. Though all of those are reason enough to be fucked up.

Cleo and Harper told her that they'd make her final six months at prep school hell. Condoms in the locker. Fucking assholes coming up to her and trying to touch her breasts. *Titty twisters.* Code for sexual assault, you *motherfuckers.*

Watching someone you care about slowly and then rapidly become scared of the world around them is like being a passenger in a car crash. With no way to pump the brakes. It's fucking hell.

And it's exponentially worse for her.

They wait for me to approach them, their bodies bathed in the front porch lights. I move a few feet closer, stopping at the base of the brick stairs. I just know that I don't want them anywhere near Daisy tonight, but I also know that I have to give her the choice.

I can't make that decision for her.

"How the fuck did you get through the neighborhood gate?" I ask, my voice rougher.

Cleo is one stair below Harper and nearer to me, but I notice the small box in Harper's hands. Wrapped with white paper and a blue bow.

The bottom of my stomach drops, thinking it can't be good. Whatever that is.

"We have friends in the neighborhood," Cleo says casually, like she owns this driveway and these stairs and the house behind her.

Fuck that. I walk past her, climbing up the fucking stairs. I stand right in front of the door. Both girls follow to the highest step, but they stay put.

Cleo has to crane her neck just to meet my eyes.

"What the fuck do you want?" I can't soften my words. Not for them.

"We came to talk to Daisy," Harper says. "We're old friends. I don't know if you remember us from her birthday party."

"Yeah, and she's told me a fucking lot about you two."

Harper exchanges worry with Cleo, and then the strawberry blonde focuses back on me.

I continue, "Daisy is—"

"Actually"—Cleo motions to Harper—"maybe you could just give this to her. It's late, and we're supposed to be at my father's dinner party in five minutes."

Harper offers the small wrapped box to me.

I take it.

Cleo departs with a forced smile, and Harper whispers in her ear, hurriedly skipping down the brick steps.

"Fuck," I mutter to myself and then retreat into the house.

I'm not that surprised when I see Daisy sitting on the staircase by herself, her chin in her hand. "Was it fairies coming to deliver chocolates?" she asks with the smallest, saddest smile, her eyes pinging to the box.

"More like two fucking devils," I mumble, shaking the box but unable to hear much of anything. "Cleo and Harper."

She's expressionless, and she must take in my confusion because she says, "I saw them through the window. I figured it was them anyway."

I raise the gift box. "We can throw it away."

She pops up from the stairs. "No." Nutty trails her heels, and she stops in the foyer, right in front of me. Her narrowed eyes pin to the box. "Let's smell it first though."

I frown. "Why?"

"There's a good likelihood it's crap." Her mouth curves upward. "And I mean literal crap."

I roll my eyes, but my body boils again. She shouldn't have to even think that someone might gift her a box filled with shit.

The world is fucked up.

"I can smell it if you don't want..." Her words die off as I raise the box to my nose.

"It doesn't smell like anything."

She barely relaxes. "Okay, so what other terrible things could they give me? A dead hamster. Bloody tampons. Crusty toenails."

"Stop." I set a hand on her head.

"I just don't want to be surprised."

"I can look first," I suggest.

She contemplates this idea before putting her hand on mine, her fingers skimming the box. "I want to do it together."

That sounds good to me. She picks at the paper while I hold the box. I tell her, "Whatever this is, it's probably not as bad as Lily's mail."

I know it's a weak comment. Cleo and Harper were Daisy's best friends, not random sick fucks. She's known Cleo since she was six.

Daisy nods. "Connor told me that Lily once got a used condom in the mail."

I don't even fucking ask for the context of that conversation between Connor and Daisy. I'm sure it was to explain something or make a point.

Daisy unties the ribbon and then lifts the lid.

Her mouth falls, and she plucks out a very expensive diamond bracelet. "I don't...understand." Her hands shake, probably thinking it's a fucking trick.

I grab the bracelet from her, and the box slips and thuds to the floor. A note flutters out. I pick it up and go to hand it to her, but she dazedly returns to the staircase, plopping down next to Nutty.

The white husky nudges Daisy's legs until her eyes focus on the dog. No longer faraway and lost.

"Read it," she tells me.

"You okay?" I ask, eyeing her pale skin.

"Just confused."

With a knot in my chest, I turn to the letter. "*Hi Daisy,*" I start. "*It's been a few years since prep school, and we've had a lot of time to think and grow up since then. We know you have too. We know your family is planning another reality show, and we'd love to be a part of it. It could definitely help us repair the friendship we lost. We miss you, truly!*—for fuck's sake," I curse, their words tasting fucking foul in my mouth.

"Keep going," Daisy prods.

I shift my weight and read with an agitated voice, "*And congratulations on snagging Ryke Meadows. We always knew you were into older guys.*" I look up at Dais like *this is bullshit.* I hope she sees that too, but she's expressionless again. I glance at the letter "They do a wink face right there. And then they end with, *please give us a chance. Love you always, Cleo and Harper.*"

Daisy lets out a breath and rubs her cheeks like her face is clammy. "They're just trying to get in on a non-existent reality show." She shakes her head once.

The Calloway sisters have been approached multiple times for a second season of *Princesses of Philly*. It's nothing new. But Cleo and Harper didn't get the memo that it's never going to fucking happen.

I walk forward and put my hands on the top of her head. She stares up at me, wide-eyed and beautiful. I want to fucking protect her from the pain that her friends bring, but I can't shield her from people. I couldn't do that four years ago. I can't fucking do it now.

I'm just here when she needs me. Whatever she fucking wants. I'm here.

< 5 >

Daisy Calloway

Jane Eleanor Cobalt is speaking French. I should clarify: a *one-year-old* baby is uttering French words, strung together to sound like complete sentences.

"She's smarter than me," Lily declares, nodding in astonishment. Wearing a baggy muscle tee and geometric printed leggings, Lily stares in awe at the fashionable baby dressed in a light blue romper while hugging a stuffed lion.

I adjust Jane's headband that begins to fall off, something tugging inside of me. It's not a good tug. It hurts more than a little, and I try to hide any signs of this silent grief. I don't like that something so beautiful, my baby niece, brings these morose, contemplative emotions out of me.

She should only bring joy. That's what babies do. They're cute bundles of happiness with spirits livelier than every adult combined.

It's my fault. I shouldn't think about the possibility of having children when I'm with Jane.

"If it makes you feel any better," I tell Lily, "I've been to France a ton and I can't even understand her."

"I'm still stupid." Lily pops another BBQ chip in her mouth and crunches loudly. I'm about to tell my older sister that she's just as smart as me when Moffy walks towards baby Jane. He looks stylish in gray pants, a black tee, and tiny white Converses.

He plops down next to Jane, coloring book in hand. I wiggle his little foot, and I wear a smile that I know looks happy.

Moffy flips open a page and mutters to Jane, words that are clearly not English. Uh-oh.

Lily coughs on her chip. "Did he..."

I pat her back, unsure of how she'll take this news. "I think he might have spoken French," I say. "Or maybe it was Spanish." When we babysit, Ryke will read books to Moffy in Spanish. Lo and Lily don't know, but we thought they wouldn't mind.

I watch her reaction closely, and she goes from surprise to an elated smile, beaming in excitement. I even smile wider, happy that she's happy. Lily wants the absolute best for her son, and so the prospect of Maximoff Hale knowing a foreign language must make her proud.

"Hey." Willow waves to us after climbing down the stairs.

"Hi," Lily and I say in unison.

Willow pushes her black-rimmed glasses further up the bridge of her nose. She tucks her phone in a pocket of her worn overalls, and then heads for the kitchen, disappearing out of sight. My stomach tosses, uneasy about last night's truth.

Ryke and I didn't even go to bed until four in the morning. I was maxed out on excited energy from the proposal and nervous energy from Cleo and Harper's impromptu visit. Instead of lying awake in silence—attempting and failing at falling asleep—Ryke hugged me on the bed and explained his father's news.

The fact that Willow is Jonathan's daughter *and* Ryke's half-sister is crazy. Not bad crazy. Just a normal bout of crazy for the Hales.

So far, no one has any idea about Jonathan crashing our proposal night. Ryke told me that he wanted to tell his brother before he came up with a "plan" for Jonathan. The problem: Ryke's always had trouble breaking any kind of news to Lo, and I know he's just trying to find a good time.

Even if there's never going to be a perfect moment to say: *Hey, guess what, your half-sister is really your full sister and our dad wants a relationship with her. And...he wants me to help him. Surprise!*

It doesn't even sound great in my head. Plus, there are a lot of *fucks* left out of that proclamation.

Luckily for me, my friendship with Willow shouldn't really change. She's the one good friend I have in my life, especially when my old horrible friends are rising from the grave. That bracelet sits on my dresser, practically haunting me. I'm not sure what to do with it. It's too expensive to just toss in the trash, and the thought of wearing it makes me want to puke.

Like Ryke, I have my own plans to concoct, only mine involve bribery bracelets and ex-friends.

"Did his ring choice surprise you?" Lily asks, splintering my thoughts.

"Hmm?" I say distractedly.

Lily frowns, and her eyes flicker to the babies and back to me in contemplation. Her hair is chopped short at her shoulders, and it sways when she looks between us. I don't want Lily to think that being around her son makes me sad, even if it's starting to become obvious.

I smile bigger and nudge her side.

She blinks a couple times and then smiles back, pointing at my hand. "Your ring."

"Oh yeah." I stare at the diamond sun. I would've taken string, honestly, but this reminds me so much of our relationship.

"Because," Lily says, "I thought Ryke was going to give you twine or something."

"Glad to know what you fucking think of me." Ryke's rough voice emanates from the foyer. He appears with two motorcycle helmets in hand, his jeans ripped at the knee and his hair massively disheveled. Just meeting his gaze, that dark and dangerous stare, lightens solemn parts of me.

I bounce to my feet, my smile stretching.

"You gave her twine for her birthday!" Lily rebuts. "It's an honest prediction." She munches on a handful of chips.

Ryke rolls his eyes. "I gave her a fucking *hemp* bracelet. How about you stop trying to predict our futures?"

Lily pouts and mutters, "I thought I was getting good at it."

"You are." I stick up for my sis. "Julian was the worst. You predicted that, remember?"

"I did." Lily nods in triumph and points at Ryke. "Ha!"

Ryke looks between us, a glare forming at the mere mention of my ex-boyfriend. "I thought we banned his fucking name." That was Lo's declaration. He hates him almost as much as Ryke.

"Sorry." I playfully wince.

Ryke hands me a motorcycle helmet and then kisses the top of my head. "We need to talk," he says so quietly, I almost miss the words.

"Okay," I whisper back and then turn towards the living room. "Bye, Lil!"

"Bye!" she says. "Good luck!"

"Bye bye!" Moffy says with a laugh attached.

"Bye," Jane giggles.

My heart clenches, and I feel Ryke's hand on my lower back, guiding me through the foyer and out the door. We walk down the sidewalk to the driveway, two Ducati sportbikes leaning on their kickstands. Rose's Escalade is parked by the curb, the engine running.

"My sisters didn't help you pick out the ring then?" I wonder, slightly shifting the topic off babies, even though I know it's going to hit me soon. Full force. Without stop.

"I just asked Rose for your ring size." He halts in front of the red bike, his hand sliding to my hip. He draws me to his chest, and I note the seriousness in his pinched brows. "If you want to change your mind, you still can, Dais."

I'm confused. "I want to marry you." Have I acted differently to where he'd think otherwise? "I love you," I remind him, knowing I don't say it as often as him. When I do say those words, blood rushes to every one of my limbs, as though reminding me of life.

I am a living, breathing thing.

In love with him.

"I'm talking about trying for kids."

Right.

We've had two serious conversations in the past month about having babies.

One short. One long.

Each time we came to the same conclusion.

We want to try now.

"Because," he says, "I'm going to be twenty-seven. You're only twenty, and I'd fucking understand if you want to wait—"

"No," I stop him before he continues. He's said this before: *I could have kids tomorrow. I would've been okay to have kids at twenty-five. I just need to know if you are. And if you need to wait fucking longer, I'll be happy with that too.* I tuck my helmet beneath my arm.

"Dais…"

"I know what I want." These are magic words. They carry so much power.

My life has always been set on fast-forward, and while it seems idyllic to go backwards and experience a childhood I missed—I can't have that entirely. I've regained enough in the past couple of years with Ryke that I'm ready to move forward with him.

"You know what you're giving up?" he asks. "You can't do fucking cartwheels, Calloway."

I think through all of his support and encouragement, Ryke is more worried about this unknown. Before I can reply, the Escalade's windows roll down.

Rose taps her watch like *we're going to be late.*

I nod to her and then turn back to Ryke with a growing smile. "True," I say, "but do you know what I believe?"

He shakes his head once, listening closely.

"That having babies with you would be an awfully big adventure." Then I put on my helmet and flip up the visor, winking before I head to my red bike.

He wraps his arms around my waist, pulling my back into his chest, and he says, "Then let's fucking start it, sweetheart."

The sad realization: it's not going to be as easy for us. It's painfully clear by where we're headed.

A fertility doctor.

< 6 >

Daisy Calloway

"Someone say something." I can't take the tense silence anymore. I've tried to fill it with digressions about sprinkled donuts and wake boarding. No one took the bait in those conversations, staying quiet regarding my true intentions. Which doesn't involve pretty looking donuts or the thrill of water sports.

I'm nervous. Really nervous. I squirm on the hospital bed, paper crinkling beneath my ass. I dislike doctor's offices, the walls bland and space cramped. I feel confined, like sitting in a sterile box.

Connor is seated on one of two chairs, texting. He doesn't look up as he says, "Your theory about donuts sustaining the population of Mars was so senseless that I've been stunned to silence."

"Thank fucking God," Ryke says, his arms crossed as he stands beside me.

Usually it's hard to read Connor's expressions, but he purposefully shoots Ryke an annoyed look before pocketing his phone.

I swing my legs, antsy. This consultation means more than all the others. Dr. Yoshida is the best fertility doctor in New York City and the entire east coast. If he can't help me, I might as well pack up my hope and ship it away.

I feel Ryke watching my little movements in concern. I flash him a small smile, and he rubs my shoulders. His gaze drops to my thin white tee with the slogan *carpe that fucking diem* printed across the chest.

He fingers the hem.

My phone keeps vibrating on my leg, texts from my family's publicist, Corbin Nery. On the way here, paparazzi took a clear photograph of my engagement ring. *Celebrity Crush* and other tabloids keep reaching out to Corbin for a comment. We've told him to say *no comment*, but he wants us to make some big announcement or at least let him tell the media we're engaged.

Ryke isn't interested in working with Corbin or any publicist, really, so we'll probably just make an announcement on Instagram or Snapchat in our own time and our own way.

I twist my engagement ring a couple times, just fiddling with my fingers. I glance at Ryke, and his jaw hardens. He swallows and runs a hand through his hair.

I stop quickly, setting my palms flat on my knees.

"Hey there," I say with a forced smile, worried. In the back of my head, I remember how he explained Loren's *tell* to me once. I asked Ryke outright how he knew his little brother was having a bad day since he seemed like the same sarcastic, edged Loren Hale to me.

Apparently Lo spins his wedding ring when he craves alcohol, and it must have been what Ryke imagined when he watched me twist mine.

He raises his brows knowingly, and his dark gaze drifts to my sister. "What the fuck are you doing?"

She's been pacing the office, and now she's stopped, her phone pointed at the certificates and degrees hung on the wall.

"Making sure these are real," she replies, her tone snappy and full of ice.

I smile, glad that she's here.

Connor says, "I would've never recommended a doctor who cheated their way through medical school." He appears more bored than anything, his arm draped across the empty chair next to him.

Rose ignores him and retaliates by snapping three more photos, flashes going off in succession.

Connor grins. "I sense hostility."

Rose flips her hair over her shoulder and keeps her back to him. Her silence seems to be driving him stir-crazy. He shifts in the seat and glances at the door and his watch.

And then the door opens, air vacuuming out. I suck in a deep breath. *Here we go.*

Rose returns her cell to her purse but remains standing. In fact, Connor rises to his feet as Dr. Yoshida squeezes inside, round glasses perched on his nose. He smiles kindly, carrying two folders and a manila file. "Looks like we have a full room today."

I introduce everyone, not caring if he already knows us from the media. "This is my brother-in-law, Connor Cobalt."

His posture is full of unbridled confidence, and he reaches out to shake Dr. Yoshida's hand.

"My sister, Rose."

Her yellow-green eyes pierce him and her lips stay in a predatory line. He only looks a little scared, which is better than most. She does, however, offer a handshake—which is a smile in Rose Calloway's world.

Lastly, I clasp Ryke's hand next to me. "And this is my fiancé, Ryke." The corners of my mouth immediately rise, unable to hold back. *Fiancé.*

I'm someone's soon-to-be wife.

If I think about it in the context of Ryke, I almost have a head-rush. It's the sensation of never truly believing something will come to fruition but finally *feeling* the moment that it has.

Dr. Yoshida shakes Ryke's hand. "Nice to meet all of you." He raises the manila file. "Who wants the non-disclosure agreement?"

"Me." Connor steps forward and takes the file from him. Normalcy has vanished. I didn't go to my family's lawyers for help. I'm not exactly "cutting ties" but over the past year, I've been slowly distancing myself from my mother and father's "people"—I have my own accountant, not one handpicked by her. I have my own financial advisor.

Now I have my own lawyer. He wrote up the agreement for all of my physicians. There may be HIPPA laws and oaths requiring doctor-patient confidentiality, but none of us like taking those chances anymore. We've all been burned in different ways.

Dr. Yoshida pulls two ultrasound images from a folder and places them on a backlight. My ovaries displayed for everyone to see. They're gray blobs, the images difficult to read, but I wouldn't even freak out if they were detailed drawings of my reproductive system.

I grew up basically being told my human form belonged to photographers and designers, a mere canvas for other people to do whatever they please. I used to be desensitized to *my* body. It's taken me years, but I'm the owner of the skin I wear. And I feel free to take my clothes off when *I* want to now. On my terms.

No one is leaving me naked in a crowd of people. I won't let them without my consent. Not anymore.

Dr. Yoshida clears his throat before gesturing to the images. "We're most concerned with the cyst on your left ovary. It's larger than the right one." He points them out, outlining the dark patterns. "They're located deep within the ovaries, not on top of them, which makes them endometriomas." He turns to me. "Also known as chocolate cysts."

I go still, already knowing their nickname. When I first heard it, I thought someone was playing a cruel joke on me. *Chocolate cysts.* "My favorite kind," I say lightheartedly.

No one finds my humor amusing right now. Literally there is dead silence. Usually I'm better at easing the tension, but I guess I'm better at it when the topic doesn't surround *me*.

Ryke sets a hand on my thigh—a perilous and dangerous place. I begin to smile, liking it all. He asks the doctor, "Are you recommending surgery?" His tone is coarse. I like that too.

Dr. Yoshida clicks a pen. "If the cyst was smaller, I wouldn't have, but at this point, surgery is the best directive. All cases are different, and I don't like the look of the ones on her left ovary and tube. They're only going to worsen."

It's what the other doctor advised too.

Rose readjusts her purse on her arm, her collarbones jutting out as she holds in a breath. I feel winded, not able to remember the questions I should be asking.

Ryke nods to the doctor. "Can she still get pregnant if she undergoes surgery?"

That's an important one. *Thank you, Ryke.*

"It's going to be difficult, for a number of reasons, but that doesn't make it impossible." He faces me again. "Age decreases your reserve and surgery will have the same effect. During the removal of your left ovary and left tube, I'd like to take out the smaller cyst on the right ovary. If it looks too risky at the time, I won't touch the cyst. The important thing would be to preserve your right ovary while we can."

I nod, understanding based on the other doctor's explanation. Over time, they think my right ovary will match the ugliness of my left one, which will leave me with no option but removal.

"You're currently on birth control," he states, reading my file.

"I'm going off birth control today," I tell him.

Ryke adds, "We want to try to have a fucking kid." I don't think he realized he added a *fuck* in there, and I can't stop smiling.

Rose and Connor don't appear surprised by either his *fuck* or admittance. I think everyone silently knew we were going to try soon. It's just been a sad topic, so no one really ever brings it up that often.

Dr. Yoshida jots down a note in the folder. "Birth control can sometimes help suppress the development of cysts on ovaries. It's a reason why getting pregnant with preexisting cysts can be complicated." He scans the files. "Your irregular periods are most likely due to the endometriomas. Once we go through surgery, your right ovary should take over in two to three months and your periods should become more regular."

I nod again, feeling a little robotic.

"How has the pain been?"

Everyone looks at me.

"Just bad when I actually have a period and worse when I went off birth control." That part scares me since I obviously need to be off birth control to have a baby.

He nods like he expected my response. "Most of the pain should subside after surgery." I hone in on the *should*—it's more like a possibility and less like a certainty.

Ryke scratches his jaw and then asks, "How painful will it be for her to have sex?"

Dr. Yoshida flips through my charts. "Does she feel pain during intercourse now?"

I block out Connor who's hearing this information too, and I tie my hair into a high bun. "I didn't know that I had cysts, so there might've been a couple times where I thought it hurt a little just because he's big."

Ryke is rigid.

At the time, I never told him I felt any pain because it lasted maybe a minute or two and then he changed positions anyway. It didn't seem as big of a deal as it's become.

His dark eyes flit to me and then back to the doctor. He's mad. At himself for not catching sight of my pain and at me for not letting him know. He never wants to hurt me. I'd give him more details now—to show that it's in the past and unmemorable—but I don't want to paint vivid portraits of our sex life for the doctor, my sister, and *Connor*.

I touch his hand that's on my thigh, and instead of distancing himself from me, he threads his fingers with mine. It reminds me of how mature he is, never letting the little things take root.

"If I remove the right cyst, it should help with the pain," Dr. Yoshida says in thought, making another note.

Connor looks a little peeved by all the note taking and not enough sharing, but he surprisingly stays quiet.

"So I suggest surgery as soon as possible before trying to get pregnant. How does that sound?"

"Good," I tell him. I remember what Ryke and I already discussed and agreed upon during our long talk. He said that I needed to fix the endometrioma before I considered kids. That my health trumps pregnancy. Ryke's words: *Babies take the fucking backseat, sweetheart.*

I replied: *Literally. They will be sitting in the backseat if we drive our babies around.*

He threw me over his shoulder for that.

"There's always a chance that you could be infertile," the doctor says, "regardless of surgery. In that case, I'd recommend *in vitro* fertilization. There's no guarantee IVF will work, and there's a high risk of rupturing the cyst during egg retrieval. But…with your medical history, it's likely that pregnancy may be difficult on your body regardless."

He explains more, outlining pros and cons and listing giant words that cloud my head. The risks for pregnancy with endometriomas are terrifying: *pre-eclampsia, pre-term birth, antepartum hemorrhage, miscarriage, stillbirth.*

He finishes with, "So you need to decide whether to try on your own or go straight to IVF or surrogacy."

The pros for surrogacy: my body is spared all the hardships of a high-risk pregnancy. No possibilities of pain, miscarriages, or hemorrhaging.

"So," I start, trying to wrap my head around this, "if I don't go with IVF or surrogacy, then the risk will be possible infertility and maybe some pain?"

"Since you obviously need to have sex during ovulation—and that time has been painful for you in the past—it will be unavoidable when you're trying to conceive." He adds, "Like I mentioned, surgery should help." *Should.* "There are other methods to get more comfortable. Missionary position can be painful for some, so you can try doggy style and side-to-side. The penis enters at a better angle."

Do not look at Connor Cobalt.

Everyone is quiet, mulling over these options. I want to make a joke about sex, but I'm finding it hard to speak.

Dr. Yoshida retrieves the ultrasound images and shuts the folders. "I'd like to schedule your surgery, and in the meantime, you can think about your options to conceive." His gaze bounces between Ryke and me. "When you've decided on the route you want, we can go from there. I need to stress that your pregnancy *will be* high-risk if you choose to carry the baby. To avoid most of the complications, surrogacy is a great alternative."

I nod once, and he pats my shoulder before leaving us alone to discuss. My gut says to try by myself first. No IVF, no surrogacy. We haven't even seen if I'm entirely infertile yet. The surgery may help with that. I know it's the riskiest option—but when have I ever shied from a little danger?

Even thinking it, I'm certain that this will be one of the biggest risks of my life. And I'm not even racing down a road or diving off a cliff.

I'm toying with my body's capabilities, and it may not be fit to carry life into this world. Rose has told me that it doesn't make me less of a woman. I cried when she said it—because I've felt odd lately. Maybe that was why.

I keep trying to navigate these feelings, and I think *time* will be the biggest help in climbing over them. Time to cope. Time to accept the experience I may miss out on. Time to realize that I'm as much of a woman as *every* woman out there.

Before I close this chapter and settle with my fate, I want to follow what's in my heart. No playing it safe. I want to try. I want to run headfirst at a hundred-and-fifty miles per hour without braking.

I want to take this risk.

Even if it kills me.

The door shuts, and Connor speaks first, as though bursting from holding back for so long. "You need to think about the possibility of miscarrying and what that means for your mental health." He's more stern and brotherly than he has ever been with me.

I look at Ryke—no clue where his head is at, but the way he searches my eyes, I see that he recognizes what I'm leaning towards. I wear an expression full of mischief and excitement, my lips quirked up, which usually appears in the face of danger.

If this process didn't concern my health, I'd say that he'd be standing confidently on my side. However, he cares about what will happen to me. I tend to forget about myself and focus on grander things.

"You think I'm not mentally stable enough?" I ask Ryke.

"I don't fucking know," he admits.

I try to cheer him up, grabbing onto his waist while I'm still seated. "Frederick told me I was his *best* patient the other day." I wag my brows at him. "I beat Connor Cobalt. Therefore I should be fit for anything." We share the same therapist but for different reasons. I've been diagnosed with depression and PTSD, so it's safe to assume that I'd be mentally affected by a miscarriage.

Connor isn't amused. "I sincerely doubt those were Rick's exact words." He takes out his phone, probably to text Frederick.

Ryke crosses his arms, not playing around about this.

My grip tightens, fisting his shirt. "One-hundred-and-fifty miles per hour. No brakes."

His eyes redden. Our gazes are locked, all of our experiences together rushing through us, every moment where we kissed death but never tasted it. Every time we lived life so terribly—so *fully*.

And then he snatches my hairband, my brown locks tumbling out of a bun. His jaw glides across my cheek, his hand protectively on the back of my head, his breath warming my ear. And he says, "I'm right beside you, Calloway."

I smile wide, and it seems all good and well—to have Ryke firmly in agreement—but it's hard when two of the smartest people stand opposite us.

Rose violently clears her throat until we shift towards her and her husband. She has her hands on her hips, and he's pocketed his phone, his entire focus on us.

"I'm going to try to carry the baby first," I tell her.

"You can't just decide right now," she retorts, as though stating the law.

Ryke narrows his gaze. "We just fucking did."

"The doctor said to weigh your options." Rose looks more than upset, fighting actual tears. "What if something happens to you? Antepartum hemorrhaging and pre-eclampsia can be *fatal.* That's death, Daisy." The fear inside my brilliant, unabashedly confident sister almost knocks the breath out of me.

"There will always be risks for *any* pregnancy," I say, trying to stand my ground.

Rose glares. "This isn't a normal risk. This isn't jumping off a building into a pool. If you get pregnant and something happens, you're gone. Game over." Her usual dramatics are painful when directed at me, especially in the context of my hypothetical death.

I try to be more positive without sounding naïve. "This isn't the eighteenth century," I remind her. "We have doctors and technology and my chances aren't terrible. If they were, Dr. Yoshida wouldn't have recommended it."

"It's our fucking choice," Ryke adds, which makes my lips rise. He drapes his arm around my shoulders, his thumb drawing circles on my skin.

"She's my little sister."

"Rose," I whisper, "I haven't died. Please don't cry."

She gapes, nearly scoffing. "I'm *not* crying." She quickly wipes beneath her eyes, checking for involuntary tears, and then she raises her chin higher.

Connor shakes his head. Connor Cobalt—the voice of *reason*—is full of severity, his normally calm exterior disrupted by it. "I have a daughter and a wife now," he says, "so I'm going to do you the courtesy and tell you what I would tell them if they were in your situation."

Ryke's muscles flex and coil, his jaw tightening. I'm not sure I want to hear Connor's opinion either, even if it's filled with wisdom.

"You're making a mistake," he says flatly. "Both of you are."

Ryke seethes beside me. They're nearly the same age, and even though Ryke isn't a certified genius, he's worldly, intelligent and the one in love with me.

Connor directs this next statement to Ryke. "You view risks as tape you can tear through and not walls meant to block you. I'm not saying you're blind because you're not. You see your vulnerabilities. But you just don't care. Neither of you do. It's as if death is another thrill, and it's almost sick to watch."

"We didn't ask for a fucking lecture when we invited you here," Ryke growls. Connor is burrowing further into our situation. This isn't just about our choice to carry a child. It's about Ryke rock climbing.

It's both of us.

Connor never flinches or spends time defending himself. He just continues, "Your lives have value, and your deaths have none. It's not worth carrying a baby to term, climbing a rock without a harness, or every other risk you two take in your spare time."

I imagine living *forever* inside a space carved with safety. I imagine us banging at the walls, attempting to break free.

I gather my feelings and turn them to words. "Maybe those things are just worth more in *our* eyes than they are in yours."

Connor opens his mouth, but Rose touches his arm and whispers in his ear. Mild annoyance crosses his features before his composure returns, blank slate and all.

I hop off the hospital bed, my arm around Ryke's waist. "Rose," I say.

She fixes her glossy brown hair over one shoulder, her classy black dress hugging her hourglass frame. "Yes?"

"If the doctor said I could carry a baby myself, I'd planned to ask you something…" She offered to be my surrogate, but now that I might not need her like that—I do still want her to be a part of this in another way.

She listens intently.

"Would you consider trying to get pregnant the same time as me?" I wonder with a smile. It's no secret that Connor and Rose want more kids. They've been postponing because of my situation, and I don't want her to wait that much longer.

"What?" Rose blanches, her eyes orb-like and filled with confusion and questions.

"Lily had that experience with you, and a huge part of me would love to have it too." Also if she's pregnant at the same time as me, there'll be less focus on my issues—less worry and concern for everyone involved.

It seems like a peaceful solution. A happy one.

Connor is staring right at me, seeing into *all* of my intentions. I meet his eyes, and his are entirely impassive, only letting me absorb what I throw at him.

I don't like being a problem in people's lives, and I just want them to be happy. This way, if something does happen to me, they'll still end up with good news. I see good things. Doesn't he?

Rose touches her forehead, stressed about everything today. I can tell. This was bad timing. "It's okay," I say quickly. "It's not a big de—"

"We'll have to plan it really well," Rose declares, dropping her hand.

I bounce on my toes. "Really?" My chest rises, and my smile stretches. It must be contagious because she begins to smile too.

She nods and then spins to her husband. They begin talking in hushed French, indistinguishable from our vantage point.

My phone buzzes in my brown leather backpack. Ryke is closest, so I ask him to grab it since he's already halfway there.

He enters the security code and sees the new message. "From your mom." His voice is tighter. "Fucking A."

I lean into his body and read the text.

Engagement party is set up for Ryke's birthday weekend. No cancellations. You will be there. You're my last little girl. Love you. — Mom

"I can say no…" I tell him.

Ryke rubs his lips and then shakes his head. "We should give this to her."

I frown, wondering where he's going with this. "Why?"

His gaze darkens on me. "Because we haven't told your parents that we're trying to have a fucking baby."

I gasp. "The horror."

He doesn't even bat an eye or smile. He's stoic, his gaze raking my body in a flirty manner. My breath shallows, and I'm tempted to flirt back.

Ryke is the one to shut it down before it begins. "We need to give her something before we tell her." He doesn't want to enrage my mom or be on my parent's shit list again. We're all at a good place with each other, and it'd be a blow to lose all that progress because of this.

So I nod in agreement. "Are you more worried about my mom or my dad?" I wonder.

He gives me a look like *I'm not fucking worried.* Then he messes my hair, the strands frizzing. I smile, already knowing that my dad's respect means more to him. Everyone loves Greg Calloway, so when he doesn't at least *like* you back, it hurts a little more.

I'm mostly worried about what an engagement party thrown by Samantha Calloway looks like.

Knowing her, anything is possible.

< 7 >

Ryke Meadows

I run around the second-story gym track, which overlooks an indoor basketball court below. Empty at 4 a.m. on a Saturday. Rain pelts the metal roof, and my brother runs two paces behind me. He picks up his stride a couple times to catch up, but I easily double mine.

I look over my shoulder, and he scowls before giving me a dry half-fucking-smile.

I almost laugh. "Maybe you should run a lot fucking faster."

"Maybe you should break your leg," he suggests. He's beaten me before, but it doesn't mean that he does all the time. Before I focus ahead of me, I catch him yawning into his shoulder. "Or ask me to run during a normal hour. I'm only human, bro!"

I slow down to a walk, and Lo matches my pace beside me. I don't fucking speak at first. I need to tell him something—I know I can't keep this in like I used to. Instead of "expressing myself" I just follow my lane around the track.

Lo gives me a weird look, like I've grown a fucking antenna in the middle of my forehead.

"What?" I ask.

"You're breathing like you've smoked five packs of Camels." He touches his chest. "I know I'm in *much* better shape than you, but we only ran five miles. I've seen you run twice that without dry heaving."

"I'm not *dry heaving*."

"Whatever, man. You're doing this breathing thing." He mimics me, sounding like a beached whale.

I flip him off.

He mimes catching and pocketing it. "Thanks. I needed a *fuck you* for later."

"You're in a good mood." I stretch out my arm while we keep walking, my muscles tight from anxiety. I fucking suck at delivering bad news.

Lo nods. "Numbers came in yesterday, and the new baby clothes line for Hale Co. has increased our profit margin. Another upside, I get to watch Rose throw shade at some of the *foulest* fucking human beings I've ever met. Corporate America is dirty." He cringes at the thought. "Don't tell Rose that I complimented her."

I almost laugh. I'm glad their business partnership has worked out without any major fights. I don't think anyone expected it to go this well, not even Lo.

He scratches the back of his neck, his amber eyes softer but jaw still sharp. "Do you ever think about working there?" He quickly adds, "I don't want you to think that I need you. Because I don't. I'm just wondering if you'll ever come on board."

Lo is running Hale Co. on his own, and when our dad stepped down, I did have the opportunity to be CEO with him. My brother proved that he could do it alone and that he wanted the job. So I let him have it all.

Do I ever want to run a multi-billion dollar empire that sells baby products? "No," I tell Lo. "As much as I like the idea of working with you, I think we'd fucking kill each other by the end of it." I can only see a business relationship harming the trust and respect we've spent so fucking long building.

He nods a couple times in agreement. Then he stops completely, resting his arm on the balcony railing that overlooks six basketball courts below. I can hear myself breathing—*fucking Christ*. He was right.

Lo suddenly says, "I want to split my shares and give you part of the company."

"No," I immediately reject this idea.

Lo glares, his eyes drilling holes into me. "You never even told me that he didn't give you a share of the company."

People can access that information, just like Lo probably did when he took over Hale Co. "He didn't want anyone to know that I was his fucking son, Lo. He couldn't have a random fucking kid named *Jonathan Ryke Meadows* be a shareholder."

Lo lets out an agitated breath. "Then why not let me help you now?"

"Because I don't need fucking help. You've told me what's in your trust fund before—and mine is triple yours. Dad did that to make up for what I lost in shares. We're even."

Lo glances at the basketball courts, then back at me. "He has control over your trust, Ryke."

"Yeah, I know." Our dad has a huge stipulation attached to my trust that Lo is aware of, but I don't want him to worry about my finances. I may not be worth billions like him, but I still have millions—way more than enough. "Look, I've saved a lot of money from sponsorships—"

"You have to rock climb to make that," he cuts me off with a short, pained laugh. "Forget it." He starts walking again in a huff.

I catch up to him quickly, realizing what this is truly about. I make money through commercials and ads when I rock climb, currently the face of Fizzle's sports drink, *Ziff: River Rush.* "Hey," I say, resting a hand on his shoulder until he slows to a stop.

He spins around on me, eyes flashing murderously. "What?"

This is where I tell him everything in my head. Where I fucking let it out. I'm still not great at it, but I'm not about to bury it all like I used to. "I'm going to rock climb whether or not someone pays me for it. You have to fucking accept that."

He glares past me, having trouble looking me straight on. His eyes begin to redden, unblinking and tense.

"I've rock climbed practically my entire fucking life, and I can't give it up for anything." It's a part of who I am, and I don't know how to live without it. I don't know if I can.

"You're allowed to be selfish. I get that," Lo says. "I mean, I should get that, I'm the most selfish one out of all of us."

I grimace—feeling the sting from every word. I'm surprised when he doesn't launch anything about *having a kid* at me. Maybe he's holding back from stooping that low, but I'm thinking about it anyway. *Having a kid while taking these risks.* My life is in flux more now than it's ever been, and I'm not sure if I can root myself the right way.

"Let's just forget it," Lo mutters, cooling down some.

"Wait." I catch his arm before he leaves. "There's something I need to tell you." Willow. Our dad. This is the conversation that's plagued me, but it has to happen. Out of everyone, Lo deserves answers. I just don't know how he'll fucking handle them.

His brows lift in dry surprise. "Oh, you mean your dehydrated hippo routine wasn't because you're out of shape and need an oxygen tank on the ride home?"

I roll my eyes and then rest my hands on my head. "Look..."

"I'm looking." He's actually glaring—but not as much as before.

I open my mouth, ready to just get it over with.

His phone rings. *Fuck.*

I run a hand through my hair as he digs into his pocket. "It's probably just one of my annoyingly overachieving employees that need to be told how amazing they are every minute of the day." He looks at the screen. "Nope, it's not Rose." He presses a button and puts the phone to his ear. "Hey, Lil. Please tell me you recorded the new episode of *Teen Wolf*, and please tell me you haven't watched it without me."

He notices my glower and holds up a finger, his eyes soften in an apology. And then they transform to worry. "Wait, slow down, love. Take some breaths."

"What's wrong?" I ask, concerned. My split-second assumption is that she's craving sex. It takes me a moment to remember she hasn't called Lo crying about wanting sex or needing it in a long fucking while.

Lily's voice must escalate because I catch her next words. "He's got this thing on him. It's like a red patchy area and he keeps scratching. I've never seen it before. Lo, what if it's really, *really* bad?"

"I'm on my way home right now," Lo tells her, already moving towards the exit. I'm close behind him, so I can hear Lily again.

"What if I have some form of silent herpes and I accidentally gave it to him by kissing him on the cheek? What if I did this, Lo?" Her voice cracks into a sob at his name.

Lo's entire face breaks. "You don't have herpes," he whisper-hisses as we walk outside. It's still too early for people to be out, but there are some wary eyes on the sidewalk. We probably should have brought our bodyguards, but sometimes it's nice pretending to be fucking normal for a change. "And secondly," Lo continues, "you didn't do anything wrong. For Christ's sake, it's probably just a diaper rash."

"I can drive," I tell Lo as he starts towards the driver's side of his black Audi. He shakes his head and gives me a look like *not today*. I can't say I fucking blame him. Sometimes I make him more nervous when I'm behind the wheel.

I climb into the passenger seat and when he shuts the door, he puts the phone on speaker. I can hear Lily's sniffling clearly now.

"It's not…a…diaper…rash," she mumbles with her stuffy nose. "I looked…up…pictures."

"Should I call you Dr. Lily Hale now?" Lo asks, starting up the car.

"Yes." She blows her nose.

"You alone, Lil?" I question.

"Yeah."

Lo's hands tighten on the steering wheel. Moffy starts crying loudly. "It's okay, baby," Lily coos. "We're going to fix it. I promise." Her focus returns to the phone. "Could you guys keep talking to me until you get here? I just...I don't want to be by myself right now."

Lo can barely talk. His jaw sharpened, his teeth grinding, and his eyes carry so much empathy that they almost redden. I don't hesitate.

"So I know it may come as a shock, but I watched an episode of that *Teen Wolf* show last week. It wasn't fucking awful. That uh...one kid was my favorite. The goofy one with dark hair."

"Stiles," she answers for me, her voice a little lighter. "Which episode was it?"

I start explaining what I saw. Daisy and I found the show on the DVR, and she was enticed by the word *wolf,* so she played a random episode. We kept chucking pillows at each other and ended up on the fucking floor somehow. I remember maybe two scenes.

I keep talking and glancing at my brother, making sure he's alright.

When we arrive at the house, he rushes ahead, practically sprinting. It's that fucking moment that I realize I've completely forgotten to tell him about Willow. But right now, it's the last thing he needs to hear.

< *8* >

Daisy Calloway

I listen to the shower running while I lie in bed, tucked beneath our white quilt and a gray cable-knit sweater blanket. Coconut has occupied Ryke's pillow since he's been in the bathroom, and she hardly stirs.

If I strain my ears enough, I can distinguish the sounds of low, pleasured groans among water hitting tiles.

On a normal day, I'd slip into the shower with him, but trying that now, he'd be extremely upset. Ryke wheeled me out of the hospital yesterday—one less ovary and one less tube after surgery. I'm sore from hip-to-hip and can barely turn on my side without feeling an ache, but pain medication has helped some.

I'm in no condition to receive pleasure, and he wouldn't want me to give it after I just came home.

Lying here. In the quiet without Ryke beside me. I try not to think about the bad news from yesterday. It keeps flaring up. No matter how hard I close the curtains on my thoughts.

Dr. Yoshida couldn't remove the entire right cyst.

At least not without potentially scarring my last remaining ovary in the process. He said he took out as much as possible, but I can't stop imagining this monstrous *thing* attached to my reproductive organ, slowly mushrooming to destroy all that's left.

I'm not the only one with medical maladies recently. Maximoff had a crazy rash and after a few tests, they've determined it was hives. Allergy related. The doctors narrowed it down to ants, which has caused Lily to be extremely paranoid about the insect. I don't blame her though. Hearing that baby cry in discomfort is enough to break your heart.

The shower shuts off, tearing into my thoughts. I stretch my arm towards the light switch. The movement pulls at the skin on my belly, so I end up sitting on my knees to reach for it. I flick the switch, and hanging green paper lanterns illuminate, casting a warm glow throughout our messy room.

There are clothes everywhere.

Along with Nerf guns, tennis balls, Frisbees, and an actual bicycle. I can't even remember how or why that ended up in the basement with us.

The bathroom door swings open. Beads of water roll down Ryke's shoulders and abs, a white cotton towel tied very, very low on his waist. My body may not sing right now, but my mind is definitely enjoying the view.

Ryke immediately catches me kneeling on our bed. "What's wrong?" he asks, pushing his wet hair out of his face. *You are so attractive.* "Do you need more pain meds?"

Coconut perks her head, looking between us.

"Not right now." I gently ease my body against the headboard and extend my legs. I wear one of his gray cotton shirts, the hem reaching my thighs, naked beneath the fabric.

He nears his side of the bed, setting a knee on the mattress to be even closer. I hone in on what's behind his towel while he scrutinizes my body with a long sweep. "Do you need anything? I can get you a glass of fucking water or—"

"You could masturbate in front of me." I wag my eyebrows playfully.

His brows scrunch, like he's trying to make sense of whether I'm serious or just joking. I thought I was kidding, but I wonder if a part of me wishes he'd just openly rub one out rather than hide from me.

While he scrutinizes my expression, my eyes skim his intricate tattoo that's a reminder to overcome self-constraints. An inked phoenix covers his right ribs and chest, a gray chain tethered around the bird's ankles, and the start of an anchor rests by his hip, the end concealed by his towel. I don't even think he realizes how sexy the placement is.

I also notice his L-shape scar from his transplant surgery, a little reddened after his shower. It trails between both ribcages and veers off beneath one.

"Or," I say, "you could spread my legs open and take me so, *so* hard." I collapse on the bed, my head falling onto my pillow, and I theatrically put my hand to my forehead. "Take me now, Ryke Meadows. Ah!" I mock cry out for him with a heavy breath.

He's staring intently. I have no idea where his head lies—probably as much as he has no idea where mine rests right now.

"You okay with me masturbating?" he finally asks.

That's *not* what I thought he'd conclude. I prop myself on my arms. "I don't care. I never have." I'm not naïve to think he can go two months without sex *and* without jacking off.

"Something's eating at you, Dais. I can fucking see it all over you." Because I deflected with humor from the get-go.

He pushes his wet hair back again. *Ryke*…I wish I felt better.

Maybe that's it.

"I just don't like this," I whisper.

His brows knot as he listens closely.

"And I'm afraid of missing out on experiences with you…" I trail off because I know this is just a taste of what it may be like if I'm pregnant. Bed rest if it's a hard pregnancy. Lying down. Staying still. I want to believe I have it in me, and I don't want him to worry that I might not. "I'm just overthinking."

His jaw hardens, and he removes his knee from the mattress, standing six-foot-three-inches tall and towering. "What are you missing out on? Watching me masturbate?"

"So literal," I mutter with a weak smile.

"Then help me out, Dais."

"I'm trying," I whisper, unsure of how to express what I feel. I'm not good with words and neither is he, and my body is out of commission so I can't use that to say what I mean. "I don't like this," I repeat what's beating at me.

He suddenly climbs onto the bed, and I realize I'm crying, hot trails slick on my cheeks.

"Why am I crying?" I say through an avalanche of tears, my chest heaving. *I hate this.* "I hate this." He pulls me into his arms, and I cover my face with my hands.

"It's okay," he whispers in my ear and strokes my hair.

"I hate this," I say again, trying to wipe these involuntary tears. He holds me tightly, and I'm so thankful for his warm embrace, calming my flood of emotions. "I hate...being out of commission. Not even sexually. Just physically...broken."

It's everything.

It's the stupid cyst. The two months of waiting to try for a baby. The fact that my reproductive organs could fail me all over again. It's feeling like I've let *him* down somehow. Like I'm not pulling my weight.

Like he could do better with someone a little more whole.

"Hey." He tears my hands from my face and lifts my head up. My chin trembles, trying to keep it together. And he says so strongly, "You're not fucking broken."

My eyes burn. It takes me a moment to respond. I'm so quiet and still. I breathe, "Say that again."

He cups my cheek, his thumb brushing the tears beneath my wet lashes. "You're not fucking broken, sweetheart. And you're not missing out on anything with me."

I nod, rubbing my eyes. "You'll masturbate in front of me then?" I say lightly, attempting to lift the mood.

His brows rise. "You want me to?"

"I don't know…" My reddened eyes flit up to his darkened features that also hold a great deal of concern for me. I kiss him, and he instantly reciprocates earnestly, his fingers lost in my hair. I bite his lip, teasingly pulling back. He closes the distance, drawing me in, his tongue parting my lips until a noise tickles my throat.

Oxygen cages inside my lungs, but he's not even close to being out of breath.

Ryke Meadows endures all things like he was born to last forever.

His perseverance may deceive me some days. Because what he faces when he rock climbs could end him. Every time. I just don't want to look at it that way. I'd rather see the man who *lives* every second his fingers clasp rock, not the man who may die.

He breaks the kiss. To let me breathe.

My chest lowers in a heavy exhale. *I'm sorry*, I almost say in regards to my outburst. I stop myself though. I already hear his response. *Don't fucking apologize for your emotions, Calloway. You can be upset.*

"Thank you," I whisper, kissing his cheek. I slide off him so he can return to his own pursuits and not dwell on me.

His gaze drifts off for a moment and then returns to me. "When we start having sex again, you need to fucking tell me if you're in pain."

I wonder how long this has been on his mind.

I tuck a strand of hair behind my ear. "It's not easy, you know." My voice softens to a whisper. "I don't want to hurt you." Emotionally, I mean, but he knows this.

He cups my cheek, the one with the scar, enough to draw my attention off the bed and onto him. "I don't ever want you to lie there in pain because you're trying to make me happy—because you're afraid of hurting *my* feelings. That's not how this fucking works. *You matter.*"

I hear him say a version of this to me at sixteen. At seventeen. At eighteen and nineteen and now at twenty. He has tried to make me feel worth more than I've allowed myself to be. All this time.

Even when the topic was about me sleeping with other guys. Even when I shared details. He still listened.

And his response always had the same heartbeat. *You matter.*

I'm about to throw out a lighthearted joke, but the words catch in my throat and my eyes glass again. I nod repeatedly.

"Come here." He pulls me back onto his lap, his arms tightening around my frame, and I bury my head in his warm chest. "We all have parts of ourselves that bite us in the fucking ass."

I look up at him. "And what's biting my ass?"

He almost smiles. "You're too sweet, Calloway." I wish I had a better fatal flaw, something destructive like *lust* or *greed*. Kindness seems so easy to conquer, and yet I've let it rule me.

"Do you know what's biting yours?" I wonder.

"I'm too fucking stubborn. Maybe too aggressive."

"Or too attractive," I note. "Your beauty is *terribly* distracting."

He gives me the sexiest stern look that I devour with greedy eyes. "Yeah?" he says deeply.

"Yeah," I echo, "all the princesses in the land have evacuated their castles in search of this rugged blacksmith who has these hands…" I lift up his hands in mine, his palms calloused from all the rocks he climbs. "…these *manly* hands that they want slowly stroking their sensitive skin. You've unintentionally emptied kingdoms, Ryke Meadows. How do you feel about this?"

His rough exterior hardly changes. Even as he says, "I've already found my fucking princess."

"I bet she's proud to be with a man like you."

He kisses me on the lips, and I reciprocate before breaking it and letting him go by sliding off his lap again. He hesitates, checking on me and then deciding to stand. He holds the towel at his waist.

I watch him watch me, and I gently roll onto my stomach, hugging my pillow against my cheek. My body throbs, a dull ache at the new pressure but I don't want to lie on my back again.

His tanned skin is nearly dry, his dark brown hair still damp. And he continues to hold my gaze, standing about two feet from our bed.

"You shouldn't look at me like that," I tease.

"And how am I looking at you?"

"Like you love me."

"I do fucking love you." He removes his towel, using it to dry his hair. I can't contain a smile as his cock comes into view. Warm all of a sudden, I kick the quilt and blanket down towards the edge of the mattress. His shirt that I wear has rolled and bunched at my waist, leaving my ass completely exposed. His eyes drift down my body, and his movements slow as he drinks in my frame.

"Like you want to make babies with me," I add with a growing smile that lights up dim places within me.

His arousal pulsates in his brown eyes. "Tell me why I shouldn't look at you like that?"

"My boyfriend would be upset—the one with the ten-pack." I grip the hem of my gray tee, teasing the possibility of pulling it higher, revealing more of my lower back.

Ryke proceeds to dry his hair again, but his eyes bounce between my bare ass and my gaze. "Trying to make me fucking jealous, Calloway?"

"Maybe." I smile. "Is it working?"

"No," he deadpans, his eyes all dark and features all brooding. We're both silent, my body *almost* thrumming instead of throbbing. I think we're both picturing him taking me from behind, kissing me between my legs, driving into me—

The door blows open. *We forgot to lock it.*

< 9 >

Ryke Meadows

"Jesus Christ." Lo curses as soon as he barrels inside, abruptly rotating away and setting his hands on his head. "You'd think you two would know what a lock is by now. Wasn't Connor seeing you come on your girlfriend's face embarrassment enough?"

"Fuck off." I throw the nearest thing I have at him—which happens to be the fucking towel I was holding against my cock. Things I never planned to do today: flash my little brother. But he can't keep using that moment as ammunition, and truth is, I don't fucking care enough to go grab another towel.

Nutty barks once.

My focus immediately pulls to Daisy. I study her quickly, concern hardening my jaw. She sits on her ass, clutching a blanket to her chin, looking younger than usual. Like her actual age. She's not as panicked as she could be for an intruder, and I relax only slightly.

I question Lo, "What the fuck do you want? And by now, you would think you'd know what a *knock* is."

He turns and his gaze instantly lands on my dick. His irritated, amber eyes drill into me. "I don't want to see that, bro."

"Then get the fuck out."

"Gladly. I have shit to worry about anyway—shame on me for wanting to include you."

My face falls. "What does that mean?" I ask, but he already slams the door on his way out.

"*Fucking A*," I curse roughly and spin towards Daisy. "Are you—"

"I'm okay." She must see my doubt because she adds, "Not shaken but stirred." She gives me a real smile. "I have Coconut, and I might call Frederick to check in."

I like that she has better outlets to help her overcome simple fears that impede everyday life.

Nutty nudges her arm, and Daisy rubs her thick fur. "Go," Daisy tells me.

I hesitate for a brief second, scanning her one more time—making sure she's okay—before I shut the door closed behind me. I rush through the entertainment room and up the flight of stairs, only now fucking realizing that I'm buck naked.

Fucking fantastic.

I've only ever flashed Lily once since we've lived together. It was my ass. Not a full-frontal. She says her retinas still burn, but I worry about making her uncomfortable because of her addiction. It's something that fucking kills me. Because I don't want to be the cause of a bad day for her. I want her as healthy and as stress-free as my brother.

So when I go into the kitchen, no one around, I veer down a short hallway to the laundry room. I literally grab the first black item I find on the dryer. Walking back into the kitchen, I try my best to step into a pair of boxer-briefs.

They're tight as hell.

I glance at them and skid to a halt by the barstools. Tiny yellow bat prints are scattered on the fucking fabric.

What the fuck?

I think I might be wearing Lily's underwear.

Fuck it. I continue my stride, pushing through the kitchen door to the living room—too worried about my brother's comment to change. I don't give a fuck how I look anyway.

The television plays *Winnie the Pooh*, Moffy and Janie watching the film from their colorful yellow and pink beanbags. Connor and Rose are the first to see me, a straight shot from their loveseat. She has her legs propped on the cushion, sprawled over Connor's lap, heels off.

His grin begins to fucking mushroom, and I'm over it before he starts. Rose's amusement is fucking palpable too, her eyes alight with humor.

I walk further into the living room, not asking why they're here. It's clear they stopped by so their daughter could spend time with her cousin. Both kids lean close to each other, babbling and pointing at the screen. Janie giggles more than once.

"Where's Lo?" I ask.

"Where's your pants?" Connor says in his annoyingly calm voice. Rose actually laughs, the sound widening Connor's million-dollar grin.

Rose tries to control her vocal cords and narrows a piercing glare towards him. "Stop grinning like that."

"Like what?"

"Like you created my laughter, Richard."

"Didn't I? Because if I remember correctly, my words made you laugh."

She growls. "You're impossible."

"I would have gone with accurate, but we can talk about definitions for my charm later." *For fuck's sake.*

She tries to hone another glare, but her smile shines through. "I hate you."

"Say that a little louder, darling, and our daughter will grow up believing hate is actually love."

"Maybe it is," she muses, "at least for me."

He rubs her legs and then leans closer, whispering something in her ear. I sidle near the couch and finally spy my brother slouched on the fucking chair. Ignoring me.

His phone is clenched in his hand, and his gaze descends to my underwear. "And I thought a goddamn Pooh bear without pants was weird." Lo swivels more towards me, his brows furrowing. "Are those Willow's?"

My stomach drops. *What.* "They have to be Lily's," I say—but Willow does live with us too.

Lo stands. "Batman's DC."

"So…?"

Lo gives me a look like I still can't comprehend simple comic book facts after five years. "I hate DC."

Right.

"Lily doesn't own any DC apparel," he spells it out for me, even though that just clicked one step before.

Color must drain from my face because Lo frowns deeply at my reaction. It's just a little fucking weird wearing my half-sister's underwear. I've always seen Lily as a friend. One who I've known much longer.

I raise my hands to my head, actually contemplating stripping right now, but since two little kids are in the room, I trash the fucking option.

"Don't freak the fuck out," Lo says, his attempt at calming me, even with his harsh, edged voice. "It's not like she's your sister."

Fuuuck. I rub my lips, nauseous as this secret starts morphing into a lie. I planned on telling him way before now, but Daisy just had surgery and my concern has been with her for so long that I really, honestly, forgot.

I'm not about to repeat past mistakes and harbor this for longer than I should. "Actually," I say, drawing Connor and Rose's attention too. "Willow is Jonathan's daughter." In so few words I explain everything our dad revealed to me, painting a picture of my proposal night without overdetailing.

Connor and Rose straighten, listening with rapt attention at new information.

When I finish, Lo visibly cringes and starts pacing the length of the foyer to the couch, silent and white-knuckling his fucking cellphone.

The only sound comes from Piglet's whiney voice, irritating me more than that cartoon ever has. Pushing Lo to silence might be more terrifying than his outbursts. I just wasn't prepared for this.

"Hey." I grab his arm on his way back towards me, stopping him mid-stride. "Fucking talk to me."

He shoves me off and then points at his chest. "I've had bombs dropped on me for the past five years. You think I didn't question this once or twice? I did. I thought about it, and what I keep thinking now—out of everything—is that I'm glad *he* knows what it feels like to be duped for decades. Believing his familial relationships are set in stone, only to learn that it's a fucking lie. And this is all his fault. All *his* goddamn fault. So yeah, I'm happy that our dad had a daughter he never knew about."

He lets out a heavy breath, pausing for a second before adding, "Not really happy for Willow, but…yeah." His eyes redden, empathizing with her since he's been there.

I watch him stare past the hardwood floor. "You're not pissed at me?"

"For what?"

"For waiting to tell you."

He cocks his head with an annoyed expression. "Daisy just underwent surgery. You think I'm that selfish?"

He's just not the same guy he once was. He's grown up, not as resentful over the smallest things anymore. While I process this, he gives me one of his signature Loren Hale death stares, the kind that'd probably terrify all his billion-dollar corporate enemies.

"Thanks a lot," he says bitterly. He lets out a sigh and then runs a hand on the back of his neck. "Since you're now her brother too…" His face contorts like this is fucked up. It is, a little bit. "You really need to know what's going on."

The shit he's worrying about. "What is it?"

His eyes flicker to his cell. "So Willow called me about a half hour ago. She went to eat dinner with Maya." The Superheroes & Scones store manager, but more importantly she used to be Willow's roommate. They're good friends, but I don't see the upsetting part here. "Willow will be here in about five or ten minutes, but she said that she had news to tell us. And she sounded really fucking nervous."

I sit on the armrest of the Queen Anne chair. "Did you ask her what it's about?"

"She said that it was better if I didn't have any hints."

Connor chimes in, "Your previous theories about her car being stolen, moving to Maine, and the illogical one about alien abduction all seem less plausible than what Ryke brought to the table."

The alien scenario sounds more like a Lily Calloway theory. I understand what Connor is implying. "You think she knows Jonathan's her fucking father?"

Lily suddenly appears from the stairs with a big bowl of popcorn, unable to see my clothing from her vantage point. "Are you guys making a Hale family *Star Wars* alternate universe?" She lowers her voice, mimicking Darth Vader, "Willow, I am your father."

No one laughs.

A popcorn kernel falls out of Lily's mouth. "Waaaait...this wasn't a joke?"

"No, love," Lo says, his arm sliding around her shoulder. He steals a handful of popcorn from her bowl.

I stand up again, thoughts fucking rolling in my head about Willow's news.

"Think of it this way," Connor says, "if she already knows about Jonathan, you don't need to break the news to her."

"It's still shit," I tell him, "no matter which way you spell it."

"You would be the expert on four-letter words since your vocabulary consists almost entirely of them."

I cast a fucking glare his way. "Whose side are you on, Cobalt?"

"The intelligent side. Whether you come over here is yet to be seen. You usually average about forty-percent, so it's more or less up in the air."

He's already giving me a fucking headache.

"What are those?" Lily nearly screeches, eyes widened on my tight bat-printed girl's boxer-briefs, not leaving much to the imagination.

I forgot to stay seated. I'm even angled towards her, and I'm about to turn around, but her arm flies to her eyes, embarrassed red patches blooming on her neck.

She says to herself, "Wake up, Lily. Wake up!" *Fuck.*

Her chant causes Lo to shield her eyes with his hands, sliding behind her.

He guides her over to the vacant couch in front of the kids' beanbags. "I know, I feel your pain, love. It's such an ugly sight." His tone is lighthearted with his wife, and when he drops his hands from her eyes, he shows her the couch to relax.

She stays standing instead, hugging the fucking popcorn bowl. "I'm sorry, Lo," she apologizes with so much hurt in her eyes.

A pit wedges in my stomach.

Rose's back straightens like a stiff board, and she moves her legs off Connor's lap, her feet slipping into her heels. Ready to be there for her sister.

I concentrate on Lo, watching confusion warp his face. I take a few steps towards him, closer to Moffy's yellow beanbag.

Ready to be there for my brother.

"Sorry about what?" Lo asks hesitantly.

Lily licks her dried lips, guilt down-casting her eyes to the popcorn a couple times.

"Lil?" Lo says, his voice breaking a little. "Sorry about what?"

"I meant to ship them back," she says in a soft whisper. "I really did. They were so cute though. It was the internet's fault for sending me Batgirl underoos instead of Spider-Girl ones."

I think we all, collectively, let out a breath of relief, the tension immediately weakening.

Lo sinks into the couch, winded for a second. "I thought something bad happened, Lil," he almost shouts.

"I thought this was bad."

"Like bad, *bad*," he tells her, his eyes softening.

She plops down next to him. "In college, I bought a Superman phone case and you said we couldn't be friends if I called you on it."

Lo thinks hard to recall that memory, but I wonder if it's gone to alcohol.

"You also burned my Halloween bat-ears, which wasn't even a DC product."

"You were a bat on *my* birthday," he retorts. "That was worse than me lighting your little ears on fire."

"I was nine," she says, poking him in the chest, "and you ate all my favorite Pop-Tarts on purpose the day before."

"Huh, so it was a revenge bat-costume," he says like his point has been made.

Lily squints at him.

Lo begins to smile, and I'm just fucking thankful nothing serious happened. And that I'm *not* wearing my half-sister's underwear.

Footsteps clap along the hardwood, and we all see Daisy emerging through the kitchen doorway. She wears my clothes: one of my gray shirts partly tucked into my black cotton track pants. I can't even fucking explain how much I love her in them.

But my body definitely can. My muscles almost instantly constrict, blood rushing to my cock, and I swallow hard to suppress anything one degree more.

I focus on things that matter more than my fucking arousal. Whether or not she's in pain. If she needs more meds. How she's doing walking around.

As she comes closer to me, she's careful about widening her stride. When she realizes everyone is watching her, not just me, she offers her sisters a placating smile. "I'm not going to self-destruct," she says to them. "I'm just one ovary and one fallopian tube lighter."

Rose rolls her eyes. "I don't like your jokes."

"Too bad," Daisy smiles. "You're stuck with them."

My lips lift a fraction, glad that she's willing to make unpopular jokes if that's what she fucking wants to do.

Rose must feel the same way because she says, "As long as you're okay."

Daisy shrugs, pain flaring in her eyes, and it breaks my fucking heart. I can't tell if it's emotional or physical, but I want to take it all away.

I'm about to bridge the distance between us, but her attention plants to me, on my boxer-briefs. Her smile slowly elevates, and her pace quickens until she's right in front of me, my hand gently sliding across her waist.

And she says, "You know your ass says, *Bat Girl*, right?"

I didn't.

"That do it for you, Calloway?"

"It does a lot of things for me." Her silly fucking smile widens and she wags her brows suggestively, teasing about sex, even when she's not in the mood for it. Most of our friendship was flirting without an endgame. So I'm used to it in our relationship, and I don't want it to go away.

I draw her closer, her chest pressed against mine. "Like what?"

She rests her arms on my shoulders, her fingers running through the back of my hair. "Like I now feel one-hundred percent better. No more lower-whatever pain."

If that were the fucking truth, I'd be wearing this underwear every fucking day. "I have more medicine for your lower-whatever-fucking pain," I remind her.

She mock gasps. "You added a 'fucking' to my pain. How could you?" She mimes fainting, and I catch her as she falls against me.

"How'd you make it into this world on two fucking feet?" The girl never stays still, never stops. I shake my head. I love her, every minute of the day, and she doesn't even realize, doesn't even see how much.

"Are you saying I flew?" She rests her chin against my chest, and I think she's been spending too much time with Lily.

Before I can mention it, the front door unlocks and everyone goes still, Daisy stiffening in my arms. I whisper in her ear everything that happened, catching her up as quickly as I can. She relaxes some, realizing that Willow has to be in the foyer, not Cleo or Harper or any other fucking horrible person that she can imagine.

Just as Willow appears from the foyer, someone else trails closely behind her.

"What is this?" Lo asks, gesturing from Willow to Garrison, a guy that's been on all of our shit lists at one point. Even Lily and Daisy's, who can barely even accumulate five names.

We all have a lot more patience with Garrison after he started working at Superheroes & Scones with Willow. They've been friends, but I didn't think he'd join her tonight.

Garrison points at Willow. "Well, this is Willow." His voice is thick with sarcasm. "I'm Garrison Abbey. Nice to meet you." He stuffs his hands into his leather jacket, his brown hair concealed with a backwards black baseball cap.

Connor chimes in, "As far as first impressions go, you're now ranked below this one." I think he's going to motion to Lo, but his fucking finger is directed at *me*.

I flip him off with both hands.

"So I need to tell you all something," Willow speaks, rerouting everyone's attention. She pushes up her black-rimmed glasses, a strap of her overalls sliding off her shoulder. Her light brown braid is frizzy, and I notice that she shares Lo's hair color, but her eyes—they're brown with hazel around the center.

Like mine.

Maybe now, more than before, it really fucking sinks in. *She's my sister.* It suddenly means something more than it did, connects me to another person in a more meaningful way. Still, it's all uneven and fractured and rough as hell. I'm not sure how the knowledge would affect her, if it'd change her perception of me. Make it worse between us.

She continues, "I thought it'd be a good idea if Garrison was here too."

Lo stands while Lily stays seated, clutching his legs to keep him from chasing Garrison out of the house.

"Is he a part of your news?" Lo asks tentatively, and the bottom of my stomach drops.

Daisy keeps an arm around my waist, and I realize it's for the same reason that Lily is holding onto her husband.

"Yeah..." Willow pales a little, her nerves fucking apparent.

Garrison edges closer to her and clasps her hand in comfort.

"Are you pregnant?" Lo asks.

I hold my breath for a second, fucking worried, and then her eyes grow big.

"What?" she chokes on her surprise.

"Yeah, *what?*" Garrison glares and gestures to the entire room. "If anyone's knocking up anyone, it's one of you, and honestly, what the hell are you wearing?" He grimaces at me.

"Underwear," I say. It's not a big fucking deal.

"I see that, thanks," he says dryly.

Willow swallows, "So, um...this didn't really go how we thought it would."

"Why are you saying *we* like he's a part of this?" Lo snaps, pointing an accusing finger at Garrison.

"It's not what you're thinking," Willow struggles to get the words out. "I'm a..."

Garrison squeezes her hand, scrutinizing her frozen, immobile state before finishing for her, "Virgin."

Lily peers over the couch. "You're a virgin?"

Garrison groans. "No, *she's* a virgin. Good God, it's like tuning into five different radio stations at once when I come here. Don't you all ever get tired of each other?"

"I'm mostly tired of you," Lo slings back, a shot right to the fucking head.

It hurts Garrison more than I think he's letting on, his stance closing off. "Whatever," he says.

Regret tightens my brother's gaze, but he tries to just focus on his sister—or *our* sister. "Your news can't be that you're a virgin and your friend isn't one, so what is it? Because I keep thinking you're leaving—"

"I'm not leaving," Willow says. "I don't have plans to move back to Maine. I promise I'd tell you if I was even thinking about it."

He nods slowly. "Is it...about something else with your parents?"

It's cagey enough, but she shakes her head, dismissing it so fucking quickly. She has no clue that Jonathan Hale is her father. That's not what this is about.

"Then what?" Lo asks.

"We're together," Willow suddenly says, briefly lifting her hand up with Garrison's.

My face mirrors Lo's scrunched up expression like *this can't be a good fucking thing*. I've heard him say some derogatory things towards women before. I can let it pass as word vomit in the heat of the moment— maybe he's grown up since then. But I still have no idea how he treats women. If he'd hurt Willow, physically, emotionally.

That's all I care about. Her safety. Her wellbeing.

"What do you mean together?" Lo retorts.

Connor sets his arm behind Rose on the loveseat. "They mean it in the colloquial sense. They're an item, going steady, boyfriend-girlfriend, baes—"

"What the fuck is a bae?" I interject.

"One of the stupidest internet trends," Garrison answers, "and I'm pro-internet and pro-memes, so you know it's gotta be fucking awful."

The fact that Connor is up-to-date on slang is actually kind of fucking terrifying. He's usually a step behind Lily and Lo on pop culture. I'd rather Connor Cobalt *not* be all-knowing.

"I kinda liked baes," Lily says solemnly, as though she's lowering the term into the grave as she fucking speaks.

"This is ridiculous," Rose announces. "They just declared their relationship status, and everyone's more concerned about a made-up word." It's clear she had no idea what it meant before now, but I doubt she'll admit it out loud, not with Connor here.

"Not me," Lo snaps, his malice directed at Garrison.

"It's only been a week," Willow explains quickly. "I know it's not a long time, but I really didn't want to sneak around, especially since I live with some of you."

Garrison gauges her emotions, his concern for her pretty apparent. It *minutely* eases my fucking worry.

"We have rules," Lo starts.

"Have fun," Lily declares, her smile overwhelming. She's predicted this relationship a couple of times, but no one really wanted to talk about its possible fruition. Now here we are.

"No, not have fun—what the hell, Lily?" Lo gawks at his wife.

"They're eighteen."

"Yeah, we're eighteen," Garrison echoes.

Lo glares. "Last I remember, you're still in high school." He flunked out of his senior year and has to repeat.

Garrison sighs heavily. "You're not her fucking father."

"You're right," Lo says, "I'm her brother and the *first* person she should trust while she's in Philadelphia." He takes a step closer to Garrison. "She's my responsibility, and while I trust you with a lot of things, I don't want you upstairs in her room past two a.m.—and two a.m. is more than I'd give any kid of mine." Another step. "And keep the door open."

I like the fucking rule.

Although I'd probably make it midnight, but it's not my place.

Willow relaxes some against the wall, not that put off by this declaration. Maybe she's nervous by the prospect of something more intimate. I think, if what Daisy has told me is right, this would be her first boyfriend. I'm not even sure if she's been kissed yet.

I'm in the fucking mode to protect her, almost angled to show Garrison the fucking door earlier rather than later. I think he senses her uneasiness because he backs off too, their hands slowly disconnecting.

He nods to her. "I'll text you, okay?"

She nods back. "Will you check my gifs before you go to bed? I want to post them, but I think one isn't working."

Garrison almost smiles. "Yeah. I'll do it first thing." He acknowledges the rest of us with a curt wave and then heads out the door.

"When? Where? How?" Lily blurts out first to Willow.

Willow smiles and relaxes some. "So you're all not upset?" She lingers on Lo.

"You can do better," Lo tells her.

Daisy steps forward. "She knows Garrison in a way that none of us do, so we should really trust her instincts." Willow looks appreciative at Daisy, and they exchange smiles.

"You know what I don't trust?" Lo says, "An eighteen-year-old horny motherfucking guy's instincts."

"Same," I add.

"That's why there are rules, right?" Willow says. "So nothing should go wrong?"

If that doesn't fucking hit you right in the heart—what would?

Garrison Abbey better not pressure her or push her further or faster than she wants to go. Maltreatment of women might just be my number one boiling point, and if he sets it off—surrounding my sister no less—I'm going to lose my shit.

< *10* >

Daisy Calloway

Did you get the present? — Cleo

I keep opening the text, tormenting myself. After the fiftieth time staring at it, I click *delete*. An insignificant weight eases itself off my shoulders. Like a dust particle vacating a sand dune of anxiety. I don't want to trudge through my past friendships and unearth those feelings. There's no kindling left to reignite anything with Cleo or Harper. They've destroyed everything there ever was, proving my theory right after all.

Friends aren't forever. They're not even for a while.

It's a theory I hate with all my might, and so I cling to the one person who has the only chance of overturning its validity.

Willow sits on the other side of the small little pink table. It's nestled in the back of FroYummy—my favorite frozen yogurt spot in Philly. I've been itching to escape the house since my surgery, and four days after, with minimal soreness down below, I've finally moved beyond my gated neighborhood.

I spot Mikey, my bodyguard, a couple tables away, spending more time flipping through a worn James Patterson paperback than paying attention to us. Not that I blame him. It's a pretty dull sight in here.

Nobody has spotted us and blabbed my whereabouts to the paparazzi, so the store only has a few bodies milling about. I award my baseball cap as the winner of disguise here. Plus, it's just way easier being discreet when I'm not out with Ryke or my sisters.

Willow stares at the opened box on the table, her eyes wide in alarm. The bracelet that Cleo and Harper gave me practically glints in the light.

"I can't believe they're bribing you," she says, shaking her head. Her face rises to me. "And I can't believe they did that stuff to you at school."

I raise my brows. "After your *amazing* senior year at Dalton Academy, you can't believe they stuffed my locker with condoms?" She's confided in me about all her tribulations at prep school. I've shared my horror stories as well, but I left out the part about most of the deeds being the indirect product of my best friends turning their backs on me.

Until now.

I didn't want her to be scared of making friends at Dalton. She had moved from Maine, and it was her chance of starting over. There had to be hope in there, right?

"Tampons stuffed in my locker doesn't seem that bad though…in hindsight," she mutters and pushes her glasses up her nose. She doesn't mention how the tampons were dipped in red dye, and I don't bring it up.

Deflecting, I say, "Rose used to buy tampons for me when I was in middle school. I was too embarrassed to go in the store and check them out." I hold up my spoon coated in chocolate froyo. "In defense, the cutest boy was always the cashier, and middle school boys are always weird about tampons." Though, Ryke was never really embarrassed by them. He told me he's always been unabashedly unashamed. It's not something he grew into. He just was.

"I feel you," Willow nods. "You're so lucky you had a big sister. I always used to buy like a magazine or something really big to hide the box in my basket. Then I'd pray for a girl to be at checkout." She cringes at her memory. "Never really worked."

"The gods of luck will bless you one day, Willow. I feel it in my bones." I take a big bite of my yogurt and then close the jewelry box beside my cup.

I've already convinced Connor to donate the bracelet, so I'm heading to his office after I drop Willow off at her work. He's sworn not to tell me where it's going, and I trust he won't accidentally let the location slip. I didn't want to put that pressure on Ryke, especially since I talk to him way more about my ex-friends than anyone else.

"So…" Willow says with an ominous tone, her eyes lighting up. "When are you going to tell me about your plan?" She scoops a heap of strawberry froyo on her spoon.

"When you tell me yours."

She already knows of my fibs, shaking her head. "Not true. You know my plans. I'm working at Superheroes & Scones long enough to afford college. Yet…I still know nothing about your plans. Just that mysterious journal you keep writing in."

My journal. It's the new item in my life where I've translated my future into lists. And these lists, they're actually being checked off. My future is being molded by my own will, and it's something exciting. I know exactly what I'm going to be doing five, ten, twenty years down the line. Even thinking about it, my chest puffs out and I could toss my hands in the air and howl.

"Due time." I lick the side of the spoon. "It's going to be a fun surprise. And anyway, I want to talk about *you*. You have major news." I have news for her too—that she's Jonathan's daughter—but it's not mine to share. I hate keeping this secret from her, but Ryke said he'd do it when it was the right time. And it's not yet. So I just have to trust him.

Willow looks confused. "What news?"

"You have a boyfriend. Did you already forget?" I nudge her elbow with mine. This is her first real boyfriend. She's never even been kissed before, and she's eighteen. A fact that I find precious. All her firsts are coming closer to reality, and I'm just really happy for her.

"Yeah, but…no news yet," she tells me with a smile. "You'll be the first I tell, though…oh wait." She grimaces.

"Lily got to you, didn't she?"

"She made me pinky promise I'd tell her first," Willow says.

"She does that. I get second though, right?"

"Definitely."

I pause for a moment, thinking about something important. Mikey stands up from his table, closes his book, and heads to the bathroom.

My thoughts morph into a question. "Are you okay with Lo's rules?" A part of me worries that Lo is being strict because of me. I've had terrible experiences with my ex-boyfriends growing up, and I'm the only little sister figure he's really had in his life. I'd hate for Willow to be affected by my past.

"We talk a lot, so he knows me pretty well," Willow explains. "I think he knew that I'd want the rules. It's just…this is new for me. I'm used to having Garrison in my room, but not as my boyfriend. And I'm worried that I might not know how to say *no*. Or not be able to." She takes another spoonful from her cup. "It's just nice being able to blame some things on a curfew or an overprotective brother."

Loren Hale. Who would have known?

I'm about to ask her about her work, but something wet and cold lands on my shoulder and slides down my chest onto my white shorts. I jump up, my chair hitting the ground behind me in a clatter.

Pink frozen yogurt.

The girl who spilled her dessert looks like she just committed an act of murder. Her eyes are saucers and her face is sheet white. "I'm… so…" Her hands fly to her mouth. "I tripped…and…" My brief panic starts to subside.

"It's okay." I say quickly. "Please don't cry." I hold up my hands in surrender when the waterworks begin. "Seriously, it's really okay."

She nods a couple times, wiping her eyes with her knuckles and then shuffling back. Before I can process what happened, two girls are approaching me with napkins in hand.

"Daisy, oh my God, are you okay?! We just walked in when we saw what happened?" *What?* The strawberry blonde hair is unmistakable.

Cleo.

My ex-best friend.

I blink like maybe I constructed her from my scarred imagination. Like maybe she's just a kind stranger and not the girl who trapped me in an elevator. Who tried to humiliate me. And scare me.

But the more I blink, the more Cleo's fish-tail braid and diamond studs come into focus.

How real she is.

How real this all is.

She reaches out, frantically trying to dab the stains on my shirt. Her hands everywhere. All at once. I raise mine in defense. *Wait...*

Harper roughly digs at the frozen yogurt on my shoulder like she's scrubbing burnt oil from a pan. "It didn't look accidental. She probably recognized you and wanted to get her fifteen minutes of fame." *What are you doing here?*

Touching me.

Their hands are everywhere. *Wait...*

My head pounds, cold icing over my veins. Cleo pats her napkin near my breast, and I trip backwards, my hands pushed out more in front of me.

"Careful," Cleo says, her manicured nails clawing into my arm. "You're probably in shock. It's totally normal. Strangers are fucking weird. Fame mongers even more." She pulls my hair off my shoulder. "Oh shit, it's in your hair."

"Should we cut it?" Harper says with a coy smile.

I pale.

"Kidding," Harper tells me, tying her own dark hair off to the side. "Jesus, where'd your sense of humor go?"

"Hey." Willow—quiet, shy Willow—shoves ahead of me. "Get back." She steps in between us and their hands tear off me. I breathe through my nose, nausea building, and I only realize now that my arms and legs tremble.

I have to leave.

So many people would tell these girls to fuck off after what they did to me, but the trauma of their actions still sits with me, every day of my life. Starting a new war by shouting *fuck you* sounds like the worst idea in the world, so while fleeing may seem like the cowardly option—it's the one that calms *every* part of me.

It's the one I need.

"It's okay, honey," Harper says, "Daisy's a good friend of ours."

Friends don't humiliate other friends.

Harper reaches out to place her dirtied napkin on me again, but I step back too, stumbling against a chair. It clatters to the floor, but I spin around, heading for the exit. Blocking out their voices.

I'm not giving them the benefit of doubt. They could read my body language. I just don't think they care about how I feel. They never have.

I make it past one table. Three more to go and then the door.

Out. I just want out.

Our car is parked close to the entrance, and just as I pass the fourth table, Mikey sprints up to my side. His wide eyes suddenly tighten at the sight of the stains, all over my shirt.

"I'm getting you out of here." He places his hand on my shoulder, guiding me out.

"Daisy," Willow calls, catching up to me. I turn slightly and clasp her hand before we leave, bringing her closer while we head to the car. As soon as we climb into the back, lock the doors, tears prick my eyes.

I never wanted to see them again.

Prep school had been hard enough, and I never thought they'd be at FroYummy during the same exact time I arrived. Ready to clean my shirt with "helping" hands.

I tug at the white fabric, pink stains rubbed across the neckline and waist. I would believe, in a second, that they sent the girl in first. They told her to spill frozen yogurt on me. Just so they could act like my rescuers. They've plotted far worse and more complicated things than this, so why not?

People can change, but seeing them again, hearing their voices, was like being windswept into one of the worst times of my life.

I don't want to go back.

Willow wipes the lenses of her glasses with her sleeve before putting them on. "Are you going to be okay? I can have Garrison cover my shift."

I shake my head, my eyes swollen and burning, no tears yet. Mikey slows the car down near the Superheroes & Scones storefront. "No, it's okay," I say in a scratchy, strained voice. "I'm going to see Connor today, remember? I won't be alone."

She hesitates, eyeing my jostling legs that bounce with anxiety.

"Hey." I give her a weak smile. "You don't need to worry about me."

"Friends worry about friends," she says softly. "I mean...assuming we're friends."

My smile turns into something more genuine. "We are friends," I say, the words pumping warm blood through my veins. She knew me as a celebrity before she knew me as the regular ole Daisy, so she often questions whether someone like her could be friends with someone like me.

I couldn't think of anyone better to be my friend. I couldn't think of anything more. Willow put on a brave face for me. And I hate that she had to be my stand-in bodyguard while Mikey took a pee break. I just want her to be the kind of friend I can laugh with.

Not the kind that has to save me.

I'm grateful for her today though. "Thanks for sticking up for me."

"You'd do the same for me," she says.

It scrunches my brows a little. Was what she did too much to ask? Or was it what any kind, loyal friend would do? I'd be there for her if she was struggling in any situation, I'd try.

"Text me when you get there," Willow says as she opens her door, the car parked by the street curb.

"Promise."

She pauses, clutching the door handle, and realization lights her brown eyes. "That was Cleo and Harper, wasn't it?"

My throat swells closed, and all I can do is nod.

Her face breaks. "I'm so sorry, Daisy." She glances at her hands for a second and then leans back in her seat, tugging at a shiny silver ring on her pinky finger. "So you know the *Fourth Degree* comic books?"

I nod. They're Halway Comic's giant superhero universe much like Marvel's Avengers and X-Men. I think Lo and Lily launched the line sometime around December, and it's only grown more popular since then. Lionsgate recently bought all the film rights.

We all celebrated at Superheroes & Scones the day it was announced.

"My favorite superhero wears this ring…" She finally pulls it off and then shows me the simple silver band with a black square carved in the center. "It protects Tilly Stayzor from anyone outside of the Fourth Degree, basically her personal enemies." She flips the piece of jewelry between her fingers. "This ring is just a reminder that there are people who have your back. And we all need protection at some point." She places it in my hand. "I want you to have mine."

Now I'm crying. I brush away my tears with a small laugh, slipping the ring on my pinky, just a little tight but not enough to take off or resize. Then I reach out my hand to hers, preparing for our handshake.

She taps her knuckles to mine, and we slide our hands against one another before grabbing on with our fingers. The finger-clutch-squeeze, I call it. A small gesture in goodbye to replace a hug.

I love our handshake, which is something unique to our friendship. Something only we share, and it reminds me of Willow.

When she leaves, I turn towards the driver's seat. My eyes still sear, but no more tears fall. I kind of wish they would. It feels better when I let it all out.

My throat tries to close again, and Mikey begins driving towards Connor's office. "Mikey," I say, peeking my head between the two front seats. "Can you make a detour?"

My gaze drifts, far away, and I imagine myself at the precipice of a bridge. Plunging into icy cold waters. Weight presses on my chest, shackling me, yanking me down. I clutch onto the back of the passenger seat.

"To the beach?" Mikey asks, suspecting I may need an outlet.

I do need one, but I also *really* need to talk to someone about what happened first. Then maybe I'll go for a run with Ryke. "No," I say. "It's not really close to Connor's office either." My decision is made. I relay the address and then lie down, stretching out on the seat.

The person who has been listening to my thoughts and stories is in New York City. I can thank Connor Cobalt for lending me his therapist. Without Frederick, I'm not sure how I'd truly cope. I'd like to think I wouldn't visit a bridge or a cliff to make me weightless, but I can't know for certain.

By the end of my talks with Frederick, I always feel more prepared to confront the world and to mentally deal with Cleo and Harper.

Because right now, I see and hear and feel the panic and anxiety from prep school. Torment was my daily vitamin. The root of my problems began here. Somewhere between now and then, I'm less human in the eyes of people I grew up with.

They can touch me without thinking. They can use me without caring.

Sometimes, when I really contemplate what's happened, I feel like I've died already. Like maybe I'm just this shell moseying around, and that's what they see when they look at me.

It's a terrible thought.

I turn on my side, tucking my knees to my chest on the black leather cushion.

Wanting to cry.

Maybe then, everything will feel better.

< *11* >

Ryke Meadows

It's almost the end of September.

It's also the Saturday before my twenty-seventh birthday, and I'm speeding up the Calloway's driveway on my Ducati. A massive brick mansion looms ahead. Pink peonies in giant gold pots scatter the manicured yard, and expensive cars line the circular driveway, a valet collecting keys.

It's not exactly what I fucking predicted or expected.

Daisy sits behind me, and as we near her childhood home, she removes her helmet. "Oh no."

Guests exit their vehicles in floor-length gowns and tuxes. Suited for the Oscars, not any party with my name attached to the invitations.

It hits me.

In this fucking moment. I've been accepted into a world that has never wanted me. Not as kid. Not as a teenager, and not even as an adult. To be celebrated *formally* with Daisy by her parents, their friends—this entire social circle—it's insane.

I'm the invisible son.

Cast-out and forgotten. Being the center of anything fits me like a jacket three sizes too small, but it still has meaning that I acknowledge.

I ride on the outside of the lined cars, pulling closer to the entrance by swerving between a black Rolls-Royce. I switch the bike into neutral using the clutch and coast to a stop by the curb. Daisy hops off before I park, and I quickly remove my helmet, worried about how she's taking this.

We're underdressed. There's no fucking way around this fact.

She has on a white knit top, two teal shells printed over her chest with the words *raised by mermaids* scrawled underneath. It's really fucking cute, but in frayed jean shorts, she's not even close to formalwear. I'm not any better: a pair of jeans and a dark green shirt, the arm-cuffs short.

We both just assumed the party would be low-key and family-only when her mom texted us the details last minute. She didn't book a ballroom or a fucking castle. The location read, *Villanova*, the wealthy Philadelphia neighborhood where Greg and Samantha live.

"Hey," I call to Daisy.

She doesn't turn around.

I leave my helmet on the bike and catch up to Dais by the front stairs. Classical music filters through the door, less and less like us— everything is. But we knew today would be more about her parents than about our relationship.

I set a hand on Daisy's waist and turn her around to face me. She crosses her arms like she's cold but it's fucking hot out. Fifteen minutes ago, she was bouncing with excitement at riding a motorcycle, the first time since her surgery in August. Now she's tucked into herself, more closed off—and she keeps touching her hair, combing her fingers through the brown strands.

After Cleo and Harper confronted her at that yogurt shop weeks back, she's been a little jumpy. But I can't fucking blame her.

My brows furrow at her like *you okay?* It takes her a moment to nod in reply, and she keeps holding my gaze, like she'd rather go home but knows she can't.

"I love making her happy," she says softly. "I just wish she would listen to me, and I could've sworn I said to keep it small. She knows I won't complain, and I don't want to make waves, not over something like this."

I hug her closer to my side, and she scuffs the grass with her sandal.

Daisy has spent a long time discovering what she wants, what she desires—who she is inside. About an hour earlier, when we were getting dressed for the party, we were figuring out when to tell her parents that we're trying to have a baby.

"I don't think we should bring it up today," she said, buttoning her jean shorts.

I dried my wet hair with a towel. "You going to elaborate?"

Her voice quieted as she said, "I'm just scared that no one will listen to me. It's easy to dismiss my opinion when I'm younger than my sisters, and I also used to do what everyone else told me anyway…" She put her hands to her hips and stared up at the paper lanterns in our room. "What's the point of speaking up when no one hears you?"

It broke my heart.

I stepped closer to her. "The fucking point is for people to understand that you *have* opinions, that your voice counts, and if they don't hear you then yell louder." Her eyes flitted to mine, and I said deeply, "Never give up or back down on the things that fill your soul, Calloway. There is no worse life than a hollow one."

Imagining someone walking all over Daisy—it kills me. She's been through too much to hit that kind of roadblock.

Outside of her parent's mansion, Daisy gives me a solemn smile. "I guess it could be worse. She could've invited all my ex-boyfriends." Her smile fades rapidly, eyes widening. "Ryke, what if she—"

"No." I shut down the idea, even if Samantha Calloway has hated me for more days than she's claimed to fucking like me. I don't even want to entertain the possibility of running into Julian or the Swedish guy who took Daisy's virginity or the douchebag who backdoored her.

If Samantha brought one of them, then she must really want a fucking fistfight at this party—because I see myself swinging without enough hesitation to stop me.

Look, I've listened to detailed stories about her exes, sitting there with a grimace and a glare, thinking *God, I hope these fuckers get their dicks crushed.*

I've had to watch her date a handful of them, the worst kind of guys: ones who don't take care of their girl, who don't care about what she needs or wants. Listening to their smallest head.

My features must have darkened because a woman in a velvet blue gown says congratulations to Daisy but never even glances at me. I watch her disappear inside.

I can't be surprised that I have an unapproachable, ugly fucking glare when thinking about breaking cocks.

Before we're stuck greeting guests, I lead Daisy into her parent's foyer, my hand on her lower back. The classical music grows louder as we pass through the doorway, and her muscles tense beneath my palm.

"Hey." I twirl her around to me, her big, green doe eyes glimmering. "Don't worry about making everyone feel comfortable. That's not your fucking job tonight."

"Does this mean I can expect inappropriate acts of adventure?"

My blood heats. I raise my brows at her.

She smiles more, rocking on the tips of her toes.

I lean down, clasping the back of her head, and I whisper deeply, "Not in front of your fucking father, Calloway."

She unabashedly scans my six-foot-three build, in the flirtiest, most apparent once-over. "I thought I had you right where I wanted you, Ryke Meadows."

Her eyes twinkle impishly, and my dick throbs, my arousal gripping me. Everything about her, I want close to my body, touching her slowly. Skin against skin. I want to pick her up and toss her over my fucking shoulder.

If we were alone, I'd move aggressively.

Without second thought.

I'd have her up against the wall, legs hoisted and my tongue parting her lips fast. Rugged and intense. She always tries to meet me in the middle, wrestling midair for the same objective.

Our relationship is fucking animalistic and visceral but grounded on the trust and friendship we built first. Since we're both really physical, people may only see our sexual connection, but the latter is unbreakable. It's what I fell in love with at the start.

I walk Daisy backwards, aware of what I can and can't do in this kind of public setting. Thing is, I give no fucks most of the time—so I'm naturally going to push the boundary one inch further, stretching it without crossing it.

My stride is larger than Daisy's, and in seconds, my chest bumps into hers. She almost falls back, but I catch her easily and slip my hand down her back pocket, cupping her ass.

Her lungs expand against me, and I tug her closer, grazing her features. I watch her gaze light up, as though I've given her a slice of chocolate cake.

"That's an inappropriate act," she says, her hands moving from my biceps to my waist in a restless state.

My expression hardens like I have no idea what she's fucking talking about.

Daisy's smile expands. "How's my ass? On a scale of one to Better-Than-Chocolate."

I slip my keys into her back pocket. "Hold onto my fucking keys," I tell her before retracting my palm.

"Hold-Onto-My-Fucking-Keys kinda hot. I accept this new measurement." She curtseys.

And then a server interrupts us. "Champagne?" he asks, tray in hand.

Daisy takes a flute, and I automatically decline. As we search for Daisy's sisters among unfamiliar faces, I hear the hush of whispers and feel the fucking heat of their eyes.

I'm too calloused to let their opinions in.

They can whisper about how I'm seven years older than Dais, how I'm not right for her. They can circulate a fucking false rumor about how we slept together when she was only sixteen. They can say it all.

But it won't touch me.

Problem is, I recognize that Daisy hurts by shots at our relationship, at *me*. So I steer her away from them, hoping they don't hit her ears tonight.

It's obvious by the bar stationed next to the grand staircase that Samantha moved furniture in and out for this party. The house is packed mostly by each bar and narrow hallway.

We pass through an archway, entering the largest room in their house: vaulted ceilings, gold-draped windows, and about thirty to fifty fucking people milling around—I know less than ten of them.

A harpist and violinist play off in the corner, servers with trays of champagne and hors d'oeuvres weaving through guests.

I'm confident that I'll say the wrong thing at some point.

Small talk is not my fucking strong suit. I couldn't care less though. I'm not here to impress anyone. I just want to make sure Dais has a good time.

"There they are." Daisy bounces on her tiptoes at the sight of her three sisters and Willow. They notice her too, waving Daisy over—and I lock eyes with Willow for a millisecond before she turns her back on me and hangs her head.

It's a new reaction, something I'm not fucking used to yet. A couple days ago, Lo let it slip that she's Jonathan's daughter. I'm not pissed at him for it, especially since he's close to her. I just feel badly that I didn't tell her sooner.

But her reaction…it's not really one I expected.

She won't talk about Jonathan and she's avoiding me. It's kind of obvious when we live together and she won't even meet my eyes when we're in the same room. I just don't know why.

I scratch my jaw, unsure of fucking everything. My dad says he needs my advice to start a dialogue with her, but I'm definitely not an expert on Willow Moore.

"She may need a couple more months," Daisy tells me off my gaze.

"To what?" I ask. "I'm not going anywhere."

"It's awkward for her," Daisy explains.

I frown, not understanding. "What's awkward about it?"

Daisy tries hard not to smile.

I give her a look and set a hand on her head. "I'm not good at understanding some fucking things, Calloway. That's why I have you."

"You've always intimidated her, and I don't think she ever thought of you like a brother—so it's hard for her to switch gears. Plus, you know, she's dating for the first time and experiencing new things without parents around, but now she has *two* brothers instead of just Lo."

"I'm not going to make things fucking harder for her," I say.

"I know, but it's still awkward."

I'm just fucking glad Willow and Dais are friends. I think they both need each other in different ways.

"Daisy!" Rose shouts across the room, and somewhere else, Samantha Calloway is no doubt shooting her daughter the fucking stink-eye.

Rose waves again, tapping her high heel. All of her sisters are congregated by the fireplace, wearing gowns. I still don't know how we missed the fucking dress code.

Daisy peels away from my side to join her sisters.

And then someone pats my shoulder, hard.

< 12 >

Ryke Meadows

Hey, *little brother*, I think before I face a twenty-five-year-old with amber daggers for eyes and steel blades for a jaw. Dressed in all black with features that fucking kill, he could be the devil's son. In some ways, he is.

In other ways, so am I.

We really must be brothers. I almost smile in remembrance. I said those exact words to him the day he found out we were related.

Five years ago.

We both look older. He looks stronger. There's nowhere left to go but forward.

His hand tightens around a glass of ice water, and his gaze falls to my clothes. He laughs and pats my shoulder again. "It's been nice knowing you, bro."

I push his hand off. "Hilarious." He's referring to the third-degree Samantha Calloway will give me when she sees my fucking attire. I tug at his formal jacket. "What's this?"

Now he shoves my hand away, his water spilling on his fingers. "Shit," he curses. "It's a goddamn bunny costume. What does it look like?" His cheekbones sharpen when he wipes his hand on the side of his black slacks.

"You know we live together?"

"No, I had no idea. I just thought the Wendy's girl kept eating all the bacon and eggs in our fridge."

I give him an irritated look.

He swigs his water, staring easily at me like I'm fucking smiling at him. Clearly my *I'm-going-to-break-some-fucking-cocks* face has no effect on my little brother.

"You had enough time to tell me this is a formal event," I say. "So what the fuck?"

"You two were missing all morning."

I shake my head, trying to recall everything. We went to the quarry for a hike this morning. Daisy has finally regained her energy since her surgery. She didn't want to squander that by staying indoors—neither did I. "You could've texted me."

Lo touches his chest. "I don't text."

"Bullshit," I curse, grabbing a glass of water from a server's tray.

"Seriously," Lo says, "I thought you knew. Samantha texted Lily and Rose—I guess we just all assumed she texted Daisy too."

I take a swig of water and nod. "She did text Daisy, but she conveniently left out the number of fucking invites." I browse the room with a quick glance, spotting celebrities by another full bar: singers and an actress, maybe. I don't know them.

I barely keep up with that shit, and I usually have to remind myself that I'm a part of it too. In magazines. On entertainment news.

I deliberately try not to pay attention to any of that. It's not worth the headache.

When I observe the crowds again, I find myself searching for Daisy's exes—*fucking stop*. I rub my eyes, disliking this paranoia.

I return my attention to my brother. He's scrutinizing me like I normally do to him. I'm not used to his concern—not even a fraction of it.

He says, "I bet Samantha thought you'd ditch your own party if you knew all the details."

That sounds more like something he'd do with Lily, back when they let their addictions run their lives. I wouldn't have ditched this event if it meant something to Daisy.

I'm surprised that he's making excuses for Samantha, but I don't say anything about it. I just chug the rest of my water. The same time that he finishes off his.

He checks the empty glass, clenching his teeth. I can tell he wishes his drink had bite. Whiskey or bourbon.

"You okay?" I ask on impulse. Usually his brows will furrow in irritation.

They still do.

That hasn't fucking changed but his self-assured posture has. "I'm better than you fucking look." He raises his glass in bitter cheers. When he takes a sip from the empty glass, he mumbles, "Jesus Christ."

"This is yours." Connor appears next to Lo with a full glass of ice water. My brother sets his empty one on a passing tray.

"Appreciated, love." Lo takes a sip.

Of course he didn't offer me a fucking glass. I don't expect Connor to give me anything other than a hard time.

He holds his one-year-old daughter to his side, her brown hair tied in a tiny pony, her cheek resting against her dad's arm. Janie's deep blue eyes match Connor's. Both sets are currently pinned to me.

"You showed up." His calm voice instantly heightens my aggravation, his whole unruffled, arrogant demeanor always grating on me. "Color me surprised."

He doesn't sound remotely surprised.

Connor Cobalt looks bored.

Even Janie, in a pale blue dress, watches the party and me with disinterest—and she's *one*.

I'm about to ask him why he didn't find a babysitter, but I haven't spoken to Connor that much since the doctor's appointment in August. He can share his beliefs, but I don't want him to patronize me like I'm seven years old.

He's not my conscience.

He's not my parent.

He's my fucking *friend*.

I understand every risk I take. I know what it all means, so he doesn't need to reiterate them like I can't fucking hear or see.

I switch out my water glass from another passing server, blatantly avoiding Connor. Passive aggressive bullshit really isn't my normal tactic, but it irritates Connor more than yelling.

"This whole silent treatment is a bit infantile." Connor acts like it's not affecting him, like it's all just the same, but in the creases of his eyes, I notice his frustration matching mine.

I angle my body towards my brother. "Where's Moffy?"

"Garrison is babysitting."

I connect the dots, how Lily and Lo must trust him enough to let him watch their kid, but Connor doesn't.

"Moffy?" Janie says hopefully, looking up at her dad.

We all stare down at her, and Connor's kid tugs at my fucking heart when she claps her hands, giddy for her cousin's appearance.

"Moffy isn't here," Connor tells her in his usual calm voice.

"Moffy!" she giggles, not understanding.

My brother is smiling more than he does in a year's time. He catches me staring, and he glares. "What?"

"I didn't say a fucking thing."

"My son is cool. The baby genius thinks so."

I let out an incensed breath. "Why do you have to inflate his fucking head?" He could have left out the word "genius"—even if Janie is a little advanced for her age.

"Because I like his face." Lo flashes me a smile.

I shake my head, feeling Connor's blinding grin behind me.

"Ryke," Connor says while Janie rests her cheek against his arm.

I reluctantly give him more of my attention.

"What do you want me to do?" he asks. "Play truth or dare again? Kiss your brother?"

I roll my eyes. Their kiss stirred up more trouble in the media than I thought it would, and I feel partly guilty for it—because I fronted the dare. He also accepted it to squash whatever beef we had at the time.

Lo stands more between us, trying to separate the tension. "Is that why we kissed?" He touches his heart. "I thought you loved me. After all this time."

Connor smiles. "Always."

I'm confused by the exchange.

My brother nods to me. "*Harry Potter* reference."

I tense. "You've read *Harry Potter*?" I ask Connor.

"Lo gave me a set in March after I asked about it."

I stare off for a second, trying not to appear hurt or jealous, even though both definitely hit me. Connor takes interest in other people's hobbies to try and understand them more, and maybe I should have taken that fucking step too. Lo is my brother.

And I hate feeling like Connor would've made a better one than me.

"Ryke," he says again, drawing my gaze to him, "I won't take back what I said at the doctor. It's the truth."

"I didn't ask for your fucking truths."

"And yet, I did you a favor by providing them."

I growl in frustration. "Just shut up for a second and listen to me." I try not to look at Janie, propped against his side. It's harder to let this out in a tone that says *this is what I mean, and I'm not backing the fuck down.*

"You can't talk to me like you did in the doctor's office, not in front of Daisy."

Connor wears a blank expression. "I didn't think you would care about how you appear."

I step closer and say lowly so only he can hear. "I'm her *fiancé* and when you question my ability to make rational decisions in front of her, I look far from fucking dependable. I don't want her to worry about the choices we make." I raise my hands, not trying to start something bigger. "I know that was your goal, but stop making goals that involve Dais and me."

He looks genuinely hurt.

It takes me aback for a moment.

"You know," he says, "if you were anyone else, I wouldn't have even cared. Not enough to offer an opinion or even spend time thinking about it." He says stiffly, "I'll keep it to myself next time."

When our personalities never mesh, it's easier just arguing and hating on each other rather than making an effort to sustain a rickety friendship. I've grown to respect Connor, and he's reciprocated that respect in return.

But if Rose ever becomes a surrogate for Daisy, it'll tie the four of us together for life, and maybe he's not seeing this. Or maybe he likes all the fucking strings that connect people to him.

I didn't grow up like that.

Before I wrap my head around how to reply, Samuel Stokes detaches from a couple older men and walks over to us. He's about thirty, thirty-one: Poppy's husband and the Chief Marketing Officer of Fizzle.

He clutches a champagne flute, and the various entertainment journalists begin to snap photos, cameras flashing in waves.

"Hey, Sammy." Lo gives him a dry smile. "You've got something hanging out of your nose."

Sam never blinks, too used to Lo's jabs.

Before ever meeting Sam, I thought he might've had a brotherly relationship with Lo. He grew up with my little brother more than I did, but I learned really fucking fast that wasn't the kind of bond they shared.

Sam had been envious of Lo's place within the Calloways, the easy acceptance because our father was Greg's best friend. Sam wished for that same inherent respect, and he resented Lo for a long time. Now that they're both older, they've let most of it go.

And they bicker like family.

"I mean," Lo continues, "I don't see why else the cameras would be so interested in you."

They're not just interested in Sam. They're attracted to all four of us. Standing together.

Sam. Connor. Loren.

They're all married to a Calloway sister. And I'm about to marry the youngest one.

At Sunday brunch, the girls like to tease us about the articles in *Celebrity Crush*—where the media apparently obsesses over our friendship like we've formed a fucking clique.

Though out of all of us, Lo is the favorite. There are thousands of fucking tweets like these:

@lilycalloways: everytime i think about loren hale the first thing that comes to mind is "what a beautiful male specimen"

@LiLoX23Hellion: I really can't say it all in 140 characters why I love Lo so much!

@lorenhaIe: LET ME SHOW YOU THE TACO WORLD LOREN

@ryshannemia: Loren Hale is the light of my life and the apple of my eye <3

@teacupsbooklove: I just want to hang out at Superheroes & Scones all day with Loren Hale. Is that too much to ask?

@lilyswampahat: Loren Hale isn't afraid of scary movies. I'm afraid of scary movies. I will watch them (but not really) as long as we can cuddle okay.

@halwaycomics: I love Lo because every time he's down he manages to get back up again.

@ThisJabberwocky: Loren Hale is like a bourbon-filled chocolate; bitter and sweet.

@Iilycalloway: I've always loved comics, but lo inspired me to read even more and he helped me find out how much I love the x-men universe!

@iHeartBigBooks: #lorenhale shows us the true meaning of soulmate love #LiLo Forever

@isaboes: loren hale, if i didnt love you with lily so much i would ask you to be mine

@52_veronica: Loren Hale is one of my children. No one hurts my children. #mamabear

@ohlilycalloway: loren hale is a precious cinnamon roll who deserves every bit of happiness he gets and more

I have no fucking idea why people call him a cinnamon roll—all the fucking time—but they never say a bad thing about him. Some will hate on Lily instead, but the girls are always picked on more than us without justifiable reason.

"You know I'm babysitting your kid next weekend," Sam replies easily to my brother. It's his way of saying: *be nicer to me, Loren.*

Lo doesn't play well with subtext, so I'm not surprised by his response. "For Lily. Because everyone knows it's not for your favorite brother-in-law." He tops it with the raise of his water glass, taking a swig like it's bourbon.

"That would be me." Connor grins, his arrogance making its fucking entrance.

I'm about to find something to eat, so I don't have to be the center of anything.

"Oh shit," Lo curses. "Father-in-law is approaching."

"Fuck." I rub my lips, my skin hot all of a sudden.

Connor isn't even near breaking a sweat, immune to most tense situations.

Sam finishes off his champagne. "Just talk about the new product commercial for Ziff's lime-aid flavor and he'll get distracted." Everyone knows I manage to put my foot in my fucking mouth when it comes to Daisy's father. Sam can actually relate on some level since he had to grovel for Greg's approval.

"Wait, you're doing another commercial?" Lo asks me with a frown.

"Yeah." I struggle to find words that'll comfort him like *it's just for the money* or *I'm not climbing that much for it* or *I won't die, little brother.* None of them escape. They all just stick to my throat.

Sam fills the scalding silence as Greg walks over. "Ziff: Citrus Breeze. So far, it's been a favorite among preteens."

Fucking fantastic. "How much sugar is in it?"

Greg completes our circle of five, casually sidling between Connor and Sam. "If you think it's too sweet, we can dilute your bottle for the commercial." His tone is friendly.

Lo rests his arm on my shoulder. "Dammit, I was hoping you'd puke on Rose's feet again."

I did that when I chugged Ziff: Blue Squall and then climbed. "Not fucking happening." I nudge his arm off my shoulder.

Greg never extends a hand out to me. His normally benign gaze narrows at my jeans and shirt. "Samantha put a lot of effort into this party. It would've been nice if you showed her a little respect by dressing appropriately."

"Next time I will, but no one told us this was fu…formal." I grimace; it took a lot of concentration not to accidentally curse.

Greg looks neither happy nor ready to kick my fucking ass. I did okay then.

"I forgot to text Ryke," Lo adds on my behalf. "My bad." I'd say that Connor is Greg's favorite if it wasn't for the media shit storm that surrounded him. Lo definitely has the most sway with the girls' father.

His shoulders relax, less arched in offense. "I want to congratulate you," he tells me. "I meant it when I said that I'm glad you're a part of this family. You've taken good care of my daughter, especially recently…" He chokes up for a second.

Every guy goes rigid, even Connor.

Even me. *Please don't bring up kids. Please don't fucking bring up kids.*

Connor, Lo, and Sam are all aware that Daisy and I are trying to have a baby, and I don't need one of them letting anything slip either.

"I think now, more than ever, she can look forward to her future," Greg says with a couple nods, probably recalling the successful parts of her surgery. "And maybe in ten years, she'll be stable with a good career and ready to have a child."

Fuck.

I'm unmoving, my muscles strained. His gaze drills into mine while he leisurely sips his champagne. I never flinch or recoil from him. I can't tell him that Daisy decided on her career path around her nineteenth birthday.

She finally figured it out, and her choice lacks stability that he'd want for her, which shouldn't even matter. She lights up every time she talks about it, and she's loved putting time into it on her own.

So far, she hasn't discussed what she wants to do with anyone but me, and it's not my news to share. No one may understand. Not unless she explains what it means to her and why she feels compelled to spend money and time doing it.

As for the fucking kid stuff...

"I don't know about ten years," I say, each word rough out of my mouth. It's all I can do without cursing.

Lo scratches the back of his neck, and I'm praying he keeps his mouth shut for me. This is one of the worst times to let the truth out to her fucking parents.

His forehead scrunches with vexed lines. "She's only twenty."

"In ten fucking years, I'll be thirty-seven." I realize I've chosen the wrong words when Connor shifts his daughter to his other side. Everything he does is purposeful, and I know he's trying to distract Greg without blatantly interjecting.

Greg's eyes fall to his granddaughter.

I understand him. He values *profitable* careers and practical investments more than my father. My dad is more of a risk-taker, who's proud when a kid follows his dreams, his ambitions, even if there's nothing in it. *"It's why I busted my ass,"* he used to say. *"I worked fucking hard so you didn't have to."*

Lo said our dad would get onto him for being lazy, but when he chose to run a comic book company, he supported him.

It's also why he rarely ever hassles me about rock climbing.

Fuck. I internally groan—knowing I'm losing it when I begin to defend my father over Greg Calloway, supposedly one of the most benevolent men.

My muscles bind.

Greg focuses back on me. "I don't want you to pressure her into having a child just because time is running out for *you*. It's not running out for her."

Fucking ironic.

Time *is* running out for her. She may lose her other ovary in a year. Then she has to go through IVF. Then it's more complicated.

"I would never fucking pressure her," I tell him. "If she wanted to wait until she was in her thirties, I'd wait."

Greg looks disbelieving. "I guess we'll see if this is true."

I breathe through my nose—and I almost fucking wonder if her parents are going to show up at our wedding if we tell them the truth. I don't want to harbor any more lies or fucking secrets again, not for that long. So I know it'll be their call in the end.

He gives all of us a brief smile. "Enjoy the party." Then he leaves towards the bar where his wife talks to that woman in a blue velvet dress.

"That went well," Connor says.

"Really?" I rub my eyes.

"No."

I glare at him beneath my hand. "I fucking hate you."

"It's mutual," Connor says, not letting me have sole ownership of my fucking hate.

Lo swishes his glass. "Greg's just butt-hurt that his youngest daughter is marrying an older guy."

I give my brother a look like *shut up*.

He continues, "If I had a daughter who brought home an older guy who said *fuck* every other word, I'd probably roast him until he shit his pants and cried himself back into his ugly pick-up truck."

I groan. "What are you, Samantha and Greg's fucking advocates today?"

"It's just different when you have a kid..." he trails off, his face tightening in remorse. I barely even have time to register that I may not have a child one day, or that his statement towards me could be insensitive.

Sam nods to Lo. "I told you, it'd change you."

"Whatever…" My brother's attention is more on me. "You'll have a kid too, Ryke. Someday."

"It's okay if I don't," I tell him, believing it more than he does.

"You *will* have one," he says, almost desperately. "Life isn't that cruel—to give an asshole like me one and not someone good like you."

Someone good like you. I nod, my eyes burning. *It's okay, Lo.* I mess his hair with a rough hand, and he pushes my arm off with a fleeting smile.

I can't lie to him and say it'll happen when it might not. I can only give him the truth now, and this kind of truth has no ending yet.

"Really though, how much shit am I going to be in with her dad?" I ask them, steering the topic away.

"When he finds out you're procreating as soon as possible," Connor muses.

Lo rephrases, "When he finds out you're impregnating his youngest daughter as we speak."

Connor arches a brow. "When he finds out you're actively having sex with the hope of your sperm meeting her egg."

"When he finds out you're—"

"I got it," I cut off my brother. I shouldn't have fucking asked.

Sam shakes his head repeatedly. "You all are weird, and the sad thing is—I'm not even fazed by it anymore."

"That is sad," Lo says, "because that means I've been spending more time with you."

Sam lets out a laugh and mutters something before switching out his drink. I glance over at Daisy, still with her sisters by the fireplace.

All the guys follow my gaze to their respective girl, but none of us head over there yet. We've always had this unspoken agreement for years.

Let the Calloway sisters have time together.

It makes our girls happy, and in the end, we all strive to please the people we truly fucking love.

< *13* >

Daisy Calloway

"Your engagement opens the door to a *hundred* more possibilities. If you don't want the wedding filmed, we should at least start shooting afterwards to capture the newlywed vibe. Don't be concerned about screen time because I already talked to GBA, and they want equal footage with all of you. No wife will get shafted in *Queens of Philadelphia*."

Christopher "Striking" Barnes—his self-given title at fourteen for being "too good-looking for this world"—finishes his pitch with a cocky, entitled smile. His brown hair is slicked back, and he holds a glass of bourbon.

If we didn't know him since we were kids, he'd probably already be iced out by Rose and even Poppy—but his family is friends with ours. He's also Rose's age and someone my mom attempted to pair me with when I turned eighteen. My dad shut it down due to *his* age.

Ironically, he's as old as Ryke.

Lily frowns. "So like a housewives reality show?"

"Yeah," Christopher says in total seriousness.

Poppy looks just as confused. "I thought you worked in stocks."

"I also take advantage of lucrative opportunities, and I see one with the four of you."

"Okay," I pipe in, agreeing quickly. My three sisters nearly go into cardiac arrest, even Willow's eyes bug.

Christopher grins and squeezes my shoulder. "I thought you'd be cool with this." I wonder why he thinks that. *Because I'm cool with anything.*

I'd do anything if someone asked.

Anything at all.

I frown internally. It's not true anymore. I can put my foot down now. I know I can.

"Daisy," Rose says my name like I've lost my mind.

I ignore Rose and set my sights on Christopher. "I have conditions."

He removes his hand from my arm. "Okay." His gaze lingers on my cheek, the scarred one, but his poker face is decent, acting the same by its existence. I could cover the scar with my hair.

I used to do that. So it made everyone feel less uncomfortable, but it never made me feel any better. In the past year, I've learned to accept these constant wary glances, and in doing so I've been able to accept every blemish and every flaw of mine.

Every day, I can feel myself growing into my own skin, and I love myself more than I ever have. Ryke is a variable in my life that has led me here. I know it.

"My conditions…" I force myself flat on my feet, not bouncing. My tone completely serious, I say, "I want fifty million dollars."

Christopher blinks a couple times. "I'm sure I can discuss that with the network; they've been receptive to my ideas so far—"

"Per episode," I declare.

Christopher narrows his baby blue eyes. "That's asking way too much."

"And I'd also like a unicorn." I'm so stern about this that Lily almost bursts out laughing. "Not a horse with a horn or a donkey with a carrot attached to his head," I tell him. "A *real* unicorn. If you can't meet my conditions, I just can't bear the thought of participating."

Rose gestures to Christopher with her champagne glass. "My contract should say, *Rose Calloway Cobalt is allowed to slit the throats of her adversaries without penalty.* I also would like free dry cleaning in case blood stains my dresses." She sips her champagne like a total badass. That's my sister.

Lily clears her throat. "I'd like a taco bar."

I laugh, and Rose gives her a strange look like she asked for something mediocre when she could've been given the sun and the moon and blazing stars.

To Lily, a taco bar is a great prize. Probably because it's something that Loren Hale would love too.

"My conditions are more complicated," Poppy says in the same tone as all of us. "I'd like world peace." She then waves at him like a pageant queen.

We all explode in laughter, enough that a lot of heads turn to us.

Christopher nods a few times, not dense enough to miss the joke. "Alright, alright." His gaze plants on mine. "You got me."

As our laughter dies down, I stare past his shoulder, noticing all four guys watching us. Ryke nods to me and mouths, *what the fuck?*

I mouth back, *I love you.*

It makes him smile.

It makes me smile more.

"Is this a firm no then?" Christopher asks, hiding his disappointment if he has any.

"Yeah," I say. "It's a definite, without-a-doubt, not-gonna-change-our-minds kind of no."

While he digests this, his eyes slowly descend down my body, probably taking note of my strange attire. Even though I love my T-shirt and shorts, my mom has taken it like a slap in the face. I still hate upsetting her, even if she's one of the hardest people to please.

I'd raid my closet upstairs but I emptied it when I moved out, and I don't want to leave Ryke alone in something casual while I wear a formal dress.

"When's the wedding?" Christopher asks, so zeroed in on me. I wish he'd open the dialogue to all of my sisters at once.

"We haven't picked a date yet," I answer honestly. With my fertility issues at the forefront, planning a wedding has taken a backseat. We're not in a huge rush. Admittedly, we're both a little worried about the drama a wedding will cause.

We even contemplated eloping, which seemed easier in theory. That discussion was shut down by his statement, *"I want my brother there."* Then mine, *"I want my sisters there as bridesmaids."*

"Will I be getting an invitation?" Christopher asks.

"I don't know," I say. "Will you be gifting me a unicorn that poops rainbows?"

He squints at me and tilts his head. "Are you flirting with me?"

Oh my God. My lips downturn, hoping no one else thinks this but him. I immediately distance myself and start to walk past him, just as Lily says, "She's not coming onto you. That's her personality."

Rose adds a perfunctory, "Christopher Snot-Nosed Barnes."

"Striking," he corrects like they're teenagers.

"No, I remember it being Snot-Nosed," Poppy says.

I smile, glad to have these older sisters—the ones who always, *always* have my back. I make a quick escape from Christopher and pluck a chocolate-covered strawberry off a server's tray. I bite all the chocolate off, headed towards the table full of bite-sized pastries.

As I unnoticeably slip between bodies, I catch parts of conversations between whomever my mom invited: socialites, celebrities, and journalists.

"I heard they're both signing prenups. I give it a month before they divorce."

The last piece of chocolate goes down rough. The naysayers aren't a new force of opposition. We've always had more doubters than supporters, more than any of my sisters' relationships.

I just can't believe this opposition is *here*, at my engagement party. I think no matter where we go, no matter how far we travel, there will *always* be people that want us to fail, to fall—to stumble harder and more often.

Ryke would tell me that it doesn't matter. That no matter how much people root against us, our own relentless belief in ourselves, in our love, trumps everything.

"I bet they don't even make it to the altar."

It stings—it stings so much that I recognize the harm in doubt and the tragedy in love that must confront it. Like Romeo. Like Juliet. Ryke can say it's enduring love, but history has shown that forbidden romance never ends well. I just wonder what our ending will be. If the past will repeat itself.

I scoot behind a couple chatty women and take another bite into my strawberry.

"Kathy told me that he forbids her from getting plastic surgery."

My shoulders stiffen, and I slow my pace, just to hear the rest. I'm about twenty feet from the pastry table, the harps and violins still playing strong but I strain my ears to overhear.

The other woman gapes. "That's awful. Samantha said that doctors could try fading her scar if she went through surgery, but I had no idea that Ryke was controlling her decision."

I almost choke on the strawberry. I swallow hard so it goes down.

"Apparently he doesn't want other men to look at her." *What?* "If he keeps her disfigured, then he has her all to himself."

My chest explodes with more anger than I've felt in a long time, my neck hot. *I* decided to forgo surgery. Me. No one else. Why is this so hard to believe? That I have a voice. That *I* make my own choices.

I'm not a confrontational person, but a giant part of my soul is *begging* to tell these women the truth. To cause a scene and alert the media, to stand on a chair and shout, "I, Daisy Petunia Calloway, refused to go through surgery of my own accord! No one swayed me, and I am happy, *truly* happy, as I am!"

I can do it. I know I can do it, and just as I take a step towards the women, I'm cut off by a *dink dink dink!* The sound of a knife tapping a champagne glass.

It's as though the universe is saying, *take a seat, Daisy Petunia Calloway. It's not your time to stand up. It's not your time to shout.*

I let out a tight breath, surrendering. I reach the pastry table while the room quiets and the music stops. I'm searching for anything chocolate when Ryke sidles next to me.

"Hey," he whispers, his fingers brushing mine, our pinkies hooking before he clasps my whole hand.

Dink, dink, dink!

"I don't see any chocolate," I say dishearteningly, glancing over my shoulder. My mother stands in the middle of the room with a champagne flute and a knife. People begin to edge away from us so she has a direct view of Ryke and me.

He grabs a doily-lined petit four off a tier and then rotates to face my mother. His left hand falls to the small of my back, and I use the dessert as a distraction, eating the chocolate decorative bow from the vanilla frosting. The inside looks like a classic yellow cake.

"Firstly," my mom begins, "I'd like to thank everyone for being here to celebrate my daughter's engagement." Then her focus pins on me. Her demeanor is strict, lips a dark shade of red, brown hair tightened in a bun, and brows penciled with high arches. Three strands of black and white pearls drape across her breastbone like pieces of her soul: good and bad.

I can't predict how she'll be today. If she'll choose to be the mom who adores me, who'd give her life protecting me, the one who attended photo shoots while I was underage to keep me safe. Or if she'll choose to be the mom who needs me, the one who pushed me too hard, who wanted a life for me that I didn't choose, to parade my beauty and wealth.

Someone hands my mother a cordless microphone. She says to me, "I'm happy that I could successfully surprise one of my daughter's with an engagement party." With a rising smile, her gaze flits over my shorts and T-shirt, further emphasizing her point.

Surprise. That's how she wants to play this off then. I had no clue about the party so I dressed casually.

It works; many people chuckle. How funny, *a surprise engagement party!* Mostly I'm reminded of how much my mom hates having egg on her face.

She adjusts her handhold on the microphone, almost to hide the emotion behind her eyes. "My fearless daughter," she says to me. "I told your father that you'd be the most trouble—that you'd break free of us faster and sooner than your sisters. Maybe that's why I held on tighter to you."

The chocolate melts in my hand, too entranced by my mom's sincerity to do much else but stare straight on. I hesitate like there's a punchline coming, like something backhanded will sting my cheek.

"You could never sit still as a child," she says, the room quiet, everyone grasping at her words. I am too. "You had this toy car, a pink convertible, and if your father and I weren't looking, you'd run outside to drive it down the street. Even at four and five years old, you were ready to race away. And you never turned back, not then and not now." She takes a breath. "There was a time where I tried to contain you from what I imagined was harm's way, but you helped me realize that I can't bottle lightning."

Tears build in my eyes, and they reflect back in my mom's.

She grazes over my features and stops on Ryke. Her neck seems to elongate, stringent and authoritative. "Greg and I often talked about what kind of man would suit Daisy, who could possibly be good enough for our youngest, most carefree daughter. The answer was always *no one.*"

People laugh again, but I'm stuck on the softness in my mother's eyes, the vulnerability in her story. She rarely shares intimate pieces of our history with me, let alone aloud to her friends.

"Ryke Meadows." My mom says his name stiffly, but I don't hear any disdain that would've been there two years ago. "We've had our ups and downs." She adjusts her grip on the microphone again.

I notice Ryke's darkened stare, but he stays quiet, waiting with the rest of us to see which way this blows.

My mom raises her head. "And at one point, I misjudged you and even called the police on you." My eyes widen at her admittance of this memory, and the room explodes in whispers. I look to Ryke and he's almost smiling—what...

I follow his gaze to my mom. Her expression mirrors his, a faint smile, zeroed in on him. Not even paying attention to the gossipy throngs of people.

"Of course you had no reason to be there," she says. "You were rightfully let go without charge, and I had to surrender what I believed was a loss. My daughter was yours, and there was nothing I could do."

She looks down in reverence, and when she returns her gaze to Ryke, there are genuine tears glassing her eyes. This is partly an apology. One that holds more meaning than simply saying *I'm sorry* to his face. She's admitting her faults in front of her friends.

"I'd forgotten that you can't bottle lightning anymore than I can," my mom says. "She chose you, and it took me time to figure out *why* and *how* you both fit together. Why are *you* the one man who's good enough for my daughter?"

My heart is in my throat.

"Then, one day, I realized that you are lightning. You can't be bottled or contained anymore than she can. And together, you both make a beautiful, perfect storm." She raises her champagne glass. "To my daughter and her husband-to-be, I hope you only know true happiness."

A hot tear slides down my cheek, the room booming with applause and cheers in agreement, hopefully most sincere.

Who would have thought that my mom of all people would see the beauty in my relationship with Ryke?

Not me, but I'm so insanely glad to finally have her on *our* side.

When she meets my gaze, I mouth, "I love you."

She touches her heart with one hand, eyes welled with tears like mine. Her speech was an apology and acceptance all in one, and I heard it loud. I felt it even stronger, and by Ryke's "almost" smile—I know he did too.

Now that my mom isn't our adversary any longer, I wonder how much time it'll take for the world to follow suit. If they ever will. The media. Our fans and foes. It's a much greater battle.

I want to say I'm ready for it, but conflict isn't my strong suit.

I can never fully prepare for the moment it hits.

< *14* >

Daisy Calloway

I stand on the front of a shopping cart and pluck the most colorful cereal boxes from the shelf. The polar bear eating chocolate crisps. The vampire devouring some purple flakes with a toothy smile.

A few employees opened the grocery store an hour early for us at 5 a.m., so we're able to shop without cellphone flashes and people crowding the aisles. We all usually prefer shopping ourselves, but during bad weeks with press, normal routines become harder.

My super relaxed bodyguard, Mikey Black, lingers at the end of the aisle. His attire: Hawaiian-floral board shorts and a neon orange shirt. At the other end, Ryke's lackadaisical forty-something bodyguard listens to a wrestling podcast, so loud the noise usually echoes out of his earbuds. Quinn always finds audiobooks and podcasts to pass the time, knowing Ryke likes space and less interference.

Right now, Ryke is busy reading the ingredients of a healthy nut cereal. He keeps hold of the cart's handle, as though liking me near. I would probably roll backwards if he let go.

"You always do this, you know," I say with a growing smile, one that lights my core.

"Do what?" He sets the cereal back and grabs a raisin mix.

"You spend five to ten minutes looking at other cereals, but you always end up with the same granola kind." I spread my hands on either side of the cart, leaning forward. I add in a breathy voice, "And it's so *irresistibly* predictable."

He gives me that dangerous, dark look. The one that says, *you don't know what the fuck you're talking about.* Then he tosses the raisin cereal into the cart, making his point without a spoken word.

"The granola isn't calling out to you?" I lean my weight backwards, attempting to rock the cart.

His grip is firm, and the cart is unmoving.

"It's not saying, *oh Ryke. Eat me.*" I breathe shallowly like I'm nearing an orgasm, not caring if Mikey or Quinn notice. "*Eat me, Ry—*"

Ryke yanks the cart to his chest. So swiftly that my abdomen knocks into the metal, breath caught in my lungs. I smile instantly, but I do spot the concern in the corners of his eyes. He doesn't want to hurt me, but we always play rough.

It's not like that has to change completely.

I also started my period last night with a side of mild cramps. Yeehaw! Seriously though, it's *very* good news. This means we can start trying to have a baby.

Ryke leans forward now, enough to lift my chin with his fingers. "You're fucking trouble, Calloway." Then he kisses me, a tender kiss that aches to become ravenous. So we kiss again, his hand sliding through my hair, his tongue skillfully teasing mine. My chest rises in a deep, longing breath.

And my pulse thumps in excitement.

I smile into the last kiss, my lips tingling beneath his. "Wow," I breathe when we break apart. "I think I'd like to get to know your mouth better." I smile. "Let's do that again."

"How well does that pickup line work for you?"

"Still to be determined."

He doesn't move in, but he's playing with my hair.

I gasp. "My pickup line has failed."

I catch sight of a fleeting smile. Then he can't resist any longer; he kisses my cheek, then the outside of my lips.

I steal the next kiss, and I whisper, "I want to have sex with you every day."

He goes rigid. My declaration has turned my fiancé to stone. His jaw hardens, and he pulls away, standing up straighter. The entire cart separates us.

"I'm serious," I tell him, just so he knows I'm not fooling around still.

"Where is this coming from?"

"My heart," I say a little too theatrically. Sometimes it's easier to just be lighthearted than express deeper sentiments.

Ryke sees right through me. "If you can't even tell me the fucking reason, then how can I consider it, Dais?"

I gather my thoughts and start from the beginning. Rose said I do this a lot—I tell an entire story before I land on the crux, the important parts. I think I just like preparing the person before delivering news. "So I kind of woke up early this morning—"

"How early?" His shoulders constrict.

"Three a.m."

"Fuck," he curses beneath his breath and looks away from me, a little pained. He knows that I didn't fall asleep until midnight, and while I have a lot of issues, my cramps were mostly to blame this time. I think.

"It's just one bad night," I tell him. "I'm okay. I feel energized. This is besides the point anyway..." I trail off as his attention returns to me.

"Alright, continue." He gestures me on.

"I was researching about my fertile window and basically mapped out when I should be ovulating—and I say *should* because it'll probably change all over the place with my weird periods." I take a much needed breath, a little more nervous about his response than I realized. "And I came to a conclusion. Pre-planning a baby is orderly and clinical. I want to be messy and spontaneous but still make sure we sleep together within that window." I pause. "So...will you have sex with me every day?"

He doesn't say anything, and my pulse pounds.

"Do I need to get down on one knee?" I ask with a smile that fades quickly out of apprehension.

He rubs his unshaven jaw, some sign of life there.

I drop off the shopping cart, shorter than him now. Then I scoot around our cart, standing more in the middle of the aisle and closer to Ryke. I grab the hem of his shirt, and he stares down at me, thoughts circulating behind his brown eyes.

I whisper, "You don't want to fuck me?"

He inhales strongly, his arousal apparent in his gaze. What's also apparent: him trying to snuff it out. "I could fuck you multiple times a day, sweetheart. I could even fuck you right now against the shelves."

That image radiates throughout my brain, nearly causing it to short-circuit and overpower. My smile gives away my satisfaction. "You would fuck me against the Lucky Charms?"

I wait for him to add, *Yeah, because I find you magically delicious.*

He's not taking the bait, even sterner.

"It's hard being serious," I tell him honestly, "because I know where you're headed, and I don't like it."

"I have to tell you straight out." He's an expert at communication in our relationship, always making sure nothing is lost in translation between us. So that I understand where he's at mentally. Even when it sucks to hear it so bluntly.

I nod for him to continue.

"For as long as we've been together, you've never been in the mood to have sex for seven successive days, let alone months on fucking end." I admittedly have always had a low sex drive, and I thought I just hadn't found the right person yet. Then I met Ryke, and while I'm more aroused with him than anyone else, there are some days it's extremely hard for Ryke to even get me off once.

I've never wanted to sit, to stay still, and add these little pieces of me together: the days where I ache to *feel* alive, to switch a light on inside of myself that's burnt out. The days where it feels impossible to do just that. The days where I can stand on the precipice of life and death and not bat an eye if I just...jumped.

There is a war inside me, where storm clouds roll over the sun and no matter how far I run, no matter how far I leap, it just grows colder and more numb. I hate feeling empty, but worse than that is the emptiness that can't be filled.

It's strange that I now have a name for this monster. I've given depression more life when I wish it would just go away.

"I don't have to be in a good mood to have sex," I say to Ryke.

"Don't fucking tell me that."

I thumb his zipper. "Ryke, you have to realize that even if we calculate when I'm ovulating, I may not be in the mood during that span of time, but we *still* have to have sex." Before he interjects, I add, "I don't want it to be a requirement anymore than you do, but I think it'll be fun if it happens more frequently."

"It sounds great in theory, Dais, but I'm just not sure how it's going to actually work out." He pauses. "Have you ever even had that much sex in your fucking life?" He has this whole *I'm now twenty-seven and a whole hell of a lot older than you and more experienced* posture about him.

"I guess I'm going to start. For the sake of our family." I smile. "What hard work, making love to you is." I want to draw him closer, but he does so instinctively, stepping near until his arms wrap around my shoulders.

He kisses my head but doesn't agree yet.

So I say one last thing in my heart. "I like the idea of being close to you every day during this process, not just for a short week every month." I look up at him. "Is that so bad?"

He shakes his head. "But it doesn't have to be every day. We can have sex every two days if you need a break."

I begin to smile. "Did you research this?"

Quietly, he says, "I'm trying to get you fucking pregnant, of course I looked it up."

I'm trying to get you fucking pregnant. My heart swells. "Say that again."

His brows rise, and his strong hand fits in the back pocket of my shorts. "If you're ever in pain, we skip that day, week, whatever you need. If you want to fight me on this, we need to do it back at our house because I'm not backing down."

It's tempting—only because our short, heated bursts end with epic sex. Our arguments never really surpass the thirty-minute mark. I'm not always the one who forfeits either. Most of the time, Ryke caves to what I want first, but topics that are this serious, he rarely concedes.

I remember that I'm on my period, and my excitement wanes. "I like these terms…" I trail off as I catch Mikey looking at his watch. "What's the time?" I ask Ryke.

He checks his own watch. "Fuck," he curses and immediately scans the items in our cart, seeing what we've forgotten. "We have five minutes before the store opens."

I climb into the cart, standing up and peering over the nearby shelf. I have a view of the entire store. "I see Rose."

My older sister stands with Connor by the checkout, their groceries yet to be placed on the belt and bagged. They square off towards one another, Rose setting a piercing glare on Connor.

He's grinning in return. When they zone in on one another, they seem to have tunnel vision, less aware of time and place.

Jane plays with Rose's statement necklace, in a pale blue dress like a brunette *Alice in Wonderland* and held in the arms of her protective mom.

Rose has adapted to motherhood like she does everything she loves. With determination, passion and poise. I hope I'm able to do the same. Adapt and conquer.

"We're going without orange juice," Ryke says before pushing the cart. I sway a little but keep my balance.

"Maybe Lo and Lily put some in their cart." I whip my head back and forth, trying to spot them. "Did they already leave?"

"What?" Ryke frowns, worried about his little brother almost instantly. He pushes the cart with one hand and takes out his phone.

"No, wait." I finally spot Lily and Lo by the milk and eggs. They emerge from the bathroom together, a diaper bag on Lily's shoulder. Both are concentrated on the little boy that walks between them, his smile out-of-this-world extraordinary and his green eyes lit up with excitement.

Maximoff Hale tries to run towards their half-filled cart, but his tiny legs don't keep up with his momentum. He skips ahead and then begins to fall. Lo scoops him up in his arms before his son face-plants.

I want that.

"Dais?" Ryke asks.

"They were changing Moffy's diaper." I cup my hands around my mouth and shout to my sister, "Lily Calloway to aisle ten!"

Lily swings her head, finding me in a quick second. I wave to her, and she squints, gawking in confusion. I must look strange, my head floating above the shelf.

Lo's brows scrunch with an added *what the fuck* glare. I'm so used to them.

I tap my wrist like *time's up* and then shout, "Do you have orange juice?!"

Lily's mouth keeps falling, not hearing me that well since we're far away. I mime chugging a carton of orange juice. I think it's important to note that I've never been good at charades. Lily's cheeks turn red, and she whispers in Lo's ear.

He pulls out his phone.

"Hey." Ryke tugs on my shirt, and I drop to my butt in the cart, squashing the wheat bread. I squat so I'm not destroying the rest of our groceries. "Lo said that Garth will grab a carton on the way out."

Lily's bodyguard is the burliest, tallest, and baldest of them all. He's also super vigilant and has seniority over the rest, so when we go out in a group, he's like the admiral of the bodyguard fleet.

Ryke is about to pocket his phone, but I ask, "Why was Lily blushing?"

"It'd be easier to ask why she's *not* fucking blushing." Ryke hesitates to text his brother since Lily does turn red a lot.

"You didn't see her," I say. "I just want to know what I did that made her uncomfortable." I pause. "We've been good about less PDA in front of her, right?" Sometimes I forget that the act of *watching* relates to sex addiction as much as the act of *doing*, and I don't want to cause her to regress.

"Yeah, I think so." He texts Lo, and I wonder if we're both guilty of spacing out when we start intensely flirting. Lily always says not to change for her, especially since she's fond of PDA with Lo and it'd be hypocritical of her to tell us *no*.

While we're roommates, I still want to be respectful and mindful of her addiction.

Ryke rolls his eyes with a brief smile before pocketing the phone. "What?"

He starts pushing the cart towards the checkout. "She thought you were making a hand-job motion."

I laugh. "Classic Calloway."

"Classic *Lily* fucking Calloway."

I gasp. "That was *my* hand-job motion. All of us should get credit."

"Cute." He messes my hair with his hand. Right when he pushes the cart down the aisle again, I grab two boxes of his favorite granola cereal, knowing he'll want them later.

We're not far from the checkout when the commotion from outside barrels into the entrance, exclamations tangled together that I think is *I love you, Loren Hale!!* Or *marry me, Ryke Meadows!!*

The most frequent shouts. As soon as the glass entry and exit doors come into view, my stomach nosedives.

I couldn't be more wrong.

"DIE, CALLOWAY SISTERS, DIE!" multiple people chant, a poster in blood red paint to match. A chill snakes down my spine, and the hairs rise on my arms. About thirty or maybe even fifty angry fans congregate outside, the entrance barred with *closed* signs.

Their hostility pummels me like a sharp kick to the ribs. I eye each volatile face, full of malice that sweeps me back. "What did we do?" I murmur, so confused.

And maybe even a little scared too.

< 15 >

Ryke Meadows

"Hey, stay with me." I tap Daisy's cheek, not softly.
She still squats in our shopping cart and stares dazedly at
the mob of people outside. I've seen her space out when settings match
the pandemonium from Paris, transporting her to the riot. Truth is,
I've been back to that place a few fucking times too, but only when I
picture Dais…lifeless in my arms, screaming her name over and ov—
stop. Fucking stop.

I don't need to be pushed there either.

"Daisy." I snap my fingers in her face.

She blinks a couple times, tearing her gaze away. Then she slowly
climbs out and stands next to me.

I look over my shoulder as Lily pushes her cart beside Rose's, all of
us near the number four checkout. Our bodyguards and Lo stand by the
entrance, talking with the employees.

"How many people do you think there are?" Daisy asks quietly. Her
voice sounds stoic, but I can tell she's fucking frightened. She sucks in a
breath and never fully exhales.

"Maybe ten," I lie.

"Your math is off," Connor says between my cart and his. "Next time, you should also use your back paws to count." He rolls up the sleeves of his black button-down, not to fight. He rarely throws a punch.

And I'm really not in the fucking mood for his quips. Maybe he can tell because he nods to Daisy. "How are you feeling?"

"I'm fine." For some reason, she appears younger right now, our seven-year age difference a little fucking clearer. It only makes me want to take care of her, and I bring her closer to my chest, my hand on her back. She clasps my waist, her fingers tightening as the shouting escalates.

Connor watches her a little longer, his expression blank. He's always been able to see through her as much as I can, but it's really obvious she's not doing that well, her skin ashen.

Lo approaches my cart. "So we have a huge problem. The bodyguards can't check every single person for a weapon because the employees are going to open the store in five minutes." His irritation furrows his brows. "Basically this is a clusterfuck." He glares at me. "This is the last time I wake up at five in the hellish morning to be greeted by a bunch of crazies."

The shouting escalates outside. "WE HATE YOU! WE HATE YOU!"

Lo points at the giant entrance window. "Those must be the Team Raisin fans."

I shoot him a look, but I can tell he's just deflecting, his gaze darting back to his son and Lily. He's trying not to scare them.

I'm going to lose my shit if anyone gets physical. With Daisy. With Lo or Lily, their son. Rose and Janie. Even Connor. I'm going to fucking lose it.

"DIE, CALLOWAY SISTERS, DIE!!" That chant is fucking killing me. I repeatedly run my hand through my thick hair.

"Why are they this mad?" Daisy asks Lily and Rose, both women busy putting foam plugs in their kids' ears.

"I don't know," Lily mutters, her cheeks red in grief as she struggles to calm Moffy. He's thrashing in the front seat of the cart, rejecting the earplugs and crying. Janie is in a similar state.

Connor and Lo both go to help their wives.

"DIE, CALLOWAY SISTERS, DIE!!"

"Jesus Christ," Lo swears and turns to Connor. "Tell me you have a plan."

Connor wipes his daughter's tears with his thumb. "I do, but it has unanswered variables."

"What the fuck does that mean?" I ask.

"It means I can't take into account the behavior of everyone outside. It's an imperfect plan."

"Great," Lo says dryly. "Anyone have anything perfect?"

I'm not about to say it out loud, but if Connor's plan is marginally fucking flawed, then there's not going to be anything else better.

From our collective silence, we all must realize that.

THREE EMPLOYEES UNLOCK THE entrance, and they wheel our carts out to Rose's Escalade and Lily's BMW, parked side-by-side near the front of the grocery store.

We have seven bodyguards. All of them escort Rose and Lily to the cars, their babies pressed to their chests, and the rest of us wait for a second, the yells piercing the fucking sky.

Daisy skims the posters, the ones that say: WORTHLESS + UNGRATEFUL + PIECES OF SHIT = CALLOWAY SISTERS. She remains calm, but her lips are downturned in hurt.

"It's easier when they're only angry at one of us," she says to me. We hang back with Lo and Connor near the potted plants and multi-colored plastic chairs for sale, all stacked near the exit.

"They'll get over it." I set a hand on her head, and she takes a step back until her shoulders rest against my chest. I wrap my arms around her collar and kiss her cheek.

"Where is she?" Lo asks, tilting his head and ducking to try to see past the throngs of people and our bodyguards. Everyone dwarfs his wife, blocked by bodies.

He's about to leave without us, and before I move a muscle, Connor grabs him by his black shirt, pulling him backwards. "Wait."

"I can't see her!" Lo shouts, pointing at the crowd.

"She's fine," Connor says coolly.

Lo spins his wedding ring a couple times, veins rising in his arms as his muscles flex.

"There she is," Daisy pipes in. We follow her gaze to the Escalade, watching Lily slip in with Moffy and shut the door. Rose climbs into the BMW with Janie, her bodyguards hovering behind her. I know why they switched cars. Lily's BMW had steering issues on the way here, and in a crisis, Rose would want her sisters in the safer vehicle.

Mikey, Quinn, and Garth head back towards us.

"Now we can go," Connor declares.

I open the exit door, and Lo saunters out first with Daisy on the other side. Connor and I walk behind. The fifty-some people disperse from our cars and sprint back to the store. To us.

"UNGRATEFUL!" someone shouts. They practically circle us, waving their posters manically so we'll read them. One almost knocks into my brother's face.

"Back up!" I shout, slapping the poster away.

Our bodyguards try to create a barrier between them and us, extending their arms, but some of these people easily slip through.

I'm tall enough that I can see over almost everyone, and there are about five or six young girls sobbing by the cart return opposite our cars. Their posters droop by their sides. I wince, instinctively wishing I could do something to make them feel better but knowing I can't.

"We loved you!" a girl tearfully screams at Daisy.

Dais wipes her clammy forehead with the back of her hand, pale. My stomach tightens. I keep a hand on her shoulder, guiding her forward.

Lo looks back at me. "What'd you two do?"

"You think this is because of us?" I glower. *We didn't do anything.*

"BITCH!"

"Hey!" I yell, searching for the hostile voice. "No one is a fucking bitch!" All of this is eating at me, and I have to concentrate on getting Daisy in one of the cars.

"WE HATE YOU TOO!" another person yells.

Mikey sidles next to me. "I'm going to escort Daisy to the Escalade. Try not to let anyone follow us." I nod, and he clasps Daisy by the elbow, pulling her back towards the Escalade. "Come on, Daisy."

"I can help them with the groceries," Daisy says as she follows Mikey.

"Don't worry about the groceries," Mikey tells her before I can. The trunks are popped, and Vic and Stephen aren't finished loading the paper bags.

Through the trunk, I watch Daisy crawl into the backseat, Lily sitting in the middle beside Moffy's carrier. My brother and I quickly help Vic fill the Escalade's trunk while Connor shuts the BMW's.

"I'm checking on Rose," he tells us before opening the passenger door and disappearing inside.

"What a weird fucking day," Lo says loudly, tossing in the eggs and bread without real thought or care.

"Take it easy, man." Stress isn't going to do anything but push him over.

He glares at me. "I can be pissed off. *You're* pissed off, Superman."

"I'm not Superman."

"You're right. You're uglier." He flashes a sardonic smile.

"You're so ungrateful!" a girl screams. We both turn and find the source. She can't be older than ten or eleven, crying while she outstretches her phone. Recording us. *What the fuck...* "You're so rude! I hate all of you! I hate you so much! We *deserve* better than you!"

"I agree," Lo tells the girl.

"Lo," I start.

He continues, "You deserve better than all of us, but *you* were the one who fell in love with us." He takes a step forward, and I grab his shoulder. "Don't fall in love with people who are human. We're going to disappoint you in the end."

She cries more. "I *hate* you..."

Before Lo opens his mouth again, I spin him back to the fucking trunk. Since this is an SUV, we're able to see Lily and Daisy, who kneel on the backseat, peering over the headrests and out at us.

"Are you crying?" I hear Lo ask as I toss diapers onto a case of water.

Lily wipes her red-splotched cheeks, more tears building. "No," she refutes.

"Calloway," I say to Dais. "Catch." I chuck another package of diapers, this time at her. It hits her square in the forehead and thuds onto the bread.

"Oops," she says, a smile in her eyes. She holds out her hands. "Do me again."

Lo tilts his head at Lily. "Really, love? Then what's that wet stuff running down your cheeks?"

"Snot." Lily reddens. "That sounded better in my head."

"I don't fucking see how," I say, throwing Dais the paper plates. She catches it this time and sets them beside her.

Lo looks infatuated with his wife, even with shrill screaming behind us.

I grab two more paper bags, and Daisy has lowered in her seat, the chants about dying Calloways gaining life again.

"Almost done," I tell her.

"You can't ignore us!" someone else shouts.

Lo and I shut the trunk at the same time, and Vic puts away the two shopping carts. We're the only three left in the parking lot from our team of seven bodyguards and friends.

I turn around with my brother, and in a single fucking moment, someone suddenly pelts him with a projectile. Like slow motion, he raises his arm to protect his face, but it *explodes* into a white, dusty cloud all over him.

I waft the air. "LO!" I scream, unsure if he's okay. I can't fucking see him.

I hear him cough repeatedly and spit. "Goddammit," he curses, squatting for a second. I bend down with him, his lips, face, shoulders, and hair are covered in the white substance. I rub it between two fingers. *Flour.*

Someone flour-bombed my little brother.

The BMW's door opens and slams quickly. Connor approaches with a water bottle, unscrewing the cap.

I'm going to lose it. While he bends down to take care of Lo, I stand up, setting my hands on my head, my gaze fucking narrowed at the girls with signs. Who did it? I scan them rapidly, unable to spot the person.

They've all quieted, about twenty phones pointed at us, recording.

"Why the *fuck* would you do that?!" I fume. It makes no sense why they'd flour-bomb my brother. He's loved by *everyone* on social media. He's the fucking favorite. For a moment, I think they missed. They meant to flour-bomb me.

Then someone says, "We supported you and *loved* you. None of you even care about us!"

"What the fuck are you talking about?!" My violent register causes three girls to shuffle back in fear. I instantly feel like shit. I hate feeling like shit when I'm not the one who just harassed another human being.

"Ryke." Lo tries to rub the flour out of his eyes, but he's making it worse.

I rotate towards him. "Don't fucking touch your eye."

"Lean your head back," Connor says in an easy-tempered voice that completely polarizes mine. I want to cool off—I just can't. Not after this.

Lo follows both of our directions, struggling to hold open his eyes, and Connor rinses them with water.

"Blink," he says.

Lo does, his eyes bloodshot and water runs down his jaw, creating trails in the flour. I pull off my T-shirt and hand it to him. He uses it as a towel, rubbing his face, and then he nods, standing up with us.

"Let's go." He tries to hand me my shirt back.

"Keep it."

He nods again and motions to Connor. "You're not going to give me your shirt too?" It's lighthearted enough to cool my boiling blood.

Lo's reddened eyes flicker to me like *it's okay.*

It's not. I don't like seeing him hurt, not even for a fucking millisecond, and if it had to be someone, I'd rather it have been me.

"Next time, darling," Connor says. "I just had this dry-cleaned." He passes him the water bottle. "We'll meet you at your place."

"You deserved it!" a woman shouts while Connor walks back to Lily's car.

I'm about to confront her, out of fucking instinct—to tell her why my brother doesn't deserve any of this shit, why those girls don't either—but Lo clasps my arm and drags me away.

"I really just want to go home," he tells me, his voice so honest that I instantly back down.

"I'm driving," I tell my brother, heading towards the driver's side. I may have wrecked his car once, but he still lets me get behind the wheel this time.

I lock the door and put my seatbelt on the same time as my brother.

"Lo!" Lily leans forward in the middle seat.

"I'm okay," Lo tells her, but she unbuckles and tries to dust off his hair and cheek.

I pull out of the parking lot behind the bodyguard's SUV, one hand on the steering wheel once we're on the street. I glance in the rearview at Daisy. She's quiet, just staring out the window.

"Calloway," I call.

It takes her a long moment to pry her gaze off the window and turn straight ahead. Her eyes are reddened, but for a different reason than my brother's.

And she says softly, "We know why they're angry at us."

< 16 >

Ryke Meadows

I tense. "Yeah?"

"*Celebrity Crush*," Lily whispers, her arms wrapped around Lo. He kisses her elbow. As much as I know he loves having her close to him like that—I need her alive.

"Put your fucking seatbelt on, Lil."

She reluctantly detaches from her husband, leaning back against the seat. Moffy babbles something to her, his legs kicking out in his carrier. She responds in hushed whispers and a big smile.

Lo shoots me an agitated look and shifts uncomfortably. "I didn't realize not wearing a seatbelt is more dangerous than rock climbing without a harness. Oh wait…" His cheekbones cut sharp.

I ignore his comment but feel the fucking sting. "What'd *Celebrity Crush* lie about?" I ask.

"They didn't lie," Daisy tells me.

I'm so fucking confused. My knuckles whiten against the steering wheel. "Then what?"

"At our engagement party," Daisy clarifies, "Christopher Barnes asked us if we wanted to do a *Queens of Philadelphia* reality show—to document our lives as housewives. We said no."

Lily adds, "And *Celebrity Crush* published an article telling everyone how we've had multiple opportunities for reality shows and we've rejected all of them. GBA even left a quote, saying they've reached out to us for years with six-figure paychecks and we've shut them down."

"I think," Daisy says, "people thought that the network didn't want anymore shows, not us, and now the fans are upset."

"We don't owe them anything," I say heatedly.

The car is quiet until Lily says, "They've supported Superheroes & Scones." The store is packed full of fans every fucking day, I realize this. Lo also has a comic book publishing company. Rose has a fashion line and boutique, not to mention their family businesses: Cobalt Inc., Hale Co., Fizzle.

Sure, these benefit from loyal fans and support, but I don't want Lily or Lo thinking they have to put *their kid* on the line as payment or that they owe millions of people. They can't live with that kind of debt on their shoulders. No one can.

"You're not indebted to anyone for that," I tell Lily. "They can buy into your product or not, and it ends there." I try to look at my brother, to see how he's handling this, but I can't stare at him and look at the fucking road too.

So I concentrate on the street, about to be stuck in morning traffic. To add insult to fucking injury, it starts raining.

"Someone say something," I interrupt the strained silence, almost wishing Connor was in this car, spouting off words that'd knock down *Celebrity Crush* and reinforce *our* choices. I'm doing a fucking piss poor job.

Daisy rests her temple against the cold window, rain rolling down the pane. "Are you all ever tired of this? Like…really exhausted by everything?"

We're all silent until Lo says, "Every damn day."

I'm not sure how much longer we drive with no more words passed between us. Not until Daisy starts talking again.

"I can't repeat *Princesses of Philly*," Daisy admits. "So if Rose, Poppy, and Lily want to—"

"I'm not doing it without you," Lily interjects.

I glance at Daisy through the rearview. She looks conflicted, wanting to be there for her sisters but *Princesses of Philly* was insane. Off camera, Daisy was upset during those six months. She was being overworked for modeling, and she felt like she had to paint on a smile every time she came home. The paparazzi grew crazy. Then she had trouble sleeping.

I don't want history to repeat itself.

The car slows to a stop in traffic, and I have time to turn to my brother.

He takes a swig of water, his brows dusted with flour. "They hate us," he says, not sounding put off about it.

Then he meets my eyes, and I see the confidence beneath his daggered amber irises, ones that seem ready for some kind of war.

"They think they're being hurtful by hating us," he says, "but I've spent more of *my* life being disliked than I have being loved. It's not new shit. It's just more shit."

"Shit," Moffy says in the backseat, rattling a toy.

Lo begins to smile. "That's right, little guy."

"So what do you want to do?" I ask my brother.

"I think we should tell them why we're not signing on to another reality show, be honest about it, and if they're all still furious—then that's their prerogative. I don't want to actively set out and make them love me. If our businesses dip a little because of it—whatever. I just want to live my life. With my family. In something close to peace." He pauses. "How's that?"

I nod a couple times, proud of my brother's decision, and even though Rose and Connor are the most ambitious ones out of all of us—I'm pretty fucking certain they'll want the same. They just love Jane more than they do their companies, and I've seen them both risk aspects of their reputations and businesses to protect her.

"What if they're physical again?" Daisy asks. "When people disliked Ryke and me, I was slushied like three times just walking into Lucky's."

My brows knot. "I thought it was just once?" One time was already a fucking lot.

"...there were other times, but they weren't memorable. Anyway," she says quickly so we don't hone in on it. "All I'm saying is that it's likely this won't end here, you know. It's not just the neighbor guys pulling pranks. This is real hate from millions of people."

"We have more bodyguards now," Lo tells her. "And most of these people are all talk anyway. Just log off social media if it's eating at you. Be done with that."

"No one's going to hurt you," I chime in. "I promise you, Dais." During *Princesses of Philly*, I was less vigilant than I could've been, and when people were tweeting *Raisy is Dead*—I could only keep up with Dais, I couldn't keep pace with the world.

I know this promise is lofty and seemingly impossible, but I'd do anything for her, for *my* family. Lily once told me that she'd "go down with the Raisy ship"—and even though I rolled my eyes, it's how I feel every day of my life.

I'd go down with Daisy, to the bitter fucking end.

< 17 >

Ryke Meadows

I watch Daisy pull off her helmet and shake out her hair, a smile already pulling her lips at our location. Up north. About five hours from the city. Our bikes parked in the middle of the forest. The weather is clear. The sun is out. I'm with a girl that I fucking love.

I inhale this moment, however simple, for all its worth.

"Where to, rock climber man?" she asks with the wag of her brows and hands on her hips. Her baggy white shirt says, *Climb My Mountain* in green cursive, the color matching her knee-high socks.

I toss her a stainless steel water bottle, and she fumbles with it before catching the thing.

"You're rock climbing too, Calloway."

She tries hard not to smile while I snap the buckles of my backpack across my chest, distributing the weight. I feel her giving me a long once-over, which pools blood to my cock. I try to concentrate on my gear and check everything before we leave.

Carabiners are clipped to a zipper strap and rattle when I walk around my bike, concealing it with a fallen branch. The leaves shroud the bright red paint on her Ducati.

She opens and closes the water bottle. "I'm only climbing if the wall doesn't look like a fucking shit show," she repeats what I told her earlier.

"Knowing Adam Sully, we could be hiking to a birthday party without the fucking cake and a piñata already broken in the corner." I've never been here. I've never even seen this rock face, but my childhood climbing friend called me up, said he found a good one, and I drove five hours with the slight hope that this deserted wall isn't riddled with loose rock and debris. That the crag is even semi-climbable.

His forest-green Jeep is hidden about five feet from our bikes, positioned between two shrubs and covered with foliage.

Daisy takes a sip of water. "What a sad metaphor. A birthday party without a cake." She smiles in thought. "Sully would be attracted to piñatas."

"Yeah, he would." I check the coordinates on my phone and point north. "You lead the fucking way."

Her smile explodes, and she gladly walks ahead of me, pushing tree limbs out of our path and stepping over rocks and fallen logs. It's denser the farther north we go.

Half a mile in, Daisy begins glancing coyly over her shoulder at me. Blood thumps in my veins and circulates in my cock, and my arousal spikes more than I'll let on.

I raise my brows at her, like she's not affecting me. "You have something to say?"

She shakes her head and tries to contain another smile. When she faces the trees again, I hone in on her ass in frayed jean shorts. She climbs over a boulder, more of her skin exposed beneath them. Sex starts occupying ninety-nine percent of my fucking brain, a carnal desire that I don't shut off.

I drop off the boulder behind her and then place a firm hand on her shoulder, guiding her towards the patch of large birch trees. Our silence spools tension, so extreme that my pulse thuds with each beat. I tower above her, watching her chest fall heavier in anticipation.

I push her body against the white trunk of a birch tree and raise her hands above her head. "Hold on."

She does, and she watches me over her shoulder. I'm behind her, my hands on her waist, and I spread her legs open like a fucking cop about to pat-down a suspect.

She senses this, her lips rising. "Am I in trouble?"

My hands dip towards the front of her shorts, and my chest melds against her back. I whisper in her ear, "So much fucking trouble." I unbutton and unzip her shorts. Pressing a palm to her lower abdomen, I push her body harder against mine.

She reciprocates, her ass grinding into me. I fucking harden, and I pull her jean shorts off. She kicks off her sneakers and then steps out of them, her hands tightening on the tree trunk.

"Ryke," she rasps in want. Her neck strains as she continues to watch my movements. I meet her eyes more than once, my body fucking begging to be right up against her. To feel her. I run my hands down her hips again, her skin smooth and soft. I pull down her gray cotton panties.

She steps out again and spins around, unclipping my backpack straps. I pull off her shirt and shrug off my backpack. She lifts my charcoal tee over my head, our hands moving faster and faster to undress each other, prolonging an inevitable kiss.

I snap her bra off, our chests pressed together, while she fumbles with the buttons on my black climbing pants. My lips near hers, and she breathes deeply. Then shallowly. I slide her bra straps off her arms, and she yanks my pants down my ass.

After I slip off my shoes, I step out of them.

In only her knee-high socks, she stands practically naked in the fucking forest. I'm in black compression shorts, and I pull her up against me, my hand combing back her brown hair, a shade lighter than her sisters' from all the time she's spent in the sun.

She smiles at me and edges close for a kiss, but I pull back, teasing her as much as she teases me. I cup her ass and push her against the tree trunk again.

She lets out a surprised noise, eagerness sparkling her green eyes. I massage her breast before my hands fall. I grip her hips, skimming her slender body with a long, fucking heady gaze.

Then I kiss her, finally, and her body curves into mine, her arms tugging at my hair. My tongue parts her lips, and she gasps. I break away quickly and drop to my knees.

"Oh my God," she breathes, eyes growing as she watches me. I lift one of her legs over my shoulder, my right hand on her ass.

Her fingers rake through my thick hair.

I'm in the perfect fucking position. I kiss her clit, slowly. I use my tongue and my mouth to send her to a new place of mind. Feeling her body tremble turns me into a fucking rock, my dick throbbing to push inside of her.

"*Ryke*." Her fingers tighten, crying out. "Ryke…" She shudders, and I look up, her gaze right on me, her mouth permanently open. Her eyelids flutter. "*Ahhhh*."

Fuck. I immediately lift her other leg on my shoulder and stand up, still sucking and kissing her, only now she's on my fucking shoulders.

She gasps again, staring up at the trees. "I can't…" She shakes her head like it's too much. "I can't…" She cries a sharp cry. Her toes curl and muscles clench. I feel her back arch against my palm, and sweat coats both of our bodies. When she comes down, I pull her off my shoulders and set her on her feet.

Daisy exhaustedly leans against me.

"We're not done, Calloway." I have to come inside of her in order to make a fucking baby, and I'm not about to drive into her without her being wet.

She clasps the band of my compressions shorts with a mischievous but tired smile. "Are you going to put your nine-inch cock inside of me?"

"Yeah," I tell her, "right here." I push two fingers into her, and she lets out a high-pitched moan that seriously almost causes me to come.

I grit my teeth, forcing down my own arousal. Her back hits the tree trunk, and I thumb her sensitive nerves while my fingers work. Daisy's gaze descends my arms and abs, drinking me in as much as I'm fucking devouring her.

She yanks my compression shorts, my hard cock in view. I step out of the last article of clothing, and she mutters something under her breath that sounds like *Oh my God.*

Her hand touches mine, the one between her legs, and she stares at the way my fingers disappear inside of her. She's stimulated visually, and it's the cutest fucking thing.

"You like my fingers inside of you, sweetheart?"

She grows so fucking wet, her breath shortening. Her hand tightens on my wrist.

"What about *my* fucking cock? You want this inside of you next, Calloway?" With my free hand, I take hers and set it on my shaft.

She hits a climax, and her knees almost buckle. "*Ahh!*" she moans. I catch her around the waist, pulling my fingers out, and I spin her around to the tree, her skin slick.

I bend down for a second, grabbing my phone from my pants, and I position her palms against the white bark. "Tell me if you're in any fucking pain," I remind her. Since her period ended, she hasn't been in any when we've slept together or during the day. And I'm hoping to continue that streak.

She's too tired to look over her shoulder for long, but she watches as I grip my erection and slide into her from behind.

The tightness fucking kills me—in the best way. She pants and looks overcome by the fullness.

"Ryke." She holds onto my wrist that clutches her hip, and I thrust deeper in—*fuck*. Using my phone I record only my dick sliding further in and out, a close-up that she can't see from this angle. After thirty-seconds of footage, I hand her the phone.

She replays it while I quicken my pace, each thrust like *fucking* the sun and sky and heaven. "Fuck," I groan lowly, not finished. Not ready to end this.

She keeps watching the phone, and she clenches around my entire cock, pulsating. "I can't," I hear her choke.

I pull her body back against mine, my arm wrapped around her waist, and I fuck her with aggression and affection, pushing up into her until we're both reaching the tallest peak of my fucking life.

"I ca—*Ryke!*"

I come, releasing inside of her, and she shudders again, releasing with me. She turns her head dazedly, and her lips near mine, I kiss her tenderly. She kisses back, almost feral, and I keep her inside of me while her hunger stirs. I've never made out with someone like I have with Dais—like the world could be burning behind us and it'd only fuel our bodies, moving faster and fucking stronger.

After a couple minutes, we finally detach, and I gently pull out of her, zoned in on her expression. She never winces. While we dress and wipe off, she says, "That was in my top five."

"Yeah?" I pull on my pants and feel a fucking smile lighten my dark features.

"I think I blacked out a minute there it was so intense." She snaps on her bra. "Two wild animals, doing what wild animals do."

"And what's that?" I put my charcoal shirt on and then reach for my backpack.

"Make love to make babies to sustain the species." She buttons her shorts. "It's the natural course of things."

I'm quiet for a second, clipping the straps over my chest and then pocketing my phone. "You know, Dais," I say, trying to pick the right words, "it's not unnatural if we can't do it that way. It's just fucking different." I don't want her to think she's less than anyone. Having a baby doesn't determine anyone's fucking worth. She could have no female reproductive organs and be just as much of a woman...but I don't need to tell her this.

I think Rose already did, and it's not something that may be easy to *feel* at first, even if she understands what it means.

"I know," she says with a pretty genuine smile. She slips on her shirt and then ties her hair into a high bun. "I just want to pretend while we can. Is that bad?"

I shake my head. "No." I walk over to her and kiss her temple. "What kind of animals are we?"

She bites my arm playfully. "You're a wolf." Then she howls, pretty fucking cute. I'm about to mess with her hair, but my phone buzzes.

I check the caller, and she picks up her water bottle. "Fuck." I press the speaker. "We're half a mile—"

"Well good because I'm heading to you. Look at what I do for you, man. Can you make a note of this in the *reasons-why-Adam-Sully-is-your-best-friend* chart? I know you have a long-lost brother and all, but my red hair and my face should give me two extra points."

"Sully," I say.

"Five extra points, you're right. I shouldn't devalue myself."

I shake my head, but Daisy is all fucking smiles. I'd ask how many energy drinks he chugged, but he's always like this. "Slow down, Sul."

"I can't, man. I can't—I have to come to you. Oh wait...there you are."

I look up and spot a tuft of red hair out of the forest and bundles of white birch trees. He waves in an awkward Adam Sully way that looks like half a salute.

"Come on," I tell Daisy, resting a hand on her lower back.

Sully outstretches his arms when we approach him. "My favorite people!"

"Hey, Sully," Daisy says before she hugs him.

He hugs back like she's a fucking stuffed animal and mouths to me, *I love her.*

I flip him off.

He laughs, and when they separate, I say, "Tell me this rock is fucking good."

"It has character." His smile stretches his face.

"Fucking fantastic." I know I'll probably still be tempted to climb it, even if it looks run down—but I don't want to scare Dais either.

"Follow me." Sully motions north.

I have no clue what he's leading us into.

< 18 >

Daisy Calloway

A one-hundred-and-fifteen-*ish* foot crag stands before us. At least, that's what Sully calls the gray cliff that rockets to the sky. In certain sections, the slab juts out with no clear-cut path, and I worry about turning upside-down and losing my grip.

The more Ryke inspects the rock from the base, the more his eyes alight. He sticks *one* finger in a crevice and lifts himself off the ground, the front of his thin climbing shoe then meets a foothold no bigger than an inch.

He climbs only about six feet before he descends. As he studies the cliff again, a smile passes through his rough exterior, lifting the corners of his lips. Mine evolves instantly to match his.

Watching Ryke surrounded by the *one* thing he has truly always loved is absolutely priceless. I've never found a passion, not like Ryke, but observing his carries me to new heights.

I'd never seek to take the place of rock climbing in his heart. What a shame it'd be, to lose this moment. It's so special. Passion.

Love. *Happiness*. Seeing it all—being a part of it—is more gratifying for me.

I hope that when I show my sisters and parents what I plan to do, they see how fulfilled I am by the project and entire feat.

I also hope they realize how badly I want to raise a child now. To be a mom. To help their passions come to fruition. I can't think of a better way to spend life.

Ryke places his palm on the rock one last time before he returns to his backpack near my feet. Without speaking more than a few words, Ryke and Sully start assembling gear. Ropes, devices, harnesses, carabiners—more than I can count and each device looks vaguely different.

Ryke searches for a specific few, and Sully tosses me a harness.

I put it on, not exactly nervous about hurting myself on the climb. I just don't want to hold them back, and I'm afraid my skill-level will do just that on this challenging rock face.

"You're going to ascend first with Sul," Ryke declares, standing with a device I've never seen.

I try not to read into why I'm not climbing with him. In the past couple of years, I've accompanied both Sully and Ryke on so many climbs, and being paired with his friend is as common as being paired with him.

I nod to the device in his hand. "What's that?"

"Anti-cross-loading locking biner." I must wear my confusion because he adds, "I have to clip it to my belay loop. It'll help catch me if I fucking fall. I'm going to solo-climb after Sully makes an anchor at the top." *Solo-climb*: the act of climbing alone but *with* safety measures. Like the device in his hand. Like his rope and harness.

Sully is busy dealing with his rope, untangling the strands. His shaggy red hair bounces as he nods, like he knew this would be the plan all along.

Whenever Ryke solo-climbs, it's usually to gain a feel for the rock. So he can redo his course without any safety measures.

His brows scrunch as he scrutinizes me. I think I even tucked a flyaway hair behind my ear, showing off my vulnerability. "What's wrong?" he asks.

I shake my head like *nothing*, but more than a few things wrestle in my mind. "Doesn't Sully usually solo-climb behind you?"

"That's only if I'm free-soloing a crag I've already safely climbed before." He shifts his weight from one foot to the other and rubs his mouth. *Free-solo*: the act of climbing without a harness or rope. No safety measures.

"You're going to free-solo this after you climb it once then?" I ask straight out.

He drops his hand, eyes fixated on the ground as he tries to find some words for me.

"Why couldn't you just tell me from the start?" I wonder. "I'm not going to forbid you from free-solo climbing, and I'm glad to help Sully set the anchor for you, or even just watch him set it."

Ryke runs a hand through his hair and then gestures to me. "I don't ever want you to feel like I fucking brought you here to work for me."

I try hard not to smile, finding him *extremely* attractive for caring so much. I've never felt how he described, not even a little bit. I *love* being a part of his process for free-soloing. At a northern rock face, I've cleaned grass out of crevices for over five hours with Sully, just so Ryke could free-solo climb with less risk of potential injury or death.

Every minute, I treasure. I neither slowed him down nor sat on the sidelines.

"You have it wrong, you know," I tell him. "You've included me in something you love, and I'm only grateful and so *happy* that you've shared this with me. I would hate it if you never told me when you're climbing or if you drove five hours without me and did everything alone."

In a low, husky voice, he says, "Vieni qui." He uses Italian with me mostly in intimate moments, muttered quietly and softly. I've heard this phrase enough to translate it without asking.

Come here.

I step closer, and his rough hand slides against my cheek with so much tender affection.

My body warms. "How do you say *hold me?*"

"Abbracciami." He wraps his arms around my shoulders, pulling me until our chests meet.

I can't contain my smile. "How do you say *give me a kiss?*"

He lowers his head and whispers, "Dammi un bacio." Then his lips press to my cheek, leaving a fiery, tingling imprint.

"What about *lick me?*" I tease.

His brows rise but there's a smile toying with this lips too. "Leccami."

Swiftly, I lick his neck and then nuzzle his jaw like a puppy.

He draws me back, only enough so he can kiss me right on the lips, like he's been aching to be there all this time. It lasts maybe a couple seconds, broken by applause behind us.

We both turn to Sully, who stops clapping but his dorky smile never shies. "Can't a guy appreciate romance? Will there be tissues at the wedding because I'm a crier. I'm not against using cloth napkins." He pauses. "That's if I'm invited." His eyes ping between us. "I'm invited, right?"

"No," Ryke deadpans at the same time that I say, "Yes."

Sully points at his friend. "Traitor."

"Loser."

Sully gapes. "Toad-face."

"Ginger root." He tosses him a carabiner, and I can almost see their friendship at eight and nine years old, right before my eyes.

Sully scoffs and pats his hair. "You just wish you were part of the Weasley clan."

Ryke almost smiles. "Don't drop my fucking fiancée."

He grows more serious as he says, "On my life, man. I won't."

I'VE MADE IT SAFELY to the top with Adam Sully. He's already set an anchor, and Ryke has solo-climbed once and repelled. Now at the base of the cliff, he sheds his gear to free-solo.

I watch from the top, the surface mostly flat and grassy. I stand near the edge, the wind whipping my hair, reminding me that today's conditions are "fair but not optimal" (Sully's words).

Ryke clips his chalk bag around his waist, about ready to climb. The tips of my climbing shoes peek off the edge, fear extinguished, but I snuff out adrenaline-fueled ideas that would do damage if I let them take hold.

Sully snatches my harness from behind. "Hey, crazy." He tugs me backwards until I'm five feet from the edge. "He can go without a rope, but you can't." He attaches a carabiner to my harness. Following the rope, I'm secured to the anchor that Ryke no longer uses. So is Sully.

I smile. "Unless," I say, "my death is imminent, in that case I could probably go without one. I'd just, you know, *die*. The tragedy of it all."

Sully shakes his head at me. "So morbid."

A giant part of me wishes I *feared* death. I fear people who'll hurt me. Who'll hurt Ryke. Who'll hurt my sisters, but I don't fear the end.

Though being a huge part of someone's life makes me stop and think and ache. I hate imagining Ryke alone, so I try not to dwell or let sadness consume me. I have so much to live for, and I'm not ready to slow down.

I nudge his side with my elbow. "Aren't you the one who said in climber life-span, you're nearing your seventies and Ryke is already a hundred and should die by next year?"

Sully ponders this by staring at the sky. "Yeah, well…death is relative to those who play with it." He meets my smile and says, "We're all a fucking morbid bunch, aren't we?"

"Seems that way." I rock on my feet. "So where've you been living?" I ask, changing topics. I have a feeling Ryke is climbing, but I don't want to disturb him by suddenly appearing by the edge.

"Everywhere and anywhere." Sully spreads his arms. "I'm a certified nomad on wheels." He still lives out of his Jeep then, climbing every day, wherever he can. He gestures to the rock face. "I only come back to Pennsylvania for this grump."

"He loves climbing more when you're here," I tell him.

Sully's lips rise. "You think?"

"Definitely," I say. "His whole demeanor is different."

"Yeah, he's surlier."

"He's happier."

Sully stares down at me. "He's happier with you too, you know."

We're both smiling for a long moment. Being the cause of someone's happiness, well—that feels like love, doesn't it?

My phone buzzes in my pocket. I check the text.

You have to reconsider the reality show, Daisy. You and your sisters are getting major heat from the tabloids. Last one I read called you a spoiled brat. Assholes. — Cleo

Since my engagement party and the dismissal of *Queens of Philadelphia*, Cleo and Harper have been texting me nonstop. Giving me updates on what Twitter and gossip mags are saying. I never asked for their opinions or updates, and I never respond to their texts. They won't take the hint.

A second later, a few more texts ping through.

Shit. Someone's started a #CallowaySistersSuck hashtag — Cleo

Don't read the newest Celebrity Crush. They took a horrible picture of you. Like you look ugly as fuck and you're a freaking super model. Or...were. — Harper

Please reconsider the show. I'm telling you this as your concerned friend. — Cleo

I've already seen Twitter, and for as many fans that hate us for
turning our backs on the show, there are still those that understand our
choices. It's just that hate tends to be louder and more volatile.

My stomach knots when Cleo sends a third text.

Love you always, girl — Cleo

I could reply, for the first time, and tell her to stop texting me. But I
don't want to open a dialogue with her, so I make a plan to change my
number. It's the option that feels right.

I'm about to put my phone away, when it pings again. My head
throbs, but as soon as I see the screen, I realize it's not my ex-friends
at all.

Bad news. Your bodyguard quit. I need you to stay at home
or have Garth go out with you until I can find you a new
one. — Dad

Why would Mikey just quit on me? Especially without telling me first?

I reread the text, my stomach sinking. Mikey doesn't *always* follow
me when I'm out with Ryke. Like today. My dad has no idea but I
doubt he'd approve. I liked everything about Mikey, and I worry his
replacement will be ten times worse.

I'd rather pick out the new bodyguard than hand this over to my
dad—

"Ryke!" a girl shouts, a voice that I've never heard.

Sully curses, and we both take off towards the edge, a lump rising
in my throat.

"Ryke, look here!" a man shouts next.

What is this? Sully pulls me down so we're both sitting, our legs dangling off the cliff. Ryke is midway up the wall, his pace slow since it's a difficult climb. He's about to reach the section where he has to be slightly inverted.

"Sul," Ryke says once, knowing his friend would appear. Sweat rolls down his forehead, and he takes one hand off to dip his fingers into chalk.

"You two!" Sully yells, my pulse rocketing. A man and woman with expensive cameras stand by our gear and Ryke's backpack, snapping photos. "You need to leave!"

I stay quiet. If I protest too, I'll add to Ryke's concern and probably break his concentration. Way more than Sully. Ryke is more used to climbing with Sul talking than with me.

The man types on his phone and then snaps a couple more pictures.

This is insane. I have no clue how they could've found us, unless they've been tailing us or tracking us with a stupid drone. We've been cautious of those every time we have sex outside after seeing one around the neighborhood.

"Ryke Meadows, look here!" the girl says again.

Frustration crosses Ryke's features, and he uncharacteristically wipes sweat from his brow using his bicep.

I whisper to Sully, "Tell them that they're going to kill your friend if they don't leave." My stomach twists. *It's not true.* It is though. I know it is.

Sully stands. "You're going to kill my friend! He has no harness on, so *leave*." Sully is so unthreatening. And so am I. This would be easier if Lo was around.

"Can you tell us about your friend?!" the man screams up to us.

"Fuck you!" Sully shouts, his face reddening. "Did you not hear what I said?! You're going to kill him!"

I suck in a breath and swallow. I stand next to Sully, my fingers twitching by my side. I knot and unknot the end of my shirt. Ryke climbs at a strange angle, his body nearly horizontal beneath a piece of rock that juts out.

Cick, flash, click, flash, click, flash, the cameras never stop.

Ryke's ribs expand and collapse with expertly controlled breathing. The flashing light must disturb a nearby cave because a swarm of bats zips out. Flapping right past Ryke.

The forest is silent. The air is motionless and the trees sit still.

Sully is lying on his stomach, hand outstretched to see if he can reach his friend. He's not close. No one is close. I lose sight of Ryke until his feet slip beneath him, only hanging on by the tips of his fingers.

He tries to swing and find a foothold so he's horizontal again. *Using your fucking feet is almost more important than your hands*, he told me on our engagement night, trying to put me to sleep. *You have to distribute your weight. You can't fucking last if you're only using your upper body.*

My eyes are as wide as saucers, burning with emotion that I'm not ready to confront just yet. "Ryke," I whisper. *Don't fall. Please don't fall.*

He screams in aggression as he uses *all* of his arm-strength to hoist himself up this rock. He's eighty feet off the ground.

Don't fall.

It hits me about this moment. When he still can't find a foothold. It hits me. That I may witness his death.

My life with him sideswipes me, knees me, rips me open—the first time he smiled at me. The first time we were alone together. The first time we kissed. All the places we've been. All the things we've seen and done. All the lonely moments we've filled with each other.

All of that is…

His foot reaches a crevice, and he climbs over the difficult section. He places his right foot too, and he shakes out his arms. Then he looks up, at me, and hot tears roll down my cheeks.

Thank you. I exhale, the relief blanketing me.

"I'm okay, Dais," he says, not too far below me. "Give me five more minutes."

"Take as long as you need," I reply, wiping my cheeks quickly. "Please don't rush for me."

Sully lets out an audible deep breath and kneels. "I'm sweating." He wafts his shirt.

Ryke grunts like *I'm the one who's fucking climbing*. He flips off his friend before slipping his fingers in a crack and lifting his body higher. Ascending. Again.

The man and woman are still there, but I don't want to even give them the time of day anymore. So I shuffle back and lie down on the grassy area, staring up at the cloudy sky.

About five minutes later, a body collapses next to me, head on the grass like mine. *He's here.* Tears almost squeeze out of my eyes again. *He's alive.* I look over at Ryke, his breath heavier than usual, and he turns his head to me.

"Hey," I whisper.

He breathes out. "Hey."

You scared me. I love you. "You're alive."

He kisses me, so hungrily, and my heart bursts, my lungs on fire. Our legs tangle and my hands slide through his damp hair. He steals my hair tie, my brown locks frizzing around my face. His tongue wrestles with mine, and my head floats off my shoulders.

He pulls apart and says, "I'm not going anywhere, Calloway. Fucking remember that?" His eyes hold a single apology like *I'm sorry I don't make it easy on you.*

He doesn't have to. "I'll remember. I promise." I kiss his cheek, my hand sliding down his unshaven jaw. I feel smaller against him, and he tucks me close like I'm what he climbed towards.

Sully suddenly plops down next to Ryke, his head on the grass. He stares at the sky as he says, "I'm beginning to realize something."

"What?" Ryke asks, his hand stroking my hair. I rest my chin on his chest.

He turns to us. "You two are seriously famous."

Ryke rolls his eyes.

"So are you airing your wedding on television too because I'm not really sure America is ready for me. Don't get me wrong. I'd still go. I just need some preparation." He's definitely not the kind of person who seeks limelight. Raised by lawyers with an older sister who followed his parent's footsteps, he's sought to live freely and privately. He says he tries to keep in touch when he can, but it's not often.

I'm so close to my sisters, and Ryke is so close to his brother. We both can't imagine losing those connections and relationships. With these trips, we can always return home. Best of both worlds.

"No one's filming our fucking wedding," Ryke tells his friend.

It seems impossible to make it private, especially after being slightly off the grid today and reporters appearing. But we have *one* plan that should help.

I elaborate in a hushed voice (just in case), "We're getting married out of the country."

Sully sits up and raises his fists in the air. "Yes! Where?" He excitedly rubs his hands together. "Venezuela? Puerto Rico? Madagascar? Lay it on me hard, Daisy Calloway."

Ryke gives him a look and kicks his shin.

Sully kicks him back.

I sit up now. "Boys." I smile. "Do I need to separate you two?"

"Yes," Sully nods.

"Fuck no," Ryke curses, sitting up with us. He pulls me onto his lap, his arm curving around my waist.

Sully is all smiles. "Italy? Spain?"

"We've narrowed it down to a continent," I tell him, "but we're still trying to pick a country."

Sully looks to Ryke for the final answer.

And he says, "South America."
We're going to be married in South America.
Somewhere safe from paparazzi.
Somewhere happiness resides.
That's the hope at least.

‹ 19 ›

Ryke Meadows

"It's not fair, and don't tell me *life's not fucking fair*. They can't cat-call you while you're climbing a hundred-foot mountain," my little brother rants through the phone's receiver. I press my cell to my ear. "What's wrong with humanity? Has everyone completely lost their shit?" He filed a complaint against *Celebrity Crush* for stalking me a week ago, but it doesn't even matter.

I was on public property. They could do whatever they wanted at the time, and they'll have to stalk me again in order to be arrested.

"Just let it go," I tell Lo. I'm fucking over being pissed about it. A local tipped off the reporters that we were in the area. They found our bikes and followed our trail by paying attention to broken twigs, crushed from our fucking soles.

"You could've *died*," he emphasizes. "Or does that not concern you anymore?" His dry, bitter voice scratches my eardrums.

I shift in the backseat of Rose's Escalade, Daisy squeezed in the middle. Willow on the other side. Lily drives, and I have a view of Rose in the passenger seat, her lips rising as she texts rapidly on her cell. To her husband, probably.

"Ryke," Lo snaps at my silence.

"I'm just not going to fucking dwell on this. I'm alive, Lo. It's okay."

"Should we start fitting you for coffins?" Connor asks calmly over the receiver.

I roll my eyes. "Have I been on speaker phone?" They both couldn't be here since it's a Wednesday, and they had meetings for Hale Co. and Cobalt Inc.—each business in Philadelphia, so they see one another throughout the day.

It was hard on me at first—to fucking know that Connor spends more time with my brother than I do. Now I just try to remember that we're not competing for his attention, even if Connor sometimes acts like we are.

I hear the crunch of a fucking chip. They're eating lunch together. This entire time. Lo says, "Yeah, and it shouldn't matter to you. You'll be dead by next month."

"Fuck off," I say lightly.

"Not gonna happen, big brother." He crunches on another chip.

My stomach fucking grumbles. "Are you eating Mexican?"

"Yep." He goes ahead and bites loudly again. "Three chicken tacos, roasted salsa, chips, and cans of Fizz." I practically hear *be goddamn jealous* attached to the end.

I'm in a car full of Calloway sisters and my half-sister who won't speak more than a couple words to me, too reserved and shy to open up. About five years ago, I pushed Lo to start a relationship with me, but he was an alcoholic who needed the biggest dose of tough love.

I can't do that with Willow. I'll just end up pushing her away, and she'll run towards Jonathan fucking Hale.

"Congratulations by the way," I tell my brother.

There's a long pause. "For what?"

"You know what." It's the first week of October. Today marks the fucking day that my little brother has been sober…for two long years.

I think he's going to say something biting in return. After another pause, he says, "Thanks, you know, for everything." His edged voice is full of sincerity.

"You did it on your own. I just stood by you."

"Yeah, well...I needed a hardass." With a mouthful of food he says, "And now I'm going to hang up on you."

The line dies, and I feel the corners of my mouth tic upward.

Rose still wears a satisfied grin, and I watch her cross her legs and sit straighter in the seat. Flirting by text with Connor Cobalt. Those two are more apparent than they'd like to believe.

"Why am I driving again?" Lily asks, hands tight on the steering wheel.

Daisy drums my thigh with her fingers, more fucking antsy the closer we are to our destination. I set an arm across her shoulders while she answers her sister.

"Because you're the best driver out of everyone here."

Eh—I'm definitely the best fucking driver.

Lily perks up at the compliment, and Daisy smiles even more.

Rose coughs dramatically into her fist. Dead air hangs where Lo would slip in a comment like *is that your inner-demon trying to escape, Rose?* or *Don't touch her. Evil is contagious.*

Not having him here is fucking strange. Being in a car full of girls is even stranger for me, but it's not bad. It's not something I'd ask to change.

Rose lets out a more aggravated sound when no one invites her into the conversation. She raises her chin. "I'm a better driver."

She does haul this mammoth car into the city and parallel parks, but she's still not better than me. And if Connor were here, he'd probably dispute the fact just to incite her.

I'm not her husband. "It's not a fucking contest," I say, ending anything before it begins.

Rose huffs and returns to her cellphone to text. She won't say it, but she misses both Connor and Lo. When they're not around, she can't argue or verbally fucking spar.

Rose swivels in her seat to face me. "You could at least tell us where we're going." Her manicured, blood red nails grip the middle console. "As your future sister-in-law, you're not earning any points by keeping me in the dark." Her yellow-green eyes pierce me, thinking she can scare me enough for the answers.

She can't.

This is a fucking surprise.

Daisy's surprise.

I'm not giving that up. "Turn back around," I say flatly.

Her lips purse, and I break eye contact before she can start a staring contest for supremacy. She concedes and turns back in her seat.

Willow flips her phone in her hand, and she pushes her black-rimmed glasses further up her nose.

"Can you check my messages?" Lily asks Rose. "I want to know how Moffy is doing." Their kids are spending time with Greg and Samantha, who think we're out shopping all day.

Rose mumbles something like, *I should be driving*. She's not used to being ordered around by Lily.

I attempt to draw Willow's attention by tapping the back of her seat, but she avoids me. Anyone who's had an easy time building a familial relationship in the middle of your life—I need some fucking help. Because it's never been clear-cut for me.

She's not angry that I didn't tell her about her father earlier, but I think she may be confused why Lo and I told her to wait a little while before she jumps into a conversation with Jonathan Hale. I think she needs to process things before she sees him.

Our dad, however, is more than ready. He keeps fucking texting me, asking when he should come over and see her. I just keep saying *wait*. But that's not something he'll do forever.

But I have a feeling that this tense silence has nothing to do with our dad. It's what Daisy said; she finds *this* awkward. Me being her brother. I'm starting to feel it too.

"Hey," I tell her.

Daisy presses her back to the seat, letting Willow have a better view of me.

She gives me a sheepish smile and then busies herself by re-braiding her light brown hair.

"How've you been?" I ask.

"Okay. Lily and Lo are giving all the employees at Superheroes & Scones a chance to create a new superhero in the Fourth Degree universe."

I've listened to my brother enough to understand *Fourth Degree*. I haven't read any yet, but their tagline, *the fourth degree from you and me*, and their original superhero called Extent (Vic Whistler) sold well beyond the expected amount.

Now they're launching more origin stories, group comics, and creating tons of fucking merchandise. I'm really proud of those two. Lily and Lo have come a long fucking way to reach this place.

"It's really competitive," Lily chimes in.

Willow nods. "The employees are taking it over-the-top serious." She passes her phone from one hand to the other. "Maya made a flow chart in her apartment." She pauses. "So…um Jonathan, or—I mean our dad, left me a voicemail yesterday."

I instantly tense. "Yeah?" I rub my mouth. "What about?" *He wouldn't wait forever.* I grit my teeth some because he might have just abandoned my advice before I even offered it. And I'm fucking afraid he's fueled by chaos and will do whatever his fucked-up brain thinks is love.

Her eyes flit to me and then back to her hands. "He wants to meet me for lunch at some country club."

The car quiets.

I hold onto the door handle, my stomach tossing at every memory I have. Where I met Jonathan Hale at a country club each Monday. Where he served me alcohol as a kid. Where I fucking revered him and then despised him.

I don't want Willow going, but I don't want to control her fucking life either.

Daisy slips her hand in mine and squeezes. She brings her feet up to the seat, legs tucked to her chest. Then she turns to Willow, "Are you going to take his offer?"

"He sounded sincere," Willow says softly, considering meeting him.

"I have some fucking reservations," I express the best I can. "He's going to pretend to be a nice guy, but he's not."

Willow lets out a breath. "All I really know about him is from the media, and it's not that great…"

I wrack my brain, remembering that Jonathan was accused of molesting Lo.

False, I believe now. I don't doubt my brother, and he said that it was all a fucking lie.

Lily adds quickly, "It's not true. None of that was true."

"I know," Willow says. "I know, but it's hard for me to see anything else. And I really, really want to since he's reaching out to me. He's my dad…"

I lean forward in my seat. "Can I go with you?" I ask her outright. I don't fucking say *let me go with you*. Or *I have to go with you*. I'm trying to do this the best way possible. If she says no, then I'll push for Lo to at least be with her.

Surprise lifts her brows and widens her eyes. "You want to go?"

I nod. "Yeah."

"I thought…Lo said that you don't like him."

"I don't, but I want to be there for you." I add, "You're my fucking sister."

Her eyes flit to her phone again. "Do you think Lo will want to come too?"

"Yeah." *Without a fucking doubt.*

"Maybe you both can be there just for like part of the time?" she asks. "Is that okay?"

I know I have to accept this, even if it's not everything I fucking wanted. "Yeah, that's fine."

"Left, Lily!" Daisy calls out.

"Shit." Lily turns the Escalade sharply to the left. The SUV behind us swerves at the last minute too. It's safer having our bodyguards around, and since Mikey quit after breaking his leg surfing (on a short trip to Malibu), Daisy has had one of Connor's bodyguards temporarily follow her.

We were going to find a replacement, but Greg called me and said, *please let me handle this.* The *please* kind of did it for me. He sounded more like the father who wanted to take care of his youngest daughter, and I wanted to respect that.

Rose swivels in the seat again, eyes blazing on me. "This"—she motions to Lily's distress and rigid posture—"better be worth it."

They have absolutely no idea what we're driving to. Not even a fucking hint. Dais wants to watch the look on their faces when we pull up to her new business venture.

Lily blows out a long breath. "I'm okay. I'm the best driver in this car." She nods resolutely, like she believes it too.

"Second best," Rose amends, repositioning the vents so air cools Lily.

"That's not what Daisy said." Lily begins to smile.

"Hmmm?" Daisy feigns confusion and then unbuckles herself.

"No!" Lily yells, eyeing her sister from the rearview. "No one unbuckles in my car. Driver rules. Click it or ticket!"

Daisy wags her brows. "Sounds exciting." She ignores her sister and starts climbing over my lap, her hand sliding over my thighs and crotch before rolling down the window.

Her mischievous, green eyes flicker to me, practically saying *how did that feel?* and *I didn't do a thing, I swear.* My blood heats as she stays on all fours, and I raise my brows at her, not taking her fucking bait. Not while we're in a car full of her sisters.

I say lowly so only she hears. "You're fucking trouble, Calloway."

She smiles, her hair already blowing as the window rolls down. "Soon you won't be able to call me Calloway, you know."

"You'll always be Calloway to me." I pull her yellow shirt down that rises up her lower back, and the fabric conceals her skin again.

This one gesture causes her chest to rise in a deep breath. She sits on my lap, hands gripping the frame of the window, and she says under her breath, audible to only me. "You're a good guy, you know that?" Her eyes flit all around my features.

I watch her watch me. "You look fucking happy, you know that?"

"I have a secret," she whispers. Then she leans close, lips to my ear, she whispers, "I am really, *really* fucking happy." And then the window rolls *up*. "Hey!" Daisy slides off me and repeatedly presses the button. It's locked.

Lily shouts, "You're not jumping out!"

"I just wanted some fresh air." Dais flashes her sister doe-eyes and a fucking cute pout. I shove her onto the middle seat, and Daisy breaks into a grin. I try to push her face, but she bites my fucking hand.

"No backseat flirting," Rose announces.

"We're not flirting," Daisy says while she stares straight at me.

I raise my brows again, wanting to throw her over my shoulder, but we're stuck in a damn car.

Rose snorts, "And I'm not Rose Calloway Cobalt."

Daisy mock gasps. "No way. Who are you?"

Rose isn't amused. "I almost brought nail polish, but I thought 'no, I don't want the fumes to asphyxiate my sisters.' Now I'm rethinking my loyalties." She shoots Daisy a look like, *I blame you for making me rethink my loyalties.*

I'm fucking hot. "Turn on the air back here?" I fiddle with the vents in front of Daisy's knees.

"Lil, another left again!" Daisy shouts. "Oh wait, you missed it…" She opens her phone.

"What?" Lily whines. "How?" her eyes flit to the rearview. "Are you two groping each other while I'm driving? New rule. No groping allowed."

"For everyone," Rose says, "in all cars." She puts on dark red lipstick, using the visor mirror.

"Wait?" Lily's eyes widen. "What? No..."

"You can't be a hypocrite about it." She smacks her lips.

"Okay." Daisy has up Google maps. "Let's just rewind. We're honestly really close." She coaches Lily through a U-turn, and less than five minutes later, we've arrived.

"Left turn and then park," Daisy announces.

Lily slows the car on a gravel road, spruce trees blanketing either side. She drives up to an unmarked lookout point. A rusted sign says `private property and residents only`.

Her sisters and Willow exchange quizzical looks.

"Unmount!" Daisy exclaims with the clap of her hands.

I climb out first, my boots meeting gravel and then grass, heading towards the ridge. The east coast mountain range is full of lush green and yellow hues, spanning as far as the eye can see. No rooftops, houses, or high-rise buildings. Untouched, unobstructed nature.

In the fall, the colors will be richer and more vibrant. I inhale crisp air, this place fucking surreal—that something this beautiful can exist just a few hours from the city.

"I don't understand," Lily says as she locks the car. The SUV rolls up and parks behind the Escalade, but the bodyguards don't exit.

"It's not even paved," Rose says. "Are you sure we should be here?"

Daisy stands on a boulder by the rusted sign, about to answer her sisters, but Lily points at `private property`.

"We're trespassing!" Lily shuffles back in this awkward fucking way. It looks like she's doing the moonwalk.

"Gather 'round." Daisy motions all of them forward.

Rose sprays bug spray around her area and then crosses her arms, her five-inch heels are firmly set on the gravel.

I hang back while her sisters and Willow approach the boulder. This display is all for them.

"I've had this grand idea for a long while," Daisy begins, hands perched on her hips. The wind takes her brunette hair, and my love for this girl just fucking floods me. "It's going to seem too big for me, but I promise I understand *everything*. Just hear me out first?"

They all listen.

Daisy extends her arms. "I bought this."

Lily's nose scrunches. "The trees?"

"The land," Rose realizes. She suddenly becomes very still, and Daisy hones in on her the most.

"There are things in life," Daisy tries to express, "that I've lost and experiences that I've never truly had, friends that I never could've made. Ryke once told me this story about a boy who spent every year counting down to summer. This boy had one lasting friendship and an experience for a *lifetime*. Can you imagine a place where friends come together and adventures are made?"

She's describing Adam Sully and me. My summer camp friend.

"I may have never been to camp," Daisy says, "but I'm more determined to build one. Where summer-long campers make new friends and live their wildest adventures."

It's the most Daisy Calloway thing in the entire fucking world. A place that brings happiness to kids through wilderness, friendship, and thrills like zip-lining and ropes courses.

Lily claps alongside Willow, and I smile as tears run down Lil's cheeks. She knows that Daisy has been through a lot, including the betrayal of close friends, and now she plans to construct a place that values friendship.

She has a giant, forgiving heart, and no matter how many times people try to burn her, she's found a way to rise above.

Daisy waves Willow and Lily to join her on the boulder, and they shuffle closer while Rose stiffly struts over to me, coldness and concern mashing together in her pointed gaze.

She stops by my side. "I need details."

I need her to be happy for Daisy. She's put a lot of her soul into this fucking project, and this is just the beginning of the camp. "She bought the land," I say gruffly.

Dais tries to help Lily up, pulling her while Willow pushes on her butt so she'll reach the top. Lily Hale has no upper-body strength.

"I heard that," Rose says, worry wrinkling her forehead for point-two seconds. "How much did it cost?"

"She had the fucking money." I'm trying not to be defensive. I know Rose's questions come from a place of love, but she has to trust her little sister.

"I know she has the money," Rose hisses, lowering her voice. "But how much of it is she using to build *this*?" She crosses her arms again.

All of it. "We're well-off," I tell Rose. "I save everything I make rock climbing—"

"It's going to wipe her out, isn't it?" Rose asks, her lips down-turning. "Everything she earned modeling?"

"Yeah." She still has a trust fund and inheritance, but the former is like an allowance and the latter is imaginary unless her parents die. "If this fails and makes *nothing* in the end, I'd still be able to support her without Greg's help."

But like the protective older sister that she is, Rose wants Daisy to be able to support herself. She's silent, and I run a hand through my hair, catching a glimpse of Willow now struggling up the boulder. Both Lily and Daisy clutch each arm and hoist her to the top.

"It's a summer camp?" she says quietly.

"Yeah. Horseback riding, a lake, cabins—all of that." I watch Rose mull this over with overbearing sisterly concern that I really understand. If that was my brother, I think I'd ask these questions too. And I'd hope that someone would show me the real fucking details. "Look at her face, Rose. Then tell me she made a mistake."

Rose doesn't move, her stubborn yellow-green eyes on me. "Why didn't she ask for my advice?"

"Because for the first time in her life," I say, pride for her filling me, "she knew what she really wanted. And she didn't need anyone's advice for it."

Her face falls in realization, and she finally turns around. Daisy stares out at the horizon, her arms over Willow and Lily's shoulders, all standing on the boulder, picturesque and beautiful.

Her smile lights up the fucking sun.

There is nothing happier in the world than this moment.

Rose can see that. She brushes a tear that falls and collects her hair onto one shoulder. "Don't tell her I was upset." Before I even respond, she hikes over to her little sister in five-inch high heels, pride flushing her cheeks.

"I won't," I say beneath my breath.

It's a promise that will be easy to keep.

‹ 20 ›

Daisy Calloway

After a rough patch of turbulence, the captain announces that we can leave our seats. Ryke and I unbuckle almost at the exact same time, and with that *I'm twenty-seven and I know what I fucking want* demeanor, Ryke clasps my hand and leads me down the aisle. Towards the bathroom.

We pass the other cream leather seats in Connor Cobalt's private jet. Everyone is here for our Christmas vacation. Well, everyone except our parents, but considering what I'm about to do, I'm *very* thankful my dad is not on this plane.

I catch sight of Jane on Rose's lap, Connor fixing a cute bow in her brown hair while Rose talks to their baby. Janie's cheeks are splotchy from sobbing, not a fan of planes yet.

At least not like Moffy who's fast asleep on his father's chest. Lo keeps a hand on the small of his back and simultaneously scrolls on his phone while reading a comic book over Lily's shoulder. Willow decided to return to Maine just for the holiday, to catch up with her little sister and mom. And then Poppy, Sam, and their eight-year-old daughter Maria piece together an art-deco puzzle at a table furthest from the bathroom.

It's hard not to hone in on the kids during family getaways. Sometimes I wonder: *is this how it will always be?*

Ryke and Daisy: the cool aunt and uncle without any burdens or responsibilities. No little ones to look after or take care of. This could be our forever-title.

Ryke glances at me over his shoulder, his rough exterior never softening. I concentrate on the moment, and the hardness of his unshaven jaw, the danger set within his masculine features. *You know what you're getting yourself into by being with me, Calloway?*

Yes. Yes, I do.

I wag my brows at him, and he turns back around, not giving into my playfulness. I like that he's not outwardly desirous by it but rather still broody and mysterious. *What are you thinking, Ryke Meadows?*

He opens the bathroom door and waits for me to slip in first, not a word passed between us in a long while. The suspense drums my core, and I watch him shut the door, the space tiny and cramped. As he walks forward, my back presses against the lip of the sink.

He sets a hand on either side of the counter, caging me. Towering above me. Staring down. Our hot gazes linked as they descend slowly over one another. I reach up and skim his shoulder with my fingers. He never flinches or melts. He's stoic, *rugged.*

My breath catches, and I fist his shirt the same time he leans forward, his rough cheek sliding against mine. He nudges my face so I lift my chin, our bodies communicating in raw fashion, pleasure heating my insides. As soon as I raise my head, his lips meet mine, and we *devour* one another, our hands everywhere.

All at once.

We explore each other so carnally that I struggle to breathe. He hikes both of my legs, my hands gripping his hair. His beneath my shirt, then lower to my jeans. He unbuttons. I nip his ear. He finds my lips and kisses me *harder.*

I moan against him, and his body presses into me, now unbuttoning my easy-access flannel shirt.

My fingers fumble with his pants, and he kisses my collar, his lips trailing a scalding line between my breasts, down my belly.

Ryke drops to his knees.

I'm breathless, leaning back on my elbows, supported by the sink. "I have this theory," I pant. He shimmies off my jeans and kisses the line above my panties before rising again. Before hiking my legs back around his waist.

With my legs split open and only in white cotton panties, I'm perfectly in line with his cock, but he stares down at me, waiting for me to declare my theory. I breathe heavily. "I lost my thought."

"Did you," he deadpans, his voice low and deep and extremely attractive.

"Wait...I have it." I almost shudder in his arms and end up clutching his biceps. *I love this man.* I'm very small against him, even my 5'11" self seems little to his six-feet and three-inches.

His hand makes the perilous descent down my inner-thigh, but his hard brows and darkened gaze stays latched onto me.

"My theory," I continue, "is that if you have sex in the air, you're one step closer to reaching god-like status."

He *almost* smiles.

I'm grinning more for the both of us. "Zeus and Hera fuck in the clouds, right?"

Ryke gives me a *what the fuck* look that I appreciate. I love it all.

"Do you want to become a god with me?" I ask, running my fingers through his hair again.

One of his hands slips down my lower back and pushes me closer to his body. A sharp breath escapes my parted lips, splitting into a short, pleasured cry. I clench, coming faster than I ever have. *Holy shit.*

He says, "I don't think fucking in the air is how gods are made."

I tremble, my chest rising and falling as I catch my breath again. "Maybe we should ask Connor Cobalt." *He's practically a god.*

Ryke glowers. "Hey, Calloway?"

"Yeah?"

"Don't say his fucking name while I'm getting you off."

I try not to smile. "What about babies?" I pant, still winded. "Can I talk about making babies with you?" I search his eyes that roam my features, and he places a hand on my cheek, cupping my face.

It's a dream-like feeling. Making love with the *hope* to procreate. Not every time has been wild or monumental and successful—I've even skipped some days out of soreness. But it's filled with sentimental value that we both can't ignore.

It's been…emotional, as much as it's been physical.

Before he answers, he kisses me strongly, his abs hard and tight against my body, and I push my waist closer to him and tug down his pants. His muscles constrict, and I wrap my arms around him. He rubs my head tenderly for a second and whispers, "Every fucking day."

I'm glad he still has some hope too, even after one failed pregnancy test and some *no's*, based on my regularly appearing period. No pain with sex, another plus. The remaining chocolate cyst has not beaten me yet.

"Stand up," Ryke instructs, his hand firmly on my ass.

I can't contain my smile. I rise onto the counter, a little unstable. I have to turn my head a little so I'm not hitting the ceiling. I pulse more than once.

He holds my hip and leg so I won't fall. His head is near my abdomen, and he fingers the band of my panties before tugging them down. Ryke kisses my hipbone before he scoops me by the waist, setting me on my feet faster than I thought he would.

He lifts my panties back up, and a pit falls in my stomach. I notice the graver look in his brown eyes, and his focus keeps falling to my panties.

"What?" I breathe and then peek inside them. I notice a couple droplets of blood immediately. I shouldn't be having a period right now.

He kisses my cheek, hugging me closer so I don't freak out. I'm two-fourths scared and two-fourths bummed by what feels like a setback.

"It's okay," he assures me. "When we land, we'll call your doctor."

"I must be spotting..." It's not enough to be a period. I'm tense, and concern is all over his face. "Maybe we should still try? I could be ovulating today. Unless, you think it's gross—"

"You know that's not fucking it," he forces. He doesn't want to hurt me.

I'm aroused though, and squandering this moment feels wrong. He must sense my mood because he kisses me again and gently eases me against the sink.

I wrap my arms around his shoulders, and he lifts me up with his upper-body strength and unparalleled endurance. Only in dark green boxer-briefs, he frees his erection and pulls part of my panties aside, pushing slowly inside of me.

I gasp against his shoulder at the fullness. "Ryke..." I look down. He's only halfway in. *Oh God.* I rock forward and tighten around his hardness. *Ahhh...ohmygod.* I pant for breath, and he thrusts forward, all the way in.

All the way in. My fingers dig into him, holding on like he's my rollercoaster. *Take me. Take me.*

His pace increases, building sweat on our skin, the friction so *amazing.*

"Dais," he grunts at one point, his hand clutching the sink for a second, knuckles white, before returning to my hip.

It feels so—

Ow. I inhale sharply, the fullness rebelling into a stabbing pain. *Ow ow ow ow.* "Ow," I wince, inhaling sharply again.

"Fuck." He stops immediately and scrutinizes my frame. "What's wrong? Dais?"

"It hurts."

He combs my damp hair out of my face and then gently pulls out of me, the pain not subsiding right away. He sets my feet on the ground, and I slowly sit on the toilet seat, shaking a little.

Neither of us liked that.

"Hey, what do you need? Talk to me." His worry grows each second I'm quiet. I must be pale too because he removes his T-shirt, soaks it in the sink, and wrings it out. He pats the cold fabric against my cheek and forehead, standing above me.

I close my eyes, the coolness calming me a bit. "I think I jinxed myself," I whisper. "The whole time I was practically cheering about the lack of pain and regular periods...now *this* happens."

"You didn't fucking *jinx* yourself," he refutes.

Just in panties and a flannel shirt, I know I need to dress but I'm hit with exhaustion. "You promise you'll still have sex with me after this? Not today, I mean, just in the future?" I can't read his hard features so I add, "I don't want you to be afraid of me."

He glares like that's furthest from the truth. "I've never been scared of you, sweetheart. That's not fucking changing now."

I smile weakly. "Good."

"Now I'm going to help you get your fucking clothes on, and then I'm going to carry you through that fucking door. How does that sound?"

I smile more. "*Fucking* good."

He messes my hair and lets me hold onto his cold shirt while he collects my jeans off the ground. His back muscles ripple, especially as he jumps into his own pair of pants and zips them.

Ryke turns around and raises his brows at me. "You fucking watching me, Calloway?"

"As much as you watch me."

He actually smiles but it fades at the sight of my panties. "Can you stand?"

I nod and do. He checks the cotton one more time, not anymore blood than there was before we had sex.

"If we were the last two people on Earth, do you think we could survive? Just you and me. No doctors around to save us."

"Seeing you hurt in any capacity is not on the fucking agenda. Doctors or no doctors. Last people on Earth or surrounded by *millions*—I don't give a fuck." He helps me step into my jeans.

"I think that's the most you've said all day."

He flips me off.

I laugh, feeling better. I'm sore, in a different way than usual, but I'm fairly certain it's just the chocolate cyst seeking revenge against me. *I'll get you next time. Before you get me.*

He buttons my flannel shirt while we stare into each other's eyes. I stand on my tiptoes and kiss him. He kisses back and then swiftly lifts me into his arms, cradling my frame.

I press the back of my hand to my forehead and mime fainting. "How shall I ever regain consciousness again?" I outstretch my hand to his face. "Apothecary, the pois—"

He slaps my hand away, skillfully keeping me in his arms before slipping his hold beneath my knees once more.

I gasp. "You're a horrible apothecary. That's *twice* you've denied me a blissful end."

"Then I've done my job fucking right."

"Yeah?"

"Yeah," he says, "you're not dying while you're with me." Then he pushes open the door, and we come face-to-face with a guy we've both just met earlier today.

While I'm still firmly in Ryke's arms, his commanding *back the fuck up* glower directed at this new guy says the most.

All I can think: how much did my new bodyguard hear?

< 21 >

Ryke Meadows

Price Kepler.

That's his fucking name. I've kept an open mind about Daisy's new bodyguard for the past three hours, but now that he's physically blocking my fucking path and listening outside the fucking bathroom—not to mention I'm holding Daisy securely in *my* arms—I'm starting to have a major *fucking* problem with him.

Add in these facts:

1. Greg Calloway hired him.

2. He has slicked-back, longish light brown hair, baby-fucking-smooth face, and he sports a navy button-down paired with slacks. Clean-cut. A decent build. Nothing like me, but something Greg would fawn over in a heartbeat.

3. He's twenty-two.

Daisy's father hired a bodyguard close to her age. He's *five years* younger than me. All day my gut said something was off about Price. He's been hovering around Daisy like the air will infect her. Now *this*. I don't believe in coincidences with that many factors.

"Is everything okay?" he asks Daisy, his gray eyes sweeping us and pinning to my wet shirt in her clutch.

"Indubitably." Daisy offers him a smile while swinging her legs. She has a habit of cutting tension before it begins, but I'm not ready to let this guy off without questioning.

He shifts his weight. "It sounded like you were hurt in there."

"Stomachache," she lies with ease and touches her belly. "I ate tuna salad this morning. Bad choices, all around."

Price finally meets my fucking glare. "It's just my job. I'm trying to look out for her. Protect and serve."

"She was in the fucking bathroom with me," I say flatly, controlling my rage that simmers my veins.

"I know."

You've got to be fucking kidding me. "Then what are you protecting her from? We're on a motherfucking *plane*."

Daisy says under her breath, "With motherfucking *snakes*."

My brows furrow at her. *What the fuck.*

"*Snakes on a Plane*? Samuel L. Jackson?" she asks. "Nothing. Not ringing a bell for you?"

"No."

"Oh Ryke." She shakes her head with a widening smile.

"This movie sounds fucking horrible."

Price says, "It's really not good."

Daisy gasps dramatically. "What a low blow, Price Kepler, already ragging on my movie choices. Next thing you know, you're going to say you've never watched *Harriet the Spy*."

"What's that?" He turns to me for answers, but this entire exchange between them has solidified my fucking bones, and I'm ready to end it.

Daisy probably senses my annoyance because she beats me to the punch, sliding out of my arms. She sways against me for a second, and I keep a hand on her hip.

Price actually takes a step closer, which is *not* what Daisy fucking wants. As hard as it is for me, I willingly let go of her. She gestures to the leather seats. "I'm going to lie down for a second."

"Cookies or chips?" I plan on grabbing her a snack before I join her later.

Her lips rise. "Both."

I kiss the top of her head before she walks away, and when Price tries to follow, I snatch him by the back of the shirt and pull him towards me.

He straightens up, gray eyes flitting *attentively* between Dais and me. "I'll get her the cookies and chips—"

"No," I force. "That's not part of your fucking job description." Or is it? I have no idea what Greg Calloway told Price. Part of me feels like this is the final test. Maybe her father still doesn't trust me as much as I thought he did.

"I'm here to help," he says, halfway sincere, halfway pushy. "I'm a second or third pair of hands. In case you both need me."

"That's the thing, you *have* to give her some fucking space."

He sighs like this sits uneasily with him. "I have to do my job here. I'm not going to just sit in a corner. If something happens to—"

"I don't think we've properly met." Connor Cobalt interrupts Price by sidling next to me, a glass of red wine cupped in his hand.

"Price Kepler," he greets. His name sounds like he comes from an aristocratic family. Does no one else find this fucking strange?

I watch Price shake Connor's hand and engage eye contact longer than most people. I run my hands through my hair, ready to fucking land already. Call Daisy's doctor. Eliminate some stress since I can't eliminate him.

"You seem very benignant for a bodyguard."

Price frowns. "Very what?" I can't tell if he truly doesn't understand the word or if he doesn't understand why Connor would call him that.

"Benign. Nonmalignant. *Harmless*," Connor replies. I almost wait for him to spout off the origin of each word. "In other words, you're shorter and younger than any of our other bodyguards. Also a little less built." He never elaborates on what this could mean or why Greg hired him of all fucking people.

"I might be young, but I'm good at what I do."

"That's yet to be seen and may rely on which definition of *good* we're using. Yours or mine." Connor sips his wine, his arrogant aura clouding my space.

Still, I'm a little fucking glad he interjected himself into this. It's not all in my head.

Connor continues, "While it pains me to agree with someone who prefers to forgo modern conveniences so he can drink milk from the carton"—I glower at him; forget everything I just thought—"Ryke has a point."

Or not.

"We're on a plane," Connor says, more calmly and eloquently than me. "Unless one of Daisy's sisters turns homicidal in the next three hours, she's safe while you sit with the other bodyguards."

Price bears down on his teeth, his face strict and tense. He nods once before heading to the back of the plane, passing through blue curtains to another side with couches.

"You're welcome," Connor says.

I roll my eyes. "I was fucking dealing with that."

"Not well."

I'm too frustrated to banter or even entertain him with words. "Fuck off."

Connor finishes off his wine with a large gulp. He places the glass on an empty tray table by the window. "While we're trading favors…" He rolls up the sleeves of his white button-down. "Since the moment you went into the bathroom to have sex—"

"I'm trying to get her fucking pregnant," I say lowly and more roughly than usual.

"I realize that." His voice is calmer, and he scrutinizes my facial muscles and posture way too long.

"Stop psycho-fucking-analyzing me," I whisper in a growl.

Connor blinks like that sentence was more annoying to him than I even realize. "My brain tries to retaliate every time you insert *fuck* into an actual word." He adds, "Is Daisy okay?"

He sees my concern. "I don't know," I answer honestly. "We'll see."

I don't give him more than that, and it's his turn to roll his eyes, which he usually just does in my presence. "Like I was saying before, since you went into the bathroom, Lo has been in the back cabin." He pauses while my adrenaline rises. "He's been on the phone with Hale Co. and I can't get him to end the call."

It's a major admittance for Connor, and my muscles bind all over again. Without even a question, I quickly walk down the aisle. We had a rule for the trip. *No work.* Everyone was supposed to delegate their duties to their assistants and advisors before we left.

It's the holidays, and if Loren and Lily can't figure out how to manage their businesses and spend time with Moffy and family *now*, then they may never find balance.

Connor keeps my pace.

"Did you try yanking the phone out of his hand?" I ask.

"I'm not going to physically pry a cellphone from his fingers, no. I asked nicely, and that didn't seem to work. So I thought you'd be useful. Your language is more uncivilized than mine." He always makes me do this with Lo. He can't bear to ruin his friendship, so he piles this shit on me.

"I'm fucking sick of being the bad guy here." I slip through the curtains, the bodyguards all chatting on the couches, some playing cards.

They look up briefly at us, but we don't say a word. I open the cabin door, not leaving much time for Connor to reply in privacy. So he stays quiet.

I imagine I'll see my brother pacing. Twisting his wedding ring. A phone to his ear, aggressively switching between glaring at the ceiling to condemning the carpet with his amber eyes.

When Lo comes into full view and the door shuts behind us—I'm... shocked.

He's sitting on the queen-sized bed, a large block toy and multi-colored block letters scattered on the sky blue comforter. His son lies on his stomach beside him, picking up various blocks with interest.

"Try these, little man." Lo passes a couple letters to Moffy. When my brother notices us, his gaze narrows at Connor. "Seriously? I thought you were the smart one, love. I told you I was fine." He rubs Moffy's dark brown hair. "Paul O'Hare was just being a helpless dickhead."

"Dickhead!" Moffy laughs excitedly and shoves the letter L into its correctly-sized slot.

Lo cringes. "I should've seen that one coming."

I turn to Connor, pissed he alarmed me for nothing. Lo is fine... but Connor is zoned in on the corner of the room, not on me. His expression is blank, hardwired to bar emotions from passing through.

I follow his gaze anyway.

Lily sits cross-legged on the ground. No chairs are in this cabin, just the bed, and she squints hard at the book in her hands. I recognize the spine—the same book she gifted Connor for Christmas. The same one he returned with his annotations. *Chronicles of Narnia.*

She focuses on the text, avoiding us.

The cabin is small, but she's still Lily. And that's still Loren. They're almost always next to each other, side-by-side, squashed with arms tangled everywhere. The queen bed is large enough that she'd normally be right beside her husband and son.

It's just fucking weird. Seeing her on the floor.

"You can both stop staring at me," she says softly, never raising her head. "I can feel your eyeballs...or the burn from them. Whatever you call it..." She hoists the book a little bit to cover her face that turns bright red in shame.

My stomach caves. "What the fuck are you doing on the floor?" I ask.

"Staying away from Lo." Then she drops the book on her lap and gently closes it. A second passes before she gains the strength to meet my eyes. "I know we had this whole 'delegation' rule before we left, but the person I delegated my work to decided on taking a last minute trip to Vegas. So I've been on the phone with *five* different Halway Comics marketing interns to see if one of them can handle the holiday ads for Vic Whistler in *Fourth Degree*. I'm putting faith in a bunch of college kids that aren't being paid and who I've never even met."

Her face reddens more at the thought, only this time I can tell it's from being upset.

"I'm going to fuck this up," she says, "I know it. I just have to stay away from Lo for a little bit because the only thing that sounds good right now is sex." She doesn't blush at the word. "And I'm pretty aware that I can't self-medicate with sex when I feel like everything is out of control. So…there." She lets out a final breath.

I've never actually seen her admit to having cravings. Not outright. Not this direct or honest. Not to a room filled with Connor, Lo, and me.

I see her fucking strength. Even if she feels like shit right now. I see it.

"If it makes you feel better," I tell her, "I had sex on the plane with Daisy, and her new bodyguard overheard us."

She tries hard not to smile. "No…"

"Fucking yes." I run a hand through my hair again. "This day fucking sucks—and *not* like that."

She smiles for real. "Isn't he…twenty-three?"

"Twenty-two," Connor corrects.

I pinch my eyes, sick of glowering at him and the floor and everything else. I feel like my little brother. "Why would Greg hire him?"

"Because it's Greg," Lo says from the bed. "He hired a disgusting pervert to be Lil's therapist without knowing." I remember that.

Lily shakes her head quickly. "He felt *really* badly about that. He even apologized to me, and I don't think he'd make the same mistake twice."

"That's yet to be proven," Connor says, leaning an arm against the wall, his ankles leisurely crossed.

Lo lets out a short, dry laugh. "This is why you're not his favorite son-in-law." No one says the real reason Connor dropped from Greg's pedestal.

Greg Calloway came to terms with the fact that Connor has slept with men in his past, but the news unfortunately slanted Greg's view of him. It never fucking changed mine. He's still the same conceited, billion-dollar douchebag that I've always hated and loved.

"He's testing me." I extend my arms. "I fucking know it. I'm about to marry his daughter, so he goes and hires some young bodyguard that could take my place. Maybe he thinks I'll be jealous and drive his daughter away or maybe he thinks Dais will cheat—anything to fucking show how we're not ready for this commitment."

I don't believe either thing will happen, but the uncertainty of Price's motivations is a stress *neither* of us need.

Everyone goes quiet, and then Lily raises her hand.

"We're not in a classroom, love," Lo says with a growing smile. He eyes her like he'd love to join her in the corner—just to be closer.

"It was really quiet," Lily mutters. She does this hair-flip thing that Rose does with more gusto. On Lily's shoulder-length hair, it's comical but maybe even more endearing. "I have an alternate theory." She clears her throat. "What if he's a spy?"

Lo starts laughing first.

Lily frowns. "Hey! It's a good guess." Dais would probably think so too. She almost puts her hands on her hips, but they fall to her lap. "Think about it. Dad isn't just losing Daisy. He's losing all of us. Rose, Poppy, and me too. We're traveling together, building families, and with fans against us, maybe he feels like he's in the dark. Having someone like Price following Daisy around is a good excuse to keep tabs on us."

Fuck.

I squat for a second, knocked in the chest—just hoping he didn't hear our talk in the bathroom. If he's supposed to be spying, he'll relay it all to Greg.

"What happened?" Lo asks me, worry spiking his voice.

I stand up and rub my mouth. "Dais and I were talking about making babies in the bathroom, and Price was outside the door."

"Making babies?" Lo looks at me like I've been hijacked. "Who says it like that?"

"He's adopting his fiancée's lingo," Connor explains.

I flip them both off with two middle fingers.

Lo raises his hand now, which causes Lily to full-blown grin. She hugs her book to her chest, probably to stop herself from catapulting onto the bed.

"One problem concerning Greg Calloway," Lo says. "When has he ever given a shit about what any of his daughters are doing?" He looks at his wife. "He's always kind of been in the dark, Lil. And yeah, the fans hate us right now, but the media is always this crazy. It doesn't change much. Greg is still a goddamn clueless softie."

"And you're his favorite," Connor says. "I think that says more about Greg's character than mine."

Fucking fantastic. "So what's your theory then?" I ask Connor.

He arches a brow but says nothing, and I realize that he's not going to "share his wisdom" with me. Because I rejected it last time at the fertility doctor's.

I'm not curious enough to pry and beg for it. Even if he tries to ease my concerns by saying, *it's probably nothing*, I'm not even sure I'd believe him. Or if he says, *he's probably spying for Greg* or *he's here to test you*, I'd go fucking insane with the knowledge.

It's probably better that he keeps his "wisdom" all to himself.

I'm no closer to knowing what Greg wants with Price. I can't just fire Price and hire a new bodyguard for Daisy. The solid footing I've gained with Greg will be crushed with the act.

I just have to be cautious of Price.

And pray he's not here to royally fuck us over.

< 22 >

Daisy Calloway

"Snow!" Moffy gleefully squeals, on all fours before his parents can snap in his skis. Nestled in so many layers, he's been waddling around the Lake Tahoe ski resort like a puffy penguin. The barren area is mostly flat for young kids to learn how to stand, not ready for the beginner's slope.

Or really any slope. Moffy and Jane are too young to even be in a ski class.

"Boos boos boos," Jane sing-songs, trying to say *boots*. Even though she's learned a ton of words by eighteen-months, she has trouble hitting the hard "t" sound.

Jane sits on her bottom, patting her boots, sans skis like Moffy.

Ryke and I stick our boards by the bunny slope, a few feet behind the babies and their parents. We usually sprint off towards the mountainsides riddled with signs like *Danger: Do not enter! YOU WILL DIE!*

Just kidding.

We're not that destructive, though we do like snowboarding down black diamond trails, but we've never seen the babies ski before. We both want to witness this historic moment.

Lo bends down to his son, snapping in the skis while Connor snaps in Janie's.

I lean my hip against Ryke and bet, "A hundred for Moffy."

"Janie has it," Ryke counters.

"Are you betting on the kids again?" Lily asks, squinting at me through the falling snowflakes. She tugs down her white fuzzy Wampa cap that matches the little one on Moffy's head.

"Me?" I try to say innocently but I yawn into my ski jacket, striped with bright pinks, oranges, lime-greens, and blues. Lo called me a child's candy cane. I took it as a compliment.

Ryke's black beanie covers his hair, goggles on his forehead. His concern shines down on me for a millisecond, and my phone buzzes in my pocket.

"Yes you." Lily perches her hands on her hips, in full-on investigative mode. "I heard you. You said…" She thinks hard but can't recall my exact words. "You said *something* I know you said something." She nods.

I love my sister, and I can't stop smiling. "Depends if Moffy stands up on his skis first," I tell her. "Then we're totally betting on them."

Ryke snaps my goggles over my eyes, and I almost laugh but I remember that I have to read my texts. There's a fifty percent chance it's Harper or Cleo flooding my inbox.

My lips downturn, and I remove my glove, clicking into my phone.

If you need to talk again, don't hesitate to call me over the holidays. I'm always free. — **Frederick**

Old text. The new one:

I can't determine whether the cyst is growing without an ultrasound. It's not something that should ruin your holiday. Wait until you come back to the east coast, and we'll check.

– Dr. Yoshida

Over the phone, he told me, "It's probably a little spotting from the cyst. Nothing to worry about." Last night, it kind of plagued me, and I texted him, asking if the cyst was enlarging.

He's saying it's not urgent, so I just need to compartmentalize this and let it drift off into oblivion for now.

Rose's icy voice suddenly cuts into my thoughts. "You're not betting on Jane?" I hear the frown in her words.

"I am." Ryke nods to her.

Rose narrows her eyes at *me* like I've betrayed the sisterhood.

Cheerfully, I declare my loyalties, "I'm Team Lily for now but Team Rose for later."

Lo gives me a sharpened side-eye. "Smooth."

I'd say Rose thinks so, but the snow totally sidetracks her from sisterhood things and revenge-plots against Loren Hale. She literally dusts melting flakes off the laces of her brand new, bold red boots. I wonder if the stresses of the holidays have made her more anxious or if it's something else.

Seeing her OCD flare up puts a sinking pit in my stomach.

"Hey, Rose." I smile wide as she meets my eyes. "I like the red color you chose."

"They were out of black," she snaps and then squats to fix the laces on her boots.

"That's a shame," Lo says, clipping in Moffy's right ski. "Now your boots don't match your heart."

She growls and reties her laces. I miss her fiery comebacks.

Connor observes his wife for a second, but Jane throws her little body at her father like she's catapulting off a trampoline.

She squeals with laugher and draws Connor's attention immediately. He lifts her up.

"Hug," she grins, her cheeks redden from the cold.

His grin matches hers. "Thank you, honey." He kisses her forehead before putting her bottom back on the snow. So he can fit her skis.

"Fuck," Ryke mutters. He's peering over his shoulder at the lodge, cafés, fire pits, and ski lift where we just left. About twenty feet from us, our bodyguards block our small area, not letting anyone approach our group.

Price has distanced himself from the fleet, nearing us.

Ryke is not happy about it.

If the media hasn't figured out where we are yet, they probably will within the hour, so we need to hurry. Capturing a photo of Moffy and Jane skiing is worthy of a tabloid's front page, and everyone wants this to be a pleasant experience for them.

Meaning no lenses up against their faces or journalists screeching questions in their ears.

"I'm okay!" I shout at Price and give him a thumbs-up.

Price hesitates more at my command than Ryke, who is sizzling beside me. Radiating heat. His tense and locked body language says enough.

I don't have much of an opinion on Price yet, other than he's nothing like Mikey, who was more of a friend and less of a...parent.

I hate to do this, but I shoo Price with the wave of my hand, adding an apologetic smile with the motion. He takes the hint and eases back with the fleet.

Ryke is unmoving.

I place one of my palms on his cold cheek. Only his head shifts, just to stare down at me. My fiancé is a stone statue. Not Adonis. Ryke is the wild boar that killed the godliest god in Greek mythology, slaying all handsome things.

Then he pulls my white pom-beanie over my eyes.

"He moves!" I lift up the beanie, and Ryke flips me off. Cellphone already in my hand, I snap a photo, immortalizing his *fuck you* to me.

Such love.

His brooding brows rise. "Seriously, Calloway?"

"As serious as pumpkin pie," I say like it makes all the sense in the world. It actually makes zero sense—maybe that's why I like it so much. I replay my words in my head and laughter builds aloud, my breath smoking the air.

He gives me a look. "What the fuck is so funny?"

"Pumpkin pie." I grip my waist, a stitch in my side, and I laugh again.

He suddenly steals my phone and snaps a pic, typing too. Just as I regain composure, he chucks the phone back at me.

I manage to catch it, and my laugh quiets as I curiously skim the screen.

His Instagram is popped up, both of our photos posted side-by-side with the caption: my someday wife #sweetheart #pumpkinpie

My chest swells because Ryke isn't big on social media, not unless I remind him.

The wind whips, chilling my nose. "Ryke—"

"CALLOWAYS SUCK!" someone shouts from afar, his voice carrying with the wind and stealing my thoughts and the moment.

"Lovely," Rose mutters, collecting her glossy brown hair onto one shoulder. She diligently scans her surroundings while Connor lifts Janie onto her skis.

Ryke scouts the area with a dark gaze too. "You'd think they'd cool the fuck down by now."

"I don't know," Lily says, helping Moffy stand onto his skis with Lo. "If I loved *Princesses of Philly* as much as I love *X-Men* then I think maybe I'd understand how upset they are. Like, if Marvel just decided to stop writing *X-Men* or stop making movies about mutants, I might riot."

"Yeah, love," Lo says, "but we wouldn't drive to Marvel and start calling them names." Moffy wiggles in their grasp, trying to stand free of them. They're both not ready to let go just yet.

Lily gapes at Lo for a long while.

Lo sighs. "Okay, maybe I would." He motions to the crowd forming behind our bodyguards. "But *that* is excessive. And no offense to you Calloway girls, but you're not goddamn cool enough to elicit that kind of reaction."

My jaw drops with Lily and Rose. We're sisters. All sisters are cool by nature of just being *sisters*.

Rose closes her mouth quickly to fasten a glare. "I take offense to that, *Loren.*"

I'm so happy she snapped at him unlike her silence before. I chime in, "So do I." I try not to smile with my declaration, but it's a mighty one that almost forces my lips up.

"Me too." Lily nods.

Lo mockingly puts a hand to his heart like she pierced him. She's too busy concentrating on Moffy to see his reaction.

"Mommy," he complains. If he knew the words *let go*, I bet he'd say them right now. I love how protective and caring both Lily and Lo are with their son. Lily is scared he's going to fall, but she reluctantly loosens her grip after Lo. Connor removes his hands from Janie, and both kids instantly fall on their butts.

It's so cute, especially since neither Moffy nor Jane has broken into a sob yet. My eyes alight, happy for their monumental first. I've learned to shelve the darker sentiments, the silent, quiet grief. I don't ever want to attach it to my niece and nephew.

Ryke watches me, and when I turn to him, so much flits beneath his gaze: reverence, love and pain.

"What?" I ask.

The muscles tic in his jaw. He can't find the word for what he feels. But I can. I know. He's such a fixer, and he can't give me a baby like a cup of hot chocolate, the shirt off his back, a hug or a kiss.

This isn't an easy fix, and it's killing him.

Before a lump rises to my throat, he shoves my arm playfully.

I nudge his arm back, harder than his push to show I mean business.

He sways and then gives me another look. "Do you know what you're fucking playing with, Calloway?"

I slink up to him. "A big...bad...wolf."

He sets a hand on my breastbone like he's going to knock me backwards. My eyes twinkle like *do it, please do it. Send me flying into the snow.*

"GO BACK TO PHILLY!" someone shouts, causing our heads to swing towards our bodyguards again.

A scribbled sign reads: **QUEENS OF PHILLY! DO IT FOR YOUR FANS!!!**

Ryke has dropped his hand off my chest, but his arm slides across my shoulders, tucking me close. Little moments between us are taking detours because of the growing masses. I wonder how different today would be if they were less vocal.

Lily notices the sign too. "Have you all ever thought about maybe doing another reality—"

"No," everyone says together.

Rose dusts off Jane's jacket. "Don't worry about them. They're trying to tug on your heartstrings. It's their ploy." She then *smiles* at her daughter who tries to stand up on her own.

"Rose is obviously immune, seeing as she has no soul," Lo pipes in.

"LOREN!!" a bodyguard yells. It sounds like Garth.

We all shift in different directions, and I focus primarily on the babies' safety while Ryke's hands protectively tighten on my shoulders. I try not to fear what I can't see.

Lo and Connor lift their kids in their arms, and I look every which way for the source of Garth's panic. Some of the bodyguard fleet blocks the crowds, but Price sprints towards me, the slap of the wind reddening his cheeks.

I instinctively glance at my feet for Coconut, but I remember that we left her in Philadelphia for this trip. Then out of the corner of my eye,

I see a figure *speeding* towards us. Skiing down the side of the mountain, his face concealed with winter gear, he fists…something in his glove.

I step back on instinct, meeting Ryke's hard body. He pushes me behind him, so that he faces the skier, but I notice Rose trying to help Lily from the snow.

She must have fallen, and Lily struggles to stand in her puffy jacket and pants.

Rose almost trips onto her. "Take my hand," Rose tells Lily.

My sisters.

The skier is headed for my sisters.

My frozen legs gain more life, and I try to hike towards them. "Rose!" I yell, feeling weighed down by the deep snow—but I realize Price is holding onto the back of my jacket.

Let go.

Ryke runs past me to help. Rose is in the direct line of fire, the skier skidding towards her. I think—no, I know. She's shielding Lily. On purpose.

"ROSE!" Connor screams, and that's when I know it's too late.

The masked skier hurls an object at her head, and a white chalky substance bursts against her face. Rose waves her hands at her cheeks like she needs to wipe it off but fears smearing the powder. Her frantic, frozen state crashes against my lungs.

Lily starts desperately helping wipe Rose with her sleeve and snow, our older sister's eyes squeezed painfully shut.

Connor runs over to Rose with Jane, just as the skier flies right past us with no intention to toss anything else. The skier's eyes briefly pin to mine, and I swear there's a smile in them.

Something furious and hurtful snaps inside of me. I charge for him, peeling out of Price's grip. "DON'T HURT MY SISTERS!" I scream, grabbing fistfuls of snow on my way down to him. I chuck loose snowballs that deteriorate before impact.

He grows further and father away.

"GET BACK HERE!" I want to hurt him like he's hurt her, and this foreign *hate* zips through me. It takes hold, burning my throat raw with the chill. I throw more snowballs while a few bodyguards chase after him too.

Someone picks me up. As he tosses me over his shoulder, I know it's Ryke.

"YOU CAN'T HURT US!" I scream so loudly, practically clawing at Ryke's back to reach the skier, a blip in the distance.

"Say that a little fucking louder, Calloway!" Ryke provokes.

"YOU CAN'T HURT US!" Tears blister my eyes. *He did hurt us. He hurt Rose.* I thrash against Ryke's restraint. "LET ME AT HIM!"

He grips me tighter and treks towards the ski lodge. "What do you want to do? Fucking hit him?" My head is near his ass, sliding down to flee, and he pulls me back, my abdomen on his shoulder.

"He hurt my sister." My voice cracks, and I go still.

I cover my eyes because I'm crying more than I wanted to, more than that masked skier deserves.

He pauses for a second; maybe he hears me crying. "Hey." He sets me on my feet and then he wraps his arms around my body, hugging me in a warm, safe cocoon.

It doesn't reverse what happened.

My older, fiercer and obsessive-compulsive sister was just flour-bombed.

< 23 >

Ryke Meadows

This is somewhere between a clusterfuck and a nightmare.

Ushered past people and locked hastily in the lodge's restroom—not the girls' (out of order and barred shut) but the fucking guys'—we're surrounded by urinals with dried piss and grimy tiled floors littered with sopping toilet paper.

Which wouldn't be that bad, but Rose recoiled from the fucking walls like she'd catch an incurable disease. I don't know how Connor did it, but he calmed her enough so she'd stick her face in the sink. Eyes forced shut, shielding her reality.

I have her fucking hair bunched in my hands, keeping the strands from touching the "repulsive" basin. Connor stands on her other side and washes a portion of her hair at a time, focusing on the strands that I'm not holding. He carefully attempts to rid as much of the flour as he can.

Never did I think I'd be washing any part of Rose with her husband. Never. Not even if you fucking told me I would.

"I'm going to kill him," Rose repeats for the fourth time, her voice shaking with ire and distress. Near the brink of tears.

My muscles burn at a standstill. "Join the fucking line."

"The police are looking for him, so why don't you all holster your revenge plans for at least another hour," Connor says, his features tenser than I've seen in a long fucking time. He catches me staring and then mouths, *Concentrate.*

I return my attention to Rose's glossy brown hair. If I drop a single fucking strand and she notices, she might fall into some kind of panic. She's only gripping the sink counter because I "sacrificed" my jacket and splayed it out. Her hands meet the fabric, not anything else.

In the background, Janie is hiccupping but has stopped crying, Daisy bouncing the baby on her hip. Moffy is crying worse than Janie after our bodyguards swarmed him outside the bathroom. Lily and Lo are doing their best to settle him down, though my brother glares murderously at every fucking object.

He looks about how I fucking feel.

Connor warms the water some.

I skim Rose's attire, flour all over her formfitting woolen skirt, gray tights or leggings—whatever the fuck they are. She removed her coat, so at least her black turtleneck is somewhat fucking clean.

Connor might be able to keep her from looking down until we return to our private cabin, about thirty minutes from the ski resort. Rose was most concerned about her hair, saying over and over *I want it out. I want it out.*

"Take a breath, Rose," Connor orders, his hands pausing on the back of her head.

She inhales, her collar even stricter.

His hands move faster, passing over mine to wash out the flour that sticks and adheres with the added water.

"Is it gone?" she asks in an abnormally high voice. "Connor?"

"Almost, darling."

Rose then shifts her hands and starts scrubbing at her face like you'd scour a pan. *Fucking*—both Connor and I pull her back from the sink almost instantly.

She pushes us off and raises her hands. "Stop." The word causes both of us to freeze. Eyes tight shut, she takes a deep, strained breath. Her wet hair soaks into her turtleneck. The air is still, and we're all fucking wondering how she's going to react when she focuses back on this reality.

Please don't be fucking panicked. Watching Rose crumble is like having the world physically assaulted by meteors and comets, impaling unpredictably, infrequently and fucking violently. It usually comes at the hands of some other force—and that's what fucking tears at me the most.

She opens her eyes.

Fucking Christ.

Her yellow-green gaze fixes in a glare.

On me.

"We have to go get them." Her words rumble with anger. "We can't just stand here and do *nothing*."

She's seeking my affirmation. Because I'm aggressive. Because if I glance at the mirror, I'd meet the severest scowl, the darkest fucking gaze—and muscles that cut like I'm ready. *I'm fucking ready to end this.*

Connor doesn't wear bloodlust, even when he collides with the same brutal sentiments as us. And Rose would only turn to Lo as a last choice.

I rake a hand through my own hair. "As soon as they give me a name, Rose"—I point behind me—"I'm out that fucking door." The police are questioning guests at the resort right this second.

"We have to go *now*," Rose counters. "I'll recognize his eyes." Veins wind along her neck as she inhales deeply.

"I'm in," Lo announces. He squats by Moffy but slowly rises to a stance. "He deserves worse than hell."

I can't fucking disagree.

Though I know what this means. When Rose, Lo, and I band together, our emotions are at the most volatile level. It never indicates the *right* mode of action. Just the most fucking passionate one.

"He deserves to be roasted over fire and burned to an unrecognizable crisp," Rose says in one of her more vivid exaggerations. Her hands shake by her sides.

As I scrutinize her, I realize that her anger has superseded mine, and I'm fucking worried because she's sharing company with my brother and me. When it comes to the three of us, I really and truly think we're better at provoking one another.

Fuck.

Connor approaches his wife, a breath away from her. I'm fucking surprised she lets him.

His six-foot-four height bears down on hers, but for some fucking reason, Rose unwinds by his closeness, her breathing more natural and shoulders less strict.

He holds her face gently, his thumb stroking her cheek. "Assieds-toi." *Sit down.*

She whispers back in French, "Nous n'avons pas le temps de nous asseoir." *We don't have time to sit.* A fire simmers beneath her words.

Connor arches a brow but his eyes uncharacteristically narrow. "Tu veux aller poursuivre un fou?" *You want to chase a madman?*

She tilts her chin up. "Peut-être, oui." *Maybe, yes.*

Unflinchingly, he says, "Alors tu es folle aussi." *Then you're mad too.*

I breathe hot fucking breaths through my nose and shake my head. "Estamos todos locos," I tell Connor in Spanish. *We're all mad.*

Surprise passes his features for a millisecond. I don't speak to him in foreign languages often, but it just felt fucking right.

He replies in the language he prefers, "Peut-être que nous le sommes, mon ami."

Maybe we are, my friend.

"It's decided." Rose switches to English and charges for the door. Connor extends his arm and grabs onto her shoulder before she can even pass him.

"There are hundreds of people at this resort." Connor breaks into our plans and sinks a heavy weight on us. "They all recognize your face. What are you planning on doing that doesn't involve everyone swarming you for autographs and selfies? Give me a better plan, and I'll let you go."

Fire brims in her glare and she noticeably shakes. "I'm not writing up a business proposal for you, Richard. I'm defending myself and our unborn child."

Unborn child.

Just like that, the meteor explodes against the fucking world.

She must catch her slip because she quickly rants, "I'm protecting Jane. And Moffy. The skier could have attacked them too. Our only chance to file a lawsuit is to catch this *monster*. We couldn't do that for the first flour-bomber, but we have an opportunity now and I'm not going to fucking waste it." She raises her chin higher like she has declared fucking law. Even though she's basically said all this before.

The air strains in the dirtied bathroom.

I take a quick glance at Daisy: brows knotted in confusion and mouth slightly ajar.

I think we're all fucking there.

Lo's cheekbones sharpen like blades, and he's the first to say it. "Your *unborn child*. Is that a new way of referring to metaphorical demonic offspring in your future or are you—"

"I'm pregnant," Rose states.

Lo lets out a large breath. "Damn."

We're usually all on the same fucking page. The six of us. Ready to be happy for one another, ready to pick each other up. To cry together. To fucking laugh together. Right now, in the silence of this bathroom, we're all just confused on what to feel.

It's too fucking complicated. All of it.

Without hesitation, I peel away from Rose and reach Daisy's side. Janie, still propped up on Daisy's hip, sleeps with tiny snores, tears all dried.

Daisy sports this weak smile. Somewhere between happiness and pain. I just want to fucking hold her—to tell her that nothing has changed. Our lives are still in step with theirs. We're not being shoved backwards.

We're not being catapulted behind our friends.

Do you really believe this, Ryke?

I fucking have to.

Daisy rests her head against my shoulder, leaning into me. I wrap an arm tightly around her waist.

"Is this a good thing?" Lily finally asks.

The facts: Connor and Rose planned to postpone trying for a baby until Daisy got pregnant. So that Rose could be her surrogate if her sister had trouble on her own. Now we can pretty much cross surrogacy off as an option for the next year or even two years.

Another fact: Connor and Rose should be happy. We should *all* be fucking happy. Adding another kid to their family—this has been one of their dreams and goals. No one should diminish their joy.

We have though, and we have to fucking rectify this.

Daisy takes the reins. "It's a good thing," she says the words from the bottom of her soul. "It is."

Rose fights tears in her bloodshot eyes.

"No, don't cry," Daisy says quickly, stepping away from me. She passes Janie off to Connor and then confronts her older sister. Face-to-face, Daisy a little taller without Rose's added heels. "I'm happy for you, Rose. Please, you have to believe that I am. I really am."

Now tears brim Daisy's eyes. *Fucking hell.*

"I'm not crying. I *don't* cry," Rose snaps, staring at the ceiling and trying to thwart all her tears by sheer will.

"I'm going to hug you now."

"Don't you dare." Rose pats her fingers beneath her eyes. "Go hug Lily."

Daisy presses her arms by her own sides. "I'm *really* happy for you, and I know it may not seem like I am but I can't think of anything happier for you than a growing, *fierce* family. It's great news, Rose. So you can't be sad for me." She reaches out and brushes away Rose's last tear.

"I'm the older sister," Rose says. "I'm here for *you.*" She didn't wait for Daisy, and I don't think Rose will ever forgive herself for that. It's not her fault.

We don't expect people to stop their lives while ours take a fucking detour.

"Yes, you are." Daisy smiles with a glassy gaze. "You *always* are. I wouldn't be able to handle any of this without you." Her voice cracks.

It impales me, but I have to stay where I am.

Rose willingly and abruptly hugs Daisy. In the same instance, Daisy reciprocates tenfold.

Lo uncrosses his arms. "Looks like Connor still has superhuman sperm."

"Actually," Connor says, "it wasn't an accident."

I don't know what I'm fucking feeling right now.

Connor trains his gaze on me. "We weren't being as careful as we could have been." He could have let me believe the entire ordeal was a fucking mistake. The honesty is nice, but I don't thank him for it.

Air strains again, an uncomfortable fucking tension.

Connor continues, relieving some of it, "Daisy designed this entire scenario of Rose and her being pregnant at the same time under false pretenses." He rotates to Daisy. "You want Rose pregnant too because you're scared of hurting her if something catastrophic happens—if you die. You don't want to cause your sister pain, so maybe this way, her own child will be a distraction if something were to happen to you."

He doesn't ask if he's right. He already knows he is.

Before Daisy has a chance to explain, Rose reaches for her sister's hands and squeezes. "I want you to know that I could *never* be happy if you died, not even if I had a baby to look forward to. I could never be okay with losing you." She blinks back tears.

I tune out every time someone says *death* and *Daisy* in the same sentence. It's white noise.

I don't live in fear of the next step. I don't prep for the *what ifs* and rewire the fucked-up variables like Connor.

I drop to my knees in front of the only girl I've ever loved. And I live in the fucking moment with her.

However short, however long we have.

I nod to Connor. "So you just ignored the fucking plan because you didn't like the reasoning behind it?"

"Yes." His word is final.

"It just seemed happy," Daisy says, eyes clouding with tears again. I let out a heavy breath. *Dais…*

Connor doesn't hesitate. "A world where there are five of us, instead of six, will never be a happy one."

Rose rests her hands on Daisy's shoulders, facing her completely. It's hard to believe minutes ago Rose was facedown in a sink, distraught.

In this moment, she stands poised and fucking assertive. So unshaken that I forget something even rattled her to begin with. "I'm always leaving surrogacy as an option for you, Daisy. *Always.*" She pauses. "Maybe this shift in timeline will be for the best." I think she's trying to convince herself of this too. "By the time you learn if you can have a baby or not on your own, I could already have had mine, and I'll be ready to be your surrogate."

In that future, Daisy is infertile. Maybe it'll come to that, but we're not ready to give up this way yet.

Daisy nods. "I just want everyone to be happy."

I cut in, "We all want *you* to be fucking happy, sweetheart." That's what this boils down to. She has to put herself first this time.

She smiles at me, tears falling down her cheeks. "I am and I will be."
I head over to her.

"What'd we learn?" Connor asks, about to get on my fucking nerves.

Lily says strongly, "That none of us want Ryke and Daisy to die." My pulse slows, and I nod to myself. *I know.*

"That flour cannot defeat me." Rose lifts Janie from Connor and into her arms.

I raise my brows at Dais, and she begins to smile, not knowing what I'm about to do.

Lo adds, "That the Cobalts will never announce a goddamn pregnancy the way ordinary people do."

Connor grins, and I practically hear him fucking say: *ordinary is boring, darling.*

I swiftly pick Daisy up by the waist and toss her over my shoulder. She laughs, her hands descending to the waistband of my pants.

"That Ryke has the best ass," she says before squeezing my fucking ass.

The corners of my mouth curve, and right as I turn towards the bathroom door, a police officer slips inside. For a second, I'd actually forgotten about the skier.

The uniformed man sullenly shakes his head at us.

What I've learned: *justice never comes easy.*

< 24 >

Daisy Calloway

Our holiday trip may not be completely ruined by the flour-bomber, but with Christmas Eve tomorrow, the mood has shifted. We're all handling the second assault differently.

Connor and Rose have called the police repeatedly, mentally active in trying to hunt down the masked skier. Lily has hoarded herself in the rented cabin, reclaiming her long-forgotten hermit status. Lo has joined her, emotionally spent.

This was reason enough for Ryke and me to take a *physical* part in catching this guy.

So it begins.

Ryke and Daisy's Grand & Daring Stakeout #1

"Send whatever you can over text. Yeah…" Ryke talks to our private investigator that we recently hired (unbeknownst to everyone else), and he's been feeding us info about the attacker.

I skim the shelves of a rundown convenience store, empty except for the cashier and us. I gather candy bars, Honey Buns, beef jerky, and other stakeout provisions. I figure we might be passing a lot of time in our rented mini-van (not Ryke's car of choice)—so I grab a stack of magazines, one of each on the rickety display.

With his cell to his ear, Ryke motions to me and then points at the drinks. "Right," he says to the PI, dipping his head in concentration. His blue baseball cap conceals most of his face.

My disguise: a platinum blonde wig cut in a bob.

I run my fingers through the coarse strands, adrenaline already pumping with our new schemes. Ryke and Daisy on the road. Ryke and Daisy trap a dreadful, no-good guy. Ryke and Daisy save the day!

I like how silly it sounds. Like the tagline in a children's adventure story.

My sisters think we're spending the day on the slopes, so no one should question our whereabouts. Since we don't trust Price yet, we told him that we'd be in bed all day. The bodyguards don't stay inside our cabin, so he wouldn't know otherwise.

In the store, I make my way to the cooler and balance a couple waters on the magazines. As I check out, Ryke says goodbye to the private investigator and pockets his phone.

"And?" I wonder.

"I'll tell you in the car." He looks hopeful.

The cashier rings us up, and Ryke fishes out a few bills, paying for our stuff. About a minute later, we settle into the silver mini-van, and Ryke drives towards…somewhere.

"Here's the fucking deal." Ryke blindly digs in one of the plastic bags on the middle console, ending up with a caramel and chocolate candy bar. "He has a lead on one guy, who was part of this disbanded social media forum…" Ryke tears open the candy bar, using his knee to keep the wheel straight for a second.

I frown. "What kind of forum?"

"He said the name changes. It used to be *Callo-Haters* but now it could be as plain as fucking *Doorknob*." He takes a large bite of the candy bar, and I notice his right hand white-knuckling the steering wheel. I think the food helps distract his anger.

I lean back and extend my legs on the dashboard.

"He doesn't fucking think the first flour-bombing on Lo is connected to this one," Ryke explains. "The first one was an actual upset fan, but this one seemed like a copycat. On the group, people fucking talked about how it'd be *funny* to replicate what happened. So they're exchanging info on where we are. Asking each other who's in the area—all of that." His eyes are dead set on the snowy road.

I set my hand on his leg. "We should know who did it then. Can't the police just track down whoever owns the accounts?"

"It's not that fucking easy. He said the IP addresses change constantly, and they keep switching where they go on the internet. A lot of them are…anonymous. It's a platform *meant* to conceal identities."

My spirit sinks. It sounds like catching a shadow.

Then I remember this all started with *hope*. "We have a lead on one guy though?"

"Yeah." Ryke nods a couple times. "He connected a couple fucking things to this guy named James B. Allen." That's when he pulls the mini-van into a rundown *Lazy Peak Motel* and he parks beside an old sedan.

I straighten up, alert on the single row of chipped green motel doors.

He digs in his pocket and flashes me his phone. The picture is of James B. Allen. Mid-twenties, sandy blonde hair and chin stubble, and these metallic blue eyes. I study that gaze and try to place it to the one in my head.

It could be a match.

"So now we wait?" I ask him.

He nods. "We wait."

Two hours later.

I flick the lock button on the door, the cramped car losing its entertainment value. Candy wrappers over the dashboard, legs crossed beneath my butt, and eyes glazed at the chipped green doors—only two guests have exited.

A guy with a 12-pack of Coors Light. A mountain man with a nine-inch beard.

"Daisy, stop," Ryke growls, annoyed at the *click click click* of the lock button.

He annoyed me a half hour ago by constantly messing with my hair. Normally I love it, but confined in a mini-van—it turned from *oh Ryke* to *ugh Ryke*.

"Here." Ryke tosses my stack of magazines onto my lap. "Read something out loud. I'll keep a lookout." He eagle-eyes the motel.

Without a doubt, he's given me the more enjoyable task of the two. I thumb through the five magazines. All tabloids. All headlined with one of us for the holidays. Maybe because they like doing variations of the story, stretching it in false ways.

In my most dramatic voice, I announce our options, "We have *Raisy Turmoil: Why Daisy Calloway will break Ryke's heart over Christmas!*" I flash him the cover. A blown-up photo outside of Lucky's Diner: me staring off in the distance with his arm over my shoulder.

"Fuck no." He tosses half his jerky at the magazine.

I smile, glad he doesn't believe in this scenario. Even if the world thinks my tastes in men change like my hair color.

Throwing aside that tabloid, I read the next one, "*Ice Cold Bedroom! All the reasons why Connor Cobalt can't satisfy Rose Calloway.*" I'd rather not embark on that super false story.

"Next," Ryke agrees.

"*Holiday Affair: Lily Calloway has her eyes on other things.*" I let out a shocked sound. "They're so rude." I turn the magazine to him. In the photo, Lily has Moffy in her arms outside a Lake Tahoe café. Beside her is a specials sign with: *Warm Chili Hot Dog.* She's *barely* even glancing at it.

Ryke scowls darkly. "Fuck 'em."

I chuck that tabloid. "This one isn't as bad..." I clear my throat and recite, "*Best Father! Loren Hale...*" I trail off, skimming the rest of the words. "Okay it gets bad. *Loren Hale wants another kid, but Lily Calloway says no.*"

Ryke shakes his head a couple times, still eyeing the motels. "That's definitely not fucking true."

"Have you talked to Lo about it?" I dust that magazine off my lap.

"Yeah. He said they're in agreement that they'll know when they know."

I tilt my head. *They'll know when they know.* That vague, unclear response actually sounds like something Lo or Lily would say. "Last one," I tell him. "Drumroll, please."

He throws a piece of gum at my face.

Ugh Ryke. I throw it back more aggressively, and it hits him in the forehead, his glower forming onto me.

I reach over and drum the steering wheel. Which actually annoys him enough to steal my last magazine from me and read, "*Three's Company...*" His voice dies out almost immediately. His face falls, and he stuffs the tabloid between his back and the seat.

"What is it?" I ease away.

"Don't fucking worry about it." His jaw tenses, but he's meeting my eyes, not the motel. "Do you want to stretch outside? We can walk around—"

Quickly, I reach behind him and retrieve the magazine.

"Daisy."

I lean against my car door and kick him back with my feet, but he grabs onto my legs and just watches me, knowing I'm going to find out one way or the other.

I silently read: THREE'S COMPANY! HOW LILY CALLOWAY JINGLES RYKE & LOREN'S BELLS THIS CHRISTMAS. The picture: Ryke's hands on her shoulders, steering her away from an icy patch at the resort's parking lot. Lo walks on her other side, their fingers laced together.

"Hey." Ryke extends his arm on the back of my seat, shifting closer to me. "No one believes this fucking garbage, and if they do—fuck them."

"I know." My voice is smaller than I hoped. The three-way rumors between Ryke, Lo, and Lily are nothing new. They've been here even before I entered the picture, but I guess I thought eventually *our* love would be strong enough to dissuade them.

It's disappointing to find out that people would rather pair him with my sister than with me. As soon as I flip through the pages, Ryke tears the magazine out of my grasp.

"Why are you upset?" he asks, his concern boring through me. He wants to fix it.

"How would you feel if *all* of these magazines said I was fucking Connor Cobalt?" I sit up straighter, my chest an inch from his. "That I love him. I *prefer* him. I couldn't care less about you." Every word stabs my core, and that pain translates in his darkened gaze.

"Don't fucking say that."

"It's the equivalent of what I see *all* the time."

He says slowly, "It's not real, Daisy."

"It doesn't mean it doesn't hurt." I watch his breathing deepen, more understanding, but he can't erase what people feel or think. Ryke has never cared about his own reputation or how other people perceive him. This is out of his wheelhouse.

"So what am I supposed to fucking do?" he asks, frustration beneath his rough voice. "There's *nothing* that can change this."

"Abbracciami," I say the Italian word he taught me not long ago. *Hold me.*

His hard eyes nearly ease. He pulls me onto his lap, my legs tucked to my chest. As he wraps his arms around my frame, I feel more like *his.* Like we belong together just this way.

I rest my chin on his shoulder, looking up at him. "Dammi un bacio." *Give me a kiss.*

His lips almost quirk upwards, but he kisses me on the nose, then the corner of my mouth. I begin to smile as he nuzzles my cheek, but it fades, my gaze drifting to the windshield. Outside.

A motel door swings open. "Ryke." I pat his arm until he follows my line of view.

Sandy blonde hair emerges, ski jacket and a pair of skis beneath his arm. Like he's en route to the resort to hit the slopes. As I watch, I realize that we never really discussed a plan *after* spotting him.

Ryke picks me off his lap, setting me on the passenger seat. Determination and urgency in his brow.

"What are you going to do?" I ask as he unlocks the car.

"Talk to him." He has his cellphone in hand. Maybe he'll record the conversation?

I'm about to go with, but for some reason, my bottom stays glued to the seat. My instincts are saying: *do not move, Daisy Petunia Calloway. Sit right there.*

Do not move.

Do not move? It's a strange impulse, but I listen to my gut, especially as Ryke shuts his door. He doesn't look over his shoulder like he expects me to join.

Is it strange that I'm worried about him? We have no idea if James will recognize Ryke. I just watch from my seat, stiff and hot. I go to turn on the air vents, especially as Ryke sprints up to the guy, waving him down.

James stops in place, confused.

The car is still off, and Ryke has the keys. I unbutton my coat. It may be in the low thirties outside, but my nervous heat won't leave me until he returns.

Ryke talks but I can't hear him. James replies. Head shakes. Nods. Hand gesticulations. I can't read the mood.

I wait for the worst.

Another three minutes, two more nods, and Ryke departs from James with a disgruntled look. He shakes his head at me like *nothing*.

The door opens. "Fuck that," Ryke says, starting up the car and slamming the door shut.

"What happened?"

"He said that he can't even remember his Facebook password—that he's never been on any forums like I described."

"Do you think he was lying?"

"I acted like I was a part of the fucking forums, so no. He seemed genuinely fucking confused." As Ryke peels out of the parking lot, I realize we're back to the drawing board. Despite coming up short, I liked the alone time and feeling mischievous *with* Ryke.

I turn to him. "Is this the last stakeout?"

His eyes flit over me, a smile behind them. "When have we ever done any-fucking-thing just once?"

‹ 25 ›

Ryke Meadows

Christmas morning. Fireplace lit, snow fucking falling. In the log cabin at Lake Tahoe, everyone is curled in fleece blankets, spread among leather furniture. We all take turns opening presents beneath an eight-foot, fully decorated fir tree.

Problem is, we start opening *couple* gifts, and Daisy and I keep pawning off our fucking turns on other people. Until no one else is left but us.

We share an oversized recliner, all four Calloway sisters dressed in red holiday onesies. Lily's idea, which Rose loved because of the sisterly togetherness aspect, and Daisy topped her outfit with an elf hat.

The pom-bells jingle as she gestures to Lily. "Doesn't Moffy have another present?"

On the floor, Lily squints at Daisy like she sees behind her façade. "It's the *couple* round. You need to share your present with Ryke and he needs to share his present with you—wait…" Her eyes widen in horror. "Did you two forget to gift each other something?" She searches beneath the tree beside her.

"Yeah we forgot," Daisy nods. "Sorry."

Lo is also on the ground, his son playing with a new Black Widow action figure, and then his gaze flits to us. "Why the secrecy? It's not like we don't know Ryke gives shit presents to you."

I outstretch my arms. "What the fuck, man?"

Lo cocks his head at me. "You gave her a *string* for her nineteenth birthday." For fuck's sake. Not Lo too.

I glower, but before I defend myself, Daisy says, "Hey, I like my bracelet." She touches the hemp rope around her wrist, which she wears almost every fucking day.

"I found it!" Lily waves an envelope in the air. *Fuck*. I rub my lips while she stands and hands the thing to me. *To my wolf*.

Daisy already whispered in my ear that I shouldn't open it in front of my brother.

"Where's her present?" Poppy asks, sipping eggnog by the fireplace with her husband and eight-year-old daughter.

On the couch, Rose is busy fixing Janie's hair with a new bow, and Connor shows her a new logic puzzle.

"Yeah, where's my sister's present," Lily says with her hands on her hips. She acts like she's investigating my motives behind my horrible gift giving.

Okay, I fucking admit, I'm not the best, but I try. It's not like I don't care. "Her fucking gift is outside, and *no*, you all can't fucking see it." I actually planned this well in advance.

Lo gives me a look. "Sex isn't a Christmas gift, bro."

Lily ponders this. "Does that mean...we're not...?"

Lo seizes her waist and pulls her onto his lap. "Of course we are, but I wouldn't just give you something that I can give you any other goddamn day."

I toss my fucking hands in the air. "It's not *sex*."

"Then what?"

"You want me to ruin her fucking surprise?" I ask my brother because he'd *never* ruin a Christmas present for Lily.

This shuts him up, and he nods to the envelope in my pinched fingers. "Open it."

Daisy shrugs at me like *maybe he'll be okay with it.*

I feel like I have no choice, so I rip open the envelope and find a plane ticket...to Norway. Without pause, I start fucking smiling. I'm about to tell her *thanks*, but Lo cranes his neck to better see what's in my hand.

"Where are you going?"

It's suspicious because it's just one fucking ticket. It's not like Daisy gifted me a couple's vacation. "Norway," I say and just let it all out. "Sully is ice climbing in March, and I talked about going but hadn't made plans yet..."

All the holiday cheer has deserted my little brother. He shoots the nastiest fucking looks at Daisy.

"Hey," I nearly shout at him. "I probably would've gone, even if she didn't buy me a fucking ticket." I love that she did—her encouragement means the fucking world to me. What I hate most is that my decision to do what I love has begun hurting the people I care about.

I can't quit. No matter how many times I tell my brother, he still doesn't get it. I don't know if he ever will.

Lo reroutes his spite and hurt onto me, but he tries to bite his tongue and trounce it. In the end, he spits out, "Go fly to your death, Jonathan Ryke Meadows—see if I care."

I rock back like he slugged me. Caught off guard by his use of my birth name. He almost *never* says it. Maybe three times in all the years I've known him. I have to remind myself that he's just upset.

Everyone is quiet except for the mumbling of Janie and Moffy.

What's worse: I've kept something from Lo for maybe...two weeks now. I didn't want to tell him today, not like this, but if he finds out I kept silent here—it'll be worse. When we fought in Utah, a huge source of his pain was about me keeping him in the dark.

I don't want to torment my brother, but I'm stuck.

Daisy stands. "Does anyone want hot chocolate or maybe cookies?" She knows what I did two weeks ago, and she's trying to lighten the fucking mood before it worsens.

"Cookies!" Moffy perks up.

Daisy mock gasps. "You like cookies too?!"

He nods vigorously.

Lily rises and lifts Moffy on her hip, following Daisy to the nearby kitchen. The air is still tense, and Lo hangs his head, breathing heavily, glaring at crumpled wrapping paper.

Before regret assaults him, I say, "I'm not…" I stop short. *Just fucking say it.*

All eyes pin to me, and I sense Daisy and Lily in the kitchen archway, lingering to watch.

I actually meet Daisy's gaze and read the words behind it, *are you sure you want to do this now?*

I nod at her. I'm fucking sure.

"You're not what?" Lo asks me.

"I'm not Jonathan Ryke Meadows anymore," I announce to the fucking room.

Rose takes an audible inhale of surprise.

"Come again?" Lo's jaw is a fucking razorblade. "Because I thought you said that you're not Jonathan Meadows anymore."

"I legally changed my name, Lo."

Lo looks homicidal and pained all at once. "Tell me you're a Hale." He knows that's not it.

"I'm just Ryke Meadows now." It took me about *ten years* to settle with this decision. I've *always* wanted to change my first name, to disassociate from my dad. To become more of the person I am and less like the person he wanted me to be. Like all things attached to Jonathan, he never made it fucking easy for me.

My inheritance and my trust fund are tied to a simple stipulation.

I couldn't legally change my first name without losing both. My father knew he couldn't control me by last my name, so he made sure he could by my first. In the end, that was all that really connected us.

Now it's gone.

"You stupid, jackass." Lo pushes up from the rug, tears burning his eyes. I rise with him—the room narrowing in my mind to just us two. He points at me. "You threw away your *entire* trust fund for pride!" He's worried about me. All of my money now comes from rock climbing.

"I threw away my entire fucking trust fund to be *free* of him. If you think I can build anything *real* with our dad when he has that kind of power over me, you're out of your fucking mind!" It ate at me after Jonathan went to the press and backstabbed Connor. After I gave him half my fucking liver and learned he can still manipulate people to acquire what he wants.

Now it's not eating at me.

It's that fucking simple in my head.

Lo pinches his eyes and then shouts at me, "Don't you fucking get it?!"

My ribs are on fire. "Lo…"

He steps closer to me, feet crushing wrapping paper and boxes. He lowers his voice. "You almost died last time you climbed."

"I didn't." I was close to falling, but I *didn't*. It's already in the fucking past.

"Do you hear yourself?" Lo laughs, fighting tears that redden his eyes. "Do you, Ryke? Because you're just fooling yourself, man. You're *fooling* yourself into thinking you're never gonna die."

"I'm fucking aware of the risks—"

"No you aren't," Lo sneers. Two more steps my way. Only a few feet apart. Heat radiates between us, and I don't know how to fucking give him what he wants. I know I can't.

"No I'm not?" I repeat, a growl in my fucking throat. "I *understand* every fucking thing you're telling me." I extend my arms. "I'm human. I can die every time I climb. There is always that chance. I know. I know. I *fucking* know."

"Then stop climbing!" Lo yells.

"I can't!" I scream back.

His face shatters. "Not even for her?" He points at Daisy in the kitchen archway.

I don't want her roped into this, so I walk past my brother, a few feet, and then rotate so my back is to Daisy and the Christmas tree. "Don't turn this around on her."

Lo spins to face me, and he lets out another short, pained laugh. "You don't think this is about her? It's not about the baby you're trying to have either? Goddammit, Ryke, if you die, you leave Daisy *alone*. You leave that kid without a father. You, of all people, should know what it's like to grow up without a dad." He pauses as these facts that I've known drive into me. "Unless that's your hope; you know, let your kid experience exactly what you did—"

"*Fuck you,*" I growl.

He shoves me. "No, fuck you!" I stumble back not even a foot. "For thinking none of us care about you. For thinking we won't be affected if you're gone. Fuck *you*, man." He pushes me again, so hard that I fucking fall against the Christmas tree.

I bring my brother down with me, fisting his shirt.

The tree careens against the walls, glass ornaments breaking and lights snapping. Half the needles go dark with unlit strands. Maria, Poppy's daughter, shrieks, and bodies fucking move *out* of the living room.

Tree limbs jut into my ribs, and ornaments crack beneath me. *Fucking fuck.* I curse in my head, maybe aloud.

Lo and I violently roll off the fucking tree and onto the rug. Smashing presents. I try to right the tree before even standing, but Lo says something about *leaving it alone* or *picking it up later*. We're not finished with this exchange, both of us too emotionally exhausted to rise to our feet.

"Fuck you," he says to me. One more time. Like I'm the cause of all his pain.

It rips into me, and we breathe heavily. Staring at each other.

A hot tear rolls down his cheek.

Something wet trails down mine. I push Lo all the time. Very few people push me. And maybe I fucking needed this—but I'm still conflicted. No one but Daisy understands what climbing truly means to me. She's never pressured me to quit. She doesn't want me to.

Quietly, I tell Lo, "You're asking me to cut myself off at the knees." I've always lived to ascend. As a kid, it was the only thing that would grind at my bones, that called me to wake up, that pushed me to go.

I have never gone a year without climbing since.

It motivated me. It challenged me. It's a part of me. The way I go at life, I go at it like a climber would—self-disciplined, aggressive, tenacious, *persistent*.

It is a part of me.

But I sit here, and I know. It's not my greatest love. It's not why I woke up today. It's not what will grind at my bones tomorrow. It won't push me to go in a year.

When I turn my head and meet Daisy's glassy eyes in the archway, she gives me a weak, tearful smile in support. She means more to me— our life *together* means more to me. I shouldn't have to quit the thing I love to prove this.

Selfish, I hear my brother call me.

This is the most selfish I've ever fucking been, and it's tearing at me because I don't think I can live without climbing. I don't know how.

Most of the girls are crying now, some in the kitchen, visible from here.

"Mommy?" Moffy whispers up to Lily, the boy hanging onto her leg. She wipes her cheeks with the sleeve of her onesie.

Lo pulls a smashed wrapped box out from beneath his ass and chucks it. After a long moment, his head swings back to me. "When you have a fucking kid, you make a lot of sacrifices, Ryke."

"Have you ever loved *something*? Not someone, but some*thing*."

"Whiskey."

I glower. "Drinking's not a hobby." Though for Lo, maybe it was.

"It's a *thing*," he snaps.

I shake my head at him. "When you love something *so much*, it feels impossible to let it go. It's like a kid. Can you understand that?" *It's a part of me, Lo. Please fucking hear me.*

His throat bobs. After a long pause, he says, "No."

I don't want to look at this like losses and gains and weigh my love for everyone against a sport. Connor Cobalt can fucking do that.

I have always stared my life straight in the fucking eye and held the line. I'm not terrified of it being cut short. I'd rather live fully and briefly than to live long and empty.

I'm just not fucking sure I can be fulfilled without rock climbing.

"So…?" Lo asks.

"I'll think about everything." Climbing is safer in other areas: sport climbing, bouldering. They've never been my fucking favorites, but they're alternatives.

Lo lets out a wounded, exhausted breath. "You're killing me here." The way he says it, it's like I've been slamming him into Christmas trees for years. He's that scared he'll lose me.

I fucking rub my eyes. "I'm sorry." I wish I could just give it up.

This would be so much fucking easier if I could just say goodbye.

< **26** >

Daisy Calloway

The emotional brotherly breakdown from two hours ago has been bulldozed by my Christmas present that is unequivocally, extraordinarily better than chocolate.

I said that to Ryke, and he rolled his eyes like I was teasing him.

I wasn't.

Currently, I sit on an iconic red sleigh in the middle of the snowy, picturesque woods. A majestic chestnut horse leads the way. I've never been on a sleigh ride. Ryke knew that. And so he conjured this postcard-worthy scene out of nowhere.

No bodyguards. No paparazzi. For now at least.

We're both seated up front on the slender bench, reins in his hands as he guides the horse. The back of the sleigh is filled with dark green blankets, and gold bells jingle as the horse trots along an unmarked path, weaving between sky-scraping fir trees.

Ryke even let me steer, but I passed the reins back after I almost overturned the entire sleigh. It's not like he rented this for us. He said,

I know a fucking guy who owns a farm and gives out sleigh rides. He's big into rock climbing. I understood instantly.

The rock climbing community is small, and everywhere we travel, I've seen Ryke call people to meet up and climb. I wasn't surprised that he knows someone here or that this person trusts him with valuable things.

Once upon a time, I'm sure this man trusted Ryke with his life. As most rock climbers eventually do.

Nestled close to Ryke in my winter clothes, his arm warming my shoulders, I watch him for a second and ask, "How did you know?"

His eyes flit from me to the powdery road, flat at the bottom of the mountain. "Know what?"

"That I'm *the one*. That this is the 'can't-eat, can't-sleep, reach-for-the-stars, over-the-fence, World Series kind of stuff,'" I quote *It Takes Two* with as much of its original gusto.

He rolls his eyes, but I'm *positive* he understands what I'm talking about this time. Because he watched the movie with me.

"Do you want to know when I knew?" I ask him, swiveling more toward his body, less towards the road, and his arm falls off my shoulder.

The sleigh slows, and when I scan my surroundings, I realize we're in a snowy field, a red barn far off in the distance. The rest is just white nothingness, a few skinny trees, and us.

He removes his beanie and fixes his flattened hair. Now it sticks up every which way. *Very, very handsome.* "How about we make a fucking pact?"

I straighten up, really curious. "Okay."

He raises his brows. "I haven't even said what it is. You may fucking hate it."

"I'm willing to take the gamble," I say with a growing smile. "The danger!"

He tosses his beanie at my face before standing up and hopping onto the ground. Then he begins unhooking the horse from the sleigh as he says, "I'll tell you when I first knew this was the 'can't-eat, can't-sleep, reach-for-the-stars, over-the-fence, World Series kind of stuff' the day we get fucking married. And you can tell me then too."

"Like our vows?" I'm really surprised he'd be willing to share this in front of everyone.

He nods and then ties the horse to one of the skinnier trees.

"Are you just trying to stall to figure out an answer?" It's an honest question. "It's okay if you are—"

"I fucking know," he cuts me off, climbing back onto the sleigh. "I've fucking known for a long time." He removes his gloves and then clasps my hand, pulling me to my feet. I feel short for some reason. Maybe it's because he's so *sure* of our relationship. Of where we stand. His confidence draws me closer.

Then he guides me to the back of the sleigh.

"Do I get a hint?" I'm even more curious. How will I survive until our wedding day without knowing *when* he knew I was the one?

"You already made the fucking pact."

I rock on the balls of my feet until he brings me down to the furry blankets. We sit side-by-side, and I scoot even closer. Our knees knock together, his masculinity cloaking me. Larger, taller, rougher.

"I have this theory," I begin, "that pacts aren't truly bound until…" I trail off with a lit-up smile.

He cups my cheek, eyeing my pink lips. "…until?" he pushes.

"Until we fuck. Have sex. Make love. All at once."

His jaw clenches in arousal, letting me see that much. Then Ryke unzips my jacket. Twenty-seven, experienced and rugged among the wilderness—I drink in his build while he drinks in mine. He handles me protectively like he wants me close in case anything happens.

"Are we going to test my theory?" I whisper as he pulls off my jacket and I unzip his, both of us beginning to shed each other's clothes.

He raises his brows at me again, the mystery alive.

Then he tugs my ankle, and my back thumps on the soft mound of blankets. My giddy smile stretches. *What an adventure.* I breathe deeply, and he hovers above me.

"I'm going to fuck you," he says, yanking off my pants. The cold nips my skin. "I'm going to have sex with you." He kisses me strongly while lifting my sweater off my head. "I'm going to make love to you." His eyes bore into mine. "All at fucking once." His gaze dances over my features. "Not because of a fucking theory. I can't think of a place I'd rather be *right now* than with you. Truth is, I can't think of a place I'd rather be in fifty fucking years than next to you."

My breath shallows, and I reach up, my hand grazing his rough, hard jawline. "You think we'll live till we're seventy?" I've never pictured us that far ahead. Besides the baby planning, we've always been such a "present moment" couple that seeing beyond a few years is foreign to me.

"Yeah," he says with a reverent nod. "We'll be fucking old with blown-out knees and aches and pains."

I sit up on my elbows, my lips so close to his. "I like this theory, but...it's missing someone."

"Yeah?" He starts shedding down to his boxer-briefs.

"Yeah," I whisper. Just as I shiver, he lowers his warm body onto mine.

His lips drift to my ear as he murmurs, "He or she?" Since I've known about my cysts, this is the first time we've ever pretended or envisioned this far-off future together where a child exists. Why now— that we feel strong enough to do this—I believe is the spark on holiday magic.

Fairytales gain such wonderful life on days like these, and I grab hold, smiling.

"She," I breathe as his thumb runs down the scar on my cheek. My legs are on either side of him, and he pulls a red flannel blanket over us, blocking the winter chill.

Ten times darker but also much warmer. I brush my hands along his biceps and arms, waist and abs, discovering every part of him all over again.

"What's her name?" he asks, combing my flyaway hairs out of my face.

I warm my feet against his legs, not thinking long. "You're better at names than I am." I named Coconut after her white fur, but Ryke named his childhood dog Kina after Mount Kinabalu, a mountain he hiked in Borneo as a kid. His had sentimental value, and I'd want that for our baby's name.

He must understand because he says, "I don't want her named after something I did alone. I fucking love Coconut's name because I see you in her."

"Even though you call her Nutty?" I ask like this is evidence that I'm not great at names.

"Nutty is a fucking nickname from Coconut. I'd rather you pick, Dais."

This is so hard, even naming an imaginary baby that may never appear.

He says, "First thing that fucking comes to you."

First thing?

"Dais."

"Minnie," I say quickly. "Minnie Meadows." I have to warn him. "It's silly." Everything I've ever named has been on the side of quirky.

He kisses me, the powerful movement rocking both of our bodies. Grinding together. *Ryke.* I hang onto his arms, bucking into him. His tongue naturally tangles with mine, his hands creating friction between my legs as much as our wandering limbs.

I barely hear him over the thump of my pulse. "It's fucking cute."

It's fucking cute. I'm smiling in the next kiss, and I grip his hair, heat gathering beneath the heavy blanket.

Many times, he treats me with tender affection, as though recognizing I'm his young girl that he doesn't want to break in two. He caresses my cheek and whispers, "On a scale of one to fucking no, tell me where you are."

I can't catch my breath and we've just been making out for a second or two. I feel wet—I wonder if I'm physically ready. *I hope so.* I think his scale is referring to *pain* from my cyst. "In terms of…you penetrating me?" I ask as my chest rises and falls.

His eyes flit to my hardened nipples then down my frame, trailing my waist and hips and legs. The hairs spike on my arms, his long once-over giving me goose bumps. My smile keeps growing.

His voice is sexily low and husky. "In terms of me pounding my cock into you for at least fifteen fucking minutes."

A noise catches in my throat, and I squirm beneath him. "One. Definitely *one.*"

Ryke puts two of his fingers in *his* mouth for a second, the action indescribably hot. Especially as he holds my gaze. Then he slips his now warm fingers between my thighs, right into—

"Fuck," I gasp, clasping his wrist with both of my hands. I clench and pulse so rapidly around his fingers, my body actually responding *nicely.* Ryke scrutinizes me for a second before understanding that this is freaking glorious and not the least bit agonizing.

He lifts me up, the blanket falling off our bodies. The cold steals my breath, a new, sudden sensation that adds to this otherworldly experience. *Ryke…*I almost lose it when his skillful movements find the most sensitive spot.

The rush of the cold. The heat of my blood. The friction of our skin against skin. It all compounds on top of me. He pulls a blanket over my shoulders, turning me so that my back is against the sleigh, like a red wooden headboard.

He stands on the wooden floor of the sleigh, but one of his knees rests on the seat. He towers over me, but his wrist is still in my possession, his fingers still disappeared inside—*oh my God…*

My legs quiver, and my back arches. "Ryke," I moan, my breath smoking the air. His breathing is so controlled, better at enduring all the elements. I bask in the winter chill, letting it take me away.

I reach out and pull down his boxer-briefs. His cock is already semi-hard, and I imagine the larger, stronger force inside of me. *Ohmygod.*

The minute I start stroking his cock, he hardens more, growing hotter and firmer. I watch his hand between my legs, and lose it at seeing all of him: his sculpted body, his cock, his coarse fingers—all of *Ryke Meadows*—right in front of me. Right in me.

I burst, and before I even collect my breath, he removes his hand and lifts me up until my lower back curves over the smooth top of the sleigh.

I'm upside-down, blood rushing to my head. Cold biting my skin. Staring at the wide snowy horizon.

I am alive! my body screams.

I can't stop smiling. It's Christmas. With Ryke.

Upside-down.

I stretch out my arms. "Good morning, California!" My face hurts with my perpetual grin. *Today's orgasm is brought to you by Ryke and Daisy.* I howl at the sky.

Ryke seizes my hips, lowering me down the back of the sleigh until my shoulders meet wood. He's still standing, and at this angle with his hands on my ass, my pelvis is in line with his pelvis.

My pulse speeds.

"Still at a *one?*" he asks me roughly, his erection *very* close to my heat. I nod.

Slowly, he pushes every single inch of his hardness inside of me, the fullness overwhelming. The second he's completely in, a slight pinch nips me. *No.*

My fingers dig into his shoulder, the nip morphing into a sharp pang. Just before he rocks in and out, I whisper, "Don't…"

He stays completely still for a second and then sweeps my body with dark concern.

Fear knots my stomach. I'm afraid...that this will hurt more. I asked Ryke not to be scared of me, but I didn't even take into account that I'd fear myself.

Ryke carefully pulls me off the back of the sleigh and presses me against his chest. He could fuck me standing up, just by holding me— no brace or support required. So he's strong enough to simply keep me in his arms like a front-piggyback. Only, he's inside of me.

I hate ruining moments, and I wonder if I've shot down and destroyed this one.

I squeeze my eyes shut, thinking about how to fix this. Instinct is telling me to tell him *I'm okay. Keep going.* I can't. Because I'm not okay, and if he keeps going, he'll hurt me.

When I was fifteen, sixteen, seventeen—I would've let a guy keep going. Only with Ryke have I learned to speak up.

Still, I can't fix this moment, can I?

"Hold onto this." Ryke tosses a furry green blanket over my shoulders, and I secure it from falling off. Then he takes a seat with me straddling his waist...and cock. I have a better view of him between my legs. His hands rest protectively on my hip and ass, ensuring less movement right now.

I tuck my hair behind my ear, struggling not to say *I'm sorry.*

"What are you at, Dais?" he asks.

Even on his lap, his lips and eyes are a bit above mine. He finishes smoothing back my hair for me while I gather a response. "A two or three," I whisper. "I'm just..." *scared.* I shiver. Cold cocoons me when we're not creating heat together. "I don't want to be afraid to have sex."

He sits up straighter, very focused on my body's reactions. "We're going to conquer your fucking fears, Calloway. You just have to decide something."

I listen earnestly.

"You're moving first or I'm moving first. What do you want?"

I set my palm on his chest, his muscles constricted and ready to work and play. "I…" I absorb my position: *on top*.

My mind zips through flashbacks. Moments in time. Guys rolling me on top of them and then waiting with this famished, gross look that only said *girl, fuck me now*.

My first time, so inexperienced, I had to figure out what to do without his help. I wished I'd been in the hands of someone with more knowledge. Who could guide me and lead me.

Someone who cared about me.

Maybe in another life I'd enjoy riding a guy, but the whole grandeur was sullied from the start.

On the sleigh, Ryke says, "Hey, where are you?"

"I don't like…" I've described my issue with being on top—or at least being the sole mover on top—a couple times to him, and it must click because he doesn't ask for my answer. He just knows.

His hand travels from my ass to my hip.

Still, I make a point to speak up this time. "I want you to move," I say quietly.

His chest brushes against mine, and he kisses my cheek before lifting me a couple inches. My heart skips, but everything feels good, the friction warming me. I nod for him to continue.

While clutching my hips, Ryke rocks his pelvis up, pushing all the way into me again. My lips break apart, the fullness better. I nod again and watch his cock dip out, only a little, before disappearing again. He repeats the melodic movement, the speed increasing each time.

I find myself lowering onto him, meeting him faster, and he tucks me against his body. *Ahh…* "Ryke," I cry.

"Fuck," he grunts, pounding into me like he promised. Taking care of me. I try to hang onto his shoulders, my body jumping each time he drives in. It lasts so much longer than I can quantify. Every minute, I think, *I'm coming now, right now*.

Then another minute arrives.

The cycle continues, pure adrenaline coursing through me. *Oh my God.*

"Fuuck," I cry in a high-pitched voice, glad I didn't let fear rule me. The sensations blind me, and my body tightens against Ryke. *Holy shit.*

I moan against his shoulder, my skin slick and hot.

"Dais," I hear his deep, gruff voice in the pit of my ear, his arms gripping me.

I explode, limbs vibrating, heart thumping. His muscles flex as he hits a similar earth-shattering peak.

He pumps into me to prolong the high, and I pant against his neck, clutching the back of his head. He holds me like he's never letting me go.

And even though the universe rarely tilts our way, in this second, on this magical sleigh, I pretend that we're going to live forever.

That we'll have a Minnie Meadows.

And no one will smite us for our love.

Just this once.

< **27** >

Ryke Meadows

The sheets are tangled at the end of our fucking bed, our hanging paper lanterns dim, and our husky is fast asleep beside our unpacked suitcases, curled on her sunshine-patterned dog cushion.

I sit naked at the edge of the mattress, one of my knees bent. Daisy is fucking naked too, only she rests against the headboard. Her long legs shift every which way until she holds onto her knee for something to do. Her skin glistens with sweat, but not as much as she should be—not as fucking much as mine.

I break the extended, tense silence. "Let's take a fucking rain check. We just got back from Tahoe—"

"Six hours ago," she reminds me. "And we can't take a rain check when you said that I'm probably ovulating."

I can tell by the color of her fucking wetness, which is *almost* nonexistent, but yeah—I think she's fucking ovulating.

"We skipped sex yesterday," she also fucking reminds me.

I rake a hand through my damp hair, torn up about this. "You're not aroused. We just fooled around for *three* fucking hours, and you're still really dry, Daisy."

I'm confident and fucking experienced in foreplay and heightening a girl's arousal, but I can't make one who's chemically and psychologically not in the mood to suddenly feel pleasure. If she's like this now, there's no way she'll hit a climax with me inside her.

I fucking hate that I can't help her, but this isn't the first time we've both decided to throw in the towel. This is just the first time we're both struggling to defy what her body is saying. *Stop. Not today. Get the fuck away, Ryke.* That's what I'm fucking hearing, and I've never disobeyed those pleas.

I let out an aggravated breath and then lift my gaze to her. "Do you know the phrase I sometimes fucking whisper to you—il tuo piacere è il mio. That means *your pleasure is my pleasure.*"

Pain flashes in her eyes. She's upset.

Fuck.

She sets her cheek on her kneecap. "I told you this might happen," she says softly, tracing a wrinkle in the sheet, her doleful green eyes eating at my fucking heart. "Do you think Rose would be pregnant already if our positions were switched?"

"Fuck no," I say forcefully. "Dais, we're giving it everything we have. We're fucking trying, and it's *not* your fault if it takes longer. There wasn't something you missed or something you forgot to fucking do. It just wasn't our time, okay?"

She nods but appears just as mournful as she did three hours ago, exhaustion in the corners of her eyes, but not the kind that'll put her to sleep. Then she lies down, her back thudding to the mattress. She extends her long legs out towards me and then breaks them open.

In a soft, begging voice she says, "Please." Her knees sway. "I don't want to fight with you on this anymore. I just want it to happen."

"Were we fucking fighting?" I ask roughly, standing from the bed.

She watches me. "I think there was a fight there."

This is probably more serious than anything else we argue about. I open the end table drawer, retrieving a red bottle of lube. Then I kneel on the bed between her legs, and she musters a smile that looks forced.

"Don't fucking do that," I tell her, rubbing lube on my hardened cock.

"Do what?" Her throat bobs, and her smile wanes so fucking fast.

"Pretend to be enjoying this." I worry that she'll start a routine of faking it, thinking it'll please me more. It does the exact opposite.

"So you just want me to lie here with a frown?"

"If that's what you're fucking feeling, then yeah."

Her chest rises in a sharp inhale. "I can turn on my stomach?"

"No." I want to be able to tell if I'm hurting her, so I need her fucking facing me.

"Please don't be mad." Her voice cracks.

I lean forward. "Hey," I say quickly, brushing a tear that squeezes out of her eye. I kiss her cheek, her forehead, her nose. "Dais, I'm not fucking angry at you. Look at me."

Her glassy eyes meet mine.

I can't soften my features. I can't rid my fucking scowl or the lines that crease my forehead. "I would never fuck you while I was mad at you." For fuck's sake, it's almost impossible to be angry at Daisy for longer than a couple minutes. I end up empathizing more with her than with anyone else.

"Tell me what I should do," she says quietly. "I want to make this more enjoyable for you."

My hand trails the outside of her smooth leg, my other forearm resting beside her head. I raise her ass just a fucking fraction of an inch, enough to be in line with my erection. "You don't have to do a fucking thing. Just relax."

She tries, her hands running along my abs, but her body is stiff, joints locked.

I push inside of Daisy, careful since she's not wet. *Fuck*. Her tightness wells pressure around me, and I fucking throb, blood pooling. I rock against her, and she clutches my biceps. I watch her closely, my temperature escalating, and she does as I asked, not pretending to be aroused.

She shuts her eyes and turns her cheek onto her pillow.

It's a sign that she's waiting for this to end, and it fucking kills me for a moment. *Don't think about it.* Instead of agonizing over her reaction, I have to increase my pace. My ass flexes each time I thrust deeper. When I kiss her temple, her eyes flutter open. Sweat beads along my body, and she watches me pump inside of her for a minute.

Then her lips meet mine. I kiss her back, more aggressively, and a weak smile pulls at her mouth. I hear her mumble, "My wolf."

She's my fucking sun, and even though she's set tonight, she means nothing less to me. I love her just as fucking madly.

My pace quickens, rapid-fire, until I come with one last thrust. She nips my lip in a feral kiss, and I tuck my hand against her head, bringing her off the pillow and kissing her strongly.

After I pull out and my heartbeat slows, I turn on my side and then draw her back to my chest. I wrap my arms around her, and she clutches them.

I'm fucking glad that's over. I'm not happy that I'll eventually have to do it again, but hopefully there'll be a time where we're holding a kid.

Where we look back in remembrance and think, *we did everything we fucking could to have this.*

< 28 >

Daisy Calloway

Three-sixty views of New York City on New Year's Eve. A sight currently held by me and hundreds of socialites at Connor Cobalt's black-tie charity event in a city high-rise. We've all gathered in the classic ballroom, waiters passing around trays of pink and gold champagne.

I drank too much water on the limo ride here, so I break from my sisters to go to the restroom. A sea of people part as though creating a runway to the bathroom, their gazes hot on me.

I tug the long sleeves of my glittering white dress that has a plunging neckline and thigh-high slit. With red lips and actual eye makeup, I probably resemble "supermodel Daisy" more than just "regular ole Daisy" but I wanted to dress up for the formal event.

Five feet from the bathroom, someone abruptly cuts off my path. I almost smack into his chest, but I take a step back.

I raise my head.

And I go cold.

Face-to-face with an ex-boyfriend.

One that was with me during the reality show, *Princesses of Philly*, and so the heat of cellphones pin to my back. People know we were once together.

Julian looks a little different, a little older. His face is boxier, clean-shaven, and his hair is slicked back with gel or product. He's still beautiful enough to be a model, and after seeing his commercial for a men's fragrance, I know the fashion world thinks so too.

"Can we talk?" he asks quietly.

I don't want to be near him, honestly. I was seventeen when I dated him. I thought, maybe, I could fall in some type of love with him. I was naïve. I trusted him, and he took advantage of me in more ways than I can count.

I know that now.

I'm strong enough to stand by my convictions, and I'm not going to placate him. I'm not going to please him. I'm not going to give him time because I *have* to be nice. I don't have to be. Not to him. Not now.

"No, Julian," I say, about to lose myself in the crowd. I'm actually *scared* to go into the bathroom now. Afraid he'll follow me. I make a move to turn away from him.

He grabs me by the arm.

I jerk back. "Don't…" A few flashes go off, and I worry about causing a scene at Connor's event.

Julian lowers his voice. "This is about those videos. I'm being *investigated*, Daisy. I don't want to be charged for statutory rape just because you gave me a blow job." That's what he's worried about? What about how I was seventeen, a minor, and Scott Van Wright filmed me without my consent while I undressed and had oral sex with Julian? What about the part where Scott saved the footage to watch repeatedly with his friends? Spanning years of time.

What about when I found out? How I felt so *violated* I could barely speak, numb to my own body. When Ryke learned what Scott had done, he lost it. I couldn't verbalize my hurt or show it right away, and Ryke seemed to channel both of our pain.

He couldn't hit Scott since he was long gone in a cop car, sentenced for child pornography, and Ryke was fuming in guttural rage. He almost decked Lo and Connor, but they steered him towards the basement gym. The next time I saw Ryke, his knuckles were busted open and a punching bag bloodied.

We spent the next week basically attached to each other, which isn't normal for us—that's a Lily and Lo thing. The event unearthed raw moments in our past, where we were split apart—where I've let some people walk all over me—and it made us hold onto each other a little harder and longer.

Before my sisters, their husbands, or Ryke notice this scene, I seek to just end it quickly. In a stilted voice, I say, "You can call my lawyer."

"This could ruin my life," he whispers, eyes angrily narrowed on me.

I'm not trying to ruin anyone's life. "My lawyer can help you. Please, I don't want to talk to you." I hate that I feel a pang of guilt, just for being harsh. It's not even as cutthroat as Rose would be. She'd slice his balls off with her icy words, and she'd raise her head. She'd only feel *triumph*.

I don't want to care, but I do care. I see the way my tone can hurt someone, and so I ache to soften it, to make them feel better, even when I feel worse.

You matter, Calloway.

I'm trying to feel that. I am.

Wasting no more time, I weave into the crowds, quick to distance myself from Julian. In New York, our social circles cross paths, so it's not alarming to see him.

It's just alarming to be confronted by him.

I bump chests with a middle-aged man, his champagne dripping down my bare collar and between my breasts.

"Sorry," I apologize the same time as him. He removes his pocket square, and I see him go to dab up the spill. "No, *no*." I quickly apologize again, make a short joke about me being so clumsy, and then I frantically cut through more people and conversations.

Searching.

Then I spot Lily by a college-aged group, most with unimpressed, Ivy League expressions and girls adorning Blair Waldorf headbands.

I clasp my older sister's hand. "Excuse me," I cut in with a bright smile. "I have to steal this one away."

They look grateful to lose her.

I'm grateful to have her.

Lily's nose crinkles in confusion, at them more than me. I take a deep breath and walk with her over to the floor-length windows.

"This party is lame," she whispers to me, hiking up her floor-length black dress. Her sneakers are visible underneath.

I smile, a more genuine smile. "Why?" We stop by the window, close enough that I feel like I'm outside, flying above the packed city streets, the annual concert down below.

"I told them my New Year's resolution and they all stared at me like I was dumb." She mutters, "Lo would have understood."

I catch a glimpse of her husband lingering by the cheese table with Ryke and Sam. Lo is dressed in all black. From his shoes, dress shirt, bow tie, suit jacket and pants. Even his cufflinks are onyx. Ryke is more casual, sporting a skinny black tie, white dress shirt, black suit jacket and pants. Sam stands opposite in a classic navy tux.

None of them seem to notice us, so I focus back on my sister, surprised that she approached strangers alone. Then again, she's been slowly crawling out of her comfort zone since the inception of Superheroes & Scones and Halway Comics.

I bump her hip with mine. "I bet Connor's guests make the same old boring resolution every year." I wave her on. "Lay yours on me."

She pulls back her shoulders, readying herself. "Okay, my New Year's resolution is to not have a New Year's resolution. That way there won't be any disappointment when it isn't fulfilled."

That's definitely not an ambitious person's mode of thinking, but I like it because it reminds me of Lily. "You're speaking my language."

She grins more and then just seems to notice how close we are to the window. "Uh…" She takes four steps back, afraid of heights. "What if someone pushes us and we fall through the glass?"

I gasp. "Will we be that lucky?"

Lily tries to narrow her eyes at me, but she's just squinting. "That's not funny."

"Just joking," I tell her, feeling a little claustrophobic. I bend down to unbuckle my strappy red heels.

"You remember the New Year's Eve at the model's flat?" Lily asks me, smiling at the memory. It was one of the very first times we hung out alone together. "You were only sixteen, I think."

"Fifteen," I correct, time flooding me in a hot wave. It seems like forever ago, details blurry since I passed out from roofie-spiked punch. Ryke showed up. And carried me out of the flat.

"At least there's no hunch punch." Lily squats to tie her shoelace and falls to her butt.

I try not to laugh. "At least Lo is here."

She blows out a hair that sticks to her lips, and her smile is blindingly cute. Loren Hale was in rehab during that New Year's, and she hasn't gone without him since.

Just as I remove my heels and rise with Lily, Rose approaches us with Poppy. I miss Willow, but she's busy babysitting Moffy and Jane. She offered to watch them since she really didn't want to go to a New Year's party. Apparently, it's her least favorite holiday.

Still, I wish she could be here. Her presence is totally missed. I end up pulling out my phone and texting this to her, just so she knows we're thinking about her.

Rose flips her hair over one shoulder, and before she speaks, Poppy says, "I saw Julian."

"*We* saw Julian," Rose amends.

Poppy takes a sip of pink champagne. "We wanted to let you know so you don't cross paths with him." My sisters are very protective of me when it comes to Julian.

The guys despise Julian, and my sisters loathe him.

I want to say, *too late*, but rehashing the short exchange sounds like adding kindling to an unnecessary fire. "As long as he doesn't come near me, I'm okay," I let them know.

Rose's hands are perched on her hips, her beautiful wine-red dress hugging her frame. "Connor is dealing with him."

Connor Cobalt is dealing with Julian. It sounds *very* ominous. I wait to be lit up by the mystery and intrigue—all those exciting things. I just feel a bit hollow, and I want to find this spark inside of me that's sort of spurting out tonight.

I smile but it's not as lively as I hoped it could feel.

Lily frowns. "What does that mean?"

I say in a hushed voice, "Didn't you know, Connor Cobalt is a hit man?"

Lily's lips part, unsure whether I'm being serious or not. "Huh?"

Rose rolls her eyes. "Connor is just talking to him, and hopefully threatening his genitals and tongue until he leaves."

"Rose," Poppy says with the shake of her head.

I add, "Sounds like a hit-man thing to do."

"Or the Rose Calloway Cobalt thing to do," Lily notes. "I thought for sure Connor Cobalt was an alien, not a hit man."

I laugh with Poppy. I try to hold onto that burst of sparkling energy in my belly. *Don't go.*

Rose looks *not* amused, her black manicured nail pointed at Lily. "If my husband is an alien, yours was born in the underworld."

"Well," I say, "Loren Hale *is* smoking hot."

Lily points at Rose. "Ha!"

Rose huffs like that is *not* what she was implying, and her attention cements to me. "How's the panda bear search going?" It sounds silly from Rose, but she confidently owns every word. If someone *dared* to make fun of her, she'd be quick to shut them up.

Panda bear is a code name for getting pregnant. It would be devastating if the media found out before I told my parents, so one night over nail polish and a *One Tree Hill* marathon, we all concocted secret terms.

"I'm not sure," I admit. "I haven't had any bamboo in like six weeks, so…I guess that's promising?"

Lily stares at the ceiling with cinched brows. "I'm lost." She forgot the code words.

Poppy whispers in her ear. My oldest sister wears a silver sequined, vintage dress—what Rose called *1920s inspired*. It suits Poppy's carefree nature.

Rose snaps her fingers at me, and I smile at her, attention regained. "Six weeks?" she states like I'm insane. "Why haven't you…" She lowers her voice. "Taken a test yet?"

I shrug. "I don't know. I guess I just want to wait. In case." I'm nervous to take one after the handful of failed tests. I can't imagine anyone would like feeling repetitious rejection.

"You need to take one," Rose tells me pointedly.

I glance at the window, the city streets alive. "Right now?" I ask, the mission more enthralling than the actual act of taking a test. *Let's go see the world. All of us together.* My lips begin to rise.

"Only if you want to."

"Will Connor mind?" I wonder. We're here in solidarity, and I wouldn't want to bail if it hurt his feelings. Though when it comes to Connor Cobalt, it's *very* hard to do just that.

Rose takes my hand. "No. Not at all."

I nod, eager to leave. She ushers me towards the large double doors, and I snatch Lily's hand to follow. She's quick to grab Poppy's.

"Where are we going?" Lily asks us.

"The drugstore," I say and then notice leering gazes. My lips lift and I raise my voice. "We're getting condoms and party blowers."

People give us the strongest side-eyes, but we don't turn back or cower. Together, all four of us, we're more invincible against the world's judgment.

But deep down I know that the night can only end in one of two ways:

Yes or No.

< **29** >

Ryke Meadows

Afourth tray of pink and gold champagne passes us, and Lo snatches the server's elbow and points at the table with cubed cheese. "Is this all the food?"

The server nods to us, in recognition, like he understands who we are from the media. "Champagne?" he offers.

"No," I say pretty fucking rudely. He must know that my little brother is a recovering alcoholic, and still, he was willing to give him a drink.

Lo sets a firm hand on my shoulder. "Pardon my brother, we both suffer from the same hereditary disease called *being a dick*. Assholes Anonymous couldn't even cure us." He gives him a half-smile that says, *good fucking bye.*

The server takes the hint.

Lo spins back to the table, and my stomach fucking grumbles.

"Connor owes me big time." He picks up a toothpick with an olive-sized meatball. "What the hell is this?" I'm just as fucking offended by the thing. "He said there would be *food* here."

Sam motions to the toothpick with his champagne. "What do you call what you're eating?" He's been hanging around us all night, most of these people acquaintances with Connor.

"A snack," Lo retorts.

I haven't seen Connor since we arrived, and I scan the crowds for any sign of him.

"Did he think we wouldn't come or something?" Lo asks. "Because teasing us by describing a five-course meal this morning was just goddamn insensitive."

I focus back on Lo. "Since when is Connor Cobalt ever fucking sensitive?"

He shrugs and eats the tiny meatball. "Did he tell you?"

I frown. "Tell me what?"

Lo hesitates before he spills the news. "Dad wrote him a letter, apologizing for what happened."

My brows furrow. "Wait, *what?*"

"I almost didn't believe it too," he says in that Loren Hale—*I'm going to always forgive my dad, even when he's fucking abusive*—way. It puts me on guard. This is just Jonathan manipulating him again. That's it.

Jonathan is not a good fucking person. If I have to keep reminding myself of this fact, does it make it less true?

Lo adds, "Connor showed me the letter."

"Where was I?" I growl.

"Dealing with your own shit," Lo snaps. "Does it really matter?"

I shake my head. "No..." I don't always have to be a part of everything like Connor and Rose. I'm okay with not carrying everyone's baggage, but I do want to be there for my little brother.

I don't know what to think of our dad's apology letter to Connor. I'm not on solid footing with Jonathan. Changing my name was a big fucking deal, and I wasn't sure how he'd react. Especially since I put off helping him with Willow—to the point where he just did his own fucking thing without my input.

He hasn't brought up my name change in our brief conversations, and part of me wonders if he's looking past it.

Just so he doesn't push me further away.

Our dad once told me that he'd be willing to do anything if it meant protecting Lo and me. His kids that he loves. He'd get sober. He'd even hurt Connor if he thought—in his deluded mind—that it'd save Lo from an enemy that never existed.

He's been handing me olive branches. I've been throwing them back in his face.

"Connor accepted his apology," Lo tells me.

My head sways in surprise. And I see the words my brother's not saying: *Why can't you be okay with him like Connor is?*

I don't know.

Maybe it's the fact that he could apologize to Connor, for hurting him, but he never apologized to me. Not once in his life has he uttered those two words to my fucking face. *I'm sorry, son. For casting you out like a bastard.*

I've never even seen his remorse for what he did.

My brother's amber judgment feels hot on me. I scratch my unshaven jaw and then loosen my tie. He rolls his eyes, dropping the conversation and searches the ballroom.

"Where's Lily?" he asks, swinging his head back and forth. I don't see any of the girls either, and my muscles begin to bind.

"I saw the girls leave about ten minutes ago," Sam just now tells us.

Lo pats him hard on the shoulder. "Thanks for letting us know ten minutes ago, Sammy."

"It looked like they wanted to be alone," Sam rebuts.

Lo picks up another toothpick. "I bet they're eating real food."

Rose wouldn't leave her husband's party for a fucking burger. I pull out my cell and send Daisy a text: Where'd you go?

I type another to Lily: If you're getting food, get something for your husband. He's practically fucking frothing at the mouth.

Just as I send the message, a man in a traditional tuxedo and fucking evening scarf approaches my little brother. I miss his name, but I hear the part where he's the CEO of an up-and-coming startup in California.

This is the reason we've segregated ourselves from the girls all night. Even though Rose and Lily are business owners, no one seeks them out for referrals or pitches like they do Sam, Lo, and Connor. Not unless it's about *Queens of Philadelphia*. It's fucking sexist, but I'm happy the girls don't have this headache on New Year's Eve.

Lo even told *me* to "get the fuck away from him and have a good time"—but I can't leave my brother. He spent the early part of the night listening to pitches, but now he's pretty much done. He procures a business card with his assistant's contacts and hands it to the man.

"Call or email me," Lo says in a tone that shuts off further conversation, even closing off his body from him. He's fucking good at that.

The man mutters, "Thanks." And he shuffles away.

Sam downs the rest of his champagne, his mild annoyance flaring in his eyes.

Lo glares. "If you want to fucking say something, Sammy, just say it."

Sam checks over his shoulder for more liquor. The nearest server is helping a cluster of women.

My phone pings.

Across the street. We're on a mission. — Daisy

Seconds later, Lily replies.

We're going to the drugstore. I can get him some snacks.
— Lily

My brows knot. The drugstore?

"I didn't ask for this, you know," Lo tells Sam. "Generally, I think I have the kind of face that says: *fuck off, don't you dare goddamn talk to me.* Apparently these people woke up blind or stupid because they're just not getting it."

I group text my next response, sending it to both Lily and Daisy.

What mission? And why the fucking drugstore?

Only Daisy replies.

Girl things. I'll tell you in a bit. — Daisy

I trust her enough to slide my phone back in my pocket, also trying to shelve my fucking worry, especially since their bodyguards should be following them...

Price. *Fuck.* Yeah, Price does not make me feel any fucking better.

When I glance at Sam, I'm surprised to see him smiling. "I would've said something like that, but I wouldn't phrase it that way."

"One less insult," Lo agrees. "You're too preciously pure for your own good, Sammy."

Sam lets out a short laugh, a pretty lighthearted exchange between them. Sam has fit into our group as much as he can. Better than he fucking used to at least.

Lo nods to me. "I'm going to find the girls and eat something."

"They're at the drugstore."

Lo gives me a weird look. "Why?" He rolls his eyes like he doesn't care. "I'll go get Doritos or something." He's about to walk off, even with the insane logic that chips are somehow better than five-star appetizers here.

Truth is, I think he just wants to see his wife.

Lo immediately spins back towards the cheese table as soon as he sees Connor. Dressed in a tailored black tux and sauntering towards us like nothing and no one can fucking touch him, he never slows or flinches.

He acts like the billions that he's worth.

I'm not as disgruntled by Connor tonight. Not when we're surrounded by at least a hundred people willing to stomp on each other to climb the preverbal corporate fucking ladder. At least Connor will flat-out tell you what he thinks of you to your face.

"Don't look him in the eyes," Lo says dryly. "Maybe he won't figure out how much we hate his party."

I greet Connor with a single head nod. He never returns it, his attention pinned to Lo who glares at the pyramid of cheese puffs—or whatever *fancy* name everyone has for them.

Connor fixes his cufflink. "I came over to say hello, but I sense an issue."

Lo spins to me. "Did you hear something?"

Usually they're ribbing me, so I take the fucking opportunity to bust Connor's balls. "Nope."

Connor tells Lo, "Feigning deafness is below you, darling."

Lo cracks, acknowledging the soon-to-be twenty-eight-year-old. "And lying is below you, love."

Connor never blinks, but he does turn to me. "It pains me to look to you for a translation, but what the hell is going on?"

"You fucking told us there'd be food here," I explain.

"And you're starving me," Lo chimes in. "Unless there's a five-course meal in the back waiting for us, I'm going to leave. Watch me go."

Connor lets an uncharacteristic frown pass over his features. "Are you talking about the New Year's dinner?"

Lo wears a *fucking duh* look. "Yeah. And *you're* supposed to be the smart one. Don't change on me."

"The dinner is on New Year's *Day*," Connor emphasizes. "You were clearly confused. Today is New Year's *Eve*. I'd say it's a common mistake, but really, it's not."

Lo sets a murderous glare on the ceiling, realizing we've been waiting for nonexistent food this entire time.

"Okay," I cut in. "Don't fucking insult Lo. You didn't make it clear, Cobalt."

Connor stoically stands his ground. "I made it clear. I said exactly what I'm saying now. If you misinterpreted the meaning of my words, maybe you should buy a dictionary."

Lo's cheekbones sharpen. "We skipped *dinner*."

"I didn't," Sam proclaims.

Lo sets his glare on him.

I'm about there, hungry as shit.

"Obviously we have different definitions of New Year's Day," Connor continues to Lo. "Mine lines up with the world, and yours lines up with yourself and...him." Connor nods his head at me.

"Fuck you," I snap, just as an unwelcome face zones in on me, about ten feet across the room. When Julian begins to walk towards me, I almost can't believe it.

"He should've left by now," Connor says, his voice so controlled that I have trouble understanding what's happening—or what happened.

"You knew he was fucking here?" I almost yell.

"Calm down," Lo tells me.

"I am." I'm not even close.

"Really? Then why are your hands in fists?"

I can't untighten them. Lo has been confronted by Lily's past hookups before, but this is different for me—I *knew* Julian. I fucking watched him date Daisy and try to take advantage of her when she was underage and practically passed out drunk.

We fought constantly, and it escalated into a fistfight in the end. Or not the fucking end...now he's here, approaching me.

"We need to talk," Julian says the minute he stops in front of me, camera phones flashing. We haven't been around each other since the reality show was cancelled. Years ago.

"No we fucking don't." I have nothing to say to him that hasn't already been said.

Connor interjects, "When I told you to leave *now*, I meant the present moment. I didn't think I'd need to delineate a word that my one-year-old understands."

Julian ignores him, fixated on me. "You have to tell Daisy to call whoever to settle this video thing, dude. It's not my fault we were filmed."

I see fucking red.

Julian continues quickly, "I was mailed some letter by a court, inquiring about what happened. It looks fucking bad for me, and I need her to fix this. It's *her* fault that I'm in this mess to begin with. I didn't ask for any of it."

"Shut the fuck up," I growl. His words claw at my skull.

Connor says something calmly to Julian about needing to leave, and I tune it out.

Lo glares. "Hey, Julius, how about you go stand in a corner for the next ten years. That way only the wall has the painful experience of staring at your shitty fucking face."

I'm glad my brother is here.

Julian wears a familiar pissed and dumbfounded look, but he's not done talking to me. "Daisy told me to call her lawyer, but I think she can clear my name with one statement—"

"You spoke to Daisy?" I step forward, and Lo puts a protective hand on my shoulder. I fucking fume in place, knowing exactly how she feels about him. If she was scared—

"Tonight, yeah," Julian says, a short smirk attached. "By the bathroom."

I'm about to fucking hit him, but Lo clutches my bicep, stopping me. My brother fights with words, but I'm a lot less verbal and a lot more impatient. "Don't ever fucking corner her again," I growl and jerk out of Lo's grasp.

"You think you're the good guy?" Julian practically shouts, so everyone can hear. "The entire time I was dating Daisy, you were all over her, dude. If anyone should be in jail for rape, it's *you*."

I fucking charge. Lo and Connor hold me back. I thrash in their arms and point at Julian, cursing up a storm. "You motherfucking *piece of shit!* Fuck you, you *fucking*—" I go on and on, not even registering *what* the fuck I'm screaming. Veins protrude in my arms, and I yell until my head pounds with excess fury.

Julian presses his finger to his chest. "*I did nothing wrong. She's the slut who couldn't keep her fucking clothes on.*" *I'm going to fucking kill him.* "I'm not going to be punished for the worst blow job I've *ever* received—that cunt can rot in hell."

Both Connor and Lo let me go.

I clock Julian in the jaw, and before he regains balance, I slug him again and *again*, my ears ringing shrilly. If rage has a frequency, I'm listening to it. Security seizes my arms first, giving Julian enough time to land one fucking punch. My lip busts open, and I lunge towards him only to be yanked back.

"Go marry that slut!" he yells with a mouthful of blood, eye swollen and cheek reddened. One guard has him by the arm.

"Fuck you, you motherfucking—" Security smacks the back of my head and threatens to cuff me. My nose flares, and I barely listen to their orders: *settle down, you need to leave now, you're out of control.*

"You can release him," Connor says calmly. Like I didn't just try to cripple one of his guests.

"We can escort him out."

I breathe deeply through my nose, my knuckles burning. Lo has a hand on my shoulder, asking me if I need ice. I rigidly shake my head.

"That's unnecessary." Connor holds the main security guard's befuddled gaze and has to add, "He's my friend. He's staying with me."

The subtext beneath his declaration hits me harder than it could anyone else. Connor is vouching for me after I punched a man at his party, meaning that he values me above his reputation.

Above these people.

His company.

His money.

I never, not in a million fucking years, thought I meant that much to him.

I thought he would've made a Rottweiler joke and pushed me out of the door beside Julian, not stood beside me.

Security complies with Connor's direction, and they just escort Julian out of the ballroom. I notice camera phones raised indiscreetly at us. The media believes Connor and I more or less hate each other, and I have a fucking feeling the world is about to see the truth behind our rocky friendship.

Lo tosses a wet rag at my face. I missed seeing who handed it to him. I press the cloth against my split lip.

"I can't believe Daisy dated that guy," Lo says. "I can't believe we *let* her date him."

"She was modeling a lot at the fucking time," I remind him, my voice coarse. She was part of an industry and a world that none of us stepped a foot into, but Julian did. He was fucking *there* with her.

"There was little we could do," Connor agrees.

My phone suddenly buzzes.

"I hope Julius runs into oncoming traffic," Lo says with edge, eyes burning with malice, and when they meet mine, I can tell his fury is partly for me and partly for Daisy.

I nod at him and mess his hair. He pushes me off with a fleeting smile. I have no fucking intention of ever seeing Julian again, and there's no way he'll get in contact with Daisy. I won't let him.

I finally take out my phone.

My face falls.

"What happened?" Lo asks.

Connor steps closer to me.

"Is it Lily?" Lo tries to see the text, but my world rotates, a sensation close to being fifty feet off the ground. No safety.

No rope.

Just my fingers gripping rock, clinging to my own lifeline. Aware of every muscle, every limb, stretching, burning and screaming. My breath leveled in my lungs. Each one keeping me strong.

It's the feeling of being alive.

I reread the text, guaranteeing this is happening.

I think I might be pregnant. — Daisy

< *30* >

Daisy Calloway

Crammed into the drugstore bathroom with my four sisters, we huddle close to the toilet so our bodyguards can't listen through the door. I slip my phone into my red clutch, the pregnancy test resting in the sink basin.

I peek at it again. "It's so faint." The two bars aren't bold and prominent. All three tests look exactly the same. Maybe I've joked too much about life that now life is finding ways to play jokes on me.

Rose is smiling and also very careful not to touch *anything* in the unisex bathroom, wet toilet paper stuck to the gray tiles.

"Your doctor will confirm the pregnancy test," she tells me, more optimistic than I've tended to be. Her rare smile in a filthy bathroom speaks for itself, already happy for me.

Lily waves a plastic stick in the air, anticipating the results. She took a pregnancy test right after me. *Just in case*, she said. With Rose pregnant, I think Lily's just worried she'll have another accident like last time.

We wait for Poppy to go pee, having an easier time with her shorter dress unlike our floor-length gowns. As long as there's not toilet paper stuck on the bottom of mine, I'm good.

"Sweet Disposition" by The Temper Trap starts playing in my clutch, and I quickly pull out my phone—the ringtone set by Ryke about a year ago. It took him *forever* to choose, and so I've never changed it.

I put the cell to my ear. "Hey."

"You okay?" Ryke asks first, his concern making me smile.

"Yeah, I'm okay. The bars are really faint on the test, but Rose seems hopeful."

"But you're not fucking hopeful?" he asks.

I shrug and then realize he can't see me. "I haven't had any morning sickness, and I don't feel any different. It just seems too good to be true." The phone is instantly plucked out of my hand.

Rose holds the speaker to her mouth. "We'll send you pictures of the test. She's being pessimistic."

"Cautious," Lily rephrases.

Poppy flushes the toilet. "Realistic."

Rose sets a fiery glare on our oldest sister. "You don't think I'm realistic?"

"I think that you want her to be pregnant at the same time as you." Poppy washes her hands.

Rose's lips downturn, not liking the reality of me not being pregnant with her, that she's carrying a baby before me. If she could, she'd switch places. I know she would, and I love her for loving me and wanting this for me. Simply because I want it to come true.

"Hey!" Ryke shouts through the phone, capturing our attention. "Are you all fucking listening?"

"Yes," Rose snaps. I gather the pregnancy sticks into the box since we're planning to toss them at our house. Rose has a large enough purse to carry them out unseen.

I hear Lo's muffled voice in the receiver before Ryke lets out a frustrated breath and asks, "When are you coming back?"

"Ten minutes," Rose says.

We exchange *see you soons* before Ryke hangs up, and then Rose hands me the cell.

A text vibrates my phone.

You're all fucking crazy. — Ryke

Then another.

Every Calloway sister. — Ryke

And another.

I love you. — Ryke

I can't contain my smile.

Lily gasps. "I'm not pregnant," she whispers excitedly. Then she jumps and does a little dance, her butt shaking a lot.

I grin more and give her a high-five.

She adds her pregnancy test to the box, and Rose stuffs it into her black Chanel bag. As soon as Poppy unlocks the door, my bodyguard nearly stumbles back, standing suspiciously close *again*.

My older sisters give him warning looks; stronger and fiercer than anything I can muster. Even Lily adds her own, and Price clears his throat, seeming a little like a twenty-two-year-old rookie. My sisters' bodyguards are spread throughout the rinky-dink drugstore.

Blending in.

I stay by the bathroom while Lily peruses a row of junk food, Rose browsing the limited selection of makeup nearby. Poppy sniffs the few candles, and the old store clerk eyes us with curiosity. We're out of place. Dressed in thousand-dollar gowns in a store with cardboard over a broken window, the neon *open* sign half burnt out, spelling *pen*.

I'd say that all of this is putting Price on high alert, but he's always been overly vigilant. I haven't had much of a chance to talk to him, and my old bodyguard I knew like a friend.

While I wait for my sisters, I try to feel out Price's intentions a little more. See if I can understand *why* he wants to be a bodyguard. "Where are you from?" I ask, realizing I don't even have this simple answer.

"Here," he says vaguely, scanning our surroundings.

"New York City?"

"No, I mean, Philadelphia, originally." Price only briefly makes eye contact, and I kind of feel like I'm interrupting him, even if he's just standing here.

I angle my body more towards Price. "Have you worn a tux before?" I'd add *it looks good on you* if I thought he'd take it as platonic, but I'm really wary to say it.

"I can send you my resume if you need it." He checks his watch and scrutinizes a young couple buying champagne.

"Will your resume tell me if you've worn a tux in your lifetime?" I bend down to check the buckles on my heels. "Or if you prefer Octopus dishes and riding motorcycles off cliffs?" I gasp. "Will I know if you put sugar cubes in your coffee?"

"Okay." His eyes drop to me with a faint smile, his brown hair smoothed back, more charming than his stick-in-the-mud personality. "I know that I'm not forthcoming, but I'm just trying to take care of you tonight."

"You're already a success. I'm in one piece." I stand back up.

"Yale," he suddenly says.

"What?"

He scans the store again, staring everywhere but at me. "I recently graduated from Yale, Magna Cum Laude in Criminal Justice. I've worn tuxes to formals. Grew up in a middleclass family home in Philadelphia.

Before my dad passed, we'd build classic cars in our garage from scratch, sometimes bikes. Your father made me ride a Ducati at the highest speed around a racetrack before hiring me. Only my mom could really guarantee my experience with cars and motorcycles, and he didn't trust her unbiased opinion. I'm fluent in French, Spanish, and German. I aspired to be in the CIA or secret service, but Greg told me how much his daughter travels, the poor security you've had in the past, and how you plan to make roots in Philly. Overall, this job seemed like a better fit for my life." Without losing a single breath, he finishes sharing personal details. Sounding self-assured by each step he's made from then to now.

"Wow," I breathe, my mind racing over everything he said, especially the part where Price lost his father and where my dad made him ride a motorcycle at breakneck speeds—before he even had the job. "I'm sorry about your dad."

"He's in a better place," Price says. "Looks like your sisters are done."

I join them by the checkout counter, Lily buying a medium-sized bag of Doritos. Her green eyes flit to Price then to me. She mouths, *Spy?*

I shrug, unsure if he's really here to be a tattletale for our dad.

Instinct tells me to trust him more, but Ryke thinks he might be here to test our relationship. That's still a possibility too. Price can ride motorcycles and knows foreign languages like Ryke. He's also so young. I'd think my dad would want to hire a veteran, not an aspiring secret service agent.

Unless there's more to the story.

Lily collects her Doritos, and Poppy's bodyguard, Dave, opens the door for us. We exit onto the narrow sidewalk. The commotion outside is much louder and heartier than when we first slipped into the drugstore. I can hear a famous pop singer on a faraway stage. People had been staggering in, the roads blocked off for the New Year's Eve chaos, but now it's jam-packed, barely any room to cross over to the other side. Where the high-rise lies.

"Stay close to me," Rose tells us while our bodyguards reiterate the same thing. No doubt, she'll be the first to push through the masses.

I bounce on my feet, and I hold Lily's hand, the closest to me. She squeezes, just as the sidewalk fills with more people, shoving in tight for a closer view of the ball drop. It's not even visible from where we are, but a nearby city screen televises GBA's *Ballin' New Year's Eve*.

Lily bites her lip, looking a little scared. I squeeze her hand and say over the cacophony, "At least there aren't any cars!"

She nods a couple times.

"LILY CALLOWAY! OH MY GOD! IT'S LILY CALLOWAY!!" someone shrieks in excitement, causing interest to veer onto us.

"Let's go!" Rose raises her head, shoulders arched, ready for battle. We follow her into the crowds, her bodyguard actually leading the way, but Rose is the first one of us to enter the unknown.

That delighted shout—well, that was the only nice one.

"You guys suck!" a man screams in my ear. His closeness puncturing me more than his words, swarmed by *people*. Even Price can't clear out groups as thick as a concert festival.

"Spoiled brats!"

"Go fuck a cock!"

Rose shouts something icy and pointed back before staying her course.

"Excuse me," Lily mumbles as we weave between people.

"Sorry," I apologize to someone else, but pretty much stop when roaming hands slide down my hips and ass. My lungs shrink, and my pulse pounds so fast.

I can't even tell who's touching me since the sly grabs happen many times. Like they can go home and say, *I touched a Calloway sister!*

It's not okay.

An elbow plows into my side, and I wince—suddenly fearful for Rose. Who's pregnant. *What if you're pregnant, Daisy?* I don't know…

"WE HATE YOU!"

"GO BACK TO PHILLY!"

"DAISY, YOU'RE SUCH A BITCH!"

Garth, the veteran bodyguard, grabs Lily and pulls her away from me, and I notice Rose far, far ahead with her own bodyguard. Poppy is out of sight, and Price flanks my right side, putting a barrier between some bodies and me.

"It's getting crazy!" I shout to him.

"Which side is worse?!" he asks.

"Left!"

He shifts to my left, just as someone spits at me, but it splats on his cheek. He's steadfast in his duty to protect me, not even grimacing or wavering for a second.

"DAISY!" someone shouts. "DAISY!"

I instinctively glance at my right, to follow the source of the voice, and the minute I turn my head, a puff of white explodes against my face. My eyes burn, my throat raw and tongue thick with...flour. *Oh my God.*

I can't see.

I can't see.

I cough repeatedly, having trouble breathing.

I can't see.

I blink and blink. Hands are on me. On my shoulders. My hips. My ass. I panic. *I'm panicking.* I run, shoving blindly through people, stumbling.

Someone touches my hair.

Stop.

I cough. *Stop.*

I can't make sense of my surroundings. I inhale flour. I run and stumble, shoving people aside. Hands on my back. On my chest. On my breast.

"Stop," I choke out into a rough cough.

I can't breathe.

My hands shake, and in the midst of my eyes *searing*, I distinguish a sliver of bright light. Flashing. Cameras. *I can't breathe. I can't see.*

"DAISY!!" Ryke screams, the sound distant like a memory. *"DAISY!!"*

I tighten my eyes closed. I wait for a two-by-four to slam and rip through my cheek. Fear paralyzes me. *I can't...*

"DAISY!" Ryke shouts, hands on my cheeks, fabric wiping roughly at my eyes and face. "It's me."

Tears slip out as I start to truly see what's in front of me. *Where...* I cough again, my throat thickened with flour. I tremble, just noticing my heels on the sidewalk and Price's hands protectively on my shoulders.

And I'm certain that he was guiding me to Ryke the entire time.

I motion to my throat, struggling for a real breath, hot from a serious panic attack. Ryke lifts me in his arms, cradling me, and I choke a couple times. He sprints into the nearest diner, the bells dinging as the door flies open.

"Bathrooms for paying customers only!" a hostess shouts.

"Then we'll fucking order something," Ryke growls before entering the women's bathroom, Price close behind.

He sets me on the checkered black and white tiles, foam green stalls lined up behind me. I rest my forearms on the sink counter, and Ryke quickly turns on the faucet. I rinse out my mouth, spitting globs of congealed flour into the basin.

I gag a few times and end up puking. Ryke pulls my hair out of my face, and I mutter an *I'm sorry*, realizing I just vomited in a sink, not a toilet, and someone will have to clean it if I don't.

"Hey, I'll fucking deal with it. Just take a couple breaths, Dais. Your heart is racing."

I clutch the counter with weakened arms and look at the mirror, eyes bloodshot and blots of flour still on my tear-streaked cheeks. My scar visible from the Paris riot.

From the two-by-four years ago.

I take a deeper breath and say, "I need you to call Frederick." I turn to Ryke, his suit jacket dusted with white flour from me. His tie already undone and his hair a ratted, hot mess. He keeps a hand on my back. Here for me. And alive.

The chaos is all in my head, and then again it's not.

Without questioning, he dials my therapist's number. Price has some flour in his hair, and he mostly stands close to a couple occupied stalls.

People are in here. I didn't notice, but I'm glad he did.

I rub my eyes with the side of my hand, and suddenly see Ryke's reddened knuckles, his lip also split. My stomach drops. "What happened?" I reach out to touch his lip, but he pushes my hand down.

"It doesn't fucking matter."

I frown. "You can't tell me?"

His jaw hardens, and he rakes a hand through his hair, trying not to crack in front of me, at least not right now. "Daisy, I know what just fucking happened to you." He gestures to the door, referring to the city streets, to something *more*.

Tears well, eyeballs past burnt. I'm surprised they haven't fallen out yet. I can't even make the joke out loud. "You do?" I whisper, emotions building because *he* was there at Paris with me. If anyone knows the pain of that night, it's Ryke.

"Yeah," he nods strongly. "I fucking do." His hand finds mine, and he draws me to his chest while my phone rings. He passes it to me.

The toilet flushes.

Another follows suit.

Two girls exit in cocktail dresses, and their eyes widen at the males in the bathroom—then at me. Price observes them while they wash their hands.

I think they're going to call me names, but the blonde girl dries her hand and asks, "Are you okay, Daisy?"

I nod.

"Do you need anything?" the other girl wonders.

"I'm alright," I assure them with a weak smile. "Thanks for asking."

They both shuffle out, and Frederick finally picks up. I put the phone to my ear. "Something happened," I tell him, pain in my chest. I try to exhale better. "Paris…and…"

"Is someone around you?" Frederick asks first. I hear GBA's telecast in the background, and then it shuts off.

"Ryke is here."

"Okay good," he says. "I'm glad you called me. Take two big breaths."

I do, tightness releasing on my chest. I've expressed to Frederick how badly I want to let go of these moments that keep terrorizing me. Cleo and Harper harassing me in an elevator. Paparazzi breaking into my bedroom. A pedestrian destroying my bike and then hitting me. The riot in Paris. Neighbor kids playing pranks. Scott Van Wright filming me.

The combination of every foul deed.

Frederick told me the mind is fragile. For as quickly as it can be broken, it can take a lifetime to be repaired. I may never truly let go, but instead of being crippled each time I'm swept back, I've found a way to grow stronger.

I talk about it. I explain to Frederick what happened, and his soothing voice relays every safety net around me. How I'm not alone. How I can persevere. How no one is going to hurt me.

It's not like I'm stoic. I'm crying right now, on the phone with my therapist, but it's better to let it out. I know that. Keeping it in hurts a thousand times more.

"I just don't like how…"

"How what?" he asks.

I rinse my eyes for a second and shut off the water. Ryke and Price act like they're not listening, for my benefit. "I just want to be treated like a person," I whisper. "Everyone was grabbing me…"

Ryke has his back turned to me, but his hands rest on his head.

Price stares far off at the ground, haunted and guilt-stricken.

"It's not anyone's fault," I add to Frederick. "I think everyone's so conditioned to see me as a *thing* and not a person. It's no one's fault."

Ryke shakes his head but never turns around.

"You can be angry, Daisy. You can want to be treated like a human being. You should be, don't you think?"

"Yeah," I breathe. "I know."

"Okay. Don't forget that."

I nod to myself and take another controlled, deep breath. "I need to go find my sisters."

"Can you call me again when you get home?" Frederick asks.

"Yeah, that'd be good." We hang up at the same time, and I crawl on top of the sink counter and then stand, towering in my heels.

"What are you doing?" Price asks, causing Ryke to spin around and see me.

I set my hands on my hips, and I say tearfully, "Will you scream with me?"

Without hesitation, Ryke easily climbs onto the counter. He has to lower his head to avoid hitting the ceiling. He stares down at me, his hands sliding against my cheeks.

My chest rises in a livelier inhale, thankful for Ryke. My pillar. My wolf.

My world. My life.

Strongly, he says, "You ready, Calloway?"

"Yes," I breathe.

And we both scream. All the darkness rippling out of me.

THE MINUTE WE PUSH through the bathroom door, I see a long red vinyl booth, filled with all of my sisters and their husbands. Chatting *loudly*. The diner is packed, and people are recording them with cellphones and snapping photos. But they're in their own bubble, uncaring about the onlookers.

I smile, so glad they're here, and when I approach, they quiet, scanning me from head to toe.

Lo is the first to speak, chewing on a straw. "I just lost fifty bucks."

"Why?" Ryke asks.

Rose and Poppy stand, letting me slide into the middle of the booth next to Lily. Connor and Sam do the same for Ryke on their side while Price sits at the nearest table with the other bodyguards.

"I thought you two were being *murdered* in the bathroom." Oh. They could hear us screaming. I started laughing with Ryke at the end, but maybe that wasn't as audible. "And I bet Lily that you weren't ever coming out."

Ryke's dark brows rise at his brother. "Thanks for betting on my fucking life."

Lo touches his chest. "I wanted to go retrieve you. Everyone else said *no.*"

Rose sips water through a straw. "That's untrue, Loren. I also voted to go get them."

"Huh," Lo says, "I forgot about you."

Rose shoots him an icy glare, but the booth falls into silence once more now that I've arrived with Ryke. Plates clatter in the noisy kitchen, the cooks screaming out orders, and most of the customers at the bar drink milkshakes.

Lily pushes the glass of water closer to me, as though to say *this is yours.*

"Thanks." I give her a smile, and she hugs my side. I unravel my silverware set, folding the napkin into an intricate flower.

Everyone is watching me.

"I'm alright," I let them know. "So hey, I haven't died yet." It's a lame joke, one that does not go over well with anyone.

They all let out a collective groan that actually makes my lips rise. I realize that no one ordered any sodas, just a couple coffees, black for Ryke and one with cream for Connor.

"Did you not get a Fizz Life?" I ask Lily, who would've definitely ordered one over water.

Her face is a little red, maybe from the cold. "They only have Coke."

"Oh…" I wince. Our dad wouldn't be pleased that a New York establishment doesn't carry Fizzle products, and there's no way we can support another brand in public.

Sam taps the table with his knife. "I'm working on it." As the Chief Marketing Officer, he's more involved and passionate about Fizzle than any of us will ever be. I think we all know that in our hearts.

I face Ryke just as he lifts his coffee mug up to his *busted* lip. His raw knuckles are in view again. "What happened?" I ask out in the open, where I know someone will spill the secret.

His gaze hardens and then he flips me off with his free hand.

I smile, and I flip him off with both of my middle fingers. The flashes are insane around us.

After he drinks his coffee, he pushes the mug towards me. I take a sip, my lips upturned while I stare at him.

Since probably my sweet sixteen, maybe even before, Ryke has always shared his food and drink with me. At first, just to urge me to eat *something* (modeling woes), but now it's such a habit between us.

"He beat up your shitty ex-boyfriend," Lo unleashes the secret all of a sudden.

My eyes widen.

"And he won't say it, but I will," Lo continues, "*You're welcome.*" He sports a half-smile. "And you have the *shittiest* taste in guys. Besides this one." He gestures with his head to his brother.

"I definitely agree," I say with a pit in my stomach because I keep imagining Julian saying gross things and Ryke defending me. "…did Julian say something to you?" I ask Ryke.

His jaw hardens and after a long moment, he gets the words out. "He mentioned that you fucking talked to him."

"Briefly. Before I could use the bathroom at the party."

"I can't fucking believe he confronted you."

"I think he just wants me to send out a tweet to clear his name."

"Don't," Ryke forces.

"I never said I would." I push his mug back to him and then continue shaping my napkin flower. "Should I make a rose or a tulip?"

"This shouldn't be a real question," Rose snaps.

"Of course a rose," I say with sincerity. "Always a rose."

They all must sense my distraction off the topic of Julian, but no one reroutes it back to him, thankfully.

It's silent again.

"Can someone say something?" I ask. "You all don't have to watch me. I'm not going anywhere, I promise."

Lily flings her gangly arms around my waist, and I just see the tears in her eyes. I hug her back, and Rose uses my rose-shaped napkin to dab beneath her eyes. I think it's Rose's way of saying she was scared, and she's mighty glad I'm doing well.

Poppy reaches an arm out, holding my shoulder in a maternal, loving gesture.

That's when two waitresses arrive with plates of pancakes, waffles, eggs and toast, an omelet, and fruit parfait. They must've ordered while Ryke and I were in the bathroom.

I laugh when a bowl of cereal is placed in front of Ryke.

He gives his brother a look.

"You can't complain. This is what you always eat, bro."

"I eat fucking eggs too…" And just as he says it, a plate of eggs sets beside his bowl.

"You were saying?"

Years ago, Lo couldn't say one good thing about Ryke. Not out loud at least. Now he loves him enough to order his favorite breakfast foods. He knows him well enough to get it right.

This means so much to Ryke. I can see it in his eyes, and he just nods at Lo, unable to speak.

I'm waiting for what I guess will be chocolate chip waffles. The last plate drops in front of Lo, a breakfast burrito with hash browns, his hunger apparent as he immediately takes a bite.

They forgot to order for me, I guess. I'm about to flag down the waitress, but they both hurry off before I can call one of them over.

Ryke slides his plate of eggs over to me.

I push it back. "I'll order something." I do steal another tiny sip of his coffee, mostly preferring energy drinks, but Dr. Yoshida said to decrease my intake of caffeine. It'll help strengthen my chances of being fertile.

Rose cranes her neck over her shoulder, motioning to the waitress. My sister's piercing stare is shriveling the meek girl.

"It's okay," I tell Rose. "I'll just wait."

No one says anything, and only Lo is eating.

"You all can eat. It might take a while…" I trail off as a waiter appears, a plate in his hand. The minute it rests in front of me, I start crying.

It's a slice of chocolate cake.

Lily scoots against my side and she says, "Cake fixes everything, remember?"

I smile through my tears. *I remember.*

"Thank you," I whisper. How silly, to think my sisters would forget about me. They haven't.

Not in a long, long time.

< 31 >

Daisy Calloway

In the mid-January cold, I strut up to the elephant exhibit at the zoo. On a high-priority mission:

Ryke and Daisy's Grand & Daring Stakeout #6

My disguise: crimped blonde wig and heart-shaped sunglasses.

Limited info about this last New Year's flour-bomber—just "zoo-worker, brown hair, gray eyes, long sideburns"—means our likelihood of finding him is around 4%. Ryke still pushed the zoo trip harder than any of the last stakeouts.

I almost wonder if he made it all up to give me some hope and a whimsical zoo adventure. I don't want to ruin the fantasy, so I don't ask.

As soon as I lean a hip against the railing, elephants slowly trudging in their manmade habitat behind me, I swivel towards a handsome man. He canvasses the area, blue baseball cap dipped kind of low over his brown eyes.

I tap his shoulder. "Hi, sir, do you know if there are chickens at this zoo?" I ask like I've never met him in my life.

Ryke lowers his broody gaze down upon me. "You want to see a fucking chicken?"

"Yeah." I try hard not to smile. "I'm a big fan of cocks."

He so stoically keeps his composure like the last *four* times I tried to pick him up. At the penguin exhibit, the polar bears, the lions, and gorillas.

I'm hoping the elephants will bring me better luck.

"What kind of fucking cocks?" he asks, his rough exterior not crumbling.

"The large kind." I motion with my hands, about a foot and a half long. "Like this big."

His brows rise. "That big?" We unconsciously draw closer, until our legs touch.

"Oh yeah. They're the best cocks. Always up to play in the morning." I pause. "You wouldn't happen to have seen this cock around, would you?"

Ryke sweeps my body, warming me in the cold, and then he pulls my heart-shaped sunglasses halfway off my nose, eyes on my eyes. "Maybe check your fucking imagination. Because there are no cocks that size."

I feign disbelief. "No, this cock is real. Its favorite thing to do is be inside a field of daisies."

He pushes my sunglasses back up my nose. "Keep your cocks to yourself."

I'm the one who ends up smiling from ear-to-ear. I love flirting with him because he shuts me down, and I spend half the time poking at him while he attempts to keep a straight face.

"That seems awfully sad. Everyone who wants to see a big cock should be able to see at least one."

A nearby mom steers her kid away from me. I pretend to call after her but keep my voice soft, "We're just talking about the chicken exhibit."

When I turn to Ryke, he's finally smiling.

I gasp. "You like cocks too?"

He hooks his arm around my shoulders, bringing me into his chest. He kisses the top of my head, and his warmth cloaks me so very protectively.

I look up at him. "So it's been decided."

"What?"

"You like cock pickup lines."

"Fuck off," but he's grinning as he says it.

I brought my A-game by the penguins. *Are you sure you're not a sheep? Because your body is unbaaaalievable.* That was a major dud with Ryke, but a teenage girl giggled next to me. She understood the greatness of that line.

We walk together to the next exhibit, my gaze drifting along all the workers in khakis. "What about him?" I don't point, but Ryke follows my gaze to a thirty-something popcorn vendor. He has slight sideburns and brown hair.

With just a quick glance at the vendor, Ryke already shakes his head. "Doesn't look like him."

I notice a group of preteens ogling us instead of the giraffes. We're more inconspicuous separated, which is partly why I've been approaching him like a stranger. The other reason: it's just really, really fun.

"Do you want to split up and meet at the next place?" I ask him, lions roaring distantly. At the zoo, every human noise is accompanied by an animal one.

"You just picked up a fucking guy and you already want to ditch him," he teases me.

I slip my fingers in his belt loops, spinning around to face him. I walk backwards while he walks forwards. "Only to pick him up again and again and *again*." I smile wider, rising on the tips of my toes. "The thrill of it all."

I only now realize that we've stopped in the middle of the path, his gaze shining down on me. Watching me while I watch him. His hand slides against my cheek.

"You like this fucking guy?" he asks me in a low, husky voice.

"More than chocolate," I whisper.

Just as he leans down to kiss me, a crowd erupts with cheers. We part like we've been electrocuted, but no one is turned towards us. Large groups of families, couples, and friends are shifted towards the nearest exhibit.

We stand about ten feet from the pandas, and a zookeeper procures a microphone. "It's a girl!" she exclaims and everyone cheers, rushing closer to the barrier to see. An old lady slams into my shoulder on her way there, and Ryke pulls me closer to his side.

The panda just had a baby.

My lips downturn, the disappointment that I've shunned to the furthest parts of my soul starts bubbling to the surface.

Ryke whispers in my ear, "Let's see the fucking birds."

I smile weakly at him. "It's okay."

It's not okay.

I'm not pregnant. Again. The New Year's Eve false test can be added to the other ones. I shouldn't have even believed it could've been true.

He cups my face. "Hey, look at me."

I must be staring at the cement. I lift my downtrodden gaze.

"It's going to be okay," he says very slowly so these words sink inside me. "Whatever road we fucking take, *it's going to be okay.*"

"How do you know?" I wonder. How can he feel this and why can't I?

"Because I fucking have you, Calloway. I don't need anyone else."

I rub my leaking eyes, tearful way more than usual these days. When we started this journey, I never realized how many times the rug would be pulled from beneath us. How many times the universe would cackle in our faces. For someone who often keeps their emotions at bay, this process has ripped them to the surface.

I couldn't do this with anyone but Ryke.

In the background, the zookeeper is describing all the ways the mama panda will care for her baby. And I suddenly say to Ryke, "I can't help but feel like I'm failing you."

"No." His nose flares. "Don't ever fucking believe that because it's *not* fucking true." His unshaven jaw sets strictly.

"If time reversed itself," I wonder, "and you knew from the *very* beginning I might be infertile—would you even kiss me in the stairwell at Paris?"

I break into heavy tears because I imagine that scenario—where he never chooses me. It drives a cold wedge through my ribs.

He holds me tightly, hand pressed caringly to the back of my head while I cry in his chest. "I'm always kissing you in Paris, Dais. Every fucking time, I'm kissing you. There is nothing that'd change my course."

I feel him plant a warm kiss on my wet cheek. I try to wipe some of my tears. I need more reassurance these days, and I apologized once for it—and he told me to never apologize again. That he'd give me as many fucking truths about *us* as I needed. All I had to do was ask.

So I don't say *I'm sorry.*

I just repeat all his words in my head, feeling his confidence in the winding road we speed down. I take off my sunglasses, and he cleans the foggy lenses with his green shirt.

"We're okay?" he asks me, like it'd kill him if I said anything but yes.

I nod. "We're okay."

"Daisy Calloway!" someone shouts.

I instinctively turn my head, and the group of preteens squeals like I handed them their final piece of evidence in an ongoing mystery.

"Uh-oh," I mutter. *Cover blown.*

Ryke grips my waist and then hoists me on his shoulders. I begin to smile, high up and out of distance from any leering hands.

I wave to the girls from up here—since they seem like nice fans—and they take photos. Ryke heads towards the exit, gripping my shins while I play with his hair. He literally walks *ten* feet before large masses of people circle us.

Snapping photos. Asking questions over one another. Pointing.

"We're trying to fucking leave," Ryke tells them, but no one seems to hear or care.

Then someone tugs on my coat so Ryke will turn around, but it *pulls* me backwards. My heart is in my throat. "Don't pull," I tell the person.

Someone else tries instead.

Ryke feels the momentum yanking him, and instantly, he lifts me off his shoulders. My boots hit the path, and he wraps his arms around me, protecting me from the onslaught of bodies and eyes.

"Back the fuck up!" he shouts. "We're trying to leave."

A nice girl tries to create a narrow exit for us, shouting for people to let us pass.

I think it's right now, when a little boy with cotton candy points up at me, that I realize I'm an animal in this zoo.

Ryke guides me through a hole in the crowd. Pushing ahead. We knock shoulders and elbow sides, but there isn't time for apologies or sorry eyes. We just want to leave safely.

By the time we reach the exit, someone familiar waits there. In an expensive black suit and sunglasses, his shoulder is propped confidently on the wall of a gift shop, ankles crossed. Surrounded by four bodyguards, he basks in the attention.

No one hassles him, though they snap photos from faraway.

"I was going to meet you by the exhibits, but I thought I'd watch how you two handle the crowds. I needed a reminder on what a clusterfuck looks like." Connor Cobalt straightens off the wall and then nods to the gift shop. "It's empty." He goes inside, his bodyguards waiting by the door.

"Are we supposed to follow him?" I ask Ryke.

"Yeah," Ryke says with agitation. "What a fucking prick." Because Connor couldn't even say *come with me*. He demonstrates a lot more power when you follow out of freewill.

Truth be told, he is kind of godly. Just not the kind that I want in my arms. I clasp Ryke's hand and we disappear inside.

✿ ✿ ✿

"MY PRIVATE INVESTIGATOR HAS been tracking your private investigator," Connor explains by the rack of plush lions. "My PI also said that you two have been stalking potential perpetrators."

Ryke scowls. "No one is fucking *stalking* anyone."

I'm so spent energy-wise that I near laughter. Of course Connor found our PI. Of *course* he has come to slap our wrists for our dangerous wrongdoings. What other scenario is there?

This is the way we all go.

I snort.

Connor arches a brow at me. "What's amusing about this—other than the fact that you two are searching in a zoo?"

I catch Ryke mouthing the words, *shut the fuck up.*

I've known all along, Ryke. We were never supposed to be in the zoo. I think I love him more for that. He just wanted to cheer me up.

"Did you find your home with the primates satisfactory?" Connor asks him. "Or were there not enough bananas for you?"

Ryke outstretches his arm. "Did you come here just to bust my fucking balls? You could have done this over the fucking phone."

"Stop searching for these flour-bombers. It will lead you both nowhere. It's a waste of time, and I'd let you both waste yours but I can't…" He takes a brief pause, lips tightening like he senses more emotion on the rise than he predicted. "I can't watch you two put your excess energy in *this* because it has no good ending, and you both need one."

He's telling us that we're chasing after shadows.

Stopping feels like an even bigger defeat. Like crumpling a treasure map. Destroying the message in a bottle before letting it float out to sea.

I'd rather keep the slightest hope alive. Even if we're fooling ourselves. Is that so bad?

"I thought you were going to keep your fucking opinions to your-self," Ryke rebuts, his tone a little less antagonistic but still pissed.

"I know. This is the last time. Consider it a bonus. I don't give those often, so take pleasure in it while you can."

Ryke must feel the same as me about the entire ordeal because he says, "Tell your PI to leave our fucking PI alone."

Connor is blank-faced. "You're a stubborn piece of work, my friend."

I smile at the *my friend* part. "Have you seen the ship names of you two on Twitter?" I ask them.

Their alpha male statures rotate fully to me.

Ryke frowns. "What the fuck do you mean?"

Connor begins, "A ship name is—"

"I know what it fucking is." Lily and Lo described it a long time ago, when the fandom culture was pretty new to all of us. "I don't understand why *we* have one together."

I pick up a plush lion with a tag that says *my name is Leo*. "During New Year's Eve," I explain, "when Connor let you stay at the party after…" I don't mention the fight but Ryke nods, understanding that part. "Willow said the Twitterverse went insane and started calling you *friends*. Now you have a ship name."

Connor wears 0% surprise.

I smile at him. "You know it, don't you?"

Ryke's brows furrow. "What the fuck is it?"

"CoKe," Connor answers in a flat tone, but mild annoyance crosses his face. Probably at the prospect of sharing *anything* with Ryke.

Ryke repeatedly shakes his head. "Unfuckingbelievable."

Coke, like Pepsi, has always been Fizzle's nemesis, and in a way, it's kind of wrong that Ryke and Connor have a ship name based on our family's competitor.

Though when you remember how much they do not mix. How much they never seem to gel. Two men who see the world in vastly different ways and vastly different colors. Forced to be around each other. Forced to cultivate something. I believe any name for Ryke and Connor would have to be a little wrong to be right. Whether they like it or not, it really fits.

And their friendship isn't as fragile or as breakable as they'd like to imagine. You see, I have this theory.

Relationships that take the most effort and the most time become the *mightiest*, most resilient bonds in the end. So if this theory proves right, their friendship will be the strongest of them all.

As the Twitter topic dies off and we're left with the lingering one of private investigators and potential flour-bombers, Connor studies my expression that I try to hide with fifty-foot high walls and iron bars.

If anyone can see through them though, it's these two men.

"I really wish you would consider waiting for Rose to be a surrogate," he says. "It's a goal that may bring you more happiness in the very end than these ones."

I joke, "You want your wife to carry Ryke's baby?"

"For you two, we'd do almost anything."

Connor was the one who discovered the child pornography tapes of me. He's why Scott Van Wright went to jail and why Scott's friends won't ever replay those videos and violate me.

I've never said *thank you* to Connor, but I'm so immeasurably grateful for what he did. I nod to him and whisper, "I know you would. Thank you."

If anyone is smart enough to see the depth of my words, it's him.

I just wish he could also offer a platter of false hope.

You'll be pregnant in no time, Daisy!

You'll catch those flour-bomb attackers and stop another one from happening, Daisy!

You'll save the day!

Why can't reality be as sweet and victorious as fairytales? I can only clasp Ryke's hand and wish upon a star that one day, it will be.

< 32 >

Ryke Meadows

Another month has passed and she's still not pregnant.

The only thing that's growing is the fucking struggle. Daisy's last period put her in excruciating pain. I had to watch her curl up into a ball and hug a pillow like she was *dying*. And I couldn't do much but carry her where she needed to go and give her a heating pad.

Neither of us said it out loud, but we know her cyst is the fucking culprit. I'm concerned about her egg reserve. When she had surgery on the left ovary, her doctor said the "chocolate fluid" polluted the quality of the eggs. So her right ovary is all she really has for surrogacy and IVF.

I've read enough and called the doctor too many fucking times to be blind to her situation. If the cyst grows to 3 cm (it's currently 2 cm), it'll need to be removed before IVF. Then the risks are exponentially higher, leading to infection and possibly decreasing her egg reserve *again*.

As the months pass us by, surrogacy seems like the safer option, but Dais isn't ready to give up. In the end, I'm just really fucking worried about her health.

She's my first priority.

And our lives have to move on *together*.

It's why I'm about to leave for Connor and Rose's house where she's currently at with my brother and Lily. I'm stuck in Fizzle headquarters with Greg Calloway, Samuel Stokes, and four other businessmen whose names I can't remember. All congregated at a long conference table. Images of the first cans of Fizz are framed on the walls behind me.

I slip on my leather bike jacket, thinking they'll take the fucking hint that I need to leave.

"This has to be the most challenging rock face that you've ever climbed," a man with a gray mustache tells me, sliding a stack of papers across the table. We've been discussing my next commercial for Ziff where I'm supposed to be free-solo climbing. They keep repeating words like "astonishing" and "jaw-dropping" and "extraordinary"— while Greg and Sam have stayed fucking quiet.

I roughly flip through the papers, grazing over some of the rock faces they've chosen. I shake my head slowly and then more rapidly. "These are fucking *impossible* to climb without a harness. It's never been done."

What I did before—the Yosemite Triple Crown—*that* was the hardest thing I've ever accomplished while free-soloing. But I wasn't the first to do it.

"That's the point," a younger man tells me. "It'll be covered on the news. It'll give the most exposure to the sports drink that *you're* promoting."

I hate how he emphasizes that word. Like reinforcing that this is a fucking job. I understand that I'm not climbing just for fun when I endorse Fizzle, but I only started doing this because Greg asked me to.

The older businessman with the mustache slides over a check. I've never been enticed by money. I'd climb if it said ten bucks, but when they're impatient to increase the difficulty, everything fucking changes.

I have to think about time. I have to think about Daisy. I have to think about consequences and my little brother. Will cash persuade me? Will it push me towards a rock face I'd *never* consider trying? I'm not sure.

And I fucking know…this is what Lo was afraid of.

I flip over the check, and it knocks me back. *Fuck.*

"You'll have that after you film the commercial," he tells me.

My life is worth ten million dollars.

"This is an annual sum," he elaborates. "You'll be paid this every year until the commercial is no longer on the air. It's the same kind of contract as your other ones."

Sam finally speaks up. "Do you think there's a cliff that you can climb that has the same…appeal as Yosemite but is easier for you?"

"I spent years practicing before I free-soloed the Triple Crown. I can't just fucking emulate the same thing without time." Challenging ascents usually tempt me, but the prep time for this kind of climb is not appealing right now.

I'm at a different place in my fucking life. I'd rather free-solo rock faces that don't take years to map out—that aren't mentally exhausting.

Greg leans forward in his leather chair. "We can't wait more than a year to film this." He laces his fingers together, brows knotted in contemplation. "What's the risk if you free-solo climb something on par with Yosemite?"

He doesn't fucking realize? I scratch my jaw and just say it. "Death."

His gaze fixes to his hands, color draining from his face. Everyone's watching him. Everyone's fucking quiet.

"I want to help you out here," I tell them as my phone buzzes.

I think it's someone chastising me for being late. I'm already worked up about it, my chair pushed back from the table, ready to storm out of here. Today isn't just an ordinary day.

I need verification that you're my boyfriend. Send me proof.
– Daisy

I almost smile, but really, the text causes me to stand the fuck up.

"Wait," Greg says, gesturing for me to take a seat.

"It's Daisy's fucking birthday," I remind him. We had breakfast with her parents this morning and they're not a part of tonight's events, so I'm not surprised that he thinks her birthday has already passed.

"Can you give us a list of comparable climbs that you think are doable in the allotted time frame?" Greg asks me.

I grip the back of my chair, still standing. "If you want me to do *anything* on the scale of the Triple Crown, I need more than a year and time that I don't fucking have."

"What are you doing?" Greg asks. "Once your wedding is over, you should be available."

My jaw hardens.

I'm trying to have a fucking baby.

I can't say it.

I've been helping Daisy with the early stages of her summer camp.

I can't say it.

In my spare time, I'd rather rock climb things that I'm pretty fucking sure won't kill me.

I can't say it.

"If this isn't important to you, just let me know," Greg says off my silence. "We can find another person to be the face of Ziff."

Is he fucking kidding me? "Do you want me to die?" I ask point-blank.

"Ryke," Sam warns like I've crossed a line. If anyone's crossed one, it's Greg.

"I want you to be committed to this company," Greg explains. "You have no other job but this one, and it's important to me that you have motivation. You're about to marry my twenty-one-year-old daughter."

All I hear is a father saying: *I don't want my youngest daughter hitched to a bum.*

I have drive for the things I fucking love, and I have medals, awards, and articles about races I've won, climbs I've done. None of that matters to him. Not even my passion for running or rock climbing.

He just cares about the check.

And he's the one supplying it.

I keep shaking my head, disagreeing with him on so many fucking points. I know my limits. I'm always confident I can make an ascent when I begin one. Anything less is fucking suicide.

"This is bullshit," I say aloud.

Greg flinches in surprise, but I don't care.

"I've said *yes* to practically everything you've thrown at me since I signed onto Ziff, and I'm fucking here on my fiancée's birthday. I'm saying *no* right now, and you're going to fucking hear me."

Sam covers his face with his hand.

I don't care about him either.

The oldest man in the room clears his throat. "How about we do more research? We can find a rock face that we all agree on?"

"It's ten million dollars a year," another businessman says like I'm an idiot.

Don't think about the money, I tell myself. My phone buzzes again.

Do you know where I can find my wolf? — Daisy

"I have to go," I say, and as I turn towards the door, Greg speaks.

"Can you check your email and answer the phone when Sam calls? We'll try to find something comparable but safer. I don't want to lose you on a climb, Ryke. I'm just trying to understand."

I nod, agreeing to this, but I know my brother will fucking hate it, even if the rock face is to my standards.

After I leave, I start walking down the carpeted hallway towards the elevators.

I text Daisy back: proof and add a photo in my camera roll that I took a couple days ago for her. Naked, a close-up on my abs and cock, beads of water rolling down after my shower.

I press send.

My phone vibrates quickly.

Omg you're totally my boyfriend! — Daisy

And then another text.

I remember that cock inside of me. I remember touching those abs. — Daisy

I almost fucking harden. While I wait for the elevator, I text her again: I'm your fucking fiancé.

I need another picture to verify that title ;) — Daisy

Cute, I text her and then I send her another picture that I've taken, similar to the other one, only with more of my face.

She's asked me before if I want her to send photos back, but I'd rather risk nudes of me appearing online. I won't fucking care if the world sees my cock, but she'd care if the world sees her body. She's really visually stimulated, so I fucking love doing it.

Just as the elevator doors open, my phone buzzes again.

You're him. I would recognize that super handsome scowl everywhere. (Even on the moon.) — Daisy

My lips rise, ready to be near her. Then I remember the plans to turn her birthday into a joint bachelor and bachelorette party.

I just hope everything about tonight doesn't go fucking wrong.

< **33** >

Daisy Calloway

I stand outside Connor and Rose's house while Coconut sniffs for a good place to do her business. I bounce on my toes, trying to warm myself since I left my green cargo jacket inside.

Coconut proudly pees on the Cobalt's frozen fountain.

"Let's just keep that between you and me," I tell Coconut.

Her tail wags, liking our secret.

Tulip trees on either side of the driveway stand skeletal in February's cold winter, but Rose and Connor's ten-bedroom mansion still captures a storybook aura that I've never felt or seen before. White siding with gray stone, colossal double doors, regal molding, and rose bushes.

I can't imagine anything fitting them better, and it's on the same street as Lily and Lo's eight-bedroom cozy house. Where I currently live.

Ryke and I haven't really talked about moving out.

Not because we don't want to or are afraid to say goodbye to my sister and his brother. It's just that there's not much for sale right now—not only on Whisper Ridge Road but in the whole gated neighborhood. For security reasons, we don't want to take our chances anywhere else.

A motorcycle revs up the driveway just as Coconut finishes peeing. She skips around the fountain.

As he slows to a stop, Ryke removes his helmet, his dark brown hair disheveled. He scans my bare arms like I'm insane. "It's fucking freezing."

I suddenly recall the pictures he sent me in text, and my neck heats. "I have this theory…" I begin.

He leans his Ducati on its kickstand. "Are you fucking barefoot?" he asks, edging up to me.

I glance at my unpolished toes. "Maybe next time I'll remember them, huh?"

He messes my hair and then wraps his arm around my shoulder. I whistle and Coconut bounds ahead of us up the stone steps.

"What's your fucking theory?" he asks as we near the front door.

Oh right. "If I stay out in the cold long enough, my eggs will freeze and last *forever,*" I say theatrically and outstretch my arms like I'm catching snowflakes.

Ryke is not amused. As we enter the house, he slams the door a little too loudly. The crystal chandelier rattles from the vaulted ceiling. We stand beneath, and Coconut plops down on the fairytale staircase beside us.

Voices echo from the nearby living room, but Ryke's focus is all on me.

"That's the stupidest fucking thing I've heard from you all week."

I set my hands on my hips. "Lily told me that Captain America was frozen for years and never aged when he woke up."

"You can't freeze your fucking eggs when they're still inside of you."

Egg retrieval and my egg reserve have been troubling me a lot, especially since pregnancy seems more unlikely without IVF. "I like Lily's logic more than yours," I say. "No offense."

He suddenly clasps my hand and leads me rapidly, almost in a sprint, down a dim hallway, towards a backdoor. My pulse picks up speed, and I already begin to smile.

Before I ask where we're going, he says, "Let's go do something fucking crazy, Calloway."

Something fucking crazy.

I like the sound of that.

< 34 >

Ryke Meadows

We're really fucking freezing now.

After catching Daisy around the waist and throwing her in the Cobalt's glacial-cold pool—I never took my arms off her, so I jumped in too—we ran back inside, straight for the laundry room. Sopping wet, teeth chattering.

Smiling.

I undress her fast, pulling off her cold clothes, and her fingers move quickly all over me. Shedding mine. We don't speak, but our hands do. Caring about her fucking warmth, I squeeze out her drenched hair and then yank off her jeans and roll down her panties. She steps out of them.

After less than thirty seconds, we're fucking naked, and I don't see any nearby towels—

"These look clean." Daisy refers to the stack of folded laundry on top of a granite counter.

I push my wet hair out of my fucking face. "Don't hand me Cobalt's underwear." I'd never hear the end of it, even more than when I wore Lily's panties.

She grins mischievously and then tosses me something black while she picks out an article of clothing for herself.

I unfold the black material. *Drawstring pants.* I quickly step into them, beads of water still rolling down my chest and abs.

Daisy shivers as she tugs on an extra-large shirt with the black and gold Fizzle logo. After living with Rose, I've seen her wear these outdated and faded nineties shirts when she cleans bathrooms. I'm not surprised one is in the stack of clothes.

As soon as the shirt falls at her thighs, I lift Daisy up onto the dryer. I throw all of our wet clothes inside, and she presses *start.* The machine rumbles to life, and I rub her arms, trying to create more fucking heat.

She kicks her feet back and forth, watching me fervently. Her hair still soaks into her shirt, by the tops of her breasts, so I twist the brown strands again. Wringing the water out.

She's fucking grinning.

And then her legs part to accommodate my body between them.

I harden, the length of my cock clear in Connor's drawstring pants. I watch her eyes dip down and then back up. She must notice mine doing the same to her, lingering on her thighs. Her skin is chilly, and I stroke her bare leg, reaching towards her ass.

We lock eyes and then I feel a tug on the strings of my pants, drawing me even fucking closer.

The laundry room is adjacent to the living room. Muffled voices filter through the closed door, but everything drowns out. Because Daisy is in front of me.

She vibrates on the dryer, eyes alight.

I hold the side of her head, my other hand caressing her thigh.

She stops shivering, color in her cheeks. Her palm slides beneath my waistband and onto my cock.

Fuck. I let out a low grunt, pressure welling in my dick, and I lean forward, my breath warming her neck. "Dais…"

"In the wild," she says, "animals use sex to heat up their bodies."

I imagine myself deep between her legs, listening to her fucking cries. The ones that puncture with *I can't*, only to be reinforced that she *can*.

I comb her cold hair out of her face. "Is that fucking so?" I ask.

She nods slowly. "Those are just the rules of the animal kingdom."

I remove her hand from my cock, not having enough control in this fucking second to let her rub me. I hold her other cheek with my hand and kiss her tenderly. Then more strongly and ardently. Parting her lips with my tongue.

My hand returns to her thigh, kneading and rubbing her flesh.

A moan catches in her throat, causing all my blood to rush down. I play with her tongue again, and then slowly, my thumb trails up and brushes her clit. Lightly. *Harder.*

She trembles against my chest, not soaked but not dry either.

I slip one finger inside her warmth.

She bucks at my touch. *Fuck, Dais.* My body grinds against hers.

"Ryke," she breathes, a cry attached to my name. She clutches onto me, and I kiss the base of her neck, her collarbone.

About to drop to my fucking knees. I freeze as my lips press to her nipple on the outside of her shirt.

Chatter, out in the living room, amplifies. Coming closer and closer. *Fuck*—and not the fucks I like. I swiftly break from her, pushing her legs closed.

Daisy's lips are puffy and red, but she gives me the biggest lopsided grin and hangs onto my waist. I keep an arm around her shoulder, just as the door swings open.

"Serious question." Lily appears, but she's on her phone staring hard at the screen. "Should I post the video of you two to Snapchat, Instagram, or Twitter?"

Daisy's eyes bug, probably thinking her sister just filmed me finger-fucking her. "What video?"

Lily looks up, puzzled for a quick moment. "Did I…interrupt something?" Her cheeks flush, and she peeks at my crotch.

I angle my body more towards the dryer—so she can't see the outline of anything.

She relaxes some but her ears turn red.

Just then, my little brother passes through the open door, a bowl of chips smothered in salsa in hand. He pops them in his mouth. "They wouldn't fuck in Connor and Rose's laundry room, love. It's far too clean in here." He motions to the spotless room, except for water puddles. "There's no dirt and there's not a view of the moon. Definitely not their thing."

"Fucking hilarious."

He flashes me a half-smile and eyes my clothing. "Looks like you love Connor enough that you'll wear his pants. They look good on you, bro."

I flip him off and then nod to Lily. "What fucking video?"

I'm not sure how many she's snapped so far, but she has permission from us to take as many and as much as she can all night. We're documenting the party for social media.

For a fucking reason.

If the world believes we're having our bachelor and bachelorette party *now*, they'll think our wedding will be within the week.

We're marrying July 15th, not even close to February. The day we chose fit around everyone's work schedules and Rose's September due date. She'll be pretty fucking pregnant by our wedding, but she says it won't bar her from flying. Her doctor has the final say-so, and we're all crossing our fingers.

And social media tonight is *our* chance to have a paparazzi-free ceremony. They'll think they missed some secret event and just move on from the topic.

Lily spins her phone to us and plays a video.

In the short clip, I pretend to toss Daisy into the pool but hold her back once, then twice. She's not fighting to stay on the cement. She kicks *towards* the water with a laugh, and then I throw her in while she's still in my arms. Her voice fades with our splash.

I can hear Lo in the background saying, *goddamn.*

Daisy smiles and tightens the strings on my pants, tying it into a bow.

"I'm thinking Twitter, but I don't know," Lily contemplates.

"Whatever is fine," I tell her, bending down to check our clothes in the dryer. My shirt is still soaked. Daisy's panties are too damp to wear, and I slam the door shut, a little pissed I didn't think to strip before we jumped.

Not like I wanted to fucking skinny dip at Connor and Rose's place.

Lo crunches on a chip. "Hashtag Raisins Need More Love."

I shoot him my middle finger again and then lift Daisy off the dryer, setting her on her feet. She quickly tugs the hem of her shirt down, covering her ass and thighs.

"The problem starts with your ship name," Lo tells us.

Lily peers up from her phone. "It's Raisy."

Here we go again.

Ignoring her, Lo says, "You know what happens when I see raisins in a cookie or a slice of bread? I think, *get the fuck away from me. You've ruined my food.* You don't want that negativity attached to your ship name."

His logic is as fucking weird as his wife's. I hate to even think it, but I'd prefer Connor's right now.

"You're called a fucking cinnamon roll," I retort like that makes as much sense as raisins. It's his favorite dessert, but Daisy said that Willow explained "cinnamon roll" had nothing to do with what he eats. Just an "amazing" coincidence.

I'm actually really fucking confused.

"Yeah," Lo rebuts, "and who doesn't love a cinnamon roll?"

Lily says to me, "Beautiful cinnamon roll, too good for this world, too pure."

That's it. Everyone's lost their fucking minds.

Daisy smiles. "It's a meme, Ryke."

"Don't try to explain it to him," Lo says. "It took him a solid six months to fully function on Twitter."

"Fuck you."

"Hashtag Raisin Hell."

"It's *Raisy*," Lily emphasizes for the millionth time since Dais and I have been together.

"Sounds like a bunch of raisins to me."

Lily, distracted, squints at her phone with a pout, taking the video post to heart way more than us. I think about all those magazine headlines about *three-ways* between Lil, my brother, and me. Sometimes, I forget how much invisible, jagged tension cuts between Lily and Daisy.

Lily feels guilty and wants to do *everything* in her fucking power to show how much "Ryke and Daisy" are meant to be. And not her and me.

Daisy feels guilty for Lily's remorse. Lily feels responsible for Daisy's pain. This vicious fucking cycle has been churning for years. I hate that these rumors and perceptions have festered this deep and this long. I don't even know if the girls can climb over it all.

Lily starts typing. "I'm going to do a hashtag with *Raisy is Alive*."

"I like it," Daisy says, giving her sister two thumbs-up.

#TeamRaisy is one of the only things that unifies them against the *three-way* shit. As much as Lo teases about *raisins*, he knows it too.

"We better go back," Lo says. "Can't keep the King and Queen waiting."

When we return to the living room, I immediately see Moffy staring at a comic book beside the unlit fireplace while Janie inspects a teal rattle toy. Moffy struggles to flip the very thin pages, and Lo sets his bowl on the coffee table to help his son.

I guide Daisy around the couch, my hands firm on her shoulders, and then stop as soon as Connor carries an overflowing plastic tub full of feather boas, tiaras, and what looks like a penis piñata. Rose appears and unleashes a flurry of pink and black balloons with the words *Blow Me* and *Pop Me*.

I watch them float to the ceiling.

"Fucking really?" I'm mostly surprised they went this all-out to help us trick the world. Then again, Rose likes the act of decorating a party more than the fucking party.

Connor sets the plastic tub beside the couch. "I'd answer you, but that would be recognizing your statement as a real, viable question. Which I don't." His eyes flit to Daisy's shirt and then my pants. Amusement lights his eyes, and his grin is fucking palpable.

"Don't fucking ask," I snap.

"I don't have to ask to know," he says easily. "And Ryke?"

"Yeah?"

"Don't cum in my pants."

Lo starts laughing so hard I think he may roll over onto the fireplace. Daisy's body vibrates with growing laughter too.

I spin her around. "You think that's funny, Calloway?" I try to pretend to be fucking serious about it but a smile toys with my lips the longer I watch her brim with enjoyment.

She tries to bottle the sentiments and put on a straight face. "That was the *un-funniest* un-funny thing I've ever heard. Who would laugh at such things?" Her lips curve up and then she snorts.

I push her shoulder, and then she pushes mine, a wicked grin rising.

Rose snaps her fingers at us. "Less flirting, more concentration." She passes silver sashes to us. *I'm the fucking bachelor* on one and *I'm the fucking bachelorette* on the other. Lily and Lo are already fixing paper crowns that say *Maid of Honor* and *Best Man* respectively.

It's like we're putting on a play, and in some way, this is theater for the outside world.

"Willow and Garrison are stuck in traffic," Lily says, her cell still cupped in her hands. "They're getting the cake." My relationship with Willow hasn't stepped out of the "awkward" phase, and I've given it a lot of fucking time to change naturally. *Don't be pushy with her*, I've told myself. Now I'm starting to wonder if it'll ever be different than what it is.

Daisy tugs my sash, capturing my attention, and the longer my features remain fixed and hard, the more she inches closer. I shove her shoulder lightly again.

She breaks into a grin and then tries to thrust me back—I seize her wrist and pull her to my chest. In seconds, I hoist Daisy over my shoulder and then slam her back onto the couch cushions. A breath catches in her throat like oxygen lashes her lungs.

I climb on top, ensuring her fucking extra-large shirt isn't rolled up. Then I place my hands on the armrest above her head. Her green eyes, full of curiosity, sparkle up at me.

Lo butts in, "Where's your phone?"

It takes me a long fucking moment to process his question, unable to tear my gaze off her. "My bike jacket."

Daisy writhes beneath me and tries to seize my arms. To pin me. I nuzzle her cheek with my jaw and scoop her waist, lifting her body up against mine.

"What's your password?" Lo asks.

"2108."

I ask Lo, "Why do you need my fucking phone?"

Daisy snatches my left wrist, our legs woven together, and then we somehow roll off the fucking couch, wrestling. Like animals.

She pants with excitement, lifting my arms, thinking she can pin me this time. Then I slide on top of her, reversing the fucking position. I rake my fingers through her hair, and she clutches my thick brown strands. I nip her ear with my teeth, and her smile stretches wider.

I keep yanking her shirt down, covering her thighs. My muscles flex, my weight almost bearing down on her, but I prop half my body off Daisy's long, slender frame.

She raises her head, her lips nearing my lips. And she whispers, "What are you going to do to me, pack leader?"

My blood heats, and in the pit of her ear, I murmur, "Make wolf pups with you."

Daisy almost lets out a breathy cry, but my hand runs over her mouth, quieting the noise.

"Goddamn, where is your photo app?" Lo asks, scrolling through my cell.

I go rigid and realize he never answered my previous question. Or maybe he did, and I just didn't hear. "You're going through my photos?" I sit up while Daisy's eyes grow wide in horror.

Lo leans against the fireplace. "We're trying to post more Raisin pics on Twitter. Lily wants your selfies."

Fuck.

I practically spring to my fucking feet. Because my "selfies" aren't the kind Lily is referring to. "Hey, get off my phone. Let me just send them to you." I haven't counted how many dick pics I have saved in my photo album, but it'd probably take him less than a fucking second to stumble over one.

I sprint across the living room to reach my brother. And then noises *blare* from my cell's speakers at loud volume.

High-pitched cries of pleasure.

Daisy's cries.

My low groan in the background.

Fuck.

Fuck.

The bottom of my stomach just drops, and dread contorts Lo's face before cementing in a cringe. By the fireplace, I go to steal my cell back, but in horror, Lo flings my phone as far from himself as possible.

Across the fucking room.

It thuds on the rug. By Connor's feet.

I catch a glimpse of Daisy, sinking into the couch with bright red cheeks, mortified.

Fuck me. I set my hands on my head, drop them, and then fucking race over to Connor to end this. The video clip plays, loudly enough that Rose is frozen in utter shock by the plastic tub of boas.

Lily covers her ears with her hands, eyes tightened shut.

"I can't…" emits from the speakers followed by a breathy gasp.

Daisy buries her face into a pillow.

"Shut it off," I tell Connor, and right as I approach him, he picks up the phone, eyes flitting to the screen, and calmly hands me the cell. Like it's nothing.

I hastily mute the fucking video, an *extreme* close-up of my cock thrusting into Daisy. I rub my face once, the silence deafening.

My main concern is Daisy, who's red hot with embarrassment.

<$ 35 $>

Daisy Calloway

W hat.
          The.
Fuck.

I open my mouth to toss out a joke, lighten the awkward tension, but my mind is a black abyss. As though to protect me from replaying one of the most embarrassing moments of my life.

Ryke gestures to the silent room. "Forget this. It never fucking happened." He grips his cell in a tight fist and his dark concern pinpoints on me.

I doubt he'd care as much if he thought I didn't care, but I can't even pretend to be nonchalant about it. Because Connor Cobalt and Loren Hale just saw a close-up of Ryke sticking his dick in me. Oh and not to mention, the *entire* room heard my orgasm.

The couch cushion undulates as Ryke sinks beside me. He holds my horror-stricken body, and I bury my face in the crook of his arm and mutter, "What the fuck." I rarely even curse but this is the most accurate phrase to describe the situation and how I feel.

What. The. Fuck.

Ryke presses his palm to my burning cheek and forehead and then kisses the top of my head.

My heart rate slows a fraction with his compassion and concern, but then, of course, someone worsens the already worst moment.

"Look, love," Lo says to Lily. "Two-thirds of us have sex tapes, and we're not one of them."

Ryke glowers. "It's not a fucking sex tape."

Lo tilts his head like *you have to be fucking kidding*. "Just because it's shitty quality doesn't mean it's not a sex tape, bro. It has audio and graphic nudity. I know porn when I see it."

Oh my God. Please stop talking about this, Lo.

Everyone begins taking seats around the room, and the penis piñata falls out of the tub. A *Blow Me* balloon pops, and I refuse to make eye contact with Connor. Besides Ryke, the safest place to look is at Rose.

She crosses her ankles on the Queen Anne chair, coming down from her initial bout of shock. "We have to move on from this."

Please, yes.

Ryke strokes my hair, and I take a deep breath.

Lo snaps, "That's easy for you to say. You didn't *see* the video or your brother's dick pics."

Ugh, the heat of this moment will not end.

"That'd be impossible," Rose retorts, "I don't *have* a brother."

Lo shoots her a sharpened glare. "Why do you always have to be such a smarty-pants, Angelica?"

"Because I loathe you." She whips her hair off her left shoulder and then clasps her hands.

No one chastises us for filming the video. If it leaked online, people wouldn't be able to tell who's in the clip, too close-up. Ryke could also run naked through Philly with paparazzi taking photos and he wouldn't even care. He told me that once, along with: "My body is *my* fucking body, even if someone sees it, it's still mine."

I realized something then. Each of us falls under different spectrums of what makes us comfortable and what makes us tic. I like that I've found my boundaries and that Ryke knows his.

The room hushes.

Through the tense silence and their brief glances at me, all I hear is, *we just saw your anatomy and Ryke's anatomy join forces in the most intimate way possible. How do you feel about that?*

Not good.

Not good at all.

If only the cake arrived right now. Cake would fix this.

I risk a peek at Connor. His brow arches at me in knowing, not uncomfortable at all.

My neck scalds, and Ryke kisses my temple, trying to fix this so I'm no longer burnt red.

"So…" Lily says on the loveseat beside her husband, her *Maid of Honor* crown crooked. "…you watch it while you…have sex?"

"Mmmm?" My mind is like *does not compute. Can't compute. Males named Connor & Loren in room.* I've made plenty of sex jokes in the past, but I totally blank when my real sex life is blown up in their faces. "Mmmhmm." I nod. "Yep. You know…all of that." I try to plaster on a smile.

Dig that grave, Daisy.

"I can't say this is something I've never seen before," Connor quips to Ryke. Since he saw Ryke come on my face? "Personally, I'd like to stop meeting your dick like this."

"Fuck off," Ryke says.

Lo begins to laugh, his comic book in hand.

Lily smacks his chest. "It's not funny. My sister is upset."

He feigns hurt, hand to his heart.

She goes for the jugular by trying to steal his comic. She only grips one end and he yanks the other, morphing into a tug-of-war. Her cheeks redden in effort while Lo barely does a thing.

"Let…go," she huffs.

"Is that a little bicep?" He squeezes her nonexistent muscle. "Damn, love, don't Hulk out on me."

"You're being an ass."

"I'm always an ass, Lily Hale, and I don't like sharing my toys." He pries the comic, and she loses her grip completely.

I clap at her valiant effort, happy for the distraction.

Rose rises on her heels and then takes center room. I straighten up, realizing that she's shifting the spotlight off me too. She has a penis wand in hand, so confident and poised.

I immediately smile, less and less mortified.

Ryke seems to relax when I begin to too.

"Bets are open," Rose declares and gestures the wand from her chest to Connor's. "We've decided not to know the gender of the baby, so you all can start guessing."

"Depends on what you want," Lo says first, "and then I'm going to bet on the exact opposite."

Rose rolls her eyes dramatically. "Juvenile as always, Loren."

Before Lo can retort, Lily cuts in with a raise of her hand. Rose points the wand at my older sister. "Go."

Lily stares at the penis wand for an extra second, her eyes narrowing— probably not used to being called on like that. At least, this is my theory.

Lily clears her throat. "Are you still leaving how many children you have up to fate?" Good question. A while back, Rose declared that she'd only have as many kids as it'd take for Jane to have a sister. That means if she has a daughter next, the Cobalt family will be finished growing.

"Yes," Rose says. "And I want whatever fate brings me." Her eyes flit to Lo. "So I'll be happy with either a boy or a girl." My older sister has *always* been superstitious and a believer in destiny and so forth, so her proclamation doesn't surprise anyone.

"And you, love?" Lo asks Connor.

He smiles. "I'd like a boy." He doesn't explain further, but we all know he wants a large family. A boy would mean they would try again for a girl. I wonder why he agreed to her whole "fate plan" if he really wants the big Cobalt empire. But then again, I think I already know. I see it in the way he looks at her, like he'd give up this one thing in his life if it'd please Rose.

It's love.

"Bets?" Rose asks, waving the penis wand around. Lily scoots back like she's scared it's going to fling in her face.

My eyes fall to Rose's belly and I frown. She looks…a little bigger than she was last time. Maybe? I don't know. It's not like I stare at Rose's pregnant belly a lot, especially not recently.

I have to ask though.

"Rose," I say with a fading smile, "have you been lying about how far along you are? It's okay if you have…"

Her face falls, and regret assails me for a hot second. I called Rose a liar, which is somewhere around "cheater" in her rings of hell.

"I'm sorry," I say with all sincerity, "I just—"

"*No*," she says firmly. "I wouldn't lie to you about my pregnancy."

I can tell I hurt her, even thinking that she would have deceived me. This is Rose Calloway. The sister who'd hop into a sinking ship with Lily and me. Just to be another pair of hands, urgently and untiringly scooping water out until we all drowned together.

And not only that—she just deflected an incredibly embarrassing moment of mine with ease and without question.

I explain myself the best I can. "It's just that you look a little bigger than last time."

Lo audibly winces. "It's been nice knowing you."

Rose raises a hand at Lo to shut up, but her strong gaze never leaves me. "I was going to tell you tomorrow. I didn't want to take away from your party."

"Okay…" I'm lost on where she's headed.

Connor wears a knowing look, but everyone else seems just as confused as me.

"Christ, don't say it," Lo interjects, "the baby has hooves."

"*Babies*," Rose amends.

My mind can barely process the word. Or even the plural form of it. Lo immediately glares. "You were going to let us bet on the gender when you're having goddamn twins? That's the dirtiest thing you two have done in a while."

I tune out the rest of their conversation, but the air coils in taut strands. I stand to go hug my sister, wanting people to keep it light. We're happy. We're all happy. I don't know why I have to keep repeating it.

Rose points that penis wand at me threateningly. "*No* hugs." She's not smiling and I wonder if it hurts her to look at me. If it will always hurt to look at me.

"Congratulations, big sis," I say, my smile rising with my joy. However dulled, it's still there for her. "I hope it's two boys, so you can have your empire."

She gives me a look like *what the fuck are you talking about* and turns the penis wand on herself, jabbing it at her chest. "*I* said nothing about an empire."

Before I can say anything more, Lily attack hugs her from the side, coming out of seemingly nowhere. Rose glowers at her like she's a barnacle that has attached itself to the S.S. Rose Calloway Cobalt.

Ryke touches the back of my thigh and I turn to see him. My smile wanes at his hardened brows and those brown eyes that reflect all our struggles. We're still trying to have one baby, and Rose was lucky enough to have *two*.

The pang of jealously slides below my happiness for her, but I can't ignore its existence. I hate that it's there, honestly. I just wish this was easier.

I slump down beside Ryke and nudge his shoulder with mine. He shoves my right shoulder with more force.

I grin and shove him back.

He pushes me down against the couch, pinning me there.

I hear his unspoken words, *wanna fucking wrestle, Calloway?*

Wanna do something fucking crazy, Calloway?

Wanna make wolf pups with me, Calloway?

With you. With you.

Only with you.

Whether fate will be on *our* side. That's another matter.

The front door bursts open and we all turn our heads. Ryke scoots a little so I can lift mine.

"Sorry we're late!" Willow calls out, carrying a cake in the shape of a giant penis. I can't tell if she's white from the cold or the fact that she's had to walk with an erect dick in her arms.

Either way, I'm glad to see her.

And the cake.

Because I have a theory that has never been proven wrong.

"I DON'T KNOW IF I can eat that," Lily says, eyes narrowed as Ryke cuts the head of the penis cake.

We're all gathered in the kitchen, and I've just finished posting a picture of the cake to Instagram with the hashtags: #bachelorettecake #naughtynaughty

"It's just fucking cake," Ryke tells her. *Fucking cake.* My heart sings for a moment, my focus diverting quickly to Willow.

She pushes up her glasses and stands near her now-boyfriend. The two of them, together, cause all of us to kind of slyly watch their budding relationship.

Well, some of us are sly.

Lily always stares with a big, silly grin on her face.

Garrison leans casually against the refrigerator, an unlit cigarette peeking from the pocket of his leather jacket. Ryke is giving him a look like *you're not sneaking upstairs with our fucking sister.* He's not very sly either, but that's purposeful.

"Why'd you take so long?" Lo asks in an accusing tone.

"We pulled over to fuck," Garrison says dryly. *Uh-oh.*

Ryke's jaw hardens. Lo's sharpens. I like when they're on the same side of things. When nothing separates them. Not anger or pain or another person.

Willow chokes on a breath. "We...didn't."

"They know that," Garrison tells her.

Connor makes a pot of coffee. "It's as though you want them to hate you."

Garrison is quiet like Connor struck the soul of his sarcasm. "That's stupid."

"You said it, not me," Connor states.

"Who wants the head?" I ask, raising a plate with a slice of cake, trying to soften whatever is about to happen.

"I'm trying to remember why I like you," Lo tells Garrison, ignoring me, "but it's all clouded by an image of me stabbing you, so be lucky I'm not holding a goddamn knife right now."

Garrison almost smiles. "You still like me?"

Lo enunciates, "*Me* stabbing you to death. Value your own life for me, so you can at least be kind of frightened."

It's sweet. How much they want to protect Willow.

While opening a tub of vanilla ice cream, Willow leans close and whispers in my ear, "I'm so embarrassed." Her cheeks are a little pale, and I definitely understand the word *embarrassed* today more than most days.

I hug her side and say super quietly, "They love you, you know?"

Her gaze flickers to Ryke, but the minute he turns towards her, she rapidly rotates back to me, even paler. They're still on awkward terms.

Ryke mouths to me, *what did I fucking do?*

I shake my head and mouth, *it's okay*. He wants to fix this relationship so badly, but it's just going to take more time. I clutch my plate with the piece of cake. I guess I'm eating the head.

Despite this party being framed for a social media ploy, it's been pretty amazing (minus the video clip). Rose hands Lily a middle portion of the cake and Lily just shakes her head. "I can't eat the shaft."

"Lil." Lo melds his body behind hers. "It's *cake*."

"It's a penis."

"No, love, *this* is a penis." He takes her hand and places it on his crotch.

"Lo!" A smile accompanies her squeal.

"Daisy!" My name causes me to shift my gaze slightly. Ryke stands by the towering penis. Swiftly, he scoops the cake in his palm—*oh no*—and chucks a piece at my face. It splats right against my nose and mouth and eyes.

My smiles stretches, tasting the sweet pink icing. It falls off my eyelashes enough to see Ryke lick chocolate cake off his finger.

I've never wasted cake like this, but I'd like to think that it's going to a fun place, even if it's not my stomach.

"This means war," I warn him.

"Come at me, Calloway."

I grab a hunk and throw it at his forehead. It hits him square in the cheek, and then the food fight explodes. We hit Lily and Lo with cake, and they join in, Lo and Ryke chucking more and more at us.

"Lo!" Lily says as he knocks off her *Maid of Honor* crown. I can't stop laughing, and Ryke seizes me around the waist, picking me up and twirling me.

I bite his shoulder, and he tosses me over it. Upside-down, I see Garrison draw a heart on Willow's cheek with icing. Then she draws a star on his.

Rose and Connor sip coffee by the pot, hand-in-hand. They remain clean and out of harm's way. "Rose," I sing-song with a wider smile. Ryke spins me so I can collect another handful of the destroyed cake.

She releases her death-grip on Connor, maybe anxious about the mess in her kitchen. She directs her manicured nail at me. "If you throw that anywhere near my outfit, you'll quickly become my least favorite sister."

"Duly noted." Then I toss the glob of mutilated cake…at her husband. It hits him square in the heart, his white button-down dirtied with chocolate cake and pink icing.

Rose breaks into a grin.

Connor hardly flinches. "Your happiness is showing."

"Good," she says.

"Even at my suffering?" His lips rise.

"Yes." She clutches his hand.

He kisses her like he loves her even more for those words.

Ryke sets me down on my feet, and I breathe heavily as we stare at each other. Our hair sticky with frosting and cake from our bachelor and bachelorette party. His smile grows, and mine matches.

I glance over at the sound of a body hitting a cabinet.

Garrison is pressed up against Willow, their eyes closed, and their lips meeting. He deepens the kiss, and her hands waver, unsure of where to go, until he lifts them up. Her palms settle on the back of head, his baseball hat tumbling to the floor. In the moment, they don't notice that or us.

It's her first kiss.

And I love that it's on my birthday. Happiness reigns today.

Ryke kisses my cheek, pulling my gaze onto him. I swing my arms around his shoulders, my smile still full and his eyes unnaturally light. Tomorrow it all could change. It probably will. But that dull ache in my heart has been stomped on for now.

He lowers his head, and his lips graze my ear.

"Happy birthday, Calloway."

< **36** >

Daisy Calloway

I stretch my legs across Ryke's lap, cramped in the front seat of my tiny sports car for three hours and counting. We parked outside of this giant mega hunting & camping store, and according to our private investigator, a potential anonymous forum member frequents it.

Blue eyes.

Medium height.

Longish brown hair.

One tattoo sleeve.

We'd go inside and linger, but we were spotted a week ago on a stakeout—and it created too much mayhem to stick around. Which brings us to:

Ryke and Daisy's Grand & Daring Stakeout #48

Five months of stakeouts and I've gravitated towards blonde wigs, but I mixed it up and chose a long, cotton candy pink one this time.

I retract my legs and cross them beneath my bottom, restless. I feel the heat of Ryke's gaze on me, but he stays relatively quiet, finishing off a water bottle. He tosses it in the backseat.

My phone buzzes, and my stomach curdles.

Where was your wedding? Can you send me some pics! Wish I could've been there. Love you. — **Cleo**

I thought I blocked her number? I have no idea how she keeps finding ways to text me, but it's discomforting. And no, my wedding hasn't happened yet. It's already May, months have passed since my February 20th birthday, and the world thinks our wedding has passed too. Ryke has to wear his ring, breaking tradition for the sake of a calm ceremony.

Without any remorse, I delete the text.

"Cleo and Harper?" Ryke asks just based off my expression. That's how much they've contacted me.

I nod. "I'll talk to the lawyer about a cease and desist again." Maybe they'll listen to it this time?

Ryke extends his arm over the back of my seat and gauges my state of being. I shelve my animosity towards my ex-friends and inspect the box of donuts on the dashboard. Jelly squirts out of the powdered ones, and we only have a single chocolate sprinkle donut left.

"So I was thinking," I begin a topic that I haven't broached yet, "do you think Coconut looks lonely?"

His brows furrow. "What do you mean?"

I shrug. "Like mopey or sad."

"She licked your fucking face this morning and practically leaped outside first chance she got—that's not a sad dog." He pulls back a couple strands of my pink wig to try and see beneath my gaze.

I don't hide all of what I feel, but I know I hide some.

"Where's this coming from?"

I shrug again. "I just thought maybe we could go to the animal shelter."

He goes rigid. "You want to get another fucking dog?" he asks like I'm suggesting relocation to Jupiter.

I tuck my legs to my chest and nod, both of us facing one another. "Don't you think she'd like another friend?"

His jaw muscles twitch, eyes darkening like an incoming storm. *I'm not afraid.* "Don't fuck with me," he says. "This isn't about another dog."

"I'm being serious," I express, my tone almost rising in a yell. "I think we should consider getting another puppy." Maybe three hours in a small confined space with almost nothing to do has switched on a silent pressure cooker.

"Why?" he growls.

"Because puppies are cute," I retort and playfully kick his arm off my seat.

His nose flares. "That's not good enough."

I sigh heavily. "Does there have to be a better reason?"

"Yeah because there *is* one, you're just not fucking saying it."

"They're really, *really* cute." I spread my arms. "My reason!" I yell it, not in a nice way.

"That's not a fucking reason!"

I let out a sound of frustration that I almost never make. "Why can't you just say *no, I don't want a dog* and end the conversation instead of nag me?"

"Because I can't fucking *hear* you."

"I'm yelling!" I shout at him, my body hot with sentiments that I don't normally ever share, with *anyone.* "How can you not hear me?!"

"You're not saying anything, Dais! *Puppies are cute* isn't what's eating at you!"

"How do you know?!" I retort, kneeling on my seat to be closer to his height. "You don't know what's going on in my head!"

"I'm trying to get you to fucking tell me!" He sets his arm back on the curvature of my seat.

I knock it off, not wanting him touching my seat for some reason. Or maybe I just want him at an exasperated, blood-boiling temperature like me.

"Daisy."

Heaviness bears on my chest. I don't like this feeling. "Just stop talking about it." I'm shutting down. "I'm sorry I brought it up, okay?"

"I'm not fucking sorry," he retorts. "What's so special about another fucking dog?"

"Stop," I plead. "Just stop." I'm ready to drop it, but Ryke is too assertive to just let something like this drift off to sea.

Seconds later, a powdered, jelly donut splats against my cheek.

I slowly turn to face him like *what have you done.*

He has the entire box of donuts on his lap, and he bites into my *last* chocolate donut. *The danger...*

I pick the jelly donut off my lap and chuck it at Ryke. I crawl halfway over the middle console and steal every single donut, pelting them one by one at him. That uncomfortable weight flies off my abdomen with each soaring pastry.

"I can't hear you, Calloway!" he shouts.

I scream so loudly, so ferociously, and gradually the sound transforms into a laugh, especially as his smile envelops his face. As the last donut hits his jaw and falls to his thigh, I hold onto his shoulders. My knees on the middle console, staring right into his brutally honest eyes. Powder and jelly sticks to his cheek, chocolate on his forehead, but I never break from his gaze.

I breathe deeply and everything that I trounced propels towards the surface. I'm just *searching* for something better. For something more. For something that may replace the grief we'll come to feel. The disappointment we've already met. I'm searching for the lightness in our worlds, and I'm afraid of never seeing the sun ascend again.

And I whisper, "I don't want another dog...I want a baby."

His gaze says, *I know, Dais.* He cups my cheek, the one with the scar.

"I'm scared," I breathe.

"I'm always going to fucking be here," he reminds me. "You won't be alone, sweetheart."

I nod repeatedly, his words comforting me. Easing me. Wrapping me tightly.

Ryke kisses me, so passionately that I careen into his body. He tastes like strawberry jelly and my lips tingle at the new friction. He pulls me, my chest to his chest, and then rolls me over, so my back lies flat on the seat. I tug at his shirt, wanting him closer and nearer. Right up against me.

My heart beats faster in this second than when standing on the precipice of a cliff or edge of a bungee jump. I want him so badly. I buck up towards him as he kisses me stronger, harder.

Beneath my lips, he mumbles, "I fucking love you." *I love you. I love you. I love you.* My soul says in kind. I try to express this through my lips, but I want him to hear the words from me too.

"I love you," I whisper in his ear. His coarse hands run down my back, and he kisses the hollow of my neck. Then he sheds my clothes, unclips my bra, and I tug off his shirt, my body singing.

My pulse screaming. I grip his hair, realizing that I'm straddling his lap now while he sits on the seat. Naked, powdered sugar and strawberry jelly all over our skin.

Our breaths tangle together and fog up the windows. Effervescing sentiments prick my eyes, water squeezes out of the corners. I coil my arm around his neck and pant against his jaw.

"Ryke."

His hands burn trails along my thighs and lower back, his tongue parting my lips. *Ryke.* I pulse and clench for him, and he rubs between my legs, lighting up the sensitive parts of my body.

Ryke lifts me up in a front-piggyback, bringing me to the passenger side. He leans the seat at a lower angle. My head dizzies, and my ragged breathing tries to catch up to his endurance. He rests my shoulders along the back of the seat, and he hovers over me, one hand clutching the headrest. He splits my legs apart with his knee, and his two fingers fill me.

I hold onto his wrist, my thighs trembling.

"Ryke," I cry.

His head hangs to avoid colliding with the ceiling. The car is so cramped, nowhere for us to go but towards one another. Thrillingly close. Ryke rests a hand on my back, lifting my body against his instead of forcing his weight on me.

What upper-body strength you have. I could smile, but I'm paddling in the heat of these bursting sentiments. Shared between us.

I cling to him, and my lips swell and tingle beneath his lips. My breasts pressed to his chest and pelvis right in line with his hardness. His fingers quicken rapidly, pricking my nerves. My toes curl and sweat builds across my skin.

I clench again and come slowly but surely.

And as I rise up the peak, I watch his erection drive all the way into me. Connecting us together. He cups my face again, and his forehead meets mine. Our parted lips ache to touch, but they linger as he rocks in and out.

Tears leak out of the corners of his eyes. The weight of our emotions crack like lightning, intensifying the way his skin touches my skin. He pounds harder, like he needs to be further, *deeper* inside. Like he is burrowing to the core of me.

I clutch his hair, breath shallow. "Ryke!" I cry. "Ryke."

"Dais." He pushes back the pink strands of my wig, choking on a groan. "*Fuck.*" Deeper. Deeper.

My eyes roll back. "Ry…" I pulsate around his cock, and when my head lolls, I see how fast, how far, how deep he goes. His erection in me. *He's inside of me.* Seeing it gets me off on another level.

His ass flexes with each thrust.

My parted lips press to his shoulder, blinded.

"*Fuck*," he grunts, hitting his own climax. He pushes more forcefully on my lower back, so I'm right up against him. He holds me there while our bodies throb with pleasure.

He kisses my cheek, and our gazes lock for a moment, both filled with acknowledgement and love. I've never had emotional sex like that, not with anyone but him. He's told me, more than once, that I'm the only one he's ever fucked this way. This deeply, this *fully*.

Even as we come down, I still feel sensitive. My skin and arms and—

Someone pounds on the steamy window.

I jump and wrap my arm around my chest. Ryke protectively pulls me closer against him and holds me, both of us sticky with sweat and strawberry jelly.

Another knock against the window and then a loud voice that says, "I need you two to step out of the vehicle. This is the county police."

Oh.

My.

God.

"Fuck," Ryke mutters, raking a hand through his hair. We search for our clothes, and he helps me dress, mostly, while he just puts on his jeans.

"Ryke," I whisper, "can we go to jail for this?" I've never been to jail, and when I said *Grand & Daring* stakeout, I meant for the potential flour-bomber to be behind bars.

Not us.

"Hey, don't worry about it, Dais." He pulls my shirt over my head and fixes my off-kilter pink wig, but never says one way or the other. "It's going to be—"

"Please step out of the vehicle." The officer raps the window again.

My stomach tightens.

"Fucking *fuck*," Ryke curses harshly before zipping up his jeans. When I'm fully clothed, Ryke opens the door, daylight bearing down on us.

A police officer has his squad car parked next to ours, a ticket book already in hand. "Do you two know what you were doing in the middle of the day?"

Yep. Multiple orgasms. *Thank you, Ryke.* I just nod, a little more than nervous since he has handcuffs on his belt. And a gun.

I sway from side to side.

Ryke's arm curves around my shoulders, reminding me that he's here.

We practically tower over the cop, who must only be five-feet and six-inches tall. For some reason, his short stature eases some of my nerves.

I smile at him.

He shoots me a stink-eye.

"I was just patrolling the parking lot and saw your fogged up windows, there, the back one clear as day." He gestures to the hunting & camping store to the right of us. "This is a *family* area."

I glance at Ryke, jelly all over his bare chest and arms. A streak of chocolate runs along his cheek. He must feel my gaze because he looks over at me. Then he swipes his finger across the top of my nose. He sucks off the strawberry jelly and raises his brows at me like *you taste fucking good, Calloway.*

My smile explodes.

"I'm talking to you two," the officer snaps, jolting me.

"We fucking heard you," Ryke says in his usual tone.

"Don't curse at me, sir." The officer asks for our licenses and all that jazz. Neither of us tries to talk our way out of a ticket or citation.

I just don't want to go to jail.

I think Ryke knows if he opens his mouth again, our outcome will worsen. Just by the way people perceive him. Alone, I can see him trying to talk more to the officer. With me in tow, he'd never risk a trip to a cell.

We pass over our identifications, and if the officer recognizes our names, he doesn't let on. I've never used the *don't you know who I am?* line, and I don't plan to start.

I tuck a strand of my pink wig behind my ear. "Are we going to jail?"

"You're both getting a ticket."

"For what?" Is there a *no public sex* citation?

Before the police officer replies, a news van rears up the curb of the hunting & camping store. My mouth hangs ajar. Our luck must like to find drain holes. I'm actually *really* worried now.

Because my *dad* will see this on the news.

He can't be naïve to think Ryke and I haven't had sex yet. I live with him. We share a bedroom. But my dad has been known to stick his head in the sand. He perceives me as young and wild, but I think he hoped I'd gravitate towards a man who'd tame me.

Not someone who'd start a donut war, bolster me to use my voice, and make love to me in a car.

God.

I love Ryke.

The news van parks almost parallel with the cop car.

Ryke rolls his eyes at the incoming journalist from a local station and mutters another *fuck* under his breath. To have this right up in my dad's face—when I haven't even unleashed *we're trying to have a baby!* and *I'm building a summer camp!* on him yet—is not good.

I just don't want to hurt him, but maybe it's inevitable that we all hurt the ones we love eventually, even if it's just a little bit.

The police officer rips the ticket and hands it to Ryke. "Public indecency. It's a serious fine."

No jail. No confinement. My joints loosen, and Ryke squeezes my shoulder.

The officer adds, "It's also expensive." Here comes the camera crew.

Ryke reads the ticket. "How expensive?"

"Five-hundred dollars each." It's a lot more than I thought it'd be.

But the officer is wrong about one thing.

Sex with Ryke—in this car, at that particular time, at this particular place—was totally and utterly *priceless*.

< 37 >

Ryke Meadows

"We need a game plan," Lo tells me as the valet takes the keys to his black Audi. I'm fucking fixated on the private country club.

I remember that gray stone and those oversized, cedar double doors. I remember these same leisure bodies that pass us now. Dressed in collared shirts, removing their golf gloves. Fixing their tennis visors. I remember the distinct fucking smell of grass clippings and suntan lotion.

Lo sets a hand on my shoulder and jostles me awake. "You look like shit."

I feel like I'm meeting a fucking ghost. "It's been ten years since I've been back here," I remind him. Every Monday, I saw my father at this country club. I stopped meeting him when I was seventeen.

"It's for a good cause," Lo says with furrowed brows like *don't leave me right now.*

I wouldn't.

I begin walking towards the doors, showing him that I'm not fucking scared of revisiting the past or letting it go.

My phone buzzes.

More pics (I'm the good-looking one) — Sully

He sent me extra ice climbing photos from March. Norway was fucking cold but really fucking fun, and even with slight guilt, knowing my brother hated me being there, I think I'd do it again.

I check the second missed text.

I found more of your old baseball cards. Do you want me to bring them to breakfast next time you come? — Mom

The message surfaces vivid memories. Of how my mom used to take me to Citizens Bank to see the Philadelphia Phillies when I was six, seven, eight, nine—all throughout my adolescence. I had this shoebox full of baseball cards, and I'd fucking insist on bringing them to every game.

I called them *my friends* because I wasn't allowed to bring actual friends out in public, not with her around. Because she had to be the mother to Loren Hale. Not to me. Because I couldn't have any real fucking friends find out our relation.

My mom. Sara Hale.

It's been five years, five fucking years, since my mom outed Lily's sex addiction to the press and harassed her over text. Five years since we were all thrust into the media. Five years since the world found out my relation to Jonathan Hale. To Sara Hale.

Five years since everything changed.

The minute I heard that my mom hurt Lily, I swore that I'd cut her from my life, but after the years began to pass, as she kept contacting me, kept trying to apologize, I decided to unbury the debris and piece together something that we both could stand on.

A text sent to say *hello.*

A phone call to speak more than a few words.

To hear that she moved back to New Jersey.

A video chat to see her face.

To watch her cry when she saw mine.

A couple coffees at Foghorn Café where she works as a waitress.

To learn that she *finally* legally removed "Hale" from her last name. To learn that Sara Meadows' bank account was wiped with the decision, thanks to my father.

One visit to Foghorn became two, then three, then too many to fucking count. About two years—that's how long I've been seeing my mom. No one knows except Daisy. Because no one dares to fucking ask and trudge up old memories.

Truth is, she's not a saint or wholesome. But she's more the kind of mom I want to remember than the one I fucking crave to forget.

The saddest thing, I can't invite her to my wedding. I wouldn't. I can *never* bridge what I have with her to what I have with everyone else. It's forever severed.

And all my life…all my fucking life, I never really imagined that *this* is the way the wind would blow. It's a painful reminder that our futures are fragile fucking things. At any moment, someone can be left behind.

I turn off my phone, not wanting to feel the vibration. I'll reply to her later, but this isn't a good time for more childhood memories to crash into me.

Lo keeps pace with my stride towards the country climb, and I tell him, "It's a little late for a fucking game plan. We're already here."

Paparazzi left us at the country club's gates. I never thought I'd care, but I'm honestly tired of the "do you have sex in cars often?!" questions. I could say *yeah, so fucking what* and they'd still repeat the question over and *over*. Not to mention the fucking peanut gallery called Loren Hale and Connor Cobalt.

The same day the media posted *Ryke Meadows & Daisy Calloway Parking Lot Sex Scandal!* (no pictures included)—Connor told me, "If you needed my advice on how to have sex in a parking lot, without getting a ticket, all you had to do was ask."

He went down on his wife in a parking lot. I really didn't need to be fucking reminded of that, not even in an effort to boost his own ego.

No one bothers us on our way to the club's double doors.

The staff must recognize us as celebrities because I thought we would've been kicked out for our casual attire. Lo's black V-neck and dark jeans are not up to par with Polo shirts and sport coats. My green muscle tee and track shorts are even fucking worse.

It's fucking hot. In the afternoon. In May.

"Just don't be a dick," Lo tells me.

I scowl. "I'm not a dick." But I know in the face of our father, I can be a fucking dick. In some instances, I'm the one with the shorter fuse.

A club employee opens the door for us. Memory brings me towards the five-star restaurant, fine dining with tablecloths and empty wine glasses already set. I waft my muscle tee off my chest, sweating.

"You're a little bit of a dick," Lo tells me. A line formed at the hostess podium bars us from entering the restaurant. While we wait, he shakes out the longer parts of his hair, the sides short.

He finally catches me fucking *glaring* at him.

Lo points at his chest. "Hey, I'm the *bastard*. I can call you a fucking dick." He frowns and takes a long pause. "I guess our sister is a bastard too. Can girls be bastards?"

"How about you don't be a dick," I suggest.

"Good call," Lo says dryly, "let's both not be dicks."

I roll my eyes at his tone. This isn't going to go well. I remind myself that we're here for Willow. To support her and protect her. That's it.

We reach the hostess podium and recognition floods her face. She grabs a couple menus, and we follow her to the back corner of the restaurant.

There's my father.

At the same fucking table. By that same fucking window. Overlooking the same fucking red and green tennis courts.

He's not alone.

I see Willow. In the chair that I always used to sit in, right across from our dad. And a chill snakes down my spine.

This was the fucking plan. We were supposed to meet her here after a half hour. So she could have time to talk alone with him.

As we come closer, I expect to see hundred-year-old scotch in front of my father. What he always drank. But only a coffee mug sits there.

He's still sober.

Yet I keep waiting for that to reverse too. For him to make a third mistake. A fourth and fifth. For the cycle to continue, and maybe I need to just *stop* for fucking once. Stop expecting the worst out of him. Even when it happens.

Lo heads out in front of me to greet our dad.

I fall in like a shadow.

"You made it," our father exclaims, seeming surprised that we showed up but his lips rise. Happy that we did. He stands to shake Lo's hand and pat him on the back.

I slide past and just take a seat next to Willow.

Her hair is tied in a neat braid, and she borrowed a blue, anchor-printed dress from Daisy. She sips ice water from her wine glass, her hand trembling. Color is lost in her face.

"You okay?" I ask under my breath.

I strain my ears to pick up her whispered response. "He's really intimidating." She shakily sets the water down. "I'm glad you're both here."

It almost takes me aback—that she'd be glad *I* arrived with Lo too, that she's more comfortable around me. At least enough to talk to me again. I whisper, "Don't feel pressured to say a fucking word. We can talk if you don't want to anymore."

She nods and cups her hands on her lap.

"Nice to see you too, Ryke." My dad's rough voice reroutes my attention, just as he takes a seat next to Lo, opposite Willow and me.

Don't be a dick, Ryke. I don't know what to fucking say.

"Although I've seen a lot more of *you* lately than you've seen of me. You know, Greg was upset by the parking lot 'sex scandal' but come on"—my father actually uses air quotes—"they didn't even have pictures. It was goddamn tame."

I'm not discussing this with him. I already spent an hour on the phone with Greg. First, it was about my reputation as the face of Fizzle's sports drinks. (He didn't fire me.) Then it quickly became a lecture on "being responsible for my daughter" and "you're about to marry her" and "you need to protect her"—that fucking blew my head off.

I love Daisy *more* than he will ever come to fucking know. Sometimes to be happy in our skins, we can't play within restrictions. We have to be a little fucking daring and climb outside of them.

I slouch in my chair, not responding to anything my dad has to say about the police thing.

Lo motions between Jonathan and Willow. "How'd this go?" He diverts the conversation. *Thanks, Lo.* "I'm guessing good. I don't see any tears."

Willow gives him a weak smile.

Our dad opens a sugar packet. "Hales are stronger than that."

Lo leans back in his chair. "Oh yeah, we're indestructible." He looks to our father. "You know what I think, Dad?"

"What?" Wariness grips his darkened eyes, waiting for Lo's punchline with the rest of us.

"Hales are made of glass. We're sharp, but we break easily."

He's not describing me. It's not the first time I've settled with the fucking fact that I'm not a Hale. I'll never be one. Not to that extent.

I expect our dad to curse, call his son a pussy, and wear a face of iron. Instead…he smiles. And laughs. He almost looks younger, less tired. Still, my pulse races like I'm waiting for a fucking curtain to fall.

"I'm glad you're here today, Loren." He pats Lo on the shoulder. It's friendly and fucking warm. His hardened eyes meet mine. "You too, Ryke." Then he looks to Willow, observing all of us here like he's painting a family portrait in his head.

We're his children. All together.

It reminds me that he fought for all of us to know each other. He wanted this, even if he was out of the picture. It's easy seeing the worst parts of my dad, and acknowledging the good parts that do exist—it's fucking hard for me. There was a time where I *only* saw the bad, but I do recognize the better man inside of Jonathan Hale.

I'm just not sure how long he'll stick around.

The waiter slices through the tension and takes our orders.

Lo waivers, staring at the menu for a longer second. "...I'll take a Fizz." He twists his wedding band.

I chug nearly all of my water and try to relax. Willow's phone starts buzzing in her purse near my chair.

"You going to fucking answer that?" I ask her with a frown.

She shakes her head once, her eyes flitting quickly to our dad, then back to me. "No phones at the table," she whispers.

Fucking A.

"Why can't she answer her fucking phone?" I ask him since he obviously jumped down her throat about it. "You take business calls all the time while we're fucking eating." He's also not the kind of person to enforce manners unless our behavior embarrasses him.

The waiter brings a hot breadbasket and our drinks.

He says, "I thought she'd call you two to come pick her up early and leave. I've never been on a path to fucking morality, but you all deserve my honesty. So there it is."

My jaw unhinges like he just fucking confessed to holding her hostage for a half hour. While Lo butters a piece of bread with a look like *thank you for your honesty*. Fuck that.

Her phone buzzes again and again, and she touches the end of her braid nervously. I'd normally grab the cell myself or push her to answer it, but I don't want to force her to do anything or overstep my fucking boundaries.

It's killing me not to.

"Who is it?" I ask.

"I think just Garrison, but I'm not sure."

Lo groans. "Jesus, does he text you a thousand times a fucking day?"

She shrugs. "We send each other Tumblr links a lot."

"Links to what?" His bread freezes near his mouth.

"Gif sets."

Lo drops the bread on his plate, grimacing and glaring. "He sends you sex gifs?"

"What?" Her eyes widen in horror.

Fucking fantastic.

Our dad drinks his coffee like it's wine, entertained by our close relationships.

"No, *no*, why would you think that?" Willow asks.

I flip a knife back and forth on the table. "Yeah, Lo, why would you fucking think that?" I'm fully aware of why he jumped to this conclusion. Lily used to scroll through Tumblr just for dirty gifs.

Lo points his fork at me. "What'd we say about being a dick?"

I'm just in a pissed off mood.

"I'm a virgin," Willow says and then adds quickly, "I mean...the links aren't sex gifs. We don't...do that. It's cool if other people want to, but it's not my thing. They're just gif sets from TV shows, you know those ones?"

"No," I say.

Lo nods and bites a chunk of his bread.

"You have a boyfriend?" our dad questions.

Willow sinks in her chair. "Yeah..."

"He's in high school," Lo says after he swallows.

"He's younger?"

Lo sips his Fizz. "Nope."

"He kind of flunked out of his last school," Willow explains, "and he was supposed to graduate in May, but they're holding him back until December since he's missed more school than he's attended."

Jonathan drums the table with two fingers. You know that saying: *if you have nothing nice to say, don't say it at all?* Yeah, Hales don't do that. "He sounds like a loser."

Lo pipes in, "I flunked out. Am I a loser, Dad?"

"Of college," he corrects his son. "And you're a Hale, which means that I love you no matter what shitty thing you do or how apathetic you are."

Willow picks up her water, her hand quaking. Ice cubes clank against the glass.

"While we're on the topic," our dad poorly segues, eyeing her drink.

"We weren't on any fucking topic," I snap. I should regret it. I'm obviously giving him a hard time, and he's being nice. But being *nice* and Jonathan Hale are two categories that almost never share space in a fucking Venn diagram.

I have to get used to this.

"It's relevant." His focus lands on Willow again. "You're nineteen, and I know what nineteen-year-olds do since I raised one."

Willow pushes her glasses up. "I'm not anything like Lo was at nineteen."

"Cheers to that." Lo raises his glass and downs his Fizz.

Jonathan rests an elbow on the table. "And how do you know what Loren was like?"

It takes her a minute to answer. "Um…I went to Dalton Academy for my senior year, and a lot of the kids had older siblings that went to school with him. They had stories…and Lo has told me some too."

Lo swishes the ice in his glass. "Only the best ones." He exchanges a smile with Willow.

I don't have constant heart-to-hearts with my little brother, but he's described his childhood to me. He was bullied. He was fucking spiteful.

He sought revenge more than once. He was willing do anything to protect Lily.

As long as he could keep drinking.

Jonathan motions to Willow with his knife. "I assume you go to parties?"

"Not really. It's just not my...cup of tea."

Our father butters a piece of bread. "This family has a history of alcohol dependency," he begins like this is a talk he's given all of us.

It isn't even fucking close.

My face begins to fall. For as long as I've known him, he's always struggled to identify with being an alcoholic. Admitting that he has a fucking problem. Talking about it. Out loud.

He continues, "You should avoid alcohol if you can. It'll be easier in the long run. Take it from someone who didn't go that route and from someone who did." His knife aims at me. "Ryke has the right idea."

I'm not sure what to do with the fucking compliment. Beneath everything, I feel proud of my dad. It's so fucking overwhelming. I just stare at my water glass while the waiter refills it.

"How long have you been sober?" Willow asks me when the waiter leaves. This might be one of the first personal questions she's ever broached to my face. She's asked me about Lo plenty of times though.

Lo crunches on an ice cube, but he won't make eye contact with me. If it hadn't been for Paris, where he handed me alcohol, I would've been sober for almost twelve years now.

It's not his fucking fault, not entirely. I knew what I was getting into that night. So I just say, "A long fucking time."

"It wasn't as hard for you since you quit early on?" she wonders.

"I didn't have the same kind of draw or temptation throughout my twenties like Lo, but quitting initially was fucking tough." I used alcohol as a way to cope with my feelings, and I ended it all by seventeen. Being consumed by track and rock climbing helped distract me from cravings.

"So do you understand?" Jonathan asks Willow.

She nods. "Yeah, Lo actually mentioned staying away from alcohol. He said there's no such thing as just one beer for people like us."

My brows scrunch at Lo like *you did?*

He shrugs, more sheepishly than usual.

I can't help but fucking smile. *I'm proud of you too.*

He rolls his eyes at me.

Willow's phone buzzes *again*. She readjusts her purse on the chair but doesn't reach for the phone. "I don't really like the taste of alcohol, so I've never planned to be a big drinker anyway." Lily is kind of like that. "So...you know I'm not in high school or college, so you don't have to worry about me stumbling on a party or being peer pressured either."

"About college—" Jonathan is cut off by Willow's vibrating phone again.

"Sorry," she apologizes, bringing the purse to her lap.

"I really want you to consider applying for one of the Ivy Leagues. I can find someone notable to write you a recommendation, and you'll be in, no matter your test scores. Graduating from Princeton or even University of Pennsylvania will give you a leg up in whatever you want to do."

"I don't have the money," she mutters, distracted as she digs around for her phone.

"Dad," Lo chimes in, "she doesn't want a fucking handout. Okay? You need to let it go. It's her choice—"

"I can stand by all of your choices, as long as they're not obnoxious or stupid. This falls somewhere in between. Why not take advantage of all your resources? Unless you plan to do something that wouldn't benefit from college?"

She shakes her head, finally obtaining her phone. "I'm...not really sure what I want to do yet."

Jonathan outstretches his arms. "What better way to find out than *college?*"

Willow pales. "I don't want to take anything. From *any* of you." Her eyes ping to Lo and then me. Before our dad speaks, she adds, "I'm just some girl from Maine who showed up on your doorstep, and I don't want to be the person who sticks around to leech off of her long lost brothers and father. It can't be like that."

I'm the first to fucking say, "You're not just some girl. You're our fucking sister."

It must hit her hard because her eyes glass behind her lenses.

"I'm not going to lie," our dad cuts in. "I don't understand ethical decisions." Then he makes a fucking point to stare straight at me. "Like my son legally changing his first name out of some absurd principle."

My jaw locks. I chose that over money, and he still can't comprehend *why*. Maybe he never will, but I feel better by it—and that's all that fucking matters to me.

"Ryke." Willow cups her cellphone, staring wide-eyed at the screen. "Daisy keeps texting me. Do you have your phone on you?"

"Fuck." I take out my phone and turn it back on. Five missed calls. More texts that say: call me. I'm really sorry for bothering you.

Fuck. I immediately stand up and dial Daisy's number.

No one fights me on it. I walk towards the full-length window and a nearby empty table, the phone to my ear. Ringing.

Just fucking ringing.

Pick up, Dais.

A tennis instructor wheels a cart full of balls towards the center court. Kids, no older than eight or nine, skip ahead with little rackets and beaming smiles. Clouds roll over the sun, casting shadows on the court, and the phone keeps on fucking ringing.

It clicks to voicemail, but I call her again.

On the second ring, she finally answers, "Ryke?" She's almost out of breath.

"Yeah, it's me."

There's a long fucking pause.

"Daisy," I force, worried out of my fucking mind.

"Can you meet me at Dr. Yoshida's?" There's a tremor in her voice.

The wind knocks out of me, and I rest a hand on the window. "Is something fucking wrong?" I ask.

Her cyst ruptured.

She's bleeding.

She has to go into surgery.

In her silence, the worst rams into me.

Over and fucking over, and then—

"I might be pregnant," she says, vacuuming my terrible thoughts.

I stand completely still.

"I was going to wait until you came home, but not knowing has been messing with me all day. I just...if it's a false test again—I don't know. I just need to rip this off like a Band-Aid, I think. I wasn't going to take you from your lunch but—"

"I'm fucking glad." All of these overpowering emotions try to surface. I have to keep them at bay. Because it's probably false, and I'd rather be with her when she finds out. She was fucking crushed last time, and I don't want her to be alone. "I'm on my way."

"If you can't come, I understand—"

"Hey, just breathe, cry if you fucking need to, and I'll be there in ten minutes."

I hear her cry, and it fucking kills me but it's better than her holding it in. I tell her that I fucking love her, and then we both hang up. I quickly return to the table.

"I have to go," I tell them.

"Why?" Jonathan wears so much fucking skepticism, and I'm not about to admit that I'm trying to have a baby. The information will go straight to Greg, his best friend.

"Daisy's in therapy, and she's really fucking emotional," I lie. Her parents know that she sees Frederick for PTSD and depression.

Without further questioning, Lo tosses me his car keys. "Try not to drive my car into another fucking car again."

"Thanks," I say, too tightly wound to flip him off or dish out a *fuck you*.

"Tell Daisy I said hi." Willow waves goodbye.

I nod and give her the best apologetic look I can fucking muster, which may be shit. Truth is, she's probably better off with Lo mediating the lunch than with me here. I almost never give Jonathan Hale the benefit of the doubt.

Even now, when he shows signs of being a decent human being, I continue to wait for him to fail. I don't know if that says more about him or me.

The keys dig into my palm while I practically sprint back to the valet, just thinking about Daisy.

My heart has never beat fucking faster.

< 38 >

Daisy Calloway

I squirm on the hospital bed, the crinkling paper filling the tense silence. I've already torn off a section of the paper and creased the edges to form a palm tree.

Ryke stands beside the bed and plays with my hair while massaging my head, but even that barely loosens my tight shoulders.

"I'm all out of jokes," I whisper, most of them flat-lining before I even uttered the words.

His brows rise, and my freefalling heart pauses midair. "Knock knock."

My small smile lifts my cheeks. "Who's there?"

"Fuck." He tucks my hair behind my ear.

"Fuck who?" I play along, my lungs lighter.

He leans his head down, lips to my ear as he whispers, "Fuck me."

My smile grows an extra inch or two. "How has that pickup line worked for you?"

He scrutinizes my features, landing on my lips that have curved upward. "Pretty fucking good."

Two minutes later, when taut silence approaches us again, I say, "I'm sorry." For the fifteenth time. I've been counting, and I wish I could retract this one too.

I'm not even deterred by his *don't fucking apologize* replies or by that dark, annoyed look he thunders down on me. Our reality is this: in a couple minutes, Dr. Yoshida will saunter back into the office and declare me barren or at the very least, *not* pregnant.

Again.

I know that I ruined Ryke's important lunch with his half-sister and father and brother for *nothing*. Willow needed him. Not me.

And it's not even nothing, actually. This will be for *terrible* news.

I find myself staring off at the worst paper palm tree I've ever made and then at the New York City landscape, dreary clouds blanketing the sky and darkening the room.

"Daisy," Ryke almost growls my name.

My wolf is going to bite me today. Maybe I'll let him.

His expression never softens. "I want to fucking be here."

My eyes are raw from crying earlier. I'm sick of being sad, but at least expelling these emotions gives me a better release than bottling them up.

"I just want to prepare you," I say slowly. "That this is ninety-nine percent nothing, and I'm sorry for that too—"

"Stop." He covers my mouth with his hand. "Fucking stop." He's upset, his gaze shattering but narrowed, still steadfast.

I touch his wrist, pulling his hand down and freeing my mouth. He lets me pretty easily. That's Ryke for you. "I should feel different if I'm pregnant, I think," I breathe. "I just feel the same."

Almost a year of trying to get pregnant. Mentally, I could try another year with Ryke, the same way we've been doing, but my body has shorter agendas. Physically, time is running out.

"It's okay," he says strongly but his reddened eyes show a different kind of story. *Tired.* We're both really tired. "Whatever fucking happens, it's okay."

I nod, the paper palm tree limp in my hands.

He rubs my back, and then the office door opens.

Dr. Yoshida carries a file, his features as impassive as Connor Cobalt, which sucks because I can't determine any sort of answer.

He greets us with a simple nod and stands close. "I hope you're both doing well."

I'm sure he's seen the news. We've been all over it.

DAISY CALLOWAY'S KINKS:
HOW MANY TIMES HAS SHE HAD SEX OUTDOORS?

DAISY CALLOWAY IS JUST LIKE HER SISTER!
SEX ADDICT IN THE MAKING!

BREAKING NEWS: LILY CALLOWAY & RYKE MEADOWS
HAD SEX IN THE CAR. IT WASN'T DAISY!

That was the worst one.

Hopefully though, Dr. Yoshida has just paid attention to the wedding headlines.

RAISY'S SECRET WEDDING! WHAT WE KNOW ABOUT IT!

They didn't know a lot. Most is speculation with fake sources claiming to have attended. Apparently there was a giant chocolate cake and we eloped in Prague. The cake is spot on. The city, not so much.

I try to sweep away the media from my mind, and everything seems to boil down to this moment. Dr. Yoshida will talk about my other options. He'll propose surrogacy. I'll have to wait a couple years, until Rose is physically ready to have another baby.

I brush a tear from the corner of my eye, before it even falls. I've played his voice in my head all morning, with these different scenarios. I can never be fully ready for the sting of the verdict, but at least Ryke is here.

My pillar, bracing me from the fall. *You'll stand up again, Daisy,* I remind myself. *You're a Calloway sister.*

I can do anything.

Dr. Yoshida pushes his glasses up the bridge of his nose. "I have some pamphlets and articles that I'd like you both to read up on."

My veins run cold, waiting for the blow. Ryke's arm wraps around my shoulders.

"These following months are going to be very important," Dr. Yoshida says. "Getting pregnant was the first step, now carrying the baby to term will be your next big challenge."

Blood drains out of my head, like I've been hung upside-down. "I don't understand."

Dr. Yoshida finally smiles. "Congratulations, Daisy, you're pregnant."

I shake my head once, feeling like a practical joke is being played on me. "I...how...are you sure?" I frown deeply, unwilling to believe in this just yet. "Are you a hundred, million percent sure?" Water builds in my eyes, scared that he's going to pull the rug beneath my feet and say, *gotcha!*

I'll fall hard.

"I ran the tests," he explains. "You are without a doubt pregnant. A little over two weeks. You'll need to come back soon for your first ultrasound. I want to do it early since this will be a high-risk pregnancy."

My heart pounds, his words flowing through me and then floating away. I turn to Ryke, his reddened eyes never leaving me. He looks as overcome as I feel. And then I watch as tears slide down his cheeks.

He's crying.

Ryke has acted very careful about the whole "family of three" concept, never outwardly jumping for joy. If it never came true, he didn't want me to feel like I wasn't good enough for him or that I denied him something he could obtain elsewhere.

I've almost forgotten how much this means to him.

"We're going to have a baby," I whisper, tears dripping down mine.

He nods and smiles, wider than almost anytime ever before, and he says, "Yeah, Calloway. We're going to have a fucking baby."

I laugh into my own tearful smile. "Say that again." I reach up, my hands disappearing in his thick hair.

He repeats his words and then draws me to his chest, pulling me off the hospital bed and in his arms. I'm dizzy inside his embrace, my mind twirling a thousand, bazillion miles an hour. He kisses the top of my head and then my cheek, pulling away only a little to meet my lips.

I kiss him just as wildly and zealously and soulfully.

My world loses focus.

And I can worry about the next big challenge, as my doctor called it, but I don't want this experience—which may be my only one—to be ruined by fear.

I've been scared of the dark, of strangers and things that go bump in the night. I never want to be scared of an unknown future, of risks. It's the *one* fear that I choose to never have.

We kiss fast and then slow, until our lips part, and then I stare deeply in his eyes.

This is the start of our next chapter.

Our next adventure.

‹ *39* ›

Daisy Calloway

Water cascades on us, and we both have a hard time concentrating on shampoo when we're so close to each other, naked. He's *extremely* fit, the lines of his muscles pelted by water droplets. I feel more feminine and shorter sharing the confined space with him, but I love taking showers with Ryke.

Bathing each other. Comfortable enough to let him explore my body and vice versa. I watch his hot gaze move across my nipples and hips.

I smile as I close my eyes, dipping my head back to wash away soapsuds. He helps, his hands combing through my brown hair.

When his palms leave me, I open one eye. He reaches for a washcloth on the ledge, and when he rotates back around, I spit water at his face like a fountain.

He wears his usual *fucking fuck* expression that's very Ryke Meadows.

Water dribbles down my chin, and I laugh into a larger smile. His lips immediately pull upwards, and he thumbs the scar on my cheek. It usually puckers in the heat, so add in my smile, and I bet it's super noticeable.

He seems to love it all the same.

Maybe even more, actually.

I run my fingers through my wet hair. "Am I showing?" I ask through the noise of water beating the tiles.

His hand slides across my abdomen. At six-weeks, there's not much of a bump, but we had our first ultrasound yesterday and heard the heartbeat of our baby. So far baby Meadows is alive and healthy. We've decided to leave the gender a mystery until the very end. Maybe just in case something bad happens, it's better not knowing.

"Not that much," he says what I already know. "You'll get fucking bigger, Dais."

"How big?" I smile widely. I'm holding onto what we have now, every day, for as long as I can.

He tosses the washcloth at me, and it splats on my face, covering my eyes.

I gasp. "I've lost my handsome boyfriend! Where for art thou, Rom—" I can barely keep the charade alive, laughing too much, and he has nothing else to throw at me.

Ryke plucks the washcloth off my face. "You realize that you're the only one laughing, Calloway?"

"Who said I was trying to amuse you?" I wag my brows. "I'm amusing myself."

He edges closer to me, six-foot-three and dangerously enigmatic. My pulse speeds at the way he's staring into me. "How amused are you?" he asks, his voice like sex.

"Very, very amused," I breathe softly, my words almost lost to the shower. I reach for another washcloth, and before I've begun washing him, his washcloth touches my bare arms. His other hand slides down my hip.

I'm so relaxed, practically melting in one spot. Steam fogs the glass shower door, and I focus on his body, my washcloth grazing the ridges of his abs.

His lips near me, just as the washcloth descends between my legs. My breath hitches at the warmth, and he nudges my face up with his, our movements speak to each other, and I respond, tilting my head until his lips meet mine.

His other hand rests on my abdomen for a second.

A moan tickles my throat. "Ryke," I smile against his lips. "Ah…" I inhale sharply, his fingers slipping into me as he drops the washcloth. *Holy shit.* His thumb rubs my bundle of nerves, electrifying my entire body.

My head lightens, and I lean my weight against him. He holds onto my frame while pleasuring me. He even lifts one of my legs higher around his waist, gaining further entry into me.

I shudder and then stare at his large cock. "You can push in," I breathe.

His expression hardens, which only arouses me more.

I moan against his shoulder, my fingers tightening. "Ryke," I cry.

He clutches my ass, and I watch his cock harden. *Oh my God.* I come against him, probably one of the fastest times I've ever gotten off.

I'm hot but not sweaty thanks to the shower.

He kisses me again, and I ask, "Does it bother you?"

His brows furrow. "Does what?"

"That we're not having sex as much as before." I've wondered this lately. In the past four weeks, we've had it considerably less. I've heard him jack off a couple times, too.

"No, Dais." He washes his fingers beneath the shower. "Il tuo piacere è il mio." *Your pleasure is my pleasure.* He'd rather only have sex with me when I'm truly aroused.

My mouth falls, feigning surprise. "You speak Italian?"

He pushes me lightly, and my back thuds against the tile wall. I laugh and he smiles. Ryke is about to drop to his knees in front of me, but I drop to mine first.

"Callo—"

"I want to," I protest, holding onto his bare thighs, his cock right in front of my mouth. It's been a long time since I gave him a blow job. I told my sisters that I'm not a fan of them and that fact reached his ears, so now I think he envisions me *hating* it whenever I try.

"You fucking hate it," he retorts. *See.* He tries to pull me to my feet.

His strength defeats mine. I place my hands on his chest. "I have this theory," I say.

"I already hate your fucking theory."

"Blow jobs are better in time."

"No," he retorts. "No fucking no. Fucking *no.*"

I frown. "But what if I didn't like them then but I like giving them now?" I can tell that this logic is starting to work on him, or maybe he's just really horny. He actually pauses to think.

And then he gives me a *what the fuck* look. "No."

Damn.

I cross my arms and lean against the tiled wall again. "Then you better fuck me," I say, spreading my legs open. "I'm not satisfied until you are, babe."

With that dark, brooding scowl, he says, "I'm going down on you, Calloway. You're going to come *again*, and then I'll push the fuck into you."

My lips pull so high. "Say that again."

Just as his mouth opens, another voice cuts into the bathroom.

"Daisy!" Price yells.

My eyes grow, and Ryke glowers at the misted shower glass. He can't be *in* here. "I locked the door," I tell Ryke. Price knocks against the bathroom door, confirming this.

Ryke barely relaxes and asks me lowly, "Did you call him?"

"No," I say. "Did you?"

"No fucking way." We've been actively leaving Price behind when we go out. Not only to our ultrasound and doctor's appointments but every single *Grand & Daring Stakeout*, we ditched him like an unwelcome friend. I almost feel badly, especially when he texted after the police parking lot incident.

> I could've kept you from being fined and from being filmed by the journalists. Please bring me along next time. I can tail you in another car. That's what I'm here for. — **Price**

I want to trust him, but I'm scared to. We've been hurt so many times by opening our arms to people, and a bodyguard sees things. Hears things. Knows things.

Things that my dad can't know or hear. We decided to tell my parents about the baby *after* our wedding. I'll be ten-weeks then, not showing too much, and I'm afraid if I tell my dad beforehand, he won't come to the ceremony.

I realize.

I suck just as badly as Ryke at delivering news that may hurt people I love. I guess it's something we both have in common.

"Daisy!" Price shouts again, knocking louder.

I turn off the shower, and Ryke steps out. When I follow, he tosses a dark green towel at me. "What is it?" I ask Price through the wood, drying off quickly and then securing a towel around my chest.

"I need the wedding itinerary! I just found out that *every* bodyguard already has one but me!"

So the wedding itineraries are so secretive that everyone has been told to *never* duplicate them, share them, or put them online. They're physical pieces of paper, and we've been stalling on sharing more info with Price.

Ryke *really* doesn't trust him. He thinks he'll leak info to the press, or at least, that's his ultimate worry.

"Hold on!" I shout back, my stomach roiling some and lightheaded from the extra steam.

"I'll wait here!"

Ryke is scowling, his towel low around his waist, but when he looks at me, his brows pinch. "You okay?" He touches my forehead.

I've thrown up a lot the past couple of weeks. For as much as morning sickness sucks, I love that I have it because it's a physical sign that the baby is okay.

I swallow down any brimming nausea and nod, and then I pale for a completely different reason. I whisper, "I think our sonogram is on the dresser." The grayish photo of our baby from the ultrasound.

"Fuck," he curses and waits for me. "Do you want me to get your clothes?"

I shake my head and tighten my towel around my chest. "I'm okay." If I felt uncomfortable, I'd tell Ryke.

He opens the door, the steam rushing out and Coconut pacing back and forth by the entrance, her tail wagging.

She never barked at Price.

Isn't that strange?

In a blue button-down and navy slacks, Price stands by our wicker chair, a half-eaten bowl of cereal on the cushion. His gaze remains solely on mine, no roaming down my body, strictly professional.

"Why didn't I get the itinerary the same time as the other bodyguards?" he asks, pissed by our constant deception. He has a right to be frustrated and angry with us, but we're just trying to protect ourselves.

My eyes flit to the dresser, the sonogram splayed flat. I don't think he can see it from where he stands.

Ryke approaches Price. "Greg may fucking trust you, but he's not the one you're following everywhere."

Price sighs in annoyance like we've been down this road. We have, but he can't possibly understand how much we've all been burned. Ryke's own mother hurt him. My friends. Ryke even had to stop talking to people from college because they kept selling stories to the press. One girl also sold his boxer-briefs on eBay.

How can we tell who the bad apples are when we only discover the rotten cores after we've bitten in? I'm sick of biting in and wanting to puke.

"That's just it, I'm not following you anywhere. You won't let me." Price looks at me. "Your bodyguard, Mikey, isn't coming back, and you need someone, so you're going to have to treat me like the others. I should've been given an itinerary the same time as them—if not *sooner*. I'm *your* bodyguard."

I try not to crumble easily, but I feel so bad.

"Hey," Ryke says roughly to Price, "this isn't like hiring a fucking accountant. We have *every* right to be cautious, especially since we didn't hire you."

I walk to the dresser, thinking I can grab some clothes and hide the sonogram at once.

Of course, Price follows me. "What else do I need to prove? I helped Daisy during New Year's. I could've diffused multiple situations before it escalated—like the one at the zoo."

I rest an elbow on the sonogram and spin around to face him. "I just need space, like for you to give me room to breathe."

He takes a couple steps back. "Is this better?" he asks in seriousness.

I nod. "Yeah."

Ryke nears the dresser too, but he takes out a pair of boxer-briefs. He whispers to me, "If we give him the itinerary the day before the wedding, he'll have less time to fucking leak it."

"If we give it to him now, it's a good test," I whisper back, slyly slipping the sonogram in my underwear drawer.

Ryke thinks about this while he pulls on his dark green boxer-briefs, hardly caring about Price's presence when it comes to being naked.

Coconut skips around my feet, her big beady blue eyes smiling up at me.

"Can I have the itinerary now?" Price asks. "I don't even know what country we're flying to."

Ryke nods from me to the walk-in closet, where we keep the itineraries. Our decision made. As I go collect one, he asks Price, "Did Greg ask you anything fucking strange during your interview?"

"What do you mean by strange?"

Ryke still thinks there's a possibility Price was hired to break us apart. "About your personal life."

I turn on the closet lights and search through a cardboard box on the floor, but I can still hear them outside, especially since Price drifts closer to me on instinct.

"He asked me if I like snowboarding and water sports. He also wanted to make sure I wasn't afraid of heights, and that I was willing to try new things." He pauses. "Of course he also asked if I'm single, my dating history—"

"What?" Ryke snaps.

"You don't understand," Price says easily. "Pairing bodyguards with celebrities is a lot like matchmaking. Daisy lives a single, unattached lifestyle—no offense."

I can feel Ryke fuming.

I hesitate on grabbing the itinerary.

"We're not in a fucking open relationship," Ryke retorts. "She's attached to *me*. She's not single! I'm not fucking her sister!" He's livid, and I peek out of the closet. Veins protrude in his neck. I didn't think that all those rumors—where I'm not really with him, where I could easily move on to another man—ate at him that much.

Maybe he didn't even realize it until now too.

Price doesn't look scared by conflict, which is probably a good bodyguard trait. He raises his hands to ease tension. "I didn't mean it like that. I just meant that she lives *on the go*. She pairs well with someone like me who's single and unattached so I can freely go where you need to go. Garth, who has three children and a wife, could never keep up with you two."

Ryke rubs his unshaven jaw and then glances over his shoulder. At me.

Should we still give him the itinerary? I ask through my eyes. This decision involves us both, and I can't do it if he's not comfortable.

Ryke thinks for a second and then he nods.

I collect the itinerary to give to my bodyguard. In this gesture I'm pleading, *please, don't break our hearts.*

< 40 >

Daisy Calloway

When we first started dating, cornstalks among us like witnesses to the moment, Ryke asked me what I wanted. In that cornfield, I told him, *I want to be fully committed to someone, to be married, probably earlier rather than later. And I do want babies. Maybe like three. I also want to travel and visit the great seven wonders and scuba dive and stand beneath a waterfall in Costa Rica, kissing you.*

I smile, remembering his reply. *Not in that order.*

Not in that order, he started giving me everything I wanted.

It's what I think as I stare out at a breathtaking mountain in Peru, the grays and browns blanketed with moss. Machu Picchu is our view for the rehearsal dinner. A long wooden table is set along the greenest grass, private and spectacular. The lodge is far behind us, lost among foliage.

Tomorrow, I'll be married right here.

Among one of the New Seven Wonders of the World.

We're so fortunate to be married in a place like this, and that fact is *never* lost on me. Ryke and I already asked our family to donate to our favorite charities instead of buying us wedding presents. Though, I suspect a couple of people will break our rules and do both.

It's also been paparazzi-free so far. It does help me trust Price a little more, but after that whole "single and unattached" conversation, Ryke still has his guards raised. Protecting me.

As night falls, torch flames flicker all around us. My parents have finished off three rare bottles of Merlot with Sam, Poppy, and Connor. Everyone seems to be at ease and stuffed full of chicken, beef, and pulled pork sliders with twice-baked mac and cheese. We consume our dessert slowly, two types on the menu for all the chocolate haters.

Lo demolishes his strawberry shortcake in record time.

For me—I just want to draw out the warm brownie experience for as long as possible.

Lo leans back, his wooden chair creaking. "It's official." He tilts his head towards his older brother. "You were born crazy." On the lawn, a projector flashes photographs to a huge white screen. The newest one: a little Ryke hanging off a red cliff with one hand. He's roped and harnessed but he can't be older than seven or eight.

"Born to be wild," I tease with a widening smile. Maybe in another world, we would've been friends that young. I would've been closer to his age. Life would've been fun growing up with him.

His arm, set on the back of my chair, suddenly falls to my shoulders.

My heart backflips at the simple touch and his closeness and that darkened, mysterious gaze. Nervous energy insulates me, and I tuck my feet beneath my bottom. Such a strange feeling. Like butterflies on a first date.

Even now, just being near this guy—six-foot-three, brooding, masculine, protective and so soulfully caring—double-thumps my pulse. Like it's the first time his fingers have grazed the skin on my arm. Like it's the first time his eyes have roamed over me and bored through me.

The hairs on the back of my neck rise. Electrifying. He lights me up, and I'm completely and totally glowing tonight.

He's touching you.

Your future husband is touching you, Daisy.

Such a silly thought, but it has me all twisted inside.

"Hey, I remember that," Sully says across the table, digging into his brownie. *Chocolate lovers for the win.* He points his fork at the screen. "Our instructor took the photo and he so conveniently cropped me out."

"You were belaying and way behind me," Ryke reminds him.

Sully shakes his head, his mop of shaggy red hair swaying with him. "It was a clear case of ginger bias. Twenty years later and you still can't cop to the facts, dude."

"Facts?" I smile.

"There are none," Ryke says.

Sully raises his finger, chugging a glass of water. Everyone waits intently since Sully is the only gateway to Ryke's childhood.

"Here's the fact," Sully says, "our instructor always paired me last with another climber."

"Because you were fucking skinny, and he wasn't sure you were skilled enough to belay someone twice your size."

Sully jabs his fork in Ryke's direction. "See, now there's *skinny* bias. I can never catch a break."

Ryke tells the table, "Don't let Sully fucking fool you. When we were able to choose ourselves, we always picked each other first for trad and sport climbs."

Sully grins into his next bite of brownie. I'm really happy that he's a part of our wedding ceremony. Ryke was a little worried that he'd be halfway across the world today and tomorrow, traveling wherever his heart took him. Luckily, his heart landed him in Peru with us this week.

The slideshow changes to a new picture. I like to call it Daisy Calloway's Sixth Halloween. I'm sliding down someone's banister with a bag of candy, my gray mustache, monocle, and yellow pants suit all the rage. At least in my mind.

"What the fuck are you supposed to be?" Ryke asks. He leans forward to try and peer at the corner of the image. "Is that Rose?"

In a slinky red dress, Rose has her arms crossed, standing and glaring on the fourth stair behind me.

"Who else would I be?" Rose snaps.

"The devil," Lo comments.

"You look scary in that picture," Lily pipes in. "Like scarier than usual."

Rose has her hands on her large baby bump, her dark blue dress molding her pregnant frame. Around thirty weeks along. She said this would be her last week in heels, her feet starting to hurt in them, but her all-consuming confidence hasn't diminished. She acts like her unborn babies are battle armor and precious rubies, nothing that wears her down or forces her into a chair.

Even when she does tire or look nauseous—which has happened a lot during this pregnancy—her supreme glare and raised chin says, *we'll be victorious, little gremlins.*

As if they're fighting with her, not against her.

I'm really grateful the doctor okayed her to fly, so I can have her here with me.

Rose fixes her yellow-green eyes on Lily. "I look angry because I broke my heel that night."

"Maybe thirteen-year-olds shouldn't be wearing heels," Lo retorts.

"Maybe twenty-six-year-olds named Loren Hale should shut up," Rose says and then whips her hair over her shoulder like *I slayed you.*

She almost did. He rebuts with, "I'm not the one who broke my heel, Miss Scarlet."

Realization passes through Ryke's features, and he turns to me. "You were Colonel Mustard?"

I nod. "We had a Mrs. Peacock from *Clue* too, but she bailed at the last minute because it was her best friend's birthday." I wiggle my brows at Lily and then smile at Lo.

They both glance at each other, like they remember Lily's Eleventh Halloween and Lo's Twelfth. Rose was the only one who agreed to go trick-or-treating with me, and despite her broken heel, I remember both of us having fun. I traded my Starbursts and Skittles for all her chocolate.

Across the table from each other, Connor asks Rose a short line in French.

I turn to Ryke to translate, too curious and a little bit concerned. I just hope she's as comfortable here as she can be this far along in her pregnancy.

In a hushed voice, Ryke tells me, "He asked her, 'te sens-tu malade?' which means, *do you feel sick?*"

We both watch Rose reply with, "Pas aujourd'hui."

Ryke whispers to me, "*Not today.*"

I saw Connor massaging Rose's neck this morning at breakfast, and if they were seated next to each other right now, I have a feeling he'd help melt all of her pregnancy kinks.

Ryke leans back from me, but his coarse hand rubs up and down my arm. I tingle, the sensation zipping through me. Followed with a shiver, the jittery anticipation does a number on me.

He dips his head down to whisper, "You alright?"

We're getting married.

My head lightens, and I dizzy as he strokes my arm again, thinking I'm cold.

Everyone has begun laughing loudly over a new photo: ten-year-old Rose, in two-inch black heels, carting a four-year-old me in a red wagon. Little eight-year-old Lily is worn out on the lawn, Lo picking a piece of grass out of her hair. I'm smiling so wide in the picture, my front tooth missing.

I answer Ryke quietly, "I'm just excited." So excited that I start grinning like a fool every time I meet his eyes. I'm so giddy.

His own smile grows. "You look lovesick, Calloway." He messes my hair.

"I think this must be the best sickness there is." My cheeks hurt; I can't contain anything.

Dink, dink, dink of a knife to a wine glass steals my attention elsewhere. My dad. He rises from the table with round rosy cheeks from all the Merlot. "Before the parents turn in, I want to share a surprise that has been in the works for some time, and hopefully there'll only be more good surprises for Ryke and Daisy in the future."

The irony is not lost upon most of the table.

Everyone—minus my parents and Jonathan and maybe nine-year-old Maria—share furtive glances. Full well knowing that I have a surprise in my oven, and it's been baking for ten-weeks.

My sisters cried when I told them, but I'm not sure my surprise constitutes as a "good" one for my father. Bodies twitch, especially Poppy and Rose, and I just think, *please, no one spill this news. Not the day before my wedding.*

My dad takes a long pause. Too long for Loren Hale.

"What's the surprise?" Lo asks. "Are we all going to be assholes and millionaires—oh wait..." He flashes a dry smile.

"Billionaire," Connor corrects. Seated beside his best friend, he holds Lo's gaze.

Lo mockingly winces. "You do realize that my profit margin is bigger than yours, love?"

Connor grins. "Mine is always bigger, darling." Then he winks.

Jonathan scrutinizes them in the flickering torchlight, but he's more relaxed than I thought he'd be. Connor and Lo are clearly *just* friends, both comfortable in their own skin.

"What's the surprise, Dad?" I ask, bringing the spotlight back to the owner.

He smiles at me, and I return it, giddiness still fluttering inside my belly.

"Come August, I was hoping we could all travel to Utah for a family trip."

There has to be a missing link somewhere because this trip to Peru is practically a family vacation with everyone here. And August is next month.

"What's in Utah?" Lo asks with a slightly pained face. I wonder if he's recalling what happened a long time ago on our road trip in Utah. A lot of "brotherly" fist fighting.

Surprisingly, Ryke answers, "Zion National Park."

Sully starts smiling like he knows what's at that national park. He mouths to Ryke, *bring me.*

Ryke rolls his eyes but nods and shakes his head like *why are you even fucking asking? Of course you're coming.*

"I'm lost," Lily proclaims, nudging her brownie with a fork.

"Am I fucking right?" Ryke asks my dad, both seemingly passing good vibes back and forth.

I lean back in my chair, relaxing more and keeping the butterflies alive.

My dad explains to the table, "Fizzle wants Ryke to free-solo Desert Shield, and we know he'll be more inclined to accept this *extremely* generous offer if everyone attends in support."

Jonathan adds to Ryke, "Don't be an idiot. This is good money and a climb you could do in your goddamn sleep."

"First off, I'm not a fucking idiot," Ryke says, jaw tensing. "Secondly, The Moonlight Buttress is a better climb in the same area. It's higher than Desert Shield." Just by his tone, I can tell that he's not as defensive about these cliffs as much as the last one they offered.

He told me that it was "fucking suicide" and he'd never step near it without a harness.

"He's kind of right," Sully tells our parents.

Jonathan narrows his eyes on Ryke. "Moonlight Buttress is a pitiful name and you've already free-soloed it."

Sam chimes in, "Fizzle wanted a new rock face for you, and Desert Shield is still a thousand foot ascension."

Lo shoves his empty strawberry shortcake plate away. "Jesus Christ, do we have to talk about this before his wedding?"

"Yes," all the parents say in unison.

"The family needs to talk about this so we can come to a conclusion," my mom clarifies. This really has been ongoing for a while, but I only want happiness today and tomorrow.

Ryke just ends it right here. "I need a week prep with Sully before I free-solo."

"What for?" my dad asks.

Sully is quick to answer. "I'll help Ryke clean his path and climb it together a few times. You don't have to pay me—"

"Sul," Ryke says. "It's a *job*. You're getting fucking paid."

Sully smiles. "Yeah but I'd do it for free."

Like a final gavel, my dad asks Ryke, "Desert Shield in August with the family there?"

With more light behind his eyes, Ryke nods. "Done deal."

My dad raises his glasses in cheers, and we all lift ours and drink. Ryke seems really happy about the cliff they chose, excited even.

Just as my dad sits down, my mom, with rosy cheeks too, makes a comment, "Anyone else have any more surprises before we call it a night?"

She can't know.

Can she?

"Do you know the gender yet?" Sam asks.

A knife hits a plate. I thought he directed that towards Rose, but no, Poppy's husband is looking me straight in the eye. His mouth slowly drops, watching Poppy make a motion like *stop, cut it out, leave the subject now, Sam.*

"Never mind," he says quickly.

I brave a look towards my parents.

Wide-eyed, my mom has her hand to her throat like she's choking.

My father is as pale as the tablecloth.

"Surprise," I say with quaky lightheartedness. "I'm pregnant." *Please don't be mad.*

Tough crowd. Dead silence. I'm bringing my A game. Ryke hugs me closer in comfort, our chairs practically a bench.

My mom now has her fingers to her mouth. "Are you positive?" she asks.

I nod again. "I'm ten-weeks."

She immediately stands, doesn't even ask who knows. Tears brim, and she comes behind my chair and gives me a side-hug. She even kisses my cheek.

Because she thought I couldn't get pregnant. "I'm so happy for you, honey." She strokes my hair, and I rub my eyes that start to water, overwhelmed by her response.

My dad is still in shock, I think. "How…I thought you couldn't…"

"We've been trying for a fucking year," Ryke explains, no more silence on our part. We're really doing this. Right before our wedding.

We're really, really crazy.

< *41* >

Daisy Calloway

My dad slowly and then more rapidly shakes his head. "You're only twenty-one, Daisy."

He had Poppy when he was in his early twenties, but he won't cop to that. He'll say, *it's different. I had built the Fizzle empire by then. I had a stable, flourishing career. You have nothing.*

He continues, "You have your *whole life* for babies. This isn't you. You've never been this type of girl. You could never just stay at home with a baby." *Never* is an awfully strong word.

All of my sisters start talking over each other to defend me, their voices muddled together.

I can't pick apart words, but Rose is pointing her finger, yellow-green eyes pierced at our dad.

"Hey!" Ryke yells, cutting into the cacophony. Everyone immediately quiets. "Let Daisy fucking talk."

Rose looks a little apologetic, and she's the first to wave me on.

"I am ready," I tell my dad. "And I'm not just a single type of girl. I'm not just Daisy Calloway, the girl who dives off cliffs. Or Daisy

Calloway, the girl who jumps into the ocean without a life vest. I'm so much more than that, and I want a family." I fight tears. "I want a little girl or boy to smile at me just because." I can almost see it far off, the unconditional love I want to give and the joy I want to share—and it's just a simple vision.

It's just Ryke on a hammock. It's just me sitting beside him. Our baby in our arms.

Happy.

Why can't I have that? Why can only certain girls be "meant" for something? It shouldn't be bad to want to be a mom. It shouldn't be bad to want to only have a career. It shouldn't be bad to strive for both or nothing at all.

We all should just be what *we* want to be.

I tell my dad, "I don't know how to show you that I'm not a little girl choosing the next hot fad or that in a month's time I'll be so totally over babies. This past year, I could've changed my mind. It would've been easier because..." I wipe my eyes. "...because it was *so hard* to reach this point."

My dad puts his hand to his lips. I can't tell if he's distraught or just shocked again. He turns towards Ryke.

"No," I say, quickly capturing his attention again. "This was *my* choice as much as it was his. He didn't have to convince me of anything."

I'm not defined by backflips and racing toy cars down the road. Do you hear me, Dad? Please.

He's staring at the napkin in his lap.

"I'm building a camp," I let this out, and the table collectively inhales like *Jesus Christ, Daisy—are you trying to give your father a goddamn heart attack.* Okay, so that's probably just Lo's thoughts.

"A what?" my dad asks.

"A summer camp for young girls and boys. The cabins are actually being built right now."

Worry pales his face. "You didn't use your trust fund..."

"I used all the money I'd made from modeling, but I'm responsible and I do have some goals." I thought, maybe, this would be more appealing to him than the baby aspect.

Instead, he touches his forehead like his brain is about to explode.

My mom peels away from my chair and hurries to his side. "Let's discuss this when we return to Philadelphia." She had no idea about the summer camp, but I think she's so happy about my pregnancy that it's of no matter to her. "We have an early morning, Greg. Let's head in for the night." She helps him stand, and Jonathan pushes his own chair from the table, following his friend.

It's ten o'clock.

"Goodnight," my dad tells everyone, and his eyes flit to me with too much emotion to unbury. "We'll talk later?"

I mutter a word in agreement.

Ryke whispers in my ear, "It's not fucking ruined."

I nod, trying to believe our wedding is still how we imagined. *It is. It is.*

My dad and Jonathan leave, but my mom lingers for a second.

"You shouldn't stay up too late either." She hones in on Ryke, as if instilling this declaration into him: *don't keep my precious little Daisy up past the witching hour, Mr. Meadows.*

She wouldn't say it like that, but it sounds cool in my head. And I feel a little better.

Tomorrow you're getting married, Daisy.

Tomorrow will be one of the happiest days of your life.

Come back, butterflies.

"We're not spending the fucking night together," Ryke says in defense.

I smile at the way he says that. His fingers disappear in my hair, and my stomach flutters. *Good feelings.* Everyone has reminded me of "tradition" for the night before my wedding, and I kind of like the theory of staying in separate rooms.

Reality can be scarier, just because we're in a foreign place. I peek beneath the table...

There's Coconut, sleeping close to Sully's feet. She's fond of him, and she opens her eyes, as though she can feel mine on her pretty baby blues.

"Hey there," I whisper. *I'm glad you're here too.*

She helps me feel safe.

"I'll let Greg know that," my mom says, as though to butter up her sullen husband with "good" news. "Who's coming to the ceremony tomorrow?"

Ryke lists out the few friends that we do have and trust. *Garrison, Frederick, my grandparents (the ones well enough to make the trip), and Eddie— one of Ryke's oldest climbing friends from Costa Rica, who only speaks Spanish.*

Before she leaves, she says, "Congratulations, Daisy." She smiles at me once more, which encourages my smile to return. I watch her hike up towards the lodge.

And all that remains at the table: Willow, Sully, my sisters, their husbands and children. Jane and Moffy are both yawning in high chairs, and Maria fell asleep when servers brought out dessert, her cheek on her father's arm.

"I'm so sorry, Daisy," Sam immediately says. "I thought—I don't know why—but I thought you already told them." He seems really upset and guilt-ridden.

Lo says, "Don't be surprised if we all put coal in your stocking next Christmas."

I laugh.

The entire table eases, just by the genuine sound coming from my lips.

Ryke watches me carefully. I have to push past this, and I will talk to my dad later, before bed. Just private words to reiterate the same thing.

I shrug at him, "It is what it is, right?"

"Right," he says firmly. He's always told me that I can't change the way my dad feels. *He's going to feel what he fucking feels.*

I think I'm just happy that I spoke for me. No one else had to.

Poppy suddenly gasps, fingers to her mouth, startled by something on her cellphone. "Oh God."

Rose plucks it from her hand, her gaze tightening.

I love the sidetrack. It also gives me good reason to move around. I spring from my seat, walking to the other side of the table.

"What is it?" Lily scoots her chair closer to Rose.

The guys are all mouthing things to each other, and even *Sully* has joined in, one of the few men sitting on the side with my sisters.

Don't let television and movies fool you.

Boys share secrets as much as girls.

Rose's eyes are unfamiliarly bright with glee. I stand behind her, hands on her chair, but I'm partially distracted by Lo, who tosses his silverware on his dish, the clatter making me jump.

"Were you in Forbes again?" Lo asks. "Or did Satan finally name you his successor?"

Her yellow-green eyes puncture a hole in his forehead. "Go choke on your dessert."

"You were in Forbes?" Sam asks sincerely.

Lo cocks his head. "Seriously, where have you been? She printed like fifteen copies of the magazine article. I'm surprised she didn't slip them underneath your door in the middle of the fucking night."

Connor interjects, "Being ranked in *Forbes 30 Under 30* is a rare and prestigious achievement. It deserves all the fanfare."

Rose starts to smile.

Connor says something to her in French, and I kneel next to Rose's chair and whisper, "What'd he say?"

Rose glances at me like *why the hell are you on the dirty ground?* I'm on the grass, but to Rose, the cement, the dirt, the grass—it's all the same.

I bat my eyes at her, hoping she'll tell me. "Please—"

She whispers back, "He said that he's proud of me."

Lily makes an audible *awww* noise that has Rose rolling her eyes. Connor wasn't even listed in Forbes this year, and that list, designed for the movers and shakers and millennials creating a difference, proved that Rose has inspired and impacted young women all over the world.

Rose waves the phone at Connor, only the lock screen showing, and she talks to him in French, the endnote sounding like a question. She must have told him what she just saw. His lips rise and he nods, as though allowing her permission.

It dawns on me.

This is about Connor.

"Gather 'round," Rose says to Lily, Willow, and me, since Connor approved of the public viewing. I wedge between Poppy and Rose's chair, my bare knees digging into the soft grass. My yellow strappy dress is safe from stains, which would probably plague Rose the most out of everyone.

"Is it bad?" Lily asks, squinting at the phone that's shielded by Rose's hand.

"No," Poppy and Rose say in unison.

Rose has that look again, verging on a snort and a grin.

Connor says something in French once more, and he procures his phone. All the guys begin to gather around him. Even Sully stands, walks around the table, and peers over Connor's shoulder. Maria yawns awake at Sam's movement, and she picks at her brownie.

Before Rose removes her hand from the screen, Sam and Ryke groan, finding the source of Rose and Poppy's amusement on Connor's cellphone before us.

Rose is peeved that they beat her, and Connor's satisfaction mushrooms, practically gloating across the table. She mouths, *I hate you.*

He mouths, *you love me.*

I nudge my older sister's shoulder. "Rose?" They distract *each other* more than anyone can possibly distract them.

She reveals the screen, lit up with a *Celebrity Crush* tabloid article.

Oh my God.

My jaw slowly drops.

Right below a photograph of Lily at the airport, carrying a wide-eyed Maximoff Hale, remains a photo of Connor Cobalt. He's stepping out of his limo, dressed in casual black plants and a blue button-down. I recognize the outfit since he wore it on the private jet to Peru.

This must've been taken at the airport a couple days ago.

The photoshopped pic includes a yellow circle drawn in after the fact—right around Connor's crotch.

The headline: CONNOR COBALT'S PENIS IS TOO BIG FOR HIS PANTS.

I bust out laughing. Lily and Willow instantly join in, my stomach in stitches.

They have a second picture, zoomed in on his crotch, the outline of the bulge *really* clear. It's mostly funny because we know Connor well enough to realize that the photo won't offend him or cross his personal boundaries.

Rose clicks into Twitter for a second, and I'm surprised to see Poppy's feed full of Coballoway shippers freaking out about this pic. She must follow these accounts:

@rosecoballoway
@rosecobalt
@connorcalcium
@ConnorCockbalt
@connorcobaltx
@caball0way
@cobaltconnor
@rosescalloway
@RoseCallowoah
@rosecalloways
@connrcobalt
@coballway
@msrosecalloway

The overwhelming response from fans: I KNEW IT #myhusband

Lo lets out a long whistle. "First Ryke, now Connor. I'd feel a little self-conscious if I didn't know you two had monster dicks."

Sam straightens up. "That's our cue to leave. Maria." He gestures for her to stand.

"What? I've heard this all before, Dad." She takes another bite of brownie.

"Great." He shoots Lo a look.

Lo touches his chest. "I'm not the one who was caught on camera with a twelve-inch—"

"Okay, okay," Sam cuts him off and then motions to Maria, though I see a flicker of a smile on his lips.

Maria turns to her mom. "Is twelve inches big?"

Uh-oh.

The table falls in utter silence, but Connor has his fingers pressed to his lips, his burgeoning, million-dollar grin a sight to behold.

Poppy is near-laughter, but Sam pinches his eyes in distress. "We'll talk about this later, but we should get to bed. We need to wake up early tomorrow."

Maria reluctantly stands, though she grabs her brownie plate and takes it with her as she leaves with her mom and dad. And then there were...still too many to count.

I like it that way. All of us here. Together.

"You're not really *that* big?" Sully asks like *come on, man, give it to me straight.*

Connor says, "Would it really be a surprise if I was?"

"No," about four people say, most of us under the same conclusion. Connor Cobalt is a god among men so he might as well have a godly penis too.

"Should I be annoyed about this for you?" Lo asks him, kicking his feet onto Sam's empty chair next to him. It's not much different than what we go through. They had pictures of my side-boob when I went without a bra in a weirdly cut dress.

I didn't think anything of it at the time. I just made a quick CVS run for nail polish.

Connor shakes his head. "I have no feelings about it, but if you really want to feel something, I'd rather it be somewhere around *awe* and *adoration*."

"I'm awed and adorated," Sully chimes in.

"Adorated isn't a word," Connor corrects.

Ryke cuts in, "Fuck off."

"So wait." Sully collects his thoughts for a second and then points at Ryke. "This happened to you too?"

Ryke has to crane his head over his shoulder to see Sully behind him. "Yeah, only I was taking Nutty for a fucking walk outside the gated neighborhood."

"In drawstring pants," Lo adds. "No underwear. Python in full view."

I remember the picture well.

The headline: RYKE MEADOWS' PENIS

It was as trite and to-the-point as he tends to be, which makes Connor's egotistical headline even more comical.

"I don't fucking care," Ryke says, "but they should be fucking careful about what guys they do this to. Because some will care, and it's not right for them to post this shit without consent."

"Cheers," Rose says in agreement, raising her glass of water.

We all pick up our drinks and clink again, the air buzzing with our better, more upbeat energies. I'm standing next to Willow's chair now, my gaze roaming Ryke as much as his begins to roam me.

"Before we head in, I want to say something." Lo rises with his water glass in hand. "Don't worry, this isn't a fucking surprise."

Who would have thought Lo would be the one to keep lightening the mood?

I smile, and we all begin to quiet. The wind whips through the vast Peruvian lands, the only noise truly audible.

Lo gestures from his older brother, then to me. "I've heard that people spend a *really* long time finding their soul mates."

I squeeze Lily's shoulder. She's been in her soul mate's arms since she was little.

"It took you two long enough, didn't it?" Lo says. "No thanks to me." He pauses. "But I want you two to know—from the bottom of my black, decaying heart—I love you both, and the *only* perfect world has Ryke standing beside Daisy and Daisy standing beside Ryke. Anything less is fucked up. Remember that, will you?"

My eyes glass.

I'll remember, Lo.

It's impossible to forget the kind of love that rattles my bones and screams *I am alive* every single day of my life.

< 42 >

Daisy Calloway

"I'll be in the bridal suite by one, I promise," I tell Lily and Rose in the hotel hallway, lingering by Ryke's room.

Both exchange a wary look—like I'll be zombie Daisy tomorrow instead of wide-eyed, fresh-faced effervescent Daisy, but they're both forgetting something. "I'm used to sleeping short spurts, but you both aren't, so don't let me keep you up, please."

I already spent thirty minutes chatting with my dad. He was mostly cordial and quiet, and he didn't voice much dissent. So I know I'll see him at the ceremony tomorrow.

I was going to ask my dad to walk me down the aisle, as an apology, but Ryke *and* Rose said I should only ask him if I want him to do so. Not just to make him feel better.

So I didn't ask him, and I'd already told him my decision weeks ago. He seemed okay with it back then. It's not that I don't love my father enough to do it. It's just that I like the idea of freely giving myself away. Without needing the final approval of anyone but my own heart and my own voice.

In the lodge's hallway, Ryke has his keycard in hand, standing rigid by his door. "I'm not letting Daisy stay in my room that fucking long, so don't worry."

"See." I spread my arms. I doubt I'd be able to sleep anyway, too wired and excited about what's to come tomorrow.

"We need to do that...*thing* tonight," Rose says vaguely. "So just be back by one a.m. and we should have time to do it before tomorrow morning."

I nod, unable to contain a smile.

"What fucking thing?" Ryke asks.

"Secret things," Lily chimes in and then Rose hooks her arm and they stroll off to the bridal suite without me.

I'll be there soon.

There's just something I need to do first.

Ryke unlocks his room and holds the door open for me. I slide into his suite and immediately dig in his travel bag on the wooden dresser. Out of the corner of my eye, I see him pulling his shirt over his head, his set of impeccably toned abs and lean muscles something only avid climbers can claim.

More giddiness fills me, lifts me. I can almost feel the hairs rise on my arms. I'm not the least bit discreet, so when he catches me staring, I just smile more.

His brows rise at me, knowing that I like to watch him. "It's fucking hot in here."

I feign confusion. "But I thought this was the start of a Ryke Meadows striptease."

"No," he states but chucks his shirt at my face.

I laugh and keep searching in his bag but I can't find *it*. "If you'd rather go to bed, I understand. You know we can always ditch this idea. It's not a requirement."

"I want to fucking do this, Calloway," Ryke replies in that stern, *don't argue with me about it* manner. I watch his lengthy stride close the gap between us. Then he unzips the front of his travel bag and brings out the portable speaker. Just what I wanted.

His close proximity double-flips my stomach, and he begins to plug in the speaker. I almost forgot to bring it, but Rose printed out a long travel list for me.

Usually I never really care about forgetting a toothbrush or underwear. It's all part of my packing process. Whatever is supposed to make the journey makes it. If I'm missing something important, I have fun finding alternatives.

Rose disliked my theory, at least not for my wedding, so that's where the list came in.

In the heat of the quiet moment, I grip the bottom of my dress and tug it off, tossing the garment on the floor. I stand comfortable in yellow cotton panties and a floral bra.

Ryke's eyes descend my body for a quick second, stopping on my belly.

My ten-week baby bump is very small but definitely noticeable without clothes. Before any grand emotion surfaces, his gaze lands back on mine.

With a mischievous smile, I say, "It's fucking hot in here." I like the idea of being half-naked with him, and he must see the thrill in my eyes because he doesn't ask for a real answer. He just swiftly begins closing the blinds, the warm glow of lamplight illuminating the hotel room.

I dock my phone on the speaker and then turn my music on shuffle, playing roulette with the song choice here.

"Are you ready?" I ask as he finishes the last window. I keep rocking back and forth on my feet, restless, nervous, but light and airy and *ready* for this moment to ignite. Maybe it already has.

Ryke nods and returns to the middle of the hotel suite, a buttoned couch on one side and a king-sized bed with gray bedding against light gold walls on the other. I can't discern the current song, but it's somewhere between fast and slow and alternative.

I mentally measure the empty space from him to me. A cavernous ten feet.

He crosses his arms, as though he's sculpted from stone.

I keep smiling because I love him so much, every part of him that says *I don't fucking dance.* It's been well documented in the years that I've known him. Ryke solidifies like a brick wall at concerts and celebrations and all weddings. For Ryke to want to practice our first dance at all is a big deal.

It's also been well documented that I'm *not* a great dancer like Lily or Lo or even Rose who can pull off a waltz. I spaced out during most of cotillion. I usually just jump to the beat, and jumping is not the best kind of partner dancing. So I'm in the same boat as Ryke.

"Alright," I say, strolling closer to my soon-to-be husband. His eyes never leave me as I glide to him. "We're going to have to loosen up." He lets me seize one of his hands, breaking his arms from the closed stance.

I hone in on the differences between his hand and mine: much larger and his palm more calloused and rough to my soft. He's staring down at me, this man who'd drop to his knees if I asked him to. Who'd take care of me. Never abuse me. Never pressure me or take advantage of me. He's treated me with more respect than I can quantify.

I almost feel the blood rushing through my veins. I'm so very, very attracted to this person in front of me.

"And then your other arm," I say in a soft breath. As I clutch his other hand, his arm joint livens and moves. "Then they go here." I put his hands on my shoulders.

He almost smiles, a twinkle in those darkened eyes.

"What?" My cheeks hurt from my own unequivocal smile, and I inhale shallowly. He's already taking my breath away, and we're only just trying to figure out how to dance together.

For the first time.

He speaks with his movements, his hands dropping from my shoulders to my wrists—his grip firm and assured. Then he lifts my arms until they're set securely on *his* shoulders.

My knees instinctively bend, bouncing on the tips of my toes. He's still stoic. He's still solid rock, but he's begun to smile.

His large, rough hands slide down my body until he holds my waist. I'm mesmerized for a second, his skin on my bare skin, so overwhelming that a sharp sound escapes from my lips. He draws me closer, his chest pressed against mine, the beat of our hearts in sync.

There's no right or wrong way in how to dance or how to move or how to *be*. We both know this in the end, and that's why we take our time and just do whatever comes to us. I bet we'll stay silent, let the music thrum through our bodies.

And then...

And then the song—it changes. We both inhale, the recognizable tune washing over us.

It's the song that always reminds me of Ryke.

"Sweet Disposition" by The Temper Trap fills the room with the smoothest, most beautiful melody.

His brown eyes, flecked with hazel, bore into me, and before I can think or breathe, we're moving. One foot first, he's leading me. Then the next. These aren't complex, professional moves. We haven't suddenly turned into the Best Dancing Couple in the Universe. His confidence, his strength has me guessing which way he'll go. I gladly and surely follow.

I'm laughing. I'm lost for breath. I feel like I'm chasing him, or he's chasing me. As we move together. Air rushes through me like a wind tunnel.

His hand on my waist. My legs brushing his. Lungs expanding.

Feet never stopping. Hearts never quitting.

Ryke sweeps me in such simple actions that contain the vastness, the fullness, of our lives and our love. It pumps my blood, and I see it alight in his eyes.

The lyrics throttle me, and we're not gliding. We're spinning madly. His eyes on mine. Like we're two feral creatures meant to be together. Until the end of time.

He dips me backwards and then lets go. My body *falls,* air whooshing out of me, and before I hit the ground, his arms catch me. My chest rises and drops heavily, my fingers digging into his biceps. Before I can rewrap my head around my limbs, he lifts me upright again, my hair splayed crazily. Like I've just stepped off a rollercoaster.

The tempo of the song slows, and Ryke brushes the strands away from my cheeks, his breathing deepening with mine. I run my fingers through his thick hair, and then my arms fall back to his shoulders.

We're moving again.

I smile. So wide. So alive.

And then the crescendo hits.

He dips me again, so low—this time holding on. And my lungs—my lungs *burst* inside of me, the world blind with love. I clutch his neck tightly.

If I fall, he'll come with me.

The intensity, the *caring* in his features pounds my heart more than the drumbeats, his gaze cloaking me in adoration and affection. I can't turn off the light that beams through me, and slowly and carefully, he lowers my back onto the floor. Hovering above me, his arm braced beside my cheek.

My wolf.

My everything.

He's a breath away from my lips as the song fades. And very softly, he says, "I'm so fucking in love with you."

I prop my body on my elbows, nearing his lips. People say you can't describe love, but I have this theory that you can. It's just subjective. Do you want to know what love feels like for me?

It's breathing and suffocating. Sobbing and smiling. Yearning and fading. To ache that much harder. To live that much larger. It's every moment. Every single, tiny one.

I've felt it all with Ryke.

And it's not solely the wild, crazed events that keep my heart pumping. It's these small, most inconceivable seconds of time spent together. Our smiles. Our tears. Our limbs shifting or standing still. The instant our lonely souls are filled.

I've never lived or loved wilder and freer than with him.

I open my mouth to say the words too, but he nods like *I see it, Dais*. He sees it in my eyes. I'm so in love with him. He kisses me gently, and I think, *this is it*.

Our first dance.

I whisper against his lips, "This moment is ours, isn't it?" I don't want to share this with anyone else. We ended up on the floor. Just like animals. I break into a smile, and his thumb strokes the long scar on my cheek.

He looks like he could spend the rest of his life on the floor, right here, tangled up with me. He nods and says against my lips, "This is fucking ours."

I run my fingers through his hair again. "I'm so happy I could scream."

His lips curve upward. "Then scream, Calloway."

I howl instead. When he joins in, when he howls with me, my world is absolutely, totally and entirely complete.

< 43 >

Ryke Meadows

6:02 a.m.

The sun just begins to rise behind Machu Picchu's sharp mountain peak, the dark sky fucking lightening with soft blues. I stand beneath a wooden arch draped with green foliage and an assortment of white flowers and yellow daisies.

My heart is fucking *pounding*. I watch Daisy's parents help her grandfather in a wooden chair before they take their seats. Sam, Maria, Garrison, my father, and Frederick are already in theirs. Off to the side, one of my oldest climbing buddies wields his zampoña, a pan flute. Eddie offered to play the music at our wedding last time I visited.

For a fifty-year-old fucking recluse in the middle of the Costa Rican rainforest, it was a grand gesture that I wouldn't refuse.

I keep raking my hands through my hair, the sleeves of my white button-down rolled to my biceps. Just black slacks and a black tie, nothing fucking over-the-top. Same for my groomsmen: my little brother and Connor.

"If you're going to puke, bro, you only have two minutes to do it." Lo is closest to my side.

I rub my forehead with my arm. *Fucking A.*

All I can think is that this has to be perfect for Daisy.

Luck slips out of our grasp every time we catch it. The minute we taste happiness or something decent and good happens, it's gone. Her theory about how she can't feel happiness in one breath, without being struck down in the second, fucking kills me.

Today, of all days, I want to prove her wrong.

I want her to feel happiness without anything else attached. Just pure unadulterated joy.

Let me give her that.

I stare up at the sky, expecting a helicopter. A fucking drone. The disruption of paparazzi to pour down on us.

A second later, a bird slices through the dim, morning light. *Okay.* I nod to myself, my shoulders loosening. *Okay.* Lo places his hand on my back. "Seriously, are you alright?"

I rotate, catching sight of Lo's foreign concern and Connor's tranquil, relaxed expression. Sully stands off to the left of the arch, hands in his slacks, his shaggy hair bobbing to the rustle of the trees. No music yet.

I never imagined myself married or a future wedding or anything past today. If I did ten years ago, I doubt it'd look anything like this. With these friends and family here. Willing to celebrate the love that Daisy and I share. This isn't a sad, lonely picture.

It's just the fucking opposite.

"I'm okay," I finally tell my brother. *Better than okay.* This is the kind of life I never thought I'd have, and seeing it all laid out like this does something to me.

"Really?" Disbelief clouds his face. "I thought we'd have to take a puke break for you."

"Fucking really," I snap back, glancing at his watch. "She's taking a long time." *Maybe she's sick.* "I should—"

"You should stay here," Lo cuts me off. "It's your only job."

"No surprise he's having trouble at it," Connor pipes in.

I roll my fucking eyes, but I'm glad that he's still here, no matter how much we grow older.

Connor checks his Rolex. "She is a little late though."

Something terrible fucking happened.

I'm going to leave.

And just as I'm about to take a step, Eddie begins blowing on his pan flute. The whimsical music breezes through the private gardens, the lodge far off and hidden behind trees.

I stand rigid, my arms at my side, and I fixate on the hedge where people should either frantically run out or gracefully walk along the aisle between wooden chairs. *Let it be the fucking latter.*

What feels like a century passes.

Real fucking concern darkens my face.

Then a canary yellow dress billows into the forefront.

Poppy emerges from behind the hedge. The fabric of her V-neck gown cascades to the grass, the layers light and combined to look like a flower petal.

I hone in on her slow pace, timed to the pan flute.

She's not running. She's not hysteric. She carries a tiny bouquet of white flowers, and just as Rose and Willow follow behind her, I notice something.

They all wear crowns made of baby's breath. It reminds me so much of Daisy. *Everything's going to be okay.* It's beginning to feel that way.

Lily, the maid of honor, brings the rear with a nervous smile. Her flower crown is slightly off-kilter. My little brother makes the Spock symbol thing at her, and her cheeks redden but her smile stretches.

She's beautiful and has more self-confidence than I ever remember her possessing. *I'm proud of you, Lil.*

In no time, all of Daisy's sisters line up on the other side of the arch, Lily closest to it. Next, two-year-old Janie and Moffy shuffle down the aisle, tossing white flower petals from their respective baskets. Then comes a chorus of "awwws" and camera flashes from Daisy's parents.

These two little kids are beyond fucking cute.

Janie runs out of flowers, and Moffy lets her grab some from his basket. They finish off at the end and then Samantha lifts Moffy on her lap, Greg picking up Janie.

Our white husky suddenly appears, her tail wagging as she hurries excitedly down the aisle, a yellow bow tied around her collar. As she reaches me, I crouch and pat her side and rub behind her ears.

Lo follows suit, only to retrieve the rings attached to her collar. Then Nutty sits calmly by Lo's feet, alert and watchful of the aisle. Like she fucking knows who's coming next.

I exhale.

In the audience, everyone begins to stand.

6:12 a.m.

The sun is rising in Peru.

I had no preconceived notions of what I'd feel today. I didn't think that fucking far ahead, but waiting for the bride to step out, *my* bride, shortens my breath. More than anyone else, I just want to see her.

And then she rounds the hedge.

I'm almost knocked back. I take an audible inhale, my gaze fixed on her unparalleled smile and her *golden blonde* hair.

Daisy stands strongly, fucking vibrantly, at the end of the aisle.

My eyes burn because I've never seen her this beautiful or this alive. Meeting her radiance head on is a collision with ten-thousand degrees of heat. The longer I watch, my gaze blazes, water welling like I may not fucking survive. And guess what.

I'm not shutting my eyes.

I'd rather die inside this moment than miss a single part.

An assortment of colorful flowers shaped in a crown is nestled in her golden hair. Her sheer white gown dusts the grass, see-through long sleeves reaching her wrists. As she begins to step forward, I notice the intricate embroidery of silver doves and vines dripping down her arms, breastbone, and waist.

When my eyes connect with hers again, she mouths, *hey there.*

I find the fucking strength to mouth back, *hey, Calloway.*

My gaze grows glassier the more I watch her, the more she watches me. Slowly nearing.

The glimmer in her green eyes, the lightness in her gait, the overwhelming smile stretching her scar—this is the look of someone who's free. Somewhere along the way, she found her voice. Somewhere along the way, she found her stride. I'm just the grateful fucking guy who was given the chance to stand by her side.

Through it all.

I don't pinch my eyes, and a couple tears slide down my cheek.

I can't look away.

Daisy spins in the center of the aisle, mid-walk, and when she faces me again, she wags her brows, continuing on.

Cute, Calloway.

I zone in on her blonde hair again. She must have dyed it last night with her sisters' help, the secret "thing" Rose and Lily teased.

Something about her *choice* to return to the shade she had when we met—it sends my whole fucking soul on an ascent. The nostalgia of first love—for both of us—flies to the forefront.

Times where we raced faster and farther. Times where we slowed down with one another.

And I see us in the sky. I see us in the sun and clouds. In the grass and trees.

I see us in everything.

"Fuck," I curse beneath my breath, rubbing my face dry for a second. I drop my hand about the same time Daisy is beside me, her sisters sniffling.

Rose is passing a box of tissues between them.

Daisy wipes beneath my eyes with her thumb.

Don't let her fool you. She's full-blown fucking crying with a weepy smile. I cup her cheeks with my hands and brush her tear-streaks away too.

Sully clears his throat, catching our attention as he stands behind us. Daisy was the one who asked Sully to officiate our wedding, which I thought he'd reject based on all the duties that came with it. Before she even asked him, she said to me, "He's your best childhood friend."

"Summer camp friend," I corrected her.

To which Sully scoffed and said, "Dude, we're *best* friends." He nodded to Daisy. "He doesn't believe me whenever I say it—thinks that I'm too good for him or something."

It was true. He climbs and meets up with more people than just me. To assume that I'm his best fucking friend has always felt false. Even if he tells me it's not.

So when Daisy asked him to officiate, he actually started crying. That's when I realized that we were best friends growing up. Still are.

"We're gathered here today," Sully begins, placing his hand on my shoulder and then Daisy's, "to witness the union between two of the craziest people on planet Earth."

Everyone starts applauding in affirmation of that and I kid you fucking not, our husky barks too.

Daisy laughs, and my hand falls to hers.

Then Sully takes a step back from us and says, "So I took a poll yesterday from your friends and family." He wears a goofy fucking smile.

I shake my head at him like *what the fuck did you do?*

"I figured something out—but I guess I already knew it." He nods to both of us. "You two have sacrificed a lot for the people you love. So now, right now, and whatever time that's left—this is *your* time to be happy. We're all here ready to watch you." He pauses. "Not in a pervy way."

We all laugh.

Then he gestures to Daisy and me, backing up to show that it's our time to speak.

I face her, and she places her palms flat on my chest, a playful smile growing.

"So," she says, "I'll go first."

I nod, my hand on her waist.

She starts, "During Christmas, I asked you when you knew that I'm *the one*, that this is the 'can't-eat, can't-sleep, reach-for-the-stars, over-the-fence, World Series kind of stuff'—do you remember that?"

"Yeah." *Like it was yesterday.* We made a promise to tell each other our answers during our wedding. I didn't write mine down because it'd take me a decade to figure out the best way to phrase it. I doubt that I'd ever find the appropriate words. I don't care how it fucking comes out anymore. The right way will be the first way.

Her restless hands move from my chest to arms. "I've thought a lot about this."

I've wondered what her response would be, but I didn't fucking try to guess.

"The simple answer," she says, "would be the moment you dove in after me, but back then I hadn't discovered the depth of your compassion, how much you truly *love* living life, and how we seem to fit, even when we shouldn't."

I pull her closer, my hand lost in her hair, and I hang onto her words.

She clutches onto my biceps. "I knew. I knew at the Alps when I *ran* so fast outside in deep snow. Barefoot. Barely clothed. You'd done so much for me before then."

I stayed by her side after she was drugged at a New Year's Eve party. I taught her how to ride a motorcycle. I'd watch movies with her until she fell asleep every night. Too frightened to be alone.

But she picked this moment.

I search her eyes that contain all the fucking reasons why.

"You always cared about me. You were always there for me, but this time felt different. You wrapped your coat around me, picked me up in your arms, and said, 'When life gets fucking hard, you can always turn to me. You need to run? I'll run with you, Calloway. Just put on some fucking shoes first.'" She smiles, tears streaming down her cheeks, and I feel another one roll down mine. "I realized then that I'd never want to be vulnerable with any other man but you. Someone that *understands* me. Respects me. Loves me—so wildly. You were the only one. You are the only one."

She was seventeen.

My whole body tightens with sentiments beyond me, and I bring her closer and whisper, "I love you." She playfully bites my shoulder, our family and friends shedding tears faster than I can count.

What I have to say is only for her, even if everyone else can hear. I hold her hips, my forehead nearly against hers as I say, "I have you fucking beat, sweetheart."

Confusion and curiosity light her big green eyes.

"I knew," I say slowly to her, "that you were the *only* girl that I'd ever fall in love with—could ever fall in love with—in Cancun, Mexico, on the boardwalk of a bungee jump."

She begins to sob, shaking her head.

I cup her face between my hands. "I knew back then, Daisy Petunia Calloway, because you were the *only* girl I'd ever met that was as deeply *caring* and as fucking lonely as me. If anyone was going to fill my heart, it was you. Only you."

She was sixteen.

Age played a huge factor in suppressing whatever feelings I could eventually have—the feelings I would have. I knew then that if there was any chance of me finding *the one*—it'd be with the girl that I felt emotionally connected to.

It was her.

I didn't believe I'd find anyone else on that level. Not for a fucking second.

Tears wet her lashes. "You never said anything before."

"I never thought I'd be with you." I feel hot trails scald my face. "I was fucking content with the idea of being alone for the rest of my life." I said as much to my brother at one point. "You want to know what I am now?"

She nods.

"I'm more than fucking happy, Dais." I lean down to her and whisper, "Thank you."

We kiss suddenly, an *I love you* and *thank you* in her lips that's beyond what words can fucking speak. I kiss her as savagely as she kisses me.

Her infectious smile rises against my lips.

Mine grows, in step with my wife.

And I vow, "Wherever you go, I'll go." As long as I'm alive, this will never fucking change.

< 44 >

Daisy Meadows

On my wedding night, pink and purple bubbles overflow the Jacuzzi tub in our hotel suite, thanks to a unicorn bath bomb. I'm chest-deep in shimmering water, leaning over the side with my cell in hand. Ryke stepped out for a moment when his phone rang, disappearing into the bedroom. His muffled voice is barely coherent from the tub.

I tap a couple buttons on my phone screen and an automated voice sounds, *"Please wait for the beep and then record your outgoing voicemail. Press one to end the message."*

I clear my throat.

BEEEEP.

"Hi, it's Daisy. Not Duck and not Duke. Definitely not Buchanan. I'm a Meadows. If you haven't misdialed then leave your name after the beep, and I'll call back when I return from the moon—"

Ryke appears in the door frame. Buck naked. My smile widens as he stands stoic and tall, letting my eyes graze all of him. Beads of water still drip down his abdomen and arms, and the full frontal view is pretty damn exquisite.

To my phone speaker, I say, "Don't wait around. It may take a while." I hit the number one and set my cell aside, resting my forearms on the tub ledge and my chin on my hands. "Husband," I test out the word. It sounds mighty powerful. "Did anyone interesting call?"

He approaches the tub, setting his phone next to mine. "Just my fucking father."

I straighten up, expecting bad news, but nothing filters through his darkened gaze besides his usual broodiness.

He returns to the warm bath water, sinking down and then sliding towards me. His knees stick out of the pinkish purple foam bubbles on either side of my frame. His arms rest on the tub's edges, my legs stretching out above his thighs. My chest is almost right up against his, the placement of our bodies a thousand times more intimate.

I instantly feel safer with him this close, this near. And I wait for him to tell me more.

After a couple minutes, my fingers drawing hearts and flowers in the foam, he finally gathers the words. "Greg and Jonathan are leaving tonight."

My face falls. "What? Why?" I retrace my steps, my words, wondering if I offended my dad by not asking him to walk me down the aisle after all, or if he's still uncomfortable about the fact that I'll be a young mom.

"Hey, don't worry about it. It's not your fucking fault—"

"I must've offended him," I realize, my face twisting in hurt. "I should call him—"

"Dais," Ryke forces my name, his hand on my cheek. "It's our fucking wedding night, and they're leaving because something about our wedding present. I don't fucking know; he wasn't making sense."

"Was he just lying to make us feel better?"

"I don't think so." His hazel-flecked eyes pin on mine.

You knew I was the one *in Cancun.* The fact pops up more than once to dizzy me.

"Promise me you won't let this ruin your night or I'm going to wish I never said a fucking thing until tomorrow."

I let it go and scoop up a handful of bubbles and dab them around my chin, jawline and upper-lip. I quirk my brow and grin at him. "Would you still love me with a pink beard?"

With his firm hand on the back of my head, he kisses me roughly, bubble beard and all. My lips tingle beneath his, his tongue parting them and sliding skillfully along mine. One of his hands cups my ass, and when he squeezes, I moan a little against his mouth.

He breaks away while I catch my breath. Ryke affectionately combs my blonde hair back, so soothing with the added warm water. I knew I wanted to return to blonde after *Grand & Daring Stakeout #32*. I just kept gravitating towards those wigs, but I decided to hold off on dyeing my hair until my wedding day.

To surprise Ryke. He was even more overcome than I imagined.

I'll never forget the way he stared at me as I neared him. Or the tears that rolled down his cheek.

I clutch his shoulders, resting my chin there for a second, his warmth comforting. I'm antsy though, so I lean back as much as I scoot forward. I end up running my hands through his hair, facing him.

"You tired tonight?" he asks. It's been a long day with an early morning wedding and then the never-ending reception that lasted until about an hour ago. Everyone has most likely conked out, and Ryke would never hold it against me if I just wanted to soak in the tub and then sleep.

I'm still wired from the adrenaline of our ceremony and then *him*, just his presence this weekend. "I want to solidify our union," I say. "Isn't it bad luck if we don't consummate the marriage?"

"We're not living in the seventeenth century, we can do whatever the fuck we want," he says in a low, husky voice, pulling me even further onto his lap. I wrap my legs tighter around his waist.

"Yeah?" I kiss his cheek so lightly, so teasingly that he finds my lips and makes up for the tenderness with an aggressive, *I'm pack leader and*

I want you right fucking now embrace. His hands push me so close against his chest that I lose breath and my thighs tremble.

His mouth drifts to my ear. "I need you to say the fucking words, sweetheart."

I instinctively grind forward, so very attracted to Ryke, and his muscles flex and coil in response, his arousal spiking. I rest my forehead against his shoulder, grasping some of his hair. "I want this." I practically pant. I lift my head, just to meet his eyes, and I say even more strongly, "I want you inside of me. Please."

Without wasting another second, Ryke stands, holding me perfectly around his waist. *The power of my voice*, I smile as his feral lips ravage mine. He steps out of the bathtub, essentially carrying me into the shower with him.

Swiftly, he turns on the showerhead, water raining down on us and washing away any foam bubbles and soapsuds. I feel like I can't catch my breath, my whole body vibrating for closer contact even though I'm wrapped around him.

In between a kiss that swells my lips, I pant, "I'm so aroused." More than usual for me. He supports me with just one hand, the other traveling between my legs. His fingers graze my clit, the sensitivity flicking on neon lights inside my brain.

I breathe heavily against him. "Ryke." I touch his wrist, wanting him to stay down there. *Oh God.* What is this?

As though he can read my mind, he says, "Hormones."

Hormones?

My smile stretches, and I rest my hand on my belly. "What a miracle baby." She or he has helped shift all these chemicals in my body that say, *nah, no sex for me, thanks*, into carnal, take-your-clothes-off Daisy.

At least for tonight.

Ryke runs his hand over my abdomen, the bump so small but he notices it well enough, and then he hoists me a little higher, more protectively. I reach over his side and shut off the shower before he carries me out. His lengthy stride and darkened gaze drives me curious and excited. I'm backwards to wherever he takes me.

"Daisy Meadows," he says huskily. "You ready to go for a fucking ride?"

My pulse races, and I stare at his hard, unshaven jaw, his hair dripping wet. "Say that again," I pant.

His lips rise. "Daisy Meadows."

I break into another smile, unable to even speak. Then he reaches behind me, and the sixty-degree temperature tonight rushes onto the balcony, washing over us. The suite is on the highest floor, all the other balconies below us.

As he turns *off* the lights and then steps outside, I crane my neck over my shoulder at the balcony railing and view. Filmy clouds hide the stars and the tip of the mountain peak. I like that nighttime and weather darkens our surroundings. No spotlight bearing down us. Shrouded from anyone's view.

I can barely even distinguish the black railing from the air, but Ryke discovers it just fine, setting my ass on cold iron.

I clutch his waist with a looser, daring grip, but he has one hand on my knee at all times, a vice that is not breaking. Our make-out slows for a second, only as I realize how perfect the height of the railing is to his hardened cock.

He spreads my knees apart, and I almost begin to *pulse* for him. Even though he hasn't slid in yet. I keep staring down, and he lifts my chin to kiss me one more time.

I ask in a shallow breath, "Can we skip foreplay?" If I'm not wet enough, it's like asking Ryke, *can you stick your nine-inch razor blade in my vagina?* He's not about that.

With his free hand, he slips two fingers into *his* mouth before he rubs them against my clit. I bite the bottom of my lip, a noise tickling my throat. *Ahhh...* "Ryke," I say softly, so no one else outside can possibly hear. His movements escalate, teasing me until his fingers slip…in and pump. His mouth trails my collar, then reaches my nipple.

I inhale sharply.

His teeth skim the sensitive bud, his fingers driving *further* inside me, and his thumb keeps rubbing. His talented lips and tongue return to my neck.

My hands dig into his waist, and my back begins to arch, my head tilting—eyes on the sky. My toes curl and a tremor ripples through my body. *RykeRykeRyke…* My mouth opens and can't shut.

I almost start to cry but restrain the noise. It feels like an orgasm of the century, and as I slowly, ever so slowly, come down, Ryke watches me with raised brows.

"Why would you want to fucking skip that?" he asks.

"Point felt," I conclude with one more exhale.

He comes closer, his erection in line with my wide-open legs, and one of his hands curves around my back. I trust him. I trust him a *thousand* times over with my life. Enough to sit on a thin railing ten-stories above the ground. Enough to lean back with that disastrous, missing link in my head. The one that numbs death and says, *it's okay to fall. Go right ahead.*

He has me.

He has me in his arms. In his soul. And he's not going to let go.

He never has.

My pulse is speeding a hundred-and-fifty miles per hour. "I love you," I breathe, my hands loose around his neck.

He nudges my cheek with his nose, just so I lift my head up enough to kiss him. I smile in the middle of it, and his hardness slowly fills me, the sensitivity electrifying my body. I shudder against him, and he assesses my state, for any signs of pain.

I nod to him a couple times like, *I'm good. I'm really good.*

He thrusts, rocking so slow, the pleasure like beautiful, electric anguish. I let out a high-pitched noise that he conceals with his large hand, so no one catches us making love outside. His other hand is tight on my knee again.

I clench around his cock as I watch it disappear inside of me, then out. Then in. My trembling hands fall to his ass, flexing beneath my palm each time he pushes *in*. I cry again, his coarse hand still covering my lips.

I mumble, "I can't...I can't..." *It's too much...*I moan, my body in a high, and I lean backwards, slicing through air, all of it rushing out through my lungs.

His hand on my mouth suddenly catches my wrist, right when I'm at a supine angle, staring straight up at the sky. He's still rocking back and forth inside of me, building me up all over again.

I can't help but smile, especially as I hear his heavy breath, attempting to restrain his climax so this'll last longer. His gaze is all over my body, exploring me.

Then he gently lets go of my wrist.

I have barely any use of my core muscles right now, so I fall further, staring upside-down at the ground like a hanging towel. I laugh, happiness floating all around me. I reach towards the grass but of course I'm ten-stories away.

The only thing keeping my ass on the railing: Ryke's sole hand on my knee. He could've held my shoulders, my waist, my bicep—anything more substantial. But he picked my knee.

Because he knew I'd love this. Right here.

When blood starts rushing to my head, I raise my arms back towards Ryke, and he clasps my wrist again, lifting my torso up. I hug him, my eyes flitting between his and the way our bodies meet.

His eyes do the same but manage to stay on mine a great deal more.

I rock my hips a little, and the pressure, the fullness, inside of me causes me to clench and then pulse all over again.

"*Fuck*," he grunts, lifting me higher off the railing, his arms underneath my legs and hand on my ass and the other on the small of my back. So he can pound faster. I moan into his chest, totally gone. I want him to do what he wants with me, and he rams rapidly. Until we both climax together.

Stay inside of me. I don't have to ask. He keeps me full, carrying me back inside and sliding the door and curtains closed. He brings me to our bed. Beneath the covers, facing one another, we kiss affectionately, my leg hiked over his waist.

We both grind into each other, his cock creating more friction inside of me. He lets me catch my breath again, our bodies talking as they meld together.

Then I hear intense feet against the hallway. Like people are running frantically back and forth. The mumbled voices are enough to cause both of us to freeze.

I don't conclude the worst like I might've three years ago. No paparazzi or crazies ready to break in and assault us. I listen closely with Ryke. "Do you hear that?" I sit up a little more, and he presses his hand on my shoulder, pushing me back down.

"Hold on, Dais," he says, carefully pulling out of me. The full feeling still lingers, even though he's gone.

Again, I listen and spot the jingling of Coconut's collar. "Coconut," I tell him. Rose offered to keep Coconut in her room tonight so "a slobbering canine won't watch you fuck" (her exact words). Something is either wrong with our dog or Rose, and since she's *very* pregnant, I'm going to choose the latter.

Both Ryke and I are out of bed in a quick second. I grab the hotel's white cotton robe and tie it around me, while he pulls on his gray drawstring pants.

I reach the door first, but hesitate for a brutal second, the anxiety of my past rattling me. *You can do this. Just you.* No one is going to hurt me.

I clasp the knob and turn.

"Which hospital is she going to?" Lo shouts into his phone, Lily and Willow racing down the hallway. They both knock repeatedly on another door.

Coconut sprints between them and Lo.

A lump lodges in my throat. Moffy crying in the hall and repeating what sounds like *Janie*. Something happened to Jane?

"Lo," Ryke says, barreling into the hallway.

Lo holds up his finger at him. "Whatever you said wasn't English," he says to the person on the phone.

I whistle at Coconut so she'll calm down, and she skips to my side and basically collapses at my feet with a heavy, lopsided smile and pant. She's the only happy one here.

I rub her belly. "Moffy," I call to the little boy dressed in red Spider-Man flannel pajamas.

He hiccups but ambles over to me, noticing Coconut in a submissive state, he pets her belly and cries against her white fur.

She senses his sorrow and licks his cheek.

Lily and Willow corral my mom from her sleep. She ties a silk robe, her face without any makeup. Her natural look contains more wrinkles and frown lines, but Lily says a few words under her breath, and my mom springs to action, walking quickly over to us.

"They came into the hallway on their own," Lo snaps, "so you can tell her to stop telling me not to fucking disturb them because they're here." His daggered eyes dart from Ryke to me. "Yeah? Just text me the directions. Stay safe." He hangs up his phone call with Connor, most likely.

"What the fuck is going on?" Ryke curses.

Lo slips his phone in his pocket. "Rose is having contractions, and she doesn't want to have a baby in the back of a limo again, so they went to the hospital. Connor thinks there's a chance she'll go into labor tonight."

She's a little early. "Should we all go to the hospital?" I ask. If our positions were switched, Rose would drop the entire globe to be there for any of us.

"We are, you aren't," Lo tells Ryke and me.

I exchange a look with Ryke, both of us struggling to accept this plan. It seems wrong.

"Hey, remember that speech your friend said today about you two being selfish?" Lo tells us. "Yeah that starts now. You're staying here. Doing what people do on wedding nights. Going to the hospital isn't one of those things."

Lo flashes a half-smile that's the equivalent of dropping the microphone and exiting stage left. No more room for discussion.

I look to Ryke and he says, "Let's stay, Dais."

I nod in agreement, deciding that Rose would probably want me to enjoy tonight.

I just hope we're making the right choice.

‹ 45 ›

Ryke Meadows

Seated in the front of Eddie's truck, the vehicle bounces along the jagged, primitive terrain. Tan crags loom on either side of us, jutting to the fucking sky.

From the bed of the truck, Sul sticks his head to the opened window between Eddie and me. "Eres horrible contando historias," Sully says to me. *You're horrible at telling stories.*

Eddie laughs.

I roll my eyes, busy checking Sully's fucking carabiners since I found a faulty gate on one. "Te dije la parte importante." *I told you the important part.* I find another ratchet fucking piece of gear and hold it up to Sul's face. "What the fuck."

"It has another climb in it," he refutes, "and I asked what happened when everyone went to the hospital for Rose. You can't just say *false labor.*" That was four days ago, which is why I'm now on the outskirts of Cusco, Peru to climb. When Dais and I picked Peru for our wedding, I'd always planned to meet with Sully at the end of the trip.

The honeymoon adventure with Daisy came to a close this morning. She flew one hour to Lima with her sisters, Connor, and Lo. In a couple of days, I'll meet Daisy back in the country's capital. Then we'll all fly home to Philly.

"I didn't go to the fucking hospital," I explain. "My brother said by the time they arrived they were already discharging Rose." She's fine. Her contractions weren't the real thing, and the doctor said that she didn't need to rush home.

Sully starts going off in Spanish about bouldering yesterday, and I tune him out to concentrate on the safety of his equipment. About a half hour later, the truck slows in front of a narrow path, wedged between two rock walls.

I step out and lug my gear off the truck while Sully hops off the back. "Qué tan lejos hasta llegar a la pared?" I ask Eddie. *How far until we reach the wall?*

He motions with his hand like *not too far* before saying, "Tal vez una caminata de quince minutos." *Maybe a fifteen minute walk.*

Sully elbows my arm. "Nada que no podamos hacer." *Nothing we can't do.* He fixes his own gear on his back. I rip off the carabiner from his sling that I fucking rejected and throw it in a grisly shrub.

Sully bristles. "Dude, that was expensive."

"I'll buy you a fucking new one."

He nods.

Then I turn back to Eddie. "Seguro que no quieres subirte a la roca?" *You sure you don't want to climb the rock?* He's frequented this remote spot since the eighties.

Eddie smiles. "Hoy no." *Not today.* "Ten cuidado, amigo." *Be careful, friend.* He reverses his truck, tires kicking up dirt before he disappears out of sight.

The sun blazes, heat gathering across my skin. My fucking shirt suctions to my abdomen, and I trudge on, sipping water from my CamelBak. Maybe a minute later, my phone vibrates. "We have signal," I tell Sul.

"You think we can order a pizza?" Sully grins.

"Sure." I retrieve my cell. "Tell the delivery guy to meet us at the summit." *Two thousand feet high.*

"He better pack a helmet—*shit.*" Sully stops midway, trampling a weed that blooms from dirt. His jaw is fucking ajar, staring past me at the desolate horizon. He dazedly pats his head.

I tense and wipe sweat off my forehead with my shirt's collar. "What?"

His worried eyes ping to me. "I left my helmet in the back of the truck."

"Fuck," I curse, spinning sideways to examine the crag on the right. Our specific route is close—just the other side of this cliff—but the unknown area poses real fucking threats like loose rock. We have no idea what we're climbing onto.

"I'll go without one." Sully unties a green bandana from his belt loop.

"No," I reject the idea almost instantly. "You can wear mine."

"No, man." He shakes his head.

"You're leading," I explain my rationale. "If a rock fucking falls, it's hitting you first." He'll climb ahead of me, the more dangerous position between the two of us.

"What if I accidentally kick a rock out?" he counters. "Then it's hitting you first."

"Don't kick a fucking rock on me," I rebut, detaching my black helmet and shoving it in his chest. My mind is made.

Regardless of how long I've known Adam Sully, he's without a doubt one of the *best* traditional climbers. Never makes critical mistakes during an ascent. Always shows up an hour early to prep. Brings extra gear, in case his one ratchet piece doesn't hold up. He's attentive to his partner and overcomes difficult odds with nothing but a positive fucking attitude.

He's someone you want on the other end of your rope. And if anyone asked me to fault him, I wouldn't. I fucking couldn't. The guy is as good as they come.

Sully reluctantly grips the helmet and trades his bandana for the protective gear. I tie the bandana around my forehead, pieces of my hair falling over the green fabric. Then I finally check my texts.

You on the rock yet? — Daisy

I reply quickly. No, what's up?

My phone vibrates just as fast.

Do you think it's too early to buy baby things? — Daisy

Another text comes through before I can respond.

I know it's definitely too early. But it'd be from Peru... — Daisy

I text back, Get it. I don't want her to freak out about this. It'll hurt if we lose the baby, regardless.

Thanks :) Have fun busting your ass on real rock! — Daisy

My lips rise.

Have fun in the city, Daisy Meadows.

I slip my phone back into my pocket, imagining her grin stretching across her face. She's in my head for the entirety of the walk, until we reach the base of our route.

We spend about fifteen to twenty minutes fixing our gear and pre-rigging rappels. The steep and sturdy tan slab is full of divots and inconsistent crevices. One of the more challenging multi-pitch trad climbs we've ever fucking taken together.

Right before we begin the climb, Sully says, "Your first ascent being a married man. How does it feel?"

I digest my surroundings, no cloud in the bright blue sky, the vastness of our landscape soon to be fucking recognized as we ascend thousands of feet together. I'm in Peru.

I married the love of my life.

I'm about to climb towards paradise.

My gaze drifts towards the sun. *I'm alive.*

TEN PITCHES OUT OF fifteen, everything has gone smooth so far. Sully places pieces into the rock, connected to a quickdraw. I grip an inch hold with two fingers, my toes supporting the majority of my weight.

My green bandana collects most of my sweat, but while I wait for Sully to set a new anchor, I still rub my face with my shoulder. At over a thousand feet ascension, the scenery tries to steal my fucking breath: the Peruvian terrain riddled with peaks and valleys. Colors like melted crayons of red, orange, and green.

Remote views like this are hard to come by, so I make sure to remember as much as I fucking can. After a minute, I peel my gaze off the horizon to check on Sully. He's careful about his anchors, but as he spends time setting one, his left leg shifts unconsciously between the rock and the rope.

"Watch your fucking leg, Sul!" I shout.

He mumbles a curse, fixing his stance. "Thanks!" Falling in that position would flip him upside-down and smack him into the wall. Headfirst.

My blood pumps harder, my brows pinched, and with my free hand, one focused on the belay, I lift my sunglasses to the top of my head. I inspect Sul again and then me. *We're okay.*

The sun has already reddened his nose and cheeks. "It's a little wet in the shade!" he calls. "It's going to take me another minute to set this one."

"What about higher?!" I notice a gap further above his current placement.

He stretches to reach it and winces, his arm-span shorter than mine. He struggles fitting the piece in on the first trial. I wait while he inspects the system we already built between each other.

"I'm going to use a cord to equalize the weight," he tells me.

We place redundant anchors in case one fucking fails, and building a third one is always a good idea, if he can manage to place the piece.

"Take your fucking time," I tell him. "I'm not going anywhere."

While Sully works, his grin stretches above me, and he calls out, "Did Ryke Meadows just make a joke?!"

I have no time to counter. I detect loose rock—tumbling along the wall—headed straight for us. "ROCK!" I scream at Sully, a hundredth-of-a-second too late. These situations that can claim your life—they happen with persistent thrust, unable to brake. To stop.

I'm at the mercy of forces beyond me.

The boulder, the size of a watermelon, *slams* on his head. The *crack* of his helmet nearly vibrates the rope, and his muffled grunt echoes against the wall. The momentum instantly jerks him from his footholds. He falls quickly with the boulder.

Two more massive chunks of loose rock follow the first.

I react instantly, my reflexes working in fucking overtime. Light on my feet, I jump backwards, off the wall, timed with his descent. His weight is being added rapidly to the rope.

The first boulder grazes my arm like being dragged across asphalt. *Burning.*

Sully raggedly cuts through ten feet of air above me. My jump softly catches Sully's fall but in doing so, it *rapidly*—so fucking rapidly—yanks *me* back into the uneven rock face. I can't stop.

My right leg smashes into a curved, jutted rock, bearing the fucking brunt force. I scream through my teeth, my throat scorching. The impact like a steel gavel tenderizing meat and bone.

Water squeezes out of my eyes.

I shift all of my weight to my left foot.

Fucking. Fuck.

Fuck.

My drenched bandana no longer keeps sweat from my face, beads dripping down my fucking temples. The second boulder crashes against the rock wall, higher than us, and skids off, launching over my body and Sully's.

Sul is pulled to a stop five feet above me, his last piece he placed catches him along with my belay.

"Sully!" I call. "*Fuck.* Sully!"

He torpidly shakes his head, leaning back in his harness, fucking disoriented. When he turns his sun-beaten face towards me, a stream of blood oozes beneath his helmet and down his forehead. With a quaking hand, he gives me a half-hearted thumbs-up.

And then the third boulder barrels downwards, faster than anything else, and bowls straight into his gut. *Fu*—the force and added weight instantly wrenches me against the wall again, my right leg and shoulder slamming back.

I clench my teeth, a wince cutting through me, and I breathe heavily through my nose. "Sully!" I shout with half a breath. I listen to his noises—the worst sound I've ever heard in my fucking life. Strangled, gurgled. Like being submerged and drowned.

"SULLY!" I scream, needing to reach him. *Escape the fucking belay.* The minute I think it, the boulder slips off his chest and aims right for me. I attempt to slide out of the way, but my right fucking leg lingers behind.

The loose rock sideswipes my battered limb. I'm almost torn off the wall, but I hang on with pinched fingers. *Motherfucking*—I scream through gritted teeth again. I scream aloud, rage and frustration fucking dousing fear, my pulse pounding in my neck. I shut my eyes tight, pain flaring from my calf to my knee to my fucking thigh.

I blink my eyes open and see straight down. Over a thousand feet. From the bottom.

Then I look up and nausea assaults me. Sully's limbs hang lifelessly by his side, barely able to support his neck. He's choking.

"SULLY!" I scream. *Hold on.* I have to find a fucking way up to him that doesn't kill us both. Lowering him to me—not an option. He would bounce along the rough angles of this rock face, injuring him more.

I can't see the topmost piece of protection. I can't ask Sully how it looks. He can't respond. That anchor sustained Sully's fall *and* the weight of loose rock.

If our last piece fails us, we're both dead. Slicing through air.

"SULLY!" I shout again, my throat dry and raw. *Fucking say something.* I just listen to him, *choking.*

I work fast, as fast as I fucking can, my fingers moving at rapid pace. "Hold the fuck on!" I call. I escape the belay (not the harness) while fixing the rope to a new anchor that I build. After securing another fucking back-up anchor in case that one fails, I ascend the somewhat vertical rope using a prusik, my muscles on fire, my head hammering.

I'm drenched in sweat, my hair, my face, my fucking shirt. I scream each fucking *inch* I pull myself up this fucking rope. My right leg shrieks in livid agony, and I breathe heavier. I breathe harder. Than I ever have before.

Don't fucking die on me. Don't fucking die on me.

I grit back the pain and ascend until I'm right next to him. "Hey, hey!" I growl, loosening the straps of his helmet that dig into his windpipe.

Sully is ashen, and it's not the helmet that cuts off his airway. He coughs. Blood spurts from his pale blue lips, staining them red.

"No," I almost shout. "Nono." I lift him quickly as he gags again, blood dripping down his chin.

He motions to his chest with a drooping hand. The last boulder crushed him, he's telling me. Internal bleeding.

"Hey, hey," I say in a softer tone. "I'm going to get you off this fucking rock, okay?"

He mumbles something, but I can't understand, the fucking *anguish* in his eyes is like nothing I've ever seen before. I concentrate on saving him. Because he's going to fucking make it.

We're both going to make it.

I finish rigging a tandem rappel for both of us, and his fingers, with whatever energy he has left, graze my shirt like they want to clench the fabric.

"...Ryke," he chokes, tears slipping out of his eyes. "No."

My knuckles whiten on the rope. "What do you fucking mean?" I know what he means.

"...leave...me," he cries. He's crying, his chin trembling.

My nose flares, my eyes clouding. I shake my fucking head. "I can't." I can't leave him here, even if it'll save my life. Without his dead weight, I can multi-pitch solo rappel, set anchors much more easily, and ensure that I have a safe decline.

With him attached to me, anything can happen on the descent.

If any of the anchors fail with our combined weight, we're both dead.

If I miscalculate the rope length, we're both dead.

If I make *any* mistake, we're both dead.

He's crying harder, his teeth stained with blood but he's stopped choking, and I say strongly, "I'm *not* fucking leaving you here to die."

"...I'm...scared."

Hot tears and sweat burn my cheeks. "This is what's going to happen." I clutch his harness, positioning him on my lap for the tandem rappel. "If you fucking die, I'm dying with you. So wherever you're going, I'm going to be there."

He keeps crying.

"Just whatever you fucking do—don't go to sleep on me." I rub my face with my arm. I have over a thousand feet to rappel down.

A thousand chances to die.

He finally nods, and after a couple more minutes checking the rappel, we begin to lower. The route isn't seamless to rappel. Calling it "roughly" vertical would be giving it more credit. I have to traverse to the left more than once—which would be difficult *without* his added weight on top of me. I reset anchors, but the longer I take, the more my adrenaline depletes—the more noticeable the pain in my leg becomes, my entire limb fucking vibrating.

My pulse is throbbing, the vein in my neck nearly fucking bursting. My heart is speeding.

Sul is a mess right in front of me, his breath short and slow.

I use an ATC rappel device, braking the rope slowly with my hand. I try to keep most pressure on my left side, but Sully's bearing down on me too much to give my right leg a fucking rest. I'm beyond dizzy.

We reach the end of the rope, knotted to brace us. We're still *hundreds* of feet above the ground. I have to build a new anchor.

"Come on," I mutter to myself, sweat running into my eyes, combined with tears—I can hardly fucking see. "*Fucking come on.*" I blow out a controlled breath and set the next anchor. I glance at Sully, his eyelids sagging but they drift towards me, coherent for now.

I tie us into the new anchor and then swiftly pull one end of the rope until it runs down to us.

Again, I tell myself.

Again.

Again.

Again. *Is he alive? Is he fucking breathing?*

Again.

My heart is beating out of my fucking chest, blood all over Sully's shirt, all over mine. He coughs again, spewing blood onto my shoulder. Onto my face. I work faster, yanking rope with determined speed, my clammy fingers hurrying over pieces, willing to be fucking careless if it shaves off time and means his survival.

"Stay with me—fucking stay with me; we're almost there." Two more rappels. I struggle with the next anchor, my hands practically convulsing and I drop—I drop the ATC. I scream in fucking frustration. *Why? Why right now?* I swallow the violent noise and breathe through my nose, thinking.

I need another rappel device. I just search Sully's gear for his, my hand suddenly stained with blood as I reach into his sling of carabiners.

He doesn't have time for your fucking mistakes.

I find his ATC and fix everything. I set a new anchor, my bloody hands tinting the rope red.

I can hardly breathe.

I move swiftly. Urgently. *Carelessly.*

To save his life. I forget about mine.

I rappel once more, but as I descend vertically down the rope, something feels different. His ATC seems off. We *zip* down much faster than normal, rope running through my brake hand. I can't catch it, and I try to hold on to slow our descent, my muscles wailing.

Fucking stop, fucking stop. Fucking stop!! Rope burns my palms, and fear engulfs me in this single fucking moment. I watch the rope slip through the anchor too fast, the end of the line fucking close. If the knot doesn't hold, we're dead.

With the amount of weight on the rope, I think I'm going to come right off it and meet the ground. Falling a hundred feet.

Falling a hundred feet.

I scream, my hands scorching, trying to stop our fall. My muscles raging.

Tears and sweat scald my eyes.

In the last moments, I see her walking down the aisle. Her smile like the sun. Radiating. *Radiating.* All around me. Watching her. Light up the world.

Before it darkens.

‹ 46 ›

Daisy Meadows

Five o'clock happy hour is less crowded in Lima than I predicted, the pub nearly empty. Price *almost* seems bored by the lack of activity, no swarms of paparazzi or crazed fans. He's seated at a table by the door with Lo and Connor's bodyguards, finally learning the great art of chilling.

I squeeze between a stool and Lo, who's bent over the bar, ordering a thousand things from the menu.

I catch his words as he says, "…chips, cheese dip, your chicken tacos, the hot wings—extra spice…" he continues like he's about to feed an army. In reality, we've dragged him shopping all day and forgot to stop for lunch.

Connor is on his other side, translating Lo's order in Spanish for the bartender. Times like these remind me of Ryke, and I miss him. He'd be right beside me, ordering food, speaking fluent Spanish, and blending in with the locals.

Wherever he is on that rock, I know it's where he's meant to be. I imagine him happy and loving every inch that he ascends, and I begin to smile, more than happy too.

"Do you want a beer?" Lo asks me.

I raise my brows without making wild gestures to my belly, the bump hidden beneath a white loose fitting shirt that says *proud to lick cake bowls* in rainbow print.

His pinpointed amber eyes descend to my stomach. "Never mind." He nods to the bartender. "That's it."

I'm not surprised he forgot I'm pregnant. Rose mostly did the shopping. I just bought a soft little, hand-crafted Peruvian doll in a red dress. Even if I have a boy, I'll still give the doll to him.

Lily and Rose bailed before the pub, both returning to the hotel to put Jane and Moffy down for a nap. Willow and Garrison left for an internet café, itching to tap into wifi.

Lo's hunger and Connor's translation skills made our next pit stop. I tagged along for the chips and adventure.

"How is the camp coming?" Connor asks me as the bartender leaves for the kitchen, placing our orders.

"The mess hall was just built." I scroll through my phone's pictures and show them the finished result, the wooden structure brand new with a green-shingled roof.

"Are you on budget?" Lo actually is the one to ask me this, more concerned about my finances since Ryke has basically returned his hefty trust fund with a *fuck you* note attached.

I fully support his decision, by the way. "I'm twenty-five million dollars over budget. The sprinkled donut structure, made out of *a trillion* donuts, just melted. Can you believe that? I had to replace them all a hundred times, and then, you know, the bears came—"

"Alright," Lo says, his glare pretty normal. "I get it."

I nudge his arm with mine. "I'm under budget. I might not be taken seriously for a lot of things, but I do know how to manage money."

Especially money that's been floating around in my bank account since I was fourteen, my modeling debut.

His brows knot. "You don't think we take you seriously?"

"I joke around a lot, so I understand that when I do say something that has more meaning, people don't listen as much." I stare between them as they open their stances between me, towering above my height.

Connor wears that impassivity, calmness that contains a great deal of understanding, and Lo has more maturity than all the years I've known him.

Time has aged them, made them stronger and tougher and better people than they might have been. I wonder if, in their eyes, that holds true for me too.

Connor speaks first. "Those people either don't know you well or they believe in static versions of people. Because when you want to be heard, we hear you, Daisy."

"All of us do," Lo chimes in.

I begin to smile. "Guess what?" I say to both of them, the guys who watched me flounder in Paris and find myself on a wild American road trip.

"What?" Lo asks.

"I've found my voice."

Connor grins while Lo feigns surprise, "Jesus Christ? Should we take you to the doctor? Is this curable?"

"No," I say, "I'm going to die an awfully peaceful death. What do you want of mine when I'm gone? Surf boards, roller skates, ticket stubs to Amour, my unicorn Pillow Pet." I gasp. "My porn stash."

Connor arches a brow.

Lo pats my head. "Ryke isn't here. Try back next time."

Yep, Ryke would've loved that one. *What fucking porn stash, Calloway?*

Connor's phone rings, and he checks the cell. I see the name *Henry Prinsloo* across the screen, probably someone from Cobalt Inc. "I'll be a second," Connor says, sliding away from the bar and towards the bodyguards to take the call.

The bartender pushes three glasses of water towards us. I hand Lo his and then raise mine. "To amber-eyed brother-in-laws, may they be happy and well-fed."

He clinks his glass against mine with a shadow of a smile, practically a grin in Loren Hale's world. I sip my water, my gaze drifting to three of the televisions across the long wall, empty tables below.

The left plays a tennis match. The middle soccer. The right national news.

I zone in on the right screen, red ticker tape scrolling across the bottom in Spanish. The screen shows Peruvian mountains with a sidebar that says *Cusco*. My stomach clenches, and I set down the water.

I narrow my sight on the ticker tape, hoping to understand a couple of the words before I jump to conclusions. And then—

"Lo," I say in horror, my body rushing blood-cold. There's his name. *Ryke Meadows*. On the news. Everything else is foreign to me.

"Connor!" Lo yells, already following my gaze. His jaw cuts to ice, sharpening to battle emotion.

I swivel towards the bar while Lo catches up to Connor. He speaks briskly into his phone, and all of our bodyguards have risen from their seats.

"Remote?" I ask the bartender, shifting my weight from one foot to the other with deep-seated panic. Clutching my ribcage. I motion to the television and mime a remote, but he understands before that, already passing it to me.

He's hurt. He's hurt. I try not to picture anything, but I fail before I've even begun.

Ryke falling…screaming…down a mountainside—my eyes well and burn. *Stop please stop.* I squeeze my eyes closed to drown these images.

He can't survive that.

He's alive.

Stop please stop.

I have to believe he's alive.

I open my eyes and rub them hastily. Then I start changing the channel, the middle television surfing through them.

"What does it say?" Lo asks Connor, pointing at the right television.

Connor plugs his ear to clearly hear the person on the phone.

"Goddammit, Connor!" Lo yells and shoves his friend's shoulder, hard, before returning to me.

Connor only sways a little, but rare hurt actually crosses his features for a split-second. *Find the channel, Daisy.* I keep clicking through them, hoping to land on GBA international news that plays in English.

I suddenly remember that Price can speak Spanish, so I swing my head towards him. He's staring at the right screen. Reading. His face strict, lines across his forehead, bunching his brows, toughening his jaw. Hiding dread.

No.

My whole chest tightens.

Two-thousand feet to the summit means two-thousand feet to the ground.

Lo steals the remote from me, flipping almost immediately to GBA international news. The reporter speaks, but the volume is muted. Closed-captioning flashes on the screen in English, thankfully.

> *Ryke Meadows and friend. . . are being. . . life-flighted to hospital in. . . Lima.*

He's coming here.

"We need to go," I'm the first to say, spinning towards the door but my head whirls five times faster, the rush disorienting. *He's hurt. He's hurt.* I grip the barstool, just recognizing the cascade of hot tears sliding down my face. I inhale choppy breaths. *Stop please stop.* I glance back at the television while Lo grabs my hand, leading me out.

We're still getting the details. . . but we know. . . that there was a serious rock. . . climbing accident. Both men are in. . . critical condition. . . we'll bring you more information . . . as we receive it.

I'm wedged between Connor and Lo in the backseat of our rental car. Price drives, Lo's bodyguard in the passenger seat, and Connor's bodyguard trails us in an identical SUV.

While I frantically update GBA news on my cellphone, Lo peers over my head, both of us waiting on edge for new information.

Connor is quiet, staring past the headrest in front of him. After a minute or two, traffic moving so sluggishly, Connor rotates towards us, resting his arm on the back of the seat.

His haunted expression chills my bones. I glance at the phone and then the road, the hospital not in plain sight yet.

Ryke will be there, cursing up a storm.

Sully will be grinning beside him, recalling their adventure of a lifetime.

Both with a few bumps and scratches.

They'll laugh together. We'll laugh too and say, *God, how scared we were. Silly us. You two have climbed far harder, far worse cliffs in your days. This one wouldn't bring you down. It couldn't.*

This is what will happen.

"Can you both look at me, please?" Connor asks in a gentle, soothing tone to ease us.

Lo is purposefully avoiding Connor like he's the harbinger of grim things. By the tension spooling between us, he might be.

I take a chance and meet Connor's deep blue eyes. I grip the seatbelt. Tugging it off my chest, but the uncomfortable pressure still remains. The weight bearing down comes from an unseen force inside of me. *Hurting.*

"Please, Lo," Connor says again. He's still not budging.

Price turns on the radio, an English-speaking news station giving a similar report. "All we know is that Ryke Meadows was climbing on the outskirts of—"

"Turn it off," Connor says, almost heatedly.

"No," I say before Price touches the button.

Price listens to me.

Lo narrows his bloodshot, desolate eyes at Connor. "What's wrong with you? We're trying to figure out what happened to our friend, *my* brother, her goddamn husband." His voice cracks.

My thighs shake, a brutal tremor ripping through my body. *Husband.* I lean forward to catch my breath.

"I think we should wait until we reach the hospital," Connor tells us.

It's like he knows already.

Lo's face sinks with this realization. "What'd that person on the phone tell you? What—do they work for a news station or something?"

Connor is silent, blank-faced. *Stop please stop.*

I cover my ears for a second, like I hear the answer even when it never comes. I shield my eyes, sick. *My husband.*

"What is it? What the fuck is it?!" Lo screams. "Just tell us?!" He's crying, raging tears dripping down his face.

I'm crying, grief-stricken ones choking me inside out.

We know.

We know.

And then the reporter from the radio says, "We have new information about the climbing accident involving Ryke Meadows." I click into my phone. I barely see the answer through a blurry gaze. I touch my throat that closes. *No, no.*

Anguish steamrolls my chest, but I keep clicking.

I keep clicking.

Why am I clicking?

My arms shake, nearly dropping the phone. I hold tight.

I see the same result over and over. Three media outlets. Four…then five, all reporting the same outcome, citing GBA who broke the news.

It's real.

I sob, throttling my body forward. *No, no.*

"On transit to the hospital," the radio says, "Ryke Meadows was pronounced dead." Price shuts off the news.

I cry into my soaked hands, agony rippling through my veins. *He's gone.* "No," I cry louder, my throat raw, my lungs screeching in pain. "He can't…" *He can. He's gone.* No, no.

Lo brings his foot up to the seat, shielding his face with his knee and hands. He bawls behind them, his body lurching each time.

I can't breathe. I tug at the collar of my shirt, crying hard as knives slide into me. *I can't breathe.* Pain twists my organs, cutting off all life support. Searing my flesh, languidly, bit by bit.

He's gone.

We just got married.

I just walked across an aisle. We just professed our love, and he said he knew—he knew that I was the one for a long, long time.

He's gone.

I'll never see him again. Never hear him curse. Never watch him run faster, farther than most men can go. Never see love lift his lips. Never spot the compassion in his soul. Never. Never. *Never.*

He'll never hold his child.

Boy or girl.

Never see her up close.

Never watch her take her first step. Or hear her voice.

I unbuckle almost instantly, nausea roiling to the surface, and I stretch far over Connor's lap. He cracks open the door, and I vomit on the street, my eyes squeezed shut. *No, no.* My throat scorches with acid and pain.

It's too soon, isn't it? We have decades yet to live. Eons left to go. Our adventure was just beginning.

I dry heave, losing energy to move my weighted limbs. Connor lifts me up and locks his door closed.

I tilt my head back, from side to side, searching for an escape to this despair that claws at me. Wrapping its vice around my throat.

The waterworks won't stop, and I shut my eyes, a cry caught between my teeth. I press the heel of my palm to my forehead, my mind packaging all these moments with Ryke and shipping them away.

Please stay.

Don't go.

Not yet. I want you here with me.

Please stay.

I can't help but think that my theory proved right. For every happy moment, a terrible one swoops down to smite us. If we never came to Peru, never got married, he'd still be alive.

If he never met me, he'd still exist in this world.

Maybe the universe has been telling us something. We were both meant to be unhappy and alone. And we were just too lovesick to listen.

Connor has his phone to his ear. "This is Connor Cobalt, I need to know if a Ryke Meadows has arrived at the hospital yet…he's my brother-in-law." A short pause, and I hear a muffled, *we've already had four Connor Cobalts call in.* He shuts off the phone, seeing the dead-end before it arrives. They must be journalists, impersonating him for updates.

Connor's eyes redden more. In a controlled voice, he tells us, "Ryke would want you both to keep your heads up."

I bury my face in my hands again, wishing he'd lie and say Ryke made it home safely. It's the only way this'll be okay.

"Christ." Lo's face twists. "My brother…that guy—" He opens his mouth but swallows hard, unable to finish.

Ryke kept him sober.

A rock lodges in my throat. I can't speak at all. Every time I try, a force strangles me, and an avalanche of tears cascades all over again. I touch my belly, sick. *Sick* and so dizzy.

Some say that you don't know what a person means to you until they're gone, but I've always been aware of the *extraordinary* impact Ryke Meadows has on people around him. And on me.

I fell in love with his heart.

Soulfully caring.

Selfless. Generous and kind.

He has his hands on my cheeks. He has his feet on the bridge next to mine. He meets me head on.

Calloway.

Stop pretending to be fine when all you really want to do is fucking scream?!

I scream, so hard that my lungs bleed and my voice punctures the air. Throttling me. I scream until it bursts into a cry, until my body is weightless and free.

I scream. Until I can't breathe.

Air struggles to return to my lungs. "I…" I choke out.

"Daisy." Connor rubs my back. "You need to breathe."

Lo drops his leg and turns to me, tear tracks across his cheeks. When I meet his eyes, sharing his grief, he nods at me like, *I know.*

Do you know? I wonder.

Can you feel the animal gnawing through me?

I open my mouth, but no sound comes out. Worry assaults Lo's features, and he puts a hand on my back, next to Connor's.

"Daisy," he forces.

Wet. Something's wet on my legs.

"Drive faster!" Connor starts to shout, his voice unnaturally loud.

Lo touches my forehead, almost tenderly, and then yells, "Fucking drive!"

My head lolls, my eyes rolling, and before everything turns black, I look down.

And see the gush of bright red blood between my legs.

< 47 >

Ryke Meadows

When my heavy, weighted eyelids try to fucking open, fluorescent light blisters them, and they close for a moment, my head thumping. I try to escape the darkness again, forcing my eyes to remain wide.

Through the harsh, accosting light, I see color.

So much bright, wild color.

Paper flowers and birds hang all above me.

Green and yellow.

Orange and pink. Blue and purple. Strung from the ceiling tiles. Twirling beneath the air vents.

Dozens of them.

Daisy. My chest swells.

I lick my lips and try to prop myself on the hospital bed, shoving my memories far down. For a second. *Just a second*. My limbs are murderously fucking sore, and an IV pumps meds into my body, numbing the pain that creeps up my right leg, hidden beneath a white blanket.

"Ryke?"

That voice.

I don't have to look far. Daisy sits on the edge of a chair, by the end of my bed. Dark sleepless circles create crescent moons beneath her fucking eyes. Handfuls of half-creased flowers and birds are strewn around her, but it's not what pumps adrenaline into me.

"Daisy?" I say, worry catching my fucking voice. I'm about to shrug off the fucking blanket and reach her side, to move closer to her. *Daisy, what the fuck—*

"Wait, stop—Ryke, don't move!" she shouts, standing almost instantly, her hospital gown more noticeable. She accidentally yanks her own IV, forgetting it's attached to her, and then she grasps the pole and rolls it with her until she's right next to me.

"Daisy." I sit up, using the strength in my core and I clutch her hip. I can't stop staring at her fucking hospital gown. Her IV...

What happened? I'm afraid to fucking ask out loud.

She tries to find the remote to my bed, so I can lean against the mattress, but I don't fucking care about that. I try to shift my legs.

"No, Ryke," she says, swatting my hands away. "Please, stop." Her tears come and she wipes them away quickly. "I'm sorry..."

I pinch my eyes. She's about eleven weeks pregnant, but that could've changed at any fucking moment.

We lost the baby.

My face is wet with tears, and I rub them away roughly, swallowing back a fucking sob. I exhale the deepest breath of my life, shaking my head, struggling.

I stare up at her with reddened eyes, my hand falling to my mouth.

"I'm okay," she tells me repeatedly, the bed screeching as the back mechanically rises with the remote. "You just got out of surgery—"

"I know," I say, not wanting to lean the fuck back, not wanting to let go of her. I didn't think I'd be able to touch her again. Now she's right here. In front of me.

I hold onto this, beyond everything else that's fucking gone.

It keeps my head up.

I watch confusion grip her green eyes, and I think—*God, she looks so young and so tired.* What'd I do to her? In the matter of a day or two.

"Ryke?"

"I was fucking awake when they brought me into surgery," I explain and then I scoot over, my hand still on her waist, gently pulling her to me.

She curls next to me, her cheek resting against my pillow. She stares into my eyes while I look into hers, soundlessly searching one another.

To have one more day to see her—means more to me than I can fucking express. Words fail me more often. Come out wrong most of the time.

We've never needed many in our relationship.

While we rest in silence, pages are being written between us. Telling the story of a crazy, sad girl and a fucking dangerous, lonely guy. I thought I lost her one last time.

I trace the long line of her scar with my thumb, and her fingers disappear into my thick hair, her chest rising raggedly.

We draw closer, her warm breath against my neck. I press my lips to the top of her head, her golden blonde hair tucked behind her ears. I slowly kiss her temple, then her cheek, her nose and lastly her lips.

She kisses back just as fucking feverishly, with as much fucking force. I stroke her hair, her tears mixing with my tears. Her lips swelling beneath my lips. My heart beating against her heart.

I break apart so she can catch her breath.

More of her tears begin to pool. "I love you," she murmurs, her voice cracking. "I really love you."

She's my wife. My sun.

The person I thought about. In the end.

"I'm not fucking leaving you." I cup her face and before she asks, I say it again. "I'm not fucking leaving you, Calloway. You're stuck with me."

She smiles into her tears. *That smile.* I pull her into my chest, hugging her carefully, unsure of her maladies. She's just as careful of touching my leg.

I kiss her all over again. "I fucking love you. I'm not going anywhere." I repeat it a couple more times, her tense joints beginning to loosen against me.

She combs a strand of my messy hair back, her smile toying with her lips, only briefly staying. I run my fingers down her spine, where her dreamcatcher tattoo is inked. I remember these moments I spent with her, and I just fucking think, *we're going to make more.*

It's not over. Not yet.

We keep examining each other, and I can tell that she's seconds from lifting the blanket off my leg. And I'm a fucking heartbeat away from looking under her hospital gown.

Then a red paper flower flutters. Landing between us.

Distracting us, for at least another second.

"Rose bought me paper yesterday, when you were admitted," Daisy explains softly. "The nurses asked if they could tack them to the ceiling this morning. I think they were worried I'd disappear beneath all of them."

I have to fucking ask now. "What happened, Dais?"

"You first?" she says like a question.

I can't fucking say it yet, and I'm too impatient and too concerned about her to wait. I sit up a little more, and she follows suit.

Before she protests, I lift the bottom of her hospital gown and see unfamiliar, oversized white underwear that reaches her belly button.

"I'm okay," she repeats what she said earlier. "*We're* okay."

My jaw hardens and brows cinch. "We're? You mean—"

Her lips part. "Ryke, you didn't think that the baby..." Realization washes over her. "When I said everything was okay with me, I meant it."

She used to always fucking say that when it wasn't okay. "Then why the fuck are you in a hospital gown? And don't sugarcoat it for me."

She almost laughs, her gaze watery. "I thought you like when I go off on tangents. You're missing out on a great tale about panda bears and pirates."

"Fuck your panda bears and pirates." My darkened fucking gaze only invigorates her smile. It brightens something deep inside of me, something that's still fighting to stay alive.

I can't hold onto the fact that the baby is okay when I'm not sure what's wrong with her in the first place. I love Daisy too fucking much.

"I bled a lot," she suddenly says. "I thought I miscarried and the doctor did too when I arrived."

My stomach is in fucking knots, and I reach down, holding her hand. I wish I could've been there, hating that she dealt with this *while* I was in surgery *while* Sully—I tighten my eyes closed, shutting it out. *For one more second, for fuck's sake, one more second.*

"It was a tiny hemorrhage, not fatal to the baby or me. Apparently some women can have them around ten to twelve weeks in, and I've been told to take it easy for the next fourteen days. The bleeding stopped this morning though, so it's looking up, really. I feel better."

It's hard to be *really* fucking happy after everything, but I'm glad. I'm so fucking glad that we're all here. All three of us.

I set my hand on the top of her head. "How much fucking sleep have you gotten?" She looks like hell. Her cheerfulness is also a little fucking fake so that I won't worry about her, and she knows I can tell.

"It's been hard these two days." She rubs her cheeks and groans a little in frustration. "I can't stop crying." She looks up at me with a tortured gaze. "I thought you died." Pain spikes her voice.

"I'm sorry—"

"No," she says, "I *really* thought you died. GBA rushed to break the news about your accident, and they misheard their source. They announced, to the entire world, that you were dead, Ryke. And then other media outlets ran with it too."

I rake a hand through my hair, digesting the gravity of this. What she must have felt because of GBA's inability to take second place in a fucking war for ratings, for the first to break the story. "You've got to be fucking kidding me," I almost yell, and then it slams against me. *My brother.* "Lo," I breathe.

He thought I died too. They all did.

"Is he...?" I can't even say it. I can't even ask if he broke his sobriety. I can't fathom a fucking world where that happens because I'm gone.

"He's doing better. He's been with Lily for the past two days. They haven't left the hospital or each other, and Moffy has made him smile a lot." At the mention of our nephew, Daisy starts crying again and presses the heels of her palms to her eyes. "I hate that I can't stop."

"I don't," I tell her. "It's fucking human, Dais. People cry. I cry. It doesn't make you pathetic or weak, alright?"

She drops her hands and sniffs. Then her eyes sweep me, as though making sure I'm really here, talking to her like this.

"I fucking hate that you thought I died." If our positions were reversed, I'd be inconsolable. "Who was with you?"

"Lo."

Fucking fantastic.

"And Connor," she says.

I relax some, my hand still on her head. "So you haven't slept in two fucking days, have you?"

"I've tried," she breathes. "Does that count?"

"Not fucking really. Take a nap with me later?"

She nods repeatedly and I kiss her head again, then I mess her hair with a rough hand.

Her smile is gone before it really appears. "If it takes you days or months or even years to tell me what happened on that rock, I understand," she says. "Or if you never share at all, that's okay too."

I nod, but I plan to share as much as I can right now. Which may be very fucking little. I just have to start speaking. First, I ask something important, "Is everyone still here?" She knows I mean my brother, Lily, Rose, Connor, and Willow. Maybe even Sam and Poppy.

"I texted them when you woke, and Rose told me that they all wanted to give us an hour alone before they bombard you. I can go get them now if you want."

"Not yet."

Where do I fucking start?

The beginning or the end?

I decide to focus on the easiest part. "I smashed my fucking leg into the wall."

She listens keenly, but I take a long pause, enough that she picks up the slack. "I talked to the surgeon when you came out. Good news is that you're a bionic man."

"Fucking fantastic." I uncover my right leg, casted from my foot to my thigh. *You shattered your lower femur,* I just barely remember the fucking doctor telling me before surgery, hardly conscious. And obviously, I broke my leg.

"There's an eight-inch plate in your femur with eleven screws," she says. "Your tibia has a rod and some pins. Also good news, he said the femur broke low enough that it shouldn't affect your hip, just your knee."

I don't ask about physical therapy or timeframes to walk, timeframes to gain my strength. I just don't fucking care.

She must sense this because she doesn't offer them.

"We almost made it to the fucking top," I suddenly say, leaning back against the bed. "We almost made it." My nose flares, and I take a deep, pained breath.

Daisy leans back too, her knees bent. I put my hand on her kneecap, feeling her scar beneath my palm. *From tripping on the wet concrete at a community pool, diving lessons in third grade*, she once told me.

I know every one of her scars.

How and when and why. I've told her every one of mine. Every memorable story, pieces of my history, I've given to my wife. The only one.

"It was a rock fall," I say lowly. "He was hurt, badly, and we had to tandem rappel if he had any chance…" I fucking falter again, and she helps me out.

"You already hurt your leg by then?"

"Yeah. We started rappelling once the rocks stopped." I squeeze her knee, one of them swinging back and forth like a pendulum. It's weirdly fucking calming. "We were about a hundred feet before the ground…"

This part is so vivid.

I replay it over and over, the rope slipping through my hands as I try to brake.

My palms are red and raw now—nothing to fucking complain about. I have both hands still.

"I thought we decked," I tell her, my eyes burning at the memory. "I thought we slipped off the end of the rope and we hit the fucking ground, falling a hundred feet. But my knot held."

Like a miracle. Because that thing shouldn't have supported that much weight. I was so fucking careless tying the end of the rope. I could barely even see straight.

"So you made it to the bottom before rescue arrived?" she asks.

I nod. "We made it to the bottom." I dragged Sully away from the crag and then called Search and Rescue. "He was unconscious by then," I say vaguely. "I tried to wake him up. I squirted water on him, tapped his face, screamed at the top of my fucking lungs…"

He wasn't moving. Was barely breathing. I checked his pulse.

I fucking cried over my friend's body.

"When the helicopter came," I say in a heavy breath, "I fucking hobbled in and that's when…" I choke on a pained laugh. "Fuck you, Sul." I shake my head, squeezing my eyes shut with my fingers. *Fuck you for dying on me.* "They stopped compressions in the fucking helicopter, and I tried to fight them on it—tried to do it my fucking self. They sedated me, and I passed out. The next time I woke up, I was being wheeled into surgery."

I lost Adam Sully at twenty-seven, and I thought I'd at least have him for another five fucking years. Not ten, not twenty, but I thought five—just give me five more years with my friend.

And we'll reach the summit again.

I'd say he's too young to die, but we know the fucking risks. We talk about them all the time. He'd be the first to tell you his life is cut in half every time he climbs.

Daisy wraps her arm around my waist, her tears dripping again, from her own sorrow. She had a lot of love for Sully. I know he'd miss her too.

"Have his parents…?"

She nods. "They flew in this morning and took his body home." Her chin trembles. "He's with his family now."

I nod. "I think he said he wanted to be fucking cremated." He also said that he'd rather die on a mountain than die any other way. It meant that he was living—truly living—his life, the life that he made for himself. The life that he loved.

I shut my eyes again, the weight of grief like shackles around me. Like the inked chain drawn on my ribcage, dragging me so far down.

Regardless of my leg.

I'm not sure I can ever climb again.

< *48* >

Ryke Meadows

When Daisy leaves my hospital room, I ask her to send in my brother alone first. I pull myself higher against the bed, my biceps and triceps doing all the fucking work. I grimace, my arms about to give out, but I adjust myself somewhat and try to relax.

I don't bother inspecting the cast on my leg. I just wait. About a minute later, the wooden door swings open and my brother slips inside, closing out everyone behind him.

I scrutinize him, about fifteen feet separating us. His bloodshot eyes dart to all the hanging paper flowers and birds, his complexion fucking pallid, a color I've only seen from him when he pukes.

He stands at the end of the bed and tugs at the collar of his black shirt, like it's stuffy and hot in here.

It's actually pretty cold.

"You were right," I suddenly say, the words closing my throat. I have no idea why I fucking say it. Maybe in the back of my mind, I truly believe this now. Or maybe I just thought it'd help him feel better.

Then again, Lo never wanted to be right. Not about this.

I shake my head before he can process my comment. "That was fucking stupid. Forget it."

"Forgotten," he says instantly. Then he approaches the plastic frame of my bed, holding onto the end. He eyes my legs—or kind of looks past them, at nothing really at all.

"You okay?" I ask my brother.

His gaze narrows to something fucking brutal, and they finally meet mine. "You're the one who fell off the side of a fucking cliff," he snaps. "We need to be focusing on *you*."

"I'm alive."

"Barely."

I don't respond to that, and the tension builds as fast as Connor Cobalt can complete a fucking Rubix cube. My relationship with my brother is one of the most precious things I have in this fucking world, and it's not easy.

Never has been.

I love complicated things, hard things—most rock climbers thrive off them, the challenges, physical and mental. Push through anything. We can.

Part of me is screaming for this, the other part...the other part is slowly, but surely, saying goodbye.

Lo clears his throat, his gaze shifting to the blankets again. "I'm sorry...about Sully. I know what he meant to you." He twists his wedding band.

I feel like I'm saying the wrong things, but I know he must feel the same exact way right now.

"Take a fucking seat," I tell him. "Actually bring it closer." I point at the chair by the foot of the bed.

He glares at the chair like it's already hounding him. Instead of sitting, he walks closer to the left side of my bed, concentrated on reading my heart rate, oxygen, and blood pressure levels on the fucking monitor. Then he glances over his shoulder, his expression so fucking familiar.

Like he's searching for a way out.

I know he's stronger now, but whatever's eating at him must be dragging him down.

"What's wrong?" I ask.

He touches his chest. "I'm a sick fuck, okay?" His words are so sharp they could be laced with glass.

"You're not," I refute.

"Yeah I am," he tells me. "I'm not exactly upset by the outcome here." His tortured fucking eyes bore into mine. "If things reversed, if you died and your friend lived…I'm just relieved, alright?" His face contorts in a pained half-smile. "How's that for the sickest fucking human on Earth?"

He looks like he's about to turn and leave, and I reach out, catching his wrist. "Hey," I say strongly, the word carrying more severity than I thought it would.

He meets my gaze again.

"You're *not* a sick fuck," I say, passionate about this truth. "I'm your brother, and you didn't really know Sully. It's a human reaction, Lo— what you're feeling, it's okay, man." I don't tell him the rest.

That Sully didn't even want me to save him. That he asked me to fucking leave him so I could save myself.

Lo lets this sink before shaking off my hand, his throat bobbing. His glare is softer than before. "I told you that we need to be focusing on you, bro."

I flip him off. "I'm done being the focus of everyone's attention."

"Maybe you shouldn't have fallen off the side of a goddamn cliff then." He grimaces almost immediately after it comes up.

I actually smile. "There he is. My little brother."

He wipes his eyes with the collar of his shirt and then nods at me. "Are you okay?"

After a long pause, I say, "No."

He nods again and then drags the chair next to my heart rate monitor. He sits down about the same time the door cracks open.

Lily peeks her head in the room, her Wampa cap covering her short brown hair, the strands barely touching her shoulders. I love that she's brave enough to wear her *Star Wars* hat here. And always be herself.

I wave her inside. "Come in, Lil."

Lily rushes in, hurriedly brushing her heavy tears away, and she removes her fuzzy white hat like she needs to be respectful in my fucking presence.

"He's not Jesus," Lo says, obviously thinking the same thing.

Lily sniffs, ignoring her husband. She flings her arms around my neck in a tight hug, and her tears drip on my shoulder. This kind of Lily Calloway almost never comes out for me.

I get the snarky fucking Lily with tons of attitude.

I've grown fucking fond of that, so this is just new.

I raise my brows at Lo while I hug her back with one arm.

He mouths, *she thought you died, man.*

Fuck.

When she pulls away, the room has suddenly filled up with friends and family. Sam and Poppy stand by a cellophane-wrapped tray of food: a sandwich and Jello. Next to them, Daisy's mom has her hands on Maria's shoulders, the young girl flipping through an entertainment magazine.

Moffy, in a Spider-Man shirt and tiny red Vans, tries to climb on Lo's lap. My brother lifts his kid up, setting him on his knee. Connor has Janie in his arms, her lips parted as she sleeps against his side. He watches Rose closely though.

She's trying to lead Daisy into the last unoccupied chair, but Daisy shakes her head, cajoling a very fucking pregnant Rose into it with hushed words and a smile.

"Daisy," Lo calls. "Take mine." He immediately stands with Moffy against his side. Then he tosses the kid over his shoulder. Moffy laughs and tries to snatch a blue dangling bird.

"Thanks," Daisy says, wheeling her IV over to the free chair by me.

I look around for someone. "Where's Willow?" I guess I thought she'd be here, not just because we're related. I thought she'd come in support of Daisy.

"Right here." Willow squeezes out from behind Sam and gives me a sheepish wave before pushing up her glasses.

"Hey," I say.

"Are you feeling better?"

I nod, being truthful about this. I stare around at everyone, seeing the faces of people who care about me. Someone else slips inside.

My father.

And then Greg, Daisy's dad.

I'm not even upset to see them. I'm kind of relieved that they'd show up. After all that's happened between us through the years. I'm used to discord. To fragmented things. I'd much rather these relationships stand whole. I don't want to chip at them.

Rose sits strictly in her chair and rests her hand on her round stomach. Her eyes flit across the monitors and IV stands. "This place is depressing."

I've known her long enough to read the subtext of what she says. *This place is depressing* actually means *I'm fucking nervous to go into labor.* Since her false contractions, she's probably more aware of her impending due date.

"It's sterilized," Lo combats. "I thought you'd love it here." He swings Moffy to the left, and the kid grabs a yellow paper daisy.

My lips lift a fraction.

Rose glowers. "Shut up, Loren," she says weakly.

Connor asks his wife, "Es-tu souffrante?" *Are you in pain?*

She says, "Un peu, dans le dos." *A little, my back.*

I'm not even sure how he fucking noticed. She seems fine besides shifting very fucking slightly in the chair.

Connor sidles behind her, one hand keeping his daughter on his side, but he rubs her shoulder and back with the other. She shuts her eyes a couple of times, obviously enjoying the massage, especially as his hand rises to her neck.

And then his gaze lands on mine.

There's something there that I understand but can't fully grasp. Whatever he has to say, I know what it is but then I'm not entirely fucking sure. It's like comprehending a ripped page of a book, and Connor holds the other half.

Maybe it boils down to this: I have no fucking clue what's going through his head. I rarely do. Not until he tells me, and for a while, I've been asking him to restrain his opinions.

I don't want your fucking wisdom, Cobalt.

I'd take it back right now.

I'd give anything for him to make an arrogant comment, interject and call me a fucking dog. His silence annoys me, grates on me, and I just need him to go back to irritating me.

That's our thing.

In this moment, everyone stares between us, Connor's blue eyes full of unwanted truths. Never leaving mine. I need to talk to him. He was the one with Daisy and my brother.

I end up asking, "You going to fucking say something?"

"What is there to say?"

My jaw muscles twitch. "I'm glad you're fucking alive, Ryke."

"I'm glad you're alive, Ryke," Connor repeats, only with his annoying passivity.

The strain inside the room thickens like an invisible haze. It must be bad enough because Daisy says, "Hey, how about we all go grab some lunch and bring it back here?" Most everyone nods in agreement. Daisy leans closer to me and whispers, "Is a sub sandwich okay or do you want chicken?"

"A sub is good." I kiss her before she leaves. Rose is too big to hold Janie, but Lily scoops the sleeping two-year-old from Connor's arms. Moffy seizes three more paper flowers as he's being carried out.

Connor rests his shoulder against the wall, arms crossed, and we both watch our friends and family exit. When the door slams closed, he doesn't hesitate to speak.

"I was the one who carried Daisy into the hospital when she was bleeding."

As hard as it is to hear, I want to know. I slowly bring up my sore left leg, setting my arm on my knee. Every action has so much resistance, my muscles fucking taut like a rubber band that refuses to stretch.

"Lo was horrible," he continues. "When we brought Daisy to the emergency room, he tried to leave me and sneak out the back. I had to literally block his exit with my body. After a couple minutes, he just... crumbled at my feet."

I run both of my hands through my hair multiple times, caught in the fucking IV lines, but I fix them. When I glance back at Connor, his eyes are glassed over.

Mine burn raw.

"I'm a man of extraordinary talents, but I need you." He swallows. "Do you hear what I'm saying?"

Pain begins to throb in my thigh. "It's kind of a fucking moot point. I don't even know if I can ever climb again, so you get what you want whether I say it or not."

"I'm not asking you to quit climbing."

My brows knot, so fucking confused.

"I heard Daisy," he says.

Those three words—*I heard Daisy*—stir more emotion in me than I can process. She's been my advocate for a long time, and she believed no one was listening to what she had to say. *Now look, Dais.*

"I heard her when we went to the fertility doctor. I understand that you don't value opportunity cost or risk and reward. I understand that we see the world differently and neither is wrong. I understand all of this. I have for a long time." He pauses. "So I'm not asking you to quit the thing that fuels you."

I drop my left leg. "Then what are you asking?"

"I'm asking you to care about your life," he says, "more than you do now. Can you do that?"

I open my mouth, about to argue—to tell him how much I care about my fucking life—but that's not exactly what he's telling me. I wonder if Connor asked Search and Rescue what happened. In fact, I'm almost fucking certain he did. He probably read the report, knew that there was a way I could have safely guided myself to the ground—even if it meant leaving my friend on the wall.

I would have been okay.

I care about my life, but not enough to choose the sounder route for myself in these situations. Not enough to find ways we both could have made it through safely. I just wanted him to live.

That's fucking it.

But if I reversed time, could I honestly return to that rock wall and leave Sully behind?

There's no fucking way.

"Ryke," Connor says in my silence. "Do you understand what I'm saying?"

Connor Cobalt used to put himself above every person in this world. Self-centered, conceited, arrogant as fuck—he's still these things but somehow he learned to be a little less selfish.

He wants the opposite for me.

The selfish man is telling me to be a little less self*less*.

He thinks it'll kill me. For fuck's sake, it almost did.

I'm lost for words. For time. And peace. And tangible fucking things. I just want to feel like I'm not breaking apart.

He takes a step closer to me and stops, and I notice that his emotions are crashing through his brick-walled exterior. In a rare moment, he drops his gaze to the floor, collecting his thoughts, before he returns his focus to me.

"There are people that love you here," he breathes. I can practically hear the shadow of his words: *I held them in my arms. I'm standing here.*

Pain rips into my chest. I know he's not being cruel. I know he understands what I lost. But I think he's here fighting for my future that I can't see.

And I know what he's fucking saying, in so few words, even if it sounds impossible in my head. In the heat of the moment, I only think about what's happening in front of me. I struggle thinking about things that I'll lose. My wife. My brother. Maybe even my child. What they'll lose. I tune it all out.

"Do you remember what I wrote in your journal?" he asks. "The part in Italian."

A Christmas or two ago, he wrote inside a journal I'd given him, all in different foreign languages, and he wrapped it and gifted it back to me. The parts I understand, I've read maybe a dozen times.

I lick my lips and say, "Ti rispetto e ti ammiro così tanto, amico mio. Mi hai aiutato ad essere altruista." *I respect and admire so much about you, my friend. You helped me be selfless.*

I always come back to those words because they surprise me—that Connor Cobalt could admire a part of me. That he saw something else besides my blunt, rough exterior.

"I meant what I said," Connor tells me. "I just didn't realize, until yesterday, that this would be your downfall."

I disagree out of instinct, shaking my head. He's saying self-lessness has been biting my ass, all along. It's good to be these things in moderation, but too much of one thing is fatal. Too much pride. Too much arrogance. Too much spite. Too much kindness.

I never thought I'd be dubbed too fucking selfless. *He's wrong.*

My stomach violently clenches. When has Connor Cobalt ever been wrong?

"All I'm asking is for you to find a way to care about your life a little more, so that you won't end up here again. I'm a genius, but I'm not offering you an equation you can't solve." With intensity in his blue gaze, he says, "Dig a little deeper."

I see the fear in his eyes. Like he's losing me to something he sees ahead. Because there's an integral piece of my soul that makes me *me*, but it's also fucking dangerous.

Dig a little deeper.

To put myself above other people, in the very end. So that I can live longer. So that I can be there for the people I love. I'm not sure if another situation will ever arise like this—I fucking hope it won't—but I hear what he's saying.

Connor grabs my empty water cup. "I'll refill this for you."

As he heads to the door, I call out, "Wait."

He stops, hand on the knob. His eyes are *full* of turmoil, letting me see more emotion than I ever fucking have. I actually think he may cry. His chest falls heavily.

"Thanks," I say, "for everything. Especially Daisy and Lo."

He collects most of his emotion, bottling it all away. "We're a better team than you think." The next words must sit on his tongue but he doesn't say them again: *I need you.*

I nod. "Next time—or hopefully there's not a fucking next time but…"

"I understand." He opens the door, inspecting the cup in his hand. "Actually, I'll send in the nurse to fill your water bowl. You'd probably like that more."

I flip him off twice, and he turns around, just to see my middle fingers. His grin rises and he nods at me and says more sincerely, "I'm glad you're alive, Ryke."

As he leaves, I exhale an even larger breath, my head thumping now. I notice a set of crutches against the wall, but I don't care about them.

I don't even care about trying to fucking stand.

Apathy is not my strong suit, but I sense it crawling into a vital part of me. I have no energy to push it out. So I just shut my eyes and lean back.

< 49 >

Daisy Meadows

One week back in Philadelphia, the end of July upon us, and I'm still under strict orders to "take it easy" after the tiny hemorrhage. My sisters devised a plan to keep me busy and indoors, making a day out of scrapbooking my wedding and their babies "firsts" with our photos.

Rose had to take leave from work when we arrived in Philly *and* she was told stay off her feet for almost every day. Meaning, no shopping and no high heels.

Expelling her hostility by cutting things also seems like a good idea.

We need extra supplies, so I volunteered to search the basement's entertainment room for more scissors and glue.

As soon as I creep down the stairs, I hear a *thwack thwack thwack* from a hammer meeting wood. In the big open space, Ryke sits on the carpet, brown wooden boards, nails, screws, and a toolbox open beside him. His casted leg is stretched out with curse words scrawled in black Sharpie. He didn't care what we wrote, so I suggested our Favorite Sayings from Ryke Meadows.

My favorite: I fucking love you.

Willow's: **I don't fucking understand Tumblr.**

Lo's: fuck you, you fucking fuck.

Lily's: Fucking fantastic.

Rose's: No means no. Better yet, fuck no.

Connor's: Connor Cobalt is a fucking narcissist.

Connor's won the night, but no one wanted to tell him that.

Ryke is currently engrossed in his own project. He was also told to "take it easy" and keep off his right leg for eight weeks. Afterwards his physical therapy begins.

"Hey, sexy," I openly flirt. My strut is more of a skip-walk, and his gaze follows me to the entertainment hutch.

Then his attention returns to the wooden board and packet of screws. He exchanges his hammer for a screwdriver. I like his intense focus, but last time a doctor told Ryke to take it easy, he was doing push-ups *in* the hospital room, hell-bent on shaving off recovery time. So he could run faster.

Climb sooner.

Now he's barely mentioned rock climbing or physical therapy or asked about his recovery.

His lack of response and his dedication to building a baby crib that shouldn't be constructed for another seven months has my stomach all twisted.

I squat and dig through one of the hutch's drawers, overflowing with miscellaneous items like tennis balls and batteries. "If you need any help," I tell him, "I heard that I'm particularly good at screwing things."

He pauses, mid-flip in the crib's directions. "Yeah? And who'd you fucking hear this from?"

"My husband." I meet his darkened eyes. "Maybe you've met him? He gives no fucks and has the *sexiest* vocabulary."

His lips *almost* rise.

So close.

I collect a tiny pair of scissors that barely fit my fingers and close the drawer. Then I kneel beside his toolbox, his crib assembly only three percent complete.

"Hey," I say softly.

"Hey." He screws two pieces of wood together, concentrating with a growing scowl.

I understand being sad in ways that don't necessarily make sense. To wake up feeling a little dimmer than the day before, a little emptier, and his grief has manifested into this leeching sorrow. I see it in his eyes. It hurts to watch someone like Ryke, stubborn and committed, suddenly slow down and sink beneath quicksand.

I can't pull him out. I want to so badly, but I can't rouse his spirits by going for a run or playing bad cop. I have to go easy because of the baby, and he needs someone who's going hard.

In the tense silence, Ryke lifts his brooding gaze to me. "How are you feeling?" he asks, his concern tightening his features.

"Better. How about you?"

"About the fucking same." He scratches his unshaven jaw, his gaze falling to his assembly. "I called your dad this morning about Desert Shield."

I straighten almost immediately, his first mention of climbing since Peru. My dad had that whole Utah, Ziff commercial planned, but I have no idea what the prognosis is now. "Is he postponing it?" I wonder.

"No." Ryke picks up the crib's directions. "I asked him to cancel the fucking thing."

I try to restrain my emotion, doing my best to ignore the arrow that he's shooting in his own heart. Since he touched the subject first, I poke at it a little. "The doctors said it'd be a hard road to climb again, but they never said it was impossible."

His jaw muscles tic and he points to his toolbox that I block. "Pass me a flat head."

I do, thinking about how the stubborn Ryke Meadows would've stretched, revolting against his own inability to move, and grabbed the thing on his own.

Saying a big *fuck you* to his leg.

He freezes up as he grips the board, staring far away. "I can't, Daisy." Another arrow into the man we both love.

"Can't what?" I breathe.

He says the words slowly, like he's thought about them a lot, but now they're final and real, "I don't think I can ever fucking climb again."

I edge closer and set my knees on either side of his lap, not putting any weight on him. Then I clutch either side of his face, staring directly into his eyes.

He holds me, wraps his arms around me.

"Wherever you go, I'll go," I whisper. "I'll be here no matter what, but I have to warn you." I layer on my best ominous voice.

"Yeah?" His lips begin to rise, something so familiar stirring inside of him. *Almost, Ryke, almost.*

"Be warned," I say, "my pickup lines aren't going anywhere. You can reject them or accept them, but they're here to stay."

He raises his brows. "As long as these pickup lines are only used on your fucking husband. I heard he can be a jealous jackass."

My smile widens, and his eyes flit all around my lips, as though feeling my smile rush through him. "My husband is also an alpha wolf, so you shouldn't mess with him. He's been known to chew up those who've wronged me." Julian at the top of the list. My lawyer has been in contact with my ex-boyfriend, and thankfully I haven't heard a peep from him since New Year's Eve.

Ryke pulls me closer to his chest, and he nuzzles his nose against my cheek. My lips stretch so far, my body airy, and I sense his aura mimicking mine. Just for this moment at least. He holds the back of my head and kisses me in that aggressive, feverish way that we both love.

"Craisins!" Lo yells and knocks on the wall.

We reluctantly part. Loren Hale stands on the fourth stair, Connor by his side. Ryke sends a dark glower their way.

"What?" Lo says. "You're both Crazy and you're both Raisins."

It's not exactly why Ryke is glowering. "*No*," he tells him. "No fucking no, I said no. The end."

"You've been stuck in this house for the whole week. The least you can do is hobble around a toy store for thirty minutes. And really, bro, have you *even* taken a shower?"

He definitely has, but he won't use it as a defense. This is the fortieth instance where Lo has asked Ryke to go out with them. This time, they're taking Moffy and Jane to the toy store. The rampant paparazzi, after the death-scare, have only just cooled down, enough to bring the kids somewhere fun.

"Just leave me the fuck alone." Ryke concentrates on the directions.

I stand off him, avoiding Lo's murderous glare that drills into his older brother. As I make my way out of the room, I pass both guys on the stairs.

Lo catches my arm. "How is he?" he asks lowly, so Ryke can't hear.

"The same." Even quieter, I say, "He needs you, Lo."

"I'm trying." His cheekbones sharpen and then he pulls me up a few more stairs so Ryke is out of the picture.

Connor follows suit, his brow arched like this is all silly, but I do wonder what he thinks right now. If he has all the answers that we just can't see.

Very faintly, Lo says, "He's not the easiest person to make *happy*. I cook Lily Darth Vader pancakes and she acts like I lit up her fucking world. For Christ's sake, Rose came over and put a *Pop-Tart* in the toaster for her and *that* made her happy. I can't see that working for my brother right now."

"You know what makes him happy," I whisper. *Hundreds of feet of ascension.*

"You're not easy either," Connor reminds Lo. "But that never stopped your brother when it came to you."

Lo glances at the bottom of the stairs, but Ryke is out of sight now. Then he nods to himself like *I get it.* "He has seven weeks of this moping around shit. After that, I'm kicking his ass."

I hear the unspoken endnote: *Just like he kicked mine.*

"HAVE YOU TWO, YOU know, since you know?" Lily asks me vaguely, drawing stars around Maximoff hale's First Christmas in her scrapbook.

"Have Ryke and I eaten ice cream since Lo and you totally cleaned out the freezer of all the mint chocolate chip?" I gasp. "No."

She tries to kick my legs from beneath the coffee table, our workstation on the floor, but I'm sitting cross-legged. Her cheeks redden with effort, and I smile at her attempt.

She gives up after a second or two. "It came out clearer in my head."

I hear the *tap tap* of Willow on her laptop between us. Poppy is absent since Maria wanted to go to an acting class this weekend, and Poppy's holed up in New York, supporting her daughter's current interest.

Rose is busy scrawling in the *neatest* handwriting over the cover of her bound book, propped on her round belly. The only one on the couch, higher than all of us. Very queenly, if I do say so.

Lily rephrases her question without blushing, "Have you two had sex since Peru?"

I shake my head. "It hasn't really been possible, more for me than him." I could be on top, if he really wanted to have sex, but after the hemorrhage, all vaginal activities have ceased for a couple weeks. I don't think it's bothering him either since I haven't heard him jacking off or anything.

I don't think sex is on his brain.

"Are you worried about it?" Lily wonders.

"No," I say. "Whatever happens, happens." I'm more concerned about Ryke's pain medication. He usually weans off of it near the start, but he's not limiting his intake. I don't want to bring this up now though.

"How does this look?" Rose asks us, flashing the cover of her scrapbook.

The Evolution of Jane Eleanor Cobalt's Style

Rose has even chronologically separated photos of Jane and then placed them in piles according to seasons and colors, obsessively organized.

It's a very Rose Calloway Cobalt thing to do.

Lily's nose crinkles and then she glances at her messy scrawl on Maximoff Hale's First Christmas. "Maybe you should write in mine."

"No," I say before Rose accepts. "I like yours, Lily." It practically howls with her personality and love for her son.

"Me too," Willow agrees. "It's cute." She looks to the couch. "Your book is pretty too, Rose."

Rose checks out her own work with a self-satisfied smile, knowing it's met her high standards, even without the added compliment.

I'm in the midst of gluing a wedding photo to a blank page. Ryke is smashing chocolate cake on my mouth. Our wedding cake seven tiers of pure heaven. It's one of my favorite pictures because he's caught mid-laugh. His face lit up with happiness.

I ask Rose, "So what's the prognosis of Jane's style?"

"She hates black," Rose says, not shocked by the outcome, and I catch her lips pulling up a little bit. "So besides the fact that she's betrayed the staple color of Calloway Couture, she's a beautiful miniature monster with a flair for crying in public." She flashes *four* photos of her bawling in bathrooms.

"You took pictures of her crying?" Lily says like she's gone mad.

"So she can see her *true* self. They're just for her. I wouldn't post them on social media." She sorts the photos back in their correct piles. "Connor and I both agreed that it's a good form of birth control. Crying baby pictures even make me reconsider a fourth child." But as her hand *affectionately* strokes her belly, it's clear she'd be content with an entire army.

Honestly, I think we're all rooting for two boys so there'll be more Cobalts to come.

I sort through a basket of scrapbook supplies and see a few issues of a celebrity magazine. It's not as salacious or popular as *Celebrity Crush*, so it's possible it came free with Rose's Vogue subscription and she didn't know. I try not to peek at their headlines, but they're staring at me.

RYKE'S ACCIDENT: HOW LILY CALLOWAY NEVER LEFT HIS BEDSIDE.

It guts me, and I really, *really* wish it wouldn't. I wish I never saw it. I shove the basket back.

"Can I ask you all something?" Willow speaks up.

I answer first, "Anything." I nudge her arm, hoping this conversation will distract my mind.

She rubs her lenses on her overalls. "It's coming up on six months since Garrison and I have been official, and he asked me if I wanted to do something special." Willow shuts her laptop. "I kind of blanked and said *sure*. Now I'm freaking out because I told Lo yesterday and he said *special* is a code work for *sex*."

Rose rolls her eyes. "Your first mistake is talking to Lo."

"Hey," Lily defends her husband. "He gives good advice."

I barely smile or chime in, my eyes glazing over at the magazine. I just don't understand why they have to pair him with my sister. And why I'm not good enough to be the one by his bedside.

Rose snaps, "Loren told me to cool down by sticking my head into the freezer. He also said I should build my home there so I can rule over the ice cubes and frozen broccoli."

Lily tries hard not to laugh.

Rose gapes. "Sisters before idiotic husbands." She's about to chuck her lipstick but thinks better than to use it as a projectile.

"I'm pro-Rose, but I'm also pro-Loren Hale," Lily reminds her. "I can be both."

Rose rolls her eyes again but doesn't argue.

RYKE'S ACCIDENT: HOW LILY CALLOWAY NEVER LEFT HIS BEDSIDE. It pounds against my head.

Rose looks to Willow. "Have you asked Garrison if it's about sex?"

"No," she says. "I don't want to ruin the 'something special' if it's not about sex." She seems more flustered, cleaning her lenses again. "Is it bad if I don't want to have sex yet?"

"No," Rose says adamantly. "There's no timeline to losing your virginity. I knew I loved Connor for a long time, and he waited until I was ready."

"How do you know when you're ready?" Willow asks.

I stare at my hands.

I think about my life. I wish I waited to have sex until my body was like *hell yeah, take me now.* I kept putting myself in uncomfortable situations, hoping for an end result that would never come.

"When you feel your strongest and most comfortable in the arms of whomever you're with," Rose says, "then you know."

Willow nods and then checks her phone, a lovesick, silly smile blossoming, one that I've experienced with Ryke Meadows.

She's in love.

Lily is beaming at Willow. "Is that Garrison?"

"He sent me this." She flashes her messages, a gif from the movie *My Girl* where the little boy and his best friend kiss.

RYKE'S ACCIDENT: HOW LILY—I stand up.

"I'm going to go outside for a second to get some fresh air. I'll be back in a minute," I tell my sisters and Willow, watching with concern.

As I reach the foyer, I hear Willow whisper, "I think she was looking at this magazine…"

I open the door, shut it, and take a seat on the second brick stair. The neighborhood road is quiet, and it's a sunny day. I inhale the crisp air, waiting to feel better.

I'm just sadder.

"Daisy?"

I turn my head just as Lily comes outside, wearing gray leggings and a black Superheroes & Scones muscle tee, no bra. I probably picked up that "no bra" habit from her, my older sister by four years.

She takes a seat next to me, and I feel younger than her today. It's not all days that I do.

"I saw the magazine," she whispers.

I cringe. "I'm sorry—"

"You didn't do anything. You can't be sorry," she tells me, her chin trembling a little but she holds her head up. I did do something. I'm upset, and it's not her fault but it has to do with her.

I shake my head adamantly. *I don't want to hurt you.* It's the phrase we've repeated to each other for years. We've both tiptoed. Her publicized addiction spurned a series of events. Like my friends antagonizing me. Like being called a "future sex addict" in the press. Being harassed.

She blames herself. I hurt from knowing that I hurt her. Even when we know all of these other people are to blame. My friends. The media. Not her. Not me.

I can't help myself. I continue the cycle and I say, "I don't want to hurt you."

Lily is quiet for a moment before she says, "I'm tougher than you think. You just need to believe in me. You know, like a fairy."

I do believe in fairies. I do. I do. The jubilant chorus from *Peter Pan* fills my ears.

I look up at her, tears in both our eyes. Is that how we end this? I trust that I can share my grief with her and that she won't crumble beneath the pain?

She nods to me like *go on. I can handle it.*

And I test the waters and say, "I just wish that people would see the person that I feel that I am instead of the one they think they know? Maybe then they'd see how much I love him, and how much I can't let him go."

I start crying, and Lily hugs me tightly, her round cheeks splotchy with tears too. And she whispers in my ear, "They don't know us, Daisy, but I know you. I watched you grow up. You made me smile when Lo was in rehab, and I saw you fall in love. We have all these moments together, and I don't want the media to take anything else away from us. Because...we deserve better. We deserve happiness. As sisters. And as friends."

I've never heard her speak with such conviction. Like the outside world can't harm her.

Seated next to each other on the front steps, I hug her back just as strongly, believing in her words. Believing in her.

"I love you," I practically cry.

I feel her tears on my shoulder. "I love you too."

Dark tides rush far away from us. Years and years of passing hurt and guilt and blame, taking ownership of scars that other people branded within us.

I feel it leave.

It's all vanquished.

It's all gone.

And I think, *Lily Calloway is very, very magical.*

< 50 >

Ryke Meadows

"Two poached eggs on wheat toast and another coffee," Connor orders after Lo and I put in ours at Lucky's Diner, the waitress leaving quickly.

My casted leg occupies one of the fucking chairs, our table squeezed in the far back corner away from the windows. Even at 8:00 a.m. the local Philadelphia hotspot is fucking packed.

It didn't used to be like this, but after *Princesses of Philly*—since we frequent the place all the time—Lucky's Diner has become a tourist destination for most out-of-towners.

It makes coming here a fucking trip—a reason why the girls stayed back. Daisy even passed, but I think she was looking forward to taking Nutty for a walk.

"Get out of Philly!" some old scruffy man grumbles at us from an adjacent booth. He also gestures to us like *fuck you*. He gripes at the influx of people, especially the ones with phones pointed at us.

You'd think people would cool off with the *I hate the Calloways and their men* comments after I almost died, but it's even worse. People want the inside story, and we're not letting them in far enough—not like they used to have with *Princesses of Philly*. When something big happens to us, they just fucking see what they missed.

Lo's eyes flash hot and murderous at the old guy. My brother is trying to bite his tongue.

"Don't fucking say it," I tell him, cupping my coffee mug.

"I've been here my entire life," Lo rebuts to me. "He looks like the old man in the sea. I wouldn't even be surprised if he was washed ashore on Coney Island." He tears open a sugar packet, aggravated, and dumps it into his coffee.

"Maybe Ryke should mark our territory." Connor clips on his Rolex watch, his deep blue eyes rising to mine. "Or do only fire hydrants excite you?"

I roll my eyes, no mood to even speak.

"We need a cardboard cutout of Daisy," Lo chimes in. "Does that excite you, Ryke?"

This is when I set down my coffee and flip him off with both fucking hands.

He leans back and then begins to slow clap.

Connor joins in.

I want to fucking kill them, but instead, I throw packets of sugar at their faces. "Fuck you. Fuck you." Connor looks at me like I've turned into a toddler.

"Goddamn," Lo swears, "the birthday boy is full of fucks today."

"All days," Connor amends, "it's an affliction in his personality. I'd send him back to the pound, but they'd probably send him back to me."

Fucking hilarious.

It's September 19th, 2017.

I'm twenty-eight.

Daisy is twenty-one.

In February, I'll be a father if everything goes right. I'm not sure it fucking will. Daisy and I clearly don't have good luck. I'm already numb about today's existence and the next day—am I counting towards February? Maybe. Time seems different than it used to.

My leg throbs right now, my muscles pulsating. Like knives pressed against my nerve endings. I shift on my chair, the cast a fucking appendage that I've been lugging around for eight weeks.

I feel my little brother's narrowed eyes latch onto my movements. Even Connor studies me more now than he ever fucking has.

"Fuck off," I tell both of them, knowing what they're thinking. Besides the moments where Daisy rouses me, I have no idea how I spend every hour. August was the slowest blur of my life. September has already mimicked those drawn out, sluggish days.

I'm dragging.

I know I fucking am, and I could drag five more months. Seven. Eight and nine. I've never been this tired or this slow, and as frustrating as it could be to *try* to move faster, I've benched myself from the fight.

Something. Something has died inside of me. And I don't think it's coming back.

I only went out for breakfast because Lo basically said, "If you don't come with me, I'm going to drink a bottle of bourbon right in front of your ugly face."

It was a cheap shot, but it also did the trick. I'm here. They both took off work on a Tuesday, today, just for me.

Even after I told them not to.

"So Lily looked it up," Lo tells me while the waitress refills Connor's coffee, then leaves, "and you can make *at minimum* half a million if you sell your cast on eBay tomorrow."

My brows scrunch. "You're fucking kidding."

"I swear." He raises his hand like an oath.

"My name is on your leg," Connor reminds me. "It's probably worth closer to a million or two."

I scowl. "Don't fucking say it like that."

"Like what?" His grin is already mushrooming, knowing exactly what I'm talking about. *"My name is on your leg* is a factual statement."

"It sounds like I'm your property, Cobalt."

Connor grins even more. "If that were true, I would've written my name larger."

Fucking A.

I glance at my casted leg, outstretched on another chair. From my thigh to my knee—visible to me and everyone else—he wrote in dark lettering:

Connor Cobalt is a fucking narcissist.

Those may be my exact words but he's the only one who managed to put *his* name on *my* fucking cast.

I shake my head a couple times, my mind taking a small detour. "Did you sell your cast?" I ask Lo. He broke his hand a long time ago; some fucking bigot purposefully dropped a dumbbell on him at the gym.

"No, I didn't need the money." He cringes a little, knowing what he's implying.

I'm not that offended. I just say the truth, "I don't need the fucking money either. Don't worry about me." I'm not climbing. I have no trust fund. My income is whatever I had, and Daisy's finances are pooled into her camp.

It's enough. It's more than enough, and he needs to see that I'll be okay. Whatever I do. It's not about money. It never was.

"Fine," Lo says, "have you fucked recently? Because maybe your grumpy goddamn self is from blue balls."

I glower.

"I'm not the only one who thinks it."

I focus on Connor, his brown hair eerily fucking perfect. "I said an overabundance of testosterone," Connor clarifies, calmly sipping his coffee.

They're waiting for me to solve the mystery of my sex life, and before I gather my words, our food arrives. As the plates are set around us, Lo says, "I can't believe you ordered an omelet." He's staring at me like I've been hijacked and replaced with someone else.

I can't say I'm the same when I feel fucking different. "I'm trying something new," I defend.

Lo has his elbow on the table, hand to his forehead, fucking distressed at the sight of me. It tears at me a little bit, and I actually contemplate ordering a bowl of cereal or sausage and scrambled eggs.

"Are you scared to have sex with her?" Connor asks as the servers leave. I watch him cut his toast and eggs with a fork and knife, my mind just barely grappling with his question and abandoning the food subject.

"Why would I be?"

"She's pregnant, and it's noticeable."

No kidding. *Celebrity Crush* and other tabloids had a riot when they caught sight of her round belly, visible from just a tank top. We haven't released a statement confirming her pregnancy, but it's fucking obvious.

"And," Connor adds, "I'm assuming this is your first time fucking a pregnant woman. At least, I would hope, but you had an eclectic taste in women."

I take a swig of lukewarm coffee and then gesture at him with the mug. "Are we friends?"

"Good friends, which is why I'm asking." He obviously knows what it's like to have sex with a pregnant girl. So does Lo.

I don't really need their advice, as much as I'm sure they're going to give it.

"It's my first time having sex with a pregnant girl," I tell them, not really a big fucking shocker there. "Since I fucked Daisy *yesterday*, no— I'm not exactly scared." I pick at the omelet with my fork and then run my hand through my disheveled hair. "It was our first time since Peru…"

They both listen more closely.

"Look, it has nothing to do with my fucking leg. I can get around it. I just haven't felt like it and neither has she."

"Until yesterday?" Lo asks, biting into his breakfast burrito.

I nod. "Yeah. She was really fucking flirty." *Blue Lagoon* was playing in our bedroom, her favorite movie. She was pretending we were stranded on an island together. Both of us seamlessly switched from playful to aroused. Almost the same time the characters started having sex in the film.

Lo nods at me. "How'd you get around your leg? Because there are only so many positions you can do while she's pregnant."

"I put all my weight on my left leg," I explain the best I can. "She was on her back, and I stood up at the end of the bed."

"No crutches?"

"No crutches." Which are currently on the floor beneath the fucking table.

Lo cocks his head at me. "So you're saying that you're willing to put in effort to stand up and fuck your wife, but you can't go out with me and hobble around more often?"

"I fucking love sex," I tell him, popping a dry piece of omelet in my mouth.

"You love climbing," he retorts.

I go rigid. "Don't, Lo." I'm not in the mood to argue with him about quitting. He's made curt comments like this for the past eight weeks. He's the one who wanted me to stop in the fucking first place. No matter what I do, he's angry.

He shuts down, but not without an added glare my way.

"When your cast comes off tomorrow," Connor says, "you can try kneeling and propping her back underneath a pillow."

I doubt I'll be able to put weight on my right knee for a while, but I don't mention it. "Have you ever been scared to have sex with Rose?" I ask since he was the one who jumped to that conclusion.

"Lo said he was when Lily was pregnant."

I've never heard this, but maybe they talked about it when their wives were pregnant around the same time.

Lo shrugs. "First, Lily isn't submissive in bed like Queen Rose. I have someone who'll legitimately jump on my back like a howler monkey." He actually breaks into a laugh, thinking about her.

Connor and I both smile because Lo's current one is pretty rare.

Lo adds, "Knowing that my unborn kid was in her body messed with my fucking head. So yeah, I was scared I'd hurt her or him."

"Fuck," I say, realizing that'll probably happen to me at least once.

"It's not that bad," Lo says, probably so I don't shun sex. "I'd do it again."

"The whole kid thing?" I ask with raised brows. This is the guy who doubted whether he'd be a good father. Who thought a child would be unlucky to have him, but Maximoff Hale is one of the most fortunate kids in this world. Because his life is full of unconditional love.

"Yeah, the whole kid thing."

I nod to Connor. "What about you? Do you feel the same as Lo?" He never said if he was scared or not, just that Lo was.

He sets down his fork and knife, picking up his coffee. "Do you want an education in what turns me on?"

I see where this is going. "Sure."

"I enjoy making Rose comfortable during sex and only pushing the boundaries that we're both okay with. She's undeniably more fragile when she's pregnant, even mentally, and it entices me. Taking care of her. Fucking her." He tells us, "I go easier than usual, but I like knowing that she trusts me to give her pleasure, not discomfort."

"What he said," Lo banters.

I actually laugh. His description sounded a hell of a lot more appealing than Lo's fear. Though, I can see myself feeling both.

My laugh dies pretty fucking fast, the constant, perpetual throbbing in my leg starting to irritate me. I dig in my short's pocket for a medicine bottle. I twist off the cap of my pain meds and dole out a couple, popping them in my mouth about the same fucking time Lo reaches across the table and *steals* the bottle.

I swallow them without water, going down like a dry lump. "What the fuck?" I growl, extending my arm for him to give the meds back.

He reads the label on the side. "How many have you taken today?"

"Lo," I say. "You're not my fucking doctor."

"No, I'm your *brother*," he says like he has to remind me. Like I've forgotten his role in my life. The thing is, I'm the one who's the hard ass, not him. "You know we're alcoholics, right?"

My jaw hardens, the pill bottle's cap in my hand. "Yeah, I'm aware."

"You know we're more likely to be addicted to pills?"

My shoulder muscles constrict.

"You know when you had your transplant surgery you didn't take *one* pain pill when you returned home?"

"That was fucking different, Lo." I glance at Connor to see if he's going to add to Lo's commentary.

He simply drinks his coffee, not coming between us.

Lo scrutinizes the bottle like it's the cause of my misery. It's not. "How is it different?" Lo asks. "You were physically hurt then. You're physically hurt now." His amber eyes drill cold into me.

"It just was."

"That's not good enough."

For fuck's sake. I glower at him, about to push my omelet away and fucking leave. "You know why it's different." I reach out for the pill bottle again. "Give it to me, Lo. I'm not playing around."

"You tell me why and I'll give it to you."

He's baiting me, and I have no other fucking cards to play.

I roll my eyes. Can I even say it? Can I really say the fucking words?

"Why is this so different? Come on, Ryke. Why does this matter so much to you—"

"He died," I almost fucking shout. "Now give me back my fucking pain meds."

He dumps all of them in his coffee.

I'm going to kill him. I stand up abruptly from the table, struggling on one leg and adjusting my other fucking one. I reach to pick up my crutches but Lo steals those from me too.

"Fuck you," I growl. *I'm going to kill my little brother.*

My blood is fucking boiling, and Connor rises, calmly setting bills on the table for our meal. Seeing that this is the end of breakfast.

"What the fuck is wrong with you?!" I shout at him, camera phones pointing at us. Clicking. Flashing. Capturing my hurt and rage.

Lo walks around the table with my crutches, edging towards me until his chest is about an inch from mine. And he says lowly, "You don't take oxycodone for emotional pain. You're stronger than this."

I grip the top of the chair, helping me balance as his words barrel through me. "Maybe I'm not," I say beneath my breath.

His jaw sharpens. "You are, and I'll tell you what else is happening. I called your physical therapist, who said you wanted to push back PT for another four months. Don't worry, I fixed that little mix-up with him. You're starting PT tomorrow, bright and early. Like you like it."

"Lo—"

"I also asked him to email me your mandatory, daily workouts when he's not with you. You're not missing a single fucking push-up, big brother." He hands me my crutches.

I'm not used to this from Lo. He's never had to play this part in my life, and I honestly never thought he would. He's apathetic, pretty lazy—I'm the one who pulls him from bed. Who drags him to the gym. Who reminds him why he's living.

I can't say anything, choked with more emotion. I put my crutches beneath my armpits. And then I notice a young kid, maybe twelve, carrying a tied paper bag. Eyes on Lo. His arm winds back.

"Lo," I start, about to step in front of him, but Connor is faster. Slipping in front of Lo, facing one another, just as the kid launches the bag.

It's not packaged like the other flour bombs. The explosion has a shorter radius, and only covers the back of Connor's black button-down and hair. His normally impassive expression is full of irritation.

Our bodyguards, who were standing outside, suddenly rush in and obtain the kid. "You suck!" the boy shouts at us.

"Classic," Lo says to the kid while trying to brush the clumpy flour out of Connor's hair. "Maybe you should insult someone who actually gives a shit."

He flips him off, being dragged towards the exit. Connor's bodyguard asks if he wants to press charges, and Connor says, "Give me time to think about it."

"He's a little kid," Lo reminds him.

"It sets a precedent. This is the first flour-bomber we've caught. If I let him go, there'll probably be another one." We need to charge someone with assault.

I'm uneasy about slapping that on a preteen, but it's not my fucking call. I nod to Connor, flour dusted on his forehead and some on his cheek. None in his eyes or mouth. "You got a little something on your face, Cobalt."

"Don't be so excited around me next time and your aim will improve," Connor says. Not even close to rattled, just a little peeved by his messy hair. He can't fix it without a shower. "I don't blame you if that's asking too much. I excite most people."

"My dick has never been fucking limper than this moment," I tell him.

He laughs.

I laugh too, but not for long.

Lo sits on the edge of the table with daggered eyes. He says to us, "We're not charging that kid."

My little brother has a soft spot for reckless, dangerous fucking kids, and it's hard to say no to him when he has these pleading but merciless eyes.

"It's Connor's call," I say, but I sincerely worry about someone flour-bombing Daisy again. Do we punish this kid for everyone else's wrongdoing? Make an example out of him? Just to benefit us.

I think five years ago, Connor would have without question, but over time, Lo has changed him. And he says, "We'll let him go."

His phone buzzes, and he checks the text. His entire demeanor alters, more serious, more alert than the few moments before. Whatever this is—it has to hold greater importance and priority to Connor than these flour-bombers.

I think I know what's happening.

"What's wrong?" Lo asks, standing up from the table.

We already begin to head out, and I use my crutches to keep pressure off my right leg.

Just as Connor pushes through the door, he says, "Rose is going into labor."

On my birthday. She's giving birth to twins.

‹ 51 ›

Daisy Meadows

Charlie Keating Cobalt and Beckett Joyce Cobalt were born September 19th, 2017 at 5 pounds 6 ounces and 5 pounds 4 ounces respectively.

Two boys.

Two bundles of cute, adorable joy. I've never seen Rose so happy to be in a hospital with doctors who confirmed her babies' good health, right on the spot.

"Are we going to take bets on how many babies they have?" I ask while I sit on the kitchen counter. We're heading over to Rose and Connor's house after our cake is finished. Their babies are already twelve days old.

How fast they grow.

I touch my baby bump, molded by my pale green mermaid tee that says *meet me under the sea*. I keep thinking my stomach will shrink back to normal. Any minute now. Poof. He or she will be gone.

Don't go just yet. Just stay a little longer.

One more day with me.

"Probably five. What's your fucking guess?" He cracks the oven, checking our vanilla cake.

The timer says three more minutes, but he's definitely the better cook between us.

The majority of my theories are cynical, but a handful stands strong in the positive circle of things. "I'd like to think if you want something badly enough, it'll happen," I tell him. "So I'm guessing eight kids." It's what Rose and Connor want in the end, even if Rose claims she'd be happy with any number.

Ryke nods and tries to squat to see the cake, gripping his cane for partial support.

I swallow, holding my breath a bit.

It's a simple action. *Bending*.

But not when his right leg and thigh have a plate, rod, and screws, his scar zipping up his leg. The cast sawed off and trashed.

It's not like he'll gain full mobility with the snap of his fingers. He's only had twelve days of physical therapy along with Lo aggravating him every night to finish his workouts. Thankfully. I don't think he'd do them without that extra push.

"Fuck," Ryke mutters under his breath, struggling to bend his right knee. He winces some.

The thing with Ryke, he prefers to do a lot on his own. I can't just butt in or else he'll be more frustrated, so I ask, "What can I do?"

His jaw muscles tense. "Just toss me the fucking oven mitt."

Without hopping off the counter, I chuck the oven mitt in his direction. He catches it with his free hand and then only bends his left knee. Slowly, he retrieves the cake from the oven and sets it on the stove to cool, leaving the mitt too.

He leans the cane against the counter and then walks slowly towards me, limping really. I never take my eyes off his, and he breathes through his nose, pain cramping his expression.

He makes it though, his hands sliding on either side of me. I wrap my arms around his shoulders, feeling how he distributes his weight towards his left side.

"I had a dream last night," I tell him, distracting him from the pain and his leg. I've tried complimenting him on his effort, and it tanks his mood more than bolsters it. He's a finicky one, that Ryke Meadows.

But he's my finicky husband and broody wolf.

And he's alive. I'm certain. He's still living somewhere in there. The spark hits his eyes every now and then, but here's the secret.

He never gives up on me, even when I disappear at night. Even when I wane like the setting sun. His love is unyielding and exists to cloak me through heartache, through misery, through laughter and pain. I love him in every moment.

In every smile. In every frown.

And I will love him after every long way down.

He can mourn. He can grieve. He can be upset for the rest of his life. And still. I will never give up on Ryke Meadows.

Like he never once gave up on me.

"An actual fucking dream?" he wonders, his brows pulling into a scowl.

"I'm not joking, I promise." I sleep so lightly that I rarely dream, but I dreamt last night, of all nights. We made love, so maybe that helped.

He scoots closer, still towering above me, and his gaze falls to my baby bump. "What about?"

I swing my legs, and he breaks them apart so they fit on either side of his waist. "I was swimming at the lake house, and I just kept swimming. I'm not really sure where I was going." I smile at the image. "I floated on my back and stared at the sky." I look up at him. "I almost forgot how beautiful dreams are."

His lips rise, his eyes smiling more than he knows. That spark, fighting. "That's all you remember?"

I think hard but nothing else comes. So I add, "And then there was a sea turtle that asked me if I wanted a ride and I said, 'I'm deeply afraid of breaking your shell, but I'll swim next you, sea turtle man.'" I wag my brows in jest.

He messes my hair until the blonde strands stick up every which way.

I bite his shoulder, hugging him. Then he lifts me off the counter and sets my feet on the ground. I don't freak about his leg, since he wouldn't attempt to pick me up if he thought he'd drop me or injure himself.

Anyway, his desirous, *I want to ravage the fuck out of you* gaze has me all hot.

My pulse thumps, and I lean my elbows back on the counter. "I have a problem," I say in a silky voice.

He watches me. Just as I always watch him. "What's that?"

"Someone knocked me up." I have a hard time keeping a straight face, but so does he.

"I didn't fucking notice," he deadpans.

"Yeah, it's been wild." I smile. "Even if I've been banned from riding my motorcycle." Doctor's orders. There are a lot of *cannots* on my list at the moment. Same goes for Ryke, though, so hey, jealousy is out the window.

He nears me, his unshaven jaw very masculine and attractive at the current moment. "I haven't asked you outright, and I'm fucking sorry I haven't yet—but are you doing okay with no bike, no backflips, no running around?"

"Yeah. I think I'm doing okay so far." I stay serious as I say, "Small moments, like these, make me happy. I can feel it." *Shaking my bones.*

And I think back to all of our *Grand & Daring Stakeouts*, and how we were never really upset if we didn't catch a potential flour-bomber. The stakeouts weren't about the future—just about staying happy and content within the moment.

To play. And to laugh. We can do that just by being together.

He clutches the counter by my hip. He pauses, grappling with his thoughts. "I honestly—I don't know how I'd fucking be if I didn't have you right now."

My lungs swell, and I nod, understanding his sentiments. Feeling them rush through me. I hook my fingers through his belt loops, pulling him towards me. "Guess what I just caught and reeled in?" I say quietly.

His brows rise, a shadow of a smile playing at his lips. "What?"

"A broody eel. Are you going to electrocute me?" My eyes alight. "Please sting me *hard*." I make a high-pitched noise, leaning my head back theatrically.

He pins me against the counter with his tall, rigid body, careful with my round belly. His large hand cups my face, his lips a breath from mine. "I'll give you fucking hard, Calloway." His jaw rubs against my cheek before he whispers, "Right here." He cups my heat. *Oh my God.*

My breath is ragged.

His hand from my cheek begins its descent to my belly and shorts—and panties.

I watch all five of his fingers disappear beneath the waistband. My arms and legs tingle, and he teases the most sensitive—*ahhh*…an audible gasp catches in my throat. I grip his arm that offers me this head-rush.

I open my eyes wide, and they land on his. As amazing as this feels, we both silently seem to come to a realization: not here, not in the kitchen that we share with Lily and Lo.

We've learned our lesson.

We gently pull apart from each other, the silence deafening. My shallow breath circulates more sexual tension. Tension that we have to step over and ignore for a minute or five. We both face the cake, our arms reaching over one another, tangling as we go for knives and icing.

I shift on either foot, my body still pulsing.

He leans his weight against the counter, angled towards me as he ices half the cake with vanilla frosting. I feel him watching me.

Heat flushes my skin, just from his masculine presence, all twenty-eight years of him to my twenty-one. We frost the cake in pure, aroused silence. His eyes graze me all over, basically building me to a peak without touching me.

As we both reach for the yellow gel icing at the same time, he says, "You're looking a little fucking hot there, sweetheart."

"Sexy hot?" I smooth the vanilla frosting.

He shakes the yellow gel icing. "Fucking hot."

I clench a little and grasp the edge of the counter. He brushes against me to toss his knife into the sink, my body reacting to his closeness like being swiftly tugged by an undertow.

I shudder, my toes curling. Muscles constricting. An orgasm pummels me, so abrupt and sudden that I nearly squat and fall to my ass, but Ryke catches me around the chest, pulling me against his.

Ryke. I gasp sharply, my head tilted back against him. He kisses the base of my neck with that rough, Ryke Meadows force. I cry, "I…" I cry in a higher pitch. *Oh my God.* I'm electrified from top to bottom, trembling.

It takes me another second, but I do come down.

Sweat clings my shirt to my body, my heart thudding loudly. I spin towards Ryke. "What was that?" I ask, more in confusion. This was new. My body did something new.

"A fucking orgasm."

"You didn't touch me."

"Welcome to being really, *really* fucking horny, Calloway."

My smile stretches. I know that this is temporary. That my mood could plummet. I could only feel this once in my lifetime. And that's okay. I bottle the moment for all its electric, spontaneous glory.

He kisses the top of my head and then spins me towards the cake. "You want to write it?"

"You can."

He has his arm protectively around my belly, my back to his chest, while he scrawls on the cake with yellow gel icing. I read the words:

sorry we fucked on your couch.

Our apology cake looks pretty good.

Yesterday, we meant to just watch a movie in the living room, but we were kind of spooning. The easy-access position, my flirting, and our combined arousal led to sex.

Lo and Lily caught us after we fell asleep, naked under covers. On their couch.

They've done worse, so they weren't upset, but we felt guilty because their son is obviously living in this house. It made Ryke question moving out sooner than we planned. He needs Lo though, and I need Lily right now. No houses are on the market in this neighborhood either, so we're here to stay.

He passes me the icing and I draw a sun above the word *fucked*.

Then a little flutter stirs in my belly. I go still, and I feel him rigid behind me. We both don't say a word. Scared it'll all go away.

I place my hand on his, resting on my lower abdomen. The second wave of movement wells my eyes. Then the third—the tossing, the extra flutters. A foot or a shoulder, maybe. Or restless, hurried arms waving. Ready to run. And scream. And shout and say, *I'm here now.*

"Wow," I breathe, rotating to face him.

There are tears in his eyes. He feels our baby kick one more time, and his shocked laugh breaks into a smile. I share it with him.

Happy tears roll down my cheeks, and I wipe them with the side of my hand. "I bet she smells our apology cake." We have no idea if she's a girl or boy, but we usually call our baby *her* more than *him*.

Either way, we'll be happy.

He kisses me and then says, "Guess what, Dais?"

"What?"

He pulls me closer and whispers, "She's alive."

She's alive.

I only hope she can stay that way.

Even if I have to go. Even if I have to say goodbye.

Just stay a little longer.

< 52 >

Ryke Meadows

The Cobalt house is fucking chaos.

"Holy shit," Daisy curses. Rose has her hands full, cradling a hysterical, swaddled newborn while cleaning up Jane's toys around her spacious living room. The mess is fucking frazzling her.

Connor has the other newborn cuddled to his chest, but the baby is also fucking hysterical. "Jane," he calls to the little two-year-old, chasing their orange tabby cat around the leather couch. "Don't irritate Sadie."

"Kitty kitty kitty," she squeals into a giggle, ignoring her father.

"Need help, Rose?" Daisy asks, setting our aluminum-foiled cake on the coffee table. She starts picking up stray stuffed animals.

"What?" Rose asks dazedly, protectively and territorially holding tighter to either Charlie or Beckett.

I lean most of my weight on my fucking cane, unable to bend my right knee that much. My face tightens in a grimace as I limp further into the room.

"Do they need fucking fed?" I ask, my gaze darting between both boys.

"No," Connor says, his newborn fussing in his arms while yawning *and* crying. "Charlie can't sleep."

"He's crying because he's tired?" I know babies are a lot of fucking work, but Connor and Rose look more spent than usual, about five empty coffee mugs strewn around end tables.

Connor nods, his deep blue eyes focusing on Rose with more and more concern. Rose pats Beckett and coos to him, but she also notices Daisy cleaning her house.

Rose snaps her fingers at her sister. "You're not here to do that."

"I could be," Daisy says with a cheerful smile, giving her two thumbs-up.

"You're *not*," Rose emphasizes. "That's not how it's going to be. I don't invite you over to clean my house."

Daisy tosses stuffed animals into a wicker bin like she's playing basketball. "You straighten up my room all the time when you stop by."

"Because I'm older," Rose notes. "And the neat one."

Fuck.

"Tu l'es toujours," Connor says smoothly. *You still are.*

She lets out a deeper breath, chin raised with more confidence, and she pats Beckett's back again, his cries puncturing my fucking eardrums.

"Jane!" Connor suddenly yells.

I glance down near my feet, and the little girl in a baby blue dress *yanks* Sadie's tail. The cat whips around, and I drop my cane, catching Janie around the waist and hoisting her up against my left side.

My right knee is on fucking fire.

Sadie hisses and swats her claws right where Janie once stood.

"Get the fuck away." I shoo the cat with my foot, and Sadie scampers beneath the couch.

Connor rubs his lips, and when I meet his eyes, he nods at me in thanks.

"I thought you were giving Sadie to Frederick again?" Daisy asks, but she watches me hold Janie and add extra fucking weight to my leg. I end up sitting on the armrest of the couch, pain shooting up my thigh.

Motherfucking...

I'm waiting.

I'm fucking waiting for it to be easier, but it's not. I feel like my leg muscles have atrophied and all that's left is titanium, steel and bone.

With Daisy twenty weeks pregnant, I just want to concentrate on her health, which should take fucking precedence. Every time.

I miss the answer about Frederick. "What was that?" I ask Daisy.

"They thought Sadie and Jane would behave, but they called Frederick yesterday to give the cat up temporarily."

Janie starts crying, as though she fucking realizes the cat will be sent away. Her cheeks and blue eyes redden, tearfully looking up at me like I can fucking fix this.

"She can't go," Janie cries, the words not that clear but I understand them. I think she also says something like, *she's my friend.*

Connor nears Janie and me, Charlie starting to settle down, yawning more tiredly this time. Beckett is still a fucking mess, and Rose sits strictly in a Queen Anne chair to calm him.

"Tu as deux choix, mon cœur," Connor tells his daughter. *You have two choices, my heart.* He squats down so he's the same height as her.

I'm not sure if she can fucking understand him, but she rubs her eyes with her fist, her hiccups lessening.

"We can either send Sadie to live with Frederick and she'll return to us in a year or we can send you away and you'll *never* see us again."

Her lips part in horror.

What is this? "That's your fucking solution?" I ask him. Connor Cobalt as a father is a fucking insane idea.

Connor completely ignores me. Like he knows better.

"She can't go," Janie blubbers.

"Toi ou elle," Connor says. *You or her.* "Who do you want to stay with us?"

She sniffs, "Moi." *Me.* She hugs tighter to my side, like she's just said goodbye to someone she loves.

I'd say Janie is too young to comprehend the entire meaning of the two choices, but she must've understood some fucking part.

I rub Janie's back, her cheek against my bicep. "You're all about the fucking choices, Cobalt."

"Always," he says, but I see the understanding in his eyes, knowing that I can't live my life like him. That when the day begins and ends, I just ride along the path that feels right. Instead of stopping and forecasting the most beneficial one.

I would've twirled my daughter around until her tears stopped.

I would've taken her mind off the cat by leading her outside to play.

Both ways are okay. Just different.

My lips rise at him, and he smiles back at me.

Janie touches my jaw and garbles something that sounds like, "Why do you have hair on your face?" She giggles a little, patting at my unshaven jaw.

"You want to answer this one?" I ask Connor.

He grins. "Not really." He's fucking entertained.

I instinctively look for Daisy. She'd have a better answer than me, but as soon as I find her, seated on the other side of the couch, my features darken in worry.

Her head is drooped towards her cellphone, her brows pinched with this twisted sort of hurt. "Dais?"

She doesn't hear me.

"Dais?" I call louder.

Just as she raises her head, Beckett spits up on Rose's shoulder, her high-collared black blouse dirtied with white vomit.

Her shoulders and neck are strict, and she collects her hair to her other shoulder. Connor distances himself from me and approaches his wife. After burping up, Beckett finally quiets.

I glance back at Daisy, and she stands, cellphone in hand. I watch her pace to the sliding door that leads to their backyard. I'm about to follow but she stops mid-step, staring at her fucking phone.

My muscles flex, and I set Janie on the couch cushion.

"It's fine," Rose tells Connor, Beckett on her lap. "I'm okay. I'm okay." She actually pulls off her dirtied blouse. Wearing a sheer black lingerie corset-looking thing underneath. A bodice? I don't know the word, but I've never seen Rose be this fucking flippant with changing clothes in front of people.

Not since maybe Comic-Con, a long time ago.

Connor has a hand on her waist, whispering to her rapidly. Her joints are stiff and unbending, her collarbone jutting out with short breaths.

He says, "Do you remember when Penn and Princeton faced Harvard at the Quiz Bowl Quarter-Finals, and we were both certain that George Lansidle was cheating?"

She nods. "It was my first year in college, and I despised you."

"And you spent two hours in the convention's banquet hall with me."

"To figure out how to expose George's treachery." Fire flames her yellow-green eyes.

His grin starts rising. "We were used to competing against one another, but this time we willingly worked together. Do you remember?"

She nods again, her gaze softening, and his hand slides into hers.

"I've loved you, always," he says. "I was just too blind to see how much and for how long. There's a nineteen-year-old boy, handing you his blazer in a bathroom, and if he could, he'd tell you this. All over again."

A tear rolls down Rose's cheek.

He kisses her forehead and then says, "Ensemble." *Together.*

"Ensemble," she whispers.

They glance down at their newborns, both fast asleep. Everything starts to calm down except for Daisy. I rise without a cane and limp slowly towards my wife.

Janie springs from the couch and races over to her parents. She hangs onto Rose's leg, and Rose says to her in a self-assured tone, "You're a sister now, Jane. At some point, your brothers will need you, and you'll need them. They're the best thing you have in this world."

Janie nods confidently, like she understands, even if she has no fucking clue.

Connor bends down and kisses her head and whispers to her in French, then Janie says to Rose, "I love you, Mommy."

Rose shoots a glare at Connor, but she's smiling. "You can't tell our children to tell me they love me, Richard."

"I can if it's the truth." He grins again.

"It's not from the heart."

"It's from someone's heart. If not theirs, then mine."

Rose rolls her eyes and says to Janie, "Your father thinks he's smart."

"Your mother thinks she's fierce."

Rose scoffs.

"Aren't we telling truths now, darling? You are fierce, and I am brilliant."

She raises her hand at him. "I called you smart, not *brilliant*."

While they're having a great fucking time, I'm sucking down shooting pain just to walk across the room. I have to hop more than once.

And with the worst limp yet, I finally reach her. "Dais?" I touch her shoulder.

She startles.

"Sorry," I say. *What the fuck is going on?*—my brain is doused with curses. I see more red than she probably does.

She blows out a breath, eyes bloodshot. "It's okay."

Calloway girls say that a lot, but they forget how much we fucking love them, how much we know them. How much we want to take care of them.

"Yeah? What is it?"

Her arms shake, and I hug her to my side while she says, "They won't stop texting me."

"Cleo and Harper?" I guess, my stomach in fucking knots.

"They said that they'll come over to our house every day to show me why I need to do *Queens of Philadelphia*. They keep getting my number, and if they show up at the house—I have to prepare. I need to call security at the gate, and I have to get our lawyer—"

"Hey, hey," I say quickly, cupping her face. I take her phone with my other hand. "I'm calling the fucking lawyer. I'll print out the texts and he'll send these girls a cease and desist again. The neighborhood security should already have their names blacklisted."

"I want to double check with security," she says.

"Okay." I nod. "I'll triple-fucking-check everything with you. Whatever you need to feel safe, we're doing."

Her fingers touch her lips, staring past me.

"Daisy, I'm right here." I comb her hair back, hoping she'll see me.

"Will it always be like this?" she asks so fucking softly.

The public is against us. Her old friends aren't listening to her protests or the law. The best she can do is ignore all of it and focus on staying healthy. "No, Calloway," I tell her fucking strongly.

Her eyes meet mine.

"It's going to be better than this, but you're tough enough to walk through shit and cheer on the other side. I know you are."

Her smile briefly toys with her lips. "Will you walk through shit with me?"

"Every fucking day of my life."

I pull her into a hug, and her arms wrap around me. That's when I see Lily and Lo in the living room, Lo peeling back the aluminum foil on the cake.

His amber eyes lift to us. "And you think we're fucking weird?"

"What does that say, Mommy?" Moffy asks.

Lily's eyes widen and she stumbles over her words before blurting, "Sorry we had fun on your couch."

"Fun is really bad," Daisy teases, her eyes a little fucking watery. "It'll eat you up and spit you out."

Lo covers Moffy's ears. "Brother, tell your wife not to confuse my son."

"It sounded fucking right to me."

Daisy smiles more. *Don't stop, sweetheart.* I kiss the top of her head, holding her so fucking close—I can feel her pulse still beating from fright.

Connor says, "Ryke and Daisy's future progeny will no doubt be a strange influence on ours."

"You're waiting for it, Cobalt. Admit it."

He smiles. "Maybe."

Daisy's phone buzzes in my closed fist. I take the risk and look.

This is all for you. We love you, Daisy. You'll be happy later.
– C & H

Fuck both of you.

I want her happy right now.

< 53 >

Ryke Meadows

"Ryke! Ryke!" Lo pounds on my bedroom door. "Ryke! Ryke!" Over and over and fucking over.

"Fucking A," I grumble, my eyes tiredly opening. I press my hands to my forehead like my brain is about to explode.

Daisy stirs next to me. *Fuck.*

I lean over her while she starts to wake. "Go back to sleep, Dais," I whisper.

She rubs her eyes and yawns.

"Daisy," I force. "You need to fucking sleep."

"Ryke! Ryke! Motherfucking Ryke!" Lo chants with his edged, pissed voice. He slams his fist against the door again and again.

I rake a hand through my hair, staring between the locked door and my pregnant wife.

"I'll try to fall back asleep," she yawns and then cuddles with Coconut who licks her cheek. She smiles. "You should see what your brother wants."

We both know what he wants.

I step off the bed with my left foot, shirtless, only wearing gray drawstring pants. I grab my wooden cane by the nightstand and limp to the fucking door.

I open it roughly, just as he screams, "RYKE!" in my ear.

I grimace. "Fuck you."

"Thanks, big brother." He touches his chest in mock gratitude. "Follow me."

I'd rather stay with Daisy and go back to sleep. I stay planted in the doorway. "You woke up Daisy."

"Maybe you should've answered me faster then," he says. "Think of it as motivation." He pats my shoulder. "Now follow me."

"Not today."

As though expecting my response, he lifts a bottle of Maker's Mark, swishing the liquid in my face. My temperature escalates, burning my fucking brain. I reach out to steal the alcohol from him, all I see is the worst thing in my brother's hand. Something that could kill him.

He hoists it behind his head, out of my reach, and I wobble on my cane.

How...?

"How'd you fucking get that?" I growl. The house is empty of alcohol. None of us drink here.

With daggered amber eyes, he tells me, "I walked into a liquor store and grabbed one of my favorite whiskeys. I paid for it, brought it home, and here we are." Not many people can possibly understand how hard it would be for Lo to just casually stroll into a liquor store.

I do.

I spent *years* helping him stay sober, talking him down, hearing his stories of almost going inside, of the *raging* pain. Like guzzling rock salt to just stay away. Why the fuck would he do this? Why *the fuck* would he do this?

"Why the fuck would you do this?!" I yell at him, fisting his fucking T-shirt. My lungs blazing.

"Why do you think?" he sneers, gesturing at me with the bottle. "If you don't care about your stupid life, then I figured you would care about our stupid lives." He licks his lips. "Am I right?"

My eyes burn.

"You can either follow me or I can take a swig of whiskey." He opens the bottle between us like a fucking grenade.

I breathe hot air through my nose. Once upon a fucking time, I broke my sobriety in a similar way. Lo was in my position. I was in his. He had the chance to stop me, but he didn't.

I can't forget the years I spent with my little brother.

I can't forget the struggle to just quit.

I can't forget the fucking agony of his relapse.

My soul hasn't died yet.

I react and rip the Maker's Mark out of his clutch, nearly falling against the wall to do it. My brother steadies me with his hands on my shoulders. I don't say another word, I just set the whiskey on the fucking floor, readjust my cane. And I limp ahead of him, out of the doorway.

"Looks like you still care about something," Lo says behind me, passing through the basement's entertainment room. When I start ascending the stairs, so fucking slowly, Lo runs ahead of me and stops at the top.

My features darken, still brewing about what he just did. His sobriety means more than rehabilitating my leg. It will *always* mean more.

I struggle on the sixth stair. "Wherever you're fucking going, I'll just meet you there."

"No," he says with finality.

My muscles flex, then my shin throbs. "What do you mean *no*?" I mutter under my breath.

"I'm waiting for you," he says, no irritation in his voice. No malice or contempt. "I'm patient." He nods in my direction. "Just like you were with me."

I scowl. "I'm not fucking patient." I'm *impatient* more than he realizes.

"You forgot already, bro?" He shakes his head, feigning disappointment.

Sweat gathers on my brow, and I lean my arm against the railing for a second. "What the fuck are you talking about?"

"You would slow down for me when we were on a track, see how I was doing, push me to run just a little faster. You'd do that *every time*. You could've stopped on day one. I yelled at you, called you the worst fucking names, and you just kept running beside me, ahead of me. Waiting for me to catch up to you. And guess what, I did." His eyes redden. "You were patient with me. So this, right here"—he gestures between me and him—"is me being patient with you."

Our history jostles me, screams at me, hugs me—and I nod a few times, sensing the way I'll go before I do. I bend my right knee just a fucking fraction, just enough to climb the stairs marginally faster. I grit my teeth.

Trying to catch up to him.

When I reach the top, he says, "Goddamn, what took you so long?" He taps my shoulder again. "This way."

I follow him...to the sliding glass door. The fucking backyard? "We could've gone outside through the basement." We didn't have to climb the steeper, narrower flight of stairs.

"I know, but I really wanted to see you Hulk out." He opens the sliding door with a bitter half-smile. There it is. Behind all of his dry talk, I know he forced me up the stairs for *me*, not for himself.

To help me.

I would've done the same thing to him.

I don't say anything as I pass him, and I spot a Yoga mat unfurled by the pool. Lily and Daisy already put out Halloween decorations, even though it's only the first week of October. Spider webs cling to the black iron fence, and plastic tombstones are staked into the grass. An orange pumpkin inner tube floats across the heated pool.

Lo unfolds my exercises that he printed out. "Your physical therapist said you haven't moved out of mobility and flexibility yet."

I nod. I can't start strengthening my muscles without improving those two first. I slowly sit down, cool morning air rushing towards me in a heavy gust. "Next time, let's do this in the fucking afternoon."

Lo stiffens. "What was that?"

"The afternoon," I tell him. "Don't wake me up this fucking early."

He rocks back like I slugged him in the jaw. I didn't think *these* words would assault him, but I watch him breathe out, his features tightening.

He squats next to me and says, "No."

I run both hands through my hair, my elbow resting on my bent left knee. "What does it matter when we do it?"

"Take a look around, Ryke," Lo tells me, his eyes fucking murderous.

I stare up at the dark sky that begins to lighten.

"This is your favorite time of day, and that hasn't changed."

Sunrise.

I woke, almost every morning, to see the horizon painted orange and muted blue. I went climbing. I ran. At the first sign of light. I married the only girl I've ever loved—the minute the sun ascended.

I can't do the things I used to. "Maybe I've changed."

"It's not physical, just mental," Lo tells me. "You're *going* to run again." He says it in that desperate tone, like he can't fathom a fucking world where I slack behind him. He has no idea the pain...he can't understand how deep it fucking runs.

I crack the strain in my neck and then lie back. "Okay." I prop myself on my elbows while Lo holds my right calf, helping me bend my knee towards my chest.

It won't go that far.

The muscle stretches, and pain starts radiating after the short movement. "Wait," I wince from discomfort.

"You went farther yesterday," he reminds me. "I've seen you bench press after someone took a portion of your liver. I had to *pry* dumbbells out of your hands back then. You can fucking do this now."

I wipe the sweat off my forehead, and I try again but stop in two fucking seconds, knives cutting into my kneecap. "You don't understand."

"I don't understand?"

I let out a heavy breath. "I can't." I shake my head over and over.

He narrows his eyes at me. "When has Ryke Meadows ever given up on himself?" He points at my ribcage, the story behind the inked chain, anchor and phoenix something I explained to him last Christmas. After we both fell into the tree, sweeping up broken ornaments together. "You have a tattoo that basically says, *don't drag yourself down*. What are you doing now?"

"I'm fighting—"

"You're dying!" he screams at me. "You're *dying* right in front of me." His furious eyes pool with tears, his vulnerability shining through. Making him seem younger. Fragile. My little brother.

I sit up. "Hey, I'm doing alright. I'm right here. I haven't died." I reach out and squeeze his shoulder.

He blinks and his tears fall. "I never understood. Not when Daisy explained it, not when you did. I didn't get it, but now I do."

My frown darkens. "What do you mean?"

"Climbing is a part of you. That's what you told me. And I look at you now without it…you're different. You're fucking lifeless compared to the person you were. The person *I* know, we all know." His chin quakes. "I miss my brother, and if you won't fight for the thing that makes you happy, then I'm going to fight for you."

I hang my head and pinch my raw eyes. I can't explain to him what I'm going through. "It's so fucking hard."

He puts a hand on my back, and after a long pause, he says, "Hard things are the right things. Remember that?"

I cry because I don't fucking know if I'll ever be the same.

He scoots closer. "One step at a time. I know it's hell. I know you want to give up. I know it fucking hurts. Just one step, one more time, Ryke. We're doing this together. You and me."

I thought he didn't understand this pain, but I know he does. It's not the kind where he needs to shatter his leg to feel it. I rub my face and then nod a couple times. Okay. *Okay*.

"Now," Lo says, "do your bastard brother a favor and lie the fuck down."

I give him a look before dropping back down. "That's not fucking funny."

He bends my knee towards my chest, and I inhale strongly. *Fuckfuckfuck*. "One more inch," he says. "You would've been here a week ago if you tried harder."

Probably.

I prop myself on my forearm, watching my knee do the simplest action with the most fucking strain. It's good, even if it's tender and sore and screeching. The further I go today, the further I go tomorrow.

"I'm in fucking hell," I grit as I keep my knee in place, the muscles adjusting.

"You're already dead, so it shouldn't make much of a difference being here," Lo quips with a smartass fucking smile.

I flip him off but my lips almost curve upward. I almost forget about the discomfort for a second. In the quiet, there are questions in my brother's eyes. Things like, *Will you wake up early tomorrow? Will you follow me, big brother? Will you ever climb again?*

Yes. *As soon as the light hits.*

Yes. *I'll chase after you, little brother.*

Will I ever climb again? *I don't fucking know.*

I'm my own anchor.

I decide when to rise again.

I don't know if I'm ready. I don't know if I'll ever be ready enough to reach for the some*thing* that I love. I already have the some*ones* with me.

Isn't that all I need in the fucking end?

< 54 >

Daisy Meadows

"Can we open it now?" I ask Ryke as he cradles a cardboard box beneath his arm, with the words: *you've ruined my birthday if you don't wear these costumes* in Loren Hale's messy handwriting.

Ryke enters our bedroom, leaning his weight on his cane, but he bends his right knee a little more each day. I've seen small changes in his mood since the beginning of October. He wakes up early every morning, without Lo pounding on the door.

He cooks breakfast again. And eats healthier. I even saw him doing resistance workouts on his own in the backyard. He wants to run. I can see it in his eyes most days, unlike before.

I don't know what Lo said to him, but whatever he did, it worked some.

"No," Ryke answers me after his slow trek to our dresser. He sets the box down. "Lo wants everyone to wait until five fucking thirty so we can't find an alternative costume and back out."

Today is Halloween.

And also Loren Hale's twenty-seventh birthday.

As a present this year, we've all let him dictate our costumes, and he's made it a mystery. In a box.

It's only 10:30 a.m. I pet a sleepy Coconut on her fuzzy green bed beneath the window. She turns away from me, too tired for love.

I stand and crawl back on the bed, wearing one of Ryke's plaid flannel button-downs. We have time to kill since we've opted out of the whole trick-or-treating with the little kids. But we're all attending some fancy celebrity party in New York later tonight.

It's Lo's plan.

He thinks we're all turning "old and unfun"—and this set Rose's bones on fire enough to accept the party challenge. Really though, if anyone needs the break, it's Connor and Rose. My parents and a trusted nanny are babysitting all the kids during our outing, so hopefully everyone feels at ease.

Ryke pulls the shirt off his head with one hand, his brown eyes on me more than once. Grazing the length of my long bare legs. I smile at him, sensing this quiet sexual tension stewing.

I can't say I'm one hundred percent in the mood or aroused, but I love seeing his, even if mine stays low. I crawl further across the bed, closer to where he stands. "What if my costume is a Daisy Meadows tigress?" I make a claw motion at him.

He stays stoic and mysterious, towering above me. In a husky voice, he says, "My brother would be fucking quicker to make me Jesus Christ than you a cute animal."

I smile wider. Jesus is actually a plausible option. "You think I'm cute?" I paw his arm.

He rests his good knee on the bed, leaning closer to me and says lowly, "Terribly fucking cute."

I untie his track pants, watching him study my gaze more than anything. Wondering if I'm really in the mood. We flirt a lot, and it doesn't always lead to sex or even foreplay.

I tug his pants down his ass, revealing his forest green boxer-briefs and the clear outline of his hard, long cock.

I'm practically on all fours, in line with his crotch. Perfect angle and everything for head. Maybe he'll let me pleasure him, even if it's just okay for me. I want to get him off, so I touch the waistband of his underwear. Then he catches my wrists together.

"I can't tell," he says honestly, "so I'm going to fucking ask."

"Okay." I know where this is going.

"Do you want to have sex, Daisy?"

"Not a hundred percent, no."

He kisses my cheek tenderly and then lets go of my wrists. I sit on my ass, watching him back away from the bed. I guess I just want to reciprocate in some way *more*. I'm just not sure how I can help without oral sex.

As he edges towards the bathroom door, he must see my faint disappointment. He stops midway, eyeing me for a second.

I rest against the headboard, my knees swinging back and forth.

He grabs lube out of the nightstand and then suddenly reroutes his course. He throws damp towels off our wicker chair. Then he drags the piece of furniture towards the foot of our bed.

Curiosity lights my eyes.

His head collides with one of our low-hanging paper lanterns. "Fuck," he mutters, setting a hand on the lamp so it'll stop swaying.

My lips pull higher.

Before Ryke sets his cane aside, he turns his back to me and sheds his boxer-briefs.

I have a straight-shot view of his toned ass and sculpted back, some of his long lasting bruises just losing their yellow-purplish tint.

He rotates and then slouches in the wicker chair all casual and assured and naked—my body rises with a deep inhale. My eyes drift *all over* Ryke, his lean muscles, his shoulders, his abs, his erection…and I feel his gaze gliding *all over* me.

He grips the base of his cock. *Holy shit.*

He's going to masturbate in front of me. *A first.*

I crane my neck, staring fixatedly.

He hasn't begun yet, not really. "Yeah?" he asks me if I'm okay with this, his brows scrunched and features dark. I think I know why, even if we talked about the possibility of this a *long* time ago.

Certain positions cause me to flashback to awful moments with guys. Me on top. Blow jobs. Maybe he's worried this will send me back to a time where someone just jacked off to my body. While I lied there disinterested. Feeling, ultimately, gross and uncomfortable.

But this is completely new for me. "Yeah," I say with a nod. "This is a first for me, ever, you know that?"

A flickering smile touches his lips. Then he grazes me again with his steely eyes, and his hand pumps up and down his hard shaft.

His movements make me more restless, and I find myself kicking blankets, swinging my legs more, shifting my hips, and running my palms along our sheets.

His breath stays controlled as he strokes his erection, but he never looks down. His eyes are always on me. I like watching him.

I've always liked watching him. The barely perceivable flexing of his abs. The tic in his jaw as he clenches his teeth. The veins spindling up his arms. And his cock that swells with cravings and desires.

I love it all.

My knees knock together, and I pop a couple buttons on my flannel shirt that stops mid-thigh. His hard gaze flits between the opening of the shirt and my eyes. I watch his hand pump a little faster, and he shifts slightly in the chair.

I totally prefer arousing him this way than by blowing him, and maybe he's beginning to realize it too. My silly, lovesick smile returns in full-force.

I pop a few more buttons and let the shirt fall off my arms. My breasts come into view, a little larger than usual. His jaw locks again, and his cock seems to harden *even more* beneath his hand.

I stir a bit, my body strangely awakening. Usually when I'm not in the mood, I stay that way, but the visual is so new. He's so attractive. And his *want* for me is clear in every tiny motion, in every pulse of his vein. In the wrinkle of his scowl. It's all saying, *I want to fuck you until sundown and come sunup, Calloway.*

He remains there, though. Respectful of my boundaries. My needs and my own desires. It makes him ten billion times more alluring and more perfect for me.

I unbutton my shirt all the way and pull it off entirely. Naked and bare, just like him. He seems to focus on my round belly.

A low grunt catches in his throat, and he clutches his cock a little tighter. His pleasured noise sends shockwaves down my spine.

I tremble. "Ryke," I say breathily.

He grips the base of his chair with his free hand, like he has to hold on as his arousal mounts. His other hand pumps faster. Harder. "Fuck…" He lets out another husky noise, eyes all over me. His heavy, weighted breath shakes my knees. I spread my legs wide open, and he groans, "Fuck…me."

His eyes roll back some, and then he comes on himself, milking the last of his climax with a few more strokes.

My mouth falls at the sight. If there's a scale that measures hotness, he's totally burned the entire thing.

The minute he locks eyes with me—before he decides to take a shower and wash off—I say, "Come inside of me. Please."

< 55 >

Ryke Meadows

Fuck.

Her high-pitched plea grips my fucking dick. I stay still for a second, gauging her reaction, if this is something she actually wants or if she's just trying to turn me on again. For me, not for her.

I'm not about to fuck Daisy if she doesn't care to have sex. It's not necessary like it used to be, and no one's fucking happier about it than me. Coming inside a girl who turns her head away from you, waiting for it to end—it rips my fucking heart out.

I don't think she'd set me up for that.

I know she wouldn't.

"I think I'm wet," she pants and then reaches down between her legs, stretching them even wider. More for herself this time. She's swollen and clearly soaked.

I harden again, almost fucking instantly. I stand up and rest my left knee on the edge of the bed; my right foot stays on the floor, the pain dull beneath heightened arousal. Better sentiments all around.

As her fingers graze her clit, she shudders and mumbles an, "Oh my God."

I clasp her ankle and yank her fast and hard to the bottom of the mattress.

Her blonde hair splays against the sheets and blankets, and her smile bursts, her chest rising and falling heavily. She's so fucking beautiful, and I want inside of her more than she can possibly comprehend. I grab a pillow and put it beneath the small of her back, hoisting her pelvis closer to me.

I feel her gaze travel across my body, landing on my erection. "I have this theory." While I have hold of her ankles, she wrestles against the mattress, her shoulders burrowing into the blankets. "That you were meant…" She loses breath, unable to tear her gaze off my cock.

"That I was meant…?" My hand runs down her long leg, clasping her hip. Her breasts are bigger, her waist more curved than usual, and her stomach round. It all just points to one fucking fact:

She's pregnant with *my* baby.

Not some repulsive prick that calls her names and treats her like shit. I didn't have to watch her go through life that way.

If someone told me on the yacht—when she just turned sixteen— that we'd end up here, I'd think they were fucking insane. I'd never think about getting Daisy Calloway pregnant. Never even picture either of us married.

Time changes people.

There was a point where it made me sick thinking about her kissing another fucking guy. Where I couldn't even contemplate the notion that she'd be married to someone else. Where she'd carry his baby. Where she'd be happy in his arms, not mine.

Having her here, with me, means every fucking thing.

I lift her hips up towards my pelvis, and she says, "You were meant to be…deep, deep inside of me from the get-go." The idea of me fucking her when she was fifteen turns her on—especially since it would erase her bad experiences. So I'm not going to squash her fucking fantasy.

I run my hand up and down her body, and she shudders more beneath my palm. Her nipples have been too sensitive, even for shower water, so I stay away. She's waiting for me to push in, and I'm teasing the fuck out of her.

My hand back on her hip. I lean forward and kiss the corner of her mouth. "You're my favorite fucking wild thing."

"Ryke," she cries, ready and writhing in my grasp.

I comb the hair out of her face and then kiss between her breasts, down her ribcage, down her round belly, blood pooling in my cock. I straighten up again, my left knee still on the bed. Her legs wrapped around my waist.

I grip my erection, pausing a second before I drive in. She's always been fragile during sex. In the sense that I can hurt her easily. If I push too hard against her cervix. If her cyst flares up. She can feel pain, but her being twenty-four weeks pregnant brings sex to another dimension.

I'm not fucking scared. I just want to read her body language correctly. I want to pay attention to every part of her, so I can give her everything she needs.

"Take me," she whispers, still staring at my cock.

I slowly push into her, and her face blankets with pleasure. "Ahhh," she breathes and clutches the bed on either side of her. Her legs vibrate on either side of me, and her tightness, so fucking swollen, grips me.

Fuck. Me. I run my fingers through my hair, *fuck.* Thrusting forward. Clutching her hip. Disappearing all the way inside of her.

Every time I rock forward, she rocks up, in sync with my movements. Coming at me as I come at her. I stare at her slender body, her baby bump, her feral fucking motions.

She slows for a second, and I see a wince in the crease of her eyes.

"Easy, Dais," I breathe, concern pumping adrenaline into me. "You don't have to fucking move."

She lets out heavy breaths and then nods. A look in her eyes that says *slower*.

I pull out and push in with an unhurried pace, drawing the tension and increasing the fucking friction. She watches closely and tries to thrust up, but I put a hand on her stomach, easing her body back down.

She nods again, her back arching and eyelids fluttering.

A groan scratches my fucking throat. *Jesus fucking*—I push deeper, slower but fucking deeper. She clenches around my cock, tight and pulsating. Her lips open and she gasps as she hits a peak.

I fucking burst, coming hard. I lean forward, my forearms on either side of her face, and I kiss her neck, hearing her cry out more as I'm buried inside her heat.

"Ryke."

I lift my head and she kisses me on the lips first. I kiss her back instantly, my tongue sliding against hers. She moans against my mouth, and I break away so she can catch her breath.

"Good?" I ask, my right foot still on the ground. My dick still in her.

"The very best," she smiles. "I think you were always meant to be right here." She wags her brows, alluding to our bodies connected together.

"You already said that, Calloway." I know what she sees when she looks at us, and it's easy to share her vision. To feel the same fucking thing. Animalistic. Meant to fuck. Meant to start a family.

Meant to be.

"The orgasm must have literally blown my mind."

"Cute." I pat her ass. "I'm going to pull out." She's no longer clenching, and I easily slide out, watching her exhale. No sign of pain.

She crawls off the bed, and my brows furrow, wondering what the fuck she's doing. I sit on the edge of the mattress and glance at my chest and abs. Fuck, I need a shower.

Daisy lifts the cardboard box with our costumes and sets it beside me. "I'm curious. Aren't you curious?"

"No," I say flatly. I planned to wait until five-thirty like Lo wanted, but post-sex, I'd do just about anything Daisy asked. Including opening a box we aren't supposed to fucking open.

I rip at the tape before she does. Her smile spreads so wide that I can feel a dark part of me brighten. She helps me finish and we both open the flaps together.

Two letters sit on top, and I pass the one that looks like Daisy's. We both wait for each other to read theirs, but I motion for her to go first.

She unfolds the letter and clears her throat, layering on her theatrical fucking voice. "'Dear One-Half Crazy Raisin.'" She sways from side to side, naked, in front of me. "'I thought about making you a nun, but you can thank your sister, the adorable one, for telling me not to be such a dick.' Thank you, Lily." Daisy curtsies.

I pull out her costume, something navy blue, silver, red, and a winged helmet.

She continues reading. "'Lil said you should be something cool since you're the coolest girl she's ever met or whatever. I thought you should be something flighty because you're all over the goddamn place. We decided on Thor—the girl Thor, which is a real thing in Marvel.'" She bounces on her toes, fucking excited.

It makes me happy seeing her this upbeat.

"'P.S.,'" she reads, "'don't abuse the hammer.'" She gasps at me. "There's a hammer?"

I toss her the plastic weapon that has a rubber band on the other end. So when she tosses it, it'll swing back towards her body. "Don't fucking hurt yourself," I say.

"I won't." She doesn't test it out yet. She waits and looks at my letter. "What's yours?"

Thing is, most years I dress as Green Arrow because I always forget to put together a new costume. Lo absolutely despises it, so he won't waste this opportunity to make me wear something different.

I read his letter. "'To the brother who's not the bastard.'—Fucking hilarious, Lo," I mutter and shake my head. "'I thought about making you Luke Skywalker since you have such daddy issues…'" I roll my eyes. "'…but I can't imagine you in a white robe. Anyway, you have a scar on your eyebrow, which makes you look more like Anakin. Just know, I could've made you a bottle of mustard or a banana, so be happy about it.'"

Daisy takes out my costume, a blackish-brown robe, tunic, and pants from *Star Wars* with a plastic lightsaber. It'll be the nerdiest fucking costume I've ever worn, but I'd wear it for Lo. I'd actually wear just about anything for him.

I glance down at the letter and silently read the last line.

p.s.
i don't think you're the villain, even if anakin is.

< 56 >

Ryke Meadows

"Mother of dragons!" Lo shouts at the Cobalt's house, all of us waiting outside for Connor and Rose. The limo parked by the fountain. I've known them for too many fucking years, and I can count on my hand the number of times they've been late to anything.

I try to call them again, but there's no answer. I'll be fucking worried when they go on ten minutes late. We're only at four right now.

"You stoleth thy lightsaber, you pesky fairy." Daisy outstretches her hammer towards Lily, who's dressed as Tinker Bell this year.

Lo is a disgruntled, peeved Peter Pan. "MOTHER OF FUCKING DRAGONS!" he yells at a quiet house.

I gave my lightsaber to Lily, both girls bored waiting, and Lily, all gangly limbs in a green tutu dress with wings, whips the blue plastic beam towards Daisy. "Prepare to meet thy doom, Thor." They battle with huge smiles, her lightsaber hitting Daisy's hammer.

Lo sighs heavily, crossing his arms and leaning against the limo like me. "Should I be prepared for you to be naked by the end of the night?" I've given away more than just my lightsaber in the past four minutes.

Daisy wears my robe, the long fabric dusting the ground as she fences with Lily.

"She was cold," I tell him, but his gaze has already drifted to our sister, who stands by the trunk of the limo with Garrison, his laptop popped open. She points at the screen and he nods, explaining something to her out of earshot.

I remember that Lily told me out of all the Superheroes & Scones employees, Garrison won the "make your own superhero" contest for the *Fourth Degree* comics. The artist and creators of the comic universe chose his concept: an anti-hero named Sorin X with teleportation powers linked to the proximity of the girl he loves. He can't teleport more than four miles away from her. And he's a recovering alcoholic.

Sounded a lot like Lo made an impact on Garrison. In some way. Some form. Enough to create a fucking superhero out of him.

Lo leans closer to me and says in a hushed voice, "Apparently this is Willow's first Halloween party, the kind that doesn't involve carnival games. It's really not her thing, so if she looks ready to bail, I think we should all just leave early."

I nod, agreeing. She's dressed as an angel in a knee-length white dress and matching wings, a circular gold wreath on her head. Garrison stands opposite in red slacks, a red T-shirt, and a red-horned headband on his dark brown hair.

I still can't believe my brother gave them couple costumes.

"Devil!" Lo shouts at our sister's boyfriend.

Garrison pries his eyes from the computer, and Willow pushes her glasses up.

"You know what happens when an angel and a devil create a bodily union?" *Okay, now I fucking get it.* "The apocalypse. Do the right thing and don't end the world tonight."

"That's definitely not how that works," Garrison says dryly.

Lo looks to me. "Do you hear this guy?"

"Yeah. I guess he doesn't understand the fucking meaning of apocalypse. Want to spell it out for him?"

Garrison crosses his arms with a look like *you too?*

She's my sister. I fucking care about her having a good time. No pressure to drink, to dance, to fuck, to do anything that she doesn't want to do.

Problem with Garrison is that he's too sarcastic to get a good read on. Whether he respects her hesitations, I have no fucking clue. Deep down, I want to think the best of people, but I'm not fucking naïve either.

"Apocalypse," Lo says, "also know as the end of your godforsaken, puny little life by the powers that be."

"Also known as *me*," I chime in.

"And me," Lo finishes with a half-smile. "Welcome to hell."

"I've seen scarier," Garrison says flatly.

My brows jump in surprise. Besides my father and my brother, I've never seen anyone as spiteful and sharp-tongued. "Who?" I ask.

"My brothers." Garrison closes off at that, returning to his computer. I don't bother him because I know what he's doing on there. Something for Daisy.

Lo watches him for a moment or two longer, and I check the phone. "They're ten fucking minutes late now."

Right when I say it, the door swings open. Rose struts out first in a long, light-blue draped dress with a gold belt, along with a platinum blonde wig.

I've seen episodes of *Game of Thrones* with Lo to figure out that she's Danaerys. Also known as the Mother of Dragons.

"Finally," Lo huffs.

I open the limo door, and Lily and Daisy are the first to climb inside, their cheeks reddened from the cold and bouncing around. Garrison and Willow slip into the limo next, his laptop still opened.

"You realize it's my birthday?" Lo asks her as she approaches us, her fiery attitude enhanced with penetrating yellow-green eyes.

"Sorry," she actually apologizes, almost unrecognizable with the platinum hair. "Connor will be out in another minute."

I stare at her a little fucking longer than usual. Always shocked when she changes her appearance, even slightly. I'm used to Rose being in high-collared black dresses. Any deviation usually throws me the fuck off. Like being whiplashed.

Lo smacks the back of my head, reprimanding me. I'm not checking her out in a sexual way—for fuck's sake.

I shove his arm lightly.

"What?" she asks me, scanning my wardrobe from head to toe. I don't think she knows what I'm supposed to be. At least not without my lightsaber, but she doesn't question it.

"What took you so fucking long?" I ask.

"Things." She collects her platinum hair on one shoulder and then lowers her voice. "How's Daisy?"

"Happy."

Her lips twitch upward.

Lo grimaces. "It smiles."

Rose glares and scrutinizes his traditional Peter Pan costume. "I hope your tights give you a wedgie."

"I hope your hair falls out."

"I hope this conversation fucking ends," I chime in.

Rose looks between the two of us, hands on her hips. "Let's make a pact. If *anyone* hassles our sisters tonight, we confront them and handle it with necessary means, according to how antagonistic they are towards us." She lifts up her dress.

"Whoa whoa," Lo says. "Jesus, Rose, no one wants to—oh."

She has a knife strapped to her thigh.

"What, you plan on fucking shanking someone tonight?" I'm suddenly worried. Uneasy. Concerned. All of the fucking above. She's clearly scared about a public outing. We all haven't taken one together in a long time, not like this. We're headed to the Hamptons where some famous singer invited us to her Halloween party, and our bodyguards have to stay outside her mansion.

Price included. After our wedding and helping Daisy reach the hospital in Lima, I've trusted him a lot more. I still don't know why Greg would hire someone that young, but I don't think Price is going to fuck us over.

"I plan on being resourceful and *cautious*." She raises her chin. "I also have a taser."

"Where?" Lo cringes. "Actually, I don't want to know."

"You're telling me that you don't have a knife?" Rose rebuts.

She has a point. I lift up my blackish-brown pants that are tucked into my boot. My brother and Rose can see the hilt of my knife. I usually always carry it around, especially after the crazed fucking media.

"Jesus Christ," Lo curses. "Am I the only one not armed?"

I don't say it out loud, but his words are basically a weapon.

"Do we have a pact?" Rose asks. "Keep an eye on them and proceed with *action*."

"We're not the ones who'd restrain you," I remind her. "Your fucking husband would pull you out of a confrontation first."

She mutters, "pacifist," under her breath.

Lily suddenly butts into our circle of three, climbing out of the limo and squeezing in the middle of us. "I think it's important to tell all of you something before we begin this journey." She has glitter all over her face and her wing keeps jabbing me in the fucking ribs. "The hot-tempered triad cannot come out to play."

We all groan.

"This is serious." She spits a strand of hair off her lips. "Don't freak out if someone hits on Daisy."

"She's fucking pregnant," I growl, narrowing my eyes at the idea. *No. Fuck no.*

"See, you're already freaking out! Don't do that, Ryke."

I glower, but she turns on Rose. "Don't freak out if someone says mean and rude things to me. I'm going to be okay."

Rose purses her lips, trying to bite her tongue, but she blurts out, "I'll slit their throats."

Me fucking too. Immediately agreeing with the metaphorical threat.

Lily spins on Lo. "And you."

"Yes, love?" Lo begins to smile which almost cracks Lily's stern demeanor.

She stands confidently though. Her Tinker Bell to his Peter Pan. "You better have the best twenty-seventh birthday ever. AndLorenHalealwaysfucksbetter," she slurs together before kissing his cheek quickly and disappearing back into the limo.

Lo looks infatuated.

"Fucking finally," I say as soon as the door opens and Connor emerges.

He's wearing a Luke Skywalker costume, all white like a fucking god.

I glare at Lo who can't stop laughing between the two of us. He put us in matching costumes. I realize that Rose knew what I was wearing. She was just putting the pieces together too—that I'm basically coupled with her fucking husband tonight.

"I fucking hate you," I tell my brother while Rose slips into the limo.

Lo pats my shoulder. "My birthday," he reminds me.

He's going to milk this all night.

Connor keeps a composed expression by the sight of my wardrobe, but I'm sure, beneath it all, he's just as irritated as me. He then tilts his head to Lo. "I see what you did there, darling."

Lo touches his heart. "Can you feel my love?"

"Immensely."

I nod to Connor. "What took you so fucking long?"

"Miss me?"

"I was worried," I say, not beating around the fucking bush. "You two are never late."

"We were busy." He uses the reflection of the limo to fix his slightly unkempt, wavy brown hair.

It clicks. "You were fucking."

"Good boy," he says. "Want a treat? Or should I stick my lightsaber into you now?"

I put my black Wayfarers on. "Don't stick your lightsaber anywhere near me, Cobalt."

He grins that billion-dollar grin.

Lo snatches my glasses off my eyes. "It's nighttime and you're a damn Jedi Knight. You don't wear sunglasses."

If we're seriously roleplaying, I would need to die by the night's end. Whatever happens—I just don't want to see any of the girls or my brother or even Connor in the hospital.

Can we avoid that? Or is it inevitable that everything will end in complete fucking disaster?

< 57 >

Daisy Meadows

"Breaker breaker," I say into my speakerphone. Loud, ominous music drowns the chatter from *hundreds* of bodies, mostly celebrities. It's been easier to blend within the costumed crowds and be an observer rather than the one observed. "We've lost Anakin and Peter. Where can we find them?"

"I can't hear you! What was that?!" Lily screams, her voice crackly in my phone. The reception in the coastal mansion sucks. I hold Willow's hand, a group of men dressed as a fraternity, push through our area by the mummy statue.

Willow scoots closer to me. "I've never seen so many people in one house."

This may be a record for me too. I squeeze her hand, but she begins coughing as a fog machine smokes out our area.

"WHERE IS PETER PAN?!" I shout into the phone. This pee break is turning into an adventure. Everyone left the velvet-lined coffin in the dining room, which was not cool after we returned.

Her voice crackles again. I give in and hang up on my sister. I waft the foggy air and then set my hands on Willow's shoulder. "Let's think about this. Where would Loren Hale go?" He's driving this party train somewhere.

"The kitchen?" Willow guesses. "He likes to eat chips at Superheroes & Scones functions a lot."

She may be right. "Then that's where we'll go, milady." I straighten her lopsided silver-winged headband thing. It was a part of my Thor costume but we swapped. A golden, angelic wreath sits on my blonde hair, the length to my collarbones.

As I lead her through the depths of chatting pirates and firemen, our track is cut short by a half-naked, forty-something man. A black cardboard "censor" sign covers his crotch.

"Hi," I say before he speaks. "We're trying to meet someone that way." I point past him.

He takes a moment to swig his mixed drink, eyeing both of us. "I can get you wherever you both need to go."

Willow has the most iconic, grossed out expression, like she's spent decades avoiding eating broccoli, and tonight, of all nights, she's confronted the foul vegetable.

I tell him, "That's not necessary, but thanks for the offer." I said *thanks* in a nice voice. Rose wouldn't care about offending him or *anyone* like this.

I know this part of me won't change. As long as it never brings me down, I think it's okay to be this way sometimes. I don't have to be just like Rose or like Ryke.

I can be me.

I know who that is now.

Before he can respond, I duck beneath his arm, towing Willow behind me. She thankfully keeps close and we escape that guy.

As soon as we enter the bare kitchen—tiny candles set along the granite countertops—Ryke rushes towards me. His scowl and concern mixed with his *Star Wars* costume has an oddly super attractive effect. He'd be the sexy, *I give no fucks* guy at a nerd convention. Who accidentally acts more like his character by just being confident.

"Where the fuck did you go pee? We've been looking for you two everywhere." He sets a protective hand on the top of my head, his cane in his other one.

"To the moon and back," I smile, hoping to relax him.

He looks to Willow for an actual answer.

"Just the first floor bathroom. No one was by the coffin when we came back."

"Told you," Garrison says to the entire group. Everyone is by the bar counter, his laptop propped on a stool. Connor stands closest to Garrison, scrutinizing him and the computer screen with more interest than he ever shows people.

"You're either *really* embodying this whole devil thing," Lo says, "or it's just in your soul." Lo's barely looking at him. He's currently raiding the house's pantry with Lily hanging onto his waist, trying to pull him away with lots of effort.

"Lo, you can't."

Ryke follows my gaze, going rigid for a second.

Lo retrieves a box of Cheez-Its. "I *can*. Maybe they should've thought about snacks, huh?" He opens the brand new box in front of her face.

Lily whispers, "Should we write an IOU?"

"Lil," he says, popping one in his mouth. "Think of it as their birthday present to me."

"It could be worse," Connor tells her, his attention split between Garrison and them. "He could have broken into their liquor cabinet and consumed a forty-thousand dollar bottle of alcohol."

I've heard this story before—of when Ryke met Lo at a Halloween party. After Lo drank some guy's expensive liquor.

Ryke adds, "And had a bunch of Ninja Turtles chase after you down the street."

"See, love," Lo says to her. "My worst is over."

She smiles and then holds out her hand.

He pours some Cheez-Its in her palm with his own growing smile.

The cuteness from Lily to Lo and Lo to Lily always makes me surprised that they pretended to be together for so long. I think, all along, they were just fooling each other. The love between them is true and rare and something I always wished I had.

I glance at Ryke, and he raises his brows at me like *hey, Calloway*.

And now I do.

His arm slides around my shoulders. "No one fucking hit on you, did they?" he asks while we head closer to our friends, Willow standing next to Garrison, who's fixated on the computer.

Without looking at her, his hand slides down her arm and fits tightly in hers. Such a sly move. Lily would be the first to give them 10 out of 10 stars.

"I'm pregnant," I remind Ryke, noticing Rose sipping her sparkling water and pacing between the doorway, hawkeyed. Shouldn't she be relaxing tonight?

"Yeah?" he says. "Your sister thinks it wouldn't fucking matter if you were pregnant or not."

Willow clears her throat. "We were approached...Daisy handled it really fast though."

Garrison's head whips towards Willow. "What?"

Ryke's jaw hardens. "What do you mean *approached?*"

She wears that grossed out expression again, like a bad taste fills her mouth. It was a short run-in, but for someone who actively avoids those situations, it must be harder to digest.

Garrison seems beyond concerned, his body language opened towards her and closed off to his computer. Ryke analyzes that, I think, because he shifts his weight on his cane, not coming to her rescue or comforting her like he would anyone who was alone.

"Did someone touch you?" he asks under his breath, but we're close enough to catch the words.

"No, no, like I said, Daisy handled it really fast. It was just…weird, I guess. He was old."

"Fucking fantastic," Ryke mutters.

"It does seem like there are more guys here than girls," Lily says, munching on Cheez-Its.

Lo nods to Willow. "You want to leave now?"

She shakes her head vigorously. "No. It wasn't that bad, honestly."

Garrison still looks worried, but he kisses her lightly on the cheek and then whispers in her ear. She nods, and he pulls her against his side, tucking her close.

I whisper to Ryke, "I know I'm not the best at telling who the good guys are."

His brows rise again like *no fucking kidding.*

I smile. "But I think Garrison is one." When someone cares about your limitations and your approval on simple things, like touching, that goes a long way. Not all people are like this.

Ryke's face washes with the same realization. "Maybe you're right."

Connor says to Garrison, "How many steps are left?"

Garrison shakes his head in a daze and then remembers his project. To help me. He licks his lips, types one thing on the computer, and says, "That's it."

"That's it?" My chest rises, and I edge closer. The screen is full of computer code that makes no sense to me.

"Whoever they had hacking into your accounts will be met with porn spam when they try again. I also increased all your security passwords, and I've written them down for you." He digs into his pocket, pulling out a packet of cigarettes and crumpled piece of paper. He hands me that. "I had to add a defense to all of your accounts, by the way." Besides us there aren't other people really lingering in the empty kitchen, so they can't hear him. "No one should be able to find your phone numbers unless you personally give it out."

A heavy, paranoid weight starts to lift off my chest. I didn't even realize it was still sitting there. *They can't call you anymore, Daisy.* I wasn't sure I'd ever reclaim that kind of privacy again.

Before I can tell Garrison *thank you* or even thank Willow for mentioning how good he is at computers, Garrison motions to Lily. "And your passcodes took me thirty seconds to hack."

Lo gives her a look.

"Whaaa…" She crinkles her nose. "It's not anything familiar to anyone, I promise."

"It is though," Garrison says. "Your favorite movie is *X-Men: First Class*. You said it in an interview, which is public knowledge. You can't use 2011xmen as your password—"

"Shhh!" she hushes him with large eyes and waves like she's swatting bees. "Someone's going to overhear and get into my work email."

"If you want, I'll help you change it tonight."

She nods repeatedly, and I leave Ryke's side, heading on the other side of the bar counter, to steal Cheez-Its from Lo's box. Ryke follows, limping more than he uses his cane. He grimaces the last step here, but he never complains.

Never brings up how much it hurts.

He perseveres.

I watch him lean his weight on the granite countertop, the kitchen darkened except for the warm glow of candles. I pass him a handful of Cheez-Its and then he throws one at my face.

I smile, and he tosses the second one at me, and I catch it in my mouth.

I raise my fists in the air. "I've saved the Cheez-It from death by floor. Rejoice!"

Ryke pops one in his mouth, his lips rising.

Connor closes his lightsaber and gestures from Garrison to the laptop. "You taught yourself code?"

"Yeah."

"Why?" Connor asks, deeply interested.

Lo lowers his voice to our huddle of four. "Anyone else think Connor looks impressed?"

Lily sticks her hand in the red box. "Maybe he farted."

We all burst out laughing, and Connor arches his brow at us. He couldn't have heard Lily from the other side of the counter, but he definitely knows that he's the source of our humor.

"I like it." Garrison shrugs at Connor. "Code makes sense to me. Does there need to be another reason?"

Connor smiles. "There could be, but the reason you gave me is the best one."

"*What can I do for you?* That's your opening line?" Rose suddenly says, so loudly that we all turn towards her. Her arms are crossed while a six-foot-something pale vampire stands opposite her, a wine glass in his hand.

"Look, he drinks wine just like Connor," Lo quips, eating his snack like popcorn.

Connor has zeroed in on Rose's conversation with the gothic-era vampire, who must be an actor because he's one of the better looking guys here. All clean-cut and dressed in an aristocratic black vest and button-down, like he might've had a stylist.

The guy gestures from Rose's boobs to...well just her boobs. "You are rubber. I'm glue. Whatever you say, I bet I'll fuck you."

Rose's eyes widen with hellfire.

Lo gags at the guy, and Ryke mutters, "I'm already fucking there."

Connor's expression is unreadable, but Lo whispers something about his "jealous" face. So maybe I just can't see through Connor the way that he can. Rose wouldn't be happy about Connor pissing on her territory, so it's reasonable to assume that's why he's giving her time before he interjects.

"And I bet," Rose snaps at the guy, "that you'll be masturbating at home *alone* tonight. I also bet in five years, your balls will rot and fall off."

The guy laughs and stares at her boobs *again*.

I hate this vampire.

Rose glares more. "Find something that pleases you?"

"Maybe."

"Maybe my five-inch heel in your eye socket might please you too."

He sips his wine. This is when Connor leaves his post by the barstools, his stride more urgent, as though he can tell where this conversation is headed.

"I wasn't joking." She narrows her eyes, white-knuckling her sparkling water.

The guy just tilts his head like she's still playing around. "I bet your husband likes your heel in his asshole—"

She throws her water at his face, and the guy *lunges* towards Rose. Oh my God—Connor immediately steps in front of my sister and shoves the guy so hard that he crashes into the kitchen cabinets.

"Kick his ass, Skywalker!" Lo shouts between cupped hands.

The guy rubs the back of his head, fuming at Connor who stands tall at six-foot-four.

Connor Cobalt is so calm that you wouldn't believe he was the one who slammed the guy backwards.

"She was hitting on me, you realize that?" the guy retorts.

Why do some guys blame it on girls? Rose didn't do *anything* wrong. She held a curt conversation with him. That's it.

Connor barely blinks before he says, "Normally I wouldn't even waste words on someone who I find parochial and meaningless, but maybe I pity you just enough to say this: in the next two centuries, my wife and I will still exist. We will live beyond you through minds and words and hearts. If that makes you feel weak and insignificant, then maybe you should reevaluate your own stance in the world—and not attempt to beat at mine with two flailing hands."

Wow.

The kitchen is stunned to silence except for the spooky background music, and Rose is smiling at her husband, her eyes gleaming with love.

They seem to near each other at the exact same time, both speaking hushed French. Connor clasps her hand and then kisses her forehead. He whispers another word or two, to which she whispers back. His grin envelops his face.

The vampire guy tosses the middle finger at Connor, right before shuffling away.

"Weak!" Lo yells at him, but I doubt he hears. I turn around to see if Ryke flipped the guy off, but he's not beside me.

I rotate in a big circle. Lily is gone too.

"Lo?" I question. "Where'd Lily and Ryke go?"

His half-smile fades into dire seriousness. "Lily?!" he shouts, his voice almost taking on a desperate tone. "Lily?!"

I clutch my phone and then remember…I have no cell service.

A flapper girl opens the patio door through the kitchen, speaking loudly to another 1920s flapper. "…five people snuck through security who aren't on the list. Marcie said they have a backpack full of stuff. They could've packed a gun—it's ridiculous."

"And I was going to hire this security team for my Christmas party." She shakes her head, both hurrying towards the main exit.

Five people snuck through security. I text Ryke rapidly but it won't send.

Still no cell service, I'm suddenly hot and clammy. We need to find Ryke and Lily fast. I feel a hand on my shoulder, and I jump.

It's just Rose. Right beside me. I wipe my forehead with the back of my arm.

"We're leaving," Rose says, her back arched in battle.

"We can't," I say, and then she notices the two absent bodies. "Ryke and Lily are gone."

< 58 >

Ryke Meadows

"Slow the fuck down." I limp after Lily, using my cane to lengthen my fucking stride along the second floor hallway. I still have trouble catching her as she squeezes between bodies and slips beneath arms.

"You don't have to follow me!" she calls back, squirming in her green tutu.

She needs to piss.

So badly that she left her husband's side. I'm just glad I took my eyes off Connor and Rose for a single second to see her disappear.

"You're right, I don't," I retort, "but I fucking am!" She turns towards a door and flings it open, rushing inside. As soon as I reach the doorway, she slams into my chest, trying to exit.

"Gogogogo," she slurs, her whole face beet-red.

I look over her shoulder. She entered a bedroom. Two people wrestle beneath the covers with heavy grunts and moans. "Right there! Right *there!*" a girl wails.

Fuck. I step aside as quickly as I fucking can, which is not fast at all. Lily darts around me, and I shut the door.

"Can you relax for one fucking second?" I ask.

She shoots me a narrowed look. "I have to *pee*. It's intense, and maybe you don't understand my bladder, but it's a *real* thing, Ryke."

I rake a hand through my thick hair. "I know your bladder is fucking real. Look, there has to be a bathroom down this hall, and if you run around like someone lit your ass on fire, you're going to run right past it."

Lily has my lightsaber in her hand and pokes my chest with the blue tip. "You should be looking after Lo, not me." In her green eyes, I see that she's seriously confused about why I'd choose her over my brother right now. Why I'd follow her and leave him be.

I rip the lightsaber out of her clutch, remembering when I was in my early twenties. When I first met her. I said something to her at a New Year's Eve party once. Something that I fucking regret. Because I know—right now—that it's stayed with her for a longer time than it has stayed with me.

"I care about you," I tell her like it shouldn't be that *crazy* of a notion by now. "Not because you're a part of my brother's life but because you're a part of mine. You're my fucking friend. I love you, alright?"

She crosses her ankles with an *I have to pee* face but says in all seriousness, "I know we've all grown older together, but I haven't really felt how much until now."

I was set in my ways back then, ready to pick Lo over Lily, not understanding even a fragment of her own pain, and I was so closed-minded towards her—that I almost missed one of the people I love most. Right in front of me.

I've learned a lot since then, and I'm a better fucking person because of Lily Calloway.

I nod a couple times. "We've grown older." I don't think we'll ever stop. It gives me fucking hope—that whatever I do wrong, I can fix. I can change. We all can over time.

"I have to start opening doors now." She squirms again and tentatively peeks into each door. I follow close behind.

She whips her head beneath my arm.

"What is it now?"

"Someone is following us...or is that a shadow?" she squints.

I try to spin her towards the hallway but she's really preoccupied with whoever is behind us. I glance over my shoulder, but it's pretty empty.

In fact, the whole fucking hallway is emptying. The music also shuts off. "Didn't you have to pee? Hurry the fuck up."

She sighs, "Make up your mind. Am I going too slow or too fast?"

"You're too fucking whatever," I say vaguely, glancing behind us again. There is a shadow of a person in the corner. A chill pricks my neck.

I keep a hand on Lily's shoulder as she shuffles to the next door. "What if someone heard you say that you 'love me' in the middle of the hall? Should we prepare for the blowback?" Her eyes grow big and wide up at me. "Did you pat my shoulder? I can't remember—did we hug?"

"Get it together." I need her in one piece, mentally, physically. I realize how fucking harsh my voice is right now, so I add, "In a nice way."

She peeks into another room. "Maybe we should be more aware of saying things and touching in public?" I know she doesn't want another headline about us. I don't either, but she's mended something with Daisy that's not going to crumble that quickly.

"We're just fucking friends."

I don't even realize I cursed until she cringes. She only does that when I call her a "fucking" friend. "It's not about my sister or me," she says. "Just Moffy and your baby. We don't want them to be hassled about this." Lily and I have the most platonic girl-guy relationship, but it's not a brother-sister kind. People have always twisted it out of fucking proportion.

As much as it kills me—as much as I want to say *I don't fucking care*—I really have no idea what these kinds of headlines will do to our kids. Even if they let it go, will their classmates?

"Whatever happens in the fucking future," I tell her, "it doesn't change *us*, okay?"

She nods, resolute with this idea.

I glance behind us again. This time, five guys in black clothes and zombie makeup appear, mostly just leaning against the fucking wall. One of them opens a backpack…

"Found it," Lily says, slipping into the bathroom.

I have a bad fucking feeling, and so I follow her inside and lock the door. Lily is already on the toilet, and she gasps at my sudden presence.

She didn't even shut the fucking door, so I don't know why she's surprised. "I'm peeing!"

"And I'm not fucking looking," I tell her, eyeing the light beneath the doorway. Then I grab my phone, no signal to call anyone.

I wait for a second, hearing nothing. "Lily—"

"I think I have pee fright."

For fuck's sake. "What can I do to help your pee fright?"

"Cover your ears."

Fine. I cover my ears with my hands, waiting for her to piss. About a minute or two later, she squeezes towards the sink, and I drop my hands.

The warm glow beneath the door just goes completely black. Like the hallway lights shut off. Lily dries her hands on a towel.

"Ready?" I ask, trying to stifle my fucking paranoia. *Thanks, Rose.* I remember her whole pact before we left. It's messed with my head.

"Yeah." She stands by my side, and I open the door, to be met with the flesh-eaten faces of five fucking zombies, standing mere feet from us. Before I can speak or react, they all launch something at our heads. I can't even block Lily. It smacks against my jaw and explodes.

Lily screams.

"Lily?" I cough, white clouds bursting around us. I instantly shut my eyes, the chalky substance stinging my gums and tasting like baking soda and flour.

I waft the air, footsteps banging against the floor as the five guys run away from us. Laughing. They're fucking laughing.

I could fucking kill them, but there's a twenty-six-year-old girl beside me, who was just pelted in the face too. I cough and reach for her hand. I grab air. I open my eyes, wafting the plume of white dust.

"Lily?"

She hacks up a lung on the floor.

I instinctively try to crouch. "Motherfucker," I grit, my right knee bending too far. *Motherfucker.* My eyes water from the pain.

"OhmyGod," Lily mumbles. She wipes at her face and hair. "Oh my God, Ryke."

My mouth is fucking stinging and searing. I start sweating. "Stand up," I tell her. I grip the door frame.

She wobbles to her feet. "Ryke." Her whole face is white, large clumps of flour in her hair. "My mouth…" Her tongue is caked with the shit, much more than mine.

"Spit," I tell her, both of us inhaling this. I rub beneath my nose, and she tries to spit but does a piss ass job. "Come here."

She shuffles into the bathroom, and I turn the sink on. In the mirror, I see how badly covered I am, my hair practically gray; my jaw, nose, and lips dusted. My eyes are bloodshot like Lily's.

"My face is burning," she says, waving her hands at her cheeks.

Mine too. "Stick your face beneath the water."

She's crying while the water runs, trying to rinse her mouth out.

She doesn't usually cry like this—like she's in pain. "What's wrong, Lil? Fucking talk to me." I have to lean my weight against the sink, and I keep a hand on her back, pulling her hair out of the way. I spit on the side of the counter, away from her, this shit caked in my throat.

She aggressively rubs her face. Frantic all of a sudden.

"Lily!" And then I lick my lips. Numb. My whole mouth is going numb. I can practically feel my heart pounding out of my fucking chest. I'm in a hot sweat. I've had this happen…before. Once when I was a teenager and tried something…*Fuck.*

Cocaine.

They mixed cocaine with the baking soda or flour.

We just inhaled and ate who-the-fuck-knows how much.

I realize that she already knows what this is, maybe even before I did. "Lily, calm the fuck down." I start removing my clothes, the tunic, the slacks—I don't fucking care.

I rip it all off. Just in charcoal gray boxer-briefs.

Lily drenches her hair, panting heavily. "There's a cat in the window." She touches the mirror.

Shit.

I grab a towel from a basket, wishing we were in a full bath with a shower. Not a half-bath with nothing but the sink and toilet. I push the towel at her face, a little too hard, but she's in a fucking delirious hallucination anyway.

She keeps the towel there, like it's sending her to Narnia.

I splash water at my face, getting it everywhere. The only upside to right now is that Daisy wasn't with me—but what if they found her first?

What if we were just a fucking pit stop on their way to them?

She's pregnant.

"We need to go," I tell Lily, grabbing her hand and dragging her out of the bathroom. It's only halfway down that I realize I've forgotten my cane.

I'm going to fuck up my already fucked-up leg. Because I can't feel pain anymore. Or any resistance. And it's not strong enough to carry my full weight.

"I think we're lost. I think we're going the wrong way."

"I think you need to shut the fuck up," I say. "Wait a second. Let's go this way." I tug her in a new direction. "Did we go this way?" We're both talking over each other, and I'm sweating, my hair dripping with water from the sink.

Fuck.

Fuck.

Fuck.

"Ryke!"

I grab at Lily's arm, who bumped into a wall. "Lily." I've never been so fucking disoriented. Except maybe the last time I snorted coke, which was the first time.

Lily pats her cheeks. "I can't feel anything." She spins around like she's chasing her own tail. "Zombie!"

"Where?" I spin with her.

"Jesus Christ." The familiar voice hits me before I see Lo sprinting towards us with Connor. "Lily!" Lo screams. "Lily!"

"Lo!" Lily screams back and she instantly starts crying. "Lo!"

They connect like they've lost each other for centuries. Their arms fly around each other, and he immediately lifts her up in a front-piggyback.

I keep licking my lips.

"Ryke," Connor repeats my name a couple times.

"Where's Daisy?!" I shout at him. "Where the fuck is she?!"

He clutches my face so I'll focus only on him, his expression grave. "Your pupils are dilated." He pauses. "What'd they throw at you?"

Lily is muttering in Lo's shoulder, clinging tightly to him. He rubs her back, but his concentration edges towards us.

"Ryke!" Connor shouts, my face still in his hands.

"Cocaine and flour," I say.

Lo looks like he might kill someone.

I don't think that's me hallucinating either.

My heart is on fucking broil. I breathe heavily—like I can't breathe. But I'm fucking breathing. I'm not making any sense, am I? "Where's Daisy? She's pregnant." I say like they have no fucking clue.

"She's in the limo with Rose, Garrison, and your sister. Everyone's fine except Lily and you," Connor explains quickly. "Where's your cane?"

I shake my head.

"Lean on me," Connor says. "Don't lean on your right leg." He puts his arm around my waist, and I try to rest my weight against him.

"Connor," Lo says, his voice nearly hysterical. I lift my bloodshot fucking eyes up to my little brother. And I realize he's staring right at me.

I touch my numb fucking face, and when I bring my hand down, I catch a glimpse of red on my fingers.

My nose is bleeding.

‹ 59 ›

Daisy Meadows

The emergency room is overcrowded on Halloween. I've already seen a real severed arm and an axe in a thigh from Lily and Ryke's side-by-side beds, the curtains pulled back to reveal the hustle and bustle of the hospital.

Nothing is as scary as thinking Ryke overdosed.

His heart rate is just now slowing down, after three hours. I fixate on his vitals and comb his hair out of his face. He wouldn't let me touch him until after he was sanitized in a hospital shower. Lily had to follow suit, both now in paper gowns. They were admitted overnight for observation.

There aren't enough rooms available to move out of the emergency wing yet. So we're stuck here for a while.

His brows furrow more all of a sudden.

"Your leg?" I wonder. The doctors strapped his leg on a board when he arrived, so he'd stop carelessly bending it.

"It feels like shit."

"You can probably ask for pain meds…" I trail off while he shakes his head.

"No, Dais. I won't."

I understand. He didn't let me see him struggle when he weaned off oxycodone, but he had night sweats and threw up a couple times. Ryke rarely complains, so I can only guess how dizzy and sick he felt.

Connor is on the phone with the police, closer to the nurse's station than to the hospital beds. Rose paces right beside him, on the phone with our parents. Lily has told her to leave multiple times and take care of the kids, but she's hesitating to ditch us.

Garrison and Willow left about an hour ago, so it's just the six of us.

I can't stop thinking about what happened, but maybe not more than Lo. He's been sitting at the foot of Lily's bed, staring at his Peter Pan hat in his hands.

I thought for sure he'd make a comment like *you can dress them up but you can't take them out* or *what a goddamn birthday, huh?*

He hasn't said a word about it.

"Can you sit down, Dais?" Ryke asks.

"I'm okay." I touch my baby bump. We're all okay.

"You've been standing for the past three fucking hours." He makes room on his bed and brushes some of the machine's wires out of the way.

I decide to take a seat if he'll feel better by it. "What's wrong with Lo?" I whisper to Ryke, who begins stroking my hair, cuddling me in the crook of his arm.

I'm supposed to be taking care of him, but he can't turn it off. His love for other people. Such a nurturer, that Ryke Meadows.

He stares at Lo with understanding and brotherly concern, but before he speaks, police suddenly march past the nurse's station. Both Connor and Rose hang up their cellphones and follow the police, who sidle up to Lily's bed.

Lo clutches her hand while she whispers to him, "Are they going to arrest me?"

Lo tilts his head. "You didn't do anything wrong, silly."

"Cocaine is illegal."

"It wasn't our fucking coke," Ryke retorts.

The burly police officer clears his throat, obviously hearing the tail end of that, and he gestures to Lily. "We were able to arrest three twenty-year-old men who fit the description that your friend gave us." Their gazes flit to Connor and then back to Lily. "We're here for your statements. What happened and more specifically what these men looked like."

Lily blows out a breath, her skin flushed from the whole night's ordeal. She also broke out from whatever else was in the powdery mixture, a rash creeping up her neck and forehead.

I kind of just want to hug her tight and make sure she's still okay.

"They were all really ugly," Lily begins, which lightens the mood some. Lo even cracks a smile for the first time. "The tallest one had burn marks over half his face, and one had boils over his eye—"

"We need serious statements."

"They were zombies," Ryke explains.

The police officers lose a bit of color and they whisper amongst each other.

"Not real zombies," Lily says. "The fake kind."

Ryke rubs his eyes but he actually lets out a laugh like *what the fuck is going on here? This isn't really happening.*

"What is it?" Connor asks the officer.

And then the burly one says, "Our partners detained three men dressed as fraternity guys." He checks his phone. "You'll have to excuse us for a minute. We need to make a couple calls, and then we'll come back in and get your statements."

Lily nods. Ryke pinches his eyes, more out of frustration this time.

I'm not even surprised by the idea that these five guys may escape. We're all just so used to it by now. Chasing shadows and anonymous leads. All these people just "having fun" at our expense.

I once asked Ryke when it ends—if it'll ever end. If everything will ever be better than where we stand. These are just people. Normal people. Who come after us. Old friends and ordinary citizens. Watching us online, reading about us in magazines.

We're not real in their eyes. Not to any degree that we need to be.

When Ryke drops his hand, he says to Lo, "This isn't your fucking fault. Don't sit there and think it is."

His cheekbones sharpen like ice. "I let him go."

"Who?" I ask.

"The boy who flour-bombed me," Connor clarifies. "We caught him, but he was young. Ryke, Lo, and I made a choice together and let him go—"

"*I* made the choice," Lo says, his voice rattling, his face twisting in pain. "I let him go. I didn't set a precedent. This happened because of me, so don't say anything different and try to coddle me. I don't need to hear your *lies* and your stories and your goddamn sympathy. I did this."

The bottom of my stomach drops, and I sit up, holding my bent knees. Ryke has his hand over his mouth. Everyone is upset. Every person in this room.

"I have an idea," I suddenly say. All eyes draw to me. "Please don't slam the door on it right away. Just let me explain." They listen while I try to formulate it best. What everything has been like for me and for them. "I'm really tired…I'm tired of being seen as an object, as less than human, as an emotionless, soulless being. Whether you want to believe it or not, you're all viewed that way too." I look around at them, at the only people who could understand what this has been like.

We've all been paddling in the same sinking boat. Bailing water while people put holes in our ship. They're drowning us, and I'm ready to scream as *loudly* as I can—until they hear me.

Hear me.

And see what you've done to us.

"Beyond us, how many people saw Lily afraid to leave her house for months because of the media? Because people took pictures and made comments at her? How many people know what my friends did to me?"

Ryke sets his hand on my leg, and I realize that hot, *angry* tears are running down my face.

"How many people know what Paris was like for us?" I look at Lo and then at Connor and Ryke. "I know it's hard to talk about, but maybe it's time we tell them our story. The one where *people* cause other *people* pain. The one where trauma lasts for years and never goes away."

No one knows us. Not the human, fragile parts of us.

I don't think they'll ever stop unless they see.

Lily wipes her glassy eyes with the hospital sheets. "Yes," is all she can say, choking on a sob. Lo crawls over and hugs her, but she rubs her eyes, nodding repeatedly to me like it's the right time for us.

Now it is.

We can speak loudly, together.

Rose brushes away her tears quickly and then clears her throat that's still a little raspy. "Do you have something in mind already or do we need to plan a platform for this?"

"Not a reality show," Lo immediately shuts down.

"I was thinking a docu-series, but on another network, something more unfiltered like HBO." We've been burned by GBA too many times to go crawling over to that network for help. We were also contractually obligated to them for a long time—if we filmed anything, they had first rights. Until Scott Van Wright went to jail. Our contracts were then terminated.

We can do what we want now.

It's not like we need the number one television station. We just need something, anything, to air our voice.

"We produce it," Connor chimes in, adding life to the idea. "We'll be in complete control of the edit and our message before it airs." *Unlike before.*

"We interview each other," Rose adds. "We ask the questions and are the first to receive the answers."

I smile, my tears falling to my knees.

"We can opt out at any fucking time," Ryke says, his gaze landing on me. "Say no one day, say yes the next day. We do it at our own pace."

"We can do it monthly or maybe even as little as four times a year," Lily says with a rigorous nod. "We decide how much we put out there."

I nod too, liking their additions, liking that it's as much mine as it is theirs. And then we all look to Lo, his wife's head on his chest. He hugs her like she's a part of him.

"You think this will help?" he asks us. "Because there's a lot here." He motions around the room, his eyes slowing down when he passes me. "There's a lot *here*, and..." He chokes up and a tear rolls down his cheek.

"You and Lily haven't hurt us," I say, my chin trembling. "You've given us *so much* more out of life..." I slide the heel of my palm over my wet cheeks. "It's only about their actions, not the repercussions of your addictions. Please, *please* believe in that, Lo." I know Lily already has.

It takes him a moment, but he nods a few times. "I guess it's time, isn't it?" He nods again, more assured that this is something we can do without poking holes into each other.

We've never been stronger or loved one another more than we do now.

"So," Lo says, "what are we calling this docu-series thing?"

We all look around again, and even though we haven't written out a contract to enact *this* choice yet—I feel an immense weight lift from the entire room.

And we all begin to smile.

< 60 >

Ryke Meadows

"Someone's on your ass, bro," Lo tells me in the backseat of my gray Toyota Land Cruiser, my Christmas present from Daisy. I sold my other car right after. Now it's the third of February—cold as fuck and pouring. I can hardly see five feet down the road, even with the wipers.

I check my rearview, the two-lane road narrow and slick with water. Rose drives her Escalade, presumably in front of me, but only red taillights are fucking visible.

"What kind of fucking car is behind us?" I ask, unable to tell.

Daisy cranes her neck over her shoulder, sitting in the passenger seat, the leather interior brown, rust-colored. After a short pause, she says, "It's just Price."

I notice Lily trying to relax beside my brother. We wouldn't be driving in a storm like this—with the threat of paparazzi running us off the road—unless it was a fucking important day.

And today is one of those days.

My eyes flit to Daisy. "Can you call Price and tell him to give me five fucking feet?"

She puts her phone to her ear and before she can even speak, he must start talking because her lips snap closed and she listens.

"How much farther until the courthouse?" Lily asks, biting her nails.

"Two miles," I answer. Through the rearview mirror, I see Lo grab her hand and then kiss her temple.

She smiles at him, but her anxiety tenses the fucking car. My brother keeps glancing outside, and his leg jostles while rain thrashes against the street and Land Cruiser.

I'm not going to fucking speed.

Daisy is about thirty-seven weeks pregnant, and I'm not losing her or our baby because I drove us into a fucking ditch. When Lily was pregnant, I almost made that error, just to outmaneuver paparazzi. I'm not repeating my fucking mistakes.

"Okay," Daisy says in her phone. "I will." She hangs up. "So he's on our ass because two sedans are trying to cut him off and drive beside us. He's blocking them every time they try to pass."

Fuck. I comb my fingers through my hair and set my hand back on the steering wheel. "Does everyone have their fucking seatbelts on?" I keep my focus on the road.

"You're about twenty minutes late with that question," Lo says, his voice edged. "If there's a five-car pile-up with Rose's Escalade and we all die—"

"That's not fucking happening," I cut him off.

"*If we all die,*" he enunciates since I broke off his speech, "then my son is going to be raised by Greg and Samantha Calloway. So please, *please* don't kill me." It's rare that he advocates for his own life out loud. "Or at least don't kill, Lil. She's too precious to die." He pinches her cheek.

Lily slugs his arm, and when Lo feigns a wince, I realize I need to stop looking in the rearview mirror. "You're not going anywhere," Lily says adamantly.

"Well, I am going somewhere, love." I can practically feel his half-smile behind me.

"Speaking of death," Daisy segues fucking awfully, spinning in her seat to look at her sister and brother-in-law. "You both know that if Ryke and I suddenly or tragically die somehow, you'll be the proud new parents of this little one." She rubs her round stomach, hidden beneath a burgundy tribal sweater.

I can't see their reactions.

And then Lo says abruptly, "No one's dying in this car, so you can turn around and continue thinking about bunnies and unicorns and contemplate the meaning of sprinkled donuts."

"What *is* the meaning of a sprinkled donut? Do they have feelings? Do they think about us?" Daisy says like she's auditioning for a Shakespearean play.

My lips begin to pull upward, and I reach out to hold her hand, finding hers in a second.

Lily sniffs.

"Are you crying, Lily?" I can't look.

"No," she lies. "I just...I know you said we could look after Coconut, but I didn't think you'd trust us with your baby. Lo and I are the fuck ups of the group, you know? We allow take-backs, so if you need to do a take-back—"

"No take-backs," Daisy interjects.

"Hey," I tell Lily. "We believe in you and Lo, and you're both amazing fucking parents."

"I'd die happily," Daisy proclaims.

My gaze darkens and muscles constrict. "Not anytime fucking soon." I put an end to this conversation. *I can't lose you too, Calloway.*

She just stretches her arm and runs her fingers through the back of my hair. Circles lie beneath her eyes from not feeling well the last few days. "Just uncomfortable," she's told me, averaging about three to four hours of sleep.

Yesterday I think she was mentally ready to have the baby. She's been upbeat about the whole experience, taking pictures of her growing belly every week. She even put headphones on her stomach a few times. Playing Modest Mouse, one of my favorite bands, through the speakers. She looked insanely fucking happy when using her stomach as a tray table. Eating popcorn and double fudge ice cream that way.

I can list off a million other moments where she smiled. Where she laughed and paused to intake the second, the minute—our lives.

So when she's uncomfortable enough to want this to end—that's when I fucking know she's in some kind of serious pain.

"Rose is turning right," Daisy tells me, the Escalade's blinker flashing.

The courthouse comes into view about the same time Rose turns. I follow close behind and then park between her and a black Mustang.

"Great," Lo mutters.

I see what he does as I turn off the ignition and unsnap my seatbelt. Two local news vans are here, camera equipment already set up on the courthouse stairs. I expected a lot fucking worse, but the rain probably deterred most people.

Lily grabs her purple umbrella and already squeezes outside behind Lo. I look at Dais while she rummages in her brown purse for her umbrella. Her blonde hair frizzes from the humidity, tangled around her cheeks.

She's never been scared to run in the fucking rain without a jacket or umbrella. "Hey." I angle towards her. "What's wrong, Dais?"

She takes her time fitting everything back *inside* her purse and then leans against the seat. "When I stand up, the baby feels like its head is already coming out of me. There's so much pressure down there, and I guess I'm just preparing for that feeling." She gives me a weak smile. "What if we have a courthouse baby?"

I mess her hair. "Not fucking happening." I wish I could do something more, and she must see that because she tries to put on a happy face. I shake my head at her. "If you feel like shit, you can look it." I tap her cheek a couple times, but instead of looking how she feels, she actually smiles, a genuine smile.

Maybe that is how she feels in this moment.

She taps my cheek in return, harder than I tapped her, stirring something bright inside of me. "You look handsome every day, all day. Is that how you feel, Ryke Meadows?"

Just when I look into your eyes. I raise my brows at her and then she taps my cheek again, three times with a giddy fucking smile. I hear her voice in my head: *the danger of it all.*

She pinches my nose, trying to crack my stone-cold expression. Her smile stretches her scar so fucking far. Then she rakes her nails down my jaw, and I can't hold out anymore.

I kiss her, so abruptly that a surprised gasp escapes her lips. Right against mine. I feel her smile expand before she kisses eagerly back. As I part her lips with my tongue, her fingers run through my hair. Her body producing a strong, full inhale and exhale. Breathing life into me.

When we break, she presses her fingers to her cheeks. She possesses this overwhelming, tangible radiance, and I hope, right now, she feels just how powerful she truly is.

"Has anyone told you," she says, "that you're an amazing kisser? I think I'd almost trade a piece of chocolate cake just to kiss you."

"Almost?" I toss a strand of her hair at her mouth. I could fucking kiss her for a thousand more years and live peacefully, happily—in love.

She blows the hair off her lip, trying to act serious but her smile hasn't waned yet. I live for this, with her. We're not moving fast. We're not loud.

But the air between us rumbles with a wild fucking roar.

She leans over the middle console as much as she can with her baby bump. "I don't ever have to make that trade. You know why?"

"Why?"

"You're the kind of guy who would do anything to give me both the cake and the kiss."

I think about how she's supported everything that I've ever done. Free-soloing is nothing short of death-defying, life-threatening. She never told me not to. I'd never tell her to stop either. And I know what she just said applies to herself. We want happiness so fucking badly for each other that we'd follow the other in dangerous, dark places.

She jumps. I jump right after.

She hikes her purse on her shoulder and glances in my direction, more color in her cheeks, as she opens the door. "Can he catch me?" I hear her voice taper off in the heavy rain.

She lets it soak her hair, and I quickly remove my black coat. Then I open my door, rain pelting my shoulders and head. I set my left foot on the pavement. Then my right foot.

I bear equal weight between the two.

And I walk.

Almost seven months since I shattered my thigh and broke my leg, I can sense the growth from then and now, my muscles strengthened, more durability, flexibility, mobility. Able to support pressure and resistance without giving way. I walk with an assured stride, like nothing happened, but I still feel slightly off-kilter in a way that no one can fucking see.

My ankle throbs, and at night, my leg stiffens and aches if I don't stretch. I can't go as far as I used to. Or as long. For someone who loves endurance sports, the mental challenge is as steep as the fucking physical.

I just have to be the one to push through.

I have to want it. Lo might've been right—a part of me died seven months ago—but I still have my legs.

And I'm going to run.

Maybe it'll fill the void inside of me.

In the downpour, Daisy outpaces me and then starts walking backwards along the sidewalk. Facing me with a mischievous smile. I'm not about to tell her *no*, but on the wet cement, it's fucking dangerous enough that it pushes me. And I catch up to her side.

I put my coat over her head and she spins around, both of us already drenched.

"Your limp is nearly gone," Connor says as he sidles next to me. He shares a black umbrella with Rose, both completely dry.

I nod. "Just about." As soon as we begin up the slick concrete stairs, a news anchor hovers next to us.

"Whose idea is the documentary series? Did the television station approach you or did you approach them?" We're all quiet so she asks different questions. "What can we expect from the series? What is it called? Will your children appear? Will we see the birth of your baby, Daisy?"

No one says a thing, and the minute we push into the cavernous courthouse, the doors slam shut on the news crew.

Rose pulls her hair into a tight ponytail, and Connor shakes out the wet umbrella. "The deal was made public this morning if you didn't already see it," he says.

I wring out my gray shirt. "Yeah, we did."

Back in November, we approached a premium cable channel like HBO with our idea, and the contract went through last week, so it was only a matter of time before they ran a press release.

Everything we asked for, we received in the deal.

We have complete control over almost every facet of the docuseries. We're the producers, and at the end of the fucking day, we say what gets aired.

All day people have been tweeting things like: they're doing another crappy reality show #famewhores #callowsluts.

It's not a fucking reality show.

The purpose of a reality show is to elicit drama. The purpose of a documentary is to uncover truths.

People will still refuse to call it anything else or believe in what we have to fucking say. So they can misunderstand the intent and brush off the meaning—I don't give a fuck about them.

I don't give a fuck about people who don't care to build another person up. I don't give a fuck about people whose sole purpose is to bring others down.

I squeeze Daisy's hair that soaks her sweater. She's more focused on her stomach, holding the bottom. She needs to sit the fuck down. I wrap my arm around her shoulder, leading her towards the courtroom.

Connor and Rose join us, Rose's heels tapping along the marble floors.

She eyes her little sister. "Does it feel like he's putting a fist through your vagina?"

"God, yes," Daisy says in a heavy sigh.

"It gets worse."

Daisy groans and then hugs onto my side, staring up at me with big doe eyes. "I may never have sex again."

I stroke her wet hair and nod to Rose. "Shouldn't you be encouraging her?"

"Complaining is the second best part of pregnancy," Rose says in her *take no fucking prisoners* tone. "Revel in the torment and be thankful you're not the one with back pain, headaches, and splitting pressure on your ballsac and dick."

Daisy smiles so wide, still looking up at me. "Are you reveling in my torment?"

"No, not even a fucking little bit." I kiss the top of her head and then push through the doors.

We all go quiet and our energy alters, the air stretching thin.

In the first row, Lily and Lo sit beside Garrison, Willow, and my dad. The judge hasn't arrived yet, but a man—that I've never fucking met—stays seated in the very back of the courtroom.

Dressed in jeans and a plain T-shirt, I'd guess he's in his late forties or early fifties. He's fixated on his cellphone, not even raising his head towards us as we all pass him.

My blood simmers, and a fucking rock sinks to the bottom of my stomach. I glance back at him, to see his reaction, to understand him, to get a better fucking read.

There's nothing there.

We all slip into the second row. Willow wipes the lenses of her glasses and turns around towards us. "Thanks for coming, everyone."

"Wouldn't fucking miss it," I say, prepared for the fucking worst. Like tears and heartbreak. The thing about people you give a damn about—you arrive if it's good and especially if it's bad. I have no idea what this will turn out to be, but I'm not going anywhere.

She puts her glasses on and holds my gaze, which she does more often now. "I meant to give you this." With a shaky, nervous hand, she passes me an envelope. "You can open it now or later. I already gave Lo and Dad his."

She's been calling Jonathan "dad" for the past year now, but he still lights up when she says it. Even now, sitting beside Lo, his lips lift a fraction while staring at the judge's empty bench.

Growing up, I never saw my dad as someone who appreciated love. Maybe because he was so fucking hard to love in the first place. But as our family has come together—in ways that I think he only dreamed of—it's not as hard anymore.

Personally, I'll never be as close to him as Lo. I'd never leave my kid alone with him, but I don't hate him. I'm not actively ignoring him anymore. It is what it is, and I let that rest.

"Are we doing presents already?" Lily asks.

Daisy stands. "I left Willow's in the car."

"No, it's alright," Willow tells her. "I can wait until later. The time just presented itself to give them theirs, so…"

Daisy gives her a smile. "I really want you to see it. I'll be right back, and I'll be really fast." She holds out her hand to me, asking for the car keys.

I'm worried to fucking leave her alone, especially with camera crews outside, but Rose and Lily stand, obviously going too. So I pass her the keys.

She jingles them in excitement before skipping out with Rose and Lily.

Just as they leave, I tear open the envelope.

Inside is a picture from this Christmas. At the mountain lake house. The place we all go to escape the media, off in a remote area of the Smoky Mountains. We all chipped in a couple years ago and own the property together.

I stare at the candid photo for a long fucking moment, that cold winter day rushing towards me.

That morning, Lo, Willow, and I sat on the patio around a fire. Drinking homemade, non-alcoholic Butterbeer that she made with Lily.

We're all smiling.

I flip the photo over.

She wrote on the back.

Ryke Meadows (Gryffindor), Loren Hale (Slytherin), Willow Hale (Gryffindor, like Neville Longbottom).
Thanks for caring about me, even before we were family.

My brother and sister.

I practically had no one eight years ago.

It hits me—how we've all come together in time. How alone we were before. And I can't imagine a world where we don't ever find each other.

I focus on one detail. *Willow Hale.* "You changed your name?" I ask, my voice actually fucking splitting.

"It's pending, but yeah." She fights tears. "I just hope everything goes right." Her eyes flit anxiously to the judge's bench. Still empty.

Willow chose to be a part of our lives, but the law is fucking complicated. Technically her father at the time of her birth still has legal claim. In order to establish paternity, he has to give consent to Jonathan. Even though Jonathan is her biological father.

It might not seem like a big fucking deal because she's over eighteen, but our dad wants to help her out, put her on his medical insurance, in case something happens. Willow can't afford any of that, and she's willing to accept *some* financial help now.

Though she'll be the first to tell you that's not what this is about. You'd have to be fucking dense to think it's coming from any other place than that girl's heart.

"I need to talk to you." Connor disrupts the short quiet, capturing everyone's attention. He's not speaking to Willow though.

"Me?" Garrison asks like Connor is nuts for choosing him to talk to.

"I am staring at you," Connor says, completely expressionless.

I have no idea where he's fucking going. "Let's not drag this fucking out, Cobalt."

To Garrison, he says, "I've been looking for a new investment, and I want to invest in you."

Garrison laughs, and when Connor just waits, like he fucking predicted this reaction, Garrison's face falls. "You're serious? You want to invest in *me*?" He pauses. "You do know who I am, right?"

"Garrison Abbey, proficient in tech and coding. You like Tumblr, gifs, hacking, Final Cut, classic video games, and the girl sitting next to you."

Garrison removes his leather jacket like he's hot with frustration. "I'm unreliable. I was kicked out of two high schools. I have no fucking plans to go to college—"

"You lack confidence, so I'll give you some right now. You're talented, self-motivated, and driven. If you don't see that in yourself, open your eyes and look at what you can do. All I'm asking is for you to create something, anything, and I'll back it."

Garrison blinks, dumbfounded and thunderstruck. "Why?"

"I value everything I just listed, and you need someone who believes in you. Create something brilliant, Garrison, or don't create anything at all. That's your choice."

Lo says, "Take it, man. The god has spoken."

Connor grins.

I groan. "Come on. He's a fucking six-foot-four human being with good hair."

"At least we've established one thing," Connor says. "Ryke loves my hair."

I'm ready for the girls to come back and separate him from me. "I think you want to be fucking punched in a courthouse."

Connor's grin fucking widens, but he plants his deep blue eyes back on Garrison. The guy is in deep contemplation, brows knotted, looking to Willow more than once.

"Take it," she tells him. "You can do *anything*, Garrison."

"I'll have to stay in Philadelphia?" he asks Connor.

"Yes," he says. "You've never done a start-up of any kind, and while you're creative, you need me to teach you about business."

I scratch my jaw, actually shocked. Actually hearing *what* this means. Connor rarely gives up that type of time to another human being unless it benefits himself. He must see a bright fucking future in Garrison. Even if Connor is a prick, he's a genius prick, and sometimes he notices the better path before you do.

In the first row ahead of us, Garrison angles more towards Willow.

Willow isn't just leaving Philadelphia in August; she's leaving the country. She's going to college in London, paying for the first semester herself. She said that moving to Philly was the best decision she's ever made, and she wants to push herself one more time, just for college. Lo and I are happy because it's somewhere our dad didn't choose for her, and he's okay with it too.

But if Garrison takes Connor's offer, they won't be together for the next four years.

"Take it," she repeats, her opinion unchanging. Her neck elongates, like she's holding her fucking breath. "I just want the best for you."

"The best for me is to be with you." His nose flares, restraining emotion. "I'm a better fucking person when I'm with you." He rubs his face a couple times, and any doubt I've ever had about him just fucking disappears. I can see how much they emotionally care about one another. How much they probably have this whole fucking time.

"Don't be afraid," she whispers to him. "You can do anything on your own. I know you can." Her glasses fog up and she takes them off.

His reddened eyes meet hers, and his brown hair brushes his lashes. He clasps her hand, threading their fingers. And he says, "I love you."

Tears squeeze out of her eyes.

"No matter where we are, you're always going to be my girl."

Four years is a long fucking time, but maybe it'll work.

We all can empathize with first love.

Even Connor.

The double doors open behind us, echoing against the ceiling. Then the judge's chamber door swings wide. Lily, Rose, and Daisy are back just in time.

I crane my neck over my shoulder. The man in the furthest back row stands.

To approach the bench.

< 61 >

Daisy Meadows

Seated back beside Ryke, I stuff the envelope with Willow's gift in my purse. The judge already asked Willow and Jonathan to step forward.

Willow holds her arm to her chest, timid and nervous. I wish I brought literal pompoms to cheer her on. I smile at the thought. I don't think it'd embarrass her. I'd just be shifting the judge's pointed gaze off her, and I bet she'd like that right now.

Sadly, I am without pompoms.

So I just watch the awkward tension mount and mount as she stands between Jonathan Hale and Robert Moore. She's taken two extra steps closer to Jonathan. Clearly there is a winner here in spirit, but no one knows what Robert is thinking.

We all just have facts to work with since Willow never brings him up.

Robert Moore never called Willow when she ran away from home to Philadelphia. Ryke fumed about it on the start of the car ride here, "As a fucking father, how can you not go after your daughter? She left the fucking state."

Ryke doesn't understand people who don't care.

Lo retorted, "He raised her. Jonathan didn't."

We're all on edge. I can't get comfortable on the wooden bench either. Ryke must see me fidgeting because he spreads open his legs and pulls me between them. So I can lean against his chest.

I almost let out an audible sigh. *Sweet, sweet back relief.*

The female judge motions to Robert. "Since the means of Mr. Hale outweigh most, I wanted you here in person. I need to make sure you haven't been coerced, threatened, or swayed by financial means to give consent."

The court reporter's fingers move quickly, capturing the judge's words.

Robert shrugs, hardly acknowledging Willow. "This is what it's come to. I'm not surprised."

"Are you upset by giving up your paternal rights to Willow, Mr. Moore?" the judge asks, genuinely wanting to reach the bottom of this.

I do too.

Robert shrugs again. "All along, I think I knew that she wasn't my kid. It's not just about looks, but no one in *my* family needs glasses."

Ryke mutters under his breath, "Dickfucker."

Lo grits through his teeth, and I barely catch the words, *gold star for you, motherfucker.*

My heart is taking a horrible nosedive.

Robert crosses his arms. "She doesn't act like any kid of mine." *Stop.* "She's practically mute half the time. Never went out of the house, except to movies." *Stop.* "She dresses more like a boy than a girl." *Stop it.* "She has no friends."

We all stand up at the same time, causing Willow, Jonathan, and Robert to look back at us. Willow is silently crying.

When her eyes land on mine, I mouth, *my one friend.* I make a heart with my hands, and I smile. She shares it and rubs her wet cheeks.

She is my one true friend.

And I love her. We all do.

Lo is seething and biting his tongue. He mutters something like, "I'm going to call him names in a goddamn second."

"Good," Ryke mutters back.

"Can I say something, Your Honor?" Jonathan raises his hand to the judge, his face creased with severe, strict lines.

"Yes."

Jonathan then narrows a malicious glare on Robert. I swear the air crackles with cinder and flames. "Don't ever insult my daughter again, you microscopic prick—"

"Alright, Mr. Hale—"

"In the seventeen years that she was with you—did you even talk to her?" Jonathan asks. "Did you know she's charismatic when you discuss things that interest her? Maybe you should've seen a goddamn *movie* with her—"

"Mr. Hale—"

"—instead of sitting around on your ass, you scum of this planet." He fixes his suit, as though he just finished brawling.

So that escalated quickly. Lo is smiling from ear-to-ear. He didn't have to call Robert names after all.

"Mr. Hale," the judge snaps, banging her gavel forcefully.

"I'm done," Jonathan says, and I just now really look at Robert.

He's taken five steps backwards, and his face is beet-red.

I've never wanted Willow further away from a person than from *him*.

"Let's continue. Robert Moore, do you wish to give up your legal rights as Willow's father to Jonathan Hale?"

Unflinchingly, he says, "Yes."

"Then the court recognizes Jonathan Hale as Willow's legal and biological father. Thank you all for coming today, and congratulations Willow." The judge's eyes flit heatedly to Robert before she leaves the courtroom.

I cup my hands around my mouth and make a bird noise. "Ca-Caw!"

Willow laughs a tearful laugh as she turns around, and we all start clapping. I squeeze out of the row, most everyone muttering about Robert. Watching him leave in a hurry.

I bet he's scared of Jonathan.

I approach Willow by the first row. "This is for you, and I'm totally kicking myself because it would've been awesome if you had it before... all of that." I wave at the judge's bench like it's in the past anyway.

She carefully opens the envelope, first pulling out a silver pinky ring. A square etched in the center. It's identical to the one she'd given me a long while ago.

The minute tears start flowing down her cheeks again, the dam on mine breaks all at once. We smile together as she fits the ring on her pinky.

"We all need a little protection sometimes," I tell her a version of what she once told me. "And there are a lot of people who love you here."

She has to take off her glasses. "This means...so much to me. Thank you." She fits on her glasses again.

"There's more," I say with a bigger smile.

With a trembling hand, she inspects the envelope and procures the next item. It's a picture of a tiny little willow tree next to a cabin. The sign hung over the door says, *Green Willow.*

She knows what it is, her eyes watering, but I say it anyway, "You're now officially a girl's cabin at Camp Calloway. You didn't think I missed you, did you?" We all painted signs and my sisters helped plant some of the flowers that were in season, right next to the correlating cabin name. Pink Lily. Purple Lily. Yellow Rose. White Rose. Red Poppy. Orange Daisy.

Now there's Green Willow.

I hold out my palm for our handshake, but she suddenly wraps her arms around my shoulders, light as a feather.

Before she falters, I hug her back.

Friends might not be forever, but maybe friends that you view as family have long-lasting powers, destined to stick around.

< **62** >

Daisy Meadows

I whack a pine needle away from my dad's face. He's in a suit and expensive coat, the sky overcast since the heavy rainfall yesterday. All the mountains that landscape Camp Calloway are clouded with fog. I'm not sure that the dull, grimy atmosphere exudes the magic I wanted to present.

I just need the forest to play nice for him. *Best impressions, everyone.* "This is the path to the girls' cabins," I say, my boots crunching twigs.

My dad has never been overly talkative, but I've been leading him around the grounds for an hour and a half and I've calculated the stats.

2 partial smiles.

10 head nods.

3 furrowed brows.

1 hmmm.

= *what have you done with your life, my little cupcake of a girl?!*

His disappointment is semi-better if sweets are involved. So I tell myself.

Ryke hangs back while I steer this sinking ship. Assured, rugged, he stuffs his hands in his leather coat, his hard brown eyes traveling along the cold, winter scenery. His tough, resolute presence reminds me that my dad's discontent doesn't decide my success or failure. Sure, it'll suck if he's still not on board, but this is for me. And I love everything about this project.

When my gaze meets Ryke's, he mouths, *relax, Calloway.*

I realize I'm knotting my white cable-knit sweater-dress. I let go, the dress falling back to my thighs. Gray leggings also shield my skin from the low temperature.

I pause in place as the baby kicks my left side. "Whoa," I say with a rising smile. That hurt but every time she or he moves, I can't help but think: *you're restless like me, aren't you?*

I'm already in love.

"Dais?" Ryke questions, about to pass my father to check on me.

Before he reacts, I say, "All good. We're good." I stand straighter, feeling my dad's gaze sweep me in parental worry. "Forward and onward." I point ahead, continuing our trek.

My dad steps in mud.

Okay, I thought we were making the best impressions here, forest? "It's not much farther," I say as he trudges on a couple steps behind me. I glance at Ryke for reassurance.

He shrugs at me like *you can't fucking remove the dirt from the ground, sweetheart.*

I know but failing in the eyes of a parent hurts. Even if I fool myself in believing I don't care, part of me will always want just a sliver of validation from my dad.

"I bought a thousand acres for the camp, but I'm only using about half to start with," I explain to him. "Safety inspections passed last week."

I bet this fact will bolster his spirit.

And…we have 11 head nods now.

"Our whole program is about providing a wilderness experience and building friendships." I list out just a handful of activities, some of which he's already seen. "...canoeing, kayaking, basketball, tennis, soccer, horseback riding, rock climbing, ropes courses, archery, acting, arts and crafts, and water sports. It's all based around a camper's personal interests. I'm tweaking the activity plans though."

I don't want to push anyone too far out of their comfort zones, so I'm keeping people like Willow in mind. She said that if her mom had the money, she probably would've sent her to a camp and it would've been hellish.

Kids that are forced to go, I want to take care of too, so their experience isn't miserable.

I open my mouth to add more statistics to the camp, but I stop myself. I've been rambling, haven't I?

I swallow my words, and then maybe a minute later, we finally reach the clearing with scattered log cabins. I halt next to Green Willow, the fledgling little willow tree planted nearby.

While my dad slows down in front of the cabin with Ryke, I gesture to the front door. "The inside is almost identical to the boys' cabins. We can go in if you want?"

1 shake of the head.

Uh-oh.

I try to salvage whatever I can with more rambling. "We're already fully booked for the summer this year." This has to mean something to him. It's profit. It's lucrative.

Yes, I put years into this project. Yes, I put my heart and energy and soul. If he can't see that, then maybe he sees this.

I watch him stare at each cabin one last time, and then his gaze pins to me. Oh...there it is.

1 full smile.

"It's really spectacular, Daisy."

Surprise nearly rocks me back but I begin to smile. "You think so?"

He steps closer. "I'm going to be frank. I didn't think you'd finish this. Both your mother and I thought you threw your money at all this land and you'd give up on the idea after a few months."

"I figured."

His round cheeks are pink in the cold, and his kind eyes smile back at me. "I'm proud of what you've accomplished here and that you stuck to your vision. Even if I was a…little pessimistic." He sports a look like he's very aware of how negative he's been towards my choices.

"What was your favorite part?" I ask, stifling a yawn that tries to creep its way up. I slept one hour last night. While my dad contemplates the entire camp with a faraway look, Ryke approaches my side, his hand sliding along my lower back.

He towers above me. "Take a fucking nap with me when we get home?"

I gasp. "A fuc—"

He covers my mouth with his large hand. I smile beneath it and can read his gaze. *Not in front of your fucking father.*

Flirting with Ryke Meadows is my favorite pastime.

It must be his too because his lips begin to rise.

"Hmm," my dad thinks, his gaze whipping back to me. Ryke drops his hand from my mouth. "There's a lot here, but the outside auditorium was beautiful."

"Thank you, Keith," I say aloud, even though the architect is not here at the present moment. "And thank you, trees and all the creatures willing to share your home with me."

Ryke has his hand on my head. "You forgot the sky and the fucking rocks."

"I'll thank them later," I say in a bigger yawn.

He leans down and kisses my cheek and whispers in my ear, "You have to fucking sleep."

I'm trying. It's not as easy with someone growing inside me. All I do is nod though. Ryke knows I've been doing my best.

My dad checks his watch. "I should be heading back. I have a meeting at four. Will you lead the way, Daisy?"

"Of course, forward and..." I trail off for one of them to fill in the blank. "This is where you shout *onward* and pump your fist into the air." I illustrate.

In this rare beat, my dad pumps his fist towards the sky and says, "Onward!"

My heart is soaring—that he'd even try for me. "Perfect form, Dad." I raise my hand for a high-five, and he's smiling twice as much as he has been all day. After he slaps my hand, I turn to Ryke and the way he's staring at me steals my breath.

"What is it?" I wonder, my fingers brushing my cheeks.

It's not my scar he's noticing. Or my eyes. Or my lips and hair. With tangled intensity, his hard gaze dives straight into me.

"There's no fucking way our baby won't love you."

I wonder if he can feel happiness flowing through me. I wonder if he can see how much his love empowers me. Makes me feel invincible. Incredible. Daisy Petunia Meadows, the girl who can say yes and no. Who can flap her wings and fly.

My dad coughs into his gloved fist.

I tear myself away from Ryke and trek ahead. His love never leaves me, never diminishes or retreats.

It thrums inside my soul, lifting me higher.

Thunder suddenly booms. Lightning cracks the air. We all look up, a dark gray storm cloud stretching wide.

"We better fucking hurry," Ryke says, catching up to my side to set the pace. On hikes, anywhere, I actually stop and take unnecessary detours. When I showed the guys the camp, Connor called me an overeager puppy.

Actually, he said to Ryke, "Are you aware of what your overeager puppy is doing?"

"Yeah. Let her fucking be."

The whole memory causes the corners of my mouth to curve up—but not for long. A dull throb grips my insides. I take a deep breath and block out the cramping, shelving it in a separate part of my brain. Compared to the pain from cysts, this isn't too bad.

My dad straggles ten feet behind us, but we're just retracing the path and he keeps saying, "Go ahead, go ahead."

Ryke is one step in front of me. "Falling fucking behind already, Calloway?"

"I like it back here." I unabashedly stare at his ass, molded in his dark jeans. I miss his carabiners that he used to clip to his belt loops. They always clinked together when he walked.

I haven't seen them in about seven months.

Ryke gives me a knowing look and then his gaze flits over my body. I wonder if my comment aroused him. I remember what happened last week and my neck nearly heats.

Ryke dropped to his knees in front of me, his lips pressing against my round stomach, so slowly and tenderly. Until that moment, I hadn't truly realized the depth of his attraction towards the changes in my body. Towards me carrying his baby. Me being so fertile and hormonal.

I may never have this again, but I'm just really grateful for the chance to experience it once with him.

Lightning strikes again and rain trickles down on us.

Ryke picks up his pace and reaches out for my hand. I clasp his, but I slow him down a couple times. My lower abdomen cramps fiercer, and I stifle a choked noise in my throat. Maybe this isn't my usual pain. I can't rally my hopes and dreams of giving birth today. Most likely it's a false alarm.

I don't want to feel any more dejection, so I stay quiet.

Ryke keeps scrutinizing me, his concern mounting before he says, "Are you in fucking pain?"

"Dull…" I wince at that cramp. *Ouch.*

Ryke stops abruptly and I knock into his chest. He holds me protectively.

My dad has gained five feet on us. "I meant to tell you, Daisy. Jonathan and I almost have your wedding present ready. It just wasn't possible within the constraints to give it to you sooner. It's been chaotic—"

Water gushes out of me, soaking the crotch of my leggings. I lift up my sweater-dress. *I'm going into labor.* "Ryke..." I freeze, so still as I truly see what this means. All the hope. All the excitement I trounced floods me. *I'm going to have a baby.*

"I'll call an ambulance to meet you at the parking lot," my dad says, a little nervously. "Don't wait for me."

I bend at the next cramp, the contraction stronger. "Ow," I say in a higher register than I normally use. It must scare Ryke enough because he lifts me in his arms. Cradling me. His pace is lengthy and urgent, not slowing for anything.

Stubborn, iron-willed Ryke Meadows. You can't tell him what to do.

I look up at my husband and then down at his right leg. He seems to be holding strong. No limping, but I ask anyway. "Are you okay?" The next contraction grabs at me. *Ow, ow.*

"Don't fucking ask me that. You're the one in labor."

"It's already amazing." My overwhelmed smile hurts my cheeks. *It truly is.* I reach my hands up as the rain kisses our faces. "Are you remembering this?"

I can feel his pulse racing with mine.

I shut my eyes and lean my head back. Thunder growls beneath the ground, and the naked trees creak in the robust, frigid wind. I open my eyes and the sky is nothing but darkness.

Strings that connect us to this world, to nature, to me, become apparent. We're all living and breathing. We're all terribly mighty things.

Ryke's hair dampens, rain cascading in heavy sheets upon us. "Didn't you have a fucking theory about the woods?!" he asks me over the thunder.

I smile more. *He remembered my theory.* "Magical things happens in the woods." I toss my hands in the air again and scream happily at the top of my lungs.

The way Ryke is smiling could reverse a storm and cause a heat wave.

I wish it'd stay forever, but my smile fades and his follows mine, and the next contraction pummels me like a freight train. I nearly curl into a ball against his chest, and his stride reciprocates my pain, moving faster.

I mentally time the contractions, and I realize that they're really close together. "Ryke..."

He must hear the fear leech my voice because he sets me on sopping pine needles and yanks off my boots.

"You can't deliver the baby," I say. "I'm high-risk and—" I grit my teeth at the next wave. *Oh my God.*

He tears off my leggings, his actions only accelerating. Then he breaks apart my knees and checks between my legs. Not long after, he quickly pulls down my sweater-dress to my thighs. "Come here, sweetheart." He lifts me back into his arms and continues his vigorous course again.

"What...?" *What was it?*

"I didn't see a fucking head."

Okay, we have time. "We're okay," I tell him, dizzy and light. "I can walk." I'm not sure how much weight his leg can handle. "You can set me down right there."

"Over my dead fucking body."

I push past the next contraction and say, "Some would think that you enjoy carrying me." This isn't the first instance where he's picked me up. I've lost count of how many times he's scooped me in his arms and held me like my protective shield.

Over the lightning, I barely make out his next words.

"I've always fucking loved you in my arms."

❀ ❀ ❀

I SCREAM IN TORTURED, gut-wrenching pain. *Holy shit*. The ambulance bumps along the road, the rain slowing the vehicle. I'm on the stretcher in the middle while Ryke sits close, his hand in mine.

"How much fucking farther?" Ryke asks. The three EMTs are doing their best, but the longer we take and closer I am to popping out this baby—the more all of our worry amplifies.

"Maybe forty minutes to an hour," the girl says, driving the ambulance along a windy two-lane road. A nineteen-year-old EMT takes my vitals with shaky hands. It's his third day on the job, and color drained from his face when he asked if I was Daisy Calloway.

"I'm Daisy Meadows now," I told him.

He looked shell-shocked—or I guess star struck—to the point of puking. He gagged in his fist, and the older man then explained that he was new.

Ryke's whole demeanor changed after that, sharp-eyed on every little action the new EMT takes. His alpha male aura consumes the vehicle, but I'm glad to have him here, noticing things that I don't.

The older man, late fifties maybe, retrieves his cellphone. My legs are split open, and he keeps checking—but I don't understand the phone.

"What's wrong?" Ryke asks him.

I clench my teeth awfully hard. Sweat beads my forehead as my muscles constrict. I cry a little and Ryke squeezes my hand. *Owwww*. The baby wants out. I can feel how much.

"I've only delivered a baby once," he says. "I'm going to put a doctor on the line."

"We're not going to make it to the fucking hospital?" Ryke asks, his features as dark as the roiling sky.

"I don't think so." *Am I that far along already?* He puts the phone on speaker, but I tune out the doctor's voice, my head pounding from consistent contractions, barely stopping to let me breathe.

I'm scared for the baby. "What are…the chances of a stillbirth?" I ask Ryke. *Stillbirth.* The word ensnares me like an iron vice, locked around my throat.

Stillbirth would be the worst of all.

Ryke strokes the wet hair out of my face, my drenched sweater-dress stuck to my belly. With our scars and our tangled, soaked hair, we look like we were caught in the wild. I try to focus on this fact. I try to make light of whatever fate has left to throw at us.

He leans down, his eyes diving into mine. "We're all fucking alive. All three of us."

I fight tears because I see a different outcome. "I'm scared," I whisper. I'm scared that nine months has been nothing but a trick. I'm scared that a rug will rip from under our feet again. That tomorrow morning, we'll both roll on our stomachs and we'll bury our heads in pillows. We'll scream.

Violently.

He cups my cheeks, his hands rough and strong. "A hundred-and-fifty miles per hour."

Tears slip down my cheeks and I murmur, "No brakes."

"Never any fucking brakes." He raises my hand in his and kisses my knuckles.

I inhale our exchange and bask in what it truly means.

I bottle this moment with Ryke, not worrying about the next step, the afterwards. I live for now.

And I chase. And I run and I howl. After every second, every detail, and I could raise my arms in the air again. I could say, *this is me. I exist in this great, big world.*

The older EMT sets a hand on my bent knee. "You need to lean up against something."

Ryke is quick to help. He straddles the stretcher behind me, and I rest my back against his chest. Once the EMT tells me that I actually need to start pushing, everything zooms into one action. One goal.

You'll be okay, whoever you are. I can't wait to meet you, face to face this time.

I begin pushing. Gritting my teeth, head-splitting pain latching onto me. No meds. No doctor physically present. *Don't stop.* I try as hard as I can, knowing the baby needs out.

Rain pelts the ambulance roof, the *ping ping ping* a chorus to my agonized screams. My arms quiver. Hot tears flow down my cheeks. I have no strength to contain the onslaught, the scalding waterworks. My skin heats as I try again.

And again.

Ryke wipes the tears off my face with his sleeves. He whispers encouragements in my ear, but I can barely process time or words. Woozy with exertion and discomfort, I just keep going.

Stopping only worsens the lingering pain. The next push, I scream so loudly that my throat burns raw. My muscles sear inside out. My lungs bursting. I can barely distinguish shapes ahead of me, my mind exploding with color.

And then another scream entwines with my dwindling one. All the suffering begins to eke away. I just listen to the tiny cry of a baby.

I see little arms waving, crying like *here I am; look at me.* I break into a sob, my hand trembling by my lips. The EMT cleans the baby only a little before setting the newborn on my chest.

"Here's your girl."

I place a hand on her smooth back. *How precious you are.* I look up at Ryke, tears streaming down his face as he glances between our daughter and me.

I whisper, "We made this."

He's overcome with so much that he breaks into a full-blown smile while crying with me. He kisses the top of my head. "I've never loved anything fucking more than you and her."

My core lights up with his declaration. I touch her itty-bitty fingers. "Hey there," I breathe. As soon as she clasps onto my pinky, her cries begin to fade.

She calms with regular, deep breaths. Like she understands who I am already. Ryke strokes her soft cheek, and her lips smack together.

He tells her, "It's taken a lot of fucking love to have you." He chokes on so many sentiments. He has to pinch his reddened eyes. When they meet mine again, they're consumed with this tremendous, earth-stomping joy.

I feel it too.

Teeming all around us.

I'm so happy that I can hardly speak, and I think back to every month, every day, every hour. I think back to all that we've lost and all that we've gained. There is no doubt—I know exactly who we brought into this world.

Who will one day run fast and wild.

She coos in contentment.

"Hey there," I say, "Sullivan Minnie Meadows." She stretches her left arm as though to say, *that's me*.

I lift my eyes to Ryke once more, and he nods at me, unable to contain tears, rolling down his cheeks. I stare deep into him, and he stares right back at me.

I'm lightheaded, but I hang onto him while the world recedes. I see us racing through golden stalks, my arms whipping along. Then I reach into the air. The orange horizon warms my body, and I scream madly and happily.

Nothing can stop our souls from singing. Nothing can stop our spirits from shrieking.

So whatever anyone says, whatever anyone thinks—I've lived so very long. I've been in love. I've been free.

I'd like to think, no matter where I go, I can still be found. *Just look up.*

I'll be there. That's where I'll be.

Every time the sun shines down, maybe you'll think of me.

< 63 >

Ryke Meadows

Daisy has been in surgery for two hours.

I can't fucking talk about it to anyone. After all the over-crowding, I've asked her sisters, my brother, and everyone else to just give me some fucking time alone. The nurses have me in a hospital room for the baby and "in case Daisy returns," they said.

I didn't want to be apart from either of them, but I couldn't go into surgery. They tried steering me into a waiting room, but I refused to leave Sullivan. So I watched the doctors check her, clean her, and they said she was healthy.

After I washed off, they let me have her back.

When I returned to the private room, I pulled the chair over to the window. I've been sitting here for an hour. The rain never letting up. Sullivan sleeps in my arms, swaddled in blankets. She stirs a couple of times, lips parting wider, but then rests again.

I finally talk, my voice low and raw. "I'll never love you any fucking less...whatever happens—she wouldn't want that." My throat tightens. "Even if..." I can't fucking say it. *Even if it's just you and me.*

The whole notion is fucking crippling—yet, I fucking sit here knowing it's a real possibility. She hemorrhaged. She lost an extreme amount of blood. I've blocked out everything after her eyes shut. I won't ever fucking recall it. I won't let it fucking plague me, eat at me, come back. It's gone.

I'll only remember how happy she looked. How happy we were. *How happy we are.*

I can't start crying because if I start fucking crying, I'll never fucking stop. Our child doesn't need a father who can't walk, can't breathe, can't eat. If Daisy can't be here, I'm not letting anyone else raise Sullivan but me.

The door creaks, and I look over my shoulder and see Price, of all people. I don't really acknowledge him. I just turn back and watch my daughter sleep.

I hear him come forward and then stop.

"I want you to know, Ryke," Price says, "that I'm going to be here for you and your child, no matter what..."

I'm rigid, in a fucking fog that I have trouble escaping.

"...and I asked her dad what his intentions were in hiring me. Since Daisy and you had been concerned about my age." He pauses. "I know why he chose me."

I listen but I can't respond.

"He wanted someone that would be here for the long haul. He knew you'd both build a family at some point, and he wanted you to have someone you could trust by then. I won't retire in ten years. I won't quit on you. I'll be here for as long as you and Sullivan need me. I just wanted to give you that."

Greg Calloway. Thinking ahead. Actually believing in us from the fucking start. I could laugh—how I'd been fucking paranoid for nothing. I can't laugh though. I can't do anything or say anything.

I can't move.

Then I hear the door shut. He left.

I stroke my little girl's cheek. "She named you Sullivan…"

Adam Sully would've loved it, which is why it fucking gets to me. I put my hand to my mouth. I wonder if the name was a spur of the moment idea or if she's thought about it for a while.

I'm not sure I'll ever have the chance to ask.

The door creaks again. Heavier soles strut closer, but I lack the energy to turn and see a face this time.

"…I won't pretend like I can understand what you're feeling." I would know that coarse voice, like sharp gravel, fucking anywhere. *My dad.* "We've had plenty of differences, but my love for you, son, has never changed. I've always wanted to be a father to you."

I can't get into this. I can't repeat the fucking past and scream at him until I'm blue in the fucking face. I can't tell him that he gave up on me. That he shunned me. That he made me an outcast by name, by place, by birthright. I can't fucking do this.

He nears my chair, but I'm not turning around to greet him.

And then he says, "I'm sorry, Ryke."

My nose flares, restraining fucking emotion. This is the first time he's apologized to me.

"…I've hurt you the most over time. And I'm sorry for what I did. You didn't deserve to take the fall for my actions and my reputation. I failed you, and I'm *sorry.*"

My jaw locks but something wet slides down my cheek. I wipe it before anything else crashes through.

He's so fucking stubborn. Set in his ways. I never really thought he'd admit to doing anything wrong. He can reroute history so it seems like he was saving someone—my brother, himself—but in the end, I'm the one who fucking paid.

He never cared. Never really fucking understood.

To hear that he does—I can't…I can't compute it right. I can't do anything with the apologies at the moment. So I may not be able to tell him now, but this is the past. I can let go.

I can forgive again.

When I hang my head, too spent to tear at my floodgates today, his footsteps withdraw. The door clicks closed. I shut my swollen eyes tightly, pressure bearing on me.

Nothing I do releases it, so I open my eyes, my daughter close to my chest. I kiss her forehead, just as she wakes. My thumb brushes her soft cheek.

She's so fucking small and fragile. I search her features, trying to spot Daisy in them. Maybe her delicate nose. Her wide, curious eyes.

Something like a rock lodges in my throat again.

She stirs more and lets out a weak cry about the same time the door swings open. "Ryke."

I sit straighter, my gaze darting to the nurse in white scrubs. She gently shuts the door, being quiet for Sullivan. When she approaches, I notice a bottle in her hand. I shake my head on instinct. Daisy was looking forward to breastfeeding, and I'm still thinking, *I don't want to take that from her.*

What's fucking wrong with me?

"Do you want to feed her or do you want me to?" the nurse asks. "She has to be fed now."

"I can," I barely get out. She hands me the bottle, and I tuck my daughter a little closer. I put the bottle to her lips, and she starts sucking, her wide eyes filling with contentment. I watch her for a while before focusing on the nurse again. "Do you know anything new…?"

"No." Her eyes flit to the floor. "But I promise if I hear any updates, I'll let you know."

I feel hollowed out and cold. I return my attention to Sullivan.

"I'll be back to check on her, and if you need anything, you have the buzzer over there." She points at the empty hospital bed.

It must be thirty minutes later—the bottle set aside and Sullivan asleep again—when the door cracks open one more time.

I hear footsteps. And then the feet of another chair scraping across the floor. The wooden seat pulls up right next to mine. When the person sits down, I rotate to find my brother.

He slouches and stares out at the rain, and I keep fucking looking at him. Until he meets my gaze and says, "What? You think you're alone or something?"

I inhale a ragged fucking breath, the weight of this killing me. I can't contain it any fucking longer. I break down, and he stretches his arm over my shoulder.

I fucking sob because I'm terrified to live a life without her. Where the world is nothing but dark and lonely again. I don't know how to be that light for our daughter, but I know I have to fucking try.

I know I can't give up.

I know I have to be the man that Daisy fell in love with.

< 64 >

Ryke Meadows

4:17 a.m.

My week-old daughter cries while I change her diaper in the bathroom. "I can do this in under a fucking minute, sweetie." I unsnap the bottom of her heather-gray onesie that resembles long johns, a cotton yellow hat keeping her head warm.

Her big eyes train on my features.

I raise my brows at her, and she quiets and stares so fucking curiously at them.

I love her so fucking much. "If you're looking at me like that, just wait until you see this big fucking world, Sulli."

She makes a tiny noise that digs right into my soul. I toss her dirty diaper in the bin. After finishing up with a new diaper, snapping her onesie back, I cradle her in my arms. And I shut the bathroom lights off behind me.

As I saunter back into my darkly lit bedroom, my head collides with the hanging green paper lantern. "Fuck," I swear softly and set my free hand on the lamp to freeze it in place.

"What a precious little cupcake."

I swing my head towards the bed. Daisy is tucked beneath the covers, propped on her elbow, her blonde hair wild around her cheeks. I stare at her like she's a fucking mirage. I stare at her like if I look away, she'll disappear for fucking good.

And she smiles so much that her scar stretches. "He heard me call him a cupcake," she teases. "Can I take a bite out of you?" She gasps with lively green eyes. "The thrill of it all."

Don't disappear on me.

I edge to the bed and then toss a round pillow at her face. She laughs while I climb onto the mattress, right next to her, and I set our daughter on her lap.

Daisy rests her head against my shoulder, her fingers skimming Sulli's feet, covered in tiny yellow socks. "There's nothing more precious than this, I swear," Daisy whispers. "She's like a peanut butter cupcake."

"I thought I was the fucking cupcake," I mess with her.

She looks up at me. "Have you ever heard? One cupcake makes another cupcake." She then leans forward and whispers, "Isn't your daddy just the most handsome cupcake in the world, Sulli?" Daisy brushes her nose with Sullivan's nose, and my heart just fucking melts.

Daisy leans back while Sullivan coos. "I could totally watch her do nothing for hours."

"Yeah, but you need to fucking sleep, Dais." Which is why I've tried to be as quiet as fucking possible changing and feeding her in the middle of the night. I wanted to keep her in the nursery so Daisy could sleep, but she hated the idea of our baby even being in a crib five feet away from us.

Daisy has this tiny pout on her lips, confusion in her gaze. "I thought we agreed on sharing sleepless nights?"

"That was before..." I rub my mouth, still unable to fucking recall the events from a week ago.

She had a total hysterectomy. They removed her uterus, her tubes, and her remaining ovary—along with that fucking cyst. They froze what eggs she had left, but she underwent a major surgery, not to mention losing more blood than I can even wrap my head around.

I rake my hand through my hair and ask her, "How do you feel?"

"A little lethargic."

I give her a fucking look like *see*.

"But they said it'd be that way from the blood loss." She has to take iron supplements to help with that. "I've decided to give that EMT my Ducati." She sits up straighter, glancing between me and our daughter. "I know it seems like a huge decision, but I wanted to give him something that meant a lot to me as a *thanks for saving my life*. I called his mom yesterday and she said he'd like it."

I nod a couple times, thinking about how that nineteen-year-old rookie EMT ended up being the factor in whether she made it out okay. I knew Daisy's blood type because of the Paris riot, and she needed a transfusion on the ride to the hospital. The young EMT knew his blood type.

And they were a match.

"Well if you're not going to fucking sleep, you watch her for a minute." I stand up from the bed; my right leg fucking throbs. It always does in the middle of the night.

Her eyes smile back at me. "Such a cruel job. Give it to me always."

I flip her off.

Daisy says to our baby, "That's a sign of love."

I shake my head, my lips rising. I crouch to Daisy's wooden trunk beneath the window. I can feel her watching me very fucking closely. I know what she's been putting in here, and maybe she thought I had no clue. All this time.

I have known.

This is where she's kept who I am. In case I went looking for myself again.

I unlatch the lid and then glance back at Daisy on the bed. She's not afraid. Even after everything that's happened, she only wears eagerness, light and curiosity. Brightening our entire room without the switch of a lamp.

It was a miracle, they said, that she lived.

I just keep looking at her every day. I keep holding her, and I listen to all the words she has to say. I will never take a single second of my life for granted.

After my accident, I missed August. I missed even more of September. I missed these months in a fucking daze, and I slept through them. I wandered to no fucking end. And after what happened last week, a common reaction would be to slow down, to play it safe, but I've learned that death is inevitable. I could've lost her. I could've lost my daughter.

I have another chance at this, and I refuse to waste another fucking minute of my *one life*. I refuse to be less than the person I know I am.

I've woken up.

I've seen what I used to see.

I focus on the trunk, reach inside, and pull out rope, carabiners, all of my fucking gear. Beneath them are piles and piles of magazines. She even saved my subscription to *Rock and Ice*. I pick up an old issue and stand.

I'm on the front cover, ascending a cliff in Venezuela.

When I turn to Daisy, I see her crying with the biggest fucking smile.

"Thanks for keeping this safe," I tell her. It's not going to be physically easy to start up again, but the hard things are usually the right things.

< 65 >

Daisy Meadows

"Do you see this face?" I sidestep from the kitchen sink, Sullivan set in a bath basin with an open-mouthed giddy smile, her eyes alight and tiny hands unclasping. Trying to grab hold of the warm green washcloth on her tummy.

Ryke wears a backwards baseball cap, just returning from a run with his brother. So he's also in track pants and shirtless. Though he grabbed the video camera before I could, filming Sullivan's favorite thing in the world.

Bath time.

"This is the face of two-month-old Sullivan Minnie Meadows," I narrate. "Part mermaid, part pirate." I spin back to Sulli and splash warm water on her arm. "Aye, girlie."

She beams, wiggling her legs and hands for more water. We only use soap on her bottom since we bathe her every day and don't want to dry out her skin. April is slightly warmer, but lotion has been her best friend during the cold months.

Ryke sidles next to me, and Sullivan makes a tiny squeaky noise in delight. I think she's aware that we're her mom and dad. "And what are you?" Ryke asks me. "The mermaid or the fucking pirate?"

"The pirate," I say, not missing a beat. I wash Sulli's face, leaning closer to her. "That makes Daddy the merman." I can't hold a straight face for long. I start laughing, especially since we're recording this for history's sake.

"You think you're fucking funny, Calloway?" He's totally trying not to smile right now.

"All the other pirates laughed at my stories. Maybe merpeople don't have a sense of humor." I clean our daughter's neck with warm water. "Take note Sulli, pirates have more fun."

Ryke seizes the sink hose, and without pause, he squirts me in the face.

I burst into a smile, my face doused and dripping. I try to approach him—to steal the hose, but he sprays me again. I stick my tongue out to catch a mouthful of water.

He clicks the hose off. "What were you saying, Calloway?"

"Pirates have mor—"

He squirts me again.

I laugh full-bellied laughs, my face slick and wet. "Pirates are—"

He never surrenders, only spraying my shirt that says, *donut go breaking my heart*. I practically leap onto him, trying to steal the hose this time. He raises it above my head, but it tugs to a stop, allowing me ample time to clasp the hose for myself.

I rotate the nozzle towards Ryke and spray without mercy.

Water jets out and wets his face; he's not even trying to block the stream.

"Ha ha," I hoot. "Pirate thievery wins out every—"

He kisses me, so suddenly, so strongly, that I'm almost knocked backwards. He catches me before I plummet, and I smile so wide beneath his lips.

It lasts like two-point-two seconds since someone tugs on both of our pants. Our lips break apart and our gazes descend to little Maximoff Hale. We still live with Lily and Lo, and Willow will be moving out in the summer—so run-ins with everyone is common, even with our new baby.

"Unle Ry"—he pushes his words together in haste—"daddy said big roc!" He stretches his arms out. I translate this as: *Uncle Ryke, Daddy says you're going to climb a big rock!*

"You told Lo?" I ask Ryke, setting the hose back into the sink and washing behind Sulli's ears. Ryke has upped his physical training regimen since our daughter was born. Some days I just watch him move about a room, his stride full of vigor and purpose.

I'm not nervous that he might be training too hard or too fast. He knows his limits, and he's been seeing a therapist to talk through what happened in Peru, so he can handle possible flashbacks. It's the first time he's ever sought professional help. And he's never been more awake, more conscious, of the world around him.

So when he called my dad yesterday, to discuss climbing Desert Shield—like he promised before his fall—I started crying and smiling nonstop.

His step is a little lighter. His eyes a little brighter. If you saw him now, you'd be in tears too.

Ryke removes his baseball cap and sets it backwards on my head. "On our run back, I told Lo that I was going to see if it'd be fucking possible to climb Desert Shield."

I scrutinize his expression, but I can't gauge his reaction about Lo. Whether or not his brother was happy or scared. Ryke has put the video camera on the kitchen counter, still recording and pointed at us, so I don't poke at the subject.

Ryke lifts Moffy in his arms. "Have you ever seen a fucking cliff, little guy?"

Moffy shakes his head repeatedly like Ryke just spoke about boogeymen and ghouls.

"You're going to see a really fucking big one at the end of May. It's this tall." Ryke gestures to his six-foot-three height, and Moffy goes slack-jawed like that's Mount Everest.

"Nuh-uh," Moffy says.

"Yeah fucking huh."

Lo and Lily both enter the kitchen at that, but I'm stuck on May as a deadline. Just surprised it's so close. Recently, he's had trouble climbing at the gym. Not because he can't physically ascend but because people begin filming him and trying to take photos every time he practices.

After his accident, *Celebrity Crush* interviewed random doctors to determine whether Ryke could walk again. Most said, "It'll be difficult for him to even run, and he'll *never* climb again."

Of course people are curious, and combined with my recent brush with death, the birth of our baby, and agreement to air *something* from our lives on television—we've been current news.

#RaisyIsAlive was trending for two weeks straight as well as *#RaisyBaby*. No one has pictures of Sullivan yet, but as soon as we make a grand entrance outside with her, they'll be everywhere. We don't want to sell her baby photos to a tabloid, not for any price.

So the media has officially been Team Raisy, and the world has warmed up to the idea of us on television again. It's funny though. People hated us for so long because we refused to do a reality show, and then the minute we agreed to a documentary series, people complained about us being on air *again.*

We can never please everyone. So at the end of the day, we have to worry about ourselves first.

This docu-series feels like the best direction we've ever taken.

Lo calls out, "Team Maximoff!" He roots for his son as he bickers with Ryke. Lily climbs onto a barstool and opens a packet of chocolate-glazed cookies.

Moffy tosses his fists in the air, and Ryke sets the little boy on the ground.

"Booo, you can't quit," Lo says. "The battle hasn't even begun, bro."

Ryke flips him off and slides right next to me. He grabs the bottle of baby shampoo and begins gently washing our baby's super short hair, so dark brown that we're both positive it'll be Ryke's shade.

His hands look huge compared to her teeny head.

"You okay?" he asks me, the Hale family chatting loudly behind us. I catch only bits and pieces, but I think the three of them are debating about superpowers of persuasion.

Our eyes connect before flitting back to our daughter. "About…?" I ask.

"Hormones."

I've been put on a hormone cocktail after my hysterectomy, and in March, I found out that I was allergic to a recommended cream. Thankfully this last prescription has kept my moods more level.

The best part of the surgery: no more pain. No more extremely long gushing periods and crippling cramps. No more pesky cysts to ruin sex and my everyday life.

In a way, I've been unshackled too.

Sure, the doctors warned me of the potential downsides: lack of sex drive, difficulty to orgasm. But they also said every woman's body takes to a hysterectomy differently, and there have been cases with completely opposite effects.

I think with where I was before the surgery and where I am now, I can only go up from here. Luckily, I have evidence from this morning that suggests just that.

I fill a cup with lukewarm water. "Good so far," I tell Ryke. Then I cover Sulli's forehead with my hand and rinse the shampoo out. "I didn't want to keep you from your run this morning, but you did this thing…" I trail off as he pulls our clean baby from the bath basin.

She cries a little to be kept in the sink.

He gently rests her on the white towel. "If I could, sweetie, I'd leave you in there as long as you fucking wanted." He bundles her in a green hoodie towel. When he pulls the hood over her head, little frog ears on top, she stops fussing.

Ryke leaves her wrapped tightly on the counter for a moment. "What'd I do this morning?" He shuts the camera off. I wonder if he thinks it's bad—whatever I have to say.

He combs two hands through his messy hair.

Yep, he thinks it's bad.

I lean my hip against the counter. "You let out this long groan and stretched your arms above your head." I remember how handsome in his disheveled state he looked and how content he seemed. "And then you sleepily turned over and tucked your arm around me." He even pulled me against his body. Half-asleep, drowsy Ryke Meadows wanted me closer.

His brows knot, full of "fucking" confusion.

I rest my elbow on the sink. "It made me wet." Just thinking about it now, my body pulses with a strong, aching desire. What sweet, sweet hormones.

His mouth falls. "Are you fucking serious?"

Does he think I'm teasing him? I wash away whatever flirty look I wear. "I touched myself," I say with total seriousness, "so I'm a hundred percent positive."

He lets out a shocked breath, his hand to his mouth in disbelief.

It's not about his own pleasure. It never has been for Ryke. The thought that I'd be even *less* aroused than I already was made him upset for me.

I explain, "I read that some women have increased sex drives afterwards and with the right prescriptions they can get wet too…" I suddenly realize how quiet it is in here, sensing an audience by the bar counter. Ryke must too because we both swivel.

Lily, Lo, and even Moffy—up on the counter, eating a cookie—all listen fixatedly to my arousal story.

Lily is absolutely ecstatic, but she tries to act like she heard nothing, shoving a cookie in her mouth.

Lo watches his wife with infatuation.

And Moffy asks, "What's wet?" He licks chocolate off his fingers.

Ryke opens his mouth, and Lo cuts him off before he even begins. "We all know what you're going to fucking say, and need I remind you, bro, he's not even *three*. He has to hit puberty before sex-ed class, alright?"

"Maybe next fucking time, don't listen to us talk about sex."

Lo shoots him a rather docile glare. "Trust me, no one wanted to hear that less than me."

I lift a bundled Sulli in my arms, and she rests her head against my chest. Before I leave, I need to remind them of an impending event. "Don't forget," I tell Lo and Lily, "camera operators will be here at the end of May to set up."

It'll be the first day of filming the docu-series. I think we've all decided to begin with interviews, but no one has offered to take the lead yet and be the guinea pig.

"Doomsday," Lo quips.

My face falls.

"I'm just joking," he tells me. "Don't look like I ran over your baby, Jesus Christ."

"You all want to do this, right?" I look between them, kind of worried that maybe, all this time, they agreed to the docu-series just to appease me.

Lily sits straighter. "It's my favorite idea anyone has had about this stuff. Way better than the reality show—but don't tell Rose I said that." She crinkles her nose. "And don't listen to Lo. He's being an ass."

Lo feigns hurt. "Lily Martha Hale. Where is the loyalty?"

Lily just smiles at me, and I smile back.

Calloway sisters for life.

< 66 >

Ryke Meadows

"There's more? Jesus Christ," Lo curses, watching journalists trudge through the Utah canyon with heavy camera equipment. Greg Calloway's camera crew is the only one with consent to use today's footage as commercial advertisements.

I vaguely notice the media, some even filming us now while I fix my gear about a hundred feet from the base of Desert Shield. Red rock juts towards a clear blue sky, and when I look down the canyon, my lungs fill with something bright.

Yellow wildflowers are in bloom. Daisy's favorite flowers cascade like a winding river.

I briefly make eye contact with Lo, seated on a quilt next to Lily. Close by, Moffy and Janie snoop through a wicker basket for food. Rose, Connor, their twin boys, Daisy and our daughter are all here to watch me climb.

I haven't been able to process into words what it fucking means to me yet, but I know when I stand up, I'll figure it out.

My brother starts, "If they're going to bother you—"

"Don't fucking worry about them, Lo. They're not going to stop me." In the next quiet moment, I notice everyone glancing at the media with these faraway gazes. Despite Lo's words, he's relaxed, his daggered eyes looking past the cameras and at something deeper.

There are more journalists here than when I free-soloed cliffs at Yosemite. More than my historic speed climbs. More than any achievements I've ever fucking made on rock.

And today, I'm wearing a harness. I have rope. There's nothing special about Desert Shield. Hundreds of people have climbed it the way I plan to climb it. I'm not free-soloing. I'm not banking on beating anyone's records.

I'm just climbing a challenging route.

For the first time in ten months.

Even the world has taken a bigger interest in this story, and whether or not they tell it correctly—I don't fucking care.

I stand and tighten my harness, my tattoo on my forearm visible. Daisy has an identical one in the same place. Dates written in small font, vertically lined.

9-27-14

8-12-16

7-15-17

2-4-18

The day that I kissed Daisy for the very first time. The day that I asked her to marry me. The day we became husband and wife. The day our daughter was born.

Beneath Sullivan's birthdate on my forearm, Daisy scribbled in black pen: 5-19-18

Today.

The day I climb again.

Just as I finish with my gear, I hesitate to say goodbye to my friends and family. I've done this plenty of fucking times with them. We've had these sendoffs before I climbed at Yosemite and for Ziff events. Anytime they watched me, anxiety flickered in their fucking eyes.

They were scared for me. Scared I'd fall. Scared I'd die.

Everyone except Daisy. She understood, even way back then.

I'm just preparing to meet those wary eyes again. Ones that say *are you sure you want to do this?* Or *be careful, don't die.* Or *you're doing the wrong thing here, my friend.*

I rake a hand through my thick hair, cameras recording us from a distance, my helmet in my left hand. I finally turn towards all of them, seated on the quilt.

I search for fear, for worry, for hesitation. None of them—not even my brother—wear those sentiments. Their eyes are smiling.

Every set of them.

Lo nods to me, his gaze glassy. "Do your thing."

I wipe my burning eyes with my arm. *Fuck.* I have to fucking ask because this—between all of them—is so different than anything I've met before an ascent. "You're not fucking nervous?" I ask them.

Rose actually smiles. Connor's lips pull high too, and Lily is beaming like I'm a fucking superhero. Daisy isn't staring at me, but she's glowing more than ever, busy twisting wildflowers into a crown, Sulli on her lap.

"I guess we've all realized something," Lo tells me, his son plopping down on Lily with a handful of grapes. Lo is distracted for a second, love in his eyes.

"What's that?" I ask.

Lo meets my gaze again. "You're not living when you're not climbing, big brother. None of us are going to keep you on this shitty fucking ground."

Connor adds, "Unless you want to. We'll put up with whichever Ryke Meadows you want to give us, but just so you know, I like the one in front of me the best."

I think about the last ten months. "Thanks," I say to all of them. "It's been a long fucking road." *And I needed all of you.*

I can't imagine going through what I did alone. I'd probably be dark and cold. I'd be fucking despondent and barely able to stand. I needed them, and they never gave up on me.

"Ant," Lily whisper-hisses to her husband. She hugs Moffy close to her chest, the boy unconcerned as he eats grapes, while Lo stomps on the nearby fucking ant. Moffy is still allergic to them.

I'm kind of fucking glad she's taken the heat off the moment. I notice Rose talking to Charlie who babbles incoherently, the baby cradled in her arms.

"You realize that you have my eyes, little gremlin," she says in her normal, icy voice, but the affection for her child is written all over her face. "They're the *best* eyes in the world. They can defeat your adversaries and claim victories better than your father's."

Connor hears this and begins to grin. "Have you looked into Jane's eyes recently, darling?" He has Beckett asleep on his lap.

Janie, who gazes at the clouds, rolls onto her stomach and stares at her mother with big round blue eyes.

"You're beautiful like *water*," Rose tells her daughter and then she raises Charlie. "Fire." She pats Janie's head who is full-on grinning like her fucking father. *This fucking family is still weird.* "Water."

Beckett also has yellow-green eyes but he's still fast asleep. We all can tell that the twins are fraternal. Charlie has Connor's shade of brown hair, whereas Beckett has his mother's darker color. Not to mention, their face shapes are slightly different.

"Water extinguishes fire," Connor reminds his wife.

Rose lifts her chin in defiance. "Not our fire." Though she can't contain a smile, even when she fucking tries.

Connor's billion-dollar grin consumes the canyon. And then he nods in agreement.

I check my carabiners and my knots one last time. I force myself not to make eye contact with Daisy and our daughter. Then I turn and head towards the crag, helmet in hand.

About twenty feet there, I can feel her race after me. My body heats, the sun blazing—my heart fucking speeding. I'm lit up.

In another time, another place, she's not here. I turn around to no one. The sky darkens. I scream without her. I live without her.

So as I turn around this time—I remember everything. I watch how she slows to a stop, her green eyes glittering. Boring straight through me. I touch her soft hair, wildflowers strewn throughout the blonde strands. A crown rests on Sullivan's head, our happy daughter in Daisy's arms.

I remember this moment. I remember how her scar pulls with her overpowering grin. I remember how she breathes heavily. Like she's raced miles to reach me. I remember Sullivan's giggle and kick of her legs.

I intake Daisy's soul-bearing smile and whisper, "Senza di te, il cielo non ha sole." I cup her cheek with my free hand. "*Without you, the sky has no sun.*"

Her eyes glass and shine, our bodies close, burning together. And then she reaches up and sets a flower crown on my head.

"I love you," she tells me.

I drop my helmet and clasp her other cheek. I kiss her and pull her against me. She smiles beneath my lips, and I smile beneath hers. Our daughter giggles again. I haven't even climbed yet, but I'm rising higher and fucking higher.

As our lips part, a couple tears roll down her cheek, wetting my hands. "This is why we're living," she whispers. "For these moments, right here."

I told her something similar. Way back when. In Costa Rica beneath a waterfall. "And where'd you hear that, Calloway?" I brush her tears.

"From someone very, *very* handsome."

"Have I fucking met him?"

"Oh yeah," she breathes. "He's right in front of me."

I kiss the top of her head, my body light. Then I take Sullivan in my arm, her orange onesie printed with tigers and giraffes. She runs her tiny hands along my unshaven jaw. Her smile grows like Daisy's.

"Don't quit the fucking things you love, sweetie," I tell my daughter. *It'll kill you inside.*

When I become older—when I'm fucking gray, she'll be able to recall all those times her father climbed. She'll have watched me, seen me, doing what I love. I never want her to give up on the pieces of existence that make her *her.*

I want Sullivan Minnie Meadows to race one-hundred-and-fifty miles per hour. No brakes in sight. Don't be afraid of the unknown in tomorrow. Don't be afraid of death. There is no worse life than a hollow one.

So be alive every second of every fucking day.

That's what I hope she'll do.

I hold Sulli around the waist and lift her to the sky, high above my head. She stretches out her arms and legs and laughs, a beautiful sound. She loves when I do this, and I toss her, not too fucking high, and catch her again.

Camera flashes go off, and the journalists start buzzing with chatter. I don't care about the audience. I just watch Sulli grin from ear-to-ear. She stretches her arms again like she's flying.

For as long as I fucking live, I'm never letting anyone put out your light. They'll have to crawl over my dead fucking body.

Daisy hugs me around the waist, and then I hand her our baby girl. Part of me wants to stay right here, beside both of them. The other half is being called towards the rock.

Before I leave, Daisy says, "He'd be proud of you."

"Yeah." My eyes immediately well. "I think so too." Sully never would've wanted me to quit, but looking back, there's no way I could've climbed right after his death. Not even if my leg was fine. I needed time.

I rub my face with my forearm as I walk towards the crag. Then I snap my black helmet on. After my routine setup, I pull a necklace out of my crew-neck shirt, the silver end bullet-shaped. Only Daisy knows this, but Sully had a will—this poorly written note found in the fucking glove compartment of his green Jeep.

In it, he wrote:

Give Ryke Meadows my ashes. I want to be in the clouds, and no one is going to get there but him.

His parents gave me a small portion of his ashes. The rest, they buried in the ground, so I'm going to do my fucking best to leave him in the sky.

"You're going to climb one last time with me, Sully." Then I grip the rock.

With the corners of my mouth lifting, I rise off the dirt.

< **67** >

Daisy Meadows

L o framed a *TIME* magazine on the kitchen wall. It will always draw me in, time-warping me to one of the most profound moments I've ever witnessed. Where Ryke had just reached the top of the red cliff. He positioned his right foot on a higher rock, snapped off his helmet. A flower crown nestled in his tousled hair; sweat from his climb dripped down his temples.

Then he stared up at the sky and tears crested his eyes.

That moment. Right there—where he looked unbelievably happy and overcome—has been immortalized.

Journalists posted the image on dozens of websites. Fans retweeted it millions of times. And it's been locked inside my soul.

On Desert Shield, Ryke said goodbye to his friend and hello again to a love that has been the foundation of who he is since he was six.

And I know I will dim. I will wane, but seeing Ryke happy touches a place inside of me that won't darken so quickly. It may be the only part that stays lit when depression crawls my way.

I'm thankful for that love. I hold onto it always.

"How are you feeling, Calloway?" Ryke whispers huskily in my ear. We sit side-by-side on the kitchen counter by the stove. Our three-month-old daughter is asleep in his arms, bundled in a blanket that says *chocolate over boys*. Which was Loren Hale's baby present to his niece. It's only shocking if you forget how much he loves all of us.

I rest my chin on Ryke's shoulder. *How do I feel?* Nostalgic. Overwhelmed. Maybe even nervous. As he watches me fixatedly, I begin to smile. "Will you always ask me that?" I wonder.

"Every fucking day," he promises.

Besides my sisters, I think he's the only person who really cared how I felt as a teenager, and even as I've grown, I see that won't ever change. Before I can list off reasons why I'm not scared or sad, the kitchen fills with Connor and Rose, baby monitor in hand. Then Lily and Loren. Sam and Poppy. Willow and Garrison.

We have cheese and veggie trays set out along the bar counter, a sort of tiny party since today is the first day of filming the docu-series. Cameras and lighting are already set up in the basement entertainment room, interview-style.

It's so quiet.

"I didn't realize this was a fucking funeral," Lo says as he wraps Lily in his arms. They hang by the toaster.

"It's not the end," I say with a mischievous, rising smile.

"Let me guess"—Lo tilts his head at me—"it's just the beginning?"

"It's actually the middle," I banter. "Which is the *best* part. It's neither the start nor the finish. It's all the goodness in between."

We're still young. We still have so much life left to live. I'd rather live in the middle of all the glorious things than the teasing start or the bitter end. That's just today though. Maybe my theory will change tomorrow.

Maybe everything will be new and different again. I smile at the thought.

Oh, the thrill of it all.

Lo shakes his head at me, and then he nods to Ryke. "Congratulations on marrying that one. She makes less sense than Rose's winter baby collection."

Rose shoots him a scathing side-eye. "Just because you don't know what a peplum dress is—"

"I know what a pepu dress is like," he snaps back.

"Peplum," she corrects, crossing her arms.

"Do you know what doesn't make sense? One-year-olds dressed like they're about to hit up every boring congressional meeting and leadership conference."

Rose growls. "It's cute, and I'm sorry the entire *male* staff refuses to realize that babies can have style beyond zoo animals and comic books superheroes."

"Hey," Lily and I say with smiles, knowing Rose's response to us before she even says it.

"You can dress your baby in whatever—just like *I* should be able to put Jane in a vintage romper or a well-fitted peplum cut dress. There's already a market for pandas on jammies, but there's a gap for what Calloway Couture Babies is offering."

I smile wider. "Go Rose." I clap and Lily almost joins in, but Lo pouts down at her like she's already broken his heart.

Connor soothes the situation by saying, ever so calmly, to Rose and Lo, "Let's not bring your dysfunctional board room home."

Rose spins on him. "Dysfunctional?"

"That's the word that fits Lo's week-long argument with you. If you want another, I can offer one or two or three. Four might be pushing it. For you, of course. I'd assume you're intelligent enough to understand by then." He's as much a smartass as he is a genius, and I don't think he'll ever let anyone forget it.

Rose covers his mouth with her hand. "Your voice is the most hideously, annoying thing in this kitchen. Do not talk if you wish to keep your tongue."

I can tell he's grinning.

She drops her hand.

He cocks his head. "Rose."

"Richard," she warns.

"It's still amusing—after all these years," he grins more, "that you believe you can control what I do." He leans his side against the counter, closer to her. "I know you love this part the best. When I defy you."

Rose narrows her gaze. "In your dreams."

"I don't have to dream," he breathes. "I already have you."

Rose tries not to smile, which causes most of us *to smile*. At least, Lily, Willow, Poppy, and I do. The other guys are hard to crack.

"I hate you," Rose points out.

"And I love you."

Rose's face breaks, and she almost rocks back. "That's not how it goes. You say that I'm the one who loves you."

"That's true too."

She touches a tear that threatens to fall and mutters something in French.

I look to Ryke, and he whispers lowly to me, "She said that she hates when love makes her cry."

Connor replies back in French.

Ryke rolls his eyes and divulges the secrets to me. "He quoted Shakespeare." He pauses. "*My drops of tears I'll turn to sparks of fire.*"

Those two will never change, and I think we all love them best in their intellectual, infatuated glory.

I spot Willow and Garrison by the fridge, both staring at his cellphone, cupped in his hand, with laughter on their cheeks. I bet it's a video clip, something fandom-related.

I'm sad about Willow leaving for London soon, but I know we'll keep in touch. I know she'll return in time. Maybe that's the harder thing for Garrison. Friendships that are like sisterhoods may last forever, but relationships sometimes come and go.

The strings that tie them are a little looser than the ones that tie Willow to me. I only hope their string won't be cut until they're both absolutely sure that's the right thing to do.

Sam and Poppy are on the barstools, talking quietly and eating veggies. I'm glad they decided to be a part of this, especially when they've said *no* to publicity in the past, like *Princesses of Philly.* It feels right having them here.

"You. Me," Lo says to Lily, her back to his chest, his arms draped over her shoulders and lips by her ear. "Pantry. Now."

Lily spins around to him, suspicion in her eyes. "Is this about the Ho Hos?"

I whip my head to Ryke. "There are Ho Hos in the pantry?" I gasp. "How could you eat them without me?"

He raises his brows at me, trying not to laugh. "You've eaten a h— fuck it. I can't say it."

Ryke Meadows can't say the word *hoe.*

"My older brother, ladies and gentleman," Lo says loudly, "the most decent fucking guy you'll ever meet." There's nothing but sincerity in his eyes.

Ryke flips him off.

Lo motions to his brother. "Classic Ryke Meadows."

"You give him a compliment," Connor chimes in, "and he says *fuck you.*"

"Fuck you," Ryke actually says to Connor.

All the guys laugh, and the rest of us join in too.

Lo kisses Lily's temple. "How'd you know I bought you Ho Hos?" My sister loves food and people with interesting names. I think that's a top-notch way to go in life.

This is when her cheeks redden. "I saw them this morning. Moffy ate one," she blurts out.

Lo feigns disapproval. "Are you tattling on our son, Lily Martha Hale?"

"Mmhhh," she nods quickly.

Lo gives her a look. "Who's the lying liar here?"

Lily combusts, "Okay, I ate the Ho Ho! I knew you did something nice just because—and I *ate* your surprise. *I'm* the lying liar." She exhales like it felt amazing to speak the truth and nothing but the truth. Even over something so small.

Lo wraps his arms around her waist. "I hope that Ho Ho tasted good, love."

"Really good."

I'm having trouble not bursting out laughing.

Lily raises her hands in the air. "I know it sounds sexual, everyone, but I don't care." She lifts her chin and looks right into Lo's eyes. "How was that?"

He looks like he'd ask her to marry him all over again. "Perfect," he breathes.

I'd say that I've never seen them more in love, but they've always been this way together. It's why I know they'll still be the same Lily and Lo, the same Lo and Lily, fifty years down the road.

Soon after their exchange, we all fall silent again.

Lo joked about it being a funeral in here, but no one seems sad. When we start airing this documentary series, some of our deepest wounds will be public knowledge. We're letting more people into our circle in hopes of appearing a little more human in their eyes. These memories we've sheltered together will no longer just be ours to keep safe. We're strong enough to give them away.

With that comes this bittersweet feeling. I sense all of us passing that sensation around. We're moving forward, but we also have to leave these priceless treasures behind.

Before my sisters and I start crying, Lo cuts in to shift the mood. "So what are you sharing first?" Lo asks me. "How you accidentally drank absinthe in Cancun?" *Ryke carried me in his arms.* "That one Halloween where you jumped off the roof into the pool?" *I was a flying deer.* "Or how about"—I don't like that look in his eye—"when Ryke filmed close-ups of his P in your V?"

Oh.

My God.

I cover my face with my hands, slightly mortified as Sam and Poppy hear this.

"Fucking really?" Ryke growls at his brother. He throws a dishtowel at Lo, but it lands on Lily's head.

Mission fail.

Ryke hugs me closer, probably feeling the heat of my embarrassment. I wince into his arm like that was physically painful. I thought I blocked that memory from long ago. I may joke around a lot about sex, but I can still be embarrassed like *almost* everyone.

I'm looking at you, Connor Cobalt.

Sam shakes his head repeatedly with a cringe. "I don't want any details, so please don't start giving them."

Poppy smiles. "I kind of do."

"Poppy," Lo says, "when did you get so kinky?"

She dips raw broccoli into ranch dressing. "I may be older than you, but I'm not celibate, you know."

"You have sex?" Lo feigns surprise. "Jesus Christ. I had no idea. All this time I thought your daughter was delivered by a fluffy stork."

Sam rubs his temples like Lo is giving him a migraine. "We're not opening our sex life for discussion. I'd rather discuss..." He gestures from Ryke to me.

"Fuck no." Ryke shuts that down.

"Yeah, fuck no," I pipe in, a heartier smile than before.

Thankfully we divert a lecture from Samuel Stokes—one about "not filming things that could leak on the internet"—as soon as Garrison says, "I'm going to miss hearing this shit."

Lo frowns. "Where are you going?"

Garrison turns off his phone. "You won't see as much of me around your house after Willow leaves. I just won't have a reason to stop by."

Willow pushes up her glasses, and I realize the lenses are fogging.

Everyone goes quiet again.

We all stare around at each other. Engraining this last certain kind of picture. We started out practically unknown. Then we were swept into the limelight. Years of slowly entering fame culture. Years of protecting one another. Years of growing and missteps and falling backwards.

I want to say *in the end*, but maybe this is still the middle. *In the middle*.

I've watched Lo become sober.

I've watched Lily curb a relentless addiction. *(I'm proud of you, sis.)*

I've watched Rose blaze her own trail and put fire to stereotypes.

I've watched Connor fall in love. With more than just himself.

I've watched Ryke Meadows unclip his shackles and rise again.

And me. I've discovered who I am. I'm not letting her go or hiding her to please other people. I am Daisy Petunia Meadows. And I'm here to stay.

I hop down from the counter, all attention rerouting to me. "So I'm off," I tell them. I'm the guinea pig for the documentary series interviews. The first to film. I offered since I proposed the idea. My eyes drift to Lo. "I could tell you what I'm sharing first, but it'll be more fun if you find out during episode one."

He rests his chin on Lily's shoulder, slightly hunched to do so. "If it's about me, just remember to use the word *bastard*." He flashes that half-smile. He can call himself a bastard, but I haven't heard him call himself an "idiot" in years.

Loren Hale isn't as self-hating as he used to be.

And he's less of a bastard than he may ever realize.

I promise him this, "I'll paint the most accurate picture of you." I look around. "Of all of you." They all trust me, just as I trust them. If anyone knows the many, *many* layers that cause us to run, to hide, to scream, to stay quiet—that make up *who* we are—it's all of us.

Lo, Lily, Connor, Rose, Ryke, and me.

As I step away from the counters, Ryke climbs off with our daughter in his arms. He follows me towards the basement. I glance over my shoulder, at our friends and our family.

We all wear armor made of love and time.

Together, we can defeat anything. So wicked foes, prepare your slingshots. We're ready for you. *You can't hurt us anymore.*

CAMERAS AND LIGHTING ARE pointed at the oversized leather furniture. I sit cross-legged on the couch while Ryke is out of frame behind the main camera. He cradles our daughter in the crook of his arms. She stirs a little, her tiny lips parted as she makes a cute noise.

Just watching Ryke hold her does a number on my heart. He's the most attentive, caring father that I've ever seen. He'd cradle her all hours of the day if he could, but I think he likes watching her in my arms just as much as I love watching her in his.

We made a baby together.

Shh, don't tell my sixteen-year-old self. She'd never stop smiling in front of Ryke Meadows.

"Whenever you're ready," he reminds me. He'll press record when I give him the go.

I pull my gaze off him and onto the camera lens.

There's so much that I want to say. That I *need* to tell. Words and memories tumble through me, and I trip over these significant moments in time. With friends that I thought were friends. People that I thought were kind people.

I may sound naïve. I may sound like a fool, but at the start of this journey, I was only fifteen. Do you remember that? Do you remember me?

I'm not just speaking to two girls who've wronged me over time. Cleo and Harper haven't been able to contact me since Garrison secured my accounts. They haven't been able to sneak through the neighborhood security gates—though I've heard they've tried two more times.

I'm talking to everyone. To show the truth behind the images on *Celebrity Crush* and the backlash and the hate.

I'm speaking to you.

You don't have to love me, but maybe you'll see me in a new way.

I rub my thighs, my pulse beating hard. "I'm ready," I nod to Ryke.

He turns the camera on, the red light glowing.

I take a short moment before I begin, "This is the first interview of the brand new documentary series called *We Are Calloway.*"

I pause for a second, tears welling with a powerful, unyielding sentiment.

"My name is Daisy." My eyes land on Ryke as I strongly say, "and I have this theory." My smile stretches wide as soon as his rises.

I am the biographer of my own life.

And no one can take that away from me.

< 68 >

Ryke Meadows

I run eight miles around the gated neighborhood. The end of May has brought sweltering heat, even at six in the fucking morning, so I'm shirtless, in track shorts. So is my brother.

Our breaths are controlled, in sync as we keep a steady pace. Nutty leaps next to us without a leash. I'm a couple strides behind Lo, and every time I try to fucking match him, he ups his speed. Just like I used to do to him.

I'm twenty-eight.

I met my brother six years ago.

I can never regain the time that we fucking lost together, but what we've made up has been some of the best parts of my life.

Lo turns onto Whisper Ridge Road and he bolts off into a sprint.

So we're going to play that fucking game, little brother. My lips rise as he takes off ahead of me. I push myself harder and faster, my body burning. Sweat building. My lungs contracting. Muscles stretching. We pass acres of land. The darkened sky just beginning to lighten in the early morning.

With a rigorous fucking pace, Lo glances over his shoulder at me. He's smiling and shouts, "You going to keep staring at my ass?!"

I flip him off and then grit down as I *race* towards him. It's not effortless like it used to be. I'm not even reaching the speed that I once fucking had.

I'm not giving up.

Not one fucking day will I stop.

My right leg throbs dully, then more noticeably but I push through. Sharpness scrapes along my tendons, my bones. My heart pounds and I breathe deeply through my nose.

Run.

Faster.

My muscles shriek. I can distinguish the titanium inside my limb, still foreign to my body. The pain may never leave me, and I'm not fucking bitter or furious.

I'm the lucky one.

Alive. Here today. Chasing after my brother until I can catch up to him again.

I can practically feel his fucking smile in front of me. Mine grows tenfold, seeing who will win as we near the last stretch.

I'm four long strides behind him. Both of us are going our absolute fucking hardest. As soon as he passes his mailbox, he slows like he broke through an invisible finish line.

I come to a stop beside him, Nutty following suit, her collar jingling.

He pats my shoulder and says, "Maybe one day you'll be able to outrun me."

I remember all the fucking times I've told him that. "I'd rather just run beside you."

His daggered amber eyes almost soften.

We've had a rocky start together. We've struggled with the balance of our fucking relationship, but after hitting the lowest points in my own life, I looked to Lo. He was there. I don't think

I ever imagined, at the beginning of it all, he'd be stable enough to help me.

I leaned on my brother. I was never scared to, and that's how I know we're both doing okay.

"You will," he says like he can't see any other life for me than the one that I desire. And the one that I want. Because he thinks I deserve it all.

But this guy deserves just as much for putting up with our abusive father. For battling an addiction. For never letting go of his wife.

We're both in a mindset where we're willing to do anything to facilitate the other's happiness, and that's fucking insane that we're finally, *finally* here. At this peace in our lives.

And I say, "*We* will." I nod to him. "I'll see you fucking later."

"Yeah, what time is the swim lesson?" Lo asks.

"Noon." We've been taking Sullivan to swim classes since she was four-weeks. Lily and Lo brought Moffy along to one last month. He talked about the pool non-fucking-stop, to the point where I couldn't understand what the fuck he was saying besides *water*. Now we all bring the two kids together.

Lo nods and turns around towards his house.

Instead of following, I run again down the street and whistle to Nutty. She skips ahead of me. Knowing where to go. Past his mailbox. Past the several houses along this road. My knee cramps some, but movement is fucking good for rehabilitation. It sometimes even lessens the pain.

I fly by Connor and Rose's house, pink tulip trees in bloom along their driveway. We all wonder how many kids they'll end up with, but whatever the fucking number, there's no doubt they'll be anything but great parents. Even if Connor is a narcissistic prick, they both have a way of instilling confidence in others. It's fucking invaluable.

I jog until the very end of Whisper Ridge Road, the cul-de-sac mostly green land with maple trees. Only one home straight ahead. I run towards it and then stop by the edge of the driveway.

I open the mailbox, grabbing what looks like junk mail and bills. I pat Nutty on the torso. "Good run, girl." She pants fucking happily.

I flip through the mail, heading up the driveway to what Greg Calloway called "a cottage modeled after eighteenth century architecture." Gray stone, white door—half of which is window, chimney, and a dark-slated roof resembling brick.

The four-bedroom cottage has more yard and grounds than Connor and Lo's houses combined. Greg and Jonathan apparently had this wild idea to gift Daisy and me a house for our wedding present, and they spent over a year trying to convince the owner to fucking sell this exact home.

Something tells me that they knew for a variety of reasons that we'd want this one. First, it was being used as a holiday house. The owner would return maybe once every two years. We wouldn't have felt right about making an offer—out of the blue—if a family lived here full-time.

It's not that Greg and Jonathan paid for the home. I fucking paid for it with money that I've made and will continue to make climbing.

They did the heavy lifting by persuading the owner to sell. Lo knew all along what was happening, and he said the owner was "trolling" Jonathan and Greg half the time. Pulling their legs. So they left after our wedding, earlier than planned, just to meet with him—thinking it was a done deal.

It wasn't.

I couldn't have spent the fucking time dealing with this guy, so I'm grateful and thankful they did this part for us.

It could've been another five years before anything in this neighborhood became available, and now we have our own space. Our own land. Our own home. Our own lives.

I step off the driveway. Stone is laid into the grass, leading to the front door. I dig into my pockets for the keys and enter. Boxes are stacked everywhere, no living room furniture. We haven't gone shopping yet.

It's fucking possible it'll take us three months to unpack. I head towards the kitchen and throw down the mail on the granite counter. Nutty races off to her water bowl, slurping loudly. Then I open the fridge, which we do fucking have.

I twist off the cap to the orange juice and chug from the carton.

I expect to hear Daisy somewhere, but so far, it's pretty fucking quiet besides our husky. I put the cap back on, my eyes flitting to the hardwood floor.

The first day we moved in, I fucked her right there. I can't stop replaying it or hearing her high-pitched cries. My body heats again, blood pooling.

While on top, I spread her legs apart; she'd already come three times.

She raked her fingers through my hair, and this happy, tired smile played at her lips. "Animals do it on the floor," she said. "Therefore we must be—"

I pushed deep inside of her, and her chin tilted up in a shallow breath.

"We must be…?" I whispered lowly in her ear, pumping into her, my ass tightening as I drove inside. My body was on another fucking dimension, between her legs. Having Daisy in my arms.

"Fuck," she cried.

I combed her hair back as I thrust in and out. It's not like her sex drive did a one-eighty. She doesn't crave sex every day; sometimes she could do without it for weeks. But that doesn't even fucking matter. The fact that she can be aroused at all, that she can reach that point—that matters to me. Because I know she'd want it.

I kissed her deeply until she was so fucking gone that she couldn't press her lips against mine anymore. As she began to hit a peak, I touched between her legs and rocked hard. She shuddered and cried, and I was so close to losing it, a noise caught in my own fucking throat. Cursing.

I kept going, and I leaned down to her ear again. And I said, "We must be fucking animals."

She laughed in the middle of her climax.

That did it for me, and I released harder than I ever fucking have.

I set the orange juice back into the fridge, my dick fucking throbbing. I jack off in front of Daisy more often, but hopefully I won't need to masturbate until I take a fucking shower.

The kitchen and the living room are one big open space, and I return to a box by the fireplace, deciding to stretch and unpack something at the same time. In the background, I hear Nutty crunching on her dog food.

As I take a seat on the hardwood and rip off the tape, I read the side of the box:

Fragile but amazing. Be careful with these.
I don't want to lose them.

The movers—Connor and Loren—had no fucking clue where to put half the boxes because of Daisy's labels. I didn't care. I dropped most of them around this space, and I kept finding myself reading them. Lo grimaced at me and said "you have love on your face" and he gestured to my mouth.

I was smiling. I didn't even fucking know I was.

I tuck my left foot and then reach towards my elongated right leg. Stretching a second. Then I open the flaps of the box and peek inside.

Bubble-wrapped frames. I pull a stack of them out and then as carefully as I fucking can, unfurl the bubble-wrap.

As soon as the first photo comes into view, it almost knocks me back. I rub my jaw for a second. It's of us. On the bow of a yacht in Mexico, I have her on my shoulders, and we're both caught mid-laugh. That was during her nineteenth birthday.

I pull out another. I'm sleeping on a hammock in Costa Rica. She's kissing my nose.

My chest lifts fucking high in a deep inhale, and I want to see more. So I unwrap another moment.

At a bowling alley. I'm holding her upside-down, only clutching one of her calves, and her smile has overtaken her entire fucking face. I'm staring at her like I couldn't be happier that she's happy.

Another. We're doing backflips off a roof into a pool at the same fucking time.

Another. She's on her red Ducati. I'm on my black one. I'm flipping her off as she speeds ahead of me. Lo and Lily, in the car behind us, captured the shot. I remember catching up to her that day, flirting the whole way to New York with our bikes.

Another. Cancun. Our bungee jump photo.

I pinch my eyes. I go through more. Wedding pictures. The time where Daisy stood on a fucking skateboard five-months pregnant. I was holding her waist. The moment I handed Sullivan to Daisy, when she woke up after surgery.

I have to stop myself, my eyes reddening at our lives spent together. I shut the flaps. *Fragile but amazing. Be careful with these. I don't want to lose them.*

So much fucking happiness exists inside this box. I have no doubt there'll be hundreds just like this one, all overflowing.

Nutty suddenly appears by my side, sitting down. I scratch behind her ears, wondering why she's not with Daisy. I stand, thinking maybe she's still asleep, but the chances of that are slim. Her routine sleep pattern—which was already shit—went to hell when Sulli was born.

It might take another few months to return to something better, but I know eventually we'll both get there.

"You want to find Daisy?" I ask Nutty.

She rises too but waits for me to move. I'll look in our fucking room, on the rare occasion that she's sleeping. I climb the carpeted stairs, and as soon as I reach the small second floor, something inside of me tugs my gaze.

My eyes drift out of the window. Like I just know. That's where she'll be.

With the side of my fist, I rub the morning fog off the glass. A tree house is perched between two fully-grown maples. Battery-powered lights emit an orange glow through the tree house windows, and I see the outline of Daisy and our daughter.

I don't fucking move. I just watch for a second.

The strands of her hair tangle around her face, Sullivan's head rested on her shoulder. Daisy waves this homemade wand. She said that she made it herself when she was a little girl. I've seen it: blue and green streamers and purple string hanging off a wooden stick.

Lo doesn't have to be here to tell me.

I have love on my face.

Daisy often talked about living in the wild with me. About being stranded on an island. Just the two of us. Having a baby alone in the rainforest together.

I always thought her fantasies were cute, but it's not until later in our lives that I see her and me and what she imagined and I think, *we fucking have that, Calloway.*

No matter where we are. No matter what we do.

It's *who* we are.

Fucking primal. And this wild, untamable spirit lives within us.

‹ 69 ›

Daisy Meadows

"And then the fairy disembarked for the sea to grant all the mermaids their wishes." I wave my makeshift wand side-to-side, Sulli's cheek on my bare shoulder. I may be topless, but I've run out of seashells! In actuality, I just fed her about ten minutes ago. It's much easier (and more fun) to just take everything off.

Sulli giggles this high-pitched sound of pure glee, her eyes following the blue and green streamers. She tries to reach out for the purple string but timidly retracts her hand.

"It won't bite you, my peanut butter cupcake." I tickle her nose with the streamer, and she giggles twice as exuberantly, kicking her feet. "Ah, yes, this little mermaid wishes for sweet things." I nuzzle her cheek with my nose.

I'm in love with my daughter.

Like pure, soul-bearing *I want to hold you always and forever* kind of love. It's brand new for me, and I won't let it go.

I haven't managed to decorate much of our new home yet, but the tree house was the first to get a real makeover. I spread out quilts, fuzzy pillows, hung battery lanterns and multicolored cloth tapestries, and I brought an old toy chest up as a table. Actually Ryke and Lo heaved it together. Ryke had to climb up the tree trunk's ladder (there are three-ways to reach the top). Afterwards, Lo gave me the classic Loren Hale brutal glare, followed by "you're goddamn crazy."

Totally worth it.

I set my baby on her round koala pillow, fitting her three-month-old teeny body. I dangle the wand above her head, and I gasp as I flit it away from her hold.

She observes with big round eyes, the color beginning to morph into my deep green.

"Can you believe," I whisper to her, "that you're a part of Ryke and me?"

Ryke and Daisy's baby.

I don't think many people believed we'd ever procreate. Besides my fertility troubles, we live life in the fast lane. I think they expected us to slow down, but we both just wanted another companion to ride along with us.

I smile as she does and fix her fox socks, her orange cotton bodysuit snapping below her diaper, short-sleeves and legless. Dark gray cursive across the front says: *stay curious.*

Ryke picked it out. When we went shopping for baby things, Ryke basically filled the entire cart. He was totally into it.

I comb her soft brown hair, the strands growing in. "He's already spoiling you like crazy."

Ryke is the kind of dad who will no doubt bring her cookies in bed, wish her goodnight, read her a story, tuck her in—and even sit in the hallway when she's scared.

He'll protect her with every fiber of his being. We'll teach her to rise above and to love herself *so much* that other people's hate won't drag her down.

We'll be ready for laughter. For tears. For the happiness and the sadness.

We'll bask in every small moment together. Just as I do now.

I wave the wand a little more, her gaze drifting right and left with the waft of the streamers. Not long after, the wooden rope ladder creaks. Like someone is climbing up.

I'm pretty certain it's Ryke, so I'm not nervous. I crawl over to the toy chest, pulling the koala pillow with me. Sulli makes an excited noise as she goes for a short ride.

I hear feet on the wraparound porch, and then the door begins to open. I whip my wand towards the entry. "Ryke Meadows of the House of Meadows," I introduce, watching him emerge. "House motto: *to play and protect like fucking wolves do.*"

He has to duck, but his lips rise as my words reach his ears. His hair is a little wet from his long run, his muscles rippling down his body, toned abs and arms. His shorts even hang low on his waist.

When my eyes meet his, he raises his brows at me. Knowing how much I'm checking him out. His hot gaze then rakes my body, honing in on my topless state.

His attraction seeps into me, rousing dormant hungers. My pulse thumps, and I stretch my arms behind me, giving him a better view.

His jaw muscle clenches, tension spooling.

We don't have to exchange many words. He shuts the door behind him, taking a seat in front of me. I pull Sulli closer to both of us. When he strokes her cheek, she clasps his finger and giggles enthusiastically again, almost in a fit of happiness.

"The fairy just granted this mermaid her very best wish," I tell him, Sulli's eyes sparkling with delight.

"And what was her fucking wish?"

"You." I flick the wand again. "Ta-da! He's here. Right in front of me."

Ryke looks to Sulli. "Mommy thinks she's a fucking fairy."

Sullivan kicks out her legs with another elated baby noise, grinning fully.

"Yeah, sweetie? You think she's one too?" Ryke sets his darkened eyes on me, but I see the light beneath them. "We're all in fucking agreement then."

I press my wand to my chest. "I also have the ability to grant wishes before you even know you want them." While he watches me with more intrigue, I procure a box of granola cereal, a half-gallon of milk, a bowl and spoon from behind the toy chest. I brought them up earlier this morning.

After I finish pouring cereal and milk, I scoot closer to Ryke, stretching my legs on either side of his waist.

My eyes flit up to his, passing the bowl his way, and his expression is absolutely priceless.

"You knew I'd fucking follow you here," he realizes, the bowl cupped in his large hands.

"You're the only person who will go where I go." He's the only one who ever physically chased after me. Ryke never hesitated to run towards my shadow, as I tried to reignite something that faded away.

He barely takes his hardened gaze off me, not even as he spoons a heap of granola. "Thanks, Calloway." He eats the spoonful and then passes the bowl to me.

I scoop soggy granola in my mouth. Watching him while he watches me.

I hand the bowl back, entranced by each other, just eating breakfast in a tree house. Our daughter by our sides.

In the next few minutes, the bowl travels back and forth. The quiet is tenser, and my smile expands, second by second. His stoic features have yet to shift past his darkened state. Like sharing company with a feral wolf.

The danger of it all.

His hand splays on my thigh, and I sip a spoonful of milk with this lovesick grin. He tosses a strand of my blonde hair into my face. I smile more, but he's not cracking just yet. I pass him the bowl, and he scrapes at the bottom.

We keep pulling closer to each other, only a few inches between our chests. Like nature intended us to be entangled, crazy things. I've never been happier. Never felt brighter.

Never loved my life more.

The longer my smile grows, the more his lips struggle to remain in their brooding place. I watch, so keenly, as the corners of his mouth slowly but surely rise.

Until the next bite of his cereal comes with a full-blown, effervescent smile. Unleashing all the light he wields inside his core.

Many chips had to fall in perfect place for this moment, not just us sharing a bowl of cereal, staring intently at each other, or Sulli cooing by our sides. Many facets had to go right for something simpler.

All three of us, together, existing in the world at the exact same time.

It could have been fantasy. While I love the idea of swimming with mermaids, climbing aboard a pirate ship, being the last beings on Earth—there is nothing better than my reality.

I can't think of a greater, more *magnificent* adventure.

Than this one.

TEN YEARS LATER

< Epilogue >

Ryke Meadows

On a narrow, dirt path between dense spruce trees and the call of the mountains, I run.

My legs pump and carry me. I pound the fucking earth with each step, dark skies cloaking the woods. Lights strapped around my knuckles illuminate the trail, but so does the person in front of me.

Three strides ahead, my brother runs with similar flashlights. Eight, hilly miles through the Smoky Mountains—this is our routine when we visit the lake house.

This is the way we always go.

I recall the area where trees no longer squeeze the path tight. It's coming up towards the end. So I lengthen my stride, sweat beading along my bare chest. Muscles coiling with each controlled breath. Closing the gap between him and me.

Just as I fall in line beside my brother, he picks up his speed. Our legs stretch at equal fucking distance.

Easily, I keep in step with him.

Maybe the only difference between us now is the scar that stretches from my thigh to calf. And the dull ache in my right knee. Reminding me of a day. Of a time. And a person.

Like a whisper or a fucking dream.

We both slow to a walk as the cherry red lake house pulls into view, only a few lights on inside. Around 5:39 a.m., almost everyone should be asleep.

Lo is also shirtless, his muscles as lean as mine. His cheekbones still sharp, eyes still daggered, but his feet a little fucking lighter. Right by me.

"I'm digging up that fucking root." I break the quiet, thinking about the path four miles back. I comb a hand through my thick, damp hair as we approach the lake house.

"The root didn't commit murder, it just fucking tripped me," Lo says. "Why don't you worry about more important things like your constipated face." He turns to me, just to flash a half-smile.

I flip him off.

He laughs like I'm predictable. And he's happy about that.

You know what I'm happy about—my brother, my little fucking brother—he's thirteen years sober.

Thirteen years.

After all we've been through, this is what bowls me over the most. He had a lot of chances to turn to a bottle, but he didn't. I know it was fucking hard. I was there, but as Lily said, "He's ice in the winter now. He won't melt."

I believe it every day.

I mess his hair with a rough hand, and he tries to mess mine, for a fucking change. I shove him back, and then he shoves me.

We're both smiling.

Nearing the side of the house, we reach the grassy hill that overlooks the dock and rippling lake. Red Adirondack chairs situated close by, one of the kid's sippy cups staining a ring on the armrest.

Lo stretches his quads, and I'm about to stretch mine out when the backdoor flings open in fucking haste. We both shine our lights on the wraparound porch, and a tall ten-year-old girl quickly fits on her sneakers, her dark brown hair in a sloppy pony. She missed a long strand on her neck.

She mutters, "Fuck," and hops into her sneaker on her way down to the grass.

"Careful, Sulli!" I call out.

Lo turns off his light and pats my shoulder hard. "Good luck with that one."

I roll my eyes.

"Wait up!" Sulli says, running over to us. Her limbs long and slender like Daisy. Truth is, she looks like both of us. Skin tanned from being out in the sun, constantly. Dark hair like mine. Harder jaw. But lips like her mom's. A delicate nose. Green, soulful eyes.

My daughter skids to a stop and notices our damp hair and sweat. Her face falls. "Dad," she says in a heavy breath. "You could've woken me. I was in a half-sleep, and I could've been ready really, *really* fast." Before I can answer, she says, "Uncle Lo, tell him."

Lo turns to me with crossed arms. "Yeah, Ryke. Why didn't you wake her up?" He's near laughter. He knows why.

She knows why.

"We've been through this, sweetie," I say, my tone almost always fucking gentle with her. Last summer, at Camp Calloway, she told me that she was glad I didn't kick her ass about swimming or climbing or running. That I let her do her thing.

She's seen my tough love routine at camp when I give the older teenagers climbing lessons.

Thing is, Sullivan pushes herself hard enough. She doesn't need any motivation from anyone.

"Sleep is so fucking boring," she says with a woeful sigh. "Why can't I just use an alarm clock and wake up earlier? Just one hour?"

Lo shakes his head at me. "Only your kid, man."

Daisy and I have strange fucking sleeping patterns, and Sulli mimicked us. Now she relies on naps, and she slept through all the classes she didn't like (fourth grade social studies). So this summer, she has to turn off her alarm clock and get at least seven hours straight of sleep.

Which means, I'm not fucking waking her up anymore to go run. It kills me a little bit because I know she wants to.

I put my hand on her head and she looks up at me with big doe eyes. "Go to bed fucking earlier, and you can run with us tomorrow morning."

"Will you wake me?" she asks. "Please."

"Seven fucking hours," I tell her.

She nods like *yeah, I know*. "Seven fucking hours. I'll do it."

The door opens and another kid comes out, only he's already in running gear, plus a backwards baseball cap with a Spider-Man logo.

Twelve-year-old Maximoff Hale quickly jogs over to us, his thirteenth birthday in a couple months.

I bend down to tie Sulli's untied fucking shoe.

"Dad," she says like she's not a little kid anymore and I need to stop worrying about her—*never going to fucking happen*. "I can do it."

She squats to tie her shoe but as she does, she meets my eyes, a smile in them. I mess her hair that's already a fucking mess, and her lips rise.

I love my daughter. More than the fucking world.

When I stand back up, Moffy is already talking to his dad. "I can run the trail with her. We'll bring bear spray and lights." We don't let the kids out in the woods alone when it's dark. Though Moffy sells it fucking well, not just by his words.

He stands like he's in his twenties, exuding quiet maturity that makes you pause. Makes you think, *you can carry the fucking world, Maximoff Hale*. Problem is, no matter how much he likes responsibility and being treated like a grown-up, we can't forget that he's still a kid.

Lily and Lo don't want him to carry the world. They just want him to be twelve and have fun.

Lo nods to Moffy. "Apparently there's a murderous goddamn root on the trail right now, so think of this as me saving your life."

Moffy has the same jawline as Lo. Same sharpness. Almost identical features except his green eyes and his dark brown hair. But he's not Lo.

He laughs, dimples on his cheeks. "Alright, I don't want to die yet, especially not by the Murderous Goddamn Root."

Lo nods. "Horrible way to go out."

Moffy smiles more and then looks down at his cousin. He nudges her foot with his foot while she ties her laces. "Sorry, Sul, I tried."

Sullivan rises to her feet. "Do you want to play checkers on the porch?"

"Yeah, sure." Moffy nods to her. "Race you there." He takes off with a wily fucking smile, and she determinedly follows suit, trying to beat him.

Lo and I finish stretching in five minutes, and then we both head inside, entering through the large kitchen. Lights on, almost completely silent. I shut the door behind me.

Just in drawstring pants, Connor plugs in a coffee pot, his blue eyes flickering to us as we near. We're all older, but this guy—he doesn't fucking age. Years will never wither him, never defeat him—he's still incomparably confident, his dominance like a morning wake-up call. Can't miss it. Not even before dawn.

He's not alone, by the way.

He supports a sleeping three-year-old girl on his side, only using one hand to make coffee. She drools on his shoulder, dressed in pink floral PJs.

Lo heads to the fridge for water.

I help Connor with the coffee pot, which looks fucking broken. We stand side by side, only an inch height difference, but we're both aware of how polar opposite we are—how we go at life at varied speeds and in contrasting directions.

I never stopped caring about him, and he never stopped giving me his wisdom.

He knows I like the quiet of the morning. So he doesn't hassle me. I know he likes his coffee, so I try to fix this fucked-up thing.

We just understand one another—and I remember Dais once told me a theory. The relationships that take the most effort and time become the mightiest in the end.

Maybe she was right after all.

In my quietest voice, I ask him, "She okay?" I try to turn the machine on, but the lights never glow.

Connor soothingly rubs his daughter's back, and he whispers, "She was afraid last night and didn't sleep well." His toddler is conked out now, rose-shaped clips in her red wavy hair.

Connor's mother had red hair, but not exactly the same carrot-orange that Audrey Virginia Cobalt has. She's really fucking adorable, even passed out on her dad.

A long nine years after Jane was born, Rose finally gave birth to another girl. Connor and Rose made good on their promise and stopped having children when girl number two came into the world.

Audrey is their youngest and last child. The girl that bookends the Cobalt family.

"Scared of what?" I ask quietly, having to abandon the broken coffee machine. We might have an extra in storage. I'll look later.

"*A great and terrible boogey,*" Connor whispers. "Her words."

Lo passes me a water bottle and whispers back, "What's up with this boogey? My kid was crying all last night because of the same thing."

I uncap my water. "Which kid?"

Lo has a lot.

"Kinney." His youngest girl, also three like Audrey.

"The monster is fictional," Connor tells us, "from the imagination of Eliot Alice Cobalt." He purposefully frightened the little kids with a ghost story then.

Cobalt boys.

They all have some kind of mischief running through their fucking veins. All but Beckett.

I take a swig of water and nod at them like *I'll come back soon.* To help with breakfast. As I walk away, their whispers drift in the background, but I'm certain whatever they had to say ended with *love* and *darling*.

The house is still asleep. Passing the spacious living room, dark and empty, I eye the indoor balconies. No one clamors across to annoy their siblings or chase after their cousins.

It's just still and fucking calm.

As I climb the staircase, someone else does wake. It takes me less than a fucking second to figure out who. Always in pastel colors—pinks, blues, yellows, purples and greens—tired-eyed Jane Eleanor Cobalt descends the staircase, brown hair uncombed, frizzy and tangled. Teal sleep mask on her forehead that says *meow*, a zebra sweater, and knee-high socks with pink fuzzy tassels.

Her outfits never match, but that never prods her to change.

I can't say that Janie is a spitting image of her mother, not with the brush of freckles across the tops of her cheeks and nose. I do see Rose in her longer face and her frame, but she's without a doubt a mix of both parents.

Janie inhales a lungful and stretches her arms above her head. "Is that coffee?" she asks me in the softest voice.

"Coffee pot is broken."

She sighs in a resigned way. "Merde." *Shit.*

Janie has been cursing in French for the past year. A question lingers in her eyes as we pass on the stairs. "Where's Moffy?"

"Outside playing checkers."

Just as poised as her mom would be, she descends the rest of the stairs like she's entering a royal fucking castle, not the living room of a multi-family lake house. I watch her head outside to find her best friend.

Then I continue up to the second level.

I thought she might've tried to work me over for something. I'd say Janie likes trying to pull the wool over people's eyes, but all the girls do that with me.

Yesterday, Lo said that I'm a pushover. I let his eight-year-old daughter draw an alien on my arm and stars on my cheek with Sharpie. If Luna Hale asked to pen a spaceship on my forehead, I probably would've said *just not in my eye*.

So maybe what he told me is true, but when it comes to serious shit, I always stand my ground with the kids. *No cellphones and internet here* is something I'd enforce without question or fucking hesitation.

All the kids need a mental break from the media; it keeps them healthy. A lot of them don't even put up a fight when we take their phones. It also keeps them from accidentally posting about our location.

This is the *one* place we can just exist peacefully. No paparazzi. No chaos. Just all of us, somewhere in the world, living freely. Doing commonplace things. Together.

I walk down the hall, not going far before reaching a certain door. It's cracked. In fact, most of the bedroom doors are ajar. I shake my head—the ghost story must've frightened more than a couple kids.

I slip inside, our suitcases not unpacked yet, clothes and blankets littered everywhere along the rustic room, bear-patterned rug and log-framed bed. A half-bag of dog kibble has spilled on the floorboards, *fuck*.

My sole crunches the food, and I freeze, watching the two bodies beneath the quilt. One of them stirs, the other stays fast asleep.

Curled at the end of the mattress, our thirteen-year-old white husky blinks at me and then shuts her eyes again. Nutty doesn't have a lot of energy to leap or run and play much anymore, but she seems content.

As quietly as I fucking can, I pull off my shoes and near my side of the bed. Daisy has her head on her pillow, blonde hair splayed wildly and fucking madly. Her tired eyes are already smiling at me.

My lungs practically flood. Just meeting her beautiful gaze. Pulling me towards her. Where I want to be.

She smiles like she knows. She smiles like she loves me just as much, just the same. And she whispers, "Hey there."

I crawl gently onto the bed beneath the covers. "Hey," I whisper back.

She grins more, eyes dancing over my sweaty body and damp hair. On her side, Dais reaches out and touches my unshaven jaw.

"My wolf," she yawns into a larger smile.

And I just think, *Daisy Petunia Meadows can sleep eight to ten hours. She can dream. She can feel that fucking peace.* It took a long time, but it didn't take forever. It didn't pass her by.

I lean over the tiny mound between us and kiss Daisy's cheek, then her lips. "How do you feel?" I whisper.

"Mmm, happy." While I hover over her a little bit, she runs her fingers through my hair. I watch her green orbs twinkle at me. "You must be my husband," she murmurs.

"Why?" I think she's going to make a joke about me being dirty or fucking sweaty.

Instead she says, "He asks me that every morning and every night." She grips my hair a little harder like, *don't stop. Always ask me how I feel.*

My brows rise. "That fucking so?"

"Oh yeah." There's an *I love you* in her features, and I wear my affection just as much.

I'm about to climb over to Daisy's side, to wrap her in my arms, but the tiny mound between us begins to shift. We both pull back the quilt.

A four-year-old girl in blue dolphin-print PJs squeezes a stuffed sea turtle to her chest, and she giggles as soon as she sees us, like she's been awake the entire fucking time.

Daisy mock gasps. "Who's this in our bed?" She flings the covers back over the girl's head, who giggles again, unable to hide her delight.

I can't contain a smile at that noise.

"Ryke," Daisy feigns surprise, "I think an animal has crawled into our bed." She's having trouble not laughing.

My brows rise again. "Maybe we should send her to the zoo."

"No!" the girl says with laughter attached.

"And only eat blueberries," Daisy adds ominously.

"No!" the girl shouts and gags at *blueberries*.

I say, "And never fucking see Simon the sea turtle ever again."

The girl gasps in horror. "NO!"

"Or," Daisy proposes, "we can send this animal off to the *wild* where she'll run free."

"Yes!" she kicks her feet in excitement.

We whip the quilt off the little girl, and Daisy and I both start tickling her. She squeals and rolls back and forth, tears squeezing from her eyes. We stop when she says, "I'm Winona! I'm Winona! I'm not an animal!"

Daisy combs Winona's light brown hair out of her face, the same shade as Daisy's natural color. Now this child—she's a spitting image of her mom.

Winona Briar Meadows.

Thanks to Rose's heart and generosity, we had another daughter. Daisy's frozen eggs, my sperm—they took thankfully, and surrogacy worked. Rose gave birth to our baby, and the whole nine months where Connor, Rose, Daisy, and I were linked together—it solidified something unbreakable between us.

Sullivan slips through the doorway, her pony half sagging, and then jumps on our bed. She must've finished playing checkers. "Hey, squirt," Sulli says to Winona. Then she lifts up her sister's pajama shirt and blows a raspberry on her belly.

Winona laughs, "Sulli!"

Sulli smiles and rolls onto Daisy's side. I watch Dais wrap her arms around our older daughter. Sulli lifts her head up and brushes her nose to Daisy's in a *hello*.

All my girls.

This is my family. And I swear to you—there's no shortage of love in this room. Greater and stronger than anything I experienced growing up, and I just think, *this is my life. This is my fucking life—and I'm not alone.*

I've loved every moment. Especially all the ones with them.

Sullivan yawns, which causes Winona to yawn, and then Daisy.

I stand off the bed and say, "All of you, try to go back to fucking sleep."

Winona is the only one to actually shut her eyes and start drifting again. Sulli kicks off her sneakers, and asks me, "Where are you going?"

She watches me head to the doorway.

"To the moon," Daisy banters, her smile stretching her scar.

"Only if I see you there, Calloway."

Daisy whispers, "Wherever you go, I'll go."

I hesitate to leave, but it's close to seven a.m. I'll see them all again. This isn't the last moment. The last image. The last picture. Though I remember it and I live it like it is.

I watch Sulli and Daisy turn towards one another, talking quietly while Winona sleeps on the other side of them. I force myself away and walk along the dark hall.

I peek into the second room, door ajar.

Six-year-old Ben Pirrip Cobalt hangs partially off the top wooden bunk, half the quilt with him, and he snores breathy fucking snores in deep slumber.

The boy on the lower bunk rubs his amber eyes with his fist and then turns back into his pillow. Five-year-old Xander Hale has the most photogenic face of all the fucking kids. It's been hard keeping him out of the limelight. Lo said that Xander has been counting down to the lake house.

He's the third-born of the Hale children. Maximoff, Luna, Xander, and Kinney.

I gently shut their door so they'll sleep better when kids start waking. The next darkened bedroom contains four wooden bunk beds, all occupied with boys, fast asleep.

On one top bunk, Charlie Keating Cobalt sleeps, but even though he's ten, he chose to skip two grades, in the same classes as Janie and Moffy. Truth is, he probably could've skipped more.

His twin brother sleeps in the bunk below him. I can only distinguish Beckett's dark wavy brown hair, almost curly and shaggy.

On the second top bunk lies eight-year-old Eliot Alice Cobalt. He shares his pillow with worn paperbacks of Shakespearian tragedies and comedies. His younger brother, only eleven months difference between them, sleeps below.

Tom Carraway Cobalt has his quilt pulled over his head, blocking out the world.

Just like the other room, I gently shut their door. It'd be stranger if we had one body fewer, one personality shyer of the number of Cobalts in the house now. Five boys.

Two girls.

Connor and Rose had seven children in total. An empire.

If they wanted, we all know they would've had an eighth kid—what they once hoped for—but Rose took the time to give birth to Winona instead. They altered their future for Daisy and me. I can't even express what that fucking meant to us, but we never forget their love.

We feel it every day when we hold Winona.

I head back downstairs again. The house will be more crowded tomorrow. Maria just turned twenty, and she's flying in from L.A.—she finished filming some A-list movie. I can't remember what Daisy said it's fucking called.

Janie is most excited by Maria's arrival, and the little kids can't wait for Willow to be here. We all see her often, but she bounces between England and Philly ever since she opened a Superheroes & Scones in London. It's not that the kids are hyper about Willow particularly but the little girl she brings with her.

Vada Lauren Abbey.

Garrison married Willow the same year she graduated college. He's as much a part of this family as my sister—he even created one of the most lucrative video game franchises in the world, all based off of the *Fourth Degree* comic book universe, invested by Connor.

At the bottom of the stairs, I pass the empty living room, the floor-length windows showing a lighter sky than the one before. I check the clock and then head through the kitchen.

By the fridge, Lily holds a sleepy toddler in a panda onesie, and she whispers quietly with Lo. He has this look like he's half-listening but really he's thinking about how adorable his wife fucking is, especially with his daughter right there.

I know how this'll go so I don't wait around to watch. He'll tease her by leaning in for a kiss, only to stick his tongue in Lily's ear. She'll whisper-hiss his name and then slug his shoulder.

He'll mock wince.

They'll look infatuated with each other, remembering how many years they've spent. How far their lives have come. How much love they've shared.

Their romance has never changed. We all thank the fucking world for that because there is no Lily without Lo. There is no Lo without Lily.

I notice Rose, dressed in a silk black robe, by the coffee pot. She tries to fix the machine, but Connor whispers to her too, drawing her away from the broken thing. With fire beneath her yellow-green gaze, Rose looks just as unaltered by the years. Just as fucking immortal.

Just as enduring.

Is it surprising—that they'd be equal in this measure too? It never has been to me.

As I pass them to the side door, I see their spouse's names on their lips. *Richard.*

Rose.

War and love is in their eyes.

Both entranced with battle plans, their fucking wit. Their words. In this moment, with Audrey sleeping in Connor's arms, they can't speak more than murmured whispers. War diminishes to love, and I can practically see their affection for what they've created.

Seven kids.

Their family.

With his free hand, Connor cups the back of Rose's head. He holds her piercing gaze. And then Connor presses an adoring, tender kiss to her forehead. Engrained with sentiments that Connor once believed were fake.

Rose's gaze softens a fraction, and she whispers to him, out of fucking earshot.

I've reached the side door, so I don't strain to hear. They all fade behind me, and I disappear outside. Quiet, really fucking quiet. The world is just waking, and I return to my original place. On the hill.

By the red Adirondack chairs. I take a seat on the grass and bend my knees. I trace the mountains with my eyes.

I climb weekly, still endorsed by Fizzle. People often wondered if I would ever free-solo again. I do, but nothing like I fucking used to— nothing that could kill me. I don't crave those routes, not in that way, not like I did at twenty with so much less to love.

I go at life at one-hundred-and-fifty miles an hour, but I also wake up the next day. To see this.

Right here.

Right now.

I rake my hands through my hair, the dark sky beginning to lighten. Behind the mountain peaks, an orange glow slowly crests to claim this day as today. To begin everything all over again.

Footsteps squish the grass, and before I see who, Daisy appears beside me. Without speaking, she slides between my legs, and I pull her up, until her back rests against my chest. I wrap my arms around her, both of our eyes on the horizon.

Two more people join. Without word, Lo sits down a few feet from me, Lily next to her husband. Pressed together, he holds her while she holds him. Their gazes follow ours, hushed, while warm colors paint the landscape.

Connor noiselessly walks outside and stands by a red chair near me.

Hands in his pockets. As Rose reaches him, heels sinking in the grass, he extends his hand to her, and she clasps tightly. They both turn and observe the skyline. Air weightless.

And unencumbered.

All six of us fix our eyes on the rising sun.

There are moments you remember and people you will never fucking forget. While orange light bathes us, while tension flits far, far away, how much we've felt—all that we've bled—surrenders to our collective love. Lifetimes, days, minutes spent together.

As we watch outward. As we watch upward. As our faces warm.

We live and breathe in quiet, blissful peace.

Acknowledgements

Wow. Is it over? Is this real? I think we may ask ourselves this for the next decade. The Addicted series has defined a magical part of our lives. Nine books. Six people. More than this, it's all of you. The readers, our friends—what we call the Fizzle Force. Your love for these characters, for our words will long exist in our hearts after everything else fades away. In five years, we'll think back to the start of it all. We were just dreamers, and we had a big dream—a wild, crazed dream—that you all believed in. So thank you, for believing in us. For sticking around, years later, and not giving up on us.

We want to thank our beautiful, fierce mom. You've been our Rose Calloway, always there to empower us while wearing five-inch heels. You have been such a huge support throughout our journey and a huge help at every deadline. We know we can always turn to you, just like Lily can turn to Rose. We love you so very much.

To Jenn Rohrbach—thank you for looking at us like superstars when we were nobodies from the very beginning. For being the one to gather this beautiful thing called the Fizzle Force, even when you had no idea how to run a Facebook Group, you tried your hardest because you believed in us. We hope one day you'll recognize the depth of your kindness because it's beautiful and precious and has touched more than just us.

To Lanie—oh Lanie. Our love for you will never wane. Thank you for your passion, your heart, and for keeping the Fizzle Force lively, spirited, and one of the most loving fandoms. There are days—lots of days—where we wonder how we deserved someone as sweet and generous as you. We can't imagine this journey from the start without you.

Our next thank you goes to Siiri. For your never-ending friendship. For coining Coballoway. For being one of the only friends, from before we began publishing, who stuck with us and believed in us. It has meant more than this acknowledgement will ever or could ever describe. Whatever happens in the future, we know you'll be breathing fire with passion and love in your heart.

Now to Jae—thank you for your amazing support, for your beautiful graphics, for championing Lily & Lo. Who needed lots of love, and you were never short of supply for them. To Amy and Bella Love (Lili)— thank you for creating a place on Goodreads for the Fizzle Force. For not fading away. We appreciate all that you've done for us and we love you always.

Thanks to Alexis for championing our books to foreign publishers and Audible. Thanks to the Audible team and all the narrators for the hard work and capturing the heart of the Addicted series in audio.

To all the bloggers on every Addicted series tour—we're so grateful for each and every one of you. You've added an extra heartbeat to the series, and though we don't have enough room to list you all, it doesn't mean we love you any less.

Big thanks to Olivia Danieli, Alice Tort, and Silvana Reyes for the Italian, French, and Spanish translations. The magical thing about all three of you is that you're fans of these books. Your spirit is in these pages, and we couldn't have spotlighted these beautiful languages without you.

Long, long ago, when we first began the series around Ricochet, there was just one person vocal about their love for Ryke & Daisy. Thank you, Sue. For loving them. For loving us. Raisy exists largely because you didn't give up on them, when so many people did. It's strange to think there was a time like that, but there was. And you were there. And we heard you. Thank you so much.

Now you'll have to forgive us for speeding up. This is the hardest part for us. There are so many names we want to list. So many people we want to thank. It has taken a huge army of love for this series to span this far and this long. But we only have space for a handful of names. Know that when we say the word *Fizzle Force*, we mean *you*. Yes, you. We may have never exchanged a word, but you made it here. Nine books. You loved these characters. You're a part of this lovely thing called the Fizzle Force too. Don't forget that, okay?

We like to think that a piece of each of you remains inside these pages. Because you've all impacted us. You've helped us. You've lifted our spirits higher than they've ever been. You all are the superheroes in our world. Thank you. From the bottom of our hearts. Thank you for this journey and your unyielding love.

It's not over yet. What, were you crying already? This may be the end of one era, but another will begin. Are you ready for another adventure with us? Will you go where we go? We'll lead the way. Just keep your eyes fixed on the sun.

xoxo
Krista & Becca

ALSO BY
Krista & Becca Ritchie

ADDICTED SERIES

Addicted to You

Ricochet

Addicted for Now

Thrive

Addicted After All

CALLOWAY SISTERS SERIES

Kiss the Sky

Hothouse Flower

Fuel the Fire

Long Way Down

Some Kind of Perfect

STANDALONE ROMANCE

Amour Amour

WEB SERIES

Willow & Garrison: Whatever It Takes